HIGH FLIGHT

TOR
51012-7 ★ $6.99
(CAN $7.99)

DAVID HAGBERG

NOVELS BY DAVID HAGBERG

Twister
The Capsule
Last Come the Children
Heartland
Without Honor
Countdown
Cross Fire
Critical Mass
Desert Fire
High Flight

WRITING AS SEAN FLANNERY

The Kremlin Conspiracy
Eagles Fly
The Trinity Factor
The Hollow Men
Broken Idols
False Prophets
Gulag
Moscow Crossing
The Zebra Network
Crossed Swords
Counterstrike
Moving Targets
Winner Take All

HIGH FLIGHT

DAVID HAGBERG

TOR®

A TOM DOHERTY ASSOCIATES BOOK
NEW YORK

This is a work of fiction. All the characters and events portrayed in this novel are fictitious, and any resemblance to real people or events is purely coincidental.

HIGH FLIGHT

Copyright © 1995 by David Hagberg

Cover art by Alan Ayers

Quotes from *Bushido: The Warrior's Code* by Inazo Nitobe, used with kind permission of Ohara Publications, Inc.

A Tor Book
Published by Tom Doherty Associates, Inc.
175 Fifth Avenue
New York, NY 10010

Tor Books on the World Wide Web:
http://www.tor.com

Tor® is a registered trademark of Tom Doherty Associates, Inc.

ISBN: 0-812-51012-7
Library of Congress Card Catalog Number 95-12548

First edition: August 1995
First mass market edition: August 1996

Printed in the United States of America

0 9 8 7 6 5 4 3 2 1

My apologies to the city of Portland, Oregon, and vicinity. Fact is I placed an imaginary aircraft company in a real locale. No disrespect was intended. Portland just seemed like the right place.

This book is for
LAURIE.
We too have broken the surly
bonds of earth.

HIGH FLIGHT

Oh, I have slipped the surly bonds of earth
    And danced the skies on laughter-silvered
        wings;
Sunward I've climbed, and joined the tum-
        bling mirth
Of sun-split clouds—and done a hundred
        things
You have not dreamed of—wheeled and
        soared and swung
    Hung in the sunlit silence. Hov'ring there,
I've chased the shouting wind along, and flung
    My eager craft through footless halls of air.
Up, up the long delirious, burning blue
    I've topped the windswept heights with
        easy grace
Where never lark, or even eagle flew.
    And, while with silent, lifting mind I've trod
The high untrespassed sanctity of space,
    Put out my hand, and touched the face of
        God.

*Written by RCAF Flight-Lieutenant
John Gillespie Magee, Jr., shortly
before his death at age 19.*

If he did not succeed, at least he dared greatly before he fell.

—Ovid on Phaëthon

I've tried to make the men around me feel, as I do, that we are embarked as pioneers upon a new science and industry in which our problems are so new and unusual that it behooves no one to dismiss any novel idea with the statement that "it can't be done!" Our job is to keep everlastingly at research and experiment, to adapt our laboratories to production as soon as practicable, to let no new improvement in flying and flying equipment pass us by.

—William E. Boeing, 1929

SPRING 1990

PROLOGUE

A narrow beam of light flashed suddenly in the dark confines of the airliner's electronics bay. A slightly built man dressed in the white coveralls of an American Airlines maintenance technician directed the penlight toward a particular equipment rack. The boards were all dead. Not even standby power was being supplied to the jetliner parked at the ramp. The man studied the rack, and those on either side of it in the cramped quarters, then turned his flashlight away.

Hunching down on his knees, he opened his tool kit and took out a plastic box, barely one inch on a side, laid it on the deck, then took out a screwdriver and began removing the six screws that held a narrow electronics panel marked HEAT MONITOR/ALARM, ENGINE, PORT in the center rack.

Miyazaki Oshima's movements were as precise as they were soundless. He had practiced the drill dozens of times so that he could not possibly make a mistake. When he finished he set the screwdriver aside, slid the panel out from its slot in the rack, and propped it at an angle against his knees. Holding the penlight in his mouth and directing it on the subassembly's innards, he slid the cover panel back until its spring-loaded catches released, then removed it and put it aside. The unit was crammed with electronic modules each containing one or more computer chips. Few other components or wiring were visibile from the top. A metal tag bore the legend PE171.314.LP522, INTERTECH CORP., SAN FRANCIS-CO, CA., which matched the number on the small plastic box lying beside him on the deck.

Oshima cocked his head to listen for any sound from above that might indicate someone was coming. But the equipment bay was utterly still. The air was close. It smelled of lubricating oil, hydraulic fluid, kerojet, and electronics. Irrationally he thought of this place as a coffin.

Using a special tool that looked like a four-inch plastic pry bar, he removed one of the modules from the heat monitor/alarm subassembly, and replaced it with the one from the plastic box. Both modules were identical to the naked eye, and no routine maintenance diagnostic test would tell them apart.

Making sure that the replacement module was firmly seated in its receptacle, he replaced the subassembly's cover panel, reengaging its catches, then slid the entire unit back into the equipment rack, pushing firmly to make sure the contact bar pins fully mated. Forcing himself not to speed up, not to make any mistake, he refastened the six screws holding the unit in place, returned the screwdriver, pry bar, and plastic box that now contained the original module to his tool kit, and carefully examined the area immediately around each screw head in case he had inadvertently scratched the metal. If he had, he could touch it up, but he had not, and he was satisfied.

He remained crouched for a moment or two, listening, feeling, trying to sense the essence of the jetliner and the people who would fly in her soon. And die in her.

He switched off the penlight and by touch returned it to his tool kit. The feeling of distress, he was taught, was the root of benevolence. He felt as if he was finally becoming *gishi*—a man of rectitude. Of *giri*—duty.

"It is true courage to live when it is right to live, and to die only when it is right to die." The precepts of *Bushido,* the Japanese warrior's code of honor. "But courage is a virtue only in the case of righteousness."

Hiroshima. Nagasaki. These abominations to the *Yamato Damashi*—the soul—of Japan could not be forgotten. He'd been taught that, too, from childhood. He carried the resentment like a Samurai carried his swords.

But the parliament's kowtowing to Washington over nothing more than commerce also ate at Japan's soul.

At twenty-six, Oshima was not old enough to remember Yukio Mishima, Japan's greatest post-war novelist, who committed *seppuku* in 1970 to illustrate his belief that Japan's soul could be saved only by a return to *Bushido.* But he believed in what the master had taught, and at certain times his belief was clearly visible on his face as a saintly, beatific smile. He smiled now. By being here, by doing this thing, he was helping to preserve Japan.

"I want you to have no illusions about the job you are being asked to do," Arimoto Yamagata told him six months ago. "You understand everything?"

"Hai, Yamagata-san," Oshima had answered sharply.

"If your true purpose is discovered and you are arrested, we will deny any knowledge of you. The United States authorities will punish you, and when you finally come home you will be tried again, found guilty, and will be sentenced to a very long time in prison."

"Seppuku . . ."

"There will be no honorable death for you, if you fail."

Yamagata's expression was stern, but the implication of what had gone unsaid made Oshima swell with pride. In failure there would be dishonor, but in success there would be rewards.

"I will not fail, *Yamagata-san.*"

"I'm sure you will not," Yamagata said, finally smiling. They were seated alone, fifty miles outside of Tokyo, on a broad scrubbed teak deck that overlooked a pleasant garden. The gentle sounds of running water mingled with the musical tinkling of a windchime in the single, gnarled tree in the middle of the garden. The sand had been freshly raked, and Oshima had been asked to bear witness to the placing of a new rock near the pool. Yamagata called it "future," with a second name of "hope."

"I will think of this place often," Oshima had said.

"Yes, *Oshima-san*. And here I will think of you."

Yamagata worked for the powerful Ministry of International Trade and Industry—MITI—which was the nearest thing to an intelligence agency that Japan maintained. The ministry had influence in every corner of Japanese science, business, and government, and therefore nearly unlimited resources. Training Oshima on the proper equipment, in secret, getting him to the United States on a U.S. passport as Michael Oshima, and getting him the proper credentials so that he had access to the restricted sections of Chicago's O'Hare Airport had been no problem. Nor had getting through security this morning presented any difficulties. As a technician with the proper badges and work orders his presence was barely noticed.

Now it was time to leave.

Careful to make no noise, he picked up his tool kit, got to his feet, and climbed to the top of the ladder, where he stopped a moment to listen. So far as he could tell no one was aboard the aircraft. It was before 4:30 in the morning and this plane's first scheduled flight wasn't due out until 7:30 A.M. The first of the maintenance technicians and housekeeping crew wouldn't be showing up until 5:30, which left him a full hour to get out.

Plenty of time, he told himself. But he was jumpy.

He pushed the trap door open a crack. The interior of the plane was in darkness, only a dim light came through the windows from outside. He hesitated a moment longer, then eased the trap door the rest of the way open. Laying his tool kit on the deck, he climbed up into the cockpit, careful to keep below the level of the windshield so that if someone outside happened to look this way, they would not see him.

He closed and relatched the trap door, picked up his tool kit, and scrambled back to the galley where he straightened up a few feet forward of the main hatch.

The weather was warm so the hatch was open directly onto the jetway back to the boarding gate. It had been figured into their contingency plans. If someone were on the ramp when he was ready to leave through the flight service area he could use the jetway and make his escape through the terminal.

"It will not do to simply replace the central processor," Yamagata had said. "You must not be discovered. You must make your escape."

Yamagata had shown up at Narita Airport a half-hour before Oshima's flight to Chicago. His presence came as a complete surprise and honor. Oshima had been deeply touched.

"You must know that you are part of a large team that has worked for Japan's honor for a long time. This will not be a random act of violence."

"I don't understand."

"No need for you to understand, except that you are not a terrorist."

"A warrior."

Yamagata smiled. "Yes. You will be our shield, *Oshima-san.*"

The novelist, Mishima, had maintained a private army to defend the emperor when the time came for revolt. It was called the Shield Society. Oshima was very proud that Yamagata had made such a reference even if it was obscure.

He glanced a last time back toward the cockpit, then stepped out of the galley and through the hatch into the jetway. Act of terrorism or not, he felt queasy thinking about what would happen here shortly after American's

Flight 413 took off. The crash would be blamed on a catastrophically sudden port engine overheat. The fanjet would disintegrate in midair, taking all or most of that wing with it. There would be no chance of recovery. Not one in a billion.

No one was below on the ramp. Oshima unlocked the jetway service door and hurried down the stairs. The night air smelled of burned kerojet. The flight service area was lit up, but no one was in sight.

Oshima pulled up short. A half-dozen suitcases tagged for Houston were piled on a baggage trailer. They'd not been there ten minutes ago when he'd come this way. While he'd been aboard 413, someone brought the baggage out.

Now he could hear voices from somewhere in the back. In the direction of the break room.

He stepped into the shadows. Ten minutes ago the field had been quiet. But now a pickup truck, orange lights flashing, crossed 14L toward a Delta hangar three-fourths of a mile away. The hangar's main bay doors were open, and a big jetliner, all lit up, was parked inside.

It was too early by at least an hour. No one was supposed to show up until after five. It was only 4:30. Something was wrong.

No alarms had been sounded. No airport security officers were swarming around. But that wouldn't last long. The first American Airlines supervisor he encountered would probably ask questions that Oshima couldn't answer.

He would be searched. The replacement module would be found in his tool kit. He would have failed.

"There will be no honorable *seppuku* for you," Yamagata's words came back. His comrades would not rejoice in his passing.

But he had forgotten nothing. He'd watched the airport through March and the first week of April. Timing the comings and goings of the maintenance and security staffs, the service people, the flight crews, and flights themselves until he could safely predict the day-to-day, hour-to-hour activities anywhere within the O'Hare complex.

He had picked this hour, four in the morning, on this day, Sunday, because this was the time when the airport was the quietest.

He had forgotten nothing. But the airport was coming alive an hour too early!

Somebody said something and laughed, and the swinging doors to the baggage service area opened.

Oshima sprinted back out to the ramp as a truck pulled up fifty yards away. The driver got out and went into the service area.

More service crew were coming into the baggage area, leaving Oshima no option except the route through the terminal. Forcing himself to remain calm, not to panic, he hurried upstairs, unlocked the door, and slipped into the jetway, hoping that no one had spotted him.

Somehow he had his times mixed up, although he couldn't see how that was possible. But as long as he could get away clean it wouldn't matter.

He started down the jetway toward the boarding gate when he heard voices coming his way, and he froze.

"No firearms," his trainers had told him. "If you get yourself into a situation where deadly force is needed, you will have already failed."

But he hadn't counted on being cornered like this.

He turned back to the window in time to see a man in white coveralls start up the stairs. There were no options now.

With only a few seconds leeway, Oshima reboarded the jetliner, yanked open the cockpit trap door into the electronics bay, scrambled down into the darkness, and closed and relatched the door overhead. His heart pounded, and he had to force himself to take even breaths lest someone come into the cockpit and hear him panting like a cornered animal.

At first he heard nothing, but then someone came aboard. They stopped, then came forward into the cockpit directly over his head, and Oshima held his breath.

There was silence for a few seconds, until something thumped against the hull, and a man in the cockpit spoke as if on a radio.

"That's roger. I'm bringing up standby power for one minute to finish that . . . ah, diagnostic on bus two-four-two-baker."

A second later LED indicators on a dozen electronics panels around him suddenly came to life, and he nearly fell down, his knees weak, his breath catching in his throat.

There was enough light for him to see the racks and wiring and hydraulic lines, and enough light for someone to see him if they opened the trap door.

He eased back into the darkness as far as he could go, taking care to make no noise.

Had he been stopped in the terminal he might have been able to bluff his way out of the airport. But to be caught here, like this, there would be no explanation other than the truth: He had sabotaged the airplane. But if he was trapped down here and could not get off, he would have to fly at 7:30.

He sat down on his knees and heels, set the tool kit aside, and concentrated on his breathing so that he could fight off the rising panic that threatened to block his sanity and his courage. If this were the time and place for him to die, then so be it. In a way it would be a form of *seppuku,* and therefore honorable. He would not have failed.

The panels went dead, plunging the electronics bay into complete darkness again. Oshima flinched despite himself.

"I'm down," the technician radioed. "Looks like a broken connection on f-thirty-three-fifteen-baker. That's the circuit breaker for . . . ah, the forward galley. Looks like an auxiliary. No, it's for one of the coffeemakers."

The radioed reply was too faint for Oshima to make out.

"The prep crew won't be aboard for another twenty minutes. I should have it done by then."

It was ironic, Oshima thought, that a man's life could

hinge on something so insignificant as an electric coffee-maker.

"Roger that," the technician said. "I'll set both panel clocks forward."

Oshima looked up sharply.

The technician chuckled. "It screws me up every spring, too."

Daylight saving time, the thought suddenly crystallized in Oshima's head. Since he had arrived in Chicago six weeks ago he'd been too busy to give more than cursory notice to the newspapers or the radio or television. If he had paid more attention he would have realized that on this Sunday clocks across the United States were set one hour ahead. It was not 4:30 A.M. now; it was 5:30 A.M.

That irony was even more bitter to Oshima than the coffeemaker's faulty circuit breaker, and he almost laughed out loud.

As he had promised Yamagata, he thought of the garden, and the windchime, and the rock named "future" and "hope," while with one ear he listened to the sounds from the cockpit and from the belly of the airplane as the first of the luggage was loaded aboard.

Future and hope were meant to symbolize Japan's *Yamato* spirit. The rock placed in such a setting so obviously at peace and harmony with itself was meant as a focus or catalyst for the thoughts.

Yoshida Shôin once wrote:

Full well I knew this course must end in death:
It was *Yamato* spirit urged me on
To dare whate'er betide.

Someone else came aboard the jetliner, and later others, after which the panel LED indicators came on again, and more baggage was loaded aft and below.

Oshima became calmer as his fear peeled away from him like layers of onion. He carefully examined each line of the verse that Shôin had composed on the evening before his execution for being a traitor against the turn of the century "New Japan," and he understood its meaning. He knew the fatalism that Shôin had felt, as well as the sense of inner peace that came before death.

The master had been a *bu-shi*, in the old meaning, a fighting knight. It had been his only crime against modernism.

But now in Japan the belief that the old ways were the best was coming back. Japan had lost her greatness, but she would regain it in this century, or within the first years of the next. The return to power was as inevitable as it was just and righteous.

Oshima was barely conscious of the passage of time, although he was aware of the continuing preparation for the jetliner's first and last flight of the day.

A fundamental difference between Americans and Japanese was that Americans believed anything worth doing was worth doing right. The Japanese, however, believed that anything worth doing was worth *dying* for. It was one of the reasons Japan would be victorious morally, financially, and, given the time, militarily.

Oshima was startled when the engines came to life, one at a time. The noise was loud in the equipment bay.

He could hear announcements being read over the airplane's public address system, though it was hard to pick out the exact words.

The jetliner lurched, then moved slowly backward from the boarding gate.

For a second, Oshima considered bypassing the heat monitor/alarm panel so that he could replace the original module without the flight crew becoming aware of it. But he dismissed the idea.

The airplane turned and then started forward, bumping along the uneven ramp toward the taxiway.

In the old days Samurai warriors learned to compose poetry in order to cultivate a gentleness of spirit to temper their passion for killing. Oshima had read about one ancient master who had instructed his warrior-pupil to construct a verse about the *Uguisu*, the warbler, or Japanese nightingale.

The young warrior made a first crude effort:

The brave warrior keeps apart
The ear that might listen
To the warbler's song.

The airplane stopped, then the engines roared and they accelerated down the runway, the noise rising sharply, and then even more sharply as they became airborne.

The master continued to work with the young warrior until his soul awakened, and he wrote:

Stands the warrior, mailed and strong
To hear the *Uguisu*'s song,
Warbled sweet the trees among.

The jetliner banked left as it continued to climb, and Oshima's thoughts turned again to the rock, "future" and "hope."

At twenty-three thousand feet the airplane's port engine disintegrated without warning, shearing off the entire wing to within five feet of its root, blasting a hole seven feet in diameter in the side of the hull halfway back to the tail surfaces, and taking out all electrical power to the cockpit so that neither the twenty-five-year veteran captain, nor the ten-year veteran first officer had a chance to radio Mayday.

Oshima was conscious all the way to impact in a farm field south of Joliet, and on the way down he wondered if a poem would be written about him someday.

WINTER 1997

ONE

Kirk Collough McGarvey knew that someone was coming for him again. Wishful thinking or not, he'd had the feeling all through the fall semester where he taught eighteenth-century literature at Milford College on Delaware's east coast. At the odd moment he would stop in mid-sentence and glance at the door, half expecting to see someone there. Or he would pick up the telephone in his apartment, certain that it had rung, but there'd only be the dial tone.

It had been three and a half years since he'd last had any contact with the CIA, or with anyone from official Washington, and nearly that long since he'd spoken with his ex-wife, Kathleen, although their only daughter, Elizabeth, now twenty-one, came down from New York several times a year to see him.

"What's the matter, Daddy?" she asked at Thanksgiving. But he had no answer for her. Nervousness? Simple boredom? Once a field man always a field man, that was the drill, wasn't it?

Pushing fifty, he wasn't over the hill yet. He was a tall,

muscularly built man, with a thick shock of brown hair starting to turn gray at the temples, and wide, honest eyes, sometimes green, at other times gray. He ran ten miles and swam five every day, rain or shine. He worked out with the college's fencing team to maintain his coordination. And once a month he spent an afternoon at a local gun club's firing range.

He'd not lost his edge, but as the CIA's general counsel, Howard Ryan, told him in Murphy's office three and a half years ago, he was an anachronism.

"You're a man who has outlived his usefulness," the lawyer said. "The Soviet Union is no more. The bad guys have packed up and quit. Time for the professional administrators and negotiators to take over and straighten out the mess. Thanks for a job well done, but we no longer need shooters."

Bad times, he thought, getting out of his car. He headed over the sand dunes to Slaughter Beach on the bay. It was a few minutes after three, the day cold and blustery. At the top of the last rise he stopped to watch the whitecaps march down the bay in regular rows. The wind was gusting to thirty-five knots. Spits of snow drove out of a leaden sky, and he could pick out the shape of a southbound container ship well out into the bay heading for warmer climes.

More years ago than he wanted to remember the Company had sent him to Santiago to kill a general who'd been responsible for hundreds of deaths in and around the capital. But his orders had been changed in midstream without his knowing about it. After the kill he'd returned to Washington a pariah.

He'd run then to Switzerland until he'd been called out of retirement for a brief but particularly nasty assignment. No one thanked him. There were no welcome-home parades, no presentations at the White House. He was paid and went to ground next in Paris until his call to arms had come again, as he knew it would. Ryan was just as wrong three and a half years ago as he was now. The world may have become a much safer place with the demise of the Soviet Union as a superpower, but there was still a need for a man willing to kill. A man, McGarvey sometimes thought of himself, without a past. Or, more accurately, a man driven by a past from which he was trying to escape.

Looking back toward the highway he watched until the blue Ford Taurus pulled onto the beach access road, then he headed the rest of the way down to the water's edge. The beach was deserted, as he knew it would be, and as soon as he was out of sight of the parking area, he transferred his Walther PPK automatic from the holster at the small of his back to his jacket pocket.

It was possible that someone had come from Langley to offer him another job. But it was just as likely that someone out of his past had finally come gunning for him. Lately he'd been having his old recurring nightmare in which Arkady Kurshin was climbing up out of a flooded tunnel. The Russian was impossible to kill, and he was coming for revenge.

The wind-driven spray raised a mist from the beach that smelled faintly fishy—seaweed, salt, and probably some pollution. But not an unpleasant odor. After his parents' ranch in western Kansas McGarvey preferred almost any smell other than the prairie.

He stopped a hundred yards down the beach and half turned so he could look out to sea while at the same time watch the dunes toward the parking area out of the corner of his eye. The wind was picking up, and he made mental note to take it into account if he had to make a crosswind shot. The slow-moving 7.65 mm bullet's path would be severely affected over anything but point-blank range.

A man wearing a dark, thick-collared jacket and a baseball cap topped the rise, stopped a moment, and then headed directly toward McGarvey. He was of medium height, perhaps six feet, and moved with the sure-footed grace of an athlete. But he wore gloves, so he was no immediate threat, whoever he was. You couldn't fire a gun while wearing gloves.

As he got closer, McGarvey made the judgment that the man was not from the Company. There was something about his bearing, about the way he came straight on without looking left or right, that made him seem like a soldier. The man was not a cop or field officer. But he'd asked about McGarvey on campus this afternoon. Administration had sent him over to Humanities, and Evelyn had called to warn that a visitor was on his way.

"Did he say what he wanted?" McGarvey asked.

"He said that a mutual friend sent him down to see you."

"Name?"

"David Kennedy."

McGarvey thought he might know it, but he couldn't dredge up the connection. Maybe somebody from the Company, after all, maybe not. "I'll probably just miss him," he told the dean's secretary. "My constitutional."

"He'll show up back here."

"Slaughter Bay."

"Don't catch a chill," Evelyn said. She and the dean and the chairman of the school's board were the only three on campus who knew anything about McGarvey's background. But good teachers were hard to find, and Milford wasn't Ivy League, so as long as his past didn't interfere he was accepted with open arms.

"Mr. McGarvey?" Kennedy had to shout over the wind.

McGarvey turned. "That's right."

"My name is David Kennedy," the man said. His eyes were blue, and the expression on his face was guileless, almost little boyish.

McGarvey made the connection. NASA. "You're an astronaut. A shuttle pilot."

"Until five years ago. Now I'm president of Guerin Airplane Company's Commercial Airplane Division. Portland, Oregon."

They shook hands. Guerin was the second-largest designer and manufacturer of commercial aircraft in the world behind Seattle's Boeing, with every bit as much prestige as the older company. Nearly every airline in the world flew Guerin equipment. And the United

Nations Peacekeeping Armed Forces Unit was considering Guerin's F-124 Hellfire all-weather supersonic fighter/interceptor for its primary air weapon. Not even Europe's Airbus Industrie, which was heavily subsidized with government money, could outcompete the company.

"What brings you to see me, Mr. Kennedy?"

"I'd like to offer you a job."

"Teaching your engineers about Voltaire?"

"The chairman of our board and CEO Al Vasilanti is a personal friend of Roland Murphy. Your name was mentioned."

Murphy was Director of Central Intelligence. He was a tough but fair-minded man who did not care for McGarvey. But unlike the Agency's general counsel, he understood the need for McGarvey's skills. The fact that he'd given McGarvey's name to the CEO of a civilian company was extraordinary.

"You were told about my background?"

"Mr. Murphy said that you were a . . . troubleshooter. And considering the trouble that we're having, the situation that we're facing, you might be the only man who can help us."

McGarvey looked away. The downbound container ship was nothing more than an indistinct blur on the horizon. Wherever it was headed, it had direction, a purpose. For that he envied the ship and those who sailed her.

"What else did the general tell you?"

"That your methods were not orthodox, that wherever you turned up someone would probably get hurt. And that you would be watched, and if you broke any law you would be arrested and we—the company—would find ourselves in big trouble."

McGarvey faced him. "Yet you came to offer me a job."

"Al Vasilanti is an unorthodox man. He built Guerin from the ground up, mostly on guts."

"Spare me the pep talk, Mr. Kennedy. If you know

who and what I am and you want me to do something for you, then your company must be facing something your engineers or lawyers can't handle."

Kennedy nodded.

"Unless something has changed in the past few years, I think that cargo planes and airliners are our single largest dollar-value export."

"By a wide margin."

"But Washington refuses to help. No more Chrysler-style bailouts."

"Something like that," Kennedy said. "And it concerns the Japanese. No one wants to upset the apple cart so soon before the President's economic summit next month in Tokyo."

"Did the general mention my last assignment?"

"Not in any specific terms," Kennedy said. "But he said it involved the Japanese."

A multibillionaire Japanese industrialist who'd lost his family in the destruction of Hiroshima and Nagasaki had hired a group of former East German Secret Service thugs to steal the fissionable material and parts for two nuclear devices that were to be detonated in San Francisco and Los Angeles. Except for McGarvey's interference, the plan would have succeeded. There was no love for him in Japan.

"What do you want me to do for you?"

Kennedy glanced back the way he'd come. "Could we go some place warmer? Maybe a coffee shop or something?"

"No," McGarvey said. Here on this beach their conversation was as secure as it could be.

"Then I'll get to the point. We believe that a group of Japanese corporations have formed a *zaibatsu,* which is a type of conglomerate, to try an unfriendly takeover of Guerin. We don't think this group has a government sanction, but we're not sure about that part. What we are reasonably certain of, however, is that if they're successful they mean to dismantle our company and ship it to Tokyo."

"Why?" McGarvey said. "If they wanted an airplane

manufacturing company they could build one. What has Guerin got that they want?"

Kennedy hesitated a moment. "Our company hinges on keeping what I'm about to tell you secret."

"From whom, Mr. Kennedy?"

"Anyone . . . the public."

McGarvey said nothing, and after a second the point dawned on the former astronaut.

"The Japanese wouldn't be coming after us if they didn't already know or guess," he said.

"That's a reasonable assumption. But you have a business problem on your hands, Mr. Kennedy. What do you need me for?"

"In 1990 one of our airplanes went down out of Chicago. It was an American Airlines flight. Three hundred forty-eight people were killed. No survivors."

"Sabotage?"

"We think it's a possibility. The National Transportation Safety Board disagrees. They said it was engine failure."

"That was seven years ago. What's the connection between then and the *zaibatsu* you think has been formed now? Have you come up with any evidence?"

"The flight manifest showed three hundred forty-seven passengers and crew. An extra body, parts actually—a heart, part of a skull, some tissue—were found in the vicinity of the cockpit. One of the pathologists the NTSB hired said the tissues probably came from an Oriental male. There was some question about DNA matching, and the Board shot it down. Said the body parts were from someone on the ground. A migrant farm worker probably. But the doctor disagreed, so his conjecture ended up as an addendum that was ignored."

"Have you talked to the doctor?"

"He was murdered three months later, and his office burned. The thieves were supposedly looking for drugs, but all of his paper records, as well as his computer memory, were destroyed."

"Still no connection between then and now. Maybe the doctor was wrong."

"In the past six months we've had a seven hundred percent increase in the number of job applicants of Japanese descent. In more than one-third of the cases our routine background investigations found that the applicants were lying about some very significant facts. Like where they were born, what schools they attended, their work background."

"What's your rate of faulty applications among the white population?"

"A little less."

"Among the Blacks or Hispanics?"

"A little more," Kennedy conceded the point. "But during that same time period our work-related accident rate has skyrocketed, parts and subassembly theft has become big business, and one week ago one of our structural engineers, a man who has been with the company for thirty years, was killed when a forty-pound tool box fell off a scaffold and hit him on the head. We had three guys who said they thought one of our Japanese-American employees was nearby when it happened, but now they're not so sure they saw anything."

"That's thin."

"By itself, yes. But our position on the stock market has become shaky, and there've been a couple of probing runs against us. If another of our airplanes went down now, we'd take a beating on the market."

"The Japanese would try to buy you out. But you could buy back your own stock. It's been done before. And from what I read Guerin has had a couple of very good years. You've taken customers away from Boeing and Airbus."

"We don't have the money. In fact we're so heavily leveraged that we're having trouble meeting our payroll. Eighty thousand paychecks every two weeks eats up a sizable amount of cash."

"Where did it go?"

"Research."

"Which is what the Japanese are really after."

Kennedy nodded.

"Research into what, Mr. Kennedy? What is Guerin working on that's nearly bankrupting the company and that, according to you, a group of Japanese corporations wants so badly it's willing to commit mass murder for it?"

"A new airplane."

McGarvey stared at the ex-astronaut.

"We've designated it the P/C2622. P for passenger, C for cargo, and the 2 for the twenty-first century. It's what's called 'next generation equipment.' "

"What's different about this one?"

"This one is hypersonic. Los Angeles to Tokyo in ninety minutes. But it's nothing like the Concorde, which has been a dismal failure for a lot of reasons. Our airplane creates almost no air pollution because at altitude the engines burn hydrogen, the byproduct of which is water vapor. And almost no sonic boom footprint would reach the ground because ninety-eight percent of the pressure energy is directed upward, not down. There'll be a lower passenger-per-mile cost than Boeing's 747 at current fuel prices, but with the same payloads and the same runway requirements."

"Impressive," McGarvey conceded. "But how many years will it be before your test flights begin?"

"Four weeks, maybe six weeks."

"Your prototype is already built?" McGarvey was surprised.

"All except for the hypersonic engines. Our first test flights will run to near Mach one with a cowling replacing the hydrogen engine. Rolls-Royce promises delivery within one year." Kennedy studied McGarvey. "The bottom line is that this Japanese *zaibatsu* plans to do to the commercial airplane business what has been done to the automobile business and to the consumer electronics market. And they'll stop at nothing to do it. Including the murders of a lot of innocent people. If they somehow bring down another of our airplanes, our stock will die, but so will several hundred men, women, and children. Just like 1990."

"What if you're wrong?"

"We sincerely hope we are, Mr. McGarvey. That's what we want to hire you to find out for us."

"And if you're right?"

"Then we'd like you to do whatever it takes to stop them."

"I see." McGarvey turned and started back across the beach toward the parking lot. Kennedy fell in behind him.

"Will you help us?"

McGarvey looked at him. "Why don't you sell the technology to Japan? Share it with them under license."

"We thought about it. Boeing works with the Japanese. There's precedent."

"But you can't forget 1990."

"That's right," Kennedy said.

McGarvey stopped. "In 1983 Hitachi Corporation offered to build a major engine research facility in Japan that would be shared equally by any American commercial airplane manufacturer who wanted to participate. Hitachi would put up all the money, the Americans would bring their head start in research. Guerin turned them down."

"Our prerogative," Kennedy said. "Chrysler was given the same offer before it built its billion-dollar design and research center. But Iaccoca said no: 'Chrysler is simply not for sale to the Japanese for any price.' Neither was Guerin."

Time to get out of the business for good? McGarvey wondered. He could understand Langley's hesitation to go along with the airplane company. The direction had come from the White House. Just now we were walking softly around the Japanese who held a significant percentage of our five trillion dollars plus of debt. No one wanted to upset the apple cart. Maybe America was for sale after all.

"How do I contact you, Mr. Kennedy?"

"Will you help us?"

"I'll look into it. That's all I'm saying for the moment.

Do you have a secure number in Portland where I can reach you?"

Kennedy pulled an envelope out of his pocket and handed it to McGarvey. "We have a scrambled phone system at our Gales Creek Computer Center. As long as you're calling from a phone you know has not been tapped, your message will be secure."

McGarvey pocketed the envelope. "I'd like you to stay in Washington for the next few days. Can you do that?"

"Yes."

"Can you arrange a secure meeting place in the city? Not your hotel. Maybe an apartment?"

"Dominique Kilbourne. She has an apartment in the Watergate complex. She's a lobbyist for the Airplane Manufacturers and Airlines Association. Her brother Newton is our vice president in charge of prototype development and manufacture. And she's a friend. A discreet friend."

"Are you sleeping with her?"

Kennedy reared back, but before he could reply, McGarvey cautioned him.

"Don't ever lie to me. My life may, at some point, depend upon knowing the entire truth."

"We had an affair a few years ago. It was brief, and when it was over we parted friends. That's the situation now." Kennedy handed him a thick envelope. "This is some background reading."

McGarvey nodded. "I'll be talking to you." He headed toward the parking lot. This time Kennedy did not fall in beside him.

CIA Deputy Director of Operations Phillip Carrara met McGarvey a few minutes before ten at the bar in the Four Seasons Hotel on the Georgetown side of Rock Creek. He was a barrel-chested man, with a square face, thick dark hair combed straight back, and an easy smile. As an Hispanic, he maintained that he had to work twice as hard as an Anglo to get any respect. No one in the Company took the man lightly. He was among the best.

"Did you talk to David Kennedy?" he asked when his scotch rocks came. The bar was half full, but no one was paying them any attention.

"This afternoon," McGarvey said. "I was surprised that the general mentioned my name."

Carrara smiled wanly and shook his head. "It was Ryan's suggestion actually."

"That bastard still has a hard-on for me?"

"He's got a long memory. He wants to see you dumped on your ass once and for all. Are you going to take it?"

"What have you heard?"

"Guerin's in some financial trouble. It's apparently overspent on research for the NASA space plane project, and it's vulnerable right now. It wants protection."

"Anything from Tokyo?"

"We've picked up nothing, Kirk. If there is a *zaibatsu* planning nefarious things, it's deep."

"Would you query Tokyo Station for me?"

Carrara chuckled. "Not a chance in hell, *compar.*"

"If Guerin fails it would take a hell of a big bite out of U.S. exports."

"Guerin is only one out of three. And I don't see Vasilanti or Kennedy camped out on the White House lawn. In the meantime if you'll look around you'll notice that this country is still in economic trouble. Japan holds nearly half our debt, its navy is negotiating with the Philippine government to buy our old base at Subic Bay—that by the way is privileged information—and the White House is trying to put together a package with teeth for the economic summit next month in Tokyo. Are you following me?"

"Times are tough all around. But what about the Russians? Is Yemlin still the KGB's *rezident?*"

"It's called the Foreign Intelligence Service—the SUR—these days. But Yemlin hung on."

"Is the SUR still as active in Tokyo as the KGB was? They were running a top-grade network called *Abunai,* which was a hell of a lot better than anything we were fielding."

Carrara's complexion darkened. "What's your point, Mac?"

"We've got a big problem between us and the Japanese, Phil. I'm not telling you anything new. And it's not going away. Who knows, maybe this Guerin thing is only the opening shot."

"Of what?"

McGarvey looked at his old friend. "I don't know. I really don't. Everything is different now. Everything has changed."

"You can say that again."

"Maybe a war with Japan might wake everybody up."

"Don't even think it, Mac," Carrara said. "But what about Yemlin? You knew he was here in Washington all along, didn't you?"

"If I'd wanted I could have had him anytime during the last couple of years."

Carrara nodded. "If you were going to meet with him, where would it be?"

"Is the FBI still watching him?"

"Officially yes. In actuality it's pretty loose now."

"Arlington National Cemetery. Tomorrow at noon at Kennedy's Tomb if he's clean."

"If not?"

"Thursday at one, and then Friday at ten. After that we'll have to try something else."

"Do you think he'll help you?"

McGarvey nodded. "He owes me."

Carrara smiled wanly. "And God help the poor bastard if he doesn't see it that way."

Arlington National Cemetery sprawls over more than four hundred acres across the Potomac River from the city of Washington. Established in 1864 on the Custis and Lee estates, nearly one hundred thousand people are buried there, including John F. Kennedy. On the best of days the cemetery is a grim reminder of the only true constant in war: a lot of people die. McGarvey wondered if the unthinkable were starting again. This time the stakes would be much higher and the battles would be more fierce than fifty-five years ago, but the outcome would be the same: people would die needlessly. He felt as if he were surrounded by his nightmares.

Viktor Pavlovich Yemlin stood in front of the flame at Kennedy's tomb, his hat in hand, his wispy white hair ruffling in the slight but chilly breeze. The sky was overcast, and it felt as if it might rain or even snow. The Russian wore a long, dark overcoat and a light silk scarf. In appearance he could have been Eduard Shevardnadze's younger brother, except that his shoulders were hunched, and in the old days he had been involved with some very bad people, which lent him a dark aura.

He turned as McGarvey approached, an oddly distant expression on his face, a frightened look, as if he were seeing a ghost and he was girding himself for the confrontation.

"Hello, Kirk," he said.

"It's been a long time, Viktor Pavlovich," McGarvey said.

First it had been Valentin Baranov who'd headed the KGB's Department 8 of Directorate S—the Illegals Directorate—who had given the assassin Arkady Kurshin his charter. Next, after McGarvey had killed Baranov, came General Vasili Didenko, and finally Yemlin.

Caught up in the enthusiasm of the moment, Yemlin had said. Fighting capitalism. Saving the *Rodina*. McGarvey had been allowed to read the transcripts of a National Security Agency satellite phone tap. Yemlin had been speaking with Boris Yeltsin himself, shortly after the August Kremlin coup in which Gorbachev had been arrested.

There had been deaths. Hundreds. Thousands. Tens of millions if Stalin's killed were included. Who was not guilty? Time now to go forward. Time to build on the ashes of the old.

Expedient words, McGarvey had thought at the time. But then the business, by its very nature, bred and nourished expediency.

"Are you here for revenge?" Yemlin asked.

McGarvey could hear laughter, and for a moment he

thought it was out of place here in a cemetery, but then he realized that he was remembering his sister as a young girl. She'd laughed often in those days. But afterward, after their parents died, neither of them laughed very much. Revenge, he asked himself. For what? There'd never been any hard evidence, nor did he believe the Russian was ready to offer any.

"I've taken an assignment for Guerin Airplane Company."

"That's what Phillip told me." The Russian motioned for them to walk, and they headed down a broad path away from the flame. There were very few other people visiting the cemetery.

"Guerin is concerned that a consortium of powerful Japanese corporations may be gearing up for a raid on their stock. From what I was told they've probably formed a *zaibatsu* with a lot of financial backing."

"Would Washington allow such a thing?"

"I assume their NASA and military divisions would have to be split out of the deal. But just now no one wants to rock the boat."

"I understand," Yemlin said. "But Guerin's position is strong."

"The Japanese may try to sabotage Guerin's airplanes. Blow them out of the sky, if need be. That'd knock hell out of the company's stock value. A takeover would be easy."

"They would be acquiring an essentially worthless company in that case. Unless there was something else they wanted."

"There is something else, Viktor Pavlovich," McGarvey said.

Yemlin smiled. "Can you talk about it?"

"They've been working on the next generation of commercial airplane. Just about everything flying transoceanic, or even transcontinental, will become obsolete."

"You're talking about the NASA plane?"

"They're using that as a cover project, but the other has been buried. It's one of the reasons they hired me.

They think the Japanese are desperate to buy them out for that line of development alone."

"Which they would dismantle and transport back to Japan."

"Something like that."

Yemlin stopped. "Do you honestly believe they're desperate enough to blow airplanes out of the sky? To become terrorists? To kill people? Think about it, Kirk. Japan is your country's major trading partner. It would be stupid for them to do anything to jeopardize that position. It would be disastrous for them if they were exposed."

"We don't believe the government is involved," McGarvey said. "At least Guerin's top people hope it's not."

"Those are very big stakes," Yemlin said.

"The biggest."

"What would you have us do?"

"If we can identify the individual companies that make up this consortium, and if we can get someone into a boardroom meeting, or possibly someone inside the Ministry of International Trade and Industry who could gather hard evidence that such a plan exists, Guerin's people could take it to the President and pressure would be brought directly on Tokyo."

"I ask you again, Kirk, what would you have us do?"

"Hand the project over to network *Abunai.*"

A flicker of surprise crossed the Russian's face. "What would Guerin do for us in exchange? Where is the quid pro quo?"

McGarvey had thought that out on the way in to the city. Russia was having its own trouble with Japan over the Kuril Islands and others north of Hokkaido, so whatever he offered Yemlin would have to be something Russia needed. Something very important, such as foreign exchange. He and Kennedy had discussed the situation yesterday afternoon by phone.

"It's possible that Guerin would build and equip a subassembly factory outside of Moscow."

Yemlin's eyebrows rose. "For which airplane?"

"The new one."

"What about personnel?"

"Some Russians that Guerin would train."

"Would our people be involved in the engineering?"

"I don't know, but I think something could be worked out."

Yemlin looked back the way they had come, the flame at Kennedy's Tomb just visible, and McGarvey followed his gaze. The thirty-four years since the President's assassination had been nothing short of stunning.

"It will take time," Yemlin said.

"The prototype is nearly ready to fly. If something is going to happen, we suspect it will happen very soon."

Another thought crossed Yemlin's mind. "Would Guerin be willing to pay expenses in Tokyo?"

"Within reason," McGarvey replied. The Russians' supply of hard currencies, which they needed to fund foreign intelligence operations, was very limited, and Japan was an expensive playing field.

Yemlin smiled again. "Ironic, isn't it? The SUR being hired as mercenaries for a former CIA spy?"

"We'll need action soon," McGarvey said.

"My book cable will go out this afternoon," Yemlin promised. "But I am curious about something. If this goes through, will you come to Moscow to oversee the operation?"

McGarvey shook his head. "I don't think your people would want me."

"No," Yemlin said softly. "I suppose not."

The Dassault SF-17 helicopter came in fast and low over the treetops of the Rambouillet Forest thirty miles southeast of Paris, the pilot, Pierre Gisgard, frantically searching for the field where he was supposed to land. But visibility in blowing snow was zero at times, and the gusty winds hitting forty knots buffeted the machine so violently that Gisgard thought it was going to come apart on him. He'd warned them about the weather at

Mortier, but when the colonel got a feather up his ass nothing would hold him down.

And this was the biggest feather of all. The French secret service, known as the *Service de Documentation Exteriéure et de Contre-Espionage,* or SDECE, had been chasing this group of East Germans ever since the two Germanies had been reunited. They called themselves the Berlin Hit League, and for six years the group of ex-Secret Service thugs and murderers had been terrorizing Europe: robbing banks to finance their operations, killing for hire, and sometimes to settle old scores, sabotaging bridges, power stations, radio and television transmitters, and assassinating policemen.

Three years ago members of this group shot a Swissair jetliner out of the sky over Paris with a Stinger handheld missile. Half the passengers aboard that flight had been French men, women, and children on holiday. No one in France could forget that tragedy.

Colonel Philippe Marquand, chief of the service's Anti-Terrorism Unit, had been given a literal carte blanche by the government to run them into the ground, a task which he had undertaken with zeal. Most of them were either dead or in jail now, and the last remnants of the gang—three men and one woman—had made the mistake of coming back to France and robbing the bank this afternoon at Chartres.

The local police had responded to the silent alarm not suspecting they would run into a hornet's nest. The first two officers on the scene were shot to death as they got out of their radio unit. Two other officers died when their radio unit took a direct hit from a LAW rocket.

By then the firefight had moved from the downtown bank to a roadblock on the N154 north of the city. A Chartres lieutenant of police recognized at least one of the bank robbers as a Berlin Hit League gunman by the name of Bruno Mueller. The former Stasi lieutenant colonel, whose specialties were murder and sabotage, was on France's top-ten most-wanted criminals list, his name flagged for immediate attention of the Action Service. The call had been put through to Paris as the gun battle continued up into the Rambouillet. Less than one hour earlier the bank robbers had pulled up to a stone farmhouse where apparently they were going to make their stand.

A strong gust of wind caught the chopper broadside, slewing it sharply to the left, its landing gear tangling momentarily in the tops of some trees before it went over on its side. Gisgard pulled the collective and the cyclic, hauled the stick far right, and kicked the rudder pedal hard. The machine shuddered to an upright attitude, every weld in its frame strained to the limit, and he set it down hard, chopping all power immediately.

"Nice landing, Pierre," Colonel Marquand shouted from the back.

"Yes, sir," Gisgard replied as the rear hatch was opened and Marquand and the ten men he'd brought down with him scrambled out into the snowstorm.

Colonel Marquand was a short, dark, dangerous-looking man who'd once been described as a Sherman tank with an attitude. Squinting his jet-black eyes against the driving snow, he could make out the stone farmhouse at the end of a narrow track that emerged from the woods and ran across a long, narrow field. A dozen radio units and Bureau of Criminal Investigation vans were deployed in a semicircle in front of the house. He'd been assured that the entire perimeter was secure. It meant that there would be some lost police officers wandering around in the storm, fingers on the triggers of their weapons.

"I want a scope on that house and on the woods behind it right now, René," he told his number two as they headed toward the communications truck parked just off the track. "Place your shooters no more than fifty meters from the front, left, and right."

"What about the rear?" Captain René Belleau asked, as he motioned for his people to move out. Both he and Marquand were part Corsican, and they commanded a lot of respect.

"That Chartres lieutenant has got officers back there."

"Stationary?"

"One would hope so," Marquand said. "I'll see if I can establish communications with them."

"And hostages?" Belleau said grimly. "It looks like a working farm, *hein?*"

"Just our luck," Marquand replied heavily, as they reached the comms truck. He banged on the rear door and hauled it open, as Belleau, dressed in white army camos, disappeared into the storm, a walkie-talkie to his lips.

The interior of the truck was bathed in soft red light. Three young officers were seated to the left at a long radio console, and to the right a police lieutenant and a sergeant looked up from a map spread out on a wide table.

"Lieutenant Régis?" Marquand asked, climbing up into the truck, and pulling the door closed.

"You from Paris?" the lieutenant asked. He was about forty, and looked competent.

"Marquand, Action Service."

"Pleased to meet you, sir," Régis said, holding out his hand.

Marquand ignored it, and shouldered the sergeant aside so that he could get a better look at the map. He pulled off his gloves. On this larger-scale chart he could see that the river was within twenty meters of the rear of the farmhouse, and that there were no locks or dams between here and where it joined with the much larger River Eure. From there it would be possible to take a boat all the way to Le Havre.

"What are you doing to protect the people you have deployed in front of the house?" he asked.

"Protect?" Régis asked, surprised. "I have twenty-three men, all of them heavily armed . . ."

"How many have you lost so far?"

"I . . ."

"Yes?"

"Seven dead, five wounded," the lieutenant said.

"Sergeant, I want all of those men out of their vehicles and on the ground. Pull any of them not dressed for the weather out of there."

"Yes, sir," the sergeant snapped, and he turned to the radio operators.

"Now, what about your people at the rear of the farmhouse? Are they on this side of the river, or the other?"

"The far side. We have fourteen back there, and they *are* equipped for this weather."

"I'll put four of my people with them. Radio your men and tell them what to expect."

The sergeant looked around. "We're momentarily out of communication with three of our people."

"Why is this?"

"We don't know yet."

"Sergeant, locate them as soon as possible," Marquand said.

"Yes, sir."

"Is the river frozen over?"

Régis looked surprised. "I don't know," he admitted.

"Find out," Marquand said.

"Yes, sir," the sergeant answered for him.

"Do they have any hostages in the house? Did they take any from the bank?"

"None from the bank, colonel, but we believe there are two civilians in the farmhouse. The man and the wife."

"Is the house equipped with a telephone?"

The lieutenant hesitated.

Marquand pulled out his walkie-talkie and keyed it. "René, phone line?"

"*Oui*. It has tone."

"*Bon*. Any movement in the house?"

"A few shadows, but no clear targets. What about the rear?"

"Looks as if there may be three friendlies without communications. We'll do *orange* on my signal."

"Right," Belleau radioed tersely.

"I want a link to that phone line. Send Henri over on the double."

"What about the local officers?"

"Stand by only. I didn't spot any medical units out there."

"Non, neither have I," Belleau radioed.

"They're on their way," Régis said.

"That's good," Marquand said. "Because in a few minutes we're going to have some casualties."

"Our men are dismounting now," the sergeant said. "But I'm sorry to say there is no luck so far in the rear."

"What about the river?"

"It isn't frozen, the current is too swift."

"It's an escape route. Are any of your people within sight of the river?"

"Yes, sir," the sergeant said.

"If anything moves toward the river, from whatever direction, shoot to kill."

"But, colonel, you understand three of my men are unaccounted for back there," Régis protested.

"Then let us hope they do not decide to go for a swim this evening."

The sergeant turned back to the radios to issue the orders.

"Your men are to be used for containment. If anything gets past us, it will be up to you to bring it down."

"I thought we might go in with you," the lieutenant said.

"You have lost enough brave officers. No need for more," Marquand said almost gently. "This is our fight now."

The back door opened. One of Marquand's men dressed in white camos came in and went immediately to the radio consoles. His name tag read BOUTET. "The line is isolated, and I've tied it to the auxiliary here," he said, studying the panel. He flipped a couple of switches, and picked up one of the handsets. *"Bon."*

"René," Marquand radioed.

"In position," Belleau came back.

"We go in in one minute."

"Oui."

"Inform your people," Marquand told the sergeant, and he motioned for Boutet to place the call. He remembered a half-dozen other moments similar to this one, and each time he hoped it would be the last.

"Hallo. Bonjour. This is the police, to whom am I speaking?" Boutet began. His job was to keep the hostage-takers talking for as long as possible, which would help distract them.

Marquand was about to raise the walkie-talkie to his lips, when Boutet shook his head.

"Lost him."

Belleau came on. "There's movement! They're coming out!"

"Allez-y! Allez-y!" Marquand radioed, then shoved the sergeant toward the door. "Out of here now!" he shouted. "Everybody!"

He was out the door right behind the sergeant, nearly stumbling in the snow, Boutet on his heels. Before they got ten yards, a bright flash seemed to surround them, and the communications truck exploded in a million pieces, knocking them down like a set of ten pins.

The bastards had targeted the truck from the moment they realized what it was being used for, Marquand thought, scrambling to his feet. It was a mistake that he should not have made.

Another flash about thirty meters nearer to the house took a police van. The sound of small arms fire rattled from behind the house.

"Two *mecs* down! We're going in!" Belleau radioed.

Lieutenant Régis and the three radio operators were dead, so there was no immediate way of knowing what had happened at the rear of the house.

Boutet was helping the sergeant who'd been hit by flying debris. There was nothing else to do for the moment. The action was in the farmhouse a hundred meters away.

The small arms fire died off within ninety seconds.

Belleau came back. "The farmhouse is secure. Two males and one female down and dead. The hostages, one male, one female, are both dead as well."

"That leaves one unaccounted for," Marquand radioed. "Watch yourself, René."

"Stand by."

"Merde," the sergeant swore. He was looking back at what was left of the communications truck.

"We've got movement back here," Belleau radioed excitedly. "Across the river. All right, stand by."

Boutet was looking up at him, his eyes narrow.

"All right, Philippe, it's the police. They're pulling a body out of the river about thirty or forty meters downstream."

"The third subject?" Marquand queried.

"Unknown."

"Stay put until I can establish communications with someone on that side of the river."

"Will do," Belleau responded.

Marquand had a feeling that this was going to be a very long night.

Edward R. Reid began to think of himself as the great pacifier in 1986 when in his financial newsletter *Lamplighter* he predicted the downfall of the Soviet Union and the rise of Japan as the next threat to the nation. His stated goal, and there were a lot of powerful people in and out of Washington who listened to him, was true peace through a beneficent financial domination of the world by the United States. But now at sixty-nine he felt as if he were no closer to his goal than he had been eleven years ago, and he was running out of time.

"The tragic inevitability of war can be circumvented only if we have the will," he'd written in his last newsletter. "Economic conditions in the U.S. continue to deteriorate on many fronts, the national debt spirals upward at an ever-increasing pace, and the new health care system is pushing record numbers of small businesses into bankruptcy, elements that will lead either to a decline into international obscurity for America and Americans, or war with Japan for the same reasons we went to war with them fifty-six years ago."

A war he'd missed because he was too young, he thought as he paid off his cabby at the 21st Street entrance to the State Department and shuffled across the sidewalk. He was a bulky man, with huge feet, very large, still powerful hands, a broad, almost square head with white, thinning hair, a bulbous red nose, patchwork blue and red blood vessels high on his cheeks, and brilliantly penetrating blue eyes. A Princeton class of '50 man, he'd come to work for State after a three-year stint in the Army in West Germany. In 1961 he'd returned to Princeton for dual master's and doctorate degrees with honors in political science and economics, and in 1967 any department or agency in Washington would have welcomed him with open arms, but he chose State because his first love was international affairs, especially those of West Germany. He felt it was there that the fight against communism would be won or lost.

His two disappointments in life were his wife's death in 1983 and his failure to reach the top spot, Secretary of State, rising only as far as Deputy Undersecretary for Economic Affairs.

"Every President you've served under has told you that you're more valuable where you are," Margaret, his wife of twenty-eight years, told him when he would grumble. "You're too smart to be a politician, you old poop, so quit your complaining."

He missed her, and not a day went by when he failed to wish for her counsel.

It was a few minutes before one when he stepped through the metal detector downstairs and took the elevator up to the ninth floor. His name was on the list and he was expected. The call from Thomas Bruce, who held his old job, had come at 8:00 sharp this morning. "Secretary Carter would like to have a word with you sometime today. Would one o'clock be convenient?"

"It would," Reid had said, knowing full well what the meeting would be about. They were going to jump him about his last newsletter, which was fine with him because it meant they were paying attention.

Warner MacAndrew, the State Department's official spokesperson, was just coming out of the Secretary's reception area as Reid stepped off the elevator. The man was tall and thin, all planes and angles. He looked serious.

"They're waiting for you inside, Mr. Reid," he said, stepping back and holding the door.

"That serious, is it," Reid commented, entering the office.

"I for one agree with you," MacAndrew said softly, and Reid smiled.

He was passed directly through by an assistant who opened the inner door and said, "He's here, Mr. Secretary," then stepped aside.

Secretary of State Jonathan Stearnes Carter, seated behind his desk, did not bother to get up. At fifty-one he was one of the youngest Secretaries of State in recent times, but he came highly qualified from Colgate and Cornell as a lawyer with experience on the U.S. delegation to the United Nations, various presidential commissions including law enforcement and administration of justice, and work as special and chief counsel on three different Senate subcommittees. Seated across from him were Thomas Bruce and Dietrich Kaltenberger, the State Department's General Counsel. They all looked unhappy.

"Thank you for coming over on such short notice, Edward," Secretary Carter said, motioning him to take a seat.

"My pleasure, Mr. Secretary," Reid replied. "I'm always at the service of my country."

Everyone said that Carter looked something like FDR, but there was no well-met smile on his face today.

"We won't keep you long. You're a busy man."

"As you are, Mr. Secretary. What can I do for you?"

"Simply put, we want you to stop your call to arms against Japan."

"I beg your pardon, sir, but I'm doing no such thing."

"We've read your latest," Kaltenberger said.

"Then you've not read it closely enough. If you had you would understand that I am calling for something quite different."

"What?" Carter asked bluntly, and Reid turned back to him, enjoying this more than he thought he would.

"I'm sure, Mr. Secretary, that you are aware that because of the continuing trend toward corporate downsizing, one in eleven Americans are out of work."

"What does that have to do with this?" Kaltenberger said, but Carter waved him off, and Reid continued.

"Housing starts were down sharply for the fifth quarter in a row, and yet just before I left my house a half-hour ago, the Dow Jones had reached another all-time high in very heavy trading. That cannot continue, of course. Another Black Friday is just around the corner. But it's worse. The infrastructure in this country, neglected for fifty years, is falling apart. Superhighways with potholes, bridges unsafe at any speed, mass transit systems in total shambles, factories falling apart, air pollution in some cities across this great nation so horrible that individual county health departments have begun issuing gas masks for the elderly and people with respiratory problems. But nobody cares. A malaise has infected this nation. And it's time to stop it."

"By going to war with Japan?" Kaltenberger asked.

"By avoiding war with Japan."

"How?"

"It has become an unstable economic giant that needs controlling," Reid said. "It holds a significant percentage of our debt, which, of course, it could call due at any time."

"Go on," the Secretary said, tight-lipped.

"Now that the Russians have all but shut down their military spending, and ours has been sharply cut back, the Japanese ground, air, and maritime self-defense forces, as they're called, are the fastest growing military forces in the world. Within a few months they'll be occupying our old base at Subic Bay in the Philippines— the first time since 1945 that their forces have been permanently deployed outside the home islands."

"How in the hell did you hear about that?" Kaltenberger asked, but again Carter waved him off.

"A military force, I might add, that is almost certainly nuclear capable. They've got the reactors, they've got the fuel reprocessing plants to make enriched plutonium, and they've got the second-largest space center in the world on Tanegashima Island just south of Kyushu, from where they have launched satellites into space."

"That's not to say they would be stupid enough to start a war," Bruce argued. "Come on, Ed, you sat in my chair. You know the economic ties we have with Japan. This isn't the 1930s all over again."

"Do you know how much oil Japan must import to stay alive?" Reid asked, answering his own question before Bruce could respond. "Ninety-nine-point-two percent of its needs. Its own experts agree that if its Middle East oil supply were to be cut by seventy percent for just six months three million Japanese people would die and nearly three-fourths of all Japanese property would be destroyed or heavily damaged."

"Its oil supplies are secure," Carter said.

"For how long?" Reid shot back. "Japan has to import one-hundred percent of its nickel, bauxite, manganese, molybdenum, and titanium. In fact the only natural resource Japan has is coal, and it doesn't have much of that."

"What's your bottom line, Edward?" the Secretary asked.

"The President must put together an economic par treaty. For every dollar of Japanese products we purchase, Japan must purchase one dollar of ours. For every ton of raw materials we guarantee to Japan, it must give us trade concessions."

"Japan can't possibly agree to that," Bruce said. "It would drive it into bankruptcy."

"Yes," Reid said turning to the man. "It's either them or us. So I'm suggesting that while we still have the chance, we demand its navy and air force not move out to the Philippines, and in fact be sharply cut back."

"The President has asked me to convey to you his desire that you cease and desist," Carter said.

"Cease and desist what, Mr. Secretary? Defending my country?"

"You no longer work or speak for the government," Kaltenberger said.

"No, I don't. So what are you worried about? I'm just an old man who happens to have an opinion."

"Which we would like you to keep to yourself," Kaltenberger blurted, as if he were afraid that the Secretary wouldn't go so far.

"Let me ask you something, Dietrich," Reid said. "If the United States were in the same position as Japan, what would we do?"

Nobody said a thing.

"Let me answer for you," Reid said. "We'd fight for our survival, of course. Any animal when threatened does the same."

"You're insane," the general counsel said.

"Then so is the rest of this country," Reid replied calmly. "Because a lot of people agree with me."

TWO

Algeria's fight for independence had been as big a blot on France's honor as Vietnam had been on America's. But as a young man, Philippe Marquand had made his mark with the army on the desert, and he had been fighting one war or another ever since. He'd lost some, but had won most, picking up a few scars, mental as well as physical, along the way. Now, standing in the cold just beyond the rear of the stone farmhouse, he rubbed the muscles at the base of his spine. He'd wrenched his back when he'd been thrown forward by the force of the blast and had compounded the problem by spending six hours tromping around in the cold. It was midnight, the storm had not let up, if anything it was intensifying, and they'd still not found the missing East German. It was at times like these when he seriously wondered if he could continue, or even should go on being a gun-carrying cop. The SDECE wanted him to take over the entire Service 5, an administrative post that would as surely tie him to a desk in Paris as if he been chained and padlocked to it. But until the moment when he'd entered the farmhouse and saw what had been done, he'd not even considered it. The Germans had sent them a clear message: Frogs are subhuman. The old couple, whose tiny farm this was, had been stripped naked, hung from the ceiling rafters by their ankles, and their throats slit. They'd been bled to death like pigs.

Belleau came out of the house. "The police downriver have been alerted." He had to raise his voice over the wind. "Dreux, Anet, Louviers, and even Rouen."

The body the police had fished out of the river minutes after the shooting had been one of their own. The missing East German was Bruno Mueller, the same one Lieutenant Régis had spotted and identified in Chartres.

"He's the very best, René. The most cold-blooded and ruthless. He did that to those old people in there. And enjoyed it."

Marquand had been witness to the Stasi lieutenant colonel's handiwork on more than one occasion over the past eight years. But always the aftermaths. This was the nearest he'd ever come to the man. So close, he thought, unconsciously clenching his fists. They'd searched and re-searched the house and grounds, but he was gone.

"His body will wash up somewhere downstream," Belleau said. "In this weather no one could survive for long in the water."

"He may have climbed out a hundred meters from here, walked to the highway, and flagged down a car or truck."

"There are roadblocks, Philippe. He will not escape again."

"Maybe he has found a boat," Marquand said, staring

at the small stream. "Did someone visually identify that dead police officer?"

"His name was Georges Level, and he had one bullet in his heart, two in his brain, and more in his lungs and back. His own people mistook him for Mueller."

"The ultimate joke, *hein,*" Marquand said.

"Let's go, Philippe," Belleau said gently. "There is nothing more for us to do here."

"Has the helicopter been secured?"

"*Oui.* There'll be no flying until tomorrow. Gisgard and Boutet will remain here with the machine. I have a halftrack standing by to get us to Chartres, where there's a train for us. It's the only way tonight, unless you want to stay."

"No, we'll go," Marquand said, taking a last look at the river. He could almost feel Mueller's presence. Each time he'd come close to the man there'd been a lingering stench, as if the air was tainted. Death and destruction were everywhere, and wouldn't end until Mueller was dead. Not in jail, but *dead.*

"Even if he does manage to break loose, which isn't likely, it's still all over for him," Belleau said. "There's nobody left. We know the whereabouts of most of the other ex-Stasi officers, the ones who retired and stayed retired. There's no help for him there."

"Don't be so sure, René. A man like him has friends. People who owe him favors, or people who are frightened of him. If he gets away he will strike again, I guarantee it."

McGarvey arrived at the Watergate apartment of Dominique Kilbourne a few minutes after six. The snow had finally come with the lowering afternoon temperatures. Rush-hour traffic had been all snarled up so he was a half-hour late. Kennedy would be wondering what had happened to him. But there was a lot he'd had to get straight in his own mind before he finally decided he would take this job.

He'd driven out to Chevy Chase to his ex-wife's house,

but at the last moment decided not to stop. He had nothing to say to her. She knew what he was doing, where he was teaching. Elizabeth, he was sure, gave her mother detailed reports. It was for the best, he supposed. Old wounds, when reopened, hurt the worst.

Seeing Yemlin hadn't done much for his mood either. The old days had been brought back to him in living color. The bad along with what little good there'd been. It had taken every ounce of his self-control not to kill the Russian with his bare hands. He kept telling himself that the war was over. It was done.

Yet here he was, back in the fray.

Dominique Kilbourne, dressed in a pair of blue jeans and a UCLA sweatshirt, the sleeves pushed up above her elbows, answered the door. Something was cooking in the kitchen, and whatever it was smelled wonderful.

"I hope you've made enough for dinner, because I'm going to want at least two helpings, and maybe more," McGarvey said.

Her narrow but pleasant face lit up. "Kirk McGarvey?" she asked. She was a slightly built woman with short dark hair, deep, almost coal-black eyes, and a very good, if small, figure. She looked to be in her mid- to late thirties.

"That's right. You must be Dominique Kilbourne. Kennedy didn't tell me that you were beautiful."

She laughed. "Are you a chauvinist?"

"In the worst way."

"Well, at least your candor is refreshing," she said. She stepped aside. "David's waiting in the living room. Are you going to accept his job offer?"

"Yes, I am."

"Why?"

McGarvey studied her eyes for a long moment. She was a grown-up woman doing a difficult job in what was possibly the most chaotic and arguably the most dangerous city in America. But for all of that she still had the look of an innocent. Self-confident, but naïve.

"It's what I do," he said. "Has Kennedy told you about me?"

"He has. But I have to admit I've never met anyone in your . . . profession before."

McGarvey smiled. "I'll try to keep my contact with you to a minimum," he said. He brushed past her and went down a short hall that opened into a large well-furnished living room.

David Kennedy stood at the broad windows facing the Potomac River, looking at the falling snow and the lights of the John F. Kennedy Center for the Performing Arts to the south. He was dressed casually, like Dominique, in slacks and a pullover.

"What have you decided?" he asked, turning.

McGarvey spotted a bar set up on a buffet. He went to it and poured a brandy without ice or water. "I'll need a different contact here in Washington. I don't think Ms. Kilbourne will do."

"Why is that?" she asked, perching on the arm of a long, low white couch.

"This has the possibility of getting ugly," McGarvey said.

"I'm a big girl."

"A lot of people could get hurt. I wouldn't want to see someone like you get in the middle of a firing line."

"People like me. You mean a woman."

"That's right."

She bridled. "Every major airline in this country flies Guerin equipment. I think I'm entitled to know if we're facing a threat."

McGarvey shrugged, and turned to Kennedy. "It's your call."

"But not yours?"

"We're talking about industrial espionage at the very least. That's a felony. Guerin could be hit with a hell of a fine, and the co-conspirators could go to jail. Might even involve treason, considering who we're dealing with."

"We went over that," Kennedy said. "We understand what we're getting into."

"I don't think you do, but there's 1990 to consider. If your enemies brought down that airplane, and they mean to bring down another, possibly more than one, it means they won't hesitate to kill whoever gets in their way. Me. You. Ms. Kilbourne."

"I'm a part of the industry, Mr. McGarvey, whether you like it or not," Dominique said evenly. "A lot of people trust my judgment in spite of the fact I'm a woman."

"Still your call," McGarvey told Kennedy.

The ex-astronaut hesitated for just a moment. "Unless you have some other objection to working with Dominique I'll have to go along with her. She knows your background, she knows the situation, and she has the contacts in the industry that you might need. I trust her completely."

"It's not a matter of trust," McGarvey said.

"Are you taking the job?" Kennedy asked.

"When you came to see me you said that you understood my methods were unorthodox."

"He told me he was taking the job," Dominique said.

"I spoke with someone today who might be able to help us. But we would have to give him something in return."

Kennedy's eyes were bright. "Like what?"

"Some money, maybe a couple of hundred thousand dollars, give or take."

"We won't get involved in bribery."

"This would be for operational funds," McGarvey said. "But there'd be more. I told him that if his people helped us, Guerin might be willing to build a subassembly plant."

Kennedy had a half-smile on his face. "Where?" he asked.

"Outside Moscow."

Kennedy's left eyebrow rose. "Okay," he said to cover his hesitation. "You've got my attention."

Dominique was staring at him, her mouth open.

"I met with a friend at the CIA and asked if the Agency could help out. The key is finding out who is involved with this *zaibatsu,* and then putting a man at one of their board meetings. I was turned down, as I suspected I would be, so I went to the next best organization that watches Tokyo."

"The Russians?" Dominique asked.

"Viktor Yemlin. He's the chief of Russian intelligence operations for all of North America. He and I go a long way back together, and he owes me a favor."

"You went to the Russians for help?" Dominique asked again.

"Do you still want to be a part of this, Ms. Kilbourne?" McGarvey asked.

"David, what the hell is going on?" she demanded, turning to Kennedy.

McGarvey didn't wait for the Guerin executive to reply. "Yemlin has agreed to query Moscow. If they go along with us, they'll expect you to make good on my suggestion, or at least talk to them about it. They have a network already in place in Tokyo, and if they take the job we'll have some answers fairly fast."

"I never thought you'd go to a foreign intelligence service. I don't know what to say."

"You came to me, Mr. Kennedy, with a story that your company is on the line. That there've been deaths, and that there may be more. It's your call."

Kennedy looked bleakly at Dominique then turned away to watch the blowing snow and the lights along the river. He was a former astronaut. One of the men with the right stuff. A straight shooter. A fair player. A man whose word was his bond. A simple handshake was enough.

The trouble was, McGarvey thought, the man was coming face-to-face with the real world, possibly for the first time in his life. Some of it wasn't very nice.

"The money will be no problem," Kennedy said.

"You can't be serious, David," Dominique blurted. "Think about what you're getting yourself into. Think!"

"I have," Kennedy said. "So has Al, so has your brother. We've thought about it, and we all came to the same conclusion. We need help, and we need it now, before anyone else gets hurt."

"Maybe you're right after all, Mr. McGarvey," Dominique said. "Maybe I have no business being involved."

"Then go downstairs for a drink. We'll be finished in a few minutes."

She shook her head. "No. I'm staying. As I said before, there are a lot of people in the industry who trust my judgment. If there's a threat to them, I need to know about it."

"What about the subassembly factory?" Kennedy asked, turning back. He seemed to have recovered somewhat from the shock.

"Nothing is written in stone. But what the Russians need most is foreign exchange. They've got the engineers and a trained work force, and certainly the willingness to go to work. It might make sense for you from a strictly financial point. You and I talked about it."

"Will they help us without it?" Kennedy asked.

"I don't know. But I suspect we'll have to offer them some incentive. Something they want, because they're going through a very difficult time with the Japanese. If their spying for us in Tokyo were to be exposed they'd suffer for it. It would be a severe political embarrassment for them."

"And us," Dominique said.

"Yes, and us," McGarvey agreed. "Yemlin is taking my request to his people in Moscow. If you're still interested in my help take my suggestion back to your board of directors, or whoever it is who makes these kinds of decisions for your company. But, don't screw around, Mr. Kennedy."

"Believe me, I won't screw around," Kennedy said. "I'll talk to Al Vasilanti tonight. What about you?"

"My daughter may come down from New York. I'll be with her. I'll be in touch."

"You're married?" Dominique asked.

"Ex," McGarvey said.

She looked at him oddly for a moment, then smiled wanly. "I think I can understand that."

* * *

Marine Lieutenant Stan Liskey should have been a naval officer because he knew his way around the Pacific Ocean better than he did the battlefield. In fact he'd never seen combat, but as a kid he'd sailed from California with his father and two uncles in the four-thousand-mile sleigh ride down to Tahiti and the fabled South Seas islands of Captain Cook. In the summer after his graduation from high school he single-handed a thirty-one-foot Pacific Seacraft cutter in the San Francisco-to-Honolulu race, coming in third on corrected time. He wanted to serve his country as a military officer, but he liked little boats, not big ones, so he joined the Marines. After two years at Camp Pendleton, and two more in Washington, D.C., he was stationed in Okinawa in the East China Sea three hundred miles south-southwest of the main Japanese islands, and it suited him just fine.

He was a tall, husky man, with the deeply lined and etched face of the sailor, and the square-shouldered, short-cropped look of the Marine officer, but with a smile almost always at the corners of his mouth as if he were having a little trouble taking anything too seriously. Running his hand over the section of boat bottom he'd just sanded, his smile widened a little.

"Smooth as a baby's ass," he muttered to himself, then switched on the small finishing sander and continued to work on the bottom.

She was the *Fair Winds,* a twenty-two-year-old factory-finished Westsail cutter originally out of Port Angeles, Washington. At thirty-two feet on deck, she displaced more than ten tons, and by modern standards she was considered to be so heavy and so slow that she could barely get out of her own way. But she was ruggedly built, with scantlings that even the Finns or the Taiwan boatmakers weren't building to any longer. With the proper skipper she'd stand up to just about anything that any ocean on earth could dish out.

She'd made her first circumnavigation from 1980 to 1986, by way of Hawaii, the Samoas, Australia, across the Indian Ocean to South Africa, then northwest, following the trades to the Caribbean, then the Panama Canal, and finally the long run out to Hawaii where she doubled her track, and then back home to Washington state.

A new set of owners sailed her around the world from 1987 to 1990, this time up the Red Sea, through the Suez Canal into the Mediterranean, and then across the Atlantic to Florida.

The last owners had trucked her to Vancouver where they'd sailed her up the Inside Passage to Alaska, out into the Aleutians, then down to Japan and finally Okinawa, where the wife put her foot down: "Me or the boat," she told her husband, and she won.

Liskey bought the boat two months ago, put her up on chocks at Sporty's Commercial Boatyard on the south end of the island, and had painstakingly brought her back to like-new. Now he knew every nut and bolt, every screw, every foot of wiring and plumbing, and every square inch of fiberglass, inside and out. By this afternoon the bottom would be sanded and painted and she'd be back in the water. In two days the rigging would be fully tuned, and the sea trials finished, and on Monday his and Carol's thirty-day leaves began.

Navy Lieutenant, j.g., Carol Moss popped out into the cockpit from below, where she'd been varnishing brightwork, and peered over the side. She was a plain-looking woman with short, dishwater-blonde hair, pale green eyes, and an athletic, almost stocky build. She had a devastating smile that could light up the darkest of rooms, and that could never be mistaken for anything other than what it was: sincere. At twenty-five she was five years younger than Liskey, which was, she maintained, exactly as it should be. She planned on marrying him, and she definitely wanted an older, wiser man, someone who knew more than she, and had more experience. Her father had brought her up that way.

Liskey looked up at her, and she smiled. He'd been daydreaming again. "Caught me," he said.

She laughed out loud, the sound musical. "Keep that up and you're going to sand a hole right through the hull."

"Not this one," Liskey said, thumping the side of the boat with the heel of his hand. "Are you done up there?"

"All set for the cushions, which I'll pick up tomorrow. Soon as they're in I'll start loading the provisions. Other than that we're set up here. How about you?"

"Another couple hours of sanding, and then the paint," he said. "We'll be in the water by this afternoon."

Carol smiled. The day was warm. She wore shorts and a halter top. Like Liskey, she spent a lot of time in the sun and was well-tanned. "How about a cold beer? Then I'll help you."

"Sounds like a good deal to me," Liskey said, and Carol ducked below.

He put the sander down and shaded his eyes against the sun so that he could see past the breakwater to the East China Sea. They would have thirty days together, island hopping all the way to the Japanese main islands. Isolated anchorages when they wanted them; charming little fishing villages if they wanted that sort of thing; and even bigger cities once they reached Kyushu if that was their desire. Besides the sailing, though, Liskey wanted to be with Carol. It would be a test, he figured, to see if they were compatible with each other. Thirty days alone on a small boat would see to that. The prospect of it excited and frightened him at the same time. He did not want to lose her, but he didn't want to give up sailing either.

At 0800 sharp, Foreign Intelligence Service Colonel Mikhail Amosovich Lyalin was shown into the office of the head of First Chief Directorate General Leonty Dmitrevich Polunin, and although he wore civilian clothes as most SUR officers did these days, he approached the vast desk, brought his heels together, and saluted smartly.

He'd been called upstairs because of the overnight from Washington. Yemlin's highly unusual request had caught them off guard. There'd not been a hint of anything like it. Thank Christ he happened to be here when it came in. At least he'd had a few hours to prepare himself. As chief of the First Department, which ran U.S. and Canadian operations, he was Yemlin's boss and it was expected of him.

On the surface Yemlin's message was intriguing because of the many possibilities raised, yet disturbing because of the way the Washington *rezident* had been approached and the information the Americans had about SUR operations in Tokyo. The Siberian Far East had plenty of problems without a Japanese complication. But a high-tech airplane factory in Moscow was something to think about. Lyalin had been doing nothing but for the past five hours.

General Polunin was a bear of a Russian, with a thick, square face, bushy black eyebrows, and the biggest ears Lyalin had ever seen on a human being. The saying went that what the man couldn't hear hadn't been spoken yet. He'd wanted to get into politics, but in 1991 Boris Yeltsin had promoted him to chief of the First Directorate, which was responsible for the former KGB's foreign operations, promised him the entire SUR within five years, and made him swear a personal oath of allegiance. The five years were up soon, but it didn't look as if the general would be getting his promotion. This latest development from Washington, however, Lyalin thought, might help.

"Good morning, General," Lyalin said.

"Have a seat," General Polunin said, returning the salute. "Yegorov will be here in a few minutes. Enough time for your briefing?" Colonel Yegorov was chief of the Directorate's Seventh Department, which oversaw operations in Japan and the region.

"Yes, sir," Lyalin said, again thanking Christ that he'd personally checked the overnights. "The book cable has been verified as authentic."

"I hope that was done before it was sent to me."

"It was, General. I want to assure you that this isn't some hoax or disinformation plot."

The general's eyes never left Lyalin's. "What about Yemlin? Is the man to be trusted? He hasn't gone insane?"

"He's to be trusted, and I think he's as sane as any of us. His two concerns outlined in the message were Kirk McGarvey's veracity and the man's knowledge of our Tokyo operations. Network *Abunai* is our major asset in the region."

"The name McGarvey is familiar. Why?"

"Because of the trouble we've suffered at his hand," Lyalin said. He too had heard the name, but he'd been flabbergasted when he'd pulled up the American's file. If he'd been one of General Baranov's team in the old days, he would have made damn sure that McGarvey was killed. As it was, he found it nearly impossible to fathom that Viktor Yemlin had come face-to-face with the man and lived to tell about it.

He passed McGarvey's thick file across the big desk. "It would be easier for you to look through his dossier."

"CIA?"

"A former field officer, an assassin actually. But he was fired from the Agency some years ago. Since then he's done contract work for them on an irregular basis."

General Polunin opened the file to several photographs of McGarvey. Immediate recognition dawned in his eyes. He looked up. "He killed Baranov, and Kurshin, and the others."

Lyalin nodded. "Evidently Guerin Airplane Company has hired him to straighten out this problem with the Japanese. Fascinating."

"To say the least."

"We stand to gain a great deal from this."

"Yes, or lose a lot. Is the offer legitimate?"

"Yemlin seems to think so. But I'll need approval before I can tell him to proceed."

The general thought about it for several long seconds.

"I'll talk to Yegorov first, and then I will take it upstairs. We'll see, Mikhail Amosovich. We'll see."

It would be light soon, and the farmhouse had been quiet for a full two hours. Bruno Mueller lay hidden beneath the rock wool insulation in the attic, his face pressed against the rough ceiling boards above the living room. At just under five-feet-nine, he was an unremarkable-looking man with a bland complexion, hazel eyes that sometimes watered, sand-colored hair that was thinning in back, slope shoulders, a slight paunch, and a face that was forgettable. He'd been the perfect spy, able to blend into any scene in Europe or America. He was also a complete sociopath; human life meant absolutely nothing to him.

After the cops and the Action Service *Schwein* had finally cleared out, the helicopter pilot and the other one, called Henri, had stoked the fire on the grate and had dozed off, the pilot in a big chair and the other on the couch. Mueller could see them through a crack. Stupid little men, afraid to go into the bedroom and sleep in a perfectly good bed even though the bodies of the farm couple had been removed and most of the blood cleaned up. But the pilot had to be very good to have gotten down here from Paris in the storm. Mueller had heard them talking about it. The pilot had balls, and his presence was a stroke of luck.

But even though he figured he would get out of this fix, like he'd gotten out of every other one since his childhood, he knew that there was little or nothing left for him. There were very few places where he would be welcomed. Libya, Iran, perhaps Lebanon, if he wanted, which he didn't. Nor were there any masters left worth serving, or any causes still viable enough to fight for. The religious fanaticism of the Shiites or the Hezbollah were not for him. The superpower struggle was over and his side had lost, as he'd secretly feared it might from the moment he'd seen America with his own eyes.

Born in Leipzig in 1952, he'd been a child of the Cold

War, the Berlin Wall nothing more than the fence along any frontier between two nations. His childhood was troubled, his father an alcoholic, and his mother a petty thief and sometime informant to the East German Secret Police, the Stasi. When Bruno was seventeen, lagging in school, always in trouble, he killed a homosexual one night after receiving what he said was the worst blow job of his life, and the Stasi recruited him out of jail where he was awaiting trial. He was their kind of man: young, therefore trainable; common looking, therefore the perfect chameleon; and a killer of queers, therefore pragmatic.

The Stasi owned him, and over a four-year period spared no expense in his training, both physical and mental. And he responded. He was intelligent, and he *was* pragmatic enough to know a good thing when he saw it. He was taught hand-to-hand combat, along with mathematics, physics, chemistry, psychology, philosophy, religion, and a host of other subjects. He learned about codes and ciphers, about weapons and weapons systems from handguns to short-range missiles. He learned English and French in total-immersion courses, so that by the end of his four years he could speak well enough to be identified as a citizen, possibly second generation, but of very good breeding and excellent schooling.

Ultimately the Stasi wanted to place Mueller inside the CIA, a plan that even the Service's Russian advisers thought was too ambitious for their East German friends until Mueller received some additional training at the KGB's School One outside of Moscow.

Over eighteen months Mueller learned tradecraft from the pros, from men and women who'd actually been there and returned to teach it, and from the master strategists who knew the inner workings of every intelligence agency in the world. Again no expense was spared on Mueller's training, because the Russians also thought he had great potential.

The final plan was as simple as it was time-consuming.

There was no way for Mueller to be placed directly into the CIA—he would never be able to pass as an American—nor was it believed he would survive the intense vetting he would get if he applied off the street. First his reputation had to be built.

A job as a reporter with the Frankfurt am Main newspaper was arranged for him in 1976, and one year later he applied to and was accepted for employment by the West German Secret Service, the *Bundesnachrichtendienst,* or BND. A family (all dead) had been manufactured for him in Stuttgart; schooling records at Heidelberg (Don't remember him, but this is a big school after all); and even military service with the army (Mueller? Certainly, a damned fine soldier) all stood up to the BND's background check. In that period background investigations of new recruits were supervised by Major Karl Schey, who'd been working for the Stasi for eight years.

Mueller fit in well in West Germany, catching infiltrators from the East (a task at which he received help from his Stasi masters), but it was a full ten years before he went to work as a liaison officer to the British Secret Intelligence Service . . . one step closer to the Americans.

But they had waited too long. It was 1988 by the time he was ready to go to Washington, and the beginning of 1989 by the time he got there, and the Wall was coming down, the entire Soviet sphere of influence unraveling.

He remembered his short six months of shuffling papers on the Russian desk at Langley with confusion. So much was happening at such a frenetic pace that it was impossible to keep up with it all. One memory, however, stood out clearly in his life, and that was his first sight from the air of New York City. He was awestruck. Nothing he'd been taught by his masters, nor anything he'd learned on his own, had prepared him for that sight and the sudden inner vision that the Soviets and certainly the East Germans would lose.

Mueller rose up from between the rough-hewn ceiling

joists and shook the insulation off his back, careful to make no noise. He wanted to rip off his clothes and scratch himself all over. The irritating rock wool fibers had worked their way into his pores, and he was in agony. Instead, he concentrated on his automatic pistol, an old Walther 9mm P-38, checking its action by feel to make sure it wouldn't jam up because of the insulation dust.

Control, his masters had preached. His was superb. Each minute of the ten hours he'd lain up here, motionless, barely daring to breathe, listening to the sounds of the police and Action Service below and the storm outside, he'd waited for just this moment. If there were no longer any masters to be served, he'd decided, there was always revenge.

He worked his way, joist by joist, silently to the rear of the attic where the trapdoor to the pantry behind the kitchen was still open. The cops had crawled up here. There'd been two of them, but they hadn't been very thorough in their search. They'd been put off by the rock wool.

Nothing moved below. Mueller dropped down into the pantry, landing in a crouch, as if he were a cat, and went immediately through the kitchen to the door into the living room.

Neither the pilot nor the other one, named Henri, had stirred. Everything was as Mueller had seen it from above except for a small line of dust that had filtered down from the ceiling onto the stone floor in front of the couch. Mueller stared at it. Once again he'd been lucky that neither man had awoken and spotted it.

Keeping his eye on the two sleeping men, he crossed the narrow living room to the window and looked outside. The storm had subsided a little. From here he could make out the vague form of the helicopter across the field in the lee of the woods. The sky was beginning to grow light in the east. But there was no one else out there.

Turning away from the window he crept back to the

couch and looked down at the sleeping man. His name was Henri Boutet, a sergeant in the SDECE. He looked like a boy, not a government-sponsored bully.

Mueller placed the muzzle of his pistol a half-inch from Boutet's temple and, looking over toward the pilot, fired.

Gisgard reared up from a deep sleep and clawed for his gun beneath his camos as he jumped unsteadily to his feet.

"Arretez!" Mueller shouted, bringing his gun up.

For a moment it seemed as if Gisgard would ignore the command, but coming fully awake and realizing what was happening, he stepped back, his hands moving away from his tunic.

"Ah, bon," Mueller said. "Your friend here is dead. Do you understand this?"

Gisgard nodded hesitantly.

"Good. Now if you do not wish to join him, you will do something for me."

"What?" Gisgard asked.

"Fly me out of here in your helicopter, of course."

THREE

The Japanese Maritime Self Defense Force patrol submarine SS588 *Samisho* ran submerged at one hundred fifty feet in the Tatar Strait fifty miles off the Siberian coast. It was in a run-and-drift mode, an American naval tactic in which a submarine would run at ten or fifteen knots for a half-hour, then shut down and drift for a half-hour. It gave the sonar people practice, and if there were any surface ships looking for it, the maneuver sometimes flushed them out, forcing them to make a mistake, revealing their position and interest.

These waters between Sakhalin Island and the Siberian mainland had been a subject of bitter dispute since the First World War when the newly emergent Soviet Union claimed the island and all the waters of the strait for itself. Sakhalin was historically and geologically a part of Japan, a part of the chain of islands—Kyushu, Honshu, Hokkaido, and Karafuto (Sakhalin, as the Russians renamed it)—even though the Russians may have been the first official visitors to the barren place in the mid-1600s. Since 1945 the Soviet Navy, and now the Russian Federal Navy, constantly patrolled the region. There'd been incidents in which ship-to-ship and air-to-ship weapons launches had occurred, but the Japanese had always backed down.

Let them know we're there, but avoid direct confrontation at all costs. *Samisho*'s orders were explicit, yet she carried a full complement of GRX-2 (B) torpedoes and three highly modified Sub-Harpoon antiship missiles.

It was 0700 when Lieutenant Commander Seiji Kiyoda dismounted from the compact exercise machine, his well-muscled body glistening with sweat. At five-feet-three he was short even by Japanese standards, but he looked dangerous, his eyes dark and narrow, his face cruel except when he smiled. He drew some cold water in the tiny stainless-steel sink in his cramped quarters abaft the control center and splashed it on his face. At thirty-eight his body and his mind were as hard as the NS-90 high-tensile steel of which his boat was constructed. Every day he did a strenuous physical workout that at home port at Yokosuka was directed by his *sensei*. Every day he studied the writings of Yukio Mishima, the man of steel, and of *Bushido,* the warrior's code, for which he had another *sensei* at home. Iron will and a rigid discipline tempered with an appreciation of art and beauty, for beauty's sake alone. It was the old way. The best way. The only way for Japan now that her enemies were beginning to gather.

Chi-jin-yu, wisdom, benevolence, and courage. They would need all of that in the coming days, Kiyoda thought while sponging the sweat off his body. He was up to it, and he knew that his crew was. He could only hope for the rest of his countrymen, and especially for the Diet in Tokyo.

Dressed in a crisply starched uniform he crossed the corridor to the wardroom where a steward handed him a cup of *cha,* then went into the combined control room and attack center.

At two hundred fifty feet in length with a surfaced displacement of 2,200 tons, the *Samisho* was not a small boat. Built to the 0+2+ (1) Yuushio-class standards at Kawasaki's shipyards in Kobe, she'd begun service in 1992, and last year she'd been brought back to the yards for a retrofit. Now she was state of the art, an engineering and electronics marvel even by U.S. naval standards. She was a diesel boat, but she was fast, capable of a top speed submerged of more than twenty-five knots and a published diving depth in excess of one thousand feet. Her electronic detection systems and countermeasures by Hitachi were better than anything currently in use by any navy in the world, and her new Fuji electric motors and tunnel drive were as quiet as any nuclear submarine's propulsion system, and much simpler to operate. The *Samisho* could be safely operated, even on war footing, with fifty men and ten officers—less than half the crew needed to run the Los Angeles-class boats, and one-fourth the crew needed for a sub-hunting surface vessel.

His executive officer, Lieutenant Ikuo Minori, was on duty in the attack center with the weapons control officer, Lieutenant Shuichiyo Takasaki, and four enlisted men.

"Good morning, gentlemen," Kiyoda said, ducking through the hatch.

"Kan-cho on the conn," Minori announced crisply. Captain on the conn. "Good morning, sir, You slept well?"

"Very well, thank you, *Ikuo."*

Minori was one of the most intelligent men Kiyoda knew. He'd been number one at his prep school in

Oshima, number one in engineering at Tokyo University, and number one in his class at the Maritime Academy. It was rumored that he would get first crack at the nuclear submarine, the keel of which was being laid in secret at Kobe, when it was finished in 1998. In the meantime he refused other commands, preferring to remain aboard the *Samisho,* as did the other officers and men, all of whom Kiyoda had hand picked, and all of whom shared his belief in *Bushido* and Mishima. They'd formed their own Shield Society.

"Having a combination like that makes one almost wish for a war to test them," Admiral Higashi, commander of submarine forces, had said to his wife, not daring to say such a thing to anyone else. But he knew he wasn't alone in the opinion.

Kiyoda took his command position starboard of the periscope well and keyed the intercom. "Sonar, conn, what are you showing on the surface?"

A chartlet in color of their area of operation on his CRT showed the boat's course, speed, depth, and position. Currently they were running almost due north at twelve knots. The operations clock showed they were eighteen minutes into this mode.

"Our immediate area is clear, *Kan-cho-dono.* But we're picking up a faint target about sixty thousand meters out."

"What does it look like?"

"Hard to say for certain, sir, but I'm guessing it's a Russian frigate. Probably a Krivak class."

"Course and speed?" Kiyoda asked. He recognized the sonarman's voice. It was Tsutomu Nakayama, probably the best in the MSDF. At twenty-five he still had the ears, but he also had experience.

"She's inbound. I'd say twenty knots, maybe a little less."

"Keep a sharp watch, Tsutomu. We're going up to take a look. If he changes course or speed let me know immediately."

"Yo-so-ro, Kan-cho." Will do, Captain.

"What's the weather?"

"I'm picking up surface noises. Four to five meter waves."

Kiyoda released the switch. "Bring the boat to periscope depth."

"Hai, Kan-cho, bringing the boat to periscope depth," Minori replied.

"Reduce speed to five knots, and come left to three-four-zero degrees." The winds and seas at this time of year came mostly out of the north with a slight westerly component. By turning the boat into the general direction of the wind, a much safer attitude in which to surface than abeam the seas, they would be ready to come up fast if need be. It could save time and lives in an emergency.

"Very well, reducing speed to five knots, coming *tori-kaji* to new course three-four-zero. *Yo-so-ro.*"

The problem, as Kiyoda saw it, was that Japan would lose her initiative unless she had control of the sea in the region of the home islands, as well as the sea lanes to and from her vital Middle East oil supplies, and down to the Philippines, East Indies, and Australia, where most of the rest of her natural resources came from. Japan was a manufacturing nation. Her factories produced or died. Any disaster involving her raw materials, no matter how slight, any delay, no matter how brief, would be catastrophic.

For the moment, however, Japan faced two major threats: the first from America, which to this point was being handled diplomatically, and the second from Russia, which was still so beset with internal problems that it was becoming increasingly like a wounded animal—dangerous and unpredictable. The U.S. could shut off Japan's supply lines anytime it chose, but the Russian navy, its ponderous presence always looming just off shore, threatened the actual physical security of the home islands. It was, to Kiyoda's way of thinking, intolerable.

He keyed the intercom. "ECMs, conn, we're on the way up. I want you to scan for any emissions from that bogie to our north." ECMs were Electronic Counter Measures, a submarine's electronic defense system.

"Hai, Kan-cho," Lieutenant Masaaki Kawara, their ELINT—Electronic Intelligence—officer said. "Shall I go active, let him know we're here?"

"Negative," Kiyoda said. "Just keep your ears open."

"Hai."

Among the mast-mounted sensors that could be raised above the surface when the boat was brought to periscope depth was the ZPS-8 surveillance radar antenna. If they illuminated the Russian frigate, their own radar signal would give them away. Instead, they would use a series of directional antennae and a pair of omnidirectional arrays, which would pick up and pinpoint the source of any electronic emissions within fifty nautical miles or more, depending how high out of the water they could be raised.

The new speed and course data showed up on Kiyoda's command screen, and he watched as the depth figures counted backward, a pictorial representation of the boat showing a five-degrees-up bubble. Minori was taking it slow. He was not only intelligent, he was cautious when need be. Submarines were nearly blind on the way up because of the turbulence and noises caused by blowing her ballast tanks.

"Leveling off at two-zero meters," Minori reported when they reached periscope depth.

The status panel above the periscope well showed all three ELINT masts coming up.

"The boat is steady and level on course and depth," Minori said. "My board is green."

"Very well," Kiyoda said. His intercom buzzed.

"Conn, ECMs. That bogie is talking to someone in our direction," Lieutenant Kawara reported.

Kiyoda sat forward. "Have we been detected?" He put his tea aside.

"Tie," negative, the ECMs officer replied. There was a slim chance that the Russian frigate's search radar would pick out the ELINT masts from the surface clutter and recognize them for what they were.

"Sonar, conn, what are you showing?"

"Nothing else on my screen, *Kan-cho*," Nakayama said. "Stand by."

Kiyoda figured he was about to find what he had come looking for. "Prepare for emergency dive," he ordered.

Minori didn't miss a beat. "Prepare for emergency dive, *yo-so-ro*," he said.

"Conn, sonar. That bogie is definitely a Krivak class. She's turned directly toward us and is making turns for full speed."

Was it a trap? It was as if the Russian bastards had been waiting for them. But it was what he'd come for.

"Estimated time to intercept?" Kiyoda asked.

"Fifty-four minutes, *Kan-cho*," Lieutenant Takasaki replied instantly, anticipating the request.

It meant that the Russian sub hunter would be in dangerous range soon. But if it wasn't a trap, if the Russians hadn't somehow known that the *Samisho* would be here, then it meant she'd been detected at some point earlier, possibly as she passed through the Soya Strait between Hokkaido and Sakhalin. It was suspected that the Russians had placed submarine detectors on the seabed there.

Minori was watching him.

Kiyoda keyed his intercom. "ECMs, conn. Give me one sweep overhead to thirty miles."

"*Hai*," Lieutenant Kawara said. A moment later he was back, excited. "It's a Helix, three miles out and inbound, very fast."

"Bring your masts in," Kiyoda said calmly, and he looked up at Minori. "Emergency dive. Make your depth two-zero-zero meters."

"Very well," Minori replied, his voice and manner as calm as his captain's. "Blow all tanks, flank speed forward, down full deflection. Make your depth two-zero-zero meters."

"*Yo-so-ro*." The computer-assisted helmsman/planesman repeated the order.

"Sound battle stations," Kiyoda ordered.

Minori hit the battle stations alarm, and a Klaxon horn sounded throughout the boat.

"Load torpedo tubes one and two. Make ready Harpoon one."

This time Minori's left eyebrow went up slightly, but he repeated the orders, and one by one each of the boat's battle stations reported readiness.

"Torpedoes one and two ready," the torpedoman forward said.

"Harpoon one, ready in tube three."

"Give me a continuous firing solution on the . . . intruder," Kiyoda told his weapons control officer.

"Passing four-zero meters," the dive officer said, but before Minori could reply, the intercom buzzed.

"Conn, ECMs. The helicopter has just dropped a dipping buoy."

"Belay that depth," Kiyoda told Minori. "Make it five-zero meters." A dipping buoy was a sonar unit that enabled the Russian Ka-27 Helix helicopter launched from the frigate to get a fairly accurate fix on their depth and position.

"*Yo-so-ro,* five-zero meters," Minori replied.

"ECMs, conn, put out a decoy," Kiyoda ordered. "Sonar, conn, give me a course, speed, and range to the target."

"Zero-one-zero degrees relative, speed of closure five-one knots, range just under twenty-four nautical miles."

Kiyoda instantly did the sums and subtractions in his head. "Come right ten degrees to course three-five-zero."

"*Hai,* coming *omo-kaji,* ten degrees to three-five-zero," Minori said. It put them bow on to the Russian frigate.

"Weapons, give me a final firing solution on the Harpoon," Kiyoda said. The GRX-2(B) torpedoes had an effective range of fifteen miles, but the Sub-Harpoon could be used to sixty nautical miles.

"*Kan-cho,* is this a drill?" Lieutenant Takasaki asked. Like Minori, he was one of the bright ones out of the Maritime Self Defense Force Academy, and Kiyoda had handpicked him. The man's loyalty was absolute.

Rectitude and justice, Kiyoda had learned, were the principles that it was time to die when it was right to die, and to strike when it was right to strike. His men and officers all understood that. Mishima had understood it, just as the old man, Sokichi Kamiya, understood it perfectly. Before this patrol Kiyoda had gone to see the man in the mountains outside of Tokyo. They'd sat in the garden listening to the gurgling water and the gentle music of the windchime that hung in a gnarled old tree.

"Remember that revenge is justified only on behalf of one's superiors and benefactors," *Kamiya-san* had told him. "Revenge may never be used to correct the wrongs done to yourself, your wife, or your children."

"This is not a drill," Kiyoda said. "Give me a firing solution and open torpedo door three."

"*Hai,* the solution is coming up," the weapons control officer replied.

Kiyoda hesitated. The sounds made by the opening torpedo-tube door would be picked up by the chopper's sonobuoy, and understood for what they were.

"*Kan-cho,* sonar, we've got a high-speed screw incoming," Nakayama said excitedly. "I think the Helix dropped a torpedo on us."

"ECMs, conn, get it off our tail," Kiyoda ordered, keeping his voice calm. Everything was happening as he'd planned it. The Russians were easy to manipulate, especially now. "Come left thirty degrees to new course three-two-zero, and ring for emergency stop."

There was no way they could outrun the torpedo, so their only recourse was to make it think they had by turning and slowing down while releasing a stream of bubblemakers that would drift straight ahead at the old speed long enough for the torpedo to home in on the false target.

"Give me the new solution," Kiyoda said. Minori glanced over him and a slight smile creased the corners of his mouth. He understood.

"The solution is on my board," Lieutenant Takasaki reported crisply. He too was excited.

"Conn, *Kan-cho,* the torp took the bait!"

"Hai," Kiyoda said. "Watch for the second one." The Helix carried two torpedoes. "Match bearings and shoot tube three."

Takasaki hesitated a fraction of a second, then uncaged the firing switch and flipped it. "Missile away," he called out.

"Time to impact?"

"I'm estimating forty-eight seconds after surface ignition," Takasaki said.

The Sub-Harpoon was blown out of the torpedo tube and was carried to the surface in a buoyant canister that was jettisoned when the missile came to launch position. At that point its rocket motors fired, and it accelerated toward its target at just under Mach one, its terminal radar active until lock-on. It was simple, and very effective. In this version, the warhead consisted of seven hundred fifty pounds of high explosives jacketed in a high-carbon-steel case designed to penetrate well within the bowels of a ship before it blew.

Takasaki was watching the launch clock. "Ignition now," he called out.

"Sonar, conn, what's our bogie doing?"

"Same course and speed, *Kan-cho.*"

"Watch for the torp . . ."

"Here it comes, here it comes, but it's farther away this time," the sonarman radioed. "Right on our starboard bow."

"Come right ten degrees to three-three-zero," Kiyoda said. "Target number one on that torpedo and launch when ready."

It was a tricky maneuver. Minori had the boat turning practically in its own length, and even before the turn was completed Takasaki launched their torpedo from tube one.

"Eight seconds to impact," he called out.

"Come left one-five-zero degrees to new course one-eight-zero, emergency dive to two-five-zero meters."

"Hai, coming left one-five-zero degrees to one-eight-

zero, emergency dive to two-five-zero meters," Minori repeated, and the boat heeled over to port, nose down as it accelerated.

A tremendous explosion hammered the hull.

"We got it," the sonarman reported unnecessarily, and Kiyoda laughed. It had begun.

"Give me a damage report," Minori was shouting into the intercom.

Takasaki was looking at the captain. "Shouldn't we wait to see what damage we've done to that frigate?"

"Time to impact?" Kiyoda asked.

Takasaki checked his board. "Nine seconds."

"I trust your shooting, Shuichiyo. Besides, I don't want that Helix crew picking up our sail number."

"They'll know," Minori said.

"But they fired the first shot," Kiyoda said.

The snow had tapered off in the late morning hours, and by early afternoon most of Washington, D.C., was back to normal. By 6:30, when Carrara was able to leave his office, the parking lot had been plowed, although the forecast was for more of the white stuff overnight.

He'd done a lot of thinking about what McGarvey had told him, but he wasn't in the position to do his old friend much good, although it was his understanding that the meeting with Yemlin had gone off without a hitch. He'd gotten that call from a Yemlin aide at home last night.

Deputy Director Lawrence Danielle wasn't saying much, and nothing had come down from the seventh floor. But as he told Mac, it wasn't likely that the DCI or the White House would be interested in helping out. It was a private-sector problem, and official policy was to leave it at that. After the President's economic summit in Tokyo the situation might be different, but they'd have to wait and see.

His car phone buzzed just as he was pulling out of his parking slot. He stopped and picked it up.

"Yes?"

"Mr. Danielle wanted to catch you before you got too

far," the DDCI's secretary said. "He would like you in his office as soon as possible."

"I'm still in the parking lot," Carrara said, pulling back into his slot. "Be right up."

Danielle was waiting for him in his conference room, a dozen large photographs spread out on the table. With him was the Agency's senior photo analyst, Nathan Conley, a short, slightly built man who'd come to them from the Defense Intelligence Agency after the University of Minnesota. Carrara had worked with him before.

"I don't know if this is coincidence or not, Phil, coming on the heels of Kirk McGarvey's visit, but it sure as hell is going to get the DCI's attention," Danielle said. He was an older man, stoop shouldered, with thinning white hair and a pale, almost translucent face.

"What have we got?" Carrara asked.

"These shots were taken by our KH-14 recon satellite less than an hour ago," Conley said. "Over the Tatar Strait, between the Siberian mainland and Sakhalin Island. We got lucky with the weather."

Carrara studied a few of the photographs, but it was hard to make out anything for sure, although in one sequence it seemed as if he was seeing a burning ship.

"At 2215 Zulu, a Russian Federal Navy Krivak-class frigate was attacked and sunk by what appears to be a Sub-Harpoon launch," Conley said. "We're still checking, but we think the Russian ship was the *Menshinsky,* which sailed from Vladivostok six days ago."

"We did this?" Carrara asked, hardly believing what he was being told.

"No, sir," Conley said. "We have no assets in the region at the moment. Which leaves only the Japanese."

Carrara looked up. Danielle's mood was impossible to gauge, except that he didn't seem happy. Mac would be called back, and Carrara was getting the feeling that his old friend could be right about the Japanese. It was a sobering thought.

It was midnight before Carrara could get away. There'd been no word from the Russians about the incident, but

Navy Intelligence reported that six surface vessels were converging on the location, and SOSUS—Sound Surveillance—monitors in the region had picked up the signatures of three Russian submarines, one of them a boomer—an Oscar-class cruise missile boat—with more than enough firepower to start and finish a war.

There would be nothing from Europe for another few hours, nor had Japan made any comment, although CIA's Tokyo Station reported a lot of activity at the Ministry of Foreign Affairs.

CIA Director Roland Murphy, the General, had briefed the President at 10:00 P.M. and was expected back at the White House at nine in the morning for an update. In the meantime the Agency was on emergency footing. There was no telling how the Russians would respond, or how the incident was going to affect the upcoming economic summit meeting in Tokyo.

"What the hell are the damn fools thinking about?" the DCI had asked at one point.

"Maybe it's an isolated incident," Deputy Director of Intelligence Tommy Doyle suggested. "Hell, General, it might have been nothing more than a sub-driver with an itchy finger. The fever is running high over there just now."

"I don't buy that for one minute, and neither will the President. They pick their sub skippers just as carefully as we do. For my money it was a directed action. And if the bastards wanted to stir up a hornet's nest, they sure did it."

The one stroke of good fortune was that the news media hadn't gotten the story yet, although Tokyo Station's latest cable warned that the international press corps was beginning to stir, and downstairs the Public Affairs night-duty officer had received two calls from the *Washington Post* wanting to know what was going on in Tokyo. The media couldn't be kept in the dark for long, but all the White House wanted were a few hours to figure it out before they had to start making policy and answering questions.

Before he left, Carrara went upstairs to Danielle's

office. The DCI, like nearly everyone else, was dug in for the night. "I'm going home for a couple of hours, boss."

Danielle looked up. "What about the Europeans?"

"I'll be back before they start opening up. Dan can start on the early stuff if anything comes in. I need a shower, a shave, and a clean shirt."

Danielle stared at him thoughtfully. "We need to call McGarvey on this one. He's hit too close to home. Where the hell is he getting his information?"

"He's still got friends in the business."

"Too many friends," Danielle said.

"Yes, sir," Carrara nodded.

Carrara pulled off the parkway a couple of miles south of Agency headquarters and telephoned McGarvey's hotel from a gas station pay phone. "We have to talk."

"Where are you?" McGarvey asked.

"I'm on the parkway. I'll be there in fifteen minutes." He hung up, his palms cold and wet. He was committing treason for friendship. McGarvey was owed, he told himself. Nonetheless, the headhunters, and ultimately Murphy, would have his balls nailed to the wall if and when he was tumbled. Activities prosecutable under the National Secrets Act.

All the way downriver and across the Key Bridge the same refrain played itself in his head. A betrayal of a basic position of trust. The most heinous of crimes against his country.

It had begun to snow lightly by the time Carrara pulled into the Four Seasons Hotel parking lot. McGarvey was waiting, and as soon as he got in Carrara headed for the darkest corner he could find and parked.

"Did you get word from Yemlin?" McGarvey asked.

"Not yet," Carrara replied. "But everything has changed. I just came from Langley, and I have to get back as soon as possible."

"What is it, Phil?"

"Six hours ago a Russian Navy frigate was sunk in the Tatar Strait by a sub-sea missile that was probably launched from a Japanese submarine. We've been listening to radio chatter all night. No survivors. Not one man out of a crew of two hundred plus. In the meantime, nobody is officially saying a thing. We're waiting for the Europeans to come on line in the next couple of hours, and at nine the DCI briefs the President. But the Russians are pumping one shitload of resources into the region. No one knows what the hell they're getting ready for, but it doesn't look good. The Japanese may be going after Sakhalin Island finally, and the Russians are responding."

"It's not that," McGarvey said.

"You're going to get called on this one, Mac," Carrara said. "They're going to want to know where you're getting your information."

"I read the goddamned newspapers, Phil," McGarvey said sharply. "But the Japanese aren't after Sakhalin."

"They're showing that they're able and willing to protect their home waters. We've gone all through that."

"Maybe," McGarvey said. "Maybe it's something else. Are we taking sides yet?"

"It's too soon for that."

"Was the attack unprovoked?"

"Unknown."

McGarvey looked away for a second. "What do you think?"

"We'll probably end up jumping all over the Japanese. Demand they apologize, demand they make reparations. Tokyo will deny any prior knowledge. They'll say it was a sub-driver who went berserk."

"Maybe they'll be telling the truth," McGarvey said. "How do I contact Yemlin?"

Carrara's breath caught in his throat, although he'd suspected McGarvey would ask that. "If Murphy thinks you're involved he'll come gunning for you. Won't be much I'll be able to do. Fact is, I'll probably fall with you."

"This is important," McGarvey said.

"That it is, Mac."

"I'll keep you in the loop."

"Yeah, do that," Carrara said. "It's a blind number,

untraceable. No one will answer the phone, but when the connection is made, give them your name and your message and hang up. If Yemlin wants to see you, he will."

Arlington Cemetery opened at 8:00 A.M., and fifteen minutes later Yemlin, wearing the same dark overcoat as before, came down the broad path past Kennedy's grave. Even from a distance, McGarvey could see that the Russian was troubled.

"I'm assuming you've heard the latest," Yemlin said as McGarvey fell in beside him. "The situation is very disturbing."

"Is Moscow willing to help us?"

"Yes," the SUR officer said. "But everything has changed. You can understand that my superiors want to talk with you. They have many questions."

"All right," McGarvey said. "But it'll have to be very soon, Viktor Pavlovich. With what has just happened, your superiors must understand the urgency of our request."

"There is a 2:20 flight from Dulles this afternoon. It will put us in Moscow by late morning."

McGarvey stopped short. "I'm not going to Moscow."

"It's the only way," the Russian said.

"An airplane factory worth a billion dollars is plenty of leverage. I'll meet them in Paris."

"They won't go along with that. Maybe before, but not now."

"Then the deal's off."

"I don't believe you. Think of this from our viewpoint. We're under the gun, and it's possible that you can help us more, for the moment, with the truth than with an airplane factory."

"I'll give you the truth."

"We have to be certain," Yemlin insisted. "In Paris that may be impossible. But in Moscow we believe you will tell the truth. It's up to you. We will not kidnap you."

It was up to him, McGarvey thought. But he didn't

know if he could face Moscow. Not yet. The price he'd have to pay was still too high, the dangers too great. Facing Yemlin was bad enough, but facing the others, facing his own past, could prove to be more than he could handle.

FOUR

Riding in a cab downtown from his hotel in Georgetown, McGarvey was struck by how beautiful Washington had become under a fresh blanket of snow, but he felt like a stranger here. Despite the extraordinary happenings of the past few days, he was still on the outside looking in. He was a civilian. If he got himself backed into a corner he would be on his own. There'd be no cavalry to the rescue.

After his meeting with Carrara he'd tried the Gales Creek telephone number Kennedy had given him, but the woman who answered could only tell him that Kennedy was en route back to Washington, D.C., and that she would get a message to him as soon as possible.

Against his better judgment he went to Dominique Kilbourne's Watergate apartment. He figured that if he called her first she would hold him off until morning. But he didn't have the time. He was developing an odd, between-the-shoulders feeling that something disastrous was on the verge of happening. Kennedy had come to him too late in the situation. Forces beyond anyone's control were beginning to gather, to have a life of their own.

It took a long time before Dominique answered the door and awoke sufficiently to understand who it was and let him in. She wore a thick terry-cloth bathrobe, and without makeup she looked younger, Midwestern scrubbed.

"You're not exactly a pleasant surprise, Mr. McGarvey," she said. Her voice was soft, and rounded by sleep.

"Something's come up. I need to talk to Kennedy."

"You'd better come in."

"Is he coming here?" McGarvey asked.

Her eyes widened momentarily, and her nostrils flared. "No, she said sharply. "What made you think he would be?"

"He told me that you'd been lovers."

"I see," she said evenly. "That's past tense. He's not here now." She turned and padded into the apartment.

McGarvey followed her into the kitchen where she put on the tea kettle. "Nothing for me."

"The cognac is in the same place in the living room."

"I was told Kennedy was on his way to Washington."

"He'll be touching down at eight, and after he checks in at the Hyatt Regency, he'll either come to my office, or meet with Tom Hailey at American. I imagine his afternoon will be busy too."

"I want you to meet him at the airport and set up a lunch for me at his hotel."

"Do you have a cigarette?" she asked. "I quit three years ago, but now seems to be a good time to start again."

McGarvey gave her a cigarette and held the match. "Get the message to him, Ms. Kilbourne."

"Dominique," she said, and inhaled. "I'd call him now, but that would be too public for what you've got to tell him, I think. So I'll do as you ask, and meet his flight."

"Good," McGarvey said, and he turned to go.

"In the meantime I've learned something about you since you were here last, and now I want to know more."

He turned back. It was always the same. "You're like a very bright flame," Kathleen had told him when he'd gotten back from Europe the last time. "Women are like moths around you. I don't understand it. Even your own daughter, who should know better, is blind." It was true, but he didn't know why.

"What have you learned about me?" he asked.

"Get your brandy," she said. "You were a spy for the CIA, and you still do work for them sometimes. Freelance."

"You don't have to be a part of this. Tell Kennedy that you're quitting. He can come up with another Washington contact for me."

Her eyes were bright, and she was frightened, but she was trying hard to hide it. "You were an assassin."

McGarvey was surprised that she knew what she did, but Kennedy had explained that Guerin's CEO had an in at Langley. It was disturbing though that the general would allow his chief counsel to give out such information. Or even hint at it.

"Our government does not hire assassins," he said.

"It's what you do."

"My job is saving lives," McGarvey said gently. "That's all I ever did."

"The Cold War is over, Mr. McGarvey. There's no more threat of nuclear war. The Pentagon's budget has been cut, and it'll be cut even more. But that's not good enough for you, because you enjoy it. I can see it in your eyes. You fucking love it!"

"Get out while you can, Ms. Kilbourne... Dominique," he said. "Forget you ever heard my name."

"I want to know why."

When Moses had challenged God for being too harsh, God had told him, "I am what I am." And He had left it at that. People were not gods, they were expected to change, to go with the flow, to accept the new and discard the old. But as a child he had his own set of demons that he'd never managed to exorcise. His parents were dead, the Wall was down, the Soviet Union no longer existed, but he still had his demons, stronger now in some ways than before. Probably because of the fertile ground they'd had to grow in since Kansas.

It was her last question—why?—that had sent him away. He had no answer.

The cabby dropped him off at the Hyatt Regency

Washington on D Street and New Jersey Avenue. He went inside to the atrium restaurant where David Kennedy was waiting for him. Like Dominique, the former astronaut lived in a different world than McGarvey did. What cop, after a few years on the force dealing on a daily basis with the dregs of society, could look at the world through anything but a jaundiced eye? Spies were the same; they saw conspiracies and dangers lurking everywhere. And most of the good ones he knew at Langley, and elsewhere, wore their cynicism like a badge of honor because it didn't come naturally; they'd earned it.

"Have you ordered yet?" he asked, reaching Kennedy's table.

Kennedy looked up. "I was waiting for you," he said, and they shook hands. "Dominique is shook up."

"I know," McGarvey said, sitting down. "My CIA friend stopped by last night."

"I talked to Al Vasilanti, and he said the CIA was hinting that what we were doing might not sit so well on the Hill."

McGarvey wished he could have been there. According to Dominique, Vasilanti wasn't a man to be pushed around. Guerin's annual budget, as the company's CEO liked to point out, was larger than the budgets of ninety percent of all the countries in the world. "Should give us diplomatic status."

"What'd he tell them?"

Kennedy smiled, though it was clear he was troubled. "Told them to go to hell. He's behind you one hundred percent, but he told me to tell you to watch your ass. If you get in over your head there might not be anything we can do for you."

"What else did he tell you?"

"Told me to trust my instincts or get out of the business. And since I'm not going to fire you, I'm going to take you at your word. You said that the least we could face would be charges of industrial espionage, and at the most treason. You've got to admit, Mac, that's pretty heavy going."

"Cold feet?"

"Goddamned right I've got cold feet, but you're the expert. You tell me."

Their waiter came. Kennedy ordered a tossed salad and a cup of tea. McGarvey ordered a brandy neat, no water, no ice.

"You must have had a bad night," Kennedy said when the waiter was gone.

"I've had worse," McGarvey replied. "Did Vasilanti say who he spoke with at the Agency, and when?"

"Lawrence Danielle, evidently just after you'd met with Phil Carrara."

The DCI Roland Murphy would have called Vasilanti if Danielle had brought the problem across the hall to him. But it was the DCI's style to insulate his boss. This time it would work to their advantage.

"I met with Viktor Yemlin again this morning. He's invited me to go to Moscow with him. We leave from Dulles in a few hours."

"Jesus," Kennedy said softly. He looked across the dining room as if he expected someone was listening to them. "You'll have to stall him. We'll need at least twenty-four hours to put together a negotiating team. We'll fly over on our own equipment, of course."

"They want me, David. Alone."

Kennedy looked at him. "Why?"

"Because of what happened yesterday afternoon, and because they want to make sure that I'll tell them the truth."

"What are you talking about?"

"A Japanese submarine attacked and sank a Russian naval vessel in the Tatar Strait . . . in waters the Russians are claiming as their own."

Kennedy was stunned. "There's been nothing in the news."

"There won't be, at least for the next day or two," McGarvey said. "Phil Carrara told me last night, and Yemlin confirmed it this morning. There're going to be a lot of people wanting to know why we picked just now to ask for help spying on the Japanese."

"What do we tell them?"

"The truth."

"The CIA didn't buy it, what makes you think the Russians will?" Kennedy asked. "You can't be serious about going alone to Moscow. If something happened there wouldn't be a damned thing we could do for you. And I don't think the CIA would lift a finger either."

"I know," McGarvey said. He'd gone over this with himself a dozen times in the last few hours. "But we asked for their help, and now they're willing to talk about it. So what do we do?"

"Christ, what a mess," Kennedy said looking away again.

"It's become a different world out there, David. One I don't think anyone really understands yet. Our only choice is to deal with it as best we can."

"What if you're wrong?"

"Then I'm wrong, and we go from there," McGarvey said, his gut in a knot. "But if I'm right, and if we don't even try to stop them, a lot of innocent people could get hurt."

"Yeah," Kennedy said softly.

"It's a bitch, but it was us who made it this way."

Yemlin was waiting for him in a VIP lounge at Dulles when he showed up at 2:00 P.M. An Aeroflot Ilyushin Il-86 was parked at the gate, connected to the boarding area by a jetway. The aircraft looked old, and shabby, its paint job faded and peeling. Once the largest airline in the world, the Russian carrier was in desperate straits.

"I was about to give up hope," Yemlin said. "I didn't think you were coming."

"This is important to my company, Viktor Pavlovich. I've met with my boss about the details of our offer."

Yemlin peered at him for a long beat, as if he were trying to decide what to make of what he was hearing. Something had changed since this morning. The Russian no longer seemed apologetic as before. Evidently he'd gotten further instructions from Moscow. "They'll want to talk to you about that."

"I've got nothing to hide," McGarvey said. "I came to you for help, remember?"

Taking his place beside Yemlin as the only passengers in first class, it felt like Russia already to McGarvey—even before the jumbo jet left the U.S. The interior of the aircraft was just as threadbare and chipped as the exterior had suggested, and as all of Russia was. McGarvey remembered the first time he'd come into Moscow with his chief of station. It was his first assignment. He'd had the thought that the city needed a coat of paint. A major spring cleaning that all the *babushkas* out sweeping the roads with straw brooms couldn't accomplish. The country needed refurbishing, remodeling, updating. Just as this aircraft did. Aeroflot might be having its troubles at home, but in the Western world it wouldn't last five minutes with shabby, outdated equipment like this. From a practical standpoint he had to wonder if the jetliner would make it across the Atlantic. It'd be a hell of a note, he thought wryly, to die this way.

Yemlin had a word with the crew, and even before they pulled away from the gate first class was closed off from the rest of the plane, and a good-looking young woman offered them drinks. By the time they were airborne McGarvey was on his second cognac, neat, no water, no ice, but he was still tied up in knots. He was going back, going back and back, down and down, as if he were falling into a bottomless pit with darkness all around him.

Her name was Tania Fedorovna Sorokin, and she worked as a technical translator and adviser for the government, rendering into Russian sensitive Western technical documents that she would explain in lay terms to the politicians. She was good at her job, but from the beginning she'd never trusted Brezhnev. "The man is mad for power, and he'll lead the country to nuclear holocaust before he'll step aside."

So far as she knew, or allowed herself to know, McGarvey was a dissident American scientist. An intellectual who wanted to end war once and for all by freely sharing nuclear information with anyone who wanted it. If there are no secrets there will be no wars.

There were a half-dozen of them, McGarvey told her, but in order for their struggle to have any chance of success they needed hard information about the Brezhnev government, and the extent of Brezhnev's grasp of Western technical secrets. At that time a great deal of effort was being spent on the Strategic Defense Initiative, both in the West and in the Soviet Union, and information was power.

Tania had agreed to spy for them. "But don't let me down," she'd told McGarvey. "Whoever you really work for."

They had become lovers, and McGarvey remembered that he liked lying with her in the hours just before dawn. He would awaken and watch her sleep; watch her chest rise and fall; watch her lips moving sometimes as if she were dreaming; how a few drops of sweat would form on the bridge of her nose, as if she were troubled; how when the morning light finally came the sun would illuminate the peach fuzz at the small of her back. She was a sun person and would come awake then, smiling when she saw him watching her. And they would make love, sometimes slowly with a gentle deliberation and sensitivity for each other's feelings, and at other times passionately, almost cruelly, wanting only to satisfy their own needs. It was never bad with them; sometimes better than other times, but never bad.

At home in the United States he'd been married to his first wife for four years. They'd met at Kansas State, and when he'd gone to work for the CIA he'd dragged her around the world. But it wasn't her life, and their fighting became just as passionate as their lovemaking had been. She began to smoke, mostly to irritate him, and to drink, to drown her little voices, and so he had divorced her.

No matter what she'd wanted, or thought she'd wanted by her actions, divorce had not been it. Somehow she'd secretly hoped that she could change him. Take away the hex that his parents had somehow put on him. But that was impossible. By the time she'd finally realized that it was too late, it already was. In that she and his second wife, Kathleen, were kindred spirits.

McGarvey went to Moscow alone, where he developed the network and fell in love with Tania. For that year he felt whole, the only thing missing from his life besides children (his first wife, Audrey, had not wanted them) was his parents who'd died a few years earlier. He'd wanted to show his dad what he was doing, how he was taking the fight to the Soviet Union, and how they were winning.

Walter Porterfield was his control officer. Since McGarvey was living on the economy, they'd set up a series of letter drops, two escape routes, and three face-to-face meeting points. The drops were serviced on a weekly basis, and sometimes more often because early on Tania and the others who worked in various branches of the Kremlin were supplying him with gold seam product, which was the old term for first rate intelligence information. Once a month, he and Porterfield met face-to-face, if for nothing other than moral support; it was lonely in the field, and it was nice to speak English from time to time.

During their last meeting, Porterfield had informed him that Audrey was sick, possibly very sick, and that the Company would pull him out for an emergency leave so that he could go back to the States. "It's up to you," Porterfield had said.

"She's my ex, Walt. Which means I don't go running when she calls." McGarvey remembered that decision as clearly as if he were making it at this moment. "It's probably alcohol poisoning. She'll go to a detox clinic, get clean for a month or so, then get out and start it all over again. Should I go back for that?"

Porterfield had given him an odd look. "Maybe you should get out of Moscow anyway. You know, take a little vacation. You look like shit."

McGarvey chuckled. "Thanks for the vote of confidence, but you've seen the stuff coming out of here."

"It's nothing short of fabulous, Mac. Everybody at home is shitting purple peach seeds. Vanhorne would make you President if he could find a way of pulling it off."

"Don't ask me to leave just now."

Porterfield had shaken his head. "You'll have to get out sooner or later."

"Right, but not now."

By then Tania had become something special, and she was falling in love with him. It was a common occurrence, he'd been taught at the CIA's training school. The mark, under the tremendous pressure of betraying his or her country, will transform that emotional energy into love for the agent runner. It's a life jacket for them, so be careful you don't damage that feeling, because they might grab at another straw—perhaps even their own authorities—to save themselves.

But he was vulnerable too. Rubbed raw by four years of a marriage, half of which had been spent in utter hell. The irony of it, he remembered thinking at the time, was that he still loved his ex-wife. He just couldn't live with her. So he had told Tania things, had made promises to her that he should not have made, and she believed him. Then Yemlin had arrested them, interrogated them, testified dispassionately at their trials, and had visited them once in Volodga. In the end they were all dead; most of them at the hospital, some of them on the way out, Tania in the snow just short of the Finnish border . . . and at home, Audrey.

Yemlin looked up. "Tomorrow will be a very long day. Perhaps you should try to get some sleep, Kirk."

After the Second World War the American Office of Strategic Services, which was the forerunner of the CIA, set up a new West German secret intelligence service with headquarters outside Munich. Named the *Bundesnachrichtendienst,* or Federal Intelligence Service, the

BND was started by former Nazi intelligence officers who had been politically correct enough to have fought communist Russia and not the U.S. and its Western allies. Headed by Reinhard Gehlen, Hitler's chief communist hunter, the service grew to become one of the most effective intelligence agencies in the world. But, like all such organizations on both sides of the Iron Curtain, the BND had been penetrated, and not all the penetration agents had been discovered. Among them was Karl Schey, who'd been in charge of vetting new recruits, and who from the very beginning had been an agent for the Stasi. He'd retired at the rank of brigadier general several years ago and had been among the fortunate deep-cover Stasi agents whose files had been destroyed before the Wall came down and the two Germanies were reunited. Mueller had a hand in that, and the general was aware of it. From time to time he had been of some help to the Berlin Hit League with inside information. The general still maintained powerful connections with the BND, Interpol, and all the major intelligence services across Europe, as well as Great Britain and the U.S.

Mueller stood in the cold darkness just within the tall stone walls of the general's six-acre compound south of the city, on the road to Garmisch-Partenkirchen, waiting for the last of the guests to leave in their Mercedes 560SELs, Jaguar V-12s, and Maserati sedans. Of all evenings, Schey had picked this one to entertain. But then it was a common occurrence. The general had always managed to surround himself with powerful and influential people, as if they were insurance against his being caught.

At least it had stopped snowing. Mueller shifted his weight and grunted as a sharp pain stitched his left side. He'd cracked a couple of ribs when the helicopter had come down hard in a field a few kilometers from the German border, twenty kilometers from Karlsruhe and the A8 Munich Autobahn. Wind and blowing snow had made it nearly impossible for the pilot to control the machine, and they were lucky to have gotten down alive.

"I don't think one in ten thousand pilots could have done as well," Mueller told the Frenchman.

He raised his pistol and shot the pilot in the forehead at point-blank range.

Getting across the unguarded border in any weather would have been child's play, even in daylight, but because of the snowstorm he was certain that no one had seen him, and in all likelihood the downed chopper would not be discovered for several hours, perhaps not even until the next morning.

He'd hitched a ride into Karlsruhe with a hospital linen salesman from Amsterdam, where he'd taken a Europabus to Stuttgart and from there the train to Munich, using most of his remaining German currency. At the airport he found a Volkswagen Jetta in the long-term parking lot with one back door unlocked, forced the steering lock, pried the ignition switch out of its slot, and hot-wired it.

In a shoulder bag he carried something in excess of 200,000F that they'd realized from the bank robbery (there hadn't been enough time to count it exactly), three legitimate West German passports, and a half-dozen credit cards, also still good so far as he knew. But before he went farther he had to know for sure if his documents would hold up, he had to find out where the manhunt for him was concentrated, and he had to exchange the francs for another currency, all of which the general could help him with.

General Schey was in his mid-sixties and lived alone except for a housekeeper/cook and her husband who worked as a groundskeeper, chauffeur, and occasional butler. They lived in a separate wing of the sprawling two-story orange brick house, and when the general's guests were gone they would be occupied in cleaning up.

It was well after midnight when the last automobile pulled out and headed down the long driveway, and the front lights were extinguished. Mueller, very stiff and cold, circled through the woods to the rear of the house, keeping to the deeper shadows along the edge of the six-car garage that faced a parking area. So far as he knew there were no outside guards or alarm systems. The general didn't believe in them. But the house itself was probably wired against intruders.

Light spilled from a large window onto a back porch and small trash Dumpster. Mueller could see it was the kitchen. An older woman, wearing a long white apron that was stained, was saying something to a much younger, good-looking woman who wore the black-and-white uniform of a maid. The older woman did not seem happy. A moment later the gray-haired man wearing a butler's uniform, his tie loose, came into the kitchen, took off his jacket and hung it over the back of a chair. Suddenly he got angry and shouted something at the young woman, who flipped her head, turned, and stalked out of the kitchen. The man said something else, then took a bottle of what looked like liquor from a cabinet, poured two drinks, and he and the older woman sat at the table and drank together, the bottle between them.

Mueller darted across the parking area, mounted the four steps to the porch, and flattened against the wall beside the back door, listening and waiting for an alarm to be sounded or for someone to come. When nothing happened, he tried the door. It was unlocked. He let himself into the back corridor. To the right, a door was partially open into a large pantry and storage area. Light came from under the kitchen door at the other side of the pantry. Straight ahead was a third door, which Mueller figured opened onto a main corridor that probably led to the stair hall at the front of the house. To his immediate left was a narrow staircase that led up. It would be used by the servants, but there would be a connecting hall to the general's second-floor living quarters. He took the stairs, careful to make as little noise as possible.

At the top was a bathroom and two small bedrooms, beyond which was a much larger suite of rooms including a separate bathroom. Mueller didn't know about the young woman, but one of the smaller bedrooms looked as if it had been occupied by a teenager. Clothing hung in the closet, on the backs of chairs, and over the bedposts; a robe and some other clothing hung on the back of the door, and several photographs of an old, smiling woman had been taped to a mirror above the dresser. A vanity table was filled with makeup and brushes.

Straight ahead a door opened into the second-floor corridor directly across from the stairs. Mueller was in time to see the general and the young woman enter a room to the left and shut the door.

So, Mueller thought grinning, the general was a human after all. In the BND he'd had the reputation of being "Iron Karl," the man without a weakness, the man who never smiled.

Waiting a moment to make sure no one else was coming upstairs, Mueller slipped into the corridor, hurried to the left, and let himself into the bedroom next to the general's. He laid his shoulder bag aside, took off his coat, and pressed his ear against the wall. He could hear vague, indistinct voices, but not well enough to make out what they were saying.

Mueller had been taking chances, and surviving, all of his life. He had to have the general's help, and he had to have it now, tonight, before the Action Service, and probably Interpol, tightened their net, making escape impossible.

He took out his pistol, checked the load and the safety catch, then went to the general's door and knocked softly. If he had to murder the entire house staff, he would. Their deaths would be of no consequence so long as he could get safely out of Europe.

"What is it?" the general called.

Mueller knocked softly again, glancing over his shoulder to make certain that the old man or woman from downstairs weren't coming up.

"Was ist?" the general demanded irritably and opened the door. His eyes widened slightly when he saw who it was.

Beyond the general, Mueller caught a glimpse of the young woman, the top of her dress unbuttoned, going into the bathroom.

"I'm in the next room," Mueller whispered, looking into the general's eyes for any sign that the man would betray him. There was nothing but impatience.

"I was expecting you," General Schey said. "Go back in there and I'll join you in a couple of hours."

Mueller reached out and took the general's scrawny arm by the biceps. "Get rid of her now."

"No."

"I'll kill them all, you included."

"I have no doubt that you mean it," the general said, undaunted, "in which case you'd be captured or dead within twenty-four hours. Interpol is already looking for you. The French found the helicopter at the border. They know you're in Germany."

The normally inefficient French had evidently taken umbrage with him for what he'd done and were moving much faster than normal.

"You'll be leaving before dawn, and you'll be out of Europe within twelve hours. It's all been arranged."

"But where?" Mueller asked, surprised despite himself.

"America. I have a friend in Washington who has need of your services. I talked to him a few hours ago. He's getting everything ready. Now get out of sight until I can come for you."

Mueller stepped back, the gun hanging loosely at his side. He was going back to America.

The Aeroflot Ilyushin touched down at Moscow's Sheremeteyvo Airport a few minutes before eleven in the morning, local. Surface air temperature was minus twenty degrees Fahrenheit, and as they taxied to the terminal McGarvey could see smoke rising straight up from chimneys, which meant there was no wind to make it feel colder. A black Zil was waiting for them when they parked, and a tall angular man in civilian clothes got out from the back seat.

The other passengers were held in their seats until McGarvey and Yemlin donned their coats, got their bags from the overhead, and went down the boarding steps to the apron.

"The man waiting for us by the car is my boss, Colonel Amosovich Lyalin," Yemlin said at McGarvey's side. "He's a good man, Kirk, but you will have to play straight with him if you want our help."

"If he's the highest-ranking authority I'm going to be allowed to speak to, we might as well turn around and go back to Washington," McGarvey answered.

"Not the highest, just the first."

They hurried across the apron to Colonel Lyalin, and Yemlin made the introductions.

"I can't say that it's good to be here, Colonel," McGarvey said, shaking the man's hand. "I thought I would start with General Polunin."

Lyalin's left eyebrow rose. "You and I have some things to clear up first."

McGarvey stepped closer and switched to Russian. "We're talking about a one billion dollar airplane factory, plus a long-term relationship that will generate a lot of American dollars for your economy. Lean on me, and you'll fuck the entire deal, Colonel."

Lyalin showed no reaction. It was bitterly cold, but he made no move to invite them into the warmth of the car. "How did you find out about the Japanese attack?" he asked.

"I'm not at liberty to say."

"This is important to us, Kirk," Yemlin said. "No matter what we do, the international repercussions could be damaging."

It was a rare admission on the part of a Russian, even these days, and it told McGarvey just how worried they were about the Japanese.

"It was an old friend, but I can't say anything beyond that, except that I'm here representing Guerin Airplane Company, not my government."

"You want us to spy on the Japanese for your company, Mr. McGarvey," Lyalin said patiently. "Coincident with your request, the Japanese sank one of our navy ships. All hands were lost. That's two hundred twenty men and officers . . . boys, many of them. You can understand why we are so . . . anxious to find out what you know."

"That's why I'm here. To tell you what we know and what we suspect and ask for your help to find out more, in exchange for a long-term financial investment."

"Perhaps you have come to the wrong people, Mr. McGarvey," Lyalin said after a long measure.

"If it's any consolation, Colonel, I don't think the attacks on our company, or the attack on your ship, were directed by the Japanese government. I think private interests are at work here."

"You claim not to speak for your government?"

"That's right," McGarvey said.

"Do they know that you are here?"

"By now, yes, assuming that the FBI still keeps track of who comes and goes aboard your aircraft."

Lyalin glanced at Yemlin, then nodded. "Let's not keep the general waiting."

The interior of the limousine was overheated, and wedged between Lyalin and Yemlin, McGarvey was sweating heavily by the time they had cleared the airport gate and were speeding toward the city at nearly one hundred miles per hour. There were only two speeds in all of Russia: very slow for ninety-nine-point-nine percent of the people, or very fast for the elite or the frightened.

The birch forests at the side of the road passed in a blur, the landscape gradually opening to farm fields, fallow for the winter, and factories broken down and closed because of the economy.

In 1972 the KGB constructed its new headquarters building off the circumferential highway, Outer Ring Road, that circled Moscow. Copied almost line for line after the CIA's headquarters at Langley, the seven-story structure housed the KGB's, now the SUR's, First Chief Directorate, which was responsible for all foreign operations. It was from here that the spies, the agent provocateurs, the assassins, and the terrorists trained and funded by the Soviet Union had been directed. And still were, McGarvey had no doubt. The spy business had not ended with the Cold War and the breakup of the old Soviet Union, it had merely changed. New masters perhaps, but the targets were essentially the same as they'd always been. The world, after all, was a finite place with only so many nations, armies, and intelligence agencies.

Armed guards at the gate passed them through without checking their credentials, and Colonel Lyalin led them to the seventh floor, which was the carbon of the seventh floor at Langley except that like the airplane this place was in desperate need of paint and repairs. The way everyone acted and talked, however, McGarvey didn't think any of them saw the shabbiness. It was taken for granted.

The colonel left them in an anteroom with a tall, large man who was armed, by the look of the bulge under his suit coat. His eyes never left them until Lyalin came back two minutes later and ushered them into a nicely furnished office.

General Leonty Dmitrevich Polunin, an even larger man, with thick black eyebrows and huge ears, came from behind a massive desk, his face a study in intrigue and mystery. McGarvey found himself thanking whatever gods there were that this one wasn't the director of the entire SUR, or worse, the President of the country. General Polunin, from what McGarvey knew of the man, had been Yeltsin's choice to head the Komitet, but something had gone wrong, and this was as far as he was going to rise in the hierarchy. He wore a well-cut dark gray suit and tie, with no medals or other adornment, yet it was obvious by his bearing that he had a military background and would be accustomed to being obeyed without question. The thought of Polunin facing off with Lawrence Danielle or Phil Carrara was ludicrous. The Russian would have their asses on a platter in nothing flat.

"General, this is Kirk McGarvey," Lyalin said.

"You're certainly something of a surprise, Mr. McGarvey," the general said.

McGarvey shook his hand, the general's grip firm but not crushing. "This isn't a pleasure trip."

"Nobody suspected that you would think so, not even after all these years." Polunin motioned them to a sofa and chairs across the room. "Coffee or tea?"

"Not for me," McGarvey said.

"You are presenting yourself as a man of business this time, very well."

"Within forty-eight hours a team of Guerin engineers, designers, and financial planners could be here to work with whoever will be assigned to the project, General," McGarvey said.

"I'm not a Baranov or a Didenko, but I have read your file. The *complete* file, including Kansas."

"My father loved his country, and he fought for what he believed." McGarvey looked directly into the general's eyes. "He died for his beliefs."

"We didn't kill him."

A hand clutched at McGarvey's heart. "That was a long time ago."

"Then why are you here, Mr. McGarvey? Didn't your experiences at Volodga teach you anything?"

"I don't work for the CIA."

"No?"

"If I did, I wouldn't be here making such an offer, General."

"Was it Phillip Carrara who told you about the Japanese attack?"

"No, but he made the initial contact with Viktor Pavlovich."

"Why?" Polunin shot back, his eyes narrowed.

"Perhaps because he's just as concerned about the Japanese as we are."

"We?"

"Guerin Airplane Company."

"Are you saying that it's not a view shared by Mr. Danielle or General Murphy?"

"I haven't spoken to the Director about it, but Mr. Danielle apparently does not share our concern. At least he didn't on the day before the submarine attack."

"Has he changed his mind?"

"I don't know, General, but it's certainly possible."

"Then who was it told you about the attack, Mr. McGarvey?" Polunin demanded. "We won't go any further until that mystery is cleared up."

It suddenly occurred to McGarvey that General Polunin and the others were frightened. The entire country had its collective back to the wall, and the attitudes of these three men reflected it.

"An airplane factory in what used to be East Germany would be welcomed," he said. "I think the BND might be persuaded to go along with us. I have a few friends in Munich."

The general flared. "We didn't bring you here to bargain with you like Jews."

"Nor did I come here to be threatened," McGarvey said, stiffening. "This country is no longer the superpower it once was, but the SUR has something that *may* be of commercial use to the company I represent. If you help us, we'll help you."

Polunin exchanged glances with Yemlin, then nodded. "Something can be worked out. It will be up to the negotiating team."

McGarvey sat back, surprised by the suddenness of Polunin's flip-flop in position. "I'll send word to Portland."

"The Director wishes to speak with you."

"All right," McGarvey said cautiously.

Polunin smiled wanly. "I think our relationship this time will be mutually advantageous, Mr. McGarvey. Don't you agree?"

For a secret to be kept in Washington more than twenty-four hours a miracle had to happen. But it had been more than thirty-six hours since the incident in the Tatar Strait, and by a stroke of good fortune the media was still in the dark, although there'd been a few rumblings in the *Washington Post* about strained relations between Japan and Russia. There'd also been quite a few queries to the White House about what was going on in Tokyo, which the President's press secretary, Michael Harding, had stonewalled. It would not last, of course. Sooner or later someone would leak the story, and once the floodgates were open nothing would stop the flow.

General Roland Murphy (retired) had been director of the Central Intelligence Agency for nine years, his appointment coming on the heels of the 1988 presidential election. In the old days the usual morning intelligence briefing was conducted by Agency officers for the National Security Adviser to the President. Now Murphy briefed the new President himself every weekday morning at nine sharp. Only on weekends were the summaries presented to the President's staff. Murphy liked the new arrangement because he felt it gave him much better control of the situation. If there were any nuances to be passed along to the President, they would be his, not those of his subordinates.

It was a few minutes before 9:00 A.M. when the general's chauffeured limousine pulled up at the White House's west portico and his bodyguard Ken Chapin followed him inside. Murphy was a heavyset man, with thick shoulders and surprisingly long and delicate fingers. His were the hands of a pianist. He spent as much time outdoors as he possibly could, sailing his forty-two-foot sloop on Chesapeake Bay or hunting wild boar in eastern Tennessee, so his square face was lined and tanned in fine contrast to his thick white hair. He'd been called "Bulldog" commanding a regiment in Vietnam with the same iron fist he'd brought to the joint chiefs and to Langley, but he also played classical piano and was quite good.

They were passed directly up to the second floor where the President's appointments secretary, Steve Nichols, was just coming out of the Oval Office. Chapin went down the corridor to one of the waiting rooms used by the Secret Service.

"Good morning, General," Nichols said. "Go right in, he's expecting you."

Murphy nodded curtly and entered the President's study, no longer as surprised as he'd been the first time here at how small the room was. On television it looked so much bigger, more regal, more powerful. But the design woven into the dark blue carpet was the presidential seal, and coming here never ceased to impress him. The line of presidential succession went back more than two hundred years. The Soviet Union had only lasted seventy.

The President was seated in his padded rocking chair next to his National Security Adviser, Harold Secor, on the couch. The two men were a study in contrasts. The President was tall and lanky—"Lincolnesque," the media called him—while Secor, a former professor of history and political science at Harvard, looked exactly like a professor of history: tweed jacket with leather patches at the elbows, thin pinched face and sallow complexion, wire-rimmed glasses, and a pipe-smoker's overbite and stained forefinger. Both men were brilliant. "Among the most intellectual men to hold court in the White House since Woodrow Wilson's administration," the *Post* maintained. Murphy agreed wholeheartedly, although in the first year of the President's second term, the public did not. The U.S. economy was still a mess, and everyone blamed the President, which wasn't fair considering the Congress he had to work with.

"Good morning, Roland," the President said, looking up. "Good news or bad?"

"Good morning, Mr. President. I'd say neutral for the moment," Murphy replied. He extracted a leather-bound folder from his briefcase and handed it over, then placed the briefcase on the floor beside the chair across from the President and Secor.

"That's something at least," the National Security Adviser said. "The Russians are still mum, but Tokyo has finally come out with a statement."

"What are they saying?" the DCI asked with interest.

No matter what happened the Japanese government was the key player in this instance. Current thinking was that they would have to be appeased, even if the costs were large.

"They regret the incident and they're studying it," the President said, opening the intelligence report. "Get yourself some coffee while I take a look at this."

Murphy poured a cup from the service on a cart beside the President's desk and came back and sat down. The intelligence report ran to around ten thousand words, but the President was a speed reader and would skim through it in three or four minutes. In the meantime, Secor handed over the message they'd received from Tokyo through our embassy.

Beyond the usual diplomatic verbiage, the essence of the message was contained in one paragraph.

> The government of Japan deeply regrets the recent incident in the Tatar Strait off the island of Karafuto allegedly involving a vessel of Japanese Maritime Self Defense Force and one of the Russian Federal Navy in which there may have been a loss of lives and property. Every effort is being made to quickly and fully investigate the matter to determine culpability.

"I wonder if they used that name for Sakhalin Island in their reply to Moscow," Murphy said.

Secor shrugged. "We don't even know if they've exchanged messages, official or otherwise. But I don't think the Russians are about to give up the island."

"They'd be better off offering it for sale."

Secor's eyebrows rose. "Would the Japanese consider such a proposal?"

"I don't know, Harold, but with the assets the Russians have brought to bear in those waters in the last twenty-four hours it's a safe bet the Japanese won't take the island by force." Murphy handed back the message. "Or carry the dispute over those waters any further."

The President closed the leather-bound folder. "That's the way I read this, Roland. The Japanese are simply disputing Russia's claim that all the waters of the Tatar Strait belong to them, even past the twelve-mile limit from the mainland and the island. Still leaves a lot of open water in between."

"Apparently the Russians fired first. An underwater explosion of a type consistent with a helicopter-delivered torpedo came before the missile hit."

"Moscow is going to claim that they were provoked into shooting because a Japanese submarine was operating in their waters," the President said. "But the Japanese are going to protest that they were within international waters. They were outside the twelve-mile limit, weren't they?"

"Yes, they were," Murphy said. "But we don't think Tokyo will go that route. So far as we can determine, no orders have ever been issued to test those waters. In fact standing orders are for the MSDF to stay the hell away from the strait, and to avoid any kind of confrontation at all costs."

"What are you talking about, General?" Secor asked. "Are you suggesting a renegade submarine skipper?"

"Some of my people are thinking along that line. But they pick their sub-drivers just as carefully as we do ours. It's possible that a fleet commander, or even the C-in-C of submarine operations, gave the order. Tokyo would be insulated."

The President was troubled, and it showed on his face. "What would they have to gain?"

"I don't know for sure, Mr. President, but I'd say prestige. And they'd be setting a precedent to justify an expansion out of their home waters."

"You're talking about Subic Bay?"

"Yes. The Japanese may be coming to the conclusion that we no longer have their best interests at heart. Witness what happened in the strait. We weren't there, so they had to defend themselves. Could be endemic, so they've got to begin looking out for themselves."

"We've picked up nothing like that," the President said, glancing at his National Security Adviser. Secor shook his head.

"At this point, Mr. President, it's only speculation. But we're working on it. That submarine driver will probably be fired and a very carefully worded apology will be sent to Moscow."

"Reparations?" Secor asked.

"Not likely. Tokyo will claim that although its submarine was poking its nose where it shouldn't have, its intentions were friendly. The Russian navy fired the first shot, and in the heat of the moment the submarine driver defended himself."

"So we continue to support the Japanese, while slapping the Russians on the wrist. Is that what you're suggesting?" the President asked.

"For now, until we get more information."

"At the moment there are no Japanese navy ships in the strait?"

"Not so far as we can determine."

"What about the submarine?"

"Presumably on its way home, we think to Yokosuka. We'll know for sure in a few days at the outside."

"Keep on top of this one, Roland," the President said, his gaze penetrating. "We're in a very delicate position between Tokyo and Moscow, and I don't want to be caught short. Anything that has any bearing on this subject, I want to hear about it pronto."

"Yes, sir," Murphy said.

FIVE

Dominique Kilbourne was dead tired. Parking her Corvette in the Watergate ramp, all she wanted to do was get upstairs, have a glass of white wine, take a long hot soak in her tub, and crawl into bed. Since McGarvey had left her apartment yesterday morning, she'd been on the go, which in one respect was all right. It kept her from thinking about him. She'd not gotten much sleep since his visit. Alone in bed at night she kept coming back to him, to the expression on his face, to the way he held himself. To the look in his eyes. She had tried to find him, but it was as if Washington had swallowed him. David was suddenly unavailable to her, and her brother was too busy at Gales Creek to talk.

Starting at noon yesterday when HR95831 had been proposed by William Hyde, the junior Congressman from Utah, her office had been swamped by every airline she represented, and seemingly by every journalist and television or radio reporter in town, and hundreds from across the country.

The bill proposed that a ten dollar per passenger surcharge be levied on all domestic flights, and twenty dollars on all international flights. The money was to be put into an airports and airways superfund to upgrade U.S. airports and help privatize the air-traffic control system. The bugaboo in the bill, and the one point that the Congressman and his supporters were the most adamant about, was that the tax was not to be charged back to the customer. The airlines would have to absorb this cost themselves out of their profits. But a capper to the proposal was that part of the superfund would be used to "police" the airlines, to make sure the surcharges weren't passed along to the passenger through hidden costs.

American Airlines's Tom Hailey had put it most succinctly, if indelicately. "What the hell is the dumb sonofabitch trying to do, bankrupt us all?"

There wasn't enough money in the industry to pay the extra tax. Fuel prices were going up again while the number of passengers was going down. All but a few of the nation's major airlines were hanging on by the skin of their teeth. Since 1979, the year after the government decided to end its regulation of the airlines and the airfares charged, more than half the carriers had gone out of business. Even the mighty Pan Am had fallen by the wayside. This bill, and the companion bill the Congressman was already talking about, which would add a surcharge to the cargo shipped by airlines, would kill at least two of the majors and several of the others.

"That's the minimum damage that would be done," she'd explained to the Congressman in person this afternoon.

"Maybe that wouldn't be so terrible after all, Ms. Kilbourne." Congressman Hyde smiled. "Maybe it's for the best that we pare away the dead wood in this country. Look at what the Japanese have done with themselves in the past fifty years. My God, those people started from scratch."

"With a great deal of financial and technical help from us," Dominique said, hardly believing what she was hearing.

"Certainly. Look at what we did to them in Hiroshima and Nagasaki. The innocent lives lost. Women and children, the old and infirm. Lord, it must have been horrible. A blot on our national conscience. We owed them something."

Dominique wanted to ask him if that's what his constituents wanted, but he held her off.

"We're not talking about the Japanese now. Admittedly we're having our difficulties with them, which if the President doesn't mishandle it will get straightened out. What we're talking about here is the airline industry in this country. They cried for deregulation in the seventies. Keep the government off our backs, they shouted. So, we stepped away. Have at it boys, we told them. And look what happened."

The Congressman glanced at his aide, Pat Staley, who'd been trying to get a peek up Dominique's skirt since she'd sat down, and smiled.

"I think the first smart thing they ever did was to hire a pretty spokesperson," Staley said, grinning broadly. "No offense, and don't you dare take what I'm trying to

ay as some sort of sexist remark, but you do have our
ttention."

"That's what this country is all about, I think," the
Congressman said. "Dialogue. Give and take."

It was hard to keep her temper in check. "Perhaps you
on't fully appreciate the ultimate effect this bill would
ave," Dominique said. She wanted to slap the smarmy
mile off the aide's face.

"I've talked with the experts," Hyde said.

Dominique handed him a report. "When you have the
hance take a look at this. Your bill will shut down the
veaker airlines. And maybe you have a point, maybe in
ome ways that might be for the best."

The Congressman and his aide looked surprised.

"But, when an airline goes under two things happen.
First, a lot of equipment gets auctioned at a bankruptcy
ale."

"A good deal for the stronger, better-managed air-
nes," Staley suggested.

"And secondly, because of the glut of used airplanes
nd spare parts on the market, and because there's one
ess airline to purchase new equipment, it drives our
ircraft manufacturers one step closer to bankruptcy."
Dominique sat forward. "You are aware, I'm sure,
Congressman, that there are only three major manu-
acturers of commercial aircraft left in this country.
These three account for our single largest export in terms
f dollars. If any one of them were to go out of business,
or whatever reason, it would devastate our precarious
alance of trade position, and it would throw at least
ixty thousand aircraft employees out of work. Two
undred thousand others would no longer be needed to
un the grocery stores or the department stores where
he aircraft workers shop. Truck drivers would be idled,
ontractors, real estate agents, bankers." Dominique
miled. "But I think you have the picture by now,
Congressman."

"Who do you represent, the airlines or the manufac-
urers?"

"Both, because they've become inseparable. Hurt on and the other suffers."

"My experts don't agree," the Congressman said with less certainty than before.

"Maybe they're wrong," Dominique said. "Mayb after you've read my report we can get together fo dinner."

The Congressman brightened. "I'd like that."

"Fine. I'll have a word with David Kennedy. Perhap we could make a foursome with your wife. At you convenience.

Congressman Hyde's face fell. "Sure," he mumbled.

The man was a toad, Dominique thought while ridin up in the elevator from the garage. But the disturbin thing was the support he was getting. Some powerfu members of the House were apparently behind him. An she was getting hints that the White House might b behind the bill. If that were the case, the situation woul be even less understandable to her than it was. Presi dents were known to have their own hidden agendas, bu this was stupid.

Getting off the elevator, she slipped out of her shoe and padded down the thickly carpeted corridor to he apartment. She let herself in and flipped the switch fo the hall light, but nothing happened.

"Shit," she said, flipping the switch again. It was just minor irritation, but she didn't need it tonight.

Leaving the door open so that she could see her wa into the apartment she dropped her purse and shoes b the hall table and went to a lamp in the living room.

Something dark rushed at her from the shadows knocking her aside before she could react, and then i was down the hall, moving swiftly like a jungle animal i the night.

"Hey," she shouted.

Something very hard slammed into her back, spinnin her around. It was a person, dressed in black from hea to toe, some sort of a skier's mask covering his or he features. Instinctively she reached out to stop hersel from falling and grabbed a handful of the mask. It cam off, and then she caught the edge of the coffee table with the backs of her legs and sat down hard on the floor, but not before she got a good look at the man's face . . . it was a man, she suddenly was certain, and for a second he stood there, unmoving, looking at her.

He reached down and gently, it seemed, touched the side of her neck. She felt as if she were falling into a very deep and pitch-black hole.

McGarvey was put up at the monumental Rossiya Hotel on Razin Street just off Red Square with no further word when he would be meeting with Aleksandr Karyagin, the new director of the Russian Federal Intelligence Service. But he'd been assured that he would be leaving on the 10:00 A.M. flight to Washington.

It was 4:30 in the morning, and unable to sleep he stared out of his eleventh-floor window at the fantastical domes of St. Basil's and the red brick walls of the Kremlin, a shiver rising up his spine.

Everything was different, and yet nothing had changed. The free market economy had taken hold, more or less, but there was still nothing affordable to buy in the stores. The KGB's name had been changed to the SUR, and it no longer acted as a thought police, yet the person on the street could still spot an intelligence officer a block away and steer clear. Emigration was no longer tightly controlled, and yet passing the U.S. Embassy in the back seat of General Polunin's limousine, McGarvey had seen long lines of people waiting to get inside where they could apply for visas, while uniformed militia officers watched and took notes and photographs.

Everything here was run-down. Cars, roads, buildings in the entire country had gone to hell since he'd last been here. Moscow had always been a seedy old city, but now it was worse. The place was coming apart at the seams, helped by the Russian Mafia and a growing murder rate, yet somehow McGarvey found that he wasn't glad of it. His parents would weep if they could see what was happening.

Another change that had taken place was the reopening of the churches and the young people flocking to them. Not so surprising, because through most of Russia's history its people had been deeply religious. A seventy-year atheism imposed by the communists paled to insignificance when compared to six centuries of Orthodox Catholicism.

Besides the language, McGarvey had been taught Russian history, which was his father's first love. In 1310, Moscow became the See—the seat of authority— for the Russian Orthodox Church. In 1367, the first stones of the first Kremlin were laid, and in 1448, going directly against the Council of Florence, which had finally united the western and eastern branches of the Catholic Church, the Church of Moscow became independent. Dates on dates, he remembered them all remembered having them drummed into his head.

"Without knowing where we've been how will we know where we should go . . . where we must go?" his father would ask him.

The building of the new Kremlin—1496 to 1497. War with Sweden—1502. Ivan the Terrible, the first Russian czar—1553 to 1584. The Romanovs begin in 1613 with peace between Sweden and Russia. The Pauls, the Catherines, the Alexanders and Nicholases. War and revolution. The Cheka, the White Army, the Red Guards. The Stalin years and the purges and pogroms and collectivizations. Khrushchev and Brezhnev and Molotov and Andropov . . . and on and on to Gorbachev and Yeltsin and finally this.

All the prayers and all the sacraments were for nothing, the thought passed through McGarvey's mind because throughout all their history Russians generally had less regard and less reverence for human life than even Hitler had. The sweep of Russian history was a vast panorama of death. Mind-numbing numbers of men and women and children, peasants and officers, kulaks and bankers, by the millions, even *tens of millions,* had been led off to the slaughter.

Had his father understood this? He must have.

This was a land that stretched across eleven time zones. Nearly half the earth's circumference. Oil and coal and lead and zinc, uranium and gold and platinum and diamonds. Timber stands that stretched for a thousand miles or more. Mighty rivers, at least three major mountain ranges, and coastlines that ranged from the Arctic Ocean to the Black and Caspian seas and from the Pacific to the Baltic. But it was as if a terrible dark cloud covered the entire nation or that some horrible genetic defect had somehow infected the entire people, turning them into a nation of murderers and victims.

McGarvey turned away from the window. In the dim light from outside he could see his reflection in the mirror above the dresser as a vaguely dark outline, and he could see himself as he might look in twenty or thirty years, the age his father had been at his death. But he could not make out the expression on his face, only that it was incomplete. That he was incomplete, for some reason. He was here on the first leg of a mission that he himself didn't fully understand, and that he should never have suggested. He was no longer in the business. Hadn't that been settled in his head after Volodga? Maybe Howard Ryan was right. Maybe he did not belong.

After he'd returned from the Soviet Union he'd tried to look up his first wife with the thought at the back of his head that they might get together. But she was dead. It had been breast cancer, her dying painful and lonely. She had called for him. But that's when he had begun to run.

Maybe he didn't belong anywhere, he thought grimly. At some point in his life he'd probably had the chance to take a different road, despite how he'd been raised. But he had not. And this was the result.

A truck lumbered by on the street, its exhaust white in the extreme cold. No matter how much trouble Russia continued to have it wouldn't shrivel up and die, or disappear off the face of the earth. Germany and Japan were totally devastated by 1945. Now, a half-century later, they were among the most powerful nations on earth. But they'd had help, and a lot of it. The question was, who would help the Russians? America or Japan?

Someone knocked at his door. "It's time to go." It was Yemlin.

McGarvey let him in. "How'd you know I was awake?"

Yemlin shrugged. "You know." He glanced up at the ceiling light fixture. The room was bugged. Possibly they'd even watched him with a hidden camera. It didn't matter.

"Where are we going?"

"To see the director, but from there we'll go directly to the airport, so bring your suitcase."

"This early?" McGarvey asked, putting on his tie.

"The Lubyanka is very open these days," the Russian said, smiling wryly. "Western journalists are there practically every day, but not until 8:30 in the morning."

"He should move his office."

"No." Yemlin shook his head. "Now please let's go, Kirk. General Polunin is waiting for us."

The temperature had dropped to thirty-eight below zero. The cold took McGarvey's breath away. Inside General Polunin's limousine it was roaring hot. It was a wonder that everyone over here didn't get pneumonia every winter because of the huge contrasts between outside and inside temperatures. His father explained that Russians kept their homes warm simply because they could. The warmer the better. As a nation they remembered going cold and hungry many times during their history. It was the same reason a sign of prosperity among Russian men was a pot belly. It meant the man was wealthy enough and well-connected enough to buy the necessary calories.

"I'm sorry that you didn't sleep well, Mr. McGarvey," the general said. The drive over to Dzerzhinsky Square was only a half-dozen blocks, and at this hour of the morning there was almost no traffic.

"The effects of jet lag," McGarvey answered. "I'll sleep on the way home."

"We'll make sure to get you out to the airport in plenty of time. In the meanwhile Mr. Karyagin is most interested in meeting you. He thinks, as I do, that your being here might kill two birds with one stone. That is, if you will cooperate."

"I won't spy on my country," McGarvey shot back.

"But you will have us spy on Japan for you."

"Not spy, just share your product, general. You're already spying."

"That's all we expect of you. For you to share your influence in Washington."

"Is that what Mr. Karyagin is going to ask me?"

"I don't know. I'm not the director. But your request has been discussed at the highest levels." General Polunin looked directly into McGarvey's eyes. "We take you very seriously, Mr. McGarvey. Please extend to us the same consideration."

"Believe me, General, I do," McGarvey said. "I wouldn't be here otherwise."

The black statue of Feliks Dzerzhinsky, the founder of the Cheka, which was the forerunner of the KGB and the SUR, that had stood in the courtyard of the KGB's Lubyanka headquarters, was gone, torn down in 1991 when the Soviet Union had collapsed. Even its granite base was gone now.

Aleksandr Semenovich Karyagin was a short, well-groomed dapper man in his late fifties. His hair was gray, and he wore a Western-cut suit so that he looked more like an American politician than the head of the Russian Foreign Intelligence Service.

"Good morning, Mr. McGarvey," he said. "I thought you might want breakfast before you left for the airport."

They met in the small ninth-floor dining room. An American-style breakfast of bacon and ham and sausages, eggs, toast, and fried potatoes was laid out. General Polunin came up with McGarvey, but Yemlin remained downstairs.

"Good morning, Mr. Karyagin. It's kind of you."

Because of a heart murmur, Karyagin had not served

in the military. Instead he had thrown himself into politics, first in Leningrad and later in Moscow, doing whatever was asked of him without question or complaint. Unlike many of his counterparts, however, he was intelligent and inventive and soon came to the attention of Boris Yeltsin. They had risen together. The man was generally well liked and respected in the Western intelligence community because of his professionalism.

"I understand that you still maintain ties with the CIA."

"I have a couple of friends who work for the Company. I don't see them very often, but now and then we get together for a couple of drinks. The breakfast looks good. I'm hungry."

There were four small tables each with a crisp white tablecloth and silver service in the tastefully appointed room. They served themselves from a buffet along one wall and sat at one of the tables by a large window that looked out across the city.

"When you get back to Washington ask your friends for some information," Karyagin said.

"I told General Polunin that I will not spy on my country for you," McGarvey said.

"I'm not asking you to become a traitor, merely to ask for some help."

"With what?"

"How will the United States react when the public finally learns what happened in the Tatar Strait?"

"We'll probably read about it in the *New York Times* or *Washington Post* in the next few days," McGarvey said. "But frankly I don't think the average American will give a damn. You've been our enemy since 1945, and there's no love just now for the Japanese. So I imagine that most Americans will view that attack as nothing more than a minor squabble."

"But Japan has vast economic ties with the United States."

Well put, McGarvey thought, though stranglehold might have been a more accurate choice of words. "It doesn't matter."

"By reaction, I meant the White House's reaction. How will your President respond?"

"I don't know, Mr. Karyagin," McGarvey said. "And even if I still worked for the CIA, I wouldn't know that. Only a few of the President's closest advisers would be privy to such information. And if I could get to them, which I cannot, I wouldn't do it."

"The crux of the matter is what would your country do if we retaliated in some way for the attack against us in our home waters?"

"Is that what you're planning to do?"

"It's a distinct possibility, Mr. McGarvey."

"As you say, Japan has vast economic ties with my country. They are our allies."

Karyagin stared at McGarvey without altering his expression, yet it was clear that the comment had hit home. The Russians were in a dicey situation. If they did something overtly to disturb the Americans, what aid and support they were getting from Washington and from companies like Guerin would dry up. On the other hand, if they let the Japanese incursion into waters they claimed were Russian go unchallenged, and the destruction of their naval vessel go unrevenged, it would happen again and again until their eastern border was no longer secure. The situation was intolerable.

"If Cuba attacked and sank one of your Navy or Coast Guard ships off the Florida coast, the White House would react."

"It most certainly would," McGarvey said. "But if it had happened ten years ago when Cuba was still your ally, would you have risked war to help them out?"

"I don't know."

"Neither do I, Mr. Karyagin. But I do know that we have satellites keeping a close watch on what's going on. Whatever you do we'll know about it. But how my President will react I cannot predict. In fact, your people probably have a better reading on it than I do. Yemlin runs Washington with a sharp eye."

"General Murphy is very close to the President."

McGarvey allowed himself to smile. "As I said, I'm

not privy to the President's advisers, not even the general."

"But you're concerned about the Japanese."

"Wary. We think a *zaibatsu* may have been formed to ruin Guerin Airplane Company."

"In order to acquire the technological developments that the company has made on this new airliner?"

"That's right. My government refuses to help us because it would show favoritism of one industry over another and would involve the government directly in industry."

"Foolish of them," Karyagin said. "We don't have such constraints."

Or a lot of other things, the thought occurred to McGarvey. "We believe that this Japanese group will do anything to reach its goal."

"Including murder?"

"Yes, including murder."

Karyagin glanced at General Polunin, a bleak look suddenly in his eyes. "We've heard nothing about this from our Tokyo operation?"

"That is correct, Mr. Director," Polunin said.

Karyagin turned back to McGarvey. "What will happen to our deal if we don't find out what you need to know?"

"It would be a moot point in that case," McGarvey said, "because Guerin would no longer be an American company."

"By coming here and speaking with us, you could be construed as a traitor."

"I represent a manufacturing company that wishes to make an offer to build a commercial aircraft assembly plant here, equip it, and train its personnel. Of course, before any such agreement could be finalized we would need the export licenses. But the legal people say that will present no serious problem. Will you help us?"

"Yes, of course we will," Karyagin said, as if there'd never been a doubt in anyone's mind. "But you too must understand that if the situation between us and the

Japanese government deteriorates, working with your company could become a moot point for us."

"I understand."

It had taken nearly forty-eight hours before Bruno Mueller was finally out of Europe. The automobile he had stolen from the Munich Airport had been returned in the morning by one of the general's staff, who that night drove Mueller across the border into Austria.

In Vienna, Mueller was handed over to another associate of the general, who'd driven him to Budapest, where the next afternoon, with new papers identifying him as Karl Steiner, a businessman from Stuttgart, he was able to board a Czechoslovak Airlines 747 direct to Washington's Dulles International Airport.

Customs and immigration passed him through after only a couple of very routine questions, and the Yellow cab with the roof number 659 was waiting for him as he'd been instructed. By midnight he was knocking at the door of a very large and very old farmhouse a few kilometers west of the airport, the cab's taillights disappearing in the darkness down the long driveway.

America, he thought. One week ago he would never have believed it possible. There was, however, no doubt in his mind that he was a fugitive, and that whatever opportunity the general had arranged for him was his last chance.

A bulky old man with a thick nose and white hair, wearing a moth-eaten sweater and brown corduroy trousers, answered the door. "You're Mueller?" he asked, the words slurred.

"That's right," Mueller replied in English. "The General sent me."

The old man let him in, then closed and locked the door. "Did you have any trouble getting here?"

Mueller shook his head. To the right the stair hall opened into a comfortably furnished living room. A fire was on the grate. To the left was a dining room, beyond which an open door led into the kitchen. A short corridor led to the back of the house. The place smelled pleasantly of wood smoke and pipe tobacco.

"Your room is upstairs, first on the right. Put your things away, and then come back down. I want to talk to you before I leave."

Mueller looked closer at the old man, especially his eyes, which were watery, and his complexion, which was mottled red. The man was a heavy drinker and was drunk now, or nearly drunk, he decided. Not so good, but the general never made mistakes.

"You're going away?"

"Into the city. My home is in Georgetown."

"What about this place?" Mueller asked.

"I own this house as well, but very few people know about it. I use it from time to time for . . . various things."

Mueller cocked an ear to listen, but the only sounds in the house were the crackling of the fire on the grate. "Is there anyone else here?"

"Not yet," the old man said. "But someone else will be coming to help you."

"With what?" Mueller asked.

"In due time, Colonel." The old man motioned toward the stairs. "Put your things away. I'll fix you a drink."

"What do I call you?"

The old man studied him for a second before he answered. "Edward R. Reid," he said. "Your general and I go back a long way together to when he first worked for the BND."

Mueller's eyes narrowed in surprise. "Do you know what I am?"

"You're an assassin who the West Germans would like to eliminate."

"West Germans?"

"Germans," Reid corrected himself.

"Knowing this, you have work for me?"

Reid nodded.

"Do you understand the consequences if you are discovered and arrested?"

"I'm an old man, colonel," Reid said. "And I don't frighten easily."

"I'm not an old man, and I do frighten easily, so you will be very careful for my sake. When I am cornered I fight back. If I am betrayed, I kill my betrayers. And if this is to be the time and place of my death, then I will take a great many with me. Police, soldiers, civilians . . . you."

"Put your things away," Reid said after a moment. "I believe that you will work out just fine."

"It was too easy," McGarvey said.

"Turn your back on it," Yemlin replied as their limousine was passed through the east gate at Sheremeteyvo Airport. "We have the resources and we're experts at the game. You'll be sucked in until all your choices but one will be gone."

"Is that what Karyagin means to do?"

"He's a desperate man, Kirk. You're going to have to understand how it really is with us here. General Polunin is snapping at his heels from below, just waiting for him to make a mistake. While Yeltsin and that crowd in the Kremlin are pressuring him from above for answers he simply cannot give them. And you know what happens in this country when you can't give your masters the answers they want to hear."

McGarvey looked away for a moment. A light breeze had sprung up that made for some fantastic wind-chill numbers. Yemlin had always been a pragmatist. Even during the interrogations and his later visits to the hospital at Volodga, he'd spoken only of practical matters. "What will your families do now? Can we get word to them? Are you reasonably comfortable? Are you certain that nothing can be offered you in exchange for further information?" Maybe it was still the same now.

"Why are you telling me this, Viktor?"

"I always thought you were a good man. A little ahead of your time but basically decent. You proved that by taking poor Tania as far as you did. Baranov was no friend of the *Rodina*. Let's say I want you to come into this operation with your eyes open. If it fails it could be disastrous for your company, and you personally."

"You could be fired for telling me this."

Yemlin had to smile. "I already have been. I'm no longer Washington *rezident.*"

"You're not flying back with me this morning?"

"No, Kirk. But I will be returning to Washington soon."

"To do what?" McGarvey asked him.

"To act as your handler, of course," Yemlin said. "My boss thinks that you and I have a special relationship. Sometimes this sort of a bond develops between the interrogator and his subject. It was me who you first approached for help."

"You were the logical choice."

"Maybe."

"Maybe I'll kill you when I get the chance. I have the motive."

"Then they will have been proved wrong."

"Perhaps I'll use you."

"By all means," Yemlin said. "There's nothing a great Russian loves more than intrigue. You know all about it."

"Again, why tell me this?" McGarvey asked, although he already knew the answer.

"Because you're no good to us unless your eyes are wide open. We're talking about international industrial espionage. Your company is hiring a Russian federal agency to work for it, in violation certainly of many of your laws, and even some of our own. The quid pro quo remains information in trade for information."

"In addition to the assembly factory."

"As you say, Kirk, without information for both sides, the factory becomes a moot point."

The limousine took them directly to the ramp where the same airliner that had brought them from Washington was being readied for the return flight. The other passengers were still in the terminal waiting for the first boarding call.

"Get some sleep, Kirk. I'll see you in a couple of days."

McGarvey got his single overnight bag and got out of the car. Before he walked across to the waiting aircraft he turned back.

"Perhaps I *will* kill you before this is all over, Viktor Pavlovich."

Yemlin shrugged, but it was clear that the remark bothered him. "We'll see."

Five bells went off in the operations room of the U.S. Navy Seventh Fleet's Intelligence Unit at Yokosuka, Japan, indicating a FLASH-priority message was incoming on the ready circuit from the Pentagon.

ZO72315ZJAN

TOP SECRET

FM: CINCPACCOM

TO: CINC 7TH FLEET

SUBJECT: READINESS STATUS

1. 7TH FLEET NORTHERN OPERATIONS TO INCLUDE GUAM BUT NOT XX RPT NOT XX INDIAN OCEAN DETACHMENT ARE ORDERED TO DEFCON 4.

2. THIS IS NOT XX RPT NOT XX A COMMANDWIDE UPGRADE.

3. EVIDENCE CONCENTRATED RUSSIAN NAVAL FORCES IN TATAR STRAIT VICINITY 47–42–31N XXX 140–32–00E.

4. REQUEST ID AND PRESENT WHEREABOUTS OF JAPANESE MSDF SUBMARINE RESPONSIBLE FOR ATTACK OF 04–01–97.

5. USE OF ALL APPLICABLE LOCAL RESOURCES AUTHORIZED, BUT UNDER NO CIRCUMSTANCES MUST MSDF BECOME AWARE OF YOUR INVESTIGATION.

Chief Signalman Joseph Woodmark, Jr., tore the message off the printer and hand-carried it back to the duty officer's cubicle. They'd been expecting something like this to come, and the search for the MSDF submarine had already begun. So far as the traffic Woodmark had seen coming through operations indicated, the brass was looking for the *Samisho,* which had left Yokosuka ten days ago. But no one had expected the upgraded defense condition. DEFCON 5 was normal, and DEFCON 1 meant war. Four was nothing more than a preliminary precaution, but it was on the way up.

Lieutenant, j.g. Jan Mills took the dispatch, logged it in the Top Secret control book, and shook his head. "Somebody's smoking something in D.C.," he said, picking up the phone and punching in the fleet commander's office. "First they're late asking us to look around, and then they up the ante a notch."

Last night he'd watched a video tape of the Pearl Harbor movie *Tora! Tora! Tora!* and now he felt unsettled.

SIX

Facing northeast toward the Columbia River and southwest across the city, Guerin Airplane Company's staff headquarters was housed in a sprawling glass and aluminum-framed four-story building at Portland International Airport. Nearly five thousand executives and engineers worked there. Along with the seventy-five thousand welders and riveters, tool and die makers, machinists and designers, electronics experts and metallurgists, chemists, mathematicians, and a host of other specialists in various facilities around the city and up at Forest Grove and Gales Creek, Guerin was by far Portland's largest employer. And, like Boeing in Seattle, the gigantic aircraft company dominated nearly every aspect of the city, from its taxes to its Monday-through-Friday traffic made worse this morning because of a rare snowstorm that had begun overnight. Three lanes of cars and vans streamed through the main gates into the parking lot, which was being plowed and sanded even as the day shift was showing up.

Like most upper-level Guerin executives, Kennedy had a limousine and driver at his disposal. The presidents of almost every other division made use of the privilege, claiming it gave them much needed time to and from work to review paperwork. But often he drove his own car. It gave him the time to clear his head. To get ready for the day and to come down after a long one.

This morning, however, he found it difficult to think about anything other than the Japanese, and Chairman of the Board Al Vasilanti's intransigence when it came to them. It had caused them trouble before, but they'd always managed to sidestep the issue or dig themselves out of whatever hole they'd been placed in.

During the final design stages of the P522's fly-by-wire system in the mid-eighties, Mitsubishi had come up with a new design application for its CPU that made the computer-to-sensor interface one hundred times as fast and as accurate at half the cost, as the American designed and built application.

The logical step, of course, would have been to subcontract the system to the Japanese. But Vasilanti had been adamantly against working with them, and he'd convinced the board of directors to go along with him, promising that American Micro Devices was on the verge of a better design.

AMD had come up with a system that was at least as good as Mitsubishi's. Whether by luck or by inside information, Vasilanti came out smelling like a rose.

This time there was no miracle looming six months down the road, unless McGarvey was successful, or unless Congress passed an act protecting them from a Japanese takeover—something he did not think Washington was ready to do considering the fact that the

United States had become the world's largest debtor nation and Japan had become one of the largest purchasers of that debt.

As one U.S. Senator had told him off the record last year, "We're beholden to the little bastards." It was a double-edged sword.

Parking the four-wheel-drive Range Rover in his slot in the heated executive garage, Kennedy took the elevator up to the fourth floor. Traffic on Interstate 205 had been snarled up because of the weather, and as a result he was late. He'd telephoned his secretary to have Vasilanti's meeting pushed back to nine, which had been approved, but she'd warned him that his phone was ringing off the hook. The usual spate of Monday morning problems. But there was one call from Washington that he would have to deal with personally. "I don't recommend you use the car phone."

Anyone could monitor cellular telephone conversations, and it was assumed by Guerin and every other high-tech company that such eavesdropping was common. But if the call was from McGarvey, back from Moscow, it might mean trouble.

It was 8:30 A.M. when he stepped off the elevator, crossed the broad, thickly carpeted corridor, and entered his suite of offices down the hall from the boardroom. His secretary, Nancy Nebel, was just putting down the phone.

"Let's get started," he said, going directly into his office.

"Am I glad to see you," she said, jumping up. She snatched a stack of mail, a couple of thick file folders, and a steno pad from her desk and followed him inside.

His office was large and well-appointed, with expansive windows that looked toward the airport terminal and the two main runways. From his desk Kennedy could see jetliners, many of them Guerin's, departing for and arriving from all over the world. Sometimes he felt a great sense of pride and achievement. But at other times, like this morning, he felt a sense of impending disaster.

"Mr. Vasilanti wants you in his office at nine sharp,

which gives you a half-hour," Nancy said, pouring Kennedy a cup of coffee as he hung up his overcoat in the closet. She was fifty-something and plain looking but pleasant.

"Is Gary back from Rome?"

"He got in last night." Gary Topper was Guerin's vice president in charge of sales. "Mr. Vasilanti's already talked to him along with Mr. Socrates and Mr. Soderstrom."

George Socrates was vice president in charge of new airplane design, and Jeffery Soderstrom was Guerin's chief financial officer. The old man had called all the heavy guns. This morning's meeting was going to be a council of war.

Kennedy hung his suit coat on the back of his chair, then took the cup of coffee from his secretary and sat down. She laid out a couple of legal pads and several sharpened pencils for him, along with a typed copy of his tentative schedule for the day, week, and month.

She set the stack of mail to his left. "Nothing that won't wait until this afternoon. Two queries from Washington. One from the FAA wanting a clarification on our suggested modification of the 422 rudder sensor AD that was issued in March." An AD, Airworthiness Directive, was an order from the Federal Aviation Administration requiring that a fix or modification be made to an airplane.

"And the second from Congressman Benton's office requesting our current thinking on inertial guidance systems for airliners." Benton was the new chairman of the House Subcommittee on Aviation and was interested, because of the tremendous savings for the government, in what *Aviation Week & Space Technology* was calling the "next generation" of aids to navigation.

Airliners found their way around the world using a combination of high-frequency radio beacons, radio locating networks, and a series of satellites in geostationary orbits that provided precise location information. But such systems, especially the satellites, were expensive to maintain.

Using an inertial guidance system similar to ones installed in U.S. submarines, an airliner's exact location could be entered into the navigational device on the date the set was installed. At that point the aircraft "knew" exactly where in the world it was located. Thereafter, anytime the aircraft was moved, up-down, left-right, forward-backward, even by a few feet, the movements were sensed and the airplane's true position was computed by the system.

"Engineering can handle that," Kennedy said.

"Mr. Taich bounced it back here. Said our research was too sensitive to share with Washington at this time."

Kennedy had to smile. Fred Taich, vice president in charge of engineering, was one of the true "squirrels" in the business and had probably made a reply along the lines of "Fuck the bastards!" But Nancy had cleaned it up for him.

"Send a letter to Benton's office advising them we're putting together a comprehensive study package that we'll forward soon."

"A letter to that effect is in the pile for your signature," Nancy said. "Nothing else in the mail is pressing. But I've put together two files you should look at before you see Mr. Vasilanti. The first involves the Japanese. I pulled what we had on their commercial aircraft and engine research, and Dominique's office faxed us everything they had."

"Can we get anything from the State Department updating who we might be dealing with?"

"Should be here within the hour."

Nancy had been his secretary from the day he'd started with Guerin. The third-floor junior executives called her "Attila the Hun." But it was a term of respect, not derision.

"What about this other file?" Kennedy asked.

"The project," Nancy said. "Mr. Vasilanti asked me to see that you brought it along."

He flipped the file open to the artist's rendering of the P/C2622. It looked sleek and fast.

"He's scheduled a news conference at noon sharp at Gales Creek."

Kennedy understood what the old man had in mind to counter the expected move against them by the Japanese and to prod Washington into standing up for them. NASA had used the same technique when the shuttle was in its developmental stages and Congress was dragging its heels over funding. A mockup of the space plane was shown to the public, and it made a big hit. Practically every television station, newspaper, wire service, and magazine in the world had covered the event. Congress quickly changed its mind.

The P/C2622, minus its supersonic engine, was almost ready for its first test flight at subsonic speeds. He and Vasilanti had discussed the strategy of letting the media in on the event but had rejected it for being overly sporty at a time when they could ill afford such a gamble. If the test failed Guerin would suffer. Now, however, things were different.

"What else?"

"Mr. McGarvey called from Washington and said it was urgent that you call him the moment you got in."

"Get him on the phone," Kennedy said, his chest tight. God only knew what had happened in Moscow.

Nancy left the office, closing the door softly behind her, and Kennedy swiveled in his chair so he could look out toward the airport. Snowplows and sanders were busy clearing the active runway. For the moment Portland International was open.

Another thought intruded. The Japanese weren't his only problem. His marriage was in trouble too. Last night he and Chance had fought bitterly again. Something had gone terribly wrong with their relationship in the last year or so. In part, he thought, because of the long hours he worked and the frequent absences when he had to be in Washington or Paris or London. But, like a man who wants to get off a roller coaster, he was helpless until it stopped. Until the P/C2622 was flying.

The telephone rang. He turned back and picked it up. "Mac?"

"There's no answer at his hotel room," Nancy said.

"Did you try Dominique's?"

"No answer there either, but I left a message at both places."

"All right, Nancy, call me if you get through to him, and buzz me when Mr. Vasilanti is ready."

"You have about twenty minutes."

Kennedy hung up, drew the first Japanese file to him and opened it to the first page: *Japan—A Manufacturing Nation Without Natural Resources.*

McGarvey had picked up a tail the moment he'd passed through passport control and customs at Dulles Airport. They were probably FBI, one dressed as a customs agent and the other as a terminal cop. Both of them wore uniforms, but both carried handguns in shoulder holsters beneath their jackets, something uniformed officers never did.

Outside, there'd been three pairs: one in a dark blue Ford van and a second in an electric-green Chevrolet Cavalier, alternating front and back of the Yellow cab McGarvey had taken into the city. He had the cabby slow down twice, and both times the two pairs slowed up. The third set materialized in an older brown Mercedes at the Hyatt Regency where McGarvey checked in under his own name. The driver stayed with the car, while the other agent pretended to carry on a conversation with someone on a house phone. And when McGarvey boarded the elevator to his floor, the man put down the phone and approached the registration desk.

If they wanted to charge him with something, the FBI would have picked him up by now. Which meant that to this point they were merely curious about his movements. Waiting for him to make the next move, such as meeting with his Russian control officer. If they caught him at that, he would definitely be picked up.

McGarvey did not bother going to his room. Instead, he took the service elevator down to the laundry and left the hotel by a back exit. He walked a couple of blocks to D Street and ·Third, got a cab to the Howard Johnson Downtown Motor Lodge across Virginia Avenue from the Watergate, and checked in.

Standing at his fifth-floor window, he looked across the avenue as he waited for his Portland call to go through. He thought about Dominique Kilbourne. She was attracted to him because he was a dangerous man. Race-car drivers experienced the same thing. There was a type of woman who made a career out of having affairs with men in deadly occupations. But excess baggage was the bane of the field officer. The weak link that had brought down more than one good operative. A lover was an Achilles' heel. He could write the book on that story.

He got Kennedy's secretary on the line. "McGarvey. Let me talk to David Kennedy."

"He's right here, Mr. McGarvey," Nancy said, and a moment later Kennedy came on.

"You weren't supposed to call this number."

"All the principals know who I'm working for."

Kennedy was silent for a beat. "When did you get back?"

"This morning," McGarvey said. "They agreed."

"The whole package? Both sides?"

"Everything. They're expecting our first team in the next few days."

"This is happening pretty fast," Kennedy said, cautiously. "What about their part?"

"They'll provide the site, the materials, and the construction crews, supervised by your people. They'll provide *all* the technical help they can."

"When can we start exchanging information?"

"Soon," McGarvey said. It was possible that Guerin's phones were tapped. There was no use taking unnecessary risks.

"No . . . trouble?" Kennedy asked. "No snags, or last-minute demands on their part?"

"None," McGarvey said.

"You should come out here. Al Vasilanti wants to meet you, and there are a number of things you should know about us."

"I'll be free tomorrow."

"Good. In the meantime Al has called a press conference at Gales Creek. I think he's going to unveil the new airplane."

"That's not such a good idea, David," McGarvey said. "It could push the opposition into making a move now."

"I think that's what he wants," Kennedy replied. It sounded as if he wasn't very happy about the decision. "He's up for the fight, and I think he wants to get it over with."

"I can understand that, but try to stall him if you can. Tell him that we'll be better equipped to put up a fight after we get some hard intelligence."

"He's called a council of war in his office for about two minutes from now. I'll do what I can."

"See you tomorrow," McGarvey said.

They met in the old man's office. The walls were adorned with paintings of some of the most famous commercial aircraft in the history of aviation, among them Ford's corrugated-skin Tin Goose, Douglas's DC-3, Boeing's 707 and 747, and Guerin's 422 and 522—two of the biggest-selling airplanes ever.

At seventy-seven, Alfred Vasilanti had been witness to a lot of aviation history, jumping into the industry with both feet after graduation from Harvard in 1941. Two years later he bullied his draft board into granting him an exemption because he was working in a critical industry. Not because he wanted to avoid the war, but because, as he put it, "I knew damned well I could do more to beat the Nazis and the Japs by designing and building good airplanes than by shooting at the bastards." He'd always played it close to the hip, and as a result his staff meetings were lively affairs.

The aircraft business bred contentious men, and a few women, who held strong opinions and were willing to go to the mat for them. Odd ducks. Eccentric geniuses—

"squirrels." These were the people Vasilanti surrounded himself with. As a result, the company was successful. There wasn't a national airline in any country, except Russia, that didn't fly Guerin equipment. Airplanes, he liked to point out, that except for their Rolls-Royce engines were one-hundred percent American designed and manufactured.

Kennedy was the last to arrive. The old man motioned him to his place next to George Socrates, vice president of design. The second generation Greek-American had designed and built his own two-seater rag-wing monoplane in his father's Kansas garage in 1946. He was only thirteen years old, and legally still too young to get his solo license, but he learned to fly at the town's grass-strip airport. He never became a great pilot, but he maintained that in order to design them you sure as hell better know how to fly them. He quit high school at the age of fifteen and enrolled at Kansas State University, breezing through the aeronautical engineering program in two years, after which he went to work for Cessna Aircraft Company as the youngest engineer on staff, or on the staff of any other airplane company so far as anyone knew. Since then he'd worked for every major airplane company in the U.S. designing or helping to design everything from sea planes to helicopters, and from sport aerobatic biplanes to Guerin's 322, 422, 522, and finally the P/C2622—the culmination of his life's work. He was the most respected man in the industry and could walk into any airplane design facility in the world and get a job, no questions asked, for practically any amount of money he wanted.

On Socrates's right was Newton Kilbourne, Dominique's older brother and vice president in charge of new product development and prototype manufacturing. He'd come to the aircraft industry from Detroit, where he'd started on the Ford plant's assembly line out of high school. Within the first month, realizing that being nothing more than a "wrench" wasn't good enough for him, he went to night school, finishing in six years with degrees in mechanical engineering, electrical engineering, and business administration. When Vasilanti hired him eight years ago Kilbourne was vice president in charge of manufacturing the Taurus automobile. His transition to airplanes was simple. One day he was building cars, and the next he was building jetliners.

Next to Kilbourne was Gary Topper. Topper, vice president in charge of sales, was an industry "squirrel," but his high jinks were tolerated because he sold airplanes. A former Air Force jet jockey, he'd worked for American, Pan Am, and Northwest before coming to Guerin four years ago at the age of thirty-seven. He'd been hired as a test pilot, but at a commercial air show in Buenos Aires he'd come in over the grandstands doing 400 knots in a Guerin 522 . . . upside-down, something even Socrates said was impossible for a commercial jetliner that size. Everyone was so impressed (some of them angry, but all of them impressed) that they placed their orders for the airliner with the pilot who could pull off such a stunt.

Beside him was his exact opposite, Jeff Soderstrom, Guerin's chief financial officer. A former Citibank vice president in charge of international commercial loans, he was accustomed to dealing with figures in the billions. But he was an arch conservative from a solid family, and Guerin's oftentimes precarious financial position drove him up the wall. It was the reason Vasilanti had hired the man. "We need someone to keep our feet on the ground."

"We have a lot of work to do this morning, so let's get to it," Vasilanti said when Kennedy was seated. "I've scheduled a media briefing for noon at Gales Creek. We're going to show them the 2622. And we'll let them climb aboard and take as many pictures as they want."

"So that's what this is all about," Kilbourne groaned. For the past two weeks the rush had been on to hang the aircraft's subsonic engines and the temporary cowling approximating the aerodynamic shape of the single hydrogen-burning hypersonic engine not yet ready from Rolls-Royce. "You ought to have your head examined."

"Save it until you hear everything," Vasilanti growled.

"David, give us the background on the Japanese problem . . . the entire background, including Kirk McGarvey's recommendations and actions. Is he back?"

"He's in Washington. He said it's a go."

"Back from where?" Soderstrom asked.

Kennedy looked at him, still not sure that this was the right thing to do. But he understood the old man's thinking and it was hard to fault it. "Moscow."

"You're still thinking about putting a wing assembly plant in Russia after everything I've shown you?" the CFO asked. "When they collapse—not if, but when—we'll be out a billion dollars we can't afford to toss away."

"We can't afford not to do it," Vasilanti said sharply. "Go ahead, David."

"I'll go over the details later, but simply put we think there may be a grain of truth to the rumors we've heard about a Japanese move to buy us out for our HSCT research." The acronym stood for High Speed Civil Transport, the next generation of commercial aircraft.

"We know that," Soderstrom said. "We're keeping a close watch on the market."

"We also think that they mean to do whatever it takes to drive our price per share to a favorable level by destroying the public's confidence in our equipment."

"Come off it, David. Don't you think this Japanese paranoia has gone far enough?"

"I don't know, Jeff. But the question remains that the American Airlines O'Hare crash in '90 might have something to do with the Japanese."

"Doesn't it seem coincidental to you that our troubles began *after* McGarvey was hired?" Soderstrom asked. "He may be, as you say, a bright and conscientious man, but considering his background, mightn't he be seeing boogeymen?"

Kennedy glanced at Vasilanti who sat impassively for the moment. *It's your show, you deal with it.*

"That was my first reaction," Kennedy said. "But I don't think we can safely dismiss the possibility that he's right. Not any longer."

Kilbourne sat forward. "What is it, David? What's happened?"

There was no truly innocent person, Kennedy thought. Any company this large was bound to have a few skeletons in its corporate closet. But they were about to get a tough lesson in hardball politics this morning.

"This meeting is strictly off the record. If what I'm about to share with you gets out, we could all end up in a hell of a lot of trouble."

"Then why tell us?" Soderstrom asked sharply.

"Because we're going to have to make a decision whether or not to continue with something I think we need to save this company."

No one voiced an objection, not even Soderstrom.

"Kirk McGarvey learned from his sources in Washington that a Japanese submarine attacked and sank a Russian naval vessel in the Tatar Strait just north of Hokkaido."

"Jesus Christ," Kilbourne said softly.

"There's been nothing in the news," Soderstrom objected.

"Not yet," Kennedy said. "But the story was confirmed by the Russians."

"I don't believe this," the financial officer protested, but Vasilanti cut him off.

"Go ahead, David."

"This happened a couple of days ago, but I waited for McGarvey to get back from Moscow to say anything, because I didn't have a clue what it meant, and I was hoping he would have something new."

"Does he?"

"We won't know until he gets out here tomorrow. Under the circumstances we didn't think discussing this on the telephone was very wise."

"All this may be well and good, but what does it have to do with us?" Topper asked. He was of medium height and thin. "Aren't we in the business of making and selling airplanes?"

"Yes," Kennedy said, answering him. "A business that a Japanese group may want to destroy."

"We don't know that for a fact," Soderstrom cautioned.

"No. Which is why McGarvey went to Moscow to offer the Russians the wing panel factory in exchange for information. He's asked the Russian Secret Service to spy on the Japanese for us. They've agreed."

"Jesus Christ," Kilbourne repeated himself, but Soderstrom and the others were struck dumb.

"What effect the Japanese attack is going to have on our deal, or on relations between our country and theirs remains to be seen, but for the moment we need the information to stay alive."

Vasilanti grinned wryly and shook his head. "The fat is in the fire now."

"We're talking about treason," Kilbourne said. He was a burly man whose shirt sleeves were usually rolled up to the elbows.

"I disagree, Newt," Kennedy said. "We're not spying on the U.S., nor are we giving the Russians anything we shouldn't be giving them. We'll get the proper export licenses from Washington to share our wing-section technology."

"I wondered why Howard wasn't in on this meeting," Soderstrom said a little peevishly. Howard Siegel was Guerin's general counsel. "You can't sit there and tell us that we haven't already broken the law just by approaching the intelligence agency of a foreign government. And spying on Japan? Hell, they're our allies! At the very least we could be hit with industrial espionage."

"What do you suggest?" Kennedy asked, McGarvey's warning coming back to him.

"I don't know. But it sure as hell doesn't include hiring the Russians to spy for us."

"What if it meant the survival of this company, Jeff?"

"If Washington padlocks our door because we've broken the law, there won't be any company."

"What if more of our airplanes are brought down?" Kennedy asked. "Have you thought about the people who were killed, who might be killed?"

"There's no hard evidence to that fact, David. The

NTSB found nothing. Even if it was true that the Japanese sabotaged that plane, there's nothing we can do about it. If another one goes down, however, and we can prove a Japanese group was behind it, then we'd have a leg to stand on."

"In the meantime more people would be dead, and we'd probably be ruined," Kennedy said. He and McGarvey had hashed over this same argument days ago, and this time around it still sounded unreal.

"Then so be it, but for now our hands are tied."

"No," Vasilanti said. "We'll not stand by idly if there's even the slightest chance that people might get hurt flying our equipment. The company be damned, we're talking about human lives here."

"You can have my resignation," Soderstrom said, but Vasilanti slammed his open palm on the desk top.

"I don't want your goddamned resignation. You're a fine executive, Jeff. But you're a bean counter, not an airplane man. This isn't strictly about money now."

Soderstrom shrugged. "You asked for my opinion, and I gave it. I think this course of action is wrong. But you can override me."

"Which I'm going to do this time," Vasilanti said gently.

His older brother had died on the Bataan death march in the Philippines, and he'd never lost his hatred of the Japanese. It affected his dealings with them as a businessman. But this time Kennedy didn't think the old man's hatred was his entire motivation.

"There is one point that we'd better think about this morning, and that's the press conference," Kennedy said. "Might not be such a good idea."

"Why?" Vasilanti asked.

"If it's true that we've been targeted by the Japanese because of the 2622, going public with it might goad them into some kind of action before we're ready for it."

"You mean before we've gotten any hard intelligence from the Russians," the CEO said.

"Exactly."

"We wouldn't be so dependent on Moscow, in that case," Vasilanti said bluntly. "And the fight would be out in the open. I'm going to override you too, David. We're not going to sit around waiting for them to make some move against us. We're going to take the fight to them."

"How?" Socrates asked. He was short, beefy, and very dark, but his voice was soft.

"By showing them what Americans are capable of doing."

"And daring them to do something about it," Soderstrom said, half under his breath, but everyone ignored him.

By a few minutes before noon, when the Guerin helicopter touched down at Test Facility One outside Gales Creek, the snow had tapered off. A lot of media people had made the twenty-five-mile trip from Portland to the huge center. Anything Guerin did was big news in the region. And the unveiling of a new airplane, even though it was incomplete, was the biggest news. It translated into more jobs for a sagging economy.

The governor and other VIPs would be invited to a separate, and more elaborate, unveiling ceremony in a few weeks after the jetliner passed her first FAA trials. Today's event was strictly for publicity.

Test One was a sprawling complex of hangars, concrete bunkers, and assembly halls, some that enclosed dozens of acres in which prototype commercial jetliners were assembled, and one very wide fifteen-thousand-foot runway that ran northwest-southeast along a narrow valley between the mountains. The test pilots hated the place because of the numerous unpredictable wind shears and rapidly accelerating downdrafts and the frequent bouts of very bad weather. But, as one old hand wryly observed, "Guerin Airplane Company's test pilots are the best in the world. They have to be in order to survive Gales Creek."

Saul Edwards, Facility One's operations manager, and Larry Weaver, the P/C2622's chief readiness mechanic, met the chopper in the lee of the prototype hangar and escorted Vasilanti and the other Portland brass inside. The television crews were getting set up, but they were kept at a distance from the airliner by a rope barrier and a half-dozen uniformed security people.

"Just a moment," Vasilanti said, stopping just inside the door.

The sight of a new airplane that had never flown before, state of the art so far as its designers and manufacturer could make it, was cause for awe and pride in any airline executive's breast. But this time they'd made more than a few strides, and they knew it. They had pushed the envelope over the horizon. It was unthinkable to allow Japan, or any other country, to take what they had accomplished here. Boeing's tour de force of the sixties and seventies, the humpbacked whale 747, had consisted of four-and-a-half million separate parts. The P/C2622 had nearly eleven million. When Vasilanti had first seen Socrates's engineering proposals, he'd borrowed a line from one of the 747's production managers. "We'll call this one the Savior," he said, "because every time I see it, I'm going to say, 'Jesus Christ.'"

"It's a big sonofabitch, all right," Edwards agreed.

"That it is," Vasilanti said.

With a fuselage length of four hundred twenty-one feet, it was nearly one hundred feet longer than Boeing's 747, and with a gross takeoff weight of one million pounds it was a third heavier. It could carry up to five hundred passengers and cargo, cruise above 200,000 feet at speeds in excess of Mach five, and yet take off and land on the same runways as the 747 and make less noise doing it. Nor would it become another Concorde SST that was so expensive to operate that governments had to subsidize its operations. The P/C2622 would be a paying aircraft, because it was designed to be so.

A muslin shroud completely covered the gigantic airplane. Even so, the twin-tailed, delta-winged configuration was clearly recognizable, as was the fact that this was no ordinary flying machine. This was something special, and everyone in the hangar understood it.

"Let's show it to them," Vasilanti said. He headed across the hangar floor, Kennedy and the others trailing behind him.

It was a few minutes after noon in West Hollywood. Edward R. Reid paid off his cabby at Wilshire and LaBrea and walked the last four blocks to a small diner on a side street off the main avenue. He wore brown corduroy trousers and an old green sweater under a poplin jacket. He did not stand out, which was what he wanted. In fifty years of making money (his current net worth was around $27 million) he'd become a pragmatist. He would do anything to increase his fortune. It was an aspect of him, a private aspect, that very few people knew or would understand. Even his wife had never suspected this side of him. Early in his career he'd learned that everyone had three choices: They could be poor, they could be middle class, or they could be rich. He'd made his choice and never looked back.

The first time he passed the diner he glanced in the windows at the half-dozen people eating lunch. None of them seemed suspicious, but he kept walking to the end of the block where he crossed to the opposite side of the street and started back.

He'd begun making his contacts while still in the Army in West Germany when he'd come across a cache of Nazi-vintage German Lugers wrapped in cosmoline. He'd been sent up to Kaiserlautern to evaluate an old German supply depot outside the city for possible use by the staff judge advocate's office to which he was attached. The fifteen hundred pistols had been stashed in a section of sub-basement. The week before he'd been in Munich having dinner hosted by a German army legal unit, to which a few representatives from the nearby BND headquarters had also been invited. During the evening he'd spoken at length with Karl Schey, a young Secret Service lieutenant, who'd struck him as being an eminently sensible man. Schey hated what the Nazis had been and what the communists were, but knew enough to suggest that a profit could be made by the man willing to capitalize on the aftermath.

The evening Reid discovered the pistols he'd telephoned Schey in Munich, told him what he was sitting on, and asked for help selling the cache. Schey agreed immediately, and within twenty-four hours the guns were gone, sold for one hundred dollars each. The next day a package containing $75,000 in cash was delivered to Reid's Heidelberg apartment by a cab driver.

Reid kept up his contact with Schey and others whom the German introduced him to, and they made mutual profit. Sometimes he would send items of interest, including intelligence, to Schey, and sometimes it worked the other way. But always there was money to be made.

A few months ago, he'd gone to Germany to take another look at the German stock market, and while he was there he'd driven to Munich where he and Schey had dinner together. It was like old times. They talked about a wide range of subjects, mostly dealing with the Cold War, now dead, the situation in what once had been the Soviet Union, now chaotic beyond belief, and about the rising threat to the west from Japan, very real.

"Are you planning something, my old friend?" Schey had asked.

"I think there's profit to be made, just like in the old days." Reid looked over the rim of his brandy snifter.

"It would appear that they want to buy your country in revenge for Hiroshima and Nagasaki. The Japanese do not suffer their humiliation well."

"No," Reid answered thoughtfully. "Perhaps with the right people something might be done," he mused. "Someone willing and able to carry out, shall we say, delicate operations."

"Someone who afterward you could disassociate yourself from."

"Exactly," Reid said, and Schey smiled.

"I think I might be able to help. But if he becomes

available you would have to team him up with an American group. It would seem more logical to the authorities if your . . . delicate operation were to be carried out by a Mafia family from Chicago or New York."

"Too difficult to control," Reid said. "But I have someone in mind."

Schey nodded sagely. "Where do you see the profit?"

"On the stock market."

"You have a plan after all."

"It occurred to me as we talked," Reid said. "There have been rumors that we might be able to put to good use. We would buy stocks at depressed prices and resell when they returned to normal levels."

"If they do."

"Oh, they will," Reid had assured his old friend. "I'll see to it."

Two older women entered the diner. Reid crossed the street in the middle of the block and went in after them, taking a booth in the back. He ordered coffee. A minute later a tall, skinny man who looked to be in his mid- to late thirties, with longish hair and an immense moustache under a beak of a nose, came in, walked directly back to Reid's booth, and sat down. He wore cowboy boots, faded blue jeans, and a Northwestern sweatshirt under a jean jacket. His eyes looked crazy and there were flecks of spit at the corners of his mouth.

His name was Glen Zerkel, and he was probably as crazy as a bedbug, but he was good at what he did, which was destroying things, sometimes with people still in or on them, he didn't much care one way or the other. He'd once headed a small group of terrorists who called themselves Earth Stewards. Their avowed purpose was to save the world and its resources from rape by greedy capitalists so that there'd be something left for future generations. They did this by fraying the cable on a ski lift in Idaho during a busy Thanksgiving weekend. When the lift was carrying a full load, the weakened cable broke, dumping the gondolas seventy-five feet to the ground, killing seven people, and severely injuring fifty-two others. The ski resort, which was "ruining" the pristine mountain environment, went bankrupt, was purchased by a group of courageous investors for ten cents on the dollar, and reopened. They were not bothered again.

Or by tampering with the engines, and in one case the tail rotor, of the helicopters used for Grand Canyon tours. Three of the machines went down in the same day, killing the pilots and all the passengers and ruining the tour operator's business. No one had figured who'd profited by that act, but the canyon, if littered, had been "saved" for the future.

Reid had used Earth Stewards when he wanted a new molybdenum mine shut down. A series of mysterious explosions and accidents did the trick in three months flat, after which one of Reid's blind subsidiaries profited well.

"It's really good to see you again, Mr. R.," Zerkel said. It was the only name he called Reid, although early on he'd done his homework and he knew who he was dealing with. He was crazy, not stupid.

"How have you been?"

The younger man shrugged. "Bored out of my fucking skull. Not much has been happening lately."

"You've been keeping a low profile?"

Zerkel started to laugh, but something in Reid's expression stopped him. He nodded instead. "There's no real heat for the moment, though from what I hear the feds are still poking around Coeur d'Alene."

Reid studied the man for a moment or two. He'd thought long and hard about coming out here and making contact again. There were risks. So far as he knew the FBI still had no line on Zerkel, but his source could be mistaken. If the bureau was on to the terrorist they might have followed him here to see who he was contacting. It would make for headlines.

But if Zerkel had been made, the bureau would have arrested him by now. Or shot him dead. "Mad dogs," he'd told someone once, "should never be given a second chance."

"I have a project for you," Reid said. "This one is big."

"What do you want me to do?" Zerkel asked, his eyes bright.

"We'll discuss that later. I want you in Washington tonight. Is there any reason you can't leave L.A.?"

"Money," Zerkel said. "But maybe I don't want to go anywhere until I know what's coming down."

Nobody in the diner was paying them any attention. The waitress brought Zerkel a cup of coffee and refilled Reid's cup. When she was gone Reid handed the younger man fifteen well-circulated one hundred dollar bills.

"I want you at Dulles no later than midnight. A Yellow cab with the roof number 659 will pick you up and bring you out to a place I have in the country."

"What if I don't like what I hear? I'm bored, not suicidal."

"You can get out, no hard feelings. Nothing lost. But you'll like this deal, I guarantee it."

Zerkel didn't have to think very long. "No later than midnight," he said.

"Good," Reid said, rising. "And for God's sake get your hair cut, shave off that moustache, and put on some decent clothes."

It was after six by the time Dominique Kilbourne showed up at her apartment. McGarvey watched from the stairwell door as she got off the elevator and came down the corridor. When he stepped out she stopped in her tracks, and for an instant, before she covered it up, she looked terrified.

"Are you all right?" he asked.

"Of course I am," she said sharply. "You just startled me. What are you doing here?"

"I'm going to Portland tomorrow. I wanted to talk to you before I left."

"How was Moscow?"

"You don't want to know," he said. "When I see Kennedy I'm going to tell him that I no longer need you as a contact."

"I asked you a question. I want to know how it went for you in Moscow. Did they agree? Can you give me the courtesy of answering that?" She seemed brittle.

"It looks as if they'll help."

"They said so?" she demanded sharply.

"What is it, Dominique?" McGarvey took her arm. Something was wrong with her. She was flushed.

"Well, I think we're all in danger now." She pulled away.

"What happened when I was gone?"

"They came here to my apartment the first night after you left."

"Who did?"

"Two of them, dressed in black. They broke in, but they didn't steal anything." Her lower lip was quivering. "Nothing is missing, except my security and my peace of mind. It's just that I never thought it would happen to me. I mean, what did they want?"

"Were you inside?"

"I caught them in the act," she said. She laughed nervously. "It's gotten to the point that I'm afraid to open my own goddamned door. Aren't you going to say 'I told you so?'"

"Did you call the police?"

"No."

"David?"

She shook her head. "I waited for you. This is right down your alley, isn't it?"

He took the key from her, opened her door, and ducked inside, keeping to the left. The apartment was ablaze with lights.

"I keep them on," Dominique said. "I can't come back to a dark apartment."

It was all right. There was nobody this time. "Where were they?"

"I don't know. Maybe in the bedroom."

McGarvey went into the bedroom and took apart the telephone on the nightstand. The bug, including its pickup, transmitter, and battery, was smaller than an ordinary postage stamp. It had been installed behind the mouthpiece. There was no mistaking what the device was.

He removed it, then put the phone back together and looked up. Dominique stood at the bedroom doorway.

"What was that?" she asked.

"It's a bug," McGarvey said. The time for lying to her, and keeping her out in the cold, was over. "It's a transmitter so that they can listen in on what you're saying."

"Everything that I said . . . and did . . . they listened to everything?"

McGarvey nodded. "Pack a bag. I'm getting you out of here."

Dominique's face twisted into a grimace, her eyes narrowed. "Those dirty bastards," she swore through clenched teeth.

There was something alarming in her posture and sudden anger. "Did you get a look at them? Did you recognize them?"

"No," she said. "It was dark, and it happened too fast."

McGarvey stared at her for another long moment. She was lying, but there wasn't much he could do about it now except get her out of the way.

"Get packed," he said.

Edward Reid stared at the television set in the living room of the Sterling, Virginia, farmhouse, astonished but pleasantly surprised by what he was learning. He'd expected a breakout, but not this.

The Japanese had attacked and sunk a Russian navy vessel in the Tatar Strait with a loss of all hands. The CNN news report was vague on when this had happened, but it was specific in denouncing the White House and State Department for not sharing what they knew with the American public. CNN had learned of the attack from unnamed sources in Tokyo.

Reid maintained that the Cold War with Japan began

on December 7, 1991, when the Japanese Diet in Tokyo defeated by a large margin a resolution that would have formally apologized for the sneak attack on Pearl Harbor fifty years earlier. A faction of the Japanese population still demanded an apology for Hiroshima and Nagasaki. This was the same day that President Bush had been at Pearl Harbor making a speech and dropping a wreath on the remains of the battleship *Arizona*.

He reached for his drink and took a deep pull at the straight Irish whiskey, barely tasting its harshness. The Japanese were not looking for a confrontation with the Russians. Although Siberia contained many of the natural resources that Japan desperately needed, Tokyo had never publicly considered that option. It was more interested in developing mineral recovery operations in countries along the western Pacific rim, Thailand, Vietnam, and the Malaysian peninsula. The Japanese would open mines and build towns to house the mine workers, their families, and the ancillary families who would run the grocery stores, restaurants, department stores, and public works. These people would become consumers of Japanese manufactured goods, the radios and televisions, the trucks and automobiles, and the Nintendos and digital watches. Two birds would be killed with one stone. Japan would get the mineral resources it so badly needed while creating new markets for its products. The only fly in the ointment was the United States, which wanted those markets for itself, and whose navy ruled supreme.

Reid took another long pull at his drink, finishing it. He got up and went to the sideboard where he poured another, then stood there, lost in thought.

Japan understood full well that it had no chance whatsoever to win an all-out war with the United States. Certainly not now, and very likely not for some years to come. But Japan did not want to dominate the world, as it had wanted to in the forties. It wanted control only of the western Pacific. Nothing more.

It could not win a shooting war, but knew that it would have to face increasingly tough trade agreements that could cripple its growth. It had to do something. Japan was out to finesse the United States by playing a series of cards it knew the United States could beat, but hoped it wouldn't. The attack in the Tatar Strait was the opening move.

Reid was smiling when Mueller came from the stair hall. "Zerkel is here," the German said.

"Good." Reid put down his drink. He had a few cards of his own to put in play. "Bring him right in, Bruno. We've got a lot of ground to cover tonight."

By afternoon, a light breeze sprang up, and although it was chilly the garden was still pleasant. Sokichi Kamiya sat on the broad, scrubbed teak deck, his bandy legs folded beneath him as he listened to the gurgling of the waterfall and the music of the windchime in the gnarled old tree. Kamiya, eighty-one, controlled the vast research and development *zaibatsu* called Mintori Assurance Corporation, which had been involved since shortly after the war with everything from pure electronics and electronic components research to missile development and nuclear energy.

Beside him sat his old friend and business acquaintance, Hiroshi Kobayashi, who at seventy-nine controlled the banking *zaibatsu* of Kobe, second in power and resources only to the Bank of Tokyo.

"It is gracious of our young friend, Yamagata, to share with us the pleasure of this place," Kamiya said. He had been contemplating the rock "future" and "hope" in the freshly raked garden beside the pool of golden carp, certain that its soul was at peace here, especially named as it was, and especially in this setting.

"The storm clouds are gathering, my friend," Kobayashi said.

They'd watched the CNN report on the new Guerin hypersonic transport and on the incident in the Tatar Strait. Neither had come as a surprise, but the White House remained silent, which both men took as an ominous sign. The upcoming economic summit between the United States and Japan worried both of them, not so much for its likely content, but because of the timing of the talks. They were not quite ready.

"All of what has come to pass was inevitable. We move from this point forward."

"Agreed," Kobayashi said. "But I think there will be many more dangers."

"Because of Guerin's announcement?" Kamiya asked harshly, but without raising his voice.

"It's possible they know something. Enough to offer the countermove."

"They would have gone to Washington with it. We would have heard."

"Perhaps not," Kobayashi said, apologetically. "Excuse me, I do not wish to disturb your peace, but we cannot afford to wait any longer. If we are to move, it must be now."

Kamiya composed himself. He felt a sense of frustration and loss for the spirit that had gone out of his country. "Of course you are right, my old friend."

"What will you do?"

"Send *Yamagata-san* to Washington and to Portland. He will find out for us how to stop them."

"And how much they know or suspect?"

"Yes," Kamiya said, focusing again on "future" and "hope." "We will instruct him at once. He can leave in the morning."

"We must take drastic action if this is to succeed."

"Whatever it takes, *Kobayashi-san,*" Kamiya said. He smiled, thinking about how civilized the Japanese were compared to the Americans. *Yamagata-san,* who was almost like a son to him, would have to live among the barbarians for a time. That thought gave him sadness. Still, he smiled.

McGarvey and Carrara met for breakfast at 7:30 A.M. in the Howard Johnson Motor Lodge coffee shop. For the first fifteen minutes McGarvey did all the talking. When he was done, Carrara glanced toward the entrance.

"Is she upstairs now?" he asked.

"Five-oh-three," McGarvey said. "I'm leaving for

Portland in a couple of hours, but before I go I wanted to make sure someone would keep an eye on her."

"The Bureau will watch her, and I'll have her apartment swept, but you know as well as I do, Mac, that if they want her they'll get her, unless we take her out to the Farm where she can be isolated."

"She won't do it."

"Any idea who it was?"

"No," McGarvey said. "But they left these." He handed over the three bugs he'd found in the telephones.

"I'll have Technical Services take a look," Carrara said, pocketing the devices. He sat forward. "If they were Russians I could understand it, but if they were Japanese, I'll be worried."

"Me too," McGarvey said. "In the meantime Moscow has agreed to help out."

"What else?"

"That's it, Phil, unless you'd care to tell me what the White House's reaction would be to a retaliatory strike by the Russians."

Carrara whistled long and low. "Is that what they told you?"

"Not in so many words, but they're thinking about it."

"You never were one to screw around," Carrara said.

"I'm trying to save an airplane company here, that's all."

"And maybe get us into a shooting match?"

"Or keep us from one," McGarvey said. "Think about it."

SEVEN

The black Zil limousine bearing Russian Foreign Intelligence Service director Aleksandr Karyagin glided down a narrow dirt lane through the birch forests along the Istra River east of Moscow. The only person in the car, besides his driver, was his bodyguard. Both men were personally loyal to their director, more loyal to him than even to Russia, or the Commonwealth of Independent States. He had handpicked them as his aides years ago, and even during the worst of economic times they and their families lived well.

A few kilometers off the main highway the road had not been plowed after the last snowstorm so they'd had to stop and put chains on the back wheels. The darkness of the late afternoon, the thin cut of the road through the forest, and the tinkle of the tire chains lent an air of isolation to the place, broken only by the sophisticated communications equipment built into the back seat. He was never out of touch with his staff, or with his masters at the Kremlin. Never.

Because of the crises in the Tatar Strait his leash had been pulled up short. Yeltsin and that pissant, Minister of Defense Colonel-General Vyacheslav Solovyev, had called him on the carpet for a "lack of understanding of the Japanese problem." That coming directly on the heels of the latest rounds of deep budget cuts. The KGB—Karyagin still thought of the organization by its old name—was being hamstrung by a lack of Western currencies just at a time when its foreign intelligence-gathering operations were needed the most. The fools were convinced that the new World Market rouble, which was being traded some places outside of Russia, would survive. All they had to do was look around. They could buy wheat, medical supplies, and even some other badly needed commodities. But when it came to buying technology, or tractors or heavy earth-moving equipment—durable goods—the World Market rouble was worthless. As it was worthless in Tokyo.

Yeltsin had been his mentor, but Karyagin no longer trusted the man, whom he viewed as too self-serving to be reliable. Look at the promises he had made to Polunin. Karyagin had the instincts of a politician, or at least an understanding of a politician's second sight. He

understood that he needed some insurance in the form
of advice from the one man on earth whom he trusted
without reservation to have only the best interests of the
Rodina at heart. He'd managed to get a message to the
man this noon on a secure telephone link, but still there
were risks.

"There's something blocking the road ahead, Mr.
Director," his driver said, breaking him out of his
thoughts.

His bodyguard pulled out a fifteen-shot, 9 mm Beretta
92SB pistol and switched the safety off. "Slow down," he
warned the driver. He looked in the rearview mirror to
make sure no one was behind them.

Karyagin sat forward, the automobile's powerful
headlights illuminating something about a hundred meters ahead. For a second or so his stomach tightened and
his heart quickened. This was not so much like the old
days when the only dangerous enemy that a Russian
officer or politician had was his immediate superior.
Political assassination had finally come to Russia from
the West.

But then he realized what it was. "It's all right," he
said. "The road to the dacha must be bad. They've sent a
sleigh for me."

The troika's driver stood up and waved at them. A
second figure, bundled up in an overcoat and fur hat, sat
in the back, and as they got closer Karyagin could see
that there was no one else, not even a bodyguard.

"I'll come with you, Mr. Director," Karyagin's bodyguard said.

"Very well, but put away your gun. It won't be needed
tonight. There's no reason to make them nervous."

The former President of the Soviet Union, Mikhail
Gorbachev, looking hardy and well rested, pushed back
the fur rug covering his lap as Karyagin climbed aboard
the three-horse sleigh behind his bodyguard and the
driver. When he was settled they shook hands.

"Thank you for seeing me on such short notice, Mr.
President."

Gorbachev shrugged and smiled. "Go," he said softly to his driver, and they lurched forward, the bells on the horses' harnesses sharp in the intensely cold, crisp night air.

Within minutes they were well out of sight of the limousine's headlights. Even though Karyagin was truly isolated now, he felt at ease. Gorbachev had survived a coup attempt.

"What do your Washington assets tell you?" Gorbachev asked, finally.

"I'm sorry, Mr. President, about what?"

"An American response to our retaliation for the Tatar Strait."

It was always startling when Gorbachev came directly to the point. It was un-Russian. "Nothing yet. The White House is silent, although the news story has appeared finally on CNN."

"When is our ambassador going calling?"

"Within thirty-six hours," Karyagin answered. Yeltsin had brought it up at their meeting. "We're still studying the possibilities."

Gorbachev's smile widened, as if to say *I'm sure you are studying the possibilities.* "The instructions have not yet been sent to Washington?"

"No. Everybody is expecting it, of course. But at this point there's absolutely no predicting how their President will respond. And now he has his hands full with Tokyo. The economic summit is scheduled next month, so he's in a difficult position. But so are we."

"Indeed we are. Tokyo Station was able to give no warning?"

"None . . ." Karyagin hesitated, and Gorbachev picked up on it.

"But?"

"The attack may not have been directed by the government, or even by the military as an autonomous action. It's possible that a *zaibatsu* may have been formed to foment trouble between us. The submarine captain may have been one of them."

Gorbachev looked at him sharply. "For what purpose?"

"I have no hard evidence of this, Mr. President, I'm merely speculating. But I suspect that the Americans are going to want to act as a peacekeeper in the region. They'll try to talk us and the Japanese into making concessions. If that happens, Tokyo will be in a much stronger bargaining position at the summit. It'll give a little to insure the peace, so it'd be the United States's turn to give a little."

"Japan was always the buffer against a breakout into the Pacific by our navy in case of war," Gorbachev said. "So Washington gave them anything they wanted. But now that relations between us and Washington have been normalized, Japan is no longer so important."

"Japan may be trying to bring the tensions in the region back into play."

"You said a private *zaibatsu* was involved, and not the government."

"There is a commercial interest. Without concessions from the United States, Japan is going to find itself in very difficult financial times."

Gorbachev fell silent. The frozen river was a few yards off to their left, and a light breeze had sprung up, dropping the wind chill lower.

"The Japanese apparently targeted Guerin Airplane Company for an unfriendly takeover. I met with one of the company executives yesterday. Guerin's offering to build a one billion dollar high-tech airplane-wing factory in Moscow and train our engineers and workers to run it."

"In exchange for what?"

"Information about this Japanese takeover attempt from our intelligence unit in Tokyo."

"What are you asking me, Aleksandr Semenovich?"

Karyagin needed no time to frame his question. He'd been thinking about it for a day and a night. "Who should we court as our allies? The United States or Japan?"

"We should stand alone," Gorbachev said after another long silence. "I think it would be wise if you found the *zaibatsu* behind all of these recent moves before any decision is made."

"But Boris Yeltsin is in a dream world. I don't think he understands what's really happening."

Gorbachev smiled wanly. "Would you be President?"

"No," Karyagin said.

"Then stick to intelligence gathering, Aleksandr Semenovich, so that you may better advise your President."

The rebuff stung. For the first time in Karyagin's career he felt truly alone.

In many respects Louis Zerkel was just as crazy as his half-brother Glen, the Earth Stewards terrorist. His insanity took the form of acute paranoia. Everywhere he looked, there seemed to be conspiracies. His life's mission was to counteract these conspiracies with elaborate counterplans. He was forty-six, and he'd been filling endless notebooks and computer disks with counterplots since 1963 when President Kennedy had been assassinated on Zerkel's twelfth birthday.

Another trait he shared with his half-brother was his brilliance, something they'd inherited from their father, not their mothers. The elder Zerkel had been a U.S. Army criminal investigator stationed in West Germany when he met and married his first wife, with whom he had Louis. A few years after they returned to civilian life in the States, she'd divorced him, and a couple of years later he married his second wife and they had Glen. He worked for the San Francisco Police Department as a special investigator on unsolved capital crimes. But as good an investigator as the man was, he was just as odd. Most people who came in contact with him, including his co-workers, his superiors, and even his family, shied away. There was something about his eyes, the set of his mouth, his stance that looked like a leopard's, or some feral animal that might be docile at that moment but could spring out and devour you without warning.

Police Sergeant Donald Zerkel finally put the barrel of a .357 Magnum pistol in his mouth and blew his brains out one afternoon in the bedroom of his ranch-style house as his wife and her lover watched in horror from where they lay in each other's arms.

By then Louis had graduated from the University of California at Berkeley, with a 4.0 average in electronics engineering, and was working for IBM in upstate New York. His younger brother, Glen, was in his senior year at UCLA as a physics, mathematics, and philosophy triple major with a 4.0 average.

The boys came back for the funeral, attended by a lot of people who were relieved that the man was finally dead. Afterward, at the house, the brothers got into a terrific argument about Glen's mother, who in Louis's words was nothing but a "filthy adulteress" who'd caused their father's death. That was in 1980, and they'd not seen or talked to each other since, although there'd been one news story some years ago about Glen being a suspect in an act of environmental terrorism somewhere in Montana or Idaho. Except for one interview, no police had come calling to ask Louis about his brother, and over the years he'd stopped thinking about his sibling.

A final trait he shared with his brother was a love-hate relationship with women that bordered on fear. In 1984 he took a job in the Bay Area. Many of his co-workers and neighbors were gay or lesbian, and not having the slightest clue about his own sexuality, he'd been confused. He'd always heard that you were supposed to be able to tell just by looking if a person was a homosexual. But he'd never been able to do it. Since the scare about AIDS he'd been ten times as confused. In fact one of his recent conspiracy theories involved the HIV syndrome, which he thought might be a plot by Zambia to kill off the white race so that Africans could rule the world. He conveniently turned a blind eye to the black people dying in droves because of it.

Women were a mystery to him, necessary but frightening. Except for a couple of the female engineers on staff with him, the occasional prostitute he had sex with, and Dr. Shepard, his psychiatrist, he steered clear of them.

The morning was cold and gray. Louis Zerkel pulled into the parking lot of InterTech Corporation's Alameda research center and assembly plant a few minutes before eight. At six-feet-five he was taller than his half-brother, his frame more filled out. But he had the same raw-boned look that made them appear to be the rugged, outdoors type. Women, and for that matter men, found them attractive because of that look, and because their intelligence gave them an air of self-confidence.

He tried to put his thoughts in order so he could wipe what he knew had to be a stupid grin off his face. Overnight he'd discovered a new conspiracy. This one very big, bigger in his mind than the AIDS plot, as big as the Communist Party's "Evil Empire" plot against the United States. In hindsight he should have seen this coming on the day in 1984, two months after he'd started with InterTech at its downtown office in San Francisco, when he overheard the president of the company taking orders from a pair of Japanese from Tokyo. They'd spoken in Japanese, a language that Zerkel did not know, but he'd been able to tell by the tone of their voices that the Japanese were giving an American orders. He just knew it, but he'd not done a damned thing about it, and now he was sick at heart and excited at the same time.

As a conspiracist, which is how Zerkel thought of himself, he kept abreast of world events. On a daily basis he monitored all the major television news networks and news programs, including the specials, with the help of six television sets and six video recorders. He scanned at least three dozen newspapers, news magazines, and newsletters. Once a month he flipped through the latest volumes of *Books in Print* and the *Guide to Periodical Literature* to see what was new.

Ten days ago he'd received the *Lamplighter* newsletter from Washington, D.C., which had started him thinking about the threat from Japan.

Last night he'd watched CNN's report on the incident in the Tatar Strait.

At 3:00 this morning he'd sat straight up in bed out of a sound sleep and went to his computer to look up something he'd suddenly remembered. The Japanese, who were trying to develop a new generation of commercial jetliners, had been rumored to be poised to take over Guerin Airplane Company. It had been mentioned in a short article in *Aviation Week & Space Technology* a few months ago. Zerkel had lifted the story because InterTech supplied a subassembly for Guerin. In 1990, after the crash of a Guerin airliner outside of Chicago, an NTSB investigator had shown up at InterTech to ask a few questions. It was routine, and the man had left within a half-hour, but Zerkel clearly remembered the incident.

By 3:30 A.M., he was inside InterTech's mainframe and had managed to pass through the security lockouts, something that had never occurred to him to do before now, and he'd found his first anomaly.

InterTech supplied a subassembly to Guerin that monitored critical heat measurements at a couple hundred spots in the Rolls-Royce engines. But in 1985, before the Chicago crash, one of the CPU modules had been redesigned. Searching through deeply encoded and hidden invoices revealed that the modules, along with one of the engine-mounted sensor brackets, and its complex wiring harness actually came from Japan, developed and manufactured by Tojii Corporation, a subsidiary of the Mintori Assurance Corporation.

Digging even deeper, Zerkel came up with the schematic diagrams of the subassembly, all of the diagrams, that is, except for the replacement module. Backtracking, he came up with the schematic for the old module and by comparing it with the replacement discovered that the new module used twenty-six of the mother board's thirty possible connections. Two more than the old one. One of the extra pins was wired back into the module's input section, and the second was routed directly to the wiring harness that appeared to deadend as an extra common ground connection to the engine-mounted sensor bracket that the Japanese supplied.

Something was wrong. Not only were the module connections wrong, but the fact that the Japanese were supplying some of the parts ran contrary to InterTech's contract with Guerin. It also struck Zerkel as all wrong that, except for the module change, the electronic subassembly had not been updated in nearly ten years and yet it was being used in Guerin's new project, the one unveiled yesterday.

There was a plot here, all right, and hurrying across the parking lot, Zerkel was determined to get to the bottom of it. He'd not been a part of the design team for that particular assembly, but he sure as hell could find out more about it.

By the time McGarvey deplaned at Portland International Airport and got outside to the cab ranks, it was noon. With all the east-west flying he'd done over the past few days his body clock was screwed up, and he just wanted to get some rest. But he wasn't surprised that someone had come for him.

"You look like hell," Kennedy said, as McGarvey got in the Range Rover and tossed his bag in back.

"It's not going to slack off now."

"It was Al's call, Mac," Kennedy said, pulling away from the curb and getting around a shuttle bus. "And I see his point. If there's going to be a fight, let's get it out in the open where everybody can see what's going on. Maybe Washington will finally sit up and take notice."

"For someone who's so smart, you're dumb. They're not going to mount some frontal assault. But when they hit you, and they will, it'll be decisive. Like 1990."

"I wasn't the only one who tried to talk him out of it. But he's a gutsy old bastard, and once he gets something stuck in his craw he's not about to back down. Besides, that's the way he's always fought his battles—head on."

"He's fighting this one because of a fifty-year-old grudge, and you all know it. This time there's a good chance it'll rise up and bite him in the ass."

"You can tell him that yourself tomorrow morning."

"Why not right now?"

"He's up in Seattle talking to Frank Schrontz at Boeing."

"They work with the Japanese."

"Exactly."

McGarvey shook his head. "You don't understand what you're facing. If Washington decides, for some political expediency in Tokyo next month, to sell you down the river, this President will do it without blinking an eyelash."

"He'd put more than eighty thousand voters out of work."

"He'd point them toward Boeing, and you know damned well he would," McGarvey said. "Look at them. They understand the global economy we're in, and they're prospering. Wake up to the realities, David, or you might just lose the entire shooting match."

Kennedy turned off the airport road to Interstate 205 and took the access road directly across to Guerin Headquarters.

"Well, that's a cheery thought before lunch. Are you telling me that you're writing off the Russians?"

"Not yet," McGarvey said heavily. "But we may already be in some trouble."

Kennedy looked at him. "How so?"

"Dominique Kilbourne's apartment was broken into the other night, and the place was bugged. My guess is they were Japanese, but she won't tell me. Fact is, they may have heard everything that went on there."

Kennedy was suddenly subdued. "What happened?"

"She said that she came home and caught them in the act. Apparently she wasn't hurt. She didn't call the police."

"She shouldn't stay in Washington."

"Somebody is going to look out for her, and for the moment she's staying at a hotel under an assumed name . . ." he trailed off. Kennedy was shaking his head.

"Mac, I just talked to her at her office. She was on her

way out the door. Said I could call her at home tonight. She told me to tell you not to worry."

"Shit," McGarvey said.

DCI Roland Murphy was the last to arrive for the 2:00 P.M. meeting at the White House just behind General Anthony Podvin, chairman of the Joint Chiefs. They met in the cabinet room, although the only cabinet members in attendance were Secretary of State Jonathan Carter and Secretary of Defense Paul Landry, who along with General Podvin sat on the President's left. Murphy took his place on the right with National Security Adviser Harold Secor. The afternoon sun streamed in the windows, but the mood in the room was somber.

"I would like to get this issue resolved as quickly as possible, so let's get started," the President said. "The Russian ambassador has requested a meeting for tomorrow morning at 9:00 sharp. And we all know what he's coming here to talk about, so let's start with you, Jonathan."

"Other than the first message from Tokyo the Japanese have been silent," the Secretary of State said. "We expected some announcement after CNN broke the story, and we even made a few private and discreet inquiries through unofficial channels, but there's been no word."

"Has there been anything from Moscow?" Secor asked. "Other than from their ambassador?"

"We've made a couple of back-burner inquiries at the Kremlin with the same results. Nobody is talking."

"How about the Agency?" the President asked Murphy.

"Nothing at all from the Japanese, although it's my understanding that Naval Intelligence at Yokosuka is on the lookout for the submarine."

"The *Samisho*," General Podvin said. "It was picked up by the SOSUS network in the strait, probably heading back to port. But so far the MSDF hasn't said a thing."

"What about the Russian Navy?" Murphy asked.

"That's a problem at this point. They've concentrated a lot of power in what's technically international waters but what's very close to the Japanese home islands."

"What?" Secor demanded.

"The sub has a good head start, so it's not likely the Russians will catch up with it, but their ships are going to come damned close to Hokkaido."

"What have they got out there so far?" Murphy asked.

"Two attack submarines, three boomers, and at least eight destroyers and guided-missile frigates."

"There are plenty of Russian Air Force bases and missile squadrons along the mainland coast there as well," Murphy added. "How much time do we have before it gets critical?"

"Thirty-six hours, give or take," the general said. "Question is, are the Russians willing to use all that firepower?"

"More to the point, if they do start shooting, will we come to Japan's defense?" the general's boss, Paul Landry, asked.

"That's what we're here to discuss." The President turned back to Murphy. "You said you've learned nothing about the Japanese. What about the Russians, other than their naval buildup in the strait."

One of the things Murphy liked about the President was that the man never missed a beat.

"We've gotten nothing *directly* from the Japanese, or the Russians for that matter, Mr. President, but there has been a development, of sorts, concerning both of them. My people briefed me this morning."

"Get to the point," the President warned.

"Guerin Airplane Company believes it may be the target of an unfriendly takeover attempt by a consortium of Japanese companies."

"We're not getting ourselves involved in business," the President cautioned. "Not unless it concerns our national security. Does this?"

"I'm not sure," Murphy admitted. "But a Guerin

executive hired one of our ex-field officers to go to Moscow to offer the Russians an airplane assembly plant."

The President looked sharply at his secretaries of defense and state. "We've heard nothing about this?" Both men shook their heads, mystified.

"For what type of airplane?" the National Security Adviser asked.

"From what we can tell it's to be a next-generation jetliner."

"But not a military aircraft?"

"There could be a military application, but we don't have that information yet. The point is what the Russians are apparently being asked to do in exchange for the assembly plant."

"Which is?" Secor asked.

"They want the Russians to spy on the Japanese for them. Specifically to find out about this possible takeover move."

The President sat back in his chair and stared across the table at his DCI. "Have they broken the law?"

"Damned if I know, Mr. President," Murphy said.

"Have the Russians agreed to do it?" Secor asked.

"I don't know that either," Murphy admitted. "But someone bugged the apartment here in town of Dominique Kilbourne. She runs the airlines and manufacturers' lobby, and coincidentally her brother runs Guerin's prototype and new product development division. In addition, she's had a long-standing relationship with the Guerin executive who sent our man to Moscow to negotiate the deal."

"Are you saying that the Russians are spying on her?" Secor asked.

"Not the Russians," Murphy said. "At least we don't think so. Three of the devices were taken from her apartment and were handed over to my Technical Services people who say the bugs are Japanese."

"Would Guerin's plans have been discussed in her apartment?" Secor asked.

"It's certainly possible."

"Who is this former employee of yours, General?" the President asked.

"His name is Kirk McGarvey. He was dismissed from the CIA in the eighties by mutual agreement. Since then, however, we've used his services on a contract basis."

"What services?"

Murphy had expected the discussion to lead to this point. The problem was he didn't know what to tell the President other than the truth.

"He is . . . or was . . . an assassin."

"Well," the President said. "I see."

"It shows how difficult Guerin believes the situation is."

"Do we have any control over Mr. McGarvey?"

"He is an independent operator, Mr. President," Murphy said. "But there's never been any doubt that he is anything but a completely loyal American."

"There'd be hell to pay if this got loose on the Hill."

"Yes, sir."

"You say that the Japanese are spying on us?"

"We've handed this to the Bureau. John Harding says that his counterespionage people have tracked an increasing number of industrial espionage reports, but this particular case was a new one for them."

"Will Guerin and McGarvey cooperate with you?" the President asked Murphy.

"I think so, Mr. President, if it's handled correctly."

"Then do it," the President said. "Now, what do we tell the Russians?"

"Japan is our ally," the Secretary of State answered. "We tell the Russians to back off. At the very least get their navy out of the strait until the situation cools off. As for the Japanese, we'll tell them that the Russians are backing down, but that an apology will have to be made."

"All that's reasonable," the National Security Adviser agreed. "But it'll put us on the down side when we get to Tokyo. If we force them to back off over this issue—

which is, after all, important to them—they'll want some extra consideration from us."

"Wrong," Carter disagreed. "You're forgetting something important. The Japanese will insist that this incident was a mistake. The government didn't order the attack, and its Maritime Self Defense Force continues to maintain a nonconfrontational policy with the Russians in the region."

"The Russians will back down," the President said. "Or else Guerin will never get the export licenses it needs to build its assembly plant in Moscow. But the rest of it I'll save for Tokyo, unless the Japanese do something else just as stupid. Make sure Mr. McGarvey gets the word."

"Yes, sir," Murphy said.

"Good." The President looked around the table. "Anything else?"

"What about Guerin's request that the Russians spy for it?" Murphy asked.

"We'll turn this over to the Attorney General. If anybody has broken the law, they'll be prosecuted. Otherwise it's something between the Russians and the Japanese. Something, if it comes up, I'll tell them to work out on their own." The President sat forward. "We're in a tough position here between the Russians and the Japanese. I've said it before, and I'll say it again, if we have to play rough, we will. But I'll be damned if we're going to sell out to the Japanese, or if we're going to let the Russians start a shooting war over a god-damned island in the middle of nowhere."

They'd moved aboard the boat last night, and after a late dinner of lobster and white wine went to bed in the forepeak where they made love for nearly two hours before going to sleep. The stern of the boat was facing east, and this morning the sun blasted through the open hatch.

"Another beautiful day in paradise," Carol Moss said, padding barefoot into the main saloon.

Liskey, who'd always been an early riser, stood in the

hatchway drinking his first cup of coffee for the day. He looked back at her and grinned. "If your CO could see you now, the old bag would toss you in jail and throw away the key."

Carol smiled back at him. She wore only the bottom half of a very brief bikini and a gold ankle bracelet. "Not exactly Navy issue," she said. "Anyone up and about?"

"Not for another half-hour."

"Good. I'm going for a swim. And when I get back I'll expect breakfast."

"Aye, aye, ma'am," Liskey said, moving aside so that she could get up into the cockpit. As she passed he reached out to grab her, but she nimbly avoided him, and in two quick steps was over the rail and into the water.

"Nice," she cried, breaking the surface.

"Bacon and eggs in twenty minutes," he called out to her, then went below. He switched the VHF radio to the weather channel, refilled his coffee, and started the bacon.

The local and regional weather was broadcast twenty-four hours a day in English from the U.S. Navy Meteorological Station on Okinawa, which supplemented its local data with information from ships at sea, Japanese weather stations as far as Kyushu, and U.S. weather satellites. Winds over the entire region today would be southeast at ten to fifteen knots, producing waves of three to five feet in the East China Sea, increasing to fifteen to twenty knots tonight, with seas gradually increasing to five to eight feet. The high temperatures would range from near seventy-five in the south to forty-four in the north, under partly cloudy skies with a near-zero chance of rain in the south. Perfect conditions for them to set out. By tonight they would be anchored in a quiet, secluded cove somewhere twenty-five or thirty miles north of here where Carol wouldn't have to wear so many clothes when she went in for a swim. He grinned and began to whistle the theme from Ravel's *Bolero*.

* * *

Louis Zerkel was aware that most of his co-workers and supervisors tolerated his conspiracy theories because his design and analysis work was nothing short of brilliant. Although he was unaware of his real worth, there were those in the San Francisco business office who figured he'd earned the company fifteen million dollars in excess of the salary and benefits he'd received over the years. When he spoke, people listened. You could never tell when a gem of design or application would pop out.

His psychiatrist, Dr. Jeanne Shepard, listened too. In the five years he'd been seeing her for his debilitating bouts of fear and confusion, she had picked up a number of design secrets that she passed on to a friend in Washington, D.C., for considerations, sometimes as high as twenty-five thousand dollars, always in untraceable small bills. Her specialty was dealing with what she privately called "Silicon Valley nut cases." Because of the stress that these highly brilliant men and women worked under, her office was always busy. In Zerkel's case, his stress manifested itself in conspiracy theories. It was a form of paranoia that was relatively common among people with tunnel vision—engineers, mathematicians, and researchers.

At their weekly sessions Dr. Shepard would skillfully steer his conversation back to his work. He was developing what he called a "real-time multiphasic head-up display director" for commercial jetliners. Her Washington friend was very excited about it and kept pressing her for more information.

Sitting across from Zerkel, she could see that he was even more agitated than usual. He crossed and uncrossed his legs, fiddled with the pens and colored pencils in his pocket, and darted glances out the window at the overcast afternoon.

"You're stressed out today, Louis. Would you like to talk about it?" She was a mature, attractive woman. Her friends said she looked like Candice Bergen, and she had the same, deep-throated confident voice and manner as the actress.

"There's a lot of pressure at the lab," Zerkel said. "We've hit a snag in the director. Nothing that can't be worked out. But, you know, everybody takes orders, even San Francisco.

"Who takes orders?"

"Everybody. Me, you, everybody at InterTech, and I mean *everybody*. Maybe even the U.S. one of these days unless something is done."

This was something new, Dr. Shepard thought. She'd seen him excited before, and oftentimes so fearful that it was difficult for him to speak with any coherence. During those sessions she did most of the talking. Trying to soothe him, trying to calm his fears, trying to bring him back to reality. On days like that she sometimes scheduled a second hour for him in the same week so that she could maneuver him back on track. If he ever completely broke down, he would become useless to her and she would have to cut him adrift. That was something she had no intention of allowing, even if she had to work with him every day. He was just too much of a gold mine to leave floundering.

"It's the Japanese, Dr. Shepard. They're making their move."

"I don't understand, Louis. What do you mean?"

"I want you to read something, then you'll see." He pulled a copy of the *Lamplighter* newsletter out of his coat pocket and handed it to her. "Mr. Reid knows."

Still puzzled, Dr. Shepard quickly scanned Reid's turgid prose, which, if she was catching the gist of it, seemed to suggest that a war between the United States and Japan was inevitable unless certain steps were taken immediately by a White House too unsure of itself to make the first move. It was Japanese bashing in a sophisticated forum. The newsletter's masthead identified Edward R. Reid as a Washington insider and a former undersecretary of state. "An adviser to presidents, and now an adviser to you."

She looked up. "I still don't understand. What does this have to do with you?"

Zerkel took the newsletter, carefully folded it and put it back in his pocket. "Do you watch television, read the newspaper?"

"Yes, of course."

"Then you know that a Japanese Maritime Self Defense Force submarine sank a Russian Navy ship just north of the Japanese home islands."

"What's your connection?"

"The Japanese are also trying to take over Guerin Airplane Company, something you might not know about."

"Go on."

"Well, look at it this way, Dr. Shepard. Say the Japanese do take over Guerin. Next maybe they'll go after Boeing. Or maybe General Motors, or U.S. Steel. They've got the money."

"But what does this have to do with you?" Dr. Shepard asked. She'd never seen him quite like this before. He was agitated and frightened, but he also seemed happy. He had the bit in his teeth.

"InterTech makes certain electronic assemblies for Guerin. But I found out that InterTech is being supplied, and maybe even being directed, by the Japanese. What do you think about that?"

It was another of his conspiracy theories. "Many American electronics companies work with the Japanese."

"When that Guerin airliner went down out of Chicago it could have been caused by one of our subassemblies. We even had the NTSB poking around, but it didn't find anything. Could have been sabotage though. I haven't got that part figured out yet, but it's there. What do you think about that?"

"Why would they do that? What would they have to gain?"

Zerkel smiled. "Maybe to bankrupt the company so they could take them over real cheaply, you know. Guerin is top dog right now on HSCT research. Didn't you see the unveiling of its prototype the other day?" He leaned forward. "Listen to this, Dr. Shepard. It got me thinking, why would such an advanced-design airplane use the same engine heat-monitor assembly that we designed more than ten years ago? Only thing that's never been changed is the in/out director module. What do you think about that?"

"I don't know, Louis," Dr. Shepard said, and she meant it. There was something here, but she wasn't sure what just yet. "Have you contacted Mr. Reid in Washington?"

Zerkel reared back. "Of course not," he said, and he glanced over his shoulder at the closed door to the reception room. "I'm not sure of this yet, and besides he knows what's going on. When the time comes I'll give him my help. But I don't want to be killed. They do that, you know. It could be 1941 all over again. I need more details."

Dr. Shepard delayed her next appointment for ten minutes so she could place a call to Benjamin Tallerico, her Washington friend. He ran the Fund for International Development, which worked to match U.S. and Canadian venture capital with foreign projects. Tallerico, an ex-Mafia lieutenant from Chicago, used the money to open electronics sweat shops in Taiwan, Thailand, and most recently in northern Mexico where wages were less than a dollar per hour. The work was billed out to North American and European companies, who'd ordered the subcontracts, for several dollars per hour.

Tallerico also dealt in industrial espionage, an endeavor that had grown tremendously over the past half-dozen years or so. It was he who had approached Dr. Shepard six years ago when her name came up in a conversation with a Silicon Valley technician who had information to sell. Besides telling Tallerico everything he knew about his research company's secrets, the man babbled on and on about his psychiatrist, the one person in the world whom he trusted without reservation.

"Does the name Edward R. Reid mean anything to you?" Dr. Shepard asked when she had Tallerico on his scrambled line.

"Everybody in Washington knows him, sweetie. He puts out a financial newsletter that's generally pretty close to the mark. What's up?"

"He's going after the Japanese."

Tallerico chuckled. "Big time. From what I hear the State Department is on his ass, but he won't budge."

"I've got somebody out here who thinks he's right and might have some hard evidence for him. Something that might be worth a buck."

"What've you got?"

"Has Reid got any money?"

"He's loaded."

"Good," Jeanne Shepard said. "Tell him that we might have proof that the Japanese are trying to sabotage Guerin Airplane Company so it can be bought at fire-sale prices. Think he might be interested?"

"Maybe. Who's your source?"

It was Dr. Shepard's turn to chuckle. "Talk to him, Ben, then get back to me."

The black Cadillac limousine stopped momentarily at the White House east gate, a distance of one thousand feet as the crow flies from an upper-story window in the Hay Adams Hotel on H Street, then proceeded down the drive to the east portico.

"Is it Zagorsky?" the slightly built man standing back from the window asked impatiently. The car pulled up at the White House east entryway. Someone jumped out of the front seat, ran around to the back, and opened the rear door on the passenger side.

"I think so," Toshiki Korekiyo answered. He watched through the one-thousand-millimeter camera lens set up on a tripod in the middle of the room. The license plate was of the diplomatic series used by the Russian embassy, but they had to be certain. There could be no mistakes.

They'd monitored a greatly increased flow of communications traffic between Moscow and the Russian Embassy on 16th Street over the past forty-eight hours. It had peaked early this morning, then abruptly stopped.

Russian Ambassador to the United States Yanis Yanovich Zagorsky got out of the limousine at the same time Steven Nichols, the President's appointments secretary, came out of the White House to greet him. Two Marine guards stood at ramrod attention at the door, but there was no one else. No media.

"It's him," Korekiyo said, not looking up. Zagorsky seemed nervous, ill at ease, as well the bastard should be. Korekiyo, who worked for a special research unit of the Ministry of International Trade and Industry—MITI— didn't know all the details. But he did know that Japan was no longer going to allow itself to be treated as an inferior nation. Its humiliating defeat a half-century ago had been paid for. Time now to go on. First would be the Russians, but there would be other targets.

Zagorsky and Nichols shook hands, then went inside. Korekiyo looked up. "Definitely the Russian ambassador."

Yozo Hamagachi was already on the telephone waiting for his call to Arimoto Yamagata at the embassy on Massachusetts Avenue to go through. "Who met him?"

"Nichols."

Hamagachi turned back to the telephone. "He has arrived," he said, and a moment later he turned again to Korekiyo. "Was he carrying a briefcase? Anything?"

"Nothing."

"Tie, he carried nothing."

"Good morning, Mr. President," Ambassador Zagorsky said when he was ushered into the Oval Office. He crossed to the President's desk. Secretary of State Carter and National Security Adviser Secor stood up, but the President remained seated.

"Mr. Ambassador," the President said coolly. "Mr. Carter and Mr. Secor will sit in on this."

"Of course," Zagorsky said, clearly nervous. They all sat down.

"You have something for me from your government?" the President asked.

"Yes, Mr. President, but not in writing. It was thought

in Moscow that I could open a dialogue with you in order that I might explain our difficult position."

"I'm listening."

There was no sign of any warmth or friendship among these three, Zagorsky thought. But he'd warned those idiots at the Kremlin that Yeltsin should have telephoned this President the moment they'd learned about the Tatar incident. They were not here in Washington, so they could not gauge the mood.

"Simply put, something must be done about the Japanese incursion into our waters in the Tatar Strait, and the unprovoked attack on one of our naval vessels. All hands were lost. Many of them boys."

"From what we understand, your Navy fired the first shot, and that in international waters," Harold Secor said.

"Those waters are as sensitive to our security as the Gulf of Mexico is to yours," Zagorsky replied calmly.

"But one of your anti-submarine-warfare helicopters dropped a torpedo on that Japanese submarine before it initiated the attack," Secor pressed.

"The timing was critical. I have read transcripts of the radio messages and the helicopter."

"So have we," the President said. "You fired first."

A lie? Zagorsky wondered. If not, the President had made a mistake admitting the U.S. had that level of technology in the area. "In response to the submarine's torpedo doors opening preparatory to its attack."

Before the telephone call, Arimoto Yamagata had been thinking about his home in the mountains outside of Tokyo, and about the rock "future" and "hope." He knew that under the circumstances the Western mind would consider such thinking frivolous, even silly, but it helped bring order to his thoughts. The problem his mentors had sent him to solve was so vast, and so far reaching in its implications, that it strained his abilities to contemplate. But he was truly a disciple of Mishima, and therefore capable of serenity under any condition.

Rising from the tatami where he'd taken the call from

his field officers, he left his quarters and headed to the embassy's secured communications center two floors below. At six feet two he was strikingly tall for a Japanese, and although he had had no plastic surgery, his appearance was Western. He understood that he was handsome in either world, and at forty-three experienced enough to use that knowledge to his advantage.

The Russian ambassador had called on the American president. The timing, he thought, was most interesting.

"Excuse me, but are you suggesting that we simply forget about that ship and her crew?" Zagorsky decided it was time to strike back.

"We do not want an escalation of the situation out there," the President said. So far left unspoken was the upcoming economic summit talks between the U.S. and Japan, but the President was obviously speaking with care. "I'm told that your navy continues to place warships into the strait, and some if not all of those vessels are armed with nuclear weapons. Nobody wants to see further bloodshed."

"Is it correct that two of your attack submarines are currently trying to catch up with that Japanese submarine?" Secor asked directly.

That was news to Zagorsky, but it wasn't surprising. He could understand what they were thinking in Moscow. If they allowed the Japanese to go unpunished, their entire far eastern border would be weakened. From that narrow viewpoint pursuing the *Samisho* made sense. But stepping back and looking at it from an international platform, nothing but an immense danger could be seen.

"Certain of our naval units are engaged in an exercise in the strait. But as to their exact deployment at this moment I have no direct word."

"Oh, come off it, Yanis," the President replied sharply. "You came over here this morning to tell us that you're going to retaliate for the sinking of your ship, and that we're not supposed to take such an act as a declaration of war on Japan or anyone else."

"There has not been so much as an apology."

"Has your ambassador to Japan called on the Prime Minister?"

"I don't know," Zagorsky answered. Damn those fools in the Kremlin!

"Hell, we know what this will do to the posture of your eastern defense forces. You might even lose absolute control over the strait. I'd sell them Sakhalin Island, if they want it that bad. You can use the hard cash, and they can rename the place."

Zagorsky could hardly believe what he was hearing. The President had never talked to him this way. It was almost as if they were two men sitting around a table, playing cards and drinking vodka together, but in a dangerous alliance.

"What would you tell the mothers of those boys, Mr. President?"

"I would say that they gave their lives to help secure a lasting peace."

Zagorsky looked at the President for a long moment, then lowered his eyes. "Chamberlain," he muttered. "Am I to leave this office with a piece of paper in hand— 'Peace in our time'—that I can wave toward Moscow?"

"Japan is not Nazi Germany, and this is not 1938," the President shot back. "Russia would be better off if it took care of its internal problems without seeking trouble outside its borders."

"I had hoped to open a dialogue with you, Mr. President . . ."

"Tell Mr. Yeltsin to pull your naval vessels out of the Tatar Strait for now, and I expect that the Japanese government will issue an apology. Our sources tell us that the act was not ordered by Tokyo, nor has it been condoned by the Japanese Maritime Self Defense Force."

"A renegade submarine captain?"

"A mistake. Once that boat returns to its home port the incident will be fully investigated."

"What if my government decides to proceed?" Zagorsky asked, knowing full well what the answer would be.

"We would regret that," the President said. "And we would be forced to respond." He eyed the Russian ambassador coldly. "Your country currently enjoys a Most Favored Nation trading status with us that would be affected. Certainly the export of technologies would be interrupted, as would the flow of business developmental capital."

"I see," Zagorsky said, heavily. There was no mistaking what the President was referring to. Yemlin had discussed it at length with him. "I will convey your position to my government at once." He got to his feet. "Thank you, Mr. President, for your frankness this morning."

"We've been friends for only a short while now. Let's not return to the old days."

"No, Mr. President. Let's not."

Yamagata graduated from Harvard Law School in 1978, so he understood Americans and the Western mind as well as any Japanese. From the beginning of his career, which had been guided by a mentor his father had arranged for, he'd worked ostensibly as a liaison between Japanese and American, Australian, Canadian, and British corporations. In actuality, his position with MITI was cover for his real work as a spy. He'd gone after industrial secrets—design and product as well as corporate strategies and intents. But there'd been times when he'd entered the much more dangerous political arena. Such as now.

In the early days, the trade war, as it was considered, had been primarily one of keeping up with technologies. The only real hurt anyone suffered was fiscal. Now that had changed. With the sinking of a Russian naval vessel in the Tatar Strait they could never go back.

He spoke from a soundproof booth on a secure line to Tokyo so that no one—not the Americans or the Japanese—could monitor his call. The number was direct.

"Ohayō go-zai-ma-su, Kamiya-dono," he said. "Traffic to the Russian embassy slowed down about seven hours

ago, and the ambassador called on the White House, just as you suspected would happen."

The call was not being recorded, nor did Yamagata make any notes, he simply listened as his mentor spoke, committing the old man's very precise instructions to his excellent memory. When the call was ended, Yamagata sat back and closed his eyes, trying to bring up an image of his home and its peaceful garden, but it was a full minute before he could clear his thoughts.

State Department spokesperson Warner MacAndrew entered the media briefing room at 3:00 P.M., and went directly to the podium in front of the floor-to-ceiling map of the world. A hush fell over the crowded room as he opened a buff-colored folder.

"First I'm going to read a short statement, and then I'll open it for questions," MacAndrew said. His red hair and freckled complexion seemed even more intense than usual this afternoon, which happened when something big was in the wind. Most of the press corps could read the seriousness of what was coming from the color of his face.

"Five days ago an apparent incident between what is believed to have been a Japanese Maritime Self Defense Force submarine and a Russian Krivak-class frigate in the Tatar Strait, fifty miles off the coast of Siberia, resulted in the sinking of the Russian naval vessel with a loss of all hands. In response to that incident the Japanese issued the following: 'The government of Japan deeply regrets the recent incident in the Tatar Strait off the island of Karafuto allegedly involving a vessel of the Japanese Maritime Self Defense Force and one of the Russian Federal Navy in which there may have been a loss of life and property. Every effort is being made to quickly and fully investigate the matter to determine culpability.'"

MacAndrew looked up, then continued. "This morning at 9:00 Russian Ambassador Yanis Zagorsky met here in Washington with the President to discuss the issue. One hour ago, the Russian government issued the following statement: 'The government of Russia deeply regrets the recent Tatar Strait incident involving units of the Russian and Japanese navies. During the period of our investigation all Russian military units will be unilaterally withdrawn from the strait to positions north of the fiftieth parallel. Every effort will be made to quickly and fully determine culpability.'"

Again MacAndrew looked up. "Questions?"

Everybody raised their hands, and the clamor began.

The meeting took place in Vasilanti's office, and from the moment he walked into the room, McGarvey felt as if he'd stepped into the middle of a life-or-death council of war. No one was smiling. But, as Kennedy had explained it to him on the way up, Guerin Airplane Company had never been in such a sporty position. It was literally betting the farm on the outcome of the P/C2622. The situation had become so critical that the old man had even relented on his entrenched stand that except for engines Guerin airplanes were to be entirely American designed and manufactured.

"These are extraordinary times and they call for extraordinary measures," Kennedy told the board this morning. "Pitting an enemy of seventy years against a friend of fifty may be one of them."

In the end the board had gone along with them, as Vasilanti had predicted it would. But being given such a free rein made no one very happy. This meeting now, which included Vasilanti, Kennedy, and McGarvey, plus Kilbourne, Socrates, Topper, and Soderstrom, was to be their final strategy session. Up to this moment they could have backed away from the Russian deal. But after today that would no longer be possible, and they all knew it.

"Do we go, or don't we go?" Vasilanti put it bluntly on the table after McGarvey was introduced.

Carrara had confirmed by phone this morning that the Russians were backing off from the trouble spot in the strait, and that the White House would offer no road-blocks in granting the necessary export license. *"Make it clear that a permanent solution in the strait has to be found, and soon,"* his old friend warned. Unsaid, but implied, was the warning that the licenses could be rescinded at any moment, no matter what it might do to the company. A national debt totalling in the trillions of dollars was of much greater import than Guerin's current difficulty.

"I don't see that we have much choice in the matter," Kennedy said from the sideboard where he poured a cup of coffee. "Even if Mr. McGarvey is dead wrong about the Japanese, we stand to save a considerable sum of money in tax credits."

"Congress handed us a plum with that one," Soderstrom, the chief financial officer, agreed. The U.S. aid package to Russia included a generous tax credit for companies setting up shop there. "But we're still faced with the risk of a general collapse of government which could wipe us out."

"If the 2622 fails, for whatever reason, we're dead," Topper said. "I hate to be the one to keep bringing this up, but we are in the business of manufacturing airplanes and selling them for a profit. Unit costs on the wing panels out of a Moscow facility versus our Wichita plant are one-third less. And that includes transportation. The Russians wrote the book on titanium. Makes sense to me, especially if they agree to help us with the Japanese problem, because even if there is no problem with the Japanese, we still come out ahead."

"We risk losing it all," Soderstrom responded.

Topper shrugged. "This is a risky business. And the board went along with it, didn't they, Jeff?"

"They agreed to let us shoot ourselves in the head if we want to. But they didn't recommend that we do so," Soderstrom argued.

"What about Japan?" Vasilanti asked, directing his question to McGarvey, who'd poured a brandy and stood near the window.

"They're after you, there's no question about that," McGarvey said. He glanced over at Kennedy. Apparently the old man hadn't been told about the break-in at

Dominique's apartment, and if it was brought up now, her brother Newton would probably overreact and do something stupid, causing them further problems. "They've bugged some of our telephones, which means they probably know something about our deal with Russia."

"Shit," Topper said.

"They'll make a move soon. Going public with the prototype didn't help."

"Does the CIA know this?"

"Yes."

Vasilanti looked at the others. "We have no other choice now but to get the Russians to help us while we put the prototype in the air as soon as humanly possible."

"You get her flying and I'll generate some money for this company," Topper said with enthusiasm.

"If we last that long," Soderstrom mumbled.

Edward R. Reid was drunk. But like many long-term heavy drinkers Benjamin Tallerico had known, Reid was still lucid and still very much in control of himself. At any given moment half of official Washington was in its cups, but whatever Reid's problem was it had not affected his power. When the man spoke people listened. Just now Washington was divided into two camps, and not necessarily down party lines. On one side were the White House supporters—those who agreed with the President that an appeasement with Japan was not only desirable but necessary. On the other were those who believed that a conflict between Japan and the United States was coming. It was a measure of Reid's power just how large that second faction was. What was not so widely known, however, was Reid's apparent growing fanaticism on the subject. After Jeanne Shepard's telephone call, Tallerico had dug up everything he could find on the former State Department undersecretary and had reread all the recent issues of the *Lamplighter*. He had come to the conclusion that the man was unbalanced. Nothing he'd seen or heard this evening had altered that opinion. He reached across the table and poured Reid another glass of wine. They were having dinner at the Rive Gauche, Reid's favorite restaurant.

"I'm a long-term admirer of yours, Mr. Reid. I just wanted to tell you that, before I say that I think you've never been closer to the mark than you are now."

"It's nice to hear," Reid said, eyeing the younger man over the rim of his glass. "You have some long-standing business relationships in the Far East, from what I understand. Isn't that correct?"

"Taiwan, Bangkok, Malay, but not Japan. You might say I'm in direct competition with the bastards."

"Have you had problems with them?"

"Not yet," Tallerico said. "But the time is coming. I think that's plain to see."

Reid shrugged. "You didn't invite me to dinner to tell me that you believe in what I'm writing."

"No. And you didn't accept the invitation to listen to that. What I have for you is a proposition."

"Go on."

"It has to do with Guerin Airplane Company. A Japanese group apparently wants to buy it out."

"Yes, I've heard about it. But the company is strong. I don't think there's any real danger from the Japanese."

"If the company remains strong. But if its stock were to plunge it might be a different story."

"It might."

"Let's say that Guerin airplanes started falling out of the sky for no apparent reason other than poor design, faulty workmanship. The company would head into bankruptcy."

"Won't happen. Next to Boeing it builds the best airplanes in the world."

"Unless its airplanes were sabotaged in such a way that no one would ever know about it."

Reid thought it out and came to a conclusion in under a second. Tallerico read that much from the man's eyes until a veil dropped over them.

"What is your source?"

Tallerico smiled. "My source is concerned about safety. In this day and age safety is expensive. One million dollars."

"No," Reid said without blinking.

Tallerico was not surprised by Reid's rejection of the first offer, but he was surprised by the man's abruptness. "You're not interested?"

"Not at that figure," the older man said tiredly. "Maybe not at any figure without more information up front." He sat forward. "I publish a newsletter, and you cannot believe the nut cases who write to me with offers like yours."

"This comes from California . . . Silicon Valley. A Guerin subcontractor. What we're talking about is an electronic device that can bring down airplanes." Tallerico was guessing most of that, but considering Jeanne Shepard's usual sources he didn't think he was too far off the mark.

Reid nodded. "If I could have the device, or at least the plans for it, and clear evidence linking its design back to Japan, I might pay something."

"How much?"

"I don't know yet. First find out from your source if you can meet my requirements, and then we'll discuss money."

"Fair enough," Tallerico said after a beat. The old bastard might be a drunk, but he was sharp.

EIGHT

Five minutes, Mr. McGarvey," one of the Guerin flight attendants said, passing him in the departure lounge and going outside to the P522 waiting on the company ramp.

It was after 6:00 P.M. as he waited for his call to Washington to go through. The others were already on board for the flight to Moscow's Sheremeteyvo Airport, but he'd been delayed trying to get through to Dominique. Her office said she'd been gone since this morning and they didn't know where she was. Her home phone didn't answer, and McGarvey was worried. It wasn't like her, Kennedy told him, to drop out like that.

JoAnn Carrara answered on the second ring, and she called her husband to the phone.

"Dominique is missing. No answer at home and no word from her office."

"Where are you?"

"Portland. I'm getting set to board a Guerin jet for Moscow."

"Anything from Yemlin and friends?"

"Not yet, Phil. But I want you to find Dominique for me. Get the Bureau to help out if need be. If she won't cooperate take her into protective custody."

"I don't know if I can do that," Carrara replied, his voice guarded. "Word from the seventh floor is that you're to be warned about the delicateness of the situation between us and Japan, but beyond that you're to be given all the rope you need."

"Enough to hang myself."

"But no aiding or abetting the enemy on our part. Me and you, pal."

"The bugs in Dominique's apartment were definitely of Japanese manufacture?"

"State of the art."

Kennedy came to the door and gestured for McGarvey, who waved him back.

"I need your help on this one, Phil. Find her for me, make sure she's all right. Will you do it?"

Carrara hesitated for several long seconds. "You bastard. All right. Don't take any wooden roubles over there."

Edward R. Reid had barely been able to contain his excitement after meeting with Tallerico. If what the man had told him had any basis in truth, it was the answer to his prayers.

In the beginning he'd had the idea of using Bruno Mueller and Glen Zerkel to disrupt Guerin Airplane Company by sabotaging its manufacturing and research facilities, assassinating Vasilanti and that hotshot ex-astronaut Kennedy, and blaming it on the Japanese. But now a more elegant solution was at hand if Tallerico were telling the truth and if he could be convinced to cooperate with them. From what Reid knew of the man and his business, in what amounted to international confidence games, Tallerico could very well have come up with something. And as far as gaining his cooperation was concerned . . . well, Reid didn't think there would be much trouble on that score.

The Sterling, Virginia, farmhouse was dark when he drove up and parked in front. He'd picked this place for a number of reasons, among them its isolation. There were no nearby neighbors, the house was screened from the nearest road by one thousand yards of dense woods, and yet from the back of the house there was a clear view of the main runways at Dulles Airport five miles away.

To see and not be seen. It appealed to his sensibilities. The farm had become a haven. But in the three days since Mueller and Zerkel had been here that had changed. Being near them was like being in a cage with a pair of man-eating tigers. More than once he'd had second thoughts about hiring them. Yet each time he wavered he immediately came back to his original concern about the way things were turning out for America. He wanted to go down in history as the "great pacifier." A man like Armand Hammer who'd done so much to stabilize the world during the horrible Cold War with the Soviet Union. Reid wanted to leave his mark. The world was entirely different from Hammer's time, which meant different, more drastic measures had to be taken to ensure peace. Japan had to be put in its place. There would never be another day like December 7, 1941, if he could help it.

He let himself into the dark stair hall. No fire burned on the grate in the living room, and the temperature in the house was cool. Outside under an overcast sky the night was dark, so the house was almost pitch black.

He found the hall light switch and flipped it on, but nothing happened. The feeling that he was a hunted animal suddenly rose up in his breast, and he turned. "Gentlemen . . . ?"

"Here," Mueller said softly from somewhere in the darkness.

Reid couldn't see a thing, but he was suddenly sober and clearheaded. "What the hell do you think you're doing?"

"We're getting nervous," Mueller answered. *"Alles in Ordnung,"* he called. A moment later the lights came on.

The East German stood beside the stairs, one of Reid's 7.65 mm Luger Parabellums in his hand. The gun, along with several other weapons, had been hidden in a concealed floor safe in the basement. The caged animals had gone exploring.

Glen Zerkel appeared at the basement door, a .380 Beretta automatic stuck in his belt. He was grinning. He looked like a wild man. Once again Reid wondered who was actually in control of the situation.

"We didn't know who was coming, so we hit the power at the breaker box downstairs," Zerkel said.

"It would be better if you telephoned before you came here from now on," Mueller added.

Reid realized that there had been no turning back for him from the day a few years ago when he'd written his first piece about the coming struggle between Japan and the United States. His wife had asked him if he was becoming his own creation. That was during the height of the Cold War with the Soviet Union, when even some of Reid's colleagues thought he was getting too strident. He'd answered his wife and his co-workers with some offhanded comment about it being a war, but at the odd time afterward he would stop and ask himself the same question. Like now. Except now he was an old man and running out of time, so he could not afford to fight with gloves on.

"It's a sensible precaution, providing the telephone line out here isn't tapped," Reid said, gratified by the instant look of concern on Zerkel's face. He went into the living room where he poured an Irish whiskey. The other two followed him in.

"Do you suspect your telephone is tapped?" Mueller asked calmly. He wasn't buying into it.

Reid shrugged. "You can never tell. It would be best if you kept on your toes."

Mueller studied him. "You have work for us to do?"

"Yes, tonight. The man's name is Benjamin Tallerico. He has some information that we need."

"What kind of information?"

When he told them he wanted to bring Guerin Airplane Company down and blame it on the Japanese, they were more interested in the mechanical details of the operation than the philosophy of it. Zerkel had wanted to strike directly at the company's Portland-area facilities, while Mueller wanted to know exactly how the blame would be placed on the Japanese, who in his words were a "very shrewd people."

"About the Japanese," Reid said. "It seems as if I was right on the mark. Looks like they're actually working on a plan to bring Guerin down. They weren't rumors after all."

"Tallerico has information about this plan?"

"A subcontractor in California is supposedly building a device that can bring airplanes down. He wouldn't be more specific than that, except that he wanted one million dollars for it."

Zerkel was excited, but Mueller remained deadly calm as he watched Reid drink the whiskey. "Why not let the Japanese do this themselves? It will accomplish what you want, will it not?"

Reid shook his head. "I have no way of knowing their time table. We'll help them along."

"You don't intend paying the one million, do you?"

Zerkel asked. The man was practically slavering at the bit.

"No need for it," Mueller replied, without taking his eyes from Reid. "How far do you wish for us to go?"

"I want the information. Beyond that it would not be beneficial if Mr. Tallerico were to warn his California contact, or if afterward he were to figure out who you worked for."

Mueller nodded.

"There's a Chevy Caprice in the garage, registered to Michael Larsen in Arlington . . ."

"We know," Mueller said. "Are these weapons registered to you?"

"No."

"The serial numbers?"

"Untraceable."

"Very well," Mueller said softly. For the first time he smiled.

Reid turned away, suddenly sick to his stomach.

"The next major markets will be the Far East and South America. I don't think there's any doubt about that," Kennedy said. "Both regions are developing and both have immense potential for industrial growth and consumerism. No doubt about it. Problem is both regions are halfway around the world. Big distances."

"Which means more business for the airlines, who'll in turn demand Mach-five or better airplanes," Topper added.

McGarvey sat on the opposite side of the jetliner from the others, nursing a drink and looking out the window at faint lights of some small city thirty-five thousand feet below them in the night. They were an hour out of Montreal where they would refuel for the hop across the Atlantic, and everybody was too keyed up to get any sleep. Tomorrow morning in Moscow they'd all be dead tired, but for now they were talking about the future of the industry.

He let their conversations ebb and flow around him, sometimes listening to what they were saying, sometimes drifting off into his own thoughts. There was a very big difference between the men and women he used to work with in the intelligence service and these people in the aircraft industry. Spies tended to be pessimists, while airplane people tended to be optimists. No other industry had ever progressed so far in such an incredibly short time. In 1903 the Wright brothers made the first flight of a powered airplane at Kitty Hawk—the total distance of that flight was less than the wing span of the P522—and only sixty-six years later, two Americans walked on the surface of the moon. When the P/C2622 went into regular service it would fly anyone who put up the price of a coach-class fare to the edge of space. Socrates talked about cruising altitudes at hypersonic speeds above 200,000 feet. "There the sky will be dark. The passengers will see the stars even in daylight. And they'll see the curvature of the earth."

Glancing at the men, not one of them over sixty, McGarvey couldn't help continuing the comparison between them and men such as Carrara and Danielle. Airplane people were engineers, futurists, science-fiction buffs. Technology could solve just about any problem. What we didn't know today, we'd figure out tomorrow, or the next day. An aircraft man's idea of religion was "pushing the envelope," an industry term for an expansion of knowledge usually at great financial, and even physical, risk. A lot of men and women had given their lives for the sake of flight.

Spies, on the other hand, were often very religious in the traditional sense. Why else would otherwise intelligent men and women place themselves behind enemy lines where they had to lie, cheat, and steal to stay alive, and where success meant that they'd caused someone to betray his or her country? To become a traitor for oftentimes nothing more than some esoteric ideal? Certainly as many spies had given their lives for the cause as had airplane people for theirs. If there were comparisons, he decided, they would have to be opposites, with him now in the middle.

Kennedy looked up, caught his eye, and came over to sit down beside him. "Good thoughts or bad?"

"I was just wondering what would happen if the Russians can't help us after all, and the Japanese did buy us out?"

Kennedy smiled wanly. "Guerin's demise wouldn't have any real effect on world peace or stability. At least I don't think it would."

"What about our position at the Tokyo summit?"

"The Japanese are already laughing at us, Mac. They'd just laugh a little harder, that's all."

Georgetown had an Old World charm reminiscent of Europe, but Mueller was not lulled into complacency because of the apparent similarities. On the contrary, he was even more cautious, more watchful because this was his last chance in the West.

Tallerico's house was a four-story brownstone that faced a narrow side street off Volta Place behind the Georgetown University campus.

"Here it is." Zerkel was driving. He started to pull over, but Mueller warned him off.

"Continue to the corner and then turn left."

"What's wrong?" Zerkel asked, but he did as he was told.

"I don't know," Mueller replied. He adjusted the Chevrolet's passenger-side door mirror so that he could see behind them. It was after ten and traffic was moderate. There were a few pedestrians on the sidewalks, and the upper side of the street was bumper to bumper with parked cars and vans. There was nothing out of the ordinary here, yet Mueller felt uneasy.

Zerkel turned left at the corner and at the next intersection stopped for a red light. "Did you see something?"

"No," Mueller said, watching the rearview mirror. Two cars had turned left off Volta Place behind them. "When the light changes turn right, drive one block, then turn right again."

"Okay," Zerkel said, glancing in his mirror.

The blue car continued straight, but the red Mercedes turned with them. A block later, however, when Zerkel made the second right, the Mercedes turned left.

"It's clear," Mueller said looking up. "We'll park one block away and go in on foot."

Zerkel nodded, his lip curling in a stupid grin, but the look was deceiving. Within the first six hours of knowing the man, Mueller had realized that the American was brilliant, if not a genius. But he was dedicated to whatever environmental mumbo jumbo he talked about, he was ignorant of what was happening in the world outside the United States, and he was crazy. If his ignorance or insanity became troublesome, Mueller would kill him. For now, however, he seemed to be willing to do as he was told.

They parked on P Street around the corner from Pomander Walk, a block and a half from Tallerico's brownstone, and went back to Volta Place on foot. On the first pass Mueller memorized the look of the street, including the numbers and types of parked vehicles. To his trained eye he could detect no change. Neither the blue car nor the red Mercedes that had followed them for a short distance had been among the parked vehicles, and so far as he could tell there was absolutely nothing wrong here. Yet he had a faint uneasiness in his gut. It was the fact that he was in a foreign country, he told himself. *The* foreign country, the United States, the enemy.

"Looks good," Zerkel said.

"Very well," Mueller agreed. The American had remained a fugitive from his justice system for a long time. His instincts were to be considered.

Together they crossed the street to Tallerico's house, passed through a tall iron gate, and rang the bell. From the front, the second-story windows showed light. Tallerico was home and awake.

A man's voice came from a small grille set just beneath the button. "Who is it?"

Mueller leaned forward. "Mr. Tallerico, are you alone this evening? Mr. Reid has sent us with something for you."

"Who is this?" Tallerico demanded.

"Sir, my name is of no importance. Mr. Reid asked me to speak with you about the Silicon Valley find. Am I speaking now with Mr. Tallerico?"

"I haven't had time to get an answer from my contact. Reid must know that."

"Yes, sir, he does. He's sent us to make you an offer. A firm offer, Mr. Tallerico."

"What the hell are you talking about?"

Zerkel was frustrated, but Mueller held him off. Benjamin Tallerico was a cautious man. But he had to be cautious in his business. Mueller could find no fault with it.

"Very well, Mr. Tallerico, we shan't bother you any further this evening. I'll inform Mr. Reid that you are no longer interested. Sorry to have disturbed you."

Mueller turned away from the speaker grille and started away from the door.

"Wait," Tallerico said.

Mueller stopped but did not go back. Zerkel was watching him, the stupid grin on his face again. The man was like a house dog just before its dinnertime.

"Goddammit, just hold on," Tallerico's voice came from the grille.

The stair hall lights came on a second later, and Benjamin Tallerico, wearing a dark purple dressing gown, his thick dark hair somewhat disheveled, and his eyes a little blurry as if he had been drinking heavily this evening, opened the door and eyed them both.

"Mr. Tallerico?" Mueller asked politely.

"That's right. Come in." He stepped aside to let them pass, then closed and locked the door and led them down the hall to his study at the back of the house. "Why didn't he call me? I could have told him that I didn't have an answer yet."

Mueller pulled out the Luger, thumbed the safety

catch off, and as they entered the study and Tallerico turned back to them, he raised the gun and pointed it directly at the man's head.

Tallerico, whose complexion was olive, visibly blanched. "What the fuck is this . . . ?" He stepped back.

"We would like the name and address of your source in California."

Reid had assured them that Tallerico's house would be free of any listening devices. A man in his position would make sure of it. Still, Mueller was on edge.

"Fuck you," Tallerico snarled. Reid had warned that he was a former Mafia lieutenant with connections.

Mueller pulled the pistol's toggle back with his left hand and let it snap home, cocking the hammer. He started to pull the trigger.

"Jesus Christ, you stupid fuck, back off! What the fuck do you think this is? You want to know the name of my contact? Fine, I'll tell you. It's not worth my fucking life. It's only money."

Zerkel closed the study door, and Tallerico watched him, his eyes growing wider.

"I mean it. She's a psychiatrist in San Francisco. Her name is Jeanne Shepard. One of her patients told her about it."

"What is this patient's name?"

"I don't know. She wouldn't tell me. Not until we had a deal. She's just as careful as I am. And she never makes a mistake. Never."

"How do we find her?"

"Her office is in San Francisco."

"Her home," Mueller said calmly.

"I don't know. I've never been there. I talk to her on the telephone. Sometimes she comes out here, sometimes I go out there, but we always meet on neutral territory."

Mueller said nothing.

"Fuck. Who do you think you're dealing with here? We have to be careful."

Still Mueller said nothing.

"Her office is downtown, but even if you go there you won't get anything from her."

"Where does she live, Mr. Tallerico?"

"Fucking hell! In Sausalito. She's got a goddamned houseboat in the marina. The number's seventeen-E."

"Thank you, sir," Mueller said, nodding politely, and he shot the man in the head, driving him backward off his feet, blood splattering over the desk.

"Holy shit," Zerkel said.

Mueller clicked the safety on the Luger and stuffed it in his belt beneath his coat. "Now we go to Sausalito."

"Here they come," FBI Special Agent Albert McLaren said. He watched the front of Tallerico's house through a light-intensifying 35 mm camera that lit the scene with green.

"Anybody we know?" his partner Phillip Joyce asked. They were set up across the street in a GMC conversion van with smoked-glass windows and civilian plates.

"The tall, skinny dude looks vaguely familiar. I don't know about the other one." McLaren fired off three rapid shots as the two men came through the iron gate and started toward the van. "Take a look," he said, and he moved away from the camera.

Joyce took his partner's place and snapped a half-dozen shots. "He's in the file, but I don't know about the little guy."

They passed within five feet of the van, and the shorter one looked directly at Joyce for a second as if he could see through the one-way glass. Joyce had the feeling that he'd seen that face before, although where or in what context he couldn't remember. It was bothersome. He took two more shots.

"All right, I've got them," McLaren said from the back of the van.

Joyce returned his attention to Tallerico's house. This was only the second day of their surveillance so no true pattern of behavior had been established. The man had been investigated on a similar charge of industrial espionage five years ago, but after three months of surveillance in which nothing had been found, the case was dropped. He was either innocent, or very good, although John Whitman, the chief investigating officer on the case, was convinced he was guilty of something. "Why else install the sophisticated anti-surveillance equipment he's got over there?"

"They're crossing the street," McLaren said.

Tallerico was at home. They'd watched him answer the door. He'd been upstairs when the two men arrived. He'd flipped on the front hall light, had come downstairs, and had let them in. He'd not come to the door, however, when they'd come back out.

"Did you see Tallerico when those two left?" he asked McLaren.

"No," his partner said. "They're definitely heading down Pomander."

Joyce continued to watch Tallerico's house. The visitors were gone, so why wasn't he turning off the hall light and going back upstairs?

"They're gone," McLaren said.

"Call it in, Al. I want a runner out here to pick up the film."

"Did you recognize either of them?"

"Yes and no," Joyce said. He dialed Tallerico's secured number with one of the cellular units.

"What are you going to say when he answers?"

"I got a wrong number," Joyce said, but the telephone rang twenty times before he hung up.

"Nothing?"

"Get Whitman. I want to go in."

The Russians made no special preparations for the arrival of the Guerin flight from Portland, except that upon landing the aircraft was directed away from the civilian international terminal to the VIP apron and debarking area. Visiting foreign dignitaries were met here where a more positive crowd control was possible.

But this morning there was no red carpet, only a half-dozen black limousines for the passengers and two vans for their luggage. Of the Guerin staff the only person other than McGarvey who'd ever been to Russia was Kennedy on a five-day astronaut exchange program at Baikonaur. The others were excited and nervous, except for the dour Soderstrom who had predicted disaster from day one. Vasilanti had insisted the CFO come along to make sure the entire company wasn't handed over to the Russians.

"There'll be no danger of that," he'd assured the old man.

Glancing over at him now, McGarvey could see that he was tense almost to the breaking point. He would be an ideal candidate for an entrapment scheme. He had an abundance of nervous energy and naïveté. His turning would be routine. Kennedy would have to be warned. Actually, all of them would have to be warned to keep on their guard and say nothing about the Japanese threat, especially not the Russians' part in spying on the Japanese for Guerin.

"They're going to want to start the meetings right away this morning," McGarvey told Kennedy when they came to a complete stop.

Kennedy was reaching for his bag in the overhead. "We need a couple hours, but I don't see any reason not to get started this morning before lunch."

"No," McGarvey said, and the tone of his voice caught Kennedy's attention.

"What's the problem?" Kennedy asked, leaning over the aisle seat next to McGarvey. Boarding stairs were being trundled over, and three men got out of the limousines, one of them Yemlin's boss, Colonel Lyalin.

"No one got any sleep last night, which puts us at a disadvantage. Their negotiators will be fresh and very good. They'll know everything there is to know about you, but you'll know next to nothing about them, except that some of them will be professional negotiators and others will be intelligence officers."

"What do you suggest?"

"No matter what happens, insist on taking today and tonight off. No negotiations until morning. And for every hour after 8:00 P.M. they want to keep you up eating and drinking, insist on postponing the morning meeting for one hour later than 8:00 A.M."

"We came here to talk about building a wing factory."

"We came here to ask them to spy for us," McGarvey said. "Insist on having a full twenty-fours hours of rest including twelve hours of sleep before you start. Trust me on this one, David."

Kennedy nodded after a slight hesitation.

"You're going to have to trust me on something else as well. No matter what I do or say, no matter how odd or even outrageous it seems to you at the time, I don't want you to react at all. Don't say a word, don't make a move, just act as if whatever is happening is completely normal."

"I don't understand . . ."

"You don't have to, just go along with me no matter what I do."

Again Kennedy nodded after a slight hesitation. He pulled back, but McGarvey stopped him.

"I may drop out of sight at some point. If they ask you where I am, stonewall it."

A look of consternation crossed Kennedy's features. "What the hell are you talking about? For how long? What are we supposed to do when it's time to go and you're nowhere to be found?"

"Inform the embassy that I'm overdue, and then go home."

"What do I tell the Russians?"

McGarvey shook his head. "If I'm gone that long they won't ask you about me. They'll know."

Lieutenant Commander Seiji Kiyoda, dressed in his winter blue uniform and lightweight windbreaker, waited on the ladder below the conning tower hatch for the *Samisho* to surface. They had entered the Sagami

Sea early this morning and were now just a few miles
south of the long entrance to Tokyo Bay, the peninsular
city of Misaki well off their port bow. A cold front had
settled over the area, and meteorology predicted twenty-
five- to thirty-knot winds from the northwest, with seas
running three to four meters. It would be sloppy until
they reached the protection of the bay.

A Klaxon sounded throughout the boat. Kiyoda
climbed up the ladder, spun the wheel, and pushed the
hatch open on its hydraulically sprung hinges. He lowered his head as a bucket of cold seawater cascaded
down on him, and then scrambled outside onto the
bridge. His XO, Lieutenant Minori, came up behind
him, followed by a communications man. All three of
them scanned the horizon for traffic.

The weather was cool, with low dark clouds scudding
across from the land, but it felt good to be in the fresh air
again. Kiyoda was a dedicated submariner, but he
appreciated times like these.

"I have the sea buoy three miles off our starboard
bow," Minori said.

Kiyoda swung his binoculars right, picking it up
immediately. "Come right five degrees."

"Turn right five degrees, *yo-so-ro, Kan-cho,*" the
comms man repeated the order and relayed it below.
Their bow came right.

"Secure electric motors, engage diesels ahead one-
half."

The rating relayed the order, and by the time they
passed the red sea buoy, its bell clanging erratically in
the chop, they were settled on their course and speed.
Yokosuka, barely fifteen miles into Tokyo Bay, was home
not only to the MSDF's Escort Fleet Command and two
of its flotillas plus the Japanese Maritime Self Defense
Force Academy, but to the U.S. Seventh Fleet as well.
Since before he'd given the order to shoot at the Russian
destroyer, Kiyoda had pondered his reception at home.

Yesterday, after they'd safely made their way to the
east coast of Honshu through the treacherous Tsugaru
Strait and were making their best speed submerged

south, he'd brought the boat to periscope depth, raised the main radio mast, and sent the "patrol terminated" message to flotilla headquarters. The reply had been nothing more than the "message received" code.

In one respect headquarters's silence was understandable. U.S. and Russian naval intelligence units routinely listened to MSDF traffic. What Flotilla Command had to say to him was properly for Japanese ears only, so it would wait until they docked.

In another respect, however, their silence was ominous. ELINT had detected nothing in the past twenty-four hours. Nor, now that they were this close and running on the surface, had any ship or aircraft come out to meet them as often was the case at the end of a delicate or troubled patrol. Secure communications could have been established with a dipping buoy or light signals.

Kiyoda expected that he would be relieved of his command, so he had made certain that everything he'd said and done during the attack would appear in the log as unilateral decisions that had been opposed by his officers. The blame would rest squarely on his shoulders.

But he'd expected to be met out here, his boat taken away from him *before* they docked. He was not afraid, just wary.

"Courage," his *sensei* taught, "is a virtue only in the cause of righteousness." In this instance Kiyoda knew that what he'd done was correct not only for himself and his boat, but for Nippon as well. It was *honto,* fact, that Japan's time had come again. *Chi-jin-yu.* Wisdom, benevolence, courage. It was time the world knew these things.

His father and mother were both dead, which was too bad, because they would have been pleased by what happened, and what would undoubtedly happen in the coming months if Kamiya had his way. Which Kiyoda believed the old man would. "It's our time," Kiyoda mumbled.

"Did you say something, *Kan-cho?*" Minori asked respectfully.

Kiyoda smiled wanly. "It's good to be home."

"No parades this time, I think," Minori replied, averting his eyes politely.

"You were obeying the orders of your lawful superior, Ikuo. Do not forget it."

The XO looked up. "We were with you, *Kan-cho.*"

"No."

"I beg your pardon, *Kan-cho.* I have spoken about this with the other officers, and we all know exactly how you administrated the attack, to insulate us."

"I forbid this," Kiyoda said sharply, but inside he was bursting with pride. A magnificent crew such as his could go anywhere, accomplish anything.

"I'm truly sorry, *Kan-cho,* but we are agreed."

Kiyoda glanced at the rating who was mutely scanning the horizon with his binoculars. "Listen to me very carefully, Iuko. I forbid you and the other officers to come forward with your demands. No doubt I will be placed under arrest the moment we dock . . ."

"We will go with you."

"No, my old friend, you will not. In fact you will remain here with the *Samisho* and keep the crew intact."

Minori's eyes narrowed. "What are you thinking, *Kan-cho?*"

"I must do this alone, if there's to be any hope for us to regain the sea. Do you understand this?"

Minori nodded uncertainly.

"If you are assigned another captain you will delay the boat's departure for as long as possible. The main bearings on number two are dangerously worn, and our weapons, fuel, and consumables all need replenishing."

A slight smile curled the edges of Minori's mouth. "It shall be as you order, *Kan-cho.* If need be this boat will remain in port until Mount Fuji has eroded to sand hills."

"Well, perhaps not that long," Kiyoda said, his smile warming. He turned to the rating. "Engines ahead two-thirds."

"Engines ahead two-thirds, *yo-so-ro,*" the rating relayed, but then he put a hand over his mouthpiece. *"Kan-cho, dono* we enlisted men also have spoken of this. Your crew is behind you. There is not one dissenting voice."

"Very well," Kiyoda said, his voice wanting to catch in his throat. "I will do everything in my power to deserve your trust."

Clearing the tip of the peninsula to the west, they suddenly saw the naval vessels docked at Yokosuka in the distance.

"Bridge, ELINT," Lieutenant Kawara called from below. "I'm picking up a powerful surface search radar."

Kiyoda took the bridge telephone from the rating. "Who is looking at us?"

"It's coming from the U.S. side, *Kan-cho,"* the ELINT officer said. "Seventh Fleet Intelligence. Shall I burn them?"

"No. We shall remain passive. Let them look all they want." The *Samisho* was equipped with a newly designed anti-radar weapon that took an incoming radar signal, amplified it, narrowed the beam, and sent it back to the sending station with such force that the receiver burned out.

"Hai, Kan-cho."

"We're home and everybody knows it," Minori said.

"It would appear so," Kiyoda said, but he was lost in his thoughts for the moment.

The Guerin team, including the flight crew, numbered eighteen men and five women. The entire nineteenth floor of the Rossiya Hotel had been set aside for their exclusive use. More than two hundred people could have slept there, and Topper called it their "splendid isolation." Having all that room to rattle around in made Kilbourne nervous. And Soderstrom, fearful of listening devices, had difficulty in speaking above a whisper. He felt most comfortable talking in low tones in his bathroom with water running in the tub and sink and the toilet constantly flushing.

"They want the contamination kept to a minimum," McGarvey explained after lunch. They'd gathered in a corner suite that Kennedy occupied. Everyone was keyed up and nervous.

"If Jeff keeps up his antics, the hotel is going to bill us for excessive water use," Topper quipped.

"What you're trying to do just doesn't work," McGarvey told the resentful-looking CFO. "If they want to listen to our conversations—which I guarantee they are—there's nothing we can do about it. At least not with what we brought over. So if you don't want them to hear something, don't say it."

"Hell of a way to play poker, if the other guy is going to know every card in your hand," Kilbourne grumbled.

McGarvey jotted five words on a yellow legal pad and held it up for all of them to see. IF IT'S IMPORTANT, WRITE IT.

Soderstrom started to say something, but McGarvey held him off, writing out his next instruction. He held it up.

WHEN YOU'RE DONE, BURN THE PAPER AND BURN THREE OR FOUR PAGES BENEATH THE SHEET YOU'VE WRITTEN ON.

"We've got nothing to hide," McGarvey said. "With our union problems in Wichita we need this wing factory. And considering the state of the Russian economy, I don't see any problem in getting their cooperation."

Kennedy wrote something and held it up for McGarvey to see. WHAT ABOUT INFO ABOUT THE JAPS ???

"Jeff, what's the bottom line on financing the wing factory?" Kilbourne asked.

For a second Soderstrom was nonplussed, but then he realized what was going on. "We're talking nine hundred million, maybe one billion by the time we're finished here."

"We're going to have to sell *beaucoup* airplanes to recoup that cost," Topper said.

"We will," Kennedy said. "But, Mac, what'd you mean they want to keep the contamination to a minimum?"

"Did you spot the Germans and the French in the lobby this morning?"

"I didn't notice."

"I think the word might have leaked, somehow, about why we're here. If the Germans or the French get the opportunity, they're going to pitch us. Our hosts would rather that not happen."

McGarvey wrote on his pad and held it up. THEY'RE SENSITIVE ABOUT THE JAPS NOW.

Kennedy and the others nodded. McGarvey wrote again.

IF OUR QUID PRO QUO BECAME PUBLIC THERE'D BE HELL TO PAY!!!

"Maybe it'd be better if we put the factory in Germany," Soderstrom suggested with a grin. He was actually starting to enjoy himself.

"Frankly I think the Russians will do a better job," Kennedy said. "Ukraine was the aircraft manufacturing region for the Soviet Union. Now the Russians have something to prove, and I think they'll bend over backward to show they're capable. In fact I think they'll do just about anything it takes."

"It'd be profitable for them," Soderstrom said.

Kennedy held up his note pad. He'd underlined his query: WHAT ABOUT INFO ABOUT THE JAPS???

McGarvey wrote his response and held it up. COLONEL LYALIN SAYS YEMLIN IS IN MOSCOW. WE'LL MEET BEFORE MORNING.

Kennedy reluctantly nodded. It was what they'd come for.

"Speaking of profit, it'll profit us all if we get some sleep," Kennedy said. "We've got a long day ahead of us."

It was after 5:00 A.M. before Special Agents McLaren and Joyce made it back to the J. Edgar Hoover Building on Pennsylvania Avenue. They'd managed to secure the crime scene until the Bureau's forensics team gathered most of what it needed. D.C. police had been brought into the act, and within fifteen minutes of their arrival

Volta Place was crawling with newspaper and television reporters. By then the Bureau had slipped away, so the fact that Tallerico had been under federal investigation was still secret.

"We're going to keep it that way for as long as possible," Chief Investigating Officer John Whitman told them. He looked like an IBM executive with hair graying at the temples, gold wire-rimmed glasses, and a pinched disapproving expression on his face. But he was a good cop. They met in his small office.

"That might depend on the Washington cops keeping their mouths shut," McLaren said.

"Don't worry about them. We've got another fish to fry," Whitman said. He handed across an 8 x 10 glossy photograph of the two men coming out of Tallerico's house. It was one of the shots Joyce had taken. "Recognize either one of them?"

"The tall skinny guy looks familiar. Haven't had a chance to run it down yet," McLaren said. "Don't know about the other one."

"Neither do we. But first one is probably Glen Zerkel. Earth Stewards. Environmental terrorists."

"Idaho," McLaren said.

"Right. But he dropped out of sight afterward and hasn't surfaced until now. Makes you wonder what Mr. Tallerico was up to this time."

"Doesn't fit the pattern," Joyce said.

"Maybe we never really established a pattern," Whitman said.

"This other one with him could be anybody," McLaren said, staring at the photograph. "But what have we got on Zerkel?"

"He's got a half-brother in San Francisco, which might be the connection to Tallerico. Brother's name is Louis Zerkel. Works for a high-tech electronics company as a design engineer. We checked him out just after the Idaho incident, but the field investigation at that time turned up nothing. The brothers had a falling out several years earlier and were never in touch."

"Until now?" Joyce asked.

Whitman shrugged. "It's worth a visit. I want you two on it ASAP."

"Why not just let San Francisco run with it?" Joyce asked.

"You're already familiar with the case. It'd take them a couple of days to get up to speed, and I don't want to miss anything. I've got a feeling that if we don't hustle we'll miss the boat."

Mueller rented a Ford Taurus from the Hertz counter at San Francisco International Airport under the Michael Larsen persona that Reid had supplied. Theirs was the last flight for the night, and it was well after 12:30 A.M. by the time they reached the northbound Bayshore Freeway. Zerkel drove because he was familiar with the area. He'd grown up in California, but he felt no sense of homecoming. In fact the only thing he felt was excitement that he was finally doing something. Not once did he think about his fellow Earth Stewards or about the stewardship movement. This time he was on a new quest and damned glad to be working with a real pro for a change.

Mueller had slept soundly during the flight from Dulles, and he was dozing now, his head back, his eyes closed. Zerkel glanced over at the German, his respect tinged with fear. The ex-East German Secret Service assassin was not like any of the men Zerkel had known and worked with. The instant before he'd pulled the trigger to kill Tallerico, Zerkel had watched his eyes. There'd been nothing there, not so much as a flicker of emotion to betray the fact he was about to blow away a human being.

Zerkel had examined his own feelings about the murder during the long flight west, but the only conclusion he'd come to about himself, beside the fact he was crazy, was that although he never hesitated to kill when it was necessary, he did have feelings. He did think about his victims afterward with some remorse. Mueller was clearly cut of a different cloth. Perhaps it was because he was European, or more specifically German. Those people had had plenty of practice killing each other. Maybe it was in their blood. Whatever it was, Zerkel thought, he was glad to be working with the man. It was a real education.

The urban sprawl that was San Francisco spread for miles to the north, east, and south. Millions of people, all using and spewing harsh petrochemicals into the environment, all using up the limited reserves of precious water, all of them choking the environment beyond repair. It made Zerkel sick at heart to see it again. If the Japanese took over it would be worse. Although he'd never been to Tokyo, he'd read about the city and its problems. Too many people crammed into too small a space for too many centuries had turned them into automatons. They wanted to do the same thing to the entire world. Eventually one supernational corporation would exist that would consume the world's natural resources, build the world's products, supply the world's food, drink, and entertainment, and set the world's rules and regulations. It would be *Brave New World* and *1984,* and in Zerkel's mind the only way to prevent such a thing from happening was by opposing it now with every measure at their disposal. Including sabotage and murder.

A ship was passing beneath the Golden Gate Bridge, heading out to sea, and Zerkel had the vicious thought that if it was heading for Japan he hoped it would sink in the middle of the Pacific Ocean.

Mueller opened his eyes and sat up as Zerkel pulled off the highway and headed down to the marina on Richardson Bay. The night was damp and chill with a light breeze coming out of the northwest. The marina was home to a hundred or more live-aboard houseboats, some of them two and three stories tall, and some of them elaborate. Many of them had to be in the one-million-dollar-plus range. Whatever sort of practice Dr. Jeanne Shepard ran, it had to be extremely successful.

It was late enough that no one sat on their decks or

strolled along the quay. Finger pier E was on the opposite side of the basin from the marina office.

Zerkel parked nearby. They sat in the dark car, the windows down, listening to the distant hum of traffic on the highway and the rhythmic clapping of wavelets against the boat hulls. This was a peaceful spot.

"I'm going with you," Zerkel said. He got both guns from the single bag they'd checked through.

"We'll switch pistols this time," Mueller said. "You'll take the Luger."

Together he and Mueller walked back to pier E and headed out to the houseboats on the end.

"As with Mr. Tallerico, you will be good enough not to interfere with me. You may not always understand what I am doing or why I am doing it, but these are time-honored methods that work."

"I can dig it. You're the man."

Seventeen-E was one of the more elaborate boats in the basin. Eighty feet at the waterline, she was twenty-five feet wide and rose two stories out of the water. The roof was covered by an elaborate patio garden with flowers and shrubs and what appeared to be living trees. Stepping aboard they could hear classical music from within, and Mueller motioned for Zerkel to hold up.

There were no lights. The woman had probably gone to sleep to the music.

Mueller tried the door into the main salon, but it was locked as he expected it would be. Taking out a four-inch section of ice pick that he had found at Reid's farmhouse and modified, he picked the flimsy lock in ten seconds. A cursory examination of the door and frame revealed no alarms, nevertheless he waited a full minute for lights to kick on and a siren to blast the night.

When nothing happened he stepped inside. Zerkel came in behind him and softly closed the door. The place smelled of perfume and incense. Enough light filtered through the windows for them to see that they were in a large salon. Long white couches, glass and brass coffee tables, artwork on the walls, books along one wall. Straight ahead was a fireplace, and to the right and aft, spiral stairs let up to the second floor. The soft music came from above. It was Dvořák's *New World Symphony*. The doctor had good taste.

Mueller checked the pistol, then crossed to the stairs and went up. Zerkel, careful to make no noise, followed the East German. At the top they followed the music down a hall to an open door that led into a combination sitting room/bedroom that spread across the entire width of the boat. Sliding glass doors on the aft wall opened onto a broad balcony, the railings of which were covered with weather cloths.

Dr. Jeanne Shepard, her blonde hair spilling over her pillow, the covers pulled up to her neck, was sound asleep. She was alone.

Nonchalantly, Mueller went to the stereo and turned up the music. Dr. Shepard stirred slightly but did not wake up. He went to the windows and drew the curtains, including the drapes across the sliding glass doors. Finally he flipped on the small table lamp on the nightstand.

Dr. Shepard stirred again. This time she came awake. For several moments she stared up at Mueller and Zerkel uncomprehendingly. Suddenly something connected in her head, and she sat straight up, her eyes wide, her hands flying up as if to ward off a blow.

"My God . . . who are you? What are you doing here?"

"We've come from Washington, D.C.," Mueller said pleasantly. He made no move to conceal his gun. "Mr. Tallerico supplied us with your name and address, and now we would like you to give us the name and address of a certain patient of yours."

Dr. Shepard looked from Mueller to Zerkel in disbelief. Suddenly she lunged for the telephone, but Mueller reached her in two steps, bringing the pistol up to her face.

"I don't want to kill you, but I will," he said.

Her breath caught in her throat. "I don't know what you're talking about."

Mueller gently pulled the bedcovers to the foot of the

bed. Dr. Shepard, dressed in a long, lavender-flowered nightshirt, shrank back, drawing her legs up beneath her.

"Take your nightgown off," Mueller said. He pulled the pillow out from under her and laid it aside. "Do as I say, Dr. Shepard, or I shall shoot you in the head."

"I'll give you the name . . ."

"Do as I say," Mueller insisted. He pulled the Beretta's hammer back.

"My God, this can't be happening," she cried. "I'll tell you what you want to know, it isn't that important to me . . ."

Mueller backhanded her in the face, the blow so unexpected it caught her in mid-sentence. Her head banged against the wall, and she grunted in pain.

"Take off your nightgown," Mueller said calmly.

It took her several seconds to recover. "You can't do this to me," she whimpered. But she struggled up to her knees, and hesitating a second longer, tears filling her eyes, she pulled the thin nightgown over her head. Mueller took it from her. Her breasts were large but firm, her tummy only slightly rounded, and her hips and ass looked tight.

"On your back now," the East German said, his voice still maddeningly calm. "And spread your legs."

"You're going to rape me? No . . . my God, no, please . . . you don't want to do this. God, please!"

Mueller switched the safety on the pistol, stuffed it into his belt, and then wound the nightgown around his right fist, his actions slow and very deliberate as Dr. Shepard continued to plead with him. Zerkel didn't know what was going to happen next, but he was very impressed.

"Why are you doing this to me?" Dr. Shepard asked. "I'll tell you what you want to know . . ."

Mueller smashed his nightgown-padded fist into her face, breaking her nose and knocking out two of her teeth. Her entire body was driven against the wall with a thud that shook the entire houseboat. She was dazed and offered no resistance as Mueller grabbed her ankles, pulled her flat on her back, and spread her legs.

He glanced at Zerkel. "We've found by experience that naked people, in this sort of position, tend to tell fewer lies than when they're fully clothed."

Zerkel nodded, unable to take his eyes off the woman.

"Saves time," Mueller said. He sat down at the head of the bed and watched Dr. Shepard's eyes until they came back in focus. She started to bring her legs together, but he shook his head. "Nobody wants to hurt you again, Jeanne."

She stopped, her body rigid, her eyes locked into his.

"Please tell me the name of the patient that you and Mr. Tallerico spoke of. He is the one who knows something about a device that brings down airplanes. We would like to know his place of employment and his home address."

"Louis Zerkel," she mumbled.

"No, you don't understand," Mueller said maintaining his calm. Had he misheard her?

"Wait," Zerkel interrupted. "She said *Louis* Zerkel."

"Louis Zerkel," Dr. Shepard repeated, her voice nasal. "He works for InterTech Corporation in Alameda. His apartment is there too." She gave an address. Her face was already swelling, blood oozing from her nose and her mouth.

"It's my brother, man," Zerkel was saying. "How about that shit."

"Will he cooperate with us?" Mueller asked, amazed. Only in America.

"Last time I saw him was at my old lady's funeral. He was pissed off at me. But if he was dealing with this bitch I'll be able to talk to him."

Mueller thought it out, still finding it difficult to believe the coincidence, but he played with the cards he was dealt. "Fuck her," he said, getting up.

Zerkel reared back. "What?"

"Fuck her," Mueller said matter-of-factly. "She needs to be found with semen in her vagina." He pulled out the Beretta, switched the safety catch off, wrapped the gun in the pillow, and before the stunned Jeanne Shepard could react, he shot her in the left temple at point-blank range, killing her instantly.

"Sonofabitch," Zerkel whispered.

"Now, Mr. Zerkel, fuck her, if you please. I'll wait for you in the car. When you're finished we'll go see your brother."

A weather system over Moscow deepened the overcast so that by late afternoon streetlights were on and it was necessary for cars and buses to run with their headlights. The others were asleep, but when McGarvey came to Kennedy's suite the Guerin executive was wide awake.

"Quite a mess they've got for themselves," Kennedy said from the window. From here they could see the Kremlin walls, Red Square, St. Basil's, the Moscow River, and across it to another, grimier section of the vast city.

"Having second thoughts about putting the factory here?"

"Second thoughts, third thoughts, fourth thoughts. Jeff might be right. Maybe we'd be throwing money down a bottomless pit."

McGarvey held his silence. Moscow almost always affected newcomers the same way. It was depressing. After just a few hours you began to lose hope. The grayness, the drabness everywhere got you down.

"I don't know."

"Still a big country, David," McGarvey said. "Lots of talent here even if the system is bankrupt."

Kennedy turned around. "Rather have them as friends than enemies?"

"Something like that," McGarvey said. He gestured to himself, then the door, and waved goodbye. Kennedy nodded his understanding, offered him the thumbs- up sign, and McGarvey left.

Like any building that contained as many people as the Rossiya Hotel—as many as six thousand guests could be accommodated—there were dozens of ways in and out. In the old days McGarvey had learned them all.

It was a bit of tradecraft useful for any spy in Moscow. Ten minutes after leaving Kennedy, McGarvey slipped out a basement maintenance entrance and so far as he could tell came away clean.

He was back in the field and it was affecting him the same way it always had: butterflies in the gut, tense muscles, and an almost preternatural awareness of his surroundings. And, God help him, he found that he loved it. He was alive.

Louis Zerkel's apartment was located in a faded complex a few blocks off Alameda's Central Avenue. The security system was broken or switched off so they didn't have to pick the lock to gain entry to the rear corridor.

It was a few minutes before four when Glen Zerkel knocked at his half-brother's door. Mueller stayed out of sight of the peephole. Glen was crazy and his half-brother was seeing a psychiatrist. No telling how they would react to each other.

Zerkel knocked again. He was having trouble keeping in focus. He'd never fucked a dead body before, and he didn't know how he felt.

"What do you want?" a muffled voice asked from within.

Glen Zerkel looked up. "It's me, Louis, your brother. I want to talk to you."

"What do you want with me? Why have you come here?"

Glen glanced at Mueller, then turned back to the peephole. They'd discussed just how this situation would have to be handled.

"Who's there with you?" Louis demanded.

"We talked to Dr. Shepard tonight. She told us that we should come over here to see you."

"You talked about me with Dr. Shepard?" Louis demanded loudly.

"Yes. Now let me in."

"You talked with my doctor? Goddammit, you had no right to do that."

"We need your help, Louis. With the device you're building for Guerin."

"She shouldn't have told you about that," Louis Zerkel shouted. If this kept up they would wake the neighbors and they'd have trouble.

"We came from Washington just to see you, Louis. Let us in. We need your help, and Dr. Shepard said you would do it."

"You came from Washington? Did Dr. Shepard talk to Mr. Reid after all? Did he send you to talk to me?"

Glen Zerkel glanced again at Mueller who was nodding yes. "Yes, Mr. Reid sent us. He heard about what you'd discovered and he sent us."

Mueller could hardly believe his ears. It was as if the entire scenario had been scripted. He'd never run into a situation like this in his entire career. If he had he would have immediately backed off, but he no longer had the luxury of choice. He would have to take this wherever it led.

Louis Zerkel unlocked the door and opened it. He was dressed in tattered UC-Berkeley sweats, his hair wildly disheveled. A strong odor of electronic equipment wafted out of the dark apartment, and for an instant Glen Zerkel felt as if he were a hapless victim being invited into a mad scientist's laboratory on some late-night horror flick.

"It's the Japanese. Mr. Reid is absolutely correct," Louis said excitedly. He turned back into the apartment and switched on a dim light. Computer equipment filled the living room.

Mueller locked the door as Louis brought up what appeared to be a schematic diagram on one of the computers.

"Take a look at this . . ." Louis said as he looked up, the words dying in his throat when he saw Mueller.

"Good morning, Mr. Zerkel, terribly sorry to bother you so early in the morning, but Mr. Reid thought it was very important that we come here to personally see you," Mueller said smoothly. He came across to where

Zerkel sat in front of the active screen. "What have we got here? Don't tell me that you've actually got hold of the circuit diagram for the device?"

Louis looked to his half-brother, who smiled and nodded, then back to Mueller, his enthusiasm returning. "It was Mr. Reid's articles that got me thinking, that and the fact that InterTech is owned, or at least controlled, by the Japanese."

"Could you duplicate this device for us?" Mueller asked.

"You mean build it?" Zerkel asked. He shrugged. "I suppose so, but there's more going on here than meets the eye, you know. It's the new module they switched. Could be a receiver. Have to build a transmitter to find out. But this little baby could have brought down that jet in '90. What do you think about that?"

"Brilliant, Louis. It's just brilliant. Would you be willing to come along to Washington with us and work it out?"

"When?"

"Right now. This morning."

"Holy Jesus."

"Mr. Reid would very much like to meet you and have you on our team. We're assembling only the very best, because, as you certainly understand, this is very important."

"Don't you know it," Louis Zerkel said excitedly. "What do I tell my boss? Or Dr. Shepard?"

"We'll take care of all that for you. We'd just like you to pack a few things, perhaps take the disks on which you've stored the data you might need, and we'll be on our way before the sun comes up."

"Holy Jesus, what do you think about that? It's very important."

"Very important," Mueller repeated.

"Something's got to be done."

"That's for sure."

"By God, I'll help," Zerkel said.

Mueller took out the Beretta .380, wiped it down with

his handkerchief, and held it out. "Have you ever used one of these, Mr. Zerkel?"

Louis flinched and shied away. "No."

"Well, I'd like you to hold it, for just a moment, to see what it feels like."

Zerkel hesitated, but Mueller kept holding the automatic out to him, butt first. Finally he took it, hefted it, and then handed it back.

"It's heavy," he said.

"Yes, it is," Mueller agreed. "As soon as you're ready we'll leave for the airport."

"This'll take about ten minutes," Louis Zerkel said, turning back to his computer.

Glen watched closely as Mueller stuffed the Beretta under a stack of computer printout on the floor, then using his handkerchief so that he would leave no prints, tossed one of Dr. Shepard's business cards into a wastebasket. "What do you think about that?" he said to himself.

The sun was coming up behind them as the Maryland National Guard C130 transport aircraft crossed over the city of Sacramento and started its long descent into Oakland International Airport on Bay Farm Island. Communications Technician Specialist 6 Luis Guerra called McLaren forward. "Your boss is on the horn. He wants to talk to you."

"A couple of things before you touch down," John Whitman said. "Ballistics has an ID on Tallerico's murder weapon. It's a 7.65 mm German Luger. Probably a collector's item. Registration is checking it out, but nobody's holding their breath."

"We'll be on the ground in twenty minutes," McLaren said. "Anything else?"

"The other face in the picture. The man with Glen Zerkel. But I don't know what the hell to make of it. His name is Bruno Mueller. A colonel in the former East German Secret Service. A paid assassin. The French want him in the worst way. He's the last surviving member of a gang of ex-Stasi officers who've been terrorizing the French for the past few years. Apparently he escaped after a shootout south of Paris, and they put his photo on the international wire."

"I think I saw it when it came in," McLaren said. "I just couldn't place it the other night."

"He's one tough sonofabitch, Al."

"What the hell is he doing here?"

"Unknown."

"I'll pass it along to Phil. Anything else?"

"That's it for now. Just watch yourself."

"Will do," McLaren said, and he went back to tell Joyce the good news.

NINE

The meeting was held in the Council of Ministers building great hall inside the Kremlin. Chairs were placed around a highly polished oval table forty feet long and ten feet wide. David Kennedy took his place on one side of the table, his negotiating team of fifteen men and two women seated to his left and right. Opposite him, the Russian Minister of Aviation and Aerospace Affairs, Viktor Gregorevich Matushin, and his team of fifteen men and two women took their places. Coffee, tea, and carafes of iced mineral water were served by a team of efficient stewards. For the first ten minutes as everybody was settling down, photographers were allowed in the room. Finally, however, Minister Matushin made a signal, and they cleared out.

"If this were Washington, D.C., I don't believe we would have gotten rid of the media so easily, Mr. Minister," Kennedy said pleasantly.

Matushin's translator provided the Russian simultaneously, and the minister smiled. "They're my photographers," he said in English. "Time enough for the news media later, don't you agree?"

"Wholeheartedly. We don't need the international press trying to second-guess us."

"I understand the problems you are facing, Mr. Kennedy. So long as you understand mine we will come to an agreement."

Kennedy nodded. "I think I do." Russia's new metal-backed monetary system had not gained acceptance in the world marketplace. The shortages of hard Western currencies with which to purchase desperately needed foreign foods and American or German machinery were worse than ever. Three years ago they'd begun peddling weapons and weapons systems, but so aggressively that within forty-eight months the market was glutted. Prices dropped and finally the demand slowed. There were just so many emerging nations wanting war materials. Although the threat of global thermonuclear conflict was all but eliminated, never in human history had the world been so heavily armed. "Have you been given the authority to make a final agreement here?"

"Yes, I have," Matushin answered. "What about Mr. Vasilanti and your board of directors? Will they need to vote their approval?"

"Normally, yes," Kennedy said. "But in this instance I have been given the full voice of the company. Unless I blunder badly, there'll be no problem."

Matushin and his translator exchanged some words, and Kennedy leaned over toward his translator Sally Fine.

"Mr. Matushin has asked for the correct meaning of 'blunder,'" she said.

Matushin grinned broadly. "Let us hope that neither of us blunder, Mr. Kennedy. Frankly speaking, we need this factory as badly as Guerin Airplane Company needs success with its new design."

Kennedy's ears perked up. McGarvey had warned him about just this. Ask the Russians for hard intelligence and their first move will be to gather information about the customer—the agency, or in this case, the company asking for help. Matushin had his experts advising him. Around the table this morning would be at least two FIS officers posing as either government or financial experts. He wished McGarvey were here now, if for nothing else than balance. He'd come in early this morning and had gone back out just before this meeting started. Kennedy hadn't had a chance to speak with him, nor apparently had any of the others. There was no telling where he was or what he was doing.

The Russians probably knew just how close to bankruptcy Guerin was, and therefore how important the P/C2622 had become. They also understood that the Japanese were offering the biggest threat to them, and that if Guerin went down the Russians stood to lose a substantial source of foreign exchange. But in one sentence Matushin had admitted knowing all of that. He had laid his cards on the table: We need each other. There couldn't be any other interpretation. Kennedy decided that he would never make it as a politician, but he was learning.

"Speaking just as frankly, Mr. Matushin, it's our opinion that since Russia's need for our factory is so acute, your managers, engineers, and employees will do a good job for us."

Again the Russian aerospace minister exchanged a few words with his translator, but this time they kept their voices too low for Sally Fine to catch anything. Matushin stiffened slightly, but then smiled wanly and nodded. He was a bulky man with thick eyebrows and thick, black hair, his face pockmarked by childhood chicken pox or teenage acne.

"Won't giving us this opportunity make matters worse for you with your union in Wichita?"

Bingo. There were no problems with the union at their Kansas facility. McGarvey had called it a "flag," to prove that the Russians were listening to their conversations in the hotel.

"It's nothing to worry about, Mr. Minister, I assure you. Nor will securing the necessary export licenses from my government."

"Have you already spoken with your State Department?"

"Our legal people have, and they see no impediments," Kennedy said.

Matushin and his translator spoke. "Very well, Mr. Kennedy. Will your company be posting a performance bond with us? I'm told ten percent is the norm. After all, we are exposing ourselves to just as big a risk as you are. Possibly even a bigger risk considering the tension between us and Ukraine."

Jeff Soderstrom started to object, but Kennedy held his CFO off. "That would be a point of negotiation, Mr. Matushin. Can I take it that we are agreed in principle to proceed?"

Matushin smiled. "Of course, let's proceed."

"Where is he, Bruno?" Reid asked. It was shortly after midnight.

"Upstairs setting up his computers. Apparently they're adequate," Mueller replied. Before leaving the West Coast, he'd telephoned Reid at the special number from a pay phone at the airport in San Francisco with Zerkel's list of needed computer equipment. It was extensive, but everything was waiting when they arrived at the farmhouse.

"It's hard to believe that they're brothers. The sheer coincidence is stunning, although it does have a certain internal logic, if you know what I mean. Is this one just as crazy as Glen?"

"Crazier."

"Where is Glen?"

"Upstairs watching his brother. Helping him, I think. They haven't seen each other for a long time, although it doesn't seem to bother Louis. He's only interested in his theory that the Japanese are going to purchase America outright."

"He may be correct."

"I don't care," Mueller said mildly.

"I care enough to pay one million dollars in gold if what I'm trying to do comes to pass."

Mueller turned his full attention to the older man. "What is that, Reid?"

"I'm a crusader."

Mueller dismissed the comment with a smirk. "On your white horse. First the Russians and now the Japanese. Could have been any country. Maybe Germany."

"Perhaps."

"What exactly is it you want?"

"Guerin Airplane Company driven to its knees so that the Japanese will make the buy-out attempt, and for my government to stop the deal."

"Creating a conflict between Japan and the U.S."

"Yes," Reid said. He was half-drunk again, his face puffy, his complexion mottled and his eyes watery.

"Manipulating governments would seem to be a tall order."

"Frighteningly simpler than one would expect," Reid answered. He poured another Irish whiskey at the sideboard in the living room and looked at Mueller's reflection in the mirror. "Tallerico's murder will not be connected to Louis, I presume. We're okay on that account?"

"That one will be a mystery."

Reid turned back. "Has there been another?"

"Tallerico's California contact was Louis's psychiatrist. Her murder will be blamed on him."

"The police will eventually catch up with him."

"When we no longer have need of his services, he will commit suicide."

Reid recoiled at the utter callousness of the East German. Life meant absolutely nothing to the man. Once again he was given pause to wonder if he was doing the right thing. But this was war, after all. He was fighting for nothing less than the survival of the United States of America as an entity, if not an ideal. In war there were casualties. But, like a general in the opening moments of a battle, Reid felt sorry for the destruction his plan would cause. Yet there was no other way.

"Does he know about his psychiatrist?"

"No, but if he finds out I will speak with him. Or you can. He believes you're the only man in the country who knows the truth about the Japanese."

Reid glanced toward the stairs. "He says he can actually build this device? It actually exists?"

"He says he can. But apparently there's more to it than that. Something about a transmitter, perhaps a remote control of some sort. He isn't very coherent."

"But he said the Japanese were behind it? He told you that?"

"He said InterTech, the company he works for, is either owned by the Japanese or controlled by them."

"This device he's talking about is built by InterTech?"

"Yes. On contract with Guerin."

Reid nodded thoughtfully. "My guess is that Guerin knows nothing about the Japanese connection. They've always made the claim that except for the Rolls-Royce engines they use, their airplanes are wholly American designed and built."

"Companies have lied before."

"Not this company," Reid said with assurance. "It may be one of the reasons they're in trouble." He glanced again toward the stairs. "I'll go up and meet him now."

"He's expecting you, but do you think it's wise?" Mueller asked. "To this point he has no valid claim to a connection with you. He's never met you. In case something should go wrong."

"As you say, when he is finished he will commit suicide." Reid finished his drink and set the glass down. "Get some rest. You've earned it."

All of his life Reid had been a doer, a fixer, an arranger, the man who could come up with whatever was needed, whenever it was needed, with a minimum of lead time. This applied to the information that he used for his *Lamplighter* newsletter, as well as people who were attracted to him and who did him favors (for which he helped make them money), and of course things, physical objects, such as the Lugers in Germany and the sophisticated computer equipment Zerkel had ordered.

He hesitated for a moment at the head of the stairs. The equipment that Reid's supplier had acquired for him in under six hours was mostly IBM gear designed for scientific and engineering applications. The main central processing unit was the new 18340, with a complex ultra-dense memory system of more than 950 gigabytes and the ability to handle several million operations per second, as well as ten completely different functions simultaneously. A half-dozen keyboard terminals and screens were connected to the CPU, along with two high-speed drafting machines, an ultra-high-speed modem for talking directly to other sophisticated computers, an auto-pen input, a direct-feed document reader, and a voice recognition board that would allow the operator to control many of the machine's functions with voice commands. It had cost him more than a half million dollars, but eventually he would get that back and then some, because when Guerin's stock took the plunge he was going to be one of them waiting at the bottom to buy. He would make a hundred million dollars. But even more satisfying was the thought that he'd be taking the money away from the Japanese. He would be hitting the bastards where it hurt them the most.

Louis Zerkel, his left sneaker untied, his shirt half untucked, and his long hair in disarray, was hunched over one of the terminals in the front bedroom. All the furniture had been stacked in the hall or moved to one of the other bedrooms to make room for the equipment. The window was wide open to keep the heat down, and printouts were spewing from every printer. His halfbrother Glen leaned against the door frame from the adjoining bedroom, a beer in his hand. He looked up when Reid appeared at the corridor door.

"Mr. Reid is here to see you, Louis," he called softly. At first Reid didn't think Louis heard his brother, but then the man whirled around and threw up his hands.

For just a moment Reid was afraid that the man was going to attack him. Mueller said the Zerkels were crazy, but if appearances were any judge, that was an understatement in Louis's case.

"Oh, wow, you're actually here," Louis Zerkel cried. "If it wasn't for your *Lamplighter,* Mr. Reid, I would never have figured out what was going on. It's just fate, that's all. But we'll beat the bastards. What do you think about that?"

Reid crossed the room and shook Zerkel's hand. "It's a pleasure to meet you. Your brother speaks highly of you."

"They've been planning this shit since right after the war, you can bet on it," Zerkel gushed. "From tin whistles to computer chips, what do you think about that?

"Have you got everything you need?"

"No," Zerkel said. He turned and plucked a half-dozen sheets of computer printout from atop one of the machines and handed them to Reid. "I'm going to start with the transmitter. It's that replacement chip I don't understand. I need to make an experiment."

Listed on the printouts were hundreds of electronic components, by name, function, rate value, and tolerance, along with test equipment and dozens of tools.

"Whoever got this stuff for you knows what they're doing. It's not bad. Have them pick up that shit too."

"Anything else?"

"No," Zerkel said. "Not for now." He turned back to the terminal, brought something up on screen, and was immediately lost in some incomprehensible diagram.

Finding Louis Zerkel was more difficult than McLaren or Joyce thought it would be. They wanted to keep their investigation low key in case they stumbled upon something unexpected. More than one line of inquiry had unraveled because some ham-fisted agent had unknowingly flushed the partridge or had ruined the case because of faulty evidentiary procedures. As a result it had taken them all day.

It was past 9:00 P.M. as they waited outside a white stucco, two-story apartment building for someone downtown to show up with their search warrant. In the two hours they'd been watching, there'd been no lights in Zerkel's windows, nor had there been any sign of the man. After Whitman's warning about the East German, they were taking few chances.

Earlier they'd checked Zerkel's last known address, which had turned out to be a small house in Oakland. The current renters had never heard of him, nor did the rental agency in San Francisco have a forwarding address. One of the neighbors remembered Zerkel, but only vaguely, as an "odd duck." The U.S. Post Office, Pacific Bell, and Pacific Gas & Electric had no present listing. Vehicle registration showed he owned a 1983 Chevrolet, but the address listed was for the Oakland house. It was the same at the credit bureau, and Social Security.

San Francisco S-A-C—Special Agent in Charge— Charles Colberg was pissed off that he'd not been consulted before his turf had been invaded, but once he talked to Whitman in Washington he calmed down. The local Bureau file on Zerkel had no further information, nor was there anything of value on InterTech.

By then they had run out of options, so they'd finally approached the man's employer.

"Let me get this straight," Zerkel's supervisor Bob Sutherland said, a cigar clenched in his mouth. "You're FBI, you want to talk about Louis, but this is *not* a background investigation for a government job offer?"

McLaren grinned. "You tell me, Mr. Sutherland, how many new government jobs have you heard about in the last couple of years? We're just clearing out deadwood here. Louis Zerkel has a secret clearance—we're checking it out. New program, going to save the taxpayers some money. You know how it is."

"So do a hundred other people here have clearances."

"We can only do this one at a time. Maybe if we could just take a peek at his personnel file, and then maybe have a chat with him?"

Sutherland came to a decision after a second and handed Zerkel's file over to McLaren. "You can take a look at this, but he's not here now."

McLaren flipped open the file and turned directly to the personal data section. His address was an apartment right in Alameda. Rent probably included gas and electric, which was why his name hadn't been listed with the utilities.

"Is this his day off?" Joyce was asking.

"He didn't come in," Sutherland said. "And he doesn't answer his phone or his bulletin board."

McLaren looked up. "There's no phone number listed here."

"The company provides phone lines for engineers of his level and above. The amount of data networking they do would drive their phone bills to astronomical levels."

"Does he miss work often?" Joyce asked.

"Once in a while," Sutherland said, shrugging. "Frankly I wasn't getting worried until you showed up. Is this a criminal investigation?"

"What would make you think that?" McLaren asked, his senses perking up.

"We did our own background check, and we know about his brother Glen."

"Any contact between the two of them, that you know about?"

Sutherland shook his head. "None."

Two unmarked cars and a dark blue van pulled up behind McLaren and Joyce. A dozen men and a few women jumped out. They all wore dark windbreakers and baseball caps with "FBI" stenciled on them, and they were all armed with semiautomatic pistols. Colberg's number two, A-S-A-C Gordy Behrens, came up, a serious expression on his hound-dog face. "Any activity here?" he asked.

"Nada," McLaren said. "Did you bring the warrant?"

Behrens nodded. "We're going to do this my way."

"For Christ's sake, Gordy, we just want to talk to the man."

"I talked to Whitman this afternoon," Behrens said. "We'll do this my way."

"So much for keeping our heads down," Joyce said.

"Just don't shoot him before we can ask some questions," McLaren told Behrens. "Okay?"

The first part of the meeting went well—better than anyone thought it would. Not all the details of the deal had been worked out, but the substantive points had been agreed to one after the other with such a minimum of discussion that it caught everyone off guard.

"Don't expect miracles," Soderstrom had warned them earlier. "The Russians have only had a few years to develop a capitalist mentality, so they have different expectations than we do."

Aviation Minister Matushin was anxious to see the deal go through, and it became obvious early on that someone above him was calling the shots. Authority or not, Kennedy got the definite impression that the man was on a very short leash. The wing factory was going to be built on Russian soil, and whatever it took to accomplish that goal would be done.

At the break before lunch, Kennedy and Matushin stepped over to the tall windows overlooking the brooding pile of brick that housed the Kremlin arsenal.

"The only problem that I can see is the continued stability of your government," Kennedy said, bringing up Soderstrom's concern as he promised he would if the opportunity arose.

"A legitimate question, Mr. Kennedy. But frankly it's one for which I have no satisfactory answer. Ten years ago we could not have had this conversation. It would have been unthinkable."

Kennedy had to smile. "We have an old saying: Be careful what you wish for, you might get it."

Matushin looked sharply at him. "Are you considering backing out of this deal?"

"It's not that. I meant that we in the West never really believed that the Soviet Union could fall apart in our lifetime, and we certainly never expected the economic impact it's had on the world."

"Neither did we," Matushin said distantly. "But no matter what happens we will never return to the old ways. There isn't enough blood in all of Russia to drown the new order."

"A personally held belief, Mr. Minister?"

"I'm not alone in thinking this, if that's what you're asking. But as you say, the cost is great."

"Then it's up to us to get on with it, with as many safeguards for each other as possible," Kennedy said.

The Russians were offering two thousand acres adjacent to Domodedovo Airport on the Kashira Highway thirty miles southeast of Moscow. One of the largest airports in the world, Domodedovo handled the bulk of Russia's internal flights and could handle any type of aircraft currently flying. A special rail line would link the wing-panel assembly hall with the airport so that the parts and raw materials could be flown in on modified P522s, and the finished wings could be returned to Portland the same way. The rail spur was already in place, as was a three-story building that could be used to house engineering and administration. Until ten years ago there'd been a tank factory on the site.

Russian workers would put up the assembly hall to Guerin's specifications—which would mean on-site American inspectors and supervisors—and would also supply the precision metal cutting, bending, and shaping equipment needed to build the wing components out of titanium. Most of the electrical and hydraulic parts would be U.S. designed and supplied, and Guerin would provide extensive on-the-job training for the Russian engineers and assembly workers. Within five years Guerin would be able to reduce its participation to fifty percent. Quality control would always remain strictly under Guerin's supervision, however. As Kennedy explained across the table, "If a wing fails it'd be a Guerin airplane that goes down. We'll make sure they're built correctly."

"This will be a good thing for both of us," Matushin said, lighting a cigarette. He was a chain smoker. "Admittedly your company is taking a chance by coming here, but it's one that will pay off well for you."

"We think so," Kennedy said carefully. So far there'd not been so much as a hint about the Japanese, but he wondered if that's what the Russian was referring to now. "You'll be sharing in the risk."

"When we begin exchanging dollar credits toward the purchase of airplanes from you."

"I meant that cooperating so closely with us might subject you to some criticism."

An odd, almost wistful, expression crossed Matushin's features, and he shrugged. "I don't believe I completely understand you, Mr. Kennedy. Perhaps we need the translators."

"I was merely talking about the hardliners still in your government. Maybe there is still some mistrust."

"Ah, I see what you mean," Matushin said. He shook his head. "That is absolutely nothing to worry about. As I said, we will never go back to the old ways."

Kennedy watched the Russian's eyes, but he could find nothing that might indicate something was being held back. Matushin was a professional bureaucrat, and probably very adept at saying whatever had to be said at the moment, but Kennedy prided himself on his ability to judge people. Unless he was way off the mark, he decided, the aviation minister probably knew nothing about the deal that McGarvey had cut with the SUR for information about the Japanese.

"I would hope that we could begin construction in the spring," Kennedy said. "It'll take a year to build, and possibly that long afterward before the first wing panel is completed."

"Possibly longer," Matushin replied. "Don't forget our winters. They've defeated more than one intended conqueror."

"If we can enclose the building and get heat to it before the cold weather we'll be all right. You'll have to throw enough people into the project to get it done."

Matushin nodded thoughtfully. "Providing we come to final agreement here. There are still many details, some of them quite critical, left to be worked out."

"As you say, Mr. Minister, this will be a good thing for both of us. We will make it work."

The Russian glanced over to the long conference table where several of the negotiators were already back at it, then stubbed out his cigarette in an ashtray on the broad windowsill.

"There is still time before lunch," he said. "Shall we return to the task?"

Kennedy turned. "Delivery schedules are very important to us, crucial in some instances."

"Have you figured it out yet?" Reid asked. It was 9:00 A.M., and he felt like shit. He'd been up all night arranging for the electronic components and equipment that Zerkel had requested.

The InterTech engineer was crouched over a series of schematic drawings spread out on the floor. "A relay of some type, I think. But I can tell you for sure that it doesn't belong in the circuit."

"Could it have brought down that American Airlines flight in '90?" Reid asked. Mueller had reported everything that Zerkel had talked about on the flight from San Francisco. The engineer's conspiracy theory fit with Reid's suspicions so perfectly that it was almost spooky.

"This module refit was put in place before the crash. My guess is they tried one out; when it worked they modified all the boards."

"But you still have no proof?"

Zerkel looked up. His eyes were red-rimmed and he looked as bad as Reid felt. But there was passion in them. He wasn't fooling around here. He was dead serious.

"Did you get my parts?"

"Downstairs in the van. Your brother and Bruno will bring them up." The van had been delivered to him at a supermarket parking lot in Arlington.

"I'll put together a breadboard transmitter that should

fit the frequency range of that circuit, and then run my encoding program through it until we hit the right combination."

"You're opening a lock?" Reid asked.

Zerkel grinned. "Something like that, only it's electronic, and I'm just guessing that there's a circuit internal to the new module that makes up an encoded receiver. Input the correct sequence of digital pulses, and the module will spit a signal out the other end."

"A signal to do what?"

"Trigger an explosive in the engine," the engineer said. "Maybe confuse the heat sensors into believing the engines are running too cold. If the heat builds past a critical level the turbine could fail. Might swallow a blade, blow the engine apart."

"But would it bring down the plane?"

Zerkel nodded.

Reid thought it out, careful to keep his excitement off his face. "Once you get the transmitter built, how will you know it works?"

"Simple. I'll tie into InterTech's circuit simulator and see what happens when I push the button. If the frequency is right, and I can hit the proper digital sequence, we'll see an output."

"Then what?"

"That's up to you, Mr. Reid. But if it works, and if the Japanese have installed these modules in all the heat sensors Guerin got from us, you'll be able to do the same thing the Japanese can do. And that's to bring down Guerin airplanes. What do you think about that?"

"We've got the bastard nailed," Phillip Joyce said, coming back into the autopsy theater at San Francisco General. He and McLaren had stayed with Dr. Shepard's body from the moment they'd found it on the houseboat.

"Did you talk to ballistics?" McLaren asked. He was having a cup of coffee with one of the lab technicians. The autopsy was finished, and the body had been zipped up in plastic and put in a refrigerated drawer.

"The bullet dug out of her skull was fired from the Beretta we found in Zerkel's apartment. No doubt whatsoever."

McLaren nodded tiredly. The sun was just coming up. It had been a very long night, and the new day stretched ahead of them. "They found semen in her vagina, O-positive. Same as Zerkel's blood type."

"He raped her, then killed her?"

"No. He killed her first then raped the body," the lab tech, an older man, said. "Couldn't have been very pleasant, no lubrication."

"Ah, shit," Joyce said, turning away in disgust.

"We'll put out an APB on him," McLaren said. "But I'm wondering if this has anything to do with Tallerico's murder."

"We'll ask him," Joyce snarled. Two years ago his fifteen-year-old daughter had been raped by her boyfriend. As a result, Joyce had developed a special aversion for that type of crime.

Zerkel started by drawing the transmitter wiring diagram on layout paper. He took care to trace and retrace each element of the circuit to make absolutely certain there were no mistakes before transferring it onto a sheet of etch-resistant rub-on paper and then transferring that onto the copper side of a blank printed circuit board twenty inches on a side. He was a design engineer, not a technician, so he wasn't used to working with his hands. But he understood the theory, and he forced himself to slow down, to take his time.

Across the hall in the bathroom he'd set up a plastic dishpan in the bathtub for the etching solution of ammonium persulphate. The solution had to be kept at a temperature between 90 and 115 degrees Fahrenheit, so Zerkel rigged an ordinary heat lamp just above the pan. It took him a couple of hours before he got the height of the lamp just right to keep the etch bath at the proper temperature. Once that was done he added a small amount of mercuric chloride crystals, which served as an activator for the bath, and placed the circuit board into the solution, holding it with a set of long wooden tongs so that he could keep the board in continuous motion. Where the etch-resistant wax was laid down on the circuit board, the copper would be untouched by the chemical. Everywhere else on the board the copper would be eaten away, leaving behind a complicated web of interconnected copper strips that made up the wiring of the transmitter circuit.

His brother was watching him. "How long do you have to keep that shit up?"

"About an hour."

"Then what?"

"Wash it with water, dry it off, and start wiring up the components."

"I can do this part," Glen told his brother. "You've got other shit to do."

Louis nodded. "Thanks," he said, and he went into the other room to begin assembling the parts. He hated mindless, repetitive tasks and was grateful for his brother's help. Maybe Glen wasn't so bad after all.

Darkness came early to Moscow at this time of year. Kennedy sat beneath the yellow glow of the chandelier listening to Soderstrom and Topper discuss purchase orders with Russian Federal Bank representative Ilya Lyukshin and Aeroflot Acquisitions Director Aleksei Voskoboy. They'd been at it for more than an hour but didn't seem to be any closer to an agreement than they had at the start of the meeting. Part of the problem was the transfer of credits from Washington for the deal. Guerin would get a tax break at home, but in order for Aeroflot to acquire eighty P522s and thirty P/C2622s over the next eight years, the purchases would have to be backed by U.S. loan guarantees, something Soderstrom had cautioned could be a stumbling block.

"Boeing and McDonnell Douglas could argue that Washington is subsidizing us. Could cause a glitch."

A possible way around the problem would be for the Russians to divert available Western credits from other needs to purchase the airplanes—or at least come up with the down payments that Guerin needed to survive—and get U.S. loan guarantees to replace them. The Russians were balking because if Washington decided not to go along with the loan guarantees it would create a problem for the Kremlin. Russia needed wheat, corn, and butter more than it needed high-tech jet airliners.

Dominick Grant, Guerin's tall, thin, patrician-looking government liaison, sat forward. "What if we get Washington's approval beforehand?"

Voskoboy started to say something, but Minister Matushin waved him off. "This would take time."

"Thirty-six hours," Grant replied. He turned to Kennedy. "It's a little before 9:00 A.M. in Washington. If I could get out of here tonight, I'd be at the State Department first thing tomorrow morning. Tom Bruce knows what's going on. He'll give us a reading as fast as humanly possible."

"You don't think they'll try to play politics with you, Dominick?" Kennedy asked. "We could get bogged down with this approach. It'd be harder for us to make any kind of an alternative deal later."

"They'll have their big guns, but we'll have ours. I'll take Howard and Jeff with me. Push comes to shove, Mr. Vasilanti can fly out to Washington."

"In the meantime, Mr. Minister, I assume that we can continue to negotiate here in good faith on the assumption my people will be successful."

The Russian aviation minister hesitated only long enough for his translator to finish before he smiled and nodded his massive head. "By all means, Mr. Kennedy."

"Hello, Viktor Pavlovich," McGarvey said. He stood at the open door to the Russian's apartment on Kalinin Prospekt. A stereo played softly inside.

"Yeb vas, you come as a very big surprise," Yemlin said, stepping aside. "Colonel Lyalin is threatening to have someone shot if you are not found."

"I was busy," McGarvey said. Yemlin's apartment was large by Russian standards and very nicely furnished with modern Scandinavian furniture from Helsinki. But the place had not been used for some time. Everything was dusty.

"We must know where you went last night after you disappeared from the hotel." Yemlin closed the door and followed McGarvey into the apartment.

More had changed in Russia than was visible at first glance. McGarvey's old friends, those of them he'd been able to find, and who were willing to talk to him, had been frightened. But it wasn't the SUR they were afraid of. It was starvation. There was no money or food, nor was there any way to get either except by murder, or theft, or prostitution. Even little girls and boys as young as five or six were being offered to pedophiles. Almost all moral order had broken down in Moscow.

"This is very serious, Kirk," Yemlin persisted. Like everyone else, the former Washington *rezident* was frightened.

"I went to see some old friends," McGarvey answered softly. "David Kennedy believes that the negotiations will go well. What about network *Abunai?* Heard anything yet?"

"The colonel wants to speak to you. I'll call him."

"Goddammit, what have you found out?"

Yemlin slapped the side of his leg, vexed. "It's believed that a group called Mintori Assurance Corporation may be coming after you. But at this point we have no confirmation. Nor does Tokyo Station know to what extent the Japanese are willing to go to achieve their goals, although there are rumors. Do you understand this, Kirk? These are only unconfirmed rumors, but we are trying."

"Good," McGarvey said, a measure of relief coming over him, the first in twenty-four hours. "Let's talk to Colonel Lyalin now. We're going to need more information, Viktor. And soon."

It would be a grueling flight that no one was looking forward to. Captain Peter Morrisey and his crew had gone out to the airport earlier to prep the P522, but it was well after midnight before Grant, Soderstrom, and Guerin's general counsel Howard Siegel showed up. The weather had warmed up a bit with the passage of the front, but the winds had increased, driving the wind-chill factor to nearly 100 degrees below 0 Fahrenheit.

No one said much in the van on the way out from the hotel, nor were any of them inclined to carry on a conversation as they hurried, bent against the bitter wind, across the tarmac and up the boarding stairs into the airplane. Carol Cameron, one of their two attend-ants, closed and dogged the door, and even before she came back to offer coffee or something stronger the engines were spooling up. They knew what had to be accomplished, and why. For now there was nothing to do but hang on until they got to Washington.

It took all day and most of the evening to drill tiny mounting holes in the printed circuit board and install the several hundred individual components in their proper places. A simple transmitting device would have been infinitely easier to design and build, but this circuit had to do much more. Zerkel was proud of his handi-work, and he sat back with a proffered beer from his brother.

"Is it done?" Glen asked.

"Not yet. Still has to be wired up and then tested."

The problem was coming up with the electronic code sequence that would trigger the on-board heat sensor's module. His computer could spit out millions of combi-nations per second, but the possibilities numbered in the tens of billions. He had designed a multiplex circuit internal to his transmitter that would allow one hundred encoded sequences to be broadcast simultaneously. The sophisticated circuit would speed up the search by a factor of one hundred. Not bad, Zerkel thought, for an afternoon's work.

In the morning Minister Matushin suggested they spend the day touring the proposed site at Domodedovo Air-port. Nothing would be forthcoming from Washington until the next day, so they might as well make good use of their time.

Kennedy agreed.

By 3:00 A.M., Zerkel had finished the wiring and preliminary electrical tests on the circuit board. He'd not slept in what seemed like weeks, but he felt good, fully alert. Whatever shit his brother had given him did the trick, because he was flying. He was invincible.

The interface between the transmitter and his computer decoding program took only a couple of minutes to set up, and once it was in standby he brought up a line into InterTech's mainframe in Alameda and entered the company's electronic simulator.

Operating much like the flight simulators pilots use, InterTech's sophisticated program could be loaded with the schematic diagram of an electronic device, which in turn could be operated and tested as if it were the real thing. A schematic diagram for an ordinary television set could be loaded, and the user could switch channels and receive simulated television pictures. On a higher level, simulated circuits could be tested for malfunctions, for operating characteristics under varying conditions, or even analyzed for function. In this case, Zerkel loaded the heat-sensor circuit from InterTech's files into the simulator, and then began running the encoded output into it from his transmitter.

It was a little past midnight in San Francisco, which gave him nearly eight hours on this circuit before he'd have to shut down, but a lot could be accomplished in that time. Maybe the whole enchilada.

"Guerin Airplane Company nancy-four-seven-seven-niner-echo, you are cleared for final approach and landing. Report to Dulles Ground Control on one-two-two-one-niner on touchdown."

"Roger," Captain Morrisey responded. His eyes were gritty and his back hurt like hell despite the fact he'd managed to get a few hours sleep on the last leg of the flight from Shannon. Providing the company brass didn't want a quick turnaround he'd be okay by tomorrow for the return flight. Regular commercial pilots did not fly under the same restrictions as airline jockeys. But if they wanted to return to Moscow sooner, a new crew would have to be brought from Portland.

"I'd better get back and check my charges," Lois Milliken, the second attendant said, smiling. She had come to Guerin almost directly out of Northwest's flight-attendant school and had had less than three months experience working with the general public. She liked this a lot better.

"Find out if we're heading back today," Morrisey said. "I'd like at least twenty-four hours."

"Roger that," co-pilot Joe Tobias said. He looked just as tired as Morrisey.

"Will do, Captain," Lois said. "I've got some shopping to do if we get the time."

Morrisey and Tobias exchanged glances and grinned. "We'll be on the ground in three minutes," the captain said.

"Yes, sir," Lois said, and she left the flight deck.

"Shopping," Tobias said, and he chuckled.

The encoding solution had come up more than an hour ago, but the simulated heat-sensor circuit had not responded the way Zerkel thought it would. Something was missing. Something in the module had definitely switched to the on mode. There was a tone on the output line, but that signal was being shunted to ground by a capacitive circuit tuned to that frequency. Beyond that was a second circuit that Zerkel realized almost immediately would pass only a certain frequency or combination of frequencies. What threw him off at first was the extremely low theoretical values he was coming up with.

They were in the three thousand to eight thousand cycles-per-second range.

Within the audio range, the thought suddenly occurred to him. Within the range of a human voice.

Zerkel brought up a five-thousand-cycle tone and entered it into the simulator program. Immediately a sharp spike showed up on the output line. A couple of volts, at perhaps 150 milliamps or so.

The encoding sequence was merely the key used to cock the mechanism, while the low-frequency tone provided the actual firing pulse.

His brother Glen, who'd gone downstairs a few minutes ago for some breakfast, had left his walkie-talkie behind. Reid had insisted they all keep in constant touch. It was a good idea.

He pried the back cover off the walkie-talkie, and after a quick examination found the modulation section where the voice frequencies were added to the transmitter's broadcast frequency. He clipped a wire to the input section and led it to the input section of his breadboard transmitter.

A specially built walkie-talkie would be the way to go if you wanted to bring down one airplane at a time. First an encoding tone would be transmitted that would cock the heat-sensor unit, and secondly the operator or terrorist or whatever you wanted to call him would say something into the microphone.

"Boom."

A spike showed up on the heat sensor's output line.

"What the hell was that?" Captain Morrisey shouted. They were lined up for their final approach to landing, wheels down, flaps at twenty degrees.

"It's number one engine, Captain," Tobias screamed. "It's going."

The aircraft was listing sharply to port but there was nothing Morrisey could do about it. Alarms flashed and buzzed all across the panel and overhead.

It was the port engine. The entire engine was gone, flying away in pieces! It had swallowed a blade. Something.

"Mayday, mayday, mayday," Tobias shouted into the radio.

It was no use, they were well past a ninety-degree list

to port now, the end of the runway frighteningly close, and they were still turning over.

It was just like the American Airlines flight out of Chicago in '90, Captain Morrisey thought.

The instant before they hit he said, "Fuck it!" They were the last words on the cockpit voice recorder.

Glen Zerkel came running up the stairs, Reid and Mueller pounding right after him. They'd been in the kitchen having breakfast when they saw the crash.

Louis Zerkel, his hair flying, his T-shirt untucked and dirty, his eyes wild, danced around the room, hooting and singing. In his left hand he held a walkie-talkie, its back off, wires trailing from its insides, and with his right he was pointing toward the ceiling.

"It worked!" he cried. "Did I tell you it would work? It did! It worked!"

"An airplane just crashed at the end of the runway," Glen Zerkel said in awe. "It fell over and crashed in a ball of flame."

Louis Zerkel stopped in his tracks, a large grin on his face. His brother and the others were looking at him. Waiting for him to say something. He shrugged.

"Well, what do you think about that?"

TEN

Minister Matushin put down the car phone, his face grave. "I'm afraid I have some very bad news for you, Mr. Kennedy."

The day had been gloomy. It was 5:00 and starting to snow as they returned to Moscow from touring the wing-panel factory site at Domodedovo Airport. Kennedy had been having premonitions of disaster all afternoon. "What is it?" he asked.

"You are to call Chris Bradenton as soon as you get to the hotel. Another five minutes. Do you know this name?"

"He's our director of flight operations."

"He's on his way to Washington. The hotel will help get through to him. My staff is setting it up for you now."

"Chris, on his way to Washington?" Kennedy said. "Why? What's happened?" He had an ugly feeling.

"Your company airplane crashed on landing at Dulles Airport a little more than an hour ago," the minister said. He and Kennedy rode in the back seat of the minister's Zil limousine. The others followed in an Intourist bus. "Apparently there is little chance that anyone survived. There was fire."

Kennedy slumped back in the seat, stunned. He felt as bad as he had in 1986 when he learned that the space shuttle *Challenger* had gone down with all her crew. His gut was hollow, and he found it difficult to concentrate. Such a thing was impossible to swallow in one lump. The P522 was the safest airplane that had ever flown. In her eleven-year history she'd only been involved in one fatal crash, the American Airlines accident in 1990. There'd been other minor incidents, but they were just that— nothing to be overly concerned about, although Guerin took even the smallest problems seriously.

"I'm sorry, Mr. Kennedy, I understand how you must feel," Minister Matushin said. "But let me assure you that this accident in no way diminishes our faith in your company and our desire to proceed with the project."

Kennedy looked at him. Soderstrom was gone. Despite the CFO's dour, pessimistic disposition and outlook, Guerin Airplane Company had come to depend on his counsel. Vasilanti had called him the "corporation's conscience." And the others: Siegel, Dominick Grant, the aircrew. It was impossible to believe they were gone.

"An aircraft and crew will be made available immediately to fly you and your people anywhere you need to go. We understand and sympathize. Completely."

Kennedy had made tough decisions all his life. As a

pilot and then as an astronaut when timing was often critical, his decisions had to be made instantly. But now the consequences of his judgment were more far reaching. Eighty thousand people worked for Guerin Airplane Company. Their futures rode on the future of the company, which rode on the managerial skills of its executives, from Vasilanti down. If you can't stand the heat, get out of the kitchen, the old man was fond of saying. Either manage or get the hell out of the way. Pearls of the business. "This is not an industry of fainthearted namby-pambies," Vasilanti said when he hired him. "So if you don't think you can handle it, son, let's get it on the table now and spare us all the grief later."

"Simply tragic," the Russian said. "No doubt these men were indispensable to your company. They will have to be replaced, of course, and new people brought into the talks. Which will take time, naturally. As will your government's investigation of the crash, and your own company study . . . all of it, such a waste. But we will be patient here in Moscow, no matter how long the delay. We know about these things."

Christ, Kennedy thought. He took a deep breath to clear the pressure in his chest and made his decision. He felt terrible, but there was nothing else he could do.

"Let's not get ahead of ourselves, Mr. Minister," he said, pulling himself together. "I'll need to inform my staff, and we'll need a conference room in the hotel with eight or ten reliable telephone lines, two or three competent bilingual operators, and at least three fax machines. Can that be arranged with a minimum of delay?"

"Of course," Minister Matushin said. "You're not returning to Washington?"

"I don't know yet. If there's something for us to do there, if we're needed, then we'll go. Otherwise we'll stay to continue our negotiations."

"I beg your pardon, Mr. Kennedy, but your people were to meet with State Department officials about loan guarantees."

"We'll send a new team."

They raced across the river and passed Red Square, the hotel just ahead. Minister Matushin eyed Kennedy with respect. "Life goes on," he said.

"Yes," Kennedy replied absently, his mind already ranging to the enormous problems Guerin faced because of the accident and to the distasteful job facing him of telling the others, following in the bus, what had happened.

Louis Zerkel locked himself in the front bedroom and sat cross-legged on the floor. Reid had been at him all morning, and now it was time to think about what was wanted of him. For a while he had watched all the activity over at the airport from an upstairs window. Ambulances and fire trucks and helicopters had streamed into the crash area just short of the main runway. Two hours after the P522 had gone down the stench of burned kerojet, baked metal, scorched rubber, and incinerated plastics and foams still lingered on the air. No one had survived that crash.

Zerkel knew that he was strange, probably even crazy. At this moment he wanted to talk to Dr. Shepard more than he'd ever wanted anything. All of his life he had been a law-abiding citizen. He never got traffic tickets, he always paid his taxes on time—and never cheated, even if it would have been ridiculously easy for him—nor had he ever stolen from anybody or lied. On the occasions he went with a prostitute he told himself that he really wasn't breaking any law. It was a matter of geography. If he were in Amsterdam, or Hamburg, or even Nevada the act would be perfectly legal. Simple.

But people had died in that crash, and he had made it happen. He was a murderer. He ran his fingers through his long, unruly hair. Something very odd had been done to him in the past forty-eight hours. Something had changed him from what he had been in California.

In California he had been content to study world conspiracies. Here he had become part of one. He had

no illusions now about Edward R. Reid and the others—
especially the German. They had their agendas, which
they thought they were hiding from him, but he'd seen
through their bullshit almost from the beginning. Or,
certainly he'd realized what they were up to this morning after the crash when they'd come rushing up to see
what he'd done.

Fact is, he didn't think he minded awfully much being
a killer. It didn't bother him as he thought it should. It
even fit quite well. He felt a sense of power, of brute
strength over all the sonsabitches who'd ever done a
double take in his direction. Hey, geek, what'cha think
you're doing?

Zerkel grinned.

Reid hated the Japanese because his kind needed to
hate something, but his love of making money was even
stronger. He wanted to bring Guerin airplanes crashing
to the ground and blame the Japanese government for
doing it. The company would slide toward bankruptcy,
but Washington would block the Japanese from buying
stock, so it would be up to Americans such as Edward R.
Reid to help bail the company out. There would be
hundreds of millions of dollars in profits.

Zerkel didn't mind. The question was how it could be
done, and he had already begun thinking about it. One
problem would be making sure that the blame ended up
squarely in the laps of the Japs. InterTech was the key.
The company was owned and directed by Tokyo. If
InterTech could be blamed, the guilt would transmit
directly to Japan.

Another problem was bringing down the airplanes.
There was going to be a big investigation into this
morning's accident. If another Guerin airplane went
down soon, the entire fleet might be grounded. Two
accidents might be suspicious, but they'd still be classified as accidents. If a lot of Guerin airplanes went down
all at once, or all on the same day, no one would believe
the crashes were coincidental. There would be tens of
millions of dollars in property damage and hundreds if

not thousands of lives lost. The act of terrorism would be monstrous, beyond belief. If the blame could be placed on the Japanese, it would be the end for them. The consequences would be even worse than losing the war.

There were at least two other wrinkles Zerkel could see. The first was his absence from InterTech. Someone bright out there could very well be putting together this morning's crash with his disappearance. The next time he went back into the company's computers he was going to have to be extra careful of traps.

He had to smile thinking about it. A lot of sharp people worked for InterTech, but he was smarter than all of them. Thinking about the second wrinkle, however, wiped the smile off his face.

Bruno Mueller meant to kill him as soon as he'd outlived his usefulness. It was up to Zerkel to make sure that didn't happen.

Kennedy and his staff used a conference room across the broad corridor from the Rossiya's three-thousand-seat concert hall. Phone lines and fax machines had been set up for them within the hour, but the news about the crash still hadn't sunk in. Soderstrom and the others were dead. The ones who'd been left behind felt isolated, cut off from the rest of the world. And they felt lucky and guilty because of it. Yet they had work to do, and they got to it.

Vasilanti and Bradenton were on a company jet enroute to Washington, D.C., when Kennedy finally made contact with them. "We got the news about an hour ago."

"Something's goddamned fishy, David," Vasilanti shouted. "It was the same engine as '90. Has George seen the specs?"

Kennedy glanced at Socrates standing at one of the fax machines. "I think they're coming in now," he told the old man. "What happened, Al? We haven't been able to get through to the NTSB, so we're still in the dark."

"The port engine disintegrated on the approach to landing. It's going to be just like the American Airlines crash. We'll find that the engine swallowed a blade and fell apart. A severe overheat."

"We'll take another look at the sensing system."

"You're damned right we will, but that won't turn out to be the problem. It's in the engine. I can feel it in my gut."

"Are you talking about the ceramics?" Kennedy asked. The Rolls-Royce engine used a carbon-ceramic composition for some of its turbine blades. They were lighter than steel and supposedly withstood much higher G forces and temperatures. After the crash in '90, Rolls reverted to titanium blades, but two years ago it switched to an improved ceramic composition. All of Guerin's P422s and P522s had been retrofitted.

"That's right. O'Toole is on the Concorde from London. I want you and George here. Will the Russians fly you, or should I send one of ours?"

"Al, were there any survivors?"

"No," Vasilanti said, heavily. He sounded like an old man suddenly.

"Then for now I think you should leave the crash investigation to the NTSB and to our engineers. George is setting up a go-team. There's nothing we can do for Jeff and the others."

"Except make goddamned sure it doesn't happen again," the CEO retorted.

"Our technical guys will do that. Right now you need to get Maggie Drewd and Tony Glick out to Washington." Margaret Drewd was Guerin's assistant chief financial officer, and Anthony Glick had been Howard Siegel's number two.

"They're on the plane with me. What have you got in mind, David?"

"I was sending Jeff and the others to Washington to talk to State about loan guarantees for our deal. Maggie and Tony can take over their respective departmental loads for now. But you're going to have to stand in for Dominick."

"You're staying there?"

"Until we can get a reading from State. Once that's in place, the deal will be set and I can come home."

Vasilanti took a moment to reply. When he did, his tone was guarded. "What are the Russians saying?"

"They sympathize, but Aviation Minister Viktor Matushin says our deal will not be affected. They want this just as badly as we do. They've even offered us a former tank factory and administration building at Domodedovo Airport. There's a rail spur already in place out to one of the taxiways where we can load and unload. It looks good."

Again Vasilanti hesitated. "I'll have to talk to Jeff's wife, and the others."

"Sorry, Al. I know it's something that I should be doing, but we're at a crucial point here. McGarvey has been *very* busy."

"I understand," the old man said. "This is a bad time for us."

"It is. But if we can get past this one, I think we'll be okay."

"Until the next time," Vasilanti said, the heaviness back in his voice. It was as if he personally was responsible for Guerin airplanes staying airborne and safe. It gave Kennedy an odd feeling trying to comfort the CEO. It'd always been the other way around.

"We can only take them one at a time, Al."

"Yeah," Vasilanti said. "But God help us all if this was sabotage and the Japanese were behind it."

"Al?"

"Yes?"

"It won't happen again."

"I hope not, David," Vasilanti said, a distant quality in his voice.

McGarvey came over when Kennedy hung up the telephone. His face was red from the cold.

"I just heard from one of Lyalin's people. What happened?"

"Same as '90," Kennedy said. "The port engine flew apart."

"Survivors?"

Kennedy shook his head.

McGarvey looked away for a moment. Everyone was busy, no one paid them any attention, and for the moment there were no Russians in the room. "Mintori Assurance Corporation," he said, turning back. "They're the ones after us."

"What else?" Kennedy asked.

"That's all, but the timing gets you, doesn't it?" McGarvey replied. "You guys show the world your new design, and one of your airplanes falls out of the sky."

"You don't think it was an accident?"

"No, I don't, David. And neither do you."

McGarvey took a shower and changed his clothes before he left the hotel again, this time by the front door. He picked up a tail immediately, two men in an old Moskvich station wagon who followed his cab over to the Arbat Restaurant on Kalinin Prospekt. Yemlin said it was one of the few places in the city that had anything decent to serve.

The former Washington *rezident* was waiting at a table overlooking the dance floor. "I didn't know if you'd show up after what happened in Washington. From what I understand there were no survivors."

"That's right." McGarvey sat across from him. "I hope to Christ I never find out that the FIS heard rumors and didn't pass them along."

"We heard nothing, I swear it. But we've queried Tokyo Station."

None of McGarvey's old friends had much bitterness about the old days. They were too busy trying to survive in Russia's new free-market economy. But McGarvey was still having trouble believing and trusting Yemlin or anyone else from the old KGB. Still, this was his idea, and they didn't have much choice. Especially not now.

"Do you have a name for us?" he asked.

"We know who heads the Mintori Assurance Corporation, but that's not to say he's personally involved in any sabotage attempts. He's a very old man. He may be nothing more than a titular leader."

"The Japanese don't run their corporations like that, and you know it."

"His name is Sokichi Kamiya," Yemlin said. He took an envelope out of his coat pocket and handed it across the table. "He's eighty-one years old, and by various accounts, he's the eighth or ninth richest man in Japan."

"Is there a *zaibatsu?*"

Yemlin nodded. "Kamiya is in the middle of it. Electronics, exotic materials, some petrochemicals, mostly R&D for industry. There's apparently some linkage between Mintori and a banking *zaibatsu* at Kobe. Tokyo Station is still working on that."

"Any possibility of getting inside Mintori? Bugging its boardroom?"

"I think you're expecting too much too soon, Kirk," Yemlin objected.

McGarvey sat forward. "There were no survivors of that crash, and I expect there'll be more disasters to come."

"This sort of thing takes time."

"We don't have time," McGarvey said harshly. "If need be we'll put this on the table with Minister Matushin as a condition of the deal. And you people can handle the Japanese if it gets out."

"I'll see what can be done," Yemlin replied firedly. "We can't work miracles. You can't believe how difficult it has become for us."

"After seventy years of communism it's not surprising, Viktor Pavlovich. But pardon me if I have no fucking sympathy for you. Just get the job done for us, and skip the excuses."

"Ohayō Go-zai-ma-su, Kamiya-san," Arimoto Yamagata said. He spoke on a secure phone in the Japanese consulate in San Francisco. It was a little past noon on the West Coast, which made it two in the morning in Tokyo. A very bad time for the call. But Yamagata was confused.

"Are you calling because of the crash?" the old man asked sharply.

"Yes, *Kamiya-dono*. Has it begun? Have you given the order?"

"No, of course not. It must have been a coincidence, or a technical flaw. We sent you to America to prevent such a necessity. What have you accomplished? What information are you offering me this morning?"

"I am ashamed to admit that I have very little to report. But, *Kamiya-san,* mightn't we use this incident to our advantage?"

"Of course we will. But first we must know how and why it has happened. If someone else is behind it. If someone has discovered what steps were taken seven years ago, we must know this. It may be the Russians. They have begun to spy on us through one of their crude networks here."

"For what reason, *Kamiya-san?*" The world as he understood it, as everyone had understood it, had changed in the past five or six years.

"I don't know yet, but Guerin may be behind it somehow. A number of its top executives have been meeting with the Russian Minister of Aviation in Moscow. There were some of them aboard that airplane."

"*Iie,* it was no coincidental crash in that case. But if the cause had been anything other than it was . . ."

"It gives one pause for thought, *Yamagata-san.* Now you know what must be done."

"*Hai, Kamiya-dono.* I will not fail you."

"No, you will not fail me."

Russians loved to have formal dinner gatherings at midnight—a custom, Kennedy thought, getting to his feet, his people were going to have to get used to.

Their last meeting at the Council of Ministers building in the Kremlin had been subdued because of the tragedy in Washington. Yet they'd all felt a sense of optimism because the State Department had given its approval in principle to hammer out a loan guarantee package that would work for everybody. The only proviso State had placed on the deal was that the Russians would have to work out their differences with the Japanese first. It was a provision that Kennedy had not brought up with Minister Matushin. Nor did he have any intention of doing so.

"This will remain a business deal and nothing more," he told Vasilanti. They both sidestepped the work the Russian Secret Service was doing for them for the moment.

"I would like to propose a toast," Kennedy said, raising his wine glass. Minister Matushin and the others around the table raised their glasses. This deal was going to be good for all of them, despite Soderstrom's concerns to the contrary. Kennedy could feel it.

"To our joint venture of developing and producing what will prove to be the most advanced airliner the world has ever seen. An airplane that will take us out of the twentieth century and well into the twenty-first. An airplane that will not only transport the general public in safety and comfort to the far corners of the earth with flight times of minutes rather than hours or days, but to the edge of space. An airplane that will become an important link in building the chain of trust and friendship between our two countries. Minister Matushin, ladies and gentlemen, I congratulate us all."

Everyone drained their glasses. The Russians banged theirs on the table and the waiters moved in to refill them. Minister Matushin got to his feet and raised his glass of vodka. They'd been drinking for nearly two hours, and his face was flushed, his forehead sweaty.

"I will toast to the success of our cooperation, but I will also drink to your brave executives and airplane crew who gave their lives. I make the suggestion that the Guerin-Moscow Wing Panel Development and Assembly Facility be named the Soderstrom-Grant-Siegel Assembly Facility Number One."

For a long second or two no one said a word, or made a move. The Russians watched the Americans to see their reactions, and Kennedy and his staff were caught off guard.

But then Kennedy smiled wanly and raised his glass. "It is a wonderful suggestion, Minister Matushin. One which touches us all, and one which I wholeheartedly support."

He drank his wine, put his glass down, and turned and walked out of the hall. Time now to go home, he thought, to begin picking up the pieces.

From his modest home near the Maritime Self Defense Force Academy overlooking the city of Yokosuka and the lower reaches of Tokyo Bay, Lieutenant Commander Kiyoda could see the *Samisho* at her berth. A barrier had been placed on the quay, lights had been strung up, and guards had been posted.

Within hours after the *Samisho* had docked she had been fully provisioned, and Kiyoda had been allowed to take a taxi to his home. That was forty-eight hours ago. Since then no one had been allowed in or out, nor were communications with the crew allowed.

Minori had been correct when he predicted there would be no parade for them this time. No one from the Admiralty had come to greet them or to accept their patrol report, nor had they received any communication whatsoever. It was, in Kiyoda's mind, ominous.

It was early morning, and low dark clouds continued to move in from the northwest, threatening more rain. Whitecaps marched along the broad expanse of the bay. Kiyoda shivered.

His two children were away at boarding school in Kobe, which left with him only his wife Moriko, their cook, and their gardener. Sitting on a tatami in front of the floor-to-ceiling window in his private sitting room, Kiyoda listened for their sounds as he stared down at the town and the harbor, but he could hear nothing. They were up and about, but they were being discreet for his sake.

The sinking of the Russian frigate had been in all the

newspapers and on all the television channels. Half the country was calling him a warmonger and villain, while the other half was calling him a hero, the hope for Nippon. It placed the MSDF, and in fact the entire government, in a difficult position, because no matter what action was taken half the country would find fault with it.

Yesterday, Yabe Takagi, his *sensei* from the Mishima Institute, had come to the house. They had spoken briefly about honor and about self-control, which were so necessary to a Japanese *bu-shi*.

"Dishonor is like a scar on a tree, *Kiyoda-san,*" his instructor told him. "Time will not erase this scar but only enlarge it. Understand that patience and forgiveness are a part of honor."

"I understand," Kiyoda whispered.

"To bear what you think you cannot bear, *Kiyoda-san,* is really to bear."

Kiyoda heard the car coming up the road from the city, and he sat up straighter.

The car pulled up in front and stopped. He heard two car doors open and close, and they were at the entry. Two of them. It was to be expected.

His wife Moriko came to the rice-paper door. "I am sorry for disturbing your peace, my husband, but two officers have come from the admiral. They wish to speak with you."

"They are honored guests in our home, *Moriko-san.* Please offer them tea, and bring them to me," Kiyoda said.

"As you wish, my husband," his wife said softly, and she left.

Kiyoda remained seated for five full minutes before he got to his feet and faced the open door. He wore his winter dress blues as did the two officers in the doorway. Both of them were full commanders, he was pleased to note.

"Lieutenant Commander Seiji Kiyoda, you are under arrest," the tall, fair-skinned officer said. "On orders from the Admiralty, you are requested, sir, to come with us."

"What are the charges, sir?" Kiyoda asked.

"Treason," the same officer said.

Kiyoda suppressed a smile. He had won! Kamiya had somehow pulled it off. If he had been charged with disobeying orders, he would have lost his command and gone to jail in disgrace. There was no defense against such a specification. But against the charge of treason there were a host of defenses. Half the country was behind him.

"May I be allowed to commit *seppuku?*" Kiyoda asked.

"No," the first officer said.

"Very well, then. I will accompany you."

"Prove InterTech is controlled by a Japanese firm, and we'll win," Glen Zerkel said.

"There is a more elegant solution," his brother Louis suggested. "If Mr. Reid has the stomach for it."

"I'm all ears, my dear fellow," the older man said. He'd been drinking for twenty-four hours. But like the true functioning alcoholic he wasn't falling-down drunk, just very loose.

"I believe all Guerin's P522's have been equipped with the control chip. If we can prove that, and if we can reprogram a couple of the FAA's flight service stations to send out the trigger signal on our command, we'd be able to bring a lot of airplanes down all at once."

"Wouldn't they trace the signal back here?" Reid asked.

"That's the beauty of it," Louis replied. "InterTech will send the signal, and the orders will come from Tokyo."

U.S. Navy Chief Petty Officer Clifford Talmadge had a raging hangover. His head was about to split apart, his eyes felt as if someone had thrown hot sand into them, his mouth tasted like dog shit, and he had a piss hard-on that was killing him. On top of all that, his live-in girlfriend, Susie Heidinori, was bitching at him to get up, her whiny, needling voice going on and on like an irritating insect.

Last night had started out all right at the Noncommissioned Officers Club on base. Nearly eighty percent of the Seventh was at dock, so Fleet HQ was crammed. It was party time, and when the Navy partied, everybody partied. By 2000 hours there probably wasn't a sober off-duty sailor within a hundred klicks. That's when the exodus into town began.

Yokosuka had been home to the Seventh Fleet since after the war. As a result a lot of great drinking establishments, strip joints, and whorehouses flourished just off base, although lately the city fathers were making moves to clean up the area. Apparently there was some resentment by the locals.

After last night there'd be even more resentment, Talmadge thought. There'd been fights. He'd heard that one of the after-hours clubs had been practically destroyed. And no doubt there'd been a handful of rapes and sexual assaults as well.

Susie came into the bedroom in her black lace bra, panties, garter belt, and nylons, her makeup only half finished. "Goddamn you bastard, Clifford, get your ass out of bed. We're both going to be late."

Like most Japanese women she was slightly built, with a golden complexion and tiny features. Six months ago when they'd met at a party at the NCO Club he'd thought she was the most beautiful woman he'd ever laid eyes on. But then he was new to this theatre, and the novelty had worn off quickly.

"Fuck you," Talmadge said good-naturedly, although he was starting to get mad. "It's early. We don't have to be to work until eight." He was a large man, a former Penn State running halfback, and he'd always had to watch his temper.

"Well, it's quarter 'til, you prick. Get up!" She went into the bathroom and slammed the flimsy door.

She'd stuck a hot poker up his ass. "Sonofabitch," he

roared grabbing his wristwatch. She was right. He shoved the covers back and scrambled out of bed. This would make the third time this month he was late for work. His C.O. had warned him about it last week.

"I don't care what you do on your own time, mister, until it affects my time," the old man said. "If need be I'll confine your ass to base. Is that clear?"

"Aye, aye, sir," Talmadge had replied crisply. "It won't happen again."

Susie worked on base as a bilingual secretary in Procurements. Her boss had reamed her out too.

He put on his shorts from yesterday and pulled a semi-clean set of blues out of the closet.

"For what?" he shouted in frustration. Last night had turned out shitty. He'd gotten into a squabble with a couple of bastards from Meteorology, was thrown out of at least two places he could remember, and in the end he and Susie had gotten into a terrific row about going to listen to a blues combo playing at one of the whorehouses. She liked the music, but she didn't want to go to that kind of place, and he couldn't understand. In the end they'd come back to the apartment downtown, and they tried to make love, but he couldn't do it and he blamed her.

"Christ, fuck, sonofabitch," he swore, pulling on a pair of dirty socks. For what? "Get the fuck out of the bathroom, I gotta get in there," he shouted.

Their apartment was on the third floor front, facing busy Kaigan-dori Avenue, in an old brick building that always had been used to house foreigners. Like Kamakura and Yokohama, which were part of the Tokyo megalopolis a few miles north, Yokosuka had been one of the port cities where the British and others seeking trade with Japan were isolated so as not to contaminate the purity of Nippon.

In Talmadge's opinion it was bullshit then and it was bullshit now. The Second World War had established that, all their color TVs, VCRs, stereos, and Toyotas notwithstanding. If it came to it, we'd just kick ass again.

"Get out," he shouted again, putting on his shirt. He had to shave. But his tongue felt as if it had a three-day growth of fungus on it that only a dozen hours of sleep could possibly cure.

"Just a minute," Susie yelled.

Talmadge tried the bathroom door, but it was locked. "Goddammit," he swore. She always locked the door, which really pissed him off. What the hell was she hiding that he hadn't already fucked, kissed, or licked?

Well, he was through being the nice guy. He put his shoulder to the door once very hard, the frame splintering against his 220-pound bulk. Susie, dressed now in her skirt, reared back in alarm, her eyes wide.

"I told you to get the fuck out of here," he bellowed. He grabbed her roughly by the arm, hauled her out of the tiny bathroom, and threw her against the dresser.

She cried out in pain and looked at him with hate and venom in her eyes, her jaw tight, her body rigid. This moment had been coming for weeks, and they'd both known it.

"Put on your blouse and get us a cab," Talmadge ordered. "I've got to take a piss and grab a shave, then we can shove off."

He turned to go into the bathroom when Susie, screeching in rage like a banshee, leaped on his back, biting and scratching his neck and the side of his face. She wanted to draw blood, to hurt him, like he had hurt her so often in their brief relationship. She wanted to knock him to the floor and stomp him into the dirt where he belonged, because he was a lying, bigoted sonofabitch.

The unexpectedness of her attack caught him off guard, and he was driven forward, banging his head against the door frame. Still she wouldn't let up. The bitch really wanted to hurt him.

He spun her into the wall, smashing her against the edge of the door, knocking the air out of her lungs. She grunted and lost her grip on his neck. It was enough. He grabbed her by the hair, plucked her off his back, and tossed her like a rag doll across the bed and halfway into the tiny living room.

She scrambled to her hands and knees, but Talmadge was much faster.

He came over the bed, grabbed her arm, and yanked her to her feet. "You fucking bitch," he shouted, spittle flying.

She raked his face with her free hand, her long fingernails opening three gashes in his cheek that began oozing blood.

"Goddamn you whore!" he yelled, completely out of control. He shook her so hard her head flipped back, spraining her neck.

This time she cried out in real pain. She was not angry now. Suddenly she was frightened for her life.

Talmadge was seeing red. He had crossed over the brink to where he wanted nothing more than to hurt her, to cause her pain. To blot her out of the universe.

Still violently shaking her, he shoved her backward into the living room toward the low couch that sat in front of two windows overlooking the street.

"You fucking bitch, all you want is a free ride. You want to be an American. You want us to fuck you, and then you laugh at us behind our backs. I know about you fucking superior Japs. Fucking sneaky bastards. Slant-eye fuckers! Maybe we ought to drop the fucking bomb on you again, teach you some fucking manners."

Susie was incapable of making even the smallest effort to protect herself. Physically she was no match for Talmadge, who outweighed her by more than a hundred pounds, but she was mentally stunned as well. She'd never seen him act this way, had never seen *anyone* act this way, and she was flabbergasted. She was convinced that he was going to kill her.

At the last moment, Talmadge picked her off her feet, his big, rough hands breaking three of her ribs, and he tossed her over the couch and through one of the windows, the thin bamboo-slat Venetian blinds going with her, and she was gone.

Still it wasn't enough for him. He wanted to hurt her even more, and in his insane rage he was even madder that she hadn't begged for him to stop.

In three steps he was across the living room. He yanked the door open, snapping both locks, and thundered down the dark, narrow stairs to the street. Already a crowd was gathering around Susie where she lay on her back, half off the sidewalk into the street. It was rush hour and traffic was heavy, the street clogged with cars and buses and bicycles. Many of the drivers stopped to see what was happening.

Talmadge bulled his way through the people, his rage still increasing, blind hatred choking out rational thought. He'd always had a chip on his shoulder, especially when he was drinking, and he'd always had a problem controlling it. More than one school psychologist had predicted he would do something very bad one day. But fuck 'em, something was saying at the back of his head. They'd never been laughed at like he had when he'd been a little fat boy. Fat and stupid.

"Bitch!" he shouted at the top of his lungs. He kicked Susie in the side of her rib cage with every ounce of his considerable strength, flopping her body over on its stomach without a sound from her.

She was dead, and those closest in the crowd sighed and tried to step back, but others were coming, pressing them nearer.

She was dead. The stupid bitch had gotten herself killed. He kicked her again with all of his strength, pushing her limp body completely into the street.

He was in some big shit now. There'd be nothing so simple as a Captain's Mast and a weekend in the brig. It just wasn't going to be that easy. He'd killed a woman, a fucking Japanese national, because of his foul temper, and he was going to have to pay the price.

He kicked her again, this time more in frustration than in rage.

"Yamero," someone in the crowd shouted, and someone else took it up.

Talmadge understood enough Japanese to know that they were calling for him to stop. But how could he stop? He'd already gone too far. He looked at Susie's bloody body, her arms and legs splayed out, and he felt the first stirrings of remorse mixed with a growing fear and confusion. How could he have done this thing? Christ, how could it have happened?

He looked at the crowd, some of the people jostling forward menacingly, shouting and screaming what sounded like threats. He couldn't remember from his orientation course if Japan had the death penalty, but he figured for sure he would be turned over to the civilian authorities. What he did remember was that Japanese prisons were notorious for hard time, especially for foreigners.

The blare of a police siren sounded like it was just down the street, and Talmadge stepped back a pace. It would be one thing to turn himself over to his own Shore Patrol and get a Navy hearing, but something completely different to get himself arrested by Jap cops. He wouldn't have a chance.

The crowd was pressing even closer, and the siren stopped just on the other side of them. What the hell had he done this time? He had to get to the pay phone in the downstairs hall. He could call the base.

Talmadge charged straight at the crowd, bowling the much smaller Japanese out of his way as if they were nothing. It seemed as if everyone were shouting and screaming, pummeling his back with their fists, kicking at his legs, hitting him with umbrellas, shopping bags, anything they carried.

He broke loose in front of the door to his building at the same time a uniformed cop came up the street in a run, a white plastic holster flapping at his hip.

People in the crowd shouted something to the cop, and pointed at Talmadge, who pulled up and stopped. A second cop came across the street in a dead run, and the people in the crowd shouted what sounded like a warning.

Talmadge looked toward the open door into his building and started toward it when the first cop, now just a few feet away, fumbled at his side for his night stick.

"Ugokuna," the cop shouted as he got the night stick out.

Such a stupid little toy, the thought popped into Talmadge's head, but the Jap looked like he was going to use it. Fuck, he wasn't going down this way. Not a chance in hell.

The cop was raising the night stick when Talmadge batted it out of his hand, and snatched the big automatic pistol out of the Jap's holster. Out of the corner of his eye he saw the other cop pull out his gun and bring it up.

This wasn't happening! Fucking hell, it wasn't happening!

Talmadge raised the SigSauer 9 mm automatic and pulled off four shots as fast as he could squeeze the trigger. An old woman in the crowd fell back, and then the cop went down, the right side of his head exploding.

Something hard came down on his right collarbone. His right hand instantly went numb, and he dropped the pistol. It was the first cop. The sneaking sonofabitch had hit him from behind with the night stick.

Howling in pain, Talmadge came around with his left fist, swinging it like a bludgeon, smashing the cop in the head, knocking him backward off his feet.

Still the cop tried to get up and come after him, so Talmadge scooped the pistol off the pavement with his left hand and awkwardly pumped three shots at point-blank range into the Jap's chest.

More sirens were approaching now, and despite the fact he'd killed two cops and possibly the woman, and held a gun in his hand, people kept streaming into the crowd. People screamed and shouted. Called him names, called him a killer, taunted him . . . he didn't know what, but he was frightened. He couldn't kill all of them, even if he wanted to.

But Christ, it hadn't been his fault. He had not meant to kill the bitch, but she'd gone on and on at him. He'd told her from the beginning to just leave him the fuck alone in the morning. At least until he had his coffee. And then everything would be hunky-dory. But she wouldn't let it go.

He stepped back toward the door to his building, the crowd louder now, the sirens closer.

And the cops, Christ, what the hell was he supposed to do? Let the bastards shoot him down? Well, fuck that. That part he'd do the same if he had to do it over again. It was simple self-defense, goddammit!

He turned and sprinted across the sidewalk when a bottle tossed from the crowd caught him on the back of the head, and he stumbled forward, slamming his right knee into the concrete steps, pain temporarily blotting out his vision.

"Sonofabitch," he shouted, but it only came out as a croak. He started to bring the big pistol around when it was grabbed from his hand, and someone kicked him in the side of the head.

The little bastards. Always attacking from behind.

They were kicking him in the head, in the neck, in the back. Rolling him over, kicking him in the chest and stomach and groin.

He was done. The fuckers. There were too many of them. And their blows didn't even hurt anymore, as it all began to fuzz out, coming down to a point.

ELEVEN

The Aeroflot Ilyushin Il-86 the Russians provided for the return trip to the States was a far cry from the Guerin P522 that had brought them to Russia. Even fitted out for the diplomatic service, as it was, its accommodations were narrow and cramped. Everything was chipped or worn and in need of replacement or refurbishment. The half-dozen Russian engineers and finance people who would continue to Portland to work with the plant development, design, and construction engineers didn't seem to notice the shabbiness. Neither Kennedy nor any of the other Guerin executives saw fit to point it out to them. The differences would become painfully obvious when they were given the grand tour at Gales Creek.

Heading west they would gain eight hours, so their twelve-hour flight from Moscow would put them on the ground four clock hours after they left. It made for a long day.

Socrates and his staff were huddled in deep discussion with some of the Russian engineers, while the others either slept or tried to. A pall of sadness hung over them, and it affected Kennedy more than the others because he and Socrates would stay in Washington to work with the NTSB on the accident investigation. It would be them, not their staffs, who would have to reassemble the remains of the airplane. He wasn't looking forward to it.

Sir Malcolm O'Toole, Rolls-Royce's chief designer, was already on the scene, and without a doubt the old lion was doing a lot of growling. Under most circumstances the Brit was a delight to work with. But this time would be infinitely different. Two engine failures in ten years was, on the surface, a fantastic performance record. It would be like driving an automobile for ten million miles with only two problems. But the crashes were apparently caused by the same malfunction. How many other Guerin airplanes would fall out of the sky?

They'd just finished lunch and Kennedy was seated alone with his thoughts when McGarvey sat down beside him.

"I had the flight engineer tune in the BBC's World Service. You went down four points yesterday."

"I know," Kennedy said. He'd spoken with Vasilanti about it last night just after the market closed in New York.

"I'm assuming that isn't a big enough drop for them to start the run on you."

"Not a serious run. So far as we can tell there were no big buys or institutional trading. Presuming our fleet isn't grounded, we'll start to come back in ten days or so."

"What would another crash like that do to you?"

"Don't even think it," Kennedy shuddered. "But if it happened within the next year or eighteen months we'd be in for a hell of a bad time. We might not survive even just one more crash."

"What about two crashes, or even three or more within the next ten days, before you recover from this one? Could you weather it?"

"Not a chance in hell, Mac. Unless Washington bailed us out." One of the problems was the scaled-back military establishment. Just a few years ago Guerin, McDonnell Douglas, and even Boeing depended heavily on military orders. Now that that market was all but gone the airplane manufacturers were cash poor.

"Along with our accounts payable and federal taxes outstanding, this year's drawdown on our long-term debt is running at nearly four billion dollars. Match that against our accounts receivable—for all the airplane deals we've financed for the airlines—which amounts this year to only three billion, a lot of it slow to come, and you can see we're in the hole. Al wants to spend one billion on the Moscow facility in addition to what we've already spent at Gales Creek, which means our ass is out in the wind."

"That's what they'll do."

Kennedy looked bleakly at McGarvey for a long second or two. It's a tough world out there, his father told him years ago. But sitting here now he was sure his father hadn't a clue just how tough it really was.

"It's hard to keep a handle on it," he said. "What do we do? Voluntarily ground the fleet until we can prove Mintori is on the verge of killing a lot of people? We'd go bankrupt. Or continue flying as long as the FAA allows us to, and face the risk that you are right, and that they will bring down more of our airplanes? In which case we'd also go bankrupt. Is that what you're telling me, McGarvey, that we've been placed in a no-win situation?"

"If we can prove the Japanese are behind this before something else happens we'd be able to block their takeover move and save a lot of lives."

"According to your timetable you'd have less than ten days in which to do it."

"That's right."

Kennedy looked up the aisle toward Socrates and the others—all good people who earnestly believed that designing and building safe and efficient airplanes was more important than working simply for profit. Boeing had taught them that lesson. Make a good airplane and the profits will be there. Safety first, money second. But this assault on them by the Japanese, if it was true, was so monstrous it was nearly impossible to believe. It could not be allowed to succeed. If they gave in now, more than an airplane company would have been lost. He knew that he was being melodramatic, but it was true nevertheless. When one section of the fabric of a country was torn—not altered, not exchanged for something of like value, but torn—then the entire country was diminished.

"Ten days, Mac," he said. "At the first incident, at so much as a hint that something's about to happen, I'll ground the fleet myself."

"Agreed," McGarvey said. "But it's going to get ugly."

"It couldn't get worse."

"Oh yes it could, David. And it will."

Russian Foreign Intelligence Service Director Aleksandr Semenovich Karyagin was of the new generation of Russian politicians, those who'd not been involved with the Great Patriotic War of 1940–45. At fifty-five he didn't remember the end of the war, but he clearly remembered the privations afterward, the post-Stalin years in which the gulags continued to flourish. As a result he'd become a Russian patriot as well as a practical man who knew how to bend with the times in order to survive. It was a knowledge that many of his contemporaries had not learned. Some of them were dead or still in exile, while others, like General Polunin, sitting across the desk from him, had risen as high as they would ever get. Every time Polunin came up here he fairly radiated animosity and jealousy, which was fine with Karyagin. It provided the raw energy and zeal so vital to an intelligence-gathering organization. And, in the end, Polunin would serve as a scapegoat should the situation go awry.

"What has Mr. McGarvey provided us as a quid pro quo?" Karyagin asked, looking up from the bound report Polunin had brought him. "No mention is made of it here. In fact did he tell us anything?"

"Nothing substantive, Mr. Director."

"I see," Karyagin said. He sat back and stared at his general. Polunin's jaw tightened almost imperceptibly.

"You may recall that McGarvey told us in very certain terms that he would not spy on his country, even if he did have access to the White House, or the seventh floor at Langley. Neither of which he has, so far as I understand the situation."

"What about his control officer, Colonel Yemlin?" Karyagin asked.

"He's on his way back to Washington. Should arrive within hours of the Guerin flight."

"What is his impression, General?"

"A provision of the U.S. State Department's approval of the loan package is an early settlement of the situation in the Tatar Strait."

"Were our navy or air force to retaliate, the loan guarantees would be withdrawn. Is that the substance of Colonel Yemlin's report?"

"That is the substance of his speculation, Mr. Director," Polunin said, refusing to be drawn into the trap. "I omitted it from my report because Colonel Yemlin told me that Mr. McGarvey never made a direct statement to that effect."

"Something must have been said to give him the impression."

"Generalities. Hints. Vague suggestions. Nothing more, Mr. Director." Polunin was in uniform, as if to distinguish himself from the strictly civilian element of the SUR.

"Why are they suddenly being so coy?" Karyagin asked half to himself. "If our cooperation is so necessary to the loan guarantee, then why hasn't Washington told us directly?"

"Presumably Guerin's executives want to make certain that we understand the distance between them and their own government. This is not a Washington-sponsored project, although Guerin's government must approve of the exchange of technologies."

"In other words the incident in the Tatar Strait should have nothing to do with our deal with Guerin Airplane Company."

"That is Yemlin's thinking."

Russia was in a difficult position. Unless some response were made to the Japanese attack on its frigate in Russian waters, what little credibility the eastern fleet had would evaporate, Karyagin thought. But Yeltsin was following the Guerin negotiations with a sharp eye. The deal was very important for a number of reasons, not the least of which were the jobs it would create and the influx of Western currencies it would generate. On another level the deal was important because of the ongoing tension between Russia and Ukraine. Kiev was to the former Soviet Union's aviation industry what Seattle and Portland were to America's. If Moscow could come out as a rival it would do wonders for Russian prestige, not only at home but around the world as well.

They were walking a very tight line.

"Has Tokyo Station provided us with any further information?"

"Not yet, Mr. Director."

"I want to review any new material before it is passed to Colonel Yemlin for transmittal to McGarvey."

"Of course."

"What of the airplane crash in Washington? Were the Japanese responsible?"

"Tokyo Station has no word on it, but Washington's official preliminary position is that it was an accident."

"Does Guerin Airplane Company share that view?"

"No," Polunin said. "From what was discussed among them here as well as in the air, they suspect that this Japanese *zaibatsu* may be behind it, and may be planning other accidents within the next ten days."

"If they are correct, and if they cannot prevent this from happening, their company will be ruined. Am I correct?"

"Yes, Mr. Director."

"Then I will send a personal message to Tokyo Station to make this problem their number-one priority."

So close, Karyagin mused, and yet so far. Strange how the world had changed so dramatically in the last seven years.

The timing was incredible. As Edward R. Reid watched the CNN bulletin and then the follow-up reports on the killings and the riot in Yokosuka, he could hardly believe his good fortune.

It had all the earmarks of turning out like the Rodney King incident a few years ago in Los Angeles in which a black man had been severely beaten by a group of cops. The entire country had been affected by what appeared to be a clearcut case of police brutality. When the police officers were brought to trial for use of excessive force they were acquitted, and Los Angeles was hit by the worst riots since Watts. Never mind that Rodney King was a criminal. Never mind that just minutes before the beating he'd apparently gone berserk and according to witnesses was a real threat to the cops. The glaring message Americans focused on was that a group of white cops had beat the living hell out of a lone black man.

The same could be true with this incident in Japan. So far as the early news stories were reporting, a U.S. Navy enlisted man had murdered his Japanese girlfriend, and

when the Japanese police attempted to arrest him he
disarmed one of them and shot them both to death. The
mob of civilians that had gathered went after the American and beat him to death. Probably rightly so, Reid
thought, but it wouldn't play that way.

A lone American serviceman—a boy actually—away
from home in a strange, often hostile country, is backed
into a corner by an angry, out-of-control mob, armed
men in uniforms closing in on him. He does the only
thing he can do, the only thing any reasonable red-
blooded American boy would do in the same situation—
he defends himself the best he can. He's well trained.
The U.S. military is the best-trained military in the
world. So he manages to protect himself for a few
minutes. It's all been a misunderstanding, he pleads, but
the horde has gone crazy. It was an accident, he pleads.
But it is to no avail. They swarm over him, pulling him
limb from limb, trampling him into the foreign soil so
far from home. All the training in the world could not
have protected him from the crazed mob. He was one
boy, alone, in a strange land. Now he is dead.

Americans love their melodrama.

Bruno Mueller was upstairs in a bedroom across the
corridor from Zerkel's computer room. The genius and
his brother had been tapping into computers all day
long—Federal Aviation Administration, National
Transportation Safety Board, State Department, Department of Defense, Dulles Flight Traffic Control, any
government agency that had anything even remotely to
do with the investigation. So far the crash was still being
classified as an accident. Although Guerin engineers
were questioning that preliminary finding, as was a
British design engineer from Rolls-Royce, nothing to
this point indicated sabotage.

From where he stood, smoking a cigarette, he could
look over his shoulder into the computer room, or
straight ahead out the window that faced the airport.
The accident site was lit up like a small city. So far as he
understood the procedure in this country, accident in-

vestigators would remain on site for at least a week, possibly two. They would sort through every single piece of debris, no matter how large or small, catalog it all as to its condition and precise location, and then transport the parts to a hangar where the airplane would be put back together in an effort to understand what happened.

All that would take additional time—weeks, certainly, and probably months. Long before the NTSB had reached any conclusions the next P522s would have already fallen out of the sky.

For the first time in a very long while Mueller actually felt the stirrings of interest. Killing generally meant little or nothing to him. The act of murdering a human being affected him about the same way swatting a mosquito or a fly would affect a normal person, but what Reid wanted was something different. This was murder on a very grand scale. Scores of people would die. Perhaps dozens of airplanes would crash and burn, the passengers' panic would be agonizing as their airplanes fell out of the sky and they knew they were going to die but couldn't do a thing about it. It was an interesting idea.

He had been trained to wreak havoc on the capitalists, but his training had gone to waste. His masters were all dead or gone. Even his group of former comrades was no more.

His life had been a waste. Until now.

Reid came up from downstairs. He was drunk again, but Mueller had come to appreciate the man's capacity for alcohol. No matter how much he drank he seemed to be in control of himself.

"Have you watched the news?" the older man asked.

"No. Has something interesting happened?"

Reid grinned. "You could say that. It's the Japanese—they're doing exactly what I want. There was a riot this morning in Yokosuka. A young American serviceman was killed. Pulled apart by an angry mob of civilians. That ass in the White House will have to say something this time."

"Why was this man killed?" Mueller asked, his voice soft.

"It doesn't matter. He was trying to defend himself, and the crowd went berserk. It happens. Mob psychology is a strange phenomenon."

"You say you want this?"

"Yes," Reid said. "Of course I do. First the incident in the Tatar Strait. Then the airplane crash, which the Japanese will take the blame for. Now this latest atrocity, this violent outbreak of anti-American sentiment. Soon the bastards will go completely over the edge. Something will have to be done, I tell you."

Mueller could see that Reid almost believed what he was saying. Among other things the man was a consummate actor. Glen Zerkel had told him that their host had once been a rabid anti-communist and for more than thirty years had done everything within his considerable power to keep the Cold War alive and well. "His motto is 'In conflict there is profit,'" Zerkel had explained.

"The Soviet Union was America's enemy, but Japan is your ally. It can't be so easy this time."

Zerkel had grinned. "Don't count on it. Mr. R. is what we call a mover and a shaker. If he wants to make Japan our enemy, you'd better believe it'll happen. I shit you not."

"But why Japan?" Mueller had asked.

"I don't know," Zerkel had shrugged. "I really don't. But whatever his reasons they'll be good, and there'll be more than one of them. He never does anything off the cuff. Before he makes a move he studies it three ways to Sunday. He knows what he's doing. He's never been wrong yet."

"What are you getting out of it?" Mueller had asked. It was early morning and they'd crossed paths outside.

"I get to fight back," Zerkel had said, and Mueller hadn't asked him what he meant, because he knew. He felt the same way himself.

"We'll have to move soon," Mueller told Reid.

"Louis should be finished by tomorrow, and then we'll know where we stand." Reid glanced across the corridor toward the computer room. "The FBI has issued a warrant for his arrest in Jeanne Shepard's murder."

"Has he been told?"

"Not yet. It's going to be difficult moving around the country with him. You'll have to be careful."

"It was necessary in case he tried to back out," Mueller said, but Reid held up a hand.

"I agree one-hundred percent. Nevertheless, we'll have to take care of him until he gets everything set up."

Another thought occurred to Mueller. "Do you think he suspects that once he's finished he becomes expendable?"

"He's not a stupid man, but if he does suspect I haven't seen any signs of it."

"Nor I," Mueller replied absently. Yet there was something different about Zerkel since the morning of the crash. As if the man were smirking. As if he had a secret.

"Glen will help you," Reid was saying. "He understands the stakes."

"Against his own brother?"

Reid nodded. "Without a moment's hesitation."

Mueller had no siblings, but he'd always had the vague notion that brothers, since they were of the same blood, would be staunch allies. Apparently that wasn't always so. He'd learned something new.

"We'll talk again in the morning," Reid said. "I have to go into the city to work on my newsletter."

"Have you given thought to what will happen afterward?" Mueller asked, watching Reid's eyes very carefully.

"What do you mean?" the older man asked without blinking.

"I won't be able to return to Europe for some time to come. Possibly years."

"Have you thought about what you want?"

"Not specifically."

"I suggest you do so, Herr Mueller. And when you have decided the course of your future, we will discuss my role as well as my responsibilities in it."

"Very well," Mueller said, and Reid left. From the

front window he watched the headlights of Reid's car head down the driveway, the night very dark except toward the airport where the accident investigation continued. He wondered where his life was heading.

It was the easiest headline Reid had ever written. He had been building up to this one for several months, so he did not think many of his readers, including Secretary of State Jonathan Stearnes Carter, would be surprised. Some of them, however, would scream for his blood. Everything he'd written to date was nothing but the solid-gold truth, as he saw it. No one had ever gone wrong, not financially wrong, following his advice. Not even his detractors would deny him his track record. People listened.

He maintained a suite of offices for the *Lamplighter* at the Grand Hyatt Washington, a half-dozen blocks from the White House. The weekly newsletter was written completely by him, but it was researched by a staff of a dozen people, many of whom had been editors of prison newspapers whose prison releases he had sponsored. His staff was completely loyal to him.

At three in the morning, however, he was alone in his office, working at his computer. Despite his drunkenness and tiredness, he never felt more lucid. His words flowed like a mountain stream—clear, cold, precise, and very fast.

He didn't bother with his notes, or with the latest stack of reports from his analysts, but wrote simply and directly from his heart. The passion was on him.

After this was sent to his six-thousand-plus subscribers the present relationship between Japan and the United States would change, and the change would be dramatic.

ARE WE WAITING FOR ANOTHER PEARL HARBOR? his headline demanded. And he proceeded to tell his readers why another Pearl Harbor, this one possibly a strike on the Panama Canal, bottling the Atlantic fleet, would happen. Combined with an accident at the mouth of Tokyo Bay, which would keep the Seventh Fleet from striking, the Japanese MSDF would have a free, if short, reign over the western Pacific. Wiser heads would prevail, of course, and the little war would be stopped almost immediately, but not before Japan got what it wanted, which was economic control of the western Pacific basin.

"It's coming," he warned.

The NTSB took over an old TWA maintenance hangar across Dulles field from the terminal, well away from the public's eye. Some of the wreckage had already been transported from the site three miles away, and investigators were piecing the airplane back together. It was hard enough making sense out of the tangled, burned wreckage without the intrusions of television cameras and press photographers. However, each day at noon, a media briefing that lasted exactly twenty minutes was held in one corner of the hangar. No one cared for the arrangement, but that's the way the Board did things.

Kennedy and Socrates showed up ten minutes after the briefing ended, just as Al Vasilanti and Malcolm O'Toole were emerging from one of the office trailers set up at the rear of the hangar. Vasilanti had aged ten years in the last three days, but O'Toole was an ageless English bulldog, his long white hair and muttonchops in total disarray.

"You just missed the press," Vasilanti told them. "And it's a good thing, because they're starting to smell blood."

All four men shook hands, but Socrates couldn't keep his eyes away from the remains of the P522 laid out in pieces like a corpse at a post-mortem. He shook his head. "It wasn't my airframe's fault," he muttered.

"It was an engine overheat again," O'Toole said, following the engineer's gaze. Pieces of that wing were still being picked up, whereas most of the starboard wing had been brought over and reassembled. The absence of the port wing and engine made for a stark conclusion.

"The ceramic blades again?" Socrates asked sharply.

"It would appear so, George. But I'll swear by the Queen Mother that for whatever reasons the high-pressure blisk turbine overheated, the temperatures were well within our design parameters."

"But the blades broke down?"

"Yes. It should not have happened, but it did. And it looks as if overheat was the case."

"Could it have been sabotage, Sir Malcolm?" Kennedy asked.

"I sincerely wish it were, but I've found nothing to indicate that the cat's been in the cream."

"What about the heat sensors?"

"We've found nothing on the recording tape to indicate a malfunction of the port unit. Of course it was completely destroyed. But we've got the starboard unit on the bench."

"Anything?" Kennedy asked.

Sir Malcolm shook his leonine head sadly. "Functions as designed."

"Then we're back to 1990," Socrates said bitterly.

"With one important exception," Kennedy interjected. "In '90 it was our first crash. This is the second one, apparently from the same cause. That in itself gives us a starting point."

"Rolls goes back to the Gamma titanium aluminide for its blades," Socrates shot back. "We must immediately ground the fleet and retrofit all the engines."

"That will take time and money, neither of which we can afford," Vasilanti said. The remark was so uncharacteristic that it stopped everyone dead.

"But, Mr. Vasilanti, think of the lives that might be lost," Socrates protested, recovering first.

"As long as the FAA does not issue the grounding order, we will quietly inspect each engine in the field. Our AOG teams can get the job done within the month. The airlines won't object, and they'll keep their mouths shut."

The AOG—Aircraft on the Ground—team had been Boeing's idea. Airplanes grounded because of maintenance problems were bad publicity. So Guerin, like

Boeing, fielded rapid-deployment teams of experts who could go anywhere at a moment's notice and fix virtually any problem. Each team had available to it at least one P522 equipped as a flying spare-parts store, machine shop, and electronics repair facility. On more than one occasion an AOG team had completely rebuilt a jetliner that had been so heavily damaged in an accident or hijacking or shelling by a military force that the owners had already contacted their insurance carrier to find out where the carcass should be scrapped. In many cases it was the insurance company that contacted Guerin.

"It will take us some time to supply you with replacement blades," Sir Malcolm said.

"I didn't say that we were replacing the blades. We're going to inspect each engine. Top to bottom."

"For what?"

"Booby traps. Bombs. Remote-control devices on the fuel ports or air intake ducts."

He had their attention now. Especially Socrates and Sir Malcolm.

"It would answer some fundamental questions, that," the British engine designer said.

"Our AOG teams will go out with a pair of brand-new engines from stock so there'll be no chance they will have been tampered with. We'll work one airplane at a time. Yank the old engines, replace them with the new, and before we move on, tear down the old engines. Sooner or later we'll come across another plane ready to blow."

"If there is another," Sir Malcolm said. "It has been seven years between incidents."

"There'll be another," Kennedy interjected. "Possibly more than one."

Vasilanti eyed him sharply.

"What?" Sir Malcolm asked.

"We can't assume that this crash is an isolated incident. Certain facts have come to our attention that lead me to suspect that something like this will happen again. Very soon."

"Then I agree with George, ground the fleet. In the meantime, what are these certain facts, David?"

"I'd rather not say at the moment."

"These are Rolls-Royce engines. We too have a reputation to maintain. Good Lord, man, think of the consequences if another of your birds goes down. Think of the lives lost."

"We have," Kennedy said. "Which is why we're glad that you're here. If anyone can find out how those engines are overheating, it will be you and George."

Sir Malcolm looked at Kennedy shrewdly, his lips pursed. "There've been rumors floating about that your company may be under attack. A hostile takeover of one sort or another. Any validity to this?"

"Possibly," Kennedy said carefully. This was not Rolls-Royce's fight, although the company would suffer if Guerin went under. But, if Rolls were to be officially notified that a major problem was looming on the horizon, the British government—which controlled the company—might withdraw as Guerin's primary engine supplier. That in itself would spell disaster.

"Would there be a connection to this business?"

"We hope not, Sir Malcolm, but that too is a possibility we cannot ignore."

"What a cockup," the Brit said. "Then we'd best shake a leg and keep it in the family."

The riots that began in Tokyo's Akasaka District the next morning had not been planned. Japanese newspapers and television over the past month had been filled with grisly stories about a young Japanese woman on vacation in New York who was raped and killed in Central Park. It was the eleventh murder of a Japanese citizen visiting the United States in three years, and the public was sick to death of the mindless violence. The neo-fascist organization Rising Sun, which wanted control of the Diet and wanted to take Japan back to a pre-World War II condition of international military might, took full advantage of the growing crowds in front of the

Suntory Building and nearby New Otani Hotel. The organization, which was an offshoot of the old Red Army faction, was superb. Within twenty minutes of hearing the news, the co-founders and leaders Shotoro Ashia and Takushiro Hatoyama were exhorting the crowd with bullhorns that their enemy was very near. Only blocks away, in fact, in Minato-ku at the U.S. Embassy.

The district, bounded on the northwest by the Akasaka Palace and grounds and to the east by the Imperial Palace, was a warren of federal government buildings, international business offices, and foreign embassies. They were in billionaires' row, and there were more foreigners per square hectare here than anywhere else in Japan. Which was perfect, so far as Rising Sun was concerned.

The second step, after agitating the rapidly growing crowd, was to produce an old woman who purported to be the mother of the girl killed in New York's Central Park last month *and* the young woman who'd been killed yesterday in Yokosuka.

The girls were sisters, Hatoyama claimed. The old woman's only daughters. Both of them brutally murdered by savages.

Timing the old woman's appearance perfectly, Rising Sun was able to hold the crowd from marching on the U.S. embassy until the media showed up so that everyone would know what was happening here, and why. When CNN arrived the crowd began its march to Minato-ku.

U.S. Consular Officer Philip Webb was on his way into work and had to skirt the still-growing early crowd, which he estimated to contain at least ten thousand people. He was off by a factor of ten, but he did get their purpose and destination right and managed to get into the embassy compound about five minutes ahead of the first wave.

On hearing what was coming their way, Marine Lieutenant Lloyd Robinson, chief of the A.M. security watch, called his CO, Major Bob Richards, CIA Assistant Chief of Station Stephen Pelham, and Special Assistant to the Ambassador Judy Bromme, who was the only ranking officer around this morning who could speak Japanese.

The crowd, still orderly despite its size and motivation, filled the streets immediately surrounding the embassy and spread in all directions as far as the eye could see. One official estimate placed the final number of people at one million. No one doubted that figure. Softly the crowd began to chant a single word, low, and menacing for its gentleness.

"What are they saying?" Lieutenant Robinson asked nervously from his post within the gates.

"Wakarimasen, wakarimasen," Judy Bromme repeated the ominous chant. She was frightened. "It means 'I don't understand.'"

"They don't understand what?"

"I don't know, but I think we'd better find out."

Washington's rush-hour traffic was in full swing.

McGarvey waited for Dominique Kilbourne to come out of her office just off Thomas Circle a few blocks from the Russian embassy, and he followed her across the street to the parking lot where she kept her car. It was already dark, cars and buses ran with headlights, and the streetlights had come on. She walked as if she were tired, and yet she was wary, even jumpy. He'd seen the same sort of attitude in field officers who'd lost their nerve, or who'd gone over the edge . . . or who were hiding something.

She turned and waited for him to catch up. "I saw you standing out here," she said. "Has the Board found anything yet?"

"No," McGarvey said. He'd spent most of the day at Dulles at the crash hangar. It was depressing. "How are you holding up?"

"I'm keeping busy, if that's what you mean," she said defensively. "But I sent your CIA goons away. I got tired of them following me around."

"Do you still keep all your lights on at night?" he

asked, cruelly. He wanted to get to her, cut through her bullshit.

"That's right. And I bought a gun, so I suggest the next time you want to see me you call first. I can't guarantee I won't get jumpy and pull the trigger by mistake."

"I could talk to your brother. He'd probably pull you out of here, no matter what you'd say about it. He thinks that you should be in Portland with him anyway. Kennedy would give you a job."

She laughed derisively. "I talked to him this afternoon. It's funny, you know, because he doesn't like you. He thinks that you're sleeping with me."

When she was excited color came to her cheeks. She was flushed now. He decided that she was beautiful.

"I could arrange to have you arrested and forcibly taken out of Washington."

"It won't happen," she said. "Do you want me to tell you why?"

"All right."

"Because you've come here to ask for my help." She looked back across the street. "The Japanese are demonstrating in front of our embassy in Tokyo right now. Did you know that?"

"No."

"They think we're a violent people. They want us to get out of Japan. Which is funny, if you think about what they did during the war. Their emperor is still apologizing to the Chinese."

"Now you're afraid of them."

"That's right, and it's your fault. You pointed out what they were capable of doing to us. Now every time I pick up a newspaper or watch a television news show, or even go home to my apartment, I think about them."

"It's not the Japanese government, or even the people, only one group of old men."

"What difference does it make who does it if you are violated?" She stepped closer so that he could almost feel the heat radiating from her. "They're not so far off the track. We *are* a violent people."

"What happened that night in your apartment?"

"It got broken into. You found the bugs."

"Did you recognize them? Were they Japanese?"

She turned on her heel and went across the parking lot to her low-slung yellow Corvette. It suited her.

McGarvcy followed her, even more worried than before. She was a woman with a purpose, which in this situation was very dangerous. She had no real idea to what depths of savagery people could sink.

"What makes you think I came here to ask for help?" he said.

"If you really wanted me out of the way, you would already have arranged for my arrest, and I would have been whisked out of Washington to some safe house in the country. Isn't that what you people call those kinds of places?"

"Maybe I'll do it myself."

"No."

"I don't want to see you get hurt. Can't you understand that?"

She unlocked the car, but before she opened the door she gave him a wan smile. "What do you want, Mr. McGarvey?"

"Do you know anybody at Japan Air Lines?"

"Yes."

"I want you to arrange a meeting for me as soon as possible."

"For what purpose?"

"I want to know if they are interested in purchasing a major block of shares in Guerin Airplane Company."

She held her breath, and her eyes widened.

"Tell them that Guerin is not interested in dealing with Mintori. At least not at this time."

"Do you know what you're saying? Have you talked to David?"

"How soon can you arrange the meeting?"

"They'll never agree to talk to you. You'd be wasting your time, and you'd be placing Guerin in a difficult position. Do you have any loyalties?"

"They were Japanese, the two men who broke into your apartment that night, weren't they?"

Dominique opened the car door.

"If the Japanese are implicated in the plane crash, it would make you a material witness to an act of international terrorism. I know some people who would very much like to talk to you about that."

"I'll set up your meeting tomorrow," she said.

Edward R. Reid's Georgetown home was set back in a copse off R Street. From the rear windows he could look across Oak Hill Cemetery and the Potomac River, on the other side of which was the embassy of Japan. The irony was not lost on Reid, who stood in the darkness at his bedroom window, a glass of whiskey in hand. At long last he had his *cause célèbre* and the means to do something about it.

A small noise in the corridor caused him to turn around, and his stomach did a slow roll, the liquor rebounding sourly. Bruno Mueller stood at the doorway, his slight figure outlined by the dim light filtering from the stair hall.

"Good evening, Mr. Reid," the assassin said pleasantly.

"What are you doing here?" Reid asked breathlessly. "How did you find this place?"

"You mistrust the telephones, and we must talk before I leave. As for finding your house, such things are very simple."

Reid's hand shook as he set his drink down. He reached for the table lamp.

"No light, please," Mueller cautioned.

"What do you mean, leaving? Where are you going? Are you quitting?"

"No, I am not quitting. Louis has completed his studies, and now it is time for the next phase."

"What are you talking about?" Reid asked. He was losing control of the operation.

"Louis and I will go to San Francisco. He tells me that

he needs further information from InterTech. Information that he cannot obtain via computer. In the meanwhile, Glen will travel to Portland to see what he can find out at Guerin Airplane Company."

"Traveling together like that will be risky."

"Yes, it will be."

"If you're recognized, everything that I have worked for will be jeopardized."

"Yes," Mueller said. "You would probably be arrested. But then you must have considered that possibility very carefully before you embarked on this scheme. Before you hired me."

"I don't know," Reid said indecisively. He'd not planned on seeing anybody this evening, so he'd not controlled his alcohol intake. He was drunk, and it was difficult for him to focus.

"The problem is we need more data so that we will be able to minimize your risks later."

"I can see that," Reid said.

"Your plan is very brilliant, let me tell you that, Mr. Reid. But it is also very large and very dangerous. If we are successful, which I have no doubt we will be, then many very dedicated, very professional people will be searching for us with a very great earnestness. I want to be prepared, not only for our success, but for the aftermath. Do you understand this as well?"

"Yes, I do," Reid said. For the very first time since he'd begun this campaign, as he called it, he was getting a sense of just how large and dangerous it really was.

The President, his National Security Adviser Harold Secor, his Secretary of State Jonathan Carter, and his Secretary of Defense Paul Landry were gathered in the Oval Office to watch CNN's live broadcast of Japanese Prime Minister Ichiro Enchi's speech to the Diet. It was 8:00 A.M. in Washington, which made it 10:00 P.M. that evening in Tokyo.

The White House had been informed late last night that the PM would be making what the communiqué termed a "substantive" presentation to the parliament.

Within two minutes of the start of Enchi's speech, for which CNN was providing a simultaneous translation, Secretary Carter turned to Harold Secor and said, "Substantive, my ass. This one's a bombshell."

"It would appear that an error of navigation, combined with the passions of a young crew, ultimately led to the tragedy in the Tatar Strait," the Japanese leader said. "The government of Japan deeply regrets the incident and the unnecessary loss of lives."

Prime Minister Enchi looked out at the assembly. "I too add my personal sorrow for the suffering the families of the crew of the Russian naval vessel are experiencing. I pledge that my government will leave no avenue unexplored in its effort to make amends for the loss."

"He's practically handed them the strait on a silver platter," Secretary Landry commented.

"Question is, what'll they do with it," Carter said, but the President waved him off. Prime Minister Enchi was continuing.

"In this difficult transitional era, none of us must be guilty of the errors of pride and complacency. The world has stepped away from the brink of thermonuclear war. Let us not relax our vigil, however. Here, at home, the unrest in Tokyo and Yokosuka must end."

Again the Prime Minister looked up for the benefit of the parliament as well as the international media. He was a consummate politician.

"I appeal not only to my people, but to the peoples of the world, for patience and understanding. In a measure to alleviate world tensions, to step even farther back from the brink of the unthinkable, I am proposing a new purpose for the economic summit meeting scheduled for next month here in Tokyo. I am offering to take steps that would create a Japanese free-trade zone. All trade restrictions will be lifted for a trial period of one year.

"In addition, I would like to invite every nation, not just our friends in the United States, but every nation, to attend the summit. No nation with goodwill in its heart will be turned away. We are a family of humankind. Let us begin to be a family of friends and equal partners.''

"Jesus Christ,'' Harold Secor muttered.

"You can say that again,'' the President said.

TWELVE

Karl Schey's passport was flagged at Charles de Gaulle Airport. Once he was passed through, a plainclothes Action Service officer by the name of Albert Thiers was assigned to track him to his destination.

The German's name, along with a hundred others, had been placed on the red list posted at every airport, railway station, bus terminal, water port of entry, and frontier crossing by the SDECE five years ago. Like the others, Schey was suspected of having some connection with Stasi. Each name that remained on the list was weighted with a number from one through ten. One meant that in the opinion of the Service that person was considered an important, and probably dangerous, suspect, while a ten meant that the Service was interested, but not very.

Schey's number was seven. Under other circumstances his entry into France would have been noted, but he would not have been followed. However, since the shootout near Chartres, the Action Service had increased its surveillance operations.

It took him ten minutes to make his way through customs—he had only one carry-on bag—and get to the cab ranks in front.

Thiers knew little about the man, except his number and his nationality, but it was obvious that he was, if not wealthy, at least well-to-do. His suit was English and expensive, his shoes were probably Spanish or Brazilian, and definitely handmade, and his travel bag was a Gurkha, solid, no nonsense, and pricey. So it did not surprise the Action Service officer that Schey opted for a cab into the city and not the much cheaper bus.

Memorizing the taxi's shield number, Thiers motioned for his partner, Paul Fallières, waiting in a dark green Peugeot, to move up.

"It's the taxi that just pulled out," Thiers said, getting in.

"Anyone important?" Fallières asked, merging with the light traffic.

"Il est un numéro sept."

"This will be an easy afternoon, *hein?"*

"Oui, but watch that you do not lose him. I don't want to write that kind of report."

"D'accord."

The taxi headed into the city at a high rate of speed on the Autoroute Nord, turning onto Paris's ring road, the Périphérique, and turning again onto the Avenue De Saint-Ouen.

"Well, at least we're not going to have to chase the bastard into the Left Bank."

Thiers shot his partner a sour look. He'd been a cop all his adult life, and now at forty-three he took the business very seriously. In his twenty-one-year career he'd lost five partners: one in a fiery auto crash, one stabbed to death in a dark corridor of a whorehouse, of all places, and the other three shot to death on the streets of Paris. In each case the accidents were clearly attributable to laxity.

"This bastard, as you call him, is a German. And you know what the Germans did to us at Chartres. So just watch your step, Paul."

"What's he doing here in the first place? That's all I'm asking. We go along for months without his kind coming over. But Chartres was practically an invasion. What I mean is that he's on the red list, even if he's only a seven. He knows what happened last week. So why has he come to Paris now, of all times?"

"Do you think there may be a connection? Something we should call in?"

"When you think about it, maybe we should get some help. Look what Bruno Mueller did to us down there. Made us all look like fools. The *salopard mec* hid in the attic while we were traipsing around the house. He must have had a good laugh listening to us bumping into each other. And then he kills one of our men right there in the house, has Gisgard fly him to the border, and shoots him in the head."

"What's your point?" Thiers prompted.

"We've not heard the last of Colonel Mueller. Everybody agrees to that. But the colonel has gone to ground. Now this one shows up. He's only a seven, so maybe he figures that he won't attract much attention. Maybe he's come here to set something up for Mueller."

Thiers had learned to trust a cop's instincts. This time, however, he didn't believe they had enough to go on.

"We'll just wait to make that call," he said. "First let's see where this one settles in. See if he meets anyone. Maybe he's here on business, or maybe on vacation."

The taxi turned on the Rue D'Amsterdam toward La Madeleine, and Fallières concentrated on his driving as Thiers worked at the idea like a dog worried a bone. Mueller wasn't through; he did agree with that. But the man would have to be a raving lunatic to think that he could try anything so soon on French soil. Every cop in the country was looking for the German, and there wasn't one of them who would hesitate to shoot given the chance. There'd be a promotion, a pay raise, and a commendation for the lucky bastard who gunned the terrorist down.

Mueller had lost the last of his gang in France, and he had very nearly lost his own life. He would seek revenge. If not now sometime in the future. It wasn't very likely that Karl Schey had come here to front for Mueller. But then again why not? It would be interesting to know if any others left on the red list had recently crossed into France. Say, within the past twenty-four to forty-eight hours. Paris, like any capital city in the free world, was no fortress. The city, and all who lived in her, were vulnerable to attack.

Service 5 had an enviable record. When there was trouble it was taken care of immediately with dispatch and efficiency. Its officers were enthused about what they were doing. France was a relatively small nation but shared borders with Spain, Belgium, Germany, Switzerland, and Italy. In addition she had, in effect, three separate seacoasts: the Mediterranean, the Bay of Biscay, and the English Channel. It was a lot of territory to cover, but bad people who tried to operate in France were dealt with.

Thiers had lost his last partner three years ago. Ever since then he'd held a pact with himself that he would not lose another. He would accomplish this by being very careful.

The taxi turned east on Rue Saint-Honoré and circled the block to the Rue De Castiglione, stopping in front of the elegant old Hotel Inter-Continental around the corner from the Tuileries gardens. A doorman helped Schey out of the cab and took his bag. Together they went into the hotel. A half-minute later the cab took off. Fallières had waited in front of the Godiva chocolate shop next door, and as soon as the cab was gone he pulled ahead to the hotel. Thiers got out and went inside.

Three stairs up, a broad hall led to the right into the long, narrow, ornately decorated lobby. Thiers waited before he approached the desk until the German registered and left with a bellman. He showed the clerk his SDECE identification card.

"What is the name of the gentleman who just now registered, please?"

"Karl Schey. Is there a problem, *Monsieur?*"

"What room did you give him?"

"Four-oh-five."

"I will require the use of an adjacent room. Left or right, it makes no difference. But not across the corridor."

The clerk quickly checked the register. "I am sorry, *Monsieur,* but three and seven are both currently occupied."

"Empty one of those rooms," Thiers said.

"Of course," the clerk said, his thin lips compressing. He checked the register again. "You may have four-oh-seven. Do you wish it to be made up?"

"That won't be necessary."

"It'll be just a few minutes. Can you say how long you will need use of the room?"

"How long is Herr Schey staying with you?"

"Two days."

"Then we will need the room for two days."

"Can you tell me, *Monsieur,* if there is a danger to our guests?" the clerk asked quietly.

"Absolutely no danger. The Service simply has an interest in Herr Schey's movements while he is in Paris. Nothing more. Give me the key, if you please, and I will wait five minutes before I ascend."

The clerk handed over a key, and Thiers went back to Fallières waiting in the car. "We have an adjacent room. Four-oh-seven."

"Let's call Lebrun and tell him what we are doing here," Fallières suggested. "I don't know about you, but suddenly I have a chill about this one."

"Use the radio and then come up." Thiers went back into the hotel, where he waited unobtrusively in the lobby until the clerk nodded to him that it was clear to go upstairs.

The room was small but very nicely decorated with an antique armoire and a modern, well-equipped bathroom. It looked down into a *cours,* which in summer was alive with flowers and fountains. Peaceful.

Thiers carefully opened his side of the connecting door to four-oh-five and listened. At first he could hear nothing, but then a toilet was flushed. An old man's bladder, he thought irreverently. The room fell silent again for a minute or two, until Schey began to speak. Thiers strained to catch the words, but he could make out nothing, except that the German was probably talking to someone on the telephone.

Fallières knocked at the hall door, and Thiers let him in.

"Schey is speaking on the telephone. Call downstairs and see if you can find out if he is connected to someone inside the hotel or to a number outside."

Fallières got on the telephone, and Thiers listened again at the connecting door. Schey spoke a single word, that sounded to Thiers like *oui,* and the room was silent until there was another sound, metallic. The security chain on Schey's door.

Thiers hastily closed the connecting door and opened the hall door a crack in time to see the German heading down the corridor.

"It was an outside call," Fallières said, hanging up.

"He's on the move!"

"Merde."

Schey disappeared around the corner, and Thiers rushed out into the corridor. "We'll take the stairs." He headed in a dead run down the hall to the SORTIE sign. Thank God the German hadn't taken a room on one of the upper floors. He frankly didn't know if his legs would be capable of descending ten or fifteen stories.

They reached the ground floor as Schey crossed the lobby. A corridor to the right went past the hotel bar and restaurant and then to the street doors, bypassing the lobby. Thiers and Fallières took that route.

Advertising posters were placed behind glass display units on the corridor walls. At the corner they watched Schey's reflection in the Moulin Rouge announcement go down the stairs and turn left outside toward the Place de Vendôme.

"I'll cross the street and double-tail him from the front," Thiers said as they hurried downstairs. "Keep your distance in the rear, but don't lose him."

"D'accord," Fallières agreed, and outside they immediately separated.

Schey was already twenty-five meters ahead of them.

At the corner he turned left on the much wider Rue Saint-Honoré. He moved as if he were a man in no particular hurry, heading to no particular destination. Nevertheless, Thiers had to hustle to cross the broad street then go left across the avenue to maintain his position. It became evident almost immediately that the old man was a professional. He varied his pace, he stopped at the odd moment to look at something in a shop window, sometimes he got ahead of a fellow pedestrian and remained there for a dozen meters, at other times he remained behind another for a like distance, and once he even stopped in his tracks, turned back as if he had forgotten something, pondered it for a moment, then decided against retracing his steps, turned back, and continued his stroll.

What was not immediately evident, however, to either Thiers or Fallières, was whether the German suspected that he was being followed, or if these were the normal precautions of an old field man. But an old field man from what service? Did the Action Service suspect that this might be one of the moles in the BND? Schey was an old man. Very probably he was retired, which might explain his low rating on the red list. But then what the hell was he doing practicing his tradecraft here in Paris?

The German reached a small café and went inside.

Thiers was across the street and three doors away. He motioned for Fallières to follow the German inside, then waited for a break in traffic so he could cross over.

The interval between the time Schey entered the café and the time Thiers got there was less than one minute, but already the old man was seated with a man of similar age at a small table near the back. Fallières stood at the end of the bar nearest the door. The barman poured him a glass of white wine. Thiers took the place next to him, from where he could get a good look at Schey and the man he'd come to meet.

"Monsieur?" the barman asked.

"Un café, s'il vous plaît."

"Un espres?"

"Oui," Thiers said, and the barman left.

"That one with the German, I have seen his face," Fallières said softly.

"Yes, who is he?"

"His name is Éduoard Capet. Until very recently he was the number three or four man with Airbus Industrie here in Paris."

"How do you know this, Paul?"

"He was on television last week. It was his retirement. He said the airline company would fail unless the Germans were given a much bigger part. It made me think at the time that the bastard should have been with our compatriots at Chartres if he was so much in love with the Germans."

Thiers watched the two old men for a few moments. Capet was a Frenchman. It made Thiers sick to see him sucking up to the German that way.

"What did Lebrun say?" Thiers asked. Louis Lebrun was their division supervisor.

"Nothing. Just tail and report."

"Call him again, Paul. This time I think we need help. I want to know why this bastard is here."

Éduoard Capet was saying something, and Schey was listening, but his attention was drawn to the two men at the end of the bar near the door. They looked as if they did not belong. He hadn't noticed them when he'd come in, but then he hadn't been on his guard. Not really. And now, was he simply being paranoid?

Since Mueller's visit, Schey had done a lot of serious thinking. Whatever Edward Reid was involved with was very large. Talking to his old friend some months ago he'd been struck by how excited the American had been.

The fact was that they were old men. Time now to retire from a business that was, in any event, all but played out. No enemies left these days. No causes to struggle for. Nothing to be gained by spying, except . . . what? Excitement? Money? Schey supposed he'd had enough of both in his lifetime. Yet something in Reid's voice, in his eyes had been stimulating, portending something important. Capet had confirmed Schey's suspicions that whatever was afoot might involve Guerin Airplane Company. The Japanese were on the verge of making a move against the firm. And considering what had happened last week in the Tatar Strait, Reid might be in over his head and might need help.

One of the two men at the end of the bar left while the other sipped his coffee. They were nobody.

Fallières came back from using the telephone in the tobacco shop next door. He sipped his white wine. "We have two teams on their way here for backup, a third on the way to see what secrets the old man may have stashed in his room, and the fourth to the telephone junction box beneath the street."

"Not bad for a seven," Thiers replied. The German had looked over as Paul was leaving, and again just now when he'd returned. Was there an awareness there, or simply idle curiosity?

"I got their attention because of Airbus Industrie. Louis says they're practically shitting in their pants at the Elysée Palace. Any connection with those *salaud* Germans and they want to know all about it immediately."

"Who is this German, did they say?"

"A BND general," Fallières said. "But he is retired."

"Maybe not," Thiers said absently. Something here, or were they chasing butterflies?

Schey headed back to his hotel. The day was mild and the sun quite pleasant. Capet was a fool, but he had provided a valuable insight about the international commercial airplane industry that had never occurred to Schey. There were only four companies in the world that designed and built the big jets, and all of them were in one sort of trouble or another because the international airline industry was in trouble. It wasn't as if the entire industry were going to fall apart tomorrow, but the correct nudge—it would not have to be a very big nudge—at the correct time could bring down even the largest of the players. If Reid were involved in such a scheme, Schey wanted to be a part of it. One last fling.

They would have to move with care. Capet had provided another insight as well. The airplane industry was so big that entire national governments were heavily involved. Fighting Guerin would involve fighting Washington.

Capet, who had risen so well within the Airbus Industrie based in part on intelligence that Schey had provided him, had been more than happy to cooperate. "Whatever you are involved with these days, my old friend, move with caution. My fellow Frenchmen are just now very wary of anything German."

Schey stopped in front of a small shop selling men's accessories and peered in the window at a display of brightly colored neckties. The sidewalk and street behind him were reflected in the glass. The two men from the end of the bar were nowhere in sight. There was nothing behind him but normal traffic, and yet Schey was spooked. What the hell was it?

Turning abruptly on his heel, he crossed to the other side of the street and continued at a brisk pace the last couple of blocks back toward the hotel. At the corner of the Rue De Castiglione, he stopped again and looked in a shop window. Still nothing seemed suspicious behind him.

The hotel was barely a half-block away. Two gaudily uniformed doormen stood talking at the curb. A taxicab was pulled up in the front, and the street was partially blocked by a City Engineering truck. Hazard cones were placed around an open manhole cover. Sewer problems? Paris was famous for them.

Schey hesitated a few moments longer, then turned, crossed the street, and entered a phone booth. He slid his credit card into the slot, and as he waited for the dial tone he watched the city truck. There were no workers in sight. They were probably beneath the street. Like moles burrowing into their tunnels. The French were basically nothing more than animals. Subhuman, at best.

"He's in the phone box across the street from you," Louis Lebrun radioed. "Stand by for the locator code."

"He is not calling from the hotel," Émile Pepin relayed the message to his fellow technician, Clément Deschanel. They were in the tunnel beneath the street. The hotel's telephone junction box was open. "It's the phone booth across the street."

"Shit," Deschanel swore. "What's the number?" He unscrewed the six fasteners that held the adjacent junction-box cover in place. Several hundred telephones connected to the trunk line from the one box.

"Just a second, it's coming," Pepin said. He was a short, slightly built, nervous man. He looked like a ferret.

Deschanel set the junction-box cover aside and moved his test set over from the hotel's connector board. Leads connected the monitor set to a two-way radio that would send anything picked up to a tape recorder above in the truck.

Pepin relayed the telephone box number. His partner quickly found the two terminals and connected his leads. Immediately they could hear telephone conversation between Schey and another man.

"Who am I speaking with?" Schey asked.

"I am a friend of Mr. R. Who are you?"

"I am also a friend of Mr. Reid. When will he be available?"

"How do I know who you are?"

"The fact I know this number should be proof enough for you," Schey said, obviously irritated. "Tell him an old Luger friend from Munich has called to ask about Bruno. Is he there with you?"

The line was dead for several moments, and Deschanel pressed the earphones closer to his ears. He could still hear the hiss of the long-distance connection. The two men spoke English. He was betting Schey was talking with someone in the United States.

"He's not here. He left last night."

"I see," Schey said. "Now tell me, please, when Mr. Reid will be available at this number?"

"He's in the city now, but he should be coming back out here tonight."

"Tell him . . ." Schey said, but then he stopped.

Again Deschanel held the earphones closer, and he thought he was hearing the sounds of a computer printer in the background. Not above in the telephone box, but at the distant number.

"Tell Mr. Reid that I will come there to see him. Tell him to make the usual arrangements."

"When are you coming?"

"Soon, but I'm not sure. I may have picked up a tail."

"Don't come here!" the younger man said. He was suddenly extremely agitated. "Don't lead anyone here! Are you calling from a secure number?"

"Yes," Schey said. "And do not worry. I will lead no one to you. Talk to Mr. Reid. He will tell you."

"Jesus," the younger man said. "What do you want?"

"To help with . . . the project. It sounds to me as if you need help."

"Jesus," the American said again, and the connection was broken.

Action Service Colonel Phillipe Marquand met with Tom Lynch, chief of the Paris CIA station, shortly after 6:00 P.M. at a café on the Left Bank near the Sorbonne. Lynch was a much smaller, fairer man, who'd lived in Paris nearly four years yet could not speak decent French. Marquand didn't have much respect for the man, only for his position.

"We need some help from Langley, possibly from the FBI," Marquand said.

"Is this a formal request, Colonel?" Lynch asked. *If so, why not go through proper channels?*

"Yes, it is. A German we have been following may be preparing to travel to Washington. He is, or was, in the business, and he may believe that his movements are being monitored."

"Who is this man?"

"His name is Karl Schey. Until recently he worked for the West German Secret Service. But we have reason to believe that the man in actuality worked for the Stasi as an undercover agent."

Lynch glanced toward the front of the restaurant where his bodyguard was waiting. "Has this, by chance, anything to do with the incident last week at Chartres?"

"There is a possible connection," Marquand said. He passed a small package to the American. "We monitored a portion of a telephone call that *Monsieur* Schey made to the United States. As near as we were able to determine, the call was placed to a number somewhere in the vicinity of Washington, D.C. In the conversation he speaks two names. One is Mr. Reid, and the other is Bruno."

"Bruno Mueller?" Lynch asked.

Marquand shrugged. "We do not know, but it is possible that Schey is somehow connected with Mueller. And now there may be a connection between Mueller and Schey with Mr. Reid. Do you know this last name?"

"No," Lynch admitted. "But Schey could be innocent, and therefore his call harmless."

"I lost some good men at Chartres. If Mueller is in the United States working on a project, I can guarantee it will be big and splashy."

"Our FBI is on the ball, Colonel."

Marquand nodded. "Please pass along my request to your director of operations. It is our understanding that *Monsieur* Schey will be making his move soon."

"Why don't you hand this over to your Washington bureau?"

"We don't spy in your country, Mr. Lynch."

Lynch picked up the package and pocketed it. "Is this a tape of the telephone conversation?"

"Yes."

"I'll see what we can do for you."

"Merci," Marquand said. He watched as Lynch got up and left the café. The man was a buffoon. He hoped that whoever came over next would be better.

THIRTEEN

The meeting is set for 5:00 this afternoon," Dominique Kilbourne said on the telephone.

"Where?" McGarvey asked. He was at his hotel across the street from the Watergate.

"Japan Air Lines. On Connecticut Avenue, not far from my office."

"Who will I be meeting?"

Dominique hesitated a moment. She was under a strain. McGarvey heard it in her voice. He'd telephoned Kennedy and warned the airline executive what he was going to do. Kennedy had not been happy, but he agreed to go along with whatever McGarvey asked. Since the crash everybody from Portland had become desperate for a solution. Any solution.

"I spoke with David this morning," she said. "He told me to give you anything you needed."

"But?"

"It's so goddamned futile."

"Why don't you tell me what happened that night at your apartment, Dominique?" McGarvey said. "I could come over now. Or we could go someplace where we could talk."

"You'll be meeting with Arimoto Yamagata, a special representative from the airline. He arrived from Tokyo a few days ago."

"What did you tell him?"

"That you are a special assistant to Mr. Vasilanti, and that you wished to speak with someone in authority from JAL."

"What else?"

"Nothing else. I was put through to Mr. Yamagata. It

almost seemed like he was expecting the call. He agreed without discussion."

"What do you know about him?"

"Not a thing," Dominique admitted. "I asked a few friends in the business, but all they could tell me is that he showed up at JAL sometime last week, apparently to open up new North American markets and discuss an equipment acquisition plan. No one at Guerin, or at Boeing or McDonnell Douglas, has heard from him so far."

"Who else will be at the meeting?"

"His English sounded perfect, so I'm not expecting a translator. But it's anyone's guess. After what's been happening in Tokyo this week, and the Prime Minister's announcement, the Japanese have become even more difficult to read than they usually are."

"I'd like to see you afterward," McGarvey said.

"I'll see you at the meeting."

"I don't think so."

"It's part of the deal. Yamagata is expecting me. If I don't show up he'll want to know why."

"He would be too polite to ask."

"But he would want to know why."

She had developed a real case for the Japanese, and she was putting herself into the middle of something she could not fully understand. He decided that it was coming time to get her out of the way.

"Guerin has a great security setup, Mr. R.," Glen Zerkel said. "But with eighty thousand employees in a half-dozen sites, even the best security is loose."

"Can you get in without detection?" Reid asked.

"No problem. I can think of several ways of doing it. I could apply for a job, and there's a good chance I'd get one. Word is out that they're hiring. Or I could have a plant security badge made up. Or, hell, I could sneak under the fence practically day or night."

"What's your question?"

Zerkel shrugged his narrow shoulders. His hair was getting long already, and his moustache was coming back. Reid thought he looked like a street bum, or like a goddamned hippie.

"I understand what Louis is doing, and what you want Bruno to do for us, but what I don't understand is why I'm screwing around Portland. Every day I'm out there means I'm a day closer to arrest. You gotta know, man, that sooner or later my luck is going to run out. Mr. R., I've been a damned good soldier. Don't use me as cannon fodder. Tell me what you want, and I'll figure out a way of doing it."

"Are you losing your nerve?"

Zerkel smiled wanly. "No, Mr. R., the reason I came back is because I wanted to get from you what I'm supposed to be doing. Mueller is a pro, but I can't get inside his skull. I don't know where he's coming from. He's not . . . American, do you know what I mean?"

"Of course I do, Glen. And it's my fault that you're not clear on what your role is. And it's important. We could not hope to have any success without you."

"Don't stroke me."

Reid looked over the rim of his glass at the younger man. The past twenty-four hours had been difficult. First Mueller's unexpected appearance at the Georgetown house, then Glen's return, and finally Karl's enigmatic telephone call from Paris had all served to put him off balance. It was far too late for second thoughts, but despite his excitement about what the Japanese were doing to themselves, he was frightened.

"I want you to return to Portland."

"To do what?"

"We'll need photographs of Guerin's installations. All of them, including their Gales Creek Research Facility. We're going to need maps, floor plans if you can come up with them safely, and shift-change schedules, security measures, vendor deliveries . . . all of it. Do you understand what we're after?"

"Knowledge," Zerkel said.

"That's right. The more we know about them, the easier it'll be for us to strike if my first plan doesn't work out."

"And get away," Zerkel said. "Let's not forget that part, Mr. R."

San Francisco held the key to unlocking the connection between the Japanese group targeting Guerin and the technical device that they'd designed to do the job. But San Francisco was also at the center of the search for the murderer of Dr. Jeanne Shepard. Mueller's plan was to move with extreme caution, as far as this was possible traveling with Louis, by minimizing their exposure to the city. Louis needed information, and Mueller was going to get it for him as quickly and as efficiently as possible.

They'd flown to Reno via Denver where Mueller rented a Ford Thunderbird. He traveled under the Michael Larsen identification Reid had supplied. Louis used papers his brother gave him under the name David Wolff. With his hair cut and bleached, glasses perched on the end of his nose, and a sport coat and properly knotted tie, Zerkel was a new man—unrecognizable. Mueller could almost forget the man's eccentricities. On the flight west, and then the two-hundred-mile drive up to San Francisco, Zerkel was mostly silent, either dozing or watching out the window or reading the more than a dozen magazines and newsletters he'd brought along.

Mueller took Interstate 880 into Oakland, exiting a few blocks from the Convention Center, and drove back to a Holiday Inn near the airport. He rented one of the suites for seven days, paying for it with a Michael Larsen Visa card. The hotel was exactly what he wanted: plastic, modern, indifferent, thoroughly American, and therefore anonymous. They were a pair of businessmen from out of town who enjoyed their privacy in a bit of modest luxury. No one paid them the slightest attention.

"We're about fifteen miles from the Alameda office," Zerkel told Mueller when they got up to their room.

"When can you get into the computer?"

"Soon as I'm set up. But I'm going to have to take it slow. There'll be alarms now."

"Alarms?"

Zerkel looked up, an odd, resigned expression on his face. "Yeah." He snatched a copy of *Newsweek* from his briefcase and tossed it over. "Page thirty-eight," he said, and he turned back to his laptop computer, his fingers flying over the keyboard.

The article about Dr. Jeanne Shepard's brutal rape and murder was included in a series of brief news clips under the heading "The Nation." Police were searching for Louis Zerkel, who was described as a troubled computer genius. Photographs of Dr. Shepard and Zerkel ran side by side.

"The doctor's elimination was necessary," Mueller said indifferently. It didn't make much difference to him. If Zerkel continued to work out, he would live. If he did not, his body would be found in the morning.

"You have my cooperation, *Herr* Mueller," Zerkel said. "But you are crude. Killing me won't be quite so easy, you know. What do you think about that?"

"Nobody has any intention of killing you. We need your services."

"Yes, you do. Even more than you think."

"You have a built-in safeguard somewhere?"

Zerkel smiled. "Of course. Don't you?" Zerkel went back to his computer.

Mueller wasn't surprised, though he supposed he should warn Reid. But whatever Zerkel had set up could only harm the others. They had everything to lose, whereas he had nothing. He could contemplate his own death with almost as much indifference as he could another's. That fatalism had always been his main strength, which, combined with his tradecraft, made him very good.

If this project could be taken to a successful conclusion, and if Reid made good on his promise, then retirement was possible, perhaps in the South Pacific. If not, he would see just how far it could play. The thought of many airplanes, each carrying dozens, perhaps hundreds of innocent passengers going down on the same day stirred the edge of his emotions with an erotic promise.

"Take care then, with what you are doing," Mueller said, but Zerkel had connected his computer to the telephone and was lost in the data stream flowing across his screen.

Mueller went into the bathroom where he stripped and showered. The hot water relaxed his muscles after the long trip from Washington, and when he turned the stream to all cold, his body screamed in the joy of agony. He was alive. The French had not been worthy opponents. All of his adult life he'd been trained to take the fight to America. He was here now, and he was finally taking it to them. He was going to enjoy every moment of it.

When he'd dressed in fresh clothes, Mueller went back into the sitting room. Zerkel was staring at the blank computer screen, his lips pursed.

"Did you find what you needed?"

"No," Zerkel replied absently. "InterTech's mainframe is alarmed, just like I thought it would be. But it's different."

"What do you mean?"

Zerkel shook his head. "Just different. Better than I thought, but . . . I don't know." He was grappling for a word.

"Foreign?" Mueller prompted.

The younger man looked up.

"Japanese?"

"Yes. That's it. The Japs are in. It must be something they cooked up."

"It might mean that you are on the right track after all."

"There was never any doubt of it," Zerkel said. "They're running scared. What do you think about that?"

"What do you need from the company?" Mueller asked.

"The schematic for that module."

"How about the actual unit itself?"

This time Zerkel looked up with interest. "What do you mean?"

"Wouldn't it be better if you had one of the subassemblies? The entire unit?"

"Of course."

"If you are having trouble getting into the computer, which is what they expect, maybe getting into the warehouse would be easier."

"I wouldn't know where to look."

"Who would?" Mueller asked.

Zerkel shrugged. "My boss, Bob Sutherland. He'd know."

"Do you know where he lives?"

"Yeah," Zerkel said. "As a matter of fact I do. But he won't tell us anything. I know him. He's definitely management. He'd turn me over to the cops in a New York minute."

"Allow me to worry about that aspect, Louis. Tell me, how big is this device, whatever it is? Do you know?"

"No."

"Would it weigh hundreds of kilos? Would it be difficult for us to pick up and carry?"

"Nothing like that," Zerkel said. "The CPU and its associated circuitry probably fit inside an inch-and-a-half rack. Like a drawer on slides eighteen inches on a side and an inch-and-a-half tall. We may or may not supply the cable harness that would lead out to the sensors on the engines, which in turn would be mounted on some sort of lightweight frame. The whole enchilada—the processor, the harness, and the sensor frame—would probably fit into a medium-size suitcase. Maybe weigh eight or ten kilos."

"Then we will ask Mr. Sutherland to help us acquire the device."

Zerkel looked at him owlishly. "You will have to kill him afterward."

Mueller shrugged.

"He has a wife and children. They would have to be killed if they got in the way."

"Do you have a problem with that, Louis?"

Zerkel thought about it for a moment, then shook his head, the expression on his face serious, but boyish. "No, I've got no problem with that."

It was obvious to McGarvey that Dominique Kilbourne was even more strained than she had sounded on the telephone this morning. Her complexion was sallow and her eyes were red-rimmed even behind makeup. McGarvey had spoken again about her with David Kennedy, but with everything going on the airplane executive left the decision of what to do about her up to McGarvey. The crash and subsequent grinding investigation, under the glare of the media spotlight, had pushed everything else into the background, including, for the moment, Guerin's deal with the Russians, McGarvey's investigation, and Dominique's fears.

"Everyone has a job to do" were Kennedy's parting words. "Get on with it."

"You don't have to come to this meeting, Dominique," McGarvey said.

"It's what I'm paid to do. I said it before, and I'll say it again—a lot of companies besides Guerin depend on me to keep their best interests at heart."

"This has nothing to do with your work. I'm looking for reactions, nothing more." She was brittle, McGarvey thought. Like a porcelain doll with stress fractures. "I'll send you back in the cab."

"Don't you do it!"

"You don't belong in this fight."

"I'm already in too deep," Dominique said carefully. She was holding her emotions in check. Nothing like an hysterical female to turn off her warrior. McGarvey could almost see her head working.

"That's my point. If you can't give me the truth, then you're less than worthless to me. In fact you're dangerous."

"It's the same in my business. The people I have to deal with on the Hill sometimes don't know the meaning of the word."

"Tell me about that night at your apartment."

Dominique looked at him through lidded eyes. "Later," she said. "After we meet with Yamagata I'll tell you everything you want to know."

The cabby let them off in front of the Japan Air Lines offices on Connecticut Avenue near St. Matthew's Cathedral. It was dusk and rush-hour traffic was getting into full swing. The new Congress had been in session for less than a month, and a muted hum seemed to permeate the atmosphere in the capital city. The United States was the only remaining superpower, which seemed to give the rest of the world sniping rights. Most of official Washington was kept very busy because of it.

They were directed to a third-floor reception area that was stunningly decorated in a mix of Japanese traditional and stark Western modern. Chrome and glass intermingled with lacquered wood and rice-paper screens gave a surprisingly peaceful feel to the offices and open areas. Indirect lighting simulated sunlight, which heightened the pleasant effect.

A tall, very handsome Japanese man, dressed impeccably in a well-tailored Italian silk suit, came down a broad corridor to them. He was smiling.

"Good afternoon, Mr. McGarvey, Ms. Kilbourne. Welcome to Japan Air Lines. My name is Arimoto Yamagata."

"Good afternoon. Thank you for seeing us on such short notice," Dominique said stiffly. She handed the Japanese her business card. "As I explained to you on the telephone, Mr. McGarvey is here as a spokesperson for Guerin Airplane Company."

Yamagata shook hands with Dominique and then with McGarvey and handed them both his business card. It identified him as a special representative of the president of JAL. "We are in similar positions, Mr. McGarvey." His English was perfect.

"Harvard or Yale?" McGarvey asked.

Yamagata smiled. "Harvard actually," he said. "Class of eighty."

"You don't look that old."

The Japanese chuckled. "Thanks for that. I am, but I work at it."

"What brings you to America just now?"

"To meet with people such as yourself, Mr. Mc-Garvey. You jumped the gun on me, I wasn't quite ready to set up shop. But I'm happy to start with you. Guerin is a fine company with an outstanding record."

"Yes, it is."

Yamagata's expression darkened. "If you will permit me to be un-Japanese for a moment, I will express my sorrow at your unfortunate loss. It was the hand of God, and everyone at JAL shares my condolences to you."

The man was a fool or very intelligent. Either way, McGarvey figured he was potentially dangerous. "Our engineers are working on the possibility that our aircraft was sabotaged."

"God in heaven," Yamagata said softly.

"One of the passengers may have been carrying a bomb."

"One of your own people?"

"Perhaps a Russian. The flight originated in Moscow."

The Japanese was shaking his head. "What would they have to gain?"

"We don't know, Mr. Yamagata. No demands were made. Nor has anyone made contact with us to admit responsibility."

Dominique stood still, a blank expression on her face.

"When we heard that you were in Washington I was instructed to meet with you as quickly as possible and convey two messages, the first of which concerned the crash."

"You knew that I had come to Washington, as well as my purpose in coming?"

"Everybody in the industry knows, Mr. Yamagata. It's become a small planet."

"Indeed," the Japanese replied, his expression un-readable. "What of the second message?"

Two men who sat together in deep discussion across

the large reception room glanced toward them. "Could we go someplace more private?"

"Of course. Forgive me. I was about to invite you to have something to drink and then bring you back to my office. But what you have told me has caught me off balance."

I'll bet it has, McGarvey thought. "Nothing to drink for us. Just a few moments of your time in private, Mr. Yamagata. Then we have another appointment to keep. You understand how it is."

"Certainly," the Japanese said. He led them out of the reception area to an expansive corner office with large windows that looked down Connecticut Avenue toward the White House. Photographs on the broad desk showed a pretty woman and three children.

"Your family?" McGarvey asked, as they sat down.

Yamagata glanced at the photos. "Actually this is our Washington director's office. The photographs are his."

"Pretty," McGarvey said, and he caught the slight look of irritation that crossed Yamagata's face.

"Yes, they are."

"The second message is a difficult one, Mr. Yamagata. Difficult for us as well as for you. We're asking that you keep what I'm about to tell you in strict confidence."

"Naturally."

"If it were to be known publicly, it could create additional trouble for us. Something we don't need at this point."

"I understand. Please continue."

McGarvey glanced at Dominique for effect, then smiled ingratiatingly. "The thing is we believe that a group of Japanese businessmen are getting ready to take us over. To buy us out."

Yamagata's eyes narrowed. "I can't imagine why you are telling me this, Mr. McGarvey, but do you know who these men are?"

"The Mintori Assurance Corporation." McGarvey watched the man's eyes, but there was no reaction.

"What is it you are asking us?"

"For help," McGarvey said.

"With what?"

Again McGarvey glanced over at Dominique as if he were looking for reassurances, but she said nothing. Her lack of reaction couldn't have been better if they rehearsed it. He was in trouble and on his own.

"Japan Air Lines is in a very strong position, unlike so many of our own carriers. We would like to explore the possibilities of what we might call a silent partnership."

"JAL's cash or loan guarantees to keep the Mintori group at bay, in return for what?"

"The first crack at our P/C2622, with a healthy share of stock options for a delivery guarantee at a favorable price we could both live with."

"You want to sell us some airplanes that for a time will not be offered for sale to any other airline?"

"That is the possibility my company would like to explore."

The Japanese looked at McGarvey with disdain. "The rumor is that Guerin Airplane Company has made an offer to the Russian government."

"To build a component assembly facility in Moscow," McGarvey said. "I must compliment you on your source of intelligence."

"The Russian government is unstable."

"We would save a very significant portion of the cost per aircraft if the Moscow facility works out."

Yamagata fell silent for a long moment, his expression unchanging. "What specifically are you asking me today?"

"Is JAL interested in principle in opening such a dialogue?"

"Frankly I don't know," the Japanese said. He sat forward slightly. "Would Guerin be interested, in principle, in the same sort of dialogue with a group other than JAL?"

"I don't know," McGarvey replied carefully. "Would this group have any connection with Mintori?"

"None."

"Who are they?"

"The Kobe Bank."

Gotcha, you bastard, McGarvey thought. "I'll take your offer back to my people in Portland, Mr. Yamagata."

"I will be waiting to hear from you, Mr. McGarvey."

Bob Sutherland lived in a well-maintained Spanish-style house in San Leandro, about twenty miles from the Oakland Holiday Inn. Mueller had Zerkel rent a Chevrolet Lumina from the Budget counter at the airport, and they drove out in two cars, parking the Thunderbird in the parking lot of an all-night supermarket on 14th Street.

A plain-looking woman dressed in blue jeans and a sweatshirt answered the door. A television was playing inside. Mueller smiled pleasantly.

"Mrs. Sutherland, I'm Michael Larsen with the FBI. I really hate to bother you at this hour, but could we have a word with your husband? He's at home this evening?"

She looked over her shoulder at Zerkel standing by the car. "One more time won't matter, I suppose."

"Who's at the door?" her husband called from inside.

"It's the FBI again," she answered, and she stepped back. "Come on in. No use giving the neighbors a show."

Bob Sutherland, looking as if he'd just stepped out of a heath spa in gray sweats, came around the corner at about the same moment Mueller shoved the man's wife back, stepped into the hall, and closed the door.

"What the fuck . . ." Sutherland said.

Mueller pulled out the silenced 9 mm Beretta Reid had supplied him with and pointed it at the woman.

Sutherland was struck dumb.

"I have come for some information for my friend Louis Zerkel. If you cooperate with me, Mr. Sutherland, I will not kill your wife."

Sutherland was shaking his head, and his mouth was moving, but no words were coming out. He brought his hands together as he looked at his wife.

"There is very little time," Mueller said.

Sutherland looked at him, incomprehension on his face. "Why?" he asked.

"We need information."

"But, God in heaven, who are you?"

"I will kill your children, as well, Mr. Sutherland. Are they dressed for bed?"

Sutherland looked again at his wife, and he took a half-step forward but then stopped. "What do you want from me? I'll tell you and then you can leave. My God, I don't understand."

Mueller reached back and opened the front door. A few seconds later Zerkel slipped inside and closed the door. Sutherland stared at him for a long time before recognition dawned in his eyes.

Zerkel carefully avoided looking at the man or his wife.

"What do you want?" Sutherland asked.

It seemed as if Zerkel had not heard him.

"Louis," Mueller prompted.

"I need the PE 171 subassembly. The one we supply to Guerin."

Sutherland shook his head. "The heat monitor?"

"I need both ends, including the harness if we supply it."

Sutherland was still shaking his head. "Is that what it's all about? The fucking Jap subcontract. Are you fucking people out of your minds?"

"Where do we find it, Mr. Sutherland?" Mueller asked.

Sutherland looked at him. "Shipping and receiving. The first fourteen of the new order for eighty are going out the day after tomorrow."

"Can you find that?"

"I think so," Zerkel said. "Is there anything else going to Guerin in this cycle?" he asked Sutherland.

"No."

"I can find them."

"What about security?"

"A night watchman," Sutherland said. "Take my card. It'll get you through the gate. Just get out of here now."

Mueller nodded. "Very well," he said. He shot the man in the face, then he shot the woman in the forehead. "What do you think about that?" he said.

A small child cried something from the back of the house, and Zerkel flinched.

"Wait outside in the car, Louis," Mueller said. "I'll be right out."

"You can't fight them by yourself," McGarvey said.

It was late. They'd come back to her apartment where she made them a steak and salad. Afterward they'd talked about her past, about growing up in Detroit, being raised by her brother Newton, about coming into the airline industry with him, about her brief affair with David Kennedy, and finally about the night her apartment had been broken into.

"It has nothing to do with personalities," McGarvey said.

"What then?"

"They don't care who or what you are. At this point there's little or nothing you could do to hurt them. But if you got in their way they'd destroy you as easily as they would swat a fly."

"They came in here and violated my life. It was the same thing as rape. According to you, they're responsible for the crash in '90 and now this one. All those people dead. Are we supposed to forget them?" She looked tired, used up, washed out, and very vulnerable.

"That's why I was hired," McGarvey said.

"I don't know if I can accept that."

"I could have you arrested."

"You've said that before."

"I could call your brother and ask for his help."

"Don't threaten me," she said tiredly. Her hand shook as she raised the wine glass to her lips. "I'm not going to listen to you any longer. Leave me alone."

"I can't," McGarvey said.

Dominique looked out the windows at the Kennedy Center, her profile toward McGarvey. She turned her head to look at him. Her skin glowed as if she were caught in subtle stage lighting. "Why?"

This moment had been coming since the first day he'd met her. "Because I care what happens to you."

She wanted to laugh. He could see it in the expression on her face. "What are you talking about?"

"I want to keep you out of harm's way."

"A great movie title," she said.

McGarvey went to her, took the wine glass and set it aside, and held her in his arms. For just a second she stiffened, but then she folded against him.

"Do you have someplace to go?" he asked. "Someplace where no one would think to look?"

She looked up at him and nodded. "But I don't know if I can just walk away from this."

He kissed her. This time there was no hesitation, no holding back. She responded as if she were a starving woman at a banquet table, her entire body shivering with need.

They undressed each other where they stood in front of the tall windows, and he lifted her up and entered her, her legs wrapped around his waist, her breasts crushed against his chest, her lips kissing his mouth, his face, his neck.

She was tight, her body compact and in perfect proportion, a dancer's physique, and they fit together well. He stepped back and lowered her to the carpet, their movements against each other in unison.

"I wanted you from the start," she said.

Getting inside InterTech's sprawling facility was easier than Mueller thought it would be. They drove through the unattended rear gate that opened with Sutherland's security card and parked in the shadows a few yards east of the loading dock.

Almost all of the company's sensitive work involved advanced computer programming and applications. As a result its most sophisticated security measures were geared toward protecting its computer system from unauthorized incursions. The company's mainframe was protected around the clock with armed guards, advanced electronic locks, and high-resolution, low-lux, closed-circuit television monitors. Shipping and receiving, however, was protected only by security-card-operated locks and an armed night watchman, unless Sutherland had been lying and Zerkel mistaken.

They purchased a plastic five-gallon gas can from a truck stop north of San Leandro, and in Oakland Mueller sent Zerkel on foot to get the container filled.

With the car windows down Mueller listened for several seconds, but there wasn't much to be heard except for traffic sounds from nearby Central Avenue. "Give me a minute to get inside and take care of the guard, then bring the gasoline."

Zerkel's head bobbed once. He was nervous but holding together. Both brothers had a surprising tenacity.

Mueller mounted the loading dock, and with the silenced automatic in one hand used Sutherland's card to open the steel security door. He left it ajar. A narrow vestibule opened to a small office with a couple of desks, beyond which was the shipping and receiving warehouse. A large black man, dressed in a security guard's uniform, came from the back.

"What're you doing here tonight?" the guard said, but when he realized that Mueller wasn't the person he thought he was he grabbed for his gun.

Mueller shot the man in the chest, knocking him down but not killing him.

"Shit, shit." The guard frantically grappled with his holster, trying to get the pistol loose. He looked up as Mueller loomed overhead, and his eyes bulged.

Mueller shot the man once in the forehead, then clicked the safety on his pistol and stuffed it in his belt. He took the guard's flashlight, and by the time Zerkel came in he'd found what he took to be the fourteen heat monitor/alarm subassemblies. They were loaded on a pallet near the service door, each packed in a cardboard box about thirty inches long and wide and about eight inches deep.

"Is this what we're looking for?" he asked when Zerkel joined him.

"It looks like it."

"Make sure," Mueller said. He opened the gas can and, starting in one corner, splashed gasoline over everything—cardboard cartons of parts, drums of cleaning and etching chemicals, the office area, and the guard's body.

"This is part of it," Zerkel called out. He had one of the boxes open.

"What's missing?"

"The harness and frame. They must be assembled elsewhere. This is just the monitor. But it'll do for now."

"Put it in the trunk of the car and start the engine."

Zerkel left, and Mueller splashed the last of the gasoline over the pallet, holding the remaining thirteen heat monitor subassemblies, dribbling a trail back to the door.

He waited until Zerkel had the car started and turned around, then lit a book of paper matches, tossed them in the warehouse, and slammed the door.

FOURTEEN

The extraordinary events of the past few days were testament to the power of Sokichi Kamiya.

Lieutenant Commander Seiji Kiyoda, dressed in an immaculate white kimono, sat cross-legged on a raised teak platform in the sleeping quarters of his home. The night was quiet. The children were gone, and yesterday he'd sent Moriko and the house staff away.

Better to be alone now. Moriko was a traditional wife. She understood things without lengthy explanations.

From where he sat, Kiyoda could see the Yokosuka harbor, the *Samisho,* still at her berth, still bathed in harsh lights, still guarded around the clock.

Forty-eight hours ago he'd been quietly released from prison where he awaited trial on a charge of treason. The charge stood, but he was an honorable man who would be allowed to take his confinement at home where he was to consider himself under house arrest.

For the first twenty-four hours armed guards were posted at his front gate. Last night a car had come for them, and no replacements had been sent.

Since the riots downtown and in Tokyo, his story had been dropped from the newspapers and television. It was as if the incident in the Tatar Strait had never happened. As if he had simply dropped off the face of the earth. Or, as if he had never existed. All of it was utterly fantastic, leaving him with a feeling of fatalism. He wanted his *sensei.* He wanted his boat and his crew, and he wanted the freedom of the sea. More than anything he wanted to press the fight for Nippon's rightful place in the new world order.

But he needed patience. Kamiya had many plans, many purposes. Kiyoda felt a sense of awe, thinking about his mentor. *Kamiya-san* was probably the most important man for Japan's future since Mishima, and since the Emperor Hirohito himself. He had brought Kiyoda this far, and he would not forget his faithful.

For now, Kiyoda would remain here, at peace with himself in the struggle. Content in the knowledge that forces beyond his meager understanding were at work. Content to sit in the still of an evening and watch over his boat.

It was difficult, Kiyoda decided. Almost impossible not to act. At times it was as if a billion points of light danced in his head, creating a pressure so intense, so unbearable that he could not stand it any longer. But each time he found himself at the brink of some irrational act, he stepped away from the precipice, all the stronger for it.

Something moved on the quay where the *Samisho* was berthed. Kiyoda slowly came out of his contemplative state and focused on what was happening. Two pairs of headlights moved away from the submarine. As the first vehicle passed under the streetlights he could see that it was a truck, possibly a troop transport. Moments later the second truck passed beneath the lights.

Kiyoda got to his feet and stepped outside to the broad balcony. Something was going on.

The strong lights that bathed the *Samisho* were suddenly extinguished. In one moment the submarine and the dock at which she was secured were visible, in the next they had disappeared.

A signal? Was it possible? Kiyoda crossed his sleeping chamber and in the corridor lifted the telephone to his ear. As before there was no dial tone. It was part of his isolation. But something was happening to his boat and her crew.

Returning to his sleeping quarters, he threw off his kimono and got dressed in winter blues. He contemplated the American military Beretta 9 mm automatic in its leather holster and web belt, safe in its drawer. A weapon is only as deadly as the man's will to use it.

Looking over his shoulder he could see out the broad sliding doors. The *Samisho* was still lost in darkness, while all around her the city of Yokosuka sparkled and lived. The U.S. Seventh Fleet went about its business as conqueror. No matter what colored glasses were used to look at the American naval presence here, no mistake could be made about its purpose. It was to keep Japan in her place of subservience. More specifically to keep the MSDF at bay.

Kiyoda strapped the pistol on his hip and hurried down the corridor to the entry hall. His XO Lieutenant Minori appeared out of the darkness in the front courtyard.

"*Kan-cho,* we have come for you. It is time to go," Minori called urgently.

Kiyoda's heart hammered as if he had just run up ten flights of stairs. "What is happening to my boat, Ikuo?" he said, joining his officer.

"I have a car. I'll brief you on the way. But she's ours again."

"Are we ready for sea?"

"Hai, kan-cho. We have need of only one thing."

"What is that?" Kiyoda asked as they hurried out to the car.

"Our captain," Minori said.

Kiyoda's heart wanted to burst with pride. With a crew like his, he could go anywhere in the world, vanquish any foe, meet any challenge. And they would. Starting this night.

"Is that Sam Varelis?" McGarvey asked.

The NTSB investigator he'd been talking to glanced over at a bull-necked man standing alone by the outline of the port wing chalked on the hangar floor. There was a small but growing array of parts laid out within the lines.

"That's right. He's chief investigating officer on this incident. Know him?"

"Sure do," McGarvey said, and he walked over. Varelis had his ever-present unlit cigar clamped at the corner of his mouth. McGarvey had never seen him light up, and once when he'd asked about it, Sam growled that only idiots smoked. He'd been senior to McGarvey in operations at Langley, and his had been one of the few voices raised in protest when McGarvey had been fired.

Varelis turned. "I wondered when you were going to say hello."

McGarvey shook his hand. "Long time, Sam. How's Washington treating you?"

"Tolerably. You?"

McGarvey shrugged. "I'll live." He motioned toward the wing outline. "Any early conclusions?"

"Overheat busted up Rolls's ceramic blades and the engine disintegrated."

"Same as '90?"

"That's what my people tell me."

"Any consideration being given to the possibility of sabotage?"

Varelis eyed McGarvey thoughtfully. "When I heard that Guerin had hired you, I was a little surprised, Mac. I couldn't imagine what the hell they needed your services for."

"How about now?"

"I still can't think what you're doing here."

McGarvey glanced at the wing outline. "Not much left."

"No blast marks, no external damage, nothing on the flight recorders to indicate anything malfunctioned. Every system aboard this airplane was working within its parameters."

"But it went down."

"Rolls is sending one of its engines directly off the line for us to test. We'll know better then."

"Rolls did that in '90, and Guerin's planning on sending AOG teams out to every P522 in service to replace every single engine."

"Something will show up."

"It didn't seven years ago."

"Our methods are more sophisticated now."

"By any chance was there an extra passenger aboard this flight?"

Varelis looked sharply at him. "That was a fatality on the ground, Mac. But to answer your question, no, we found no extra body parts this time. Now, if you've got something to say, say it and let me do my job. I'm busy."

"I think both planes were sabotaged."

"By whom, and for what reason?"

"By the Japanese to ruin Guerin."

Varelis nodded tightly. "There've been a few rumors floating around. For what it's worth, I hope you're wrong, because if you are right we're all going to be in deep shit."

"I think we already are, Sam."

"Watch yourself. There's a lot of money involved

here. Serious international money. National debt, balance of trade, all that."

"Have you heard something?"

Varelis shook his head. "Not a thing."

"I'd like to keep on top of this."

"It's a two-way street."

"That it is," McGarvey said, and he walked back to the office trailer set up in the hangar. Kennedy and Socrates were coming out.

"We're leaving for Portland this afternoon at three," Kennedy said. "Al flew back last night. Do you have anything for me to tell him?"

"Maybe this afternoon. Can I hitch a ride with you?"

"Of course," Kennedy said. "How did your meeting with JAL go yesterday?" His patience was worn thin. He looked haggard. They all did.

"It went okay. Does Vasilanti still want to press the fight?"

Kennedy nodded.

"I have a couple of things to take care of in town before we leave. I'll brief you on the way out."

"Better yet, I'll arrange a meeting in Portland. I think it's time that we lay all the cards on the table."

"That might not be a bad idea, because you people are going to have to make some hard decisions."

"Don't I know it," Kennedy said glumly.

On the way back to his hotel, McGarvey stopped at a gas station outside Arlington and telephoned Dominique's office. The secretary told him that Ms. Kilbourne was out of the city for several days and perhaps as long as a week. No, she did not know where Ms. Kilbourne could be reached, but she did leave a message that Mr. McGarvey was to contact Mr. Arimoto Yamagata at Japan Air Lines as soon as possible.

As a precaution, McGarvey called Dominique's apartment and left a message on her machine that he would be in Portland sometime this evening. "If anything comes up, give me a call."

Next, he telephoned Phil Carrara at CIA headquarters, catching the DDO just as he was heading upstairs to lunch with Lawrence Danielle.

"I'm leaving for Portland this afternoon, but in the meantime I need some information about a Japanese national working for Japan Air Lines here in Washington."

"I don't know if I can help, Kirk."

"His name is Arimoto Yamagata. He claims to be a special representative of JAL's president, but he was a little vague about what he was doing here in the States."

"The name doesn't ring a bell. Have you met him?"

"I asked for a loan in exchange for exclusive purchase rights to some airplanes. He didn't turn me down, but my guess is that he either works for MITI or for an organization called Mintori Assurance."

"Jesus," Carrara said.

"Check with your friends at the Bureau. See if he shows up on any of their lists."

"I'll see what I can do," the DDO said. "But something else has come up. Do you remember Phillipe Marquand, Paris?"

"Action Service."

"That's right. He's asked for help."

"Is it related?"

"No reason to think so, Kirk, but your name came to mind. A former Stasi officer who was involved a few years ago in Paris when the Swissair flight was brought down might be here in the Washington area."

McGarvey's grip tightened on the telephone. He still carried a lot of painful memories. "Who?"

"Bruno Mueller. What can you tell me about him?"

"He was a mechanic. One of the best. He worked for the BND for a few years, and even came to Langley for a few months. He should be in your files."

"He is," Carrara said. "Did you ever come up against him?"

"No. But I'm reasonably sure he's heard of me. Has he come to settle old scores?"

"Unknown, Kirk. Marquand's people picked up the trail of someone who might be an old friend not only of Mueller, but also of Edward R. Reid."

"Should I know that name?"

"He's a Washington insider. Former deputy undersecretary of state for economic affairs. He puts out a newsletter called the *Lamplighter* that at the moment is calling for the disarmament of Japanese military forces before we get into another war with them. Makes you wonder why Reid is connecting with Bruno Mueller and getting help from a former BND general whom the French think might have worked for the Stasi."

"It wouldn't be pleasant," McGarvey said, a part of his mind reaching for something, some memory, some bit of forgotten information.

"No," Carrara said.

"Anything else?"

"Not for now, *compar,* but as soon as I come up with something I'll call. How long will you be in Portland?"

"I don't know. I'll keep in touch."

"Do that," Carrara said.

Finally, McGarvey telephoned Yamagata at JAL and was put through immediately. "I just got your message. Has there been a response already?"

"As a matter of fact there has, in a manner of speaking," the Japanese said. "Are you and Ms. Kilbourne free for a late lunch?"

"Unfortunately no. Ms. Kilbourne is out of town on business, and I'm leaving within the hour for Portland. Have you anything for me that I can take back to my people?"

"I spoke with my principals last night, and they might be interested."

"JAL, or the other party?"

Yamagata hesitated. "A fourth group, not connected with JAL, Mintori, or Kobe Bank."

"You get around, Mr. Yamagata."

"Yes, thank you, I do."

"We would be interested in moving quite quickly on this," McGarvey said.

"My principals understand. Would you be willing to come to Tokyo to speak with them?"

"Who would I be meeting with?"

Again Yamagata hesitated. "It may be premature to name specific names."

"But they would like me to come to see them?"

"At their expense, of course, Mr. McGarvey."

"When?"

"At your convenience."

"I'll telephone you from Portland, Mr. Yamagata," McGarvey said.

"Until then," the Japanese replied.

"How long will these tests take you?" Reid asked.

"A few days maybe," Louis Zerkel said. "This is the actual working mechanism, not some mockup or computer-generated circuit. I have to make sure that my code generator unlocks the final switch on this unit and that my audio pulse fires the circuit."

"You've already knocked down an airplane."

"We might have been lucky. Could have been a fluke. Could be other codes." Zerkel ran his hand across the monitor. "I need to make a Faraday cage."

"What's that?" Reid asked.

"It blocks electromagnetic and electrostatic radiation. When I say the word, the spike will show up here, but it won't go any farther. What do you think about that?"

"I think you are a brilliant man," Reid answered. "And I think that you are finally using your head."

"Use it or lose it."

"Will you need more equipment to build this device?"

"Yes, but not much. A few square meters of fine-mesh copper screening and maybe a hundred feet of grounding strap. For the rest I think I can make do with what I've got here."

"Shouldn't be too difficult to obtain," Reid said.

Zerkel turned away without a word, picked up a screwdriver, and began removing the fasteners holding the heat monitor/sensor's front panel in place.

Mueller was downstairs in the kitchen making a cup of tea. Reid poured a stiff drink and joined the German at the table.

"When will he be ready for operation?" Mueller asked.

"A couple of days. He has some tests to perform." Reid watched the German's movements. Everything the man did was precise, with an economy of motion and the same smoothness and grace that a jungle cat on the hunt displayed.

"How is Glen doing in Portland?"

"There's been no word as yet, but he's competent, and well motivated."

"They're brilliant, but unstable. They'll both have to be killed."

Reid nodded. "We may have additional help," he said.

Mueller was at the counter. He turned. "What do you mean?"

"The man who arranged for you to come here is joining us."

"The general is coming here?"

"Yes," Reid said. "He called from Paris."

Mueller thought about it. "You and Karl go back a long way together, is that correct?"

"Since the fifties."

"You know his situation in Munich? His house, his staff, his . . . friends?"

"Yes."

"It is a good life."

Reid's eyes narrowed. "What are you driving at?"

"He would come here only if all of that was gone, or was about to be taken away from him. He would not take the risk otherwise."

Reid saw it at once. "Damn."

"I don't think you should stop him from coming here," Mueller said. He sipped his tea. "But make different arrangements, if that is possible, to get him here in a very roundabout manner."

"Do you think he may be followed?"

"It's a possibility."

"When he gets here, then what?"

Mueller looked over the rim of his cup at Reid. "I'll take care of it," he said, his voice as gentle as a funeral director's.

McGarvey packed his single bag, checked out of the hotel, and arrived back at the TWA hangar well before 3:00 P.M. Kennedy, Socrates, and Sir Malcolm O'Toole were in deep conversation on the floor, so without bothering them McGarvey went aboard the company P522 that had been brought around to the ramp. The stewardess stowed his bag and brought him a drink. Three minutes later a subdued Kennedy and Socrates came aboard, and within ten minutes they were airborne, climbing to the west.

Socrates stretched out on one of the couches in back, and Kennedy sat down beside McGarvey. "Did you finish your business in town?"

"All of it that was important," McGarvey said.

"I tried to call Dominique, but her office said she was out of the city."

"I sent her away. I think with what's been happening, and with what's likely to happen, she's better off out of the way."

"I suppose you're right." Kennedy looked toward the open door to the flight deck. "Sir Malcolm is worried that the sabotage might be directed at Rolls. He wants to put a hold on our engine orders."

"Even the hydrogen burner?"

"Especially the new one. That alone would be devastating to us. And he knows it."

"He's trying to save his company's skin."

"Can't say as I blame him," Kennedy admitted. "But all of this will be over, one way or the other, soon, won't it?"

"I think so," McGarvey answered. "I spoke with Yamagata again. He's invited me to Tokyo to discuss my offer."

Kennedy looked at him blankly. "What could you possibly say to them? They'll realize immediately that you aren't making a legitimate offer."

"That's the point, David. But let's wait until we get to Portland so we don't have to go over the same ground twice."

"We should be touching down around six, Pacific time. We'll meet at my house for dinner. You'll stay with us."

"That's not a very good idea," McGarvey said.

"As you wish." Kennedy stifled a yawn. "It's going to be a long night. I'm going to try to get some rest."

When Kennedy was gone, McGarvey motioned the stew for another drink. There'd be plenty of time to sleep later. He was too keyed up now. In any event he'd been fearful of sleep for a long time. He'd fought it ever since his parents died, possibly murdered, though there'd never been any proof, or suspects, and he'd inadvertently learned the truth about their lives. It was a revelation that had shaken him to the core; one he'd shared with no one, not his sister, not his wives, and especially not the Company. There was no one left from the old days, so he supposed it didn't really matter who knew, although Howard Ryan and his type would probably try to use the information against him. If that were ever to happen, he told himself, if Ryan were ever to cross swords with him in that manner, he would almost certainly kill the man.

"Sir, here's your drink."

McGarvey looked up into the young stew's pretty face. Her name tag read LINDA. "A few more and I might be able to get some rest, Linda."

She smiled. "I know what you mean, Mr. McGarvey. I get nervous flying sometimes too."

Chief Signalman Joseph Woodmark punched the five-bell designator and immediately transmitted the FLASH-priority message that had just been hand delivered from HQ and logged in two minutes ago.

Z201223ZJAN

TOP SECRET

FM: CINC 7TH FLEET

TO: CINCPACOM

SUBJECT: STATUS CHRYSANTHEMUM

1. CHRYSANTHEMUM SAILED, PRESUMABLY WITH FULL CREW AND STORES AT APPROXIMATELY 1900Z. A RELIABLE SOURCE REPORTED SEEING LT. CMDR. SEIJI KIYODA BOARDING WITH HIS XO LT. IKURO MINORI. THE BOAT WAS TRACKED OUT OF TOKYO BAY WHERE SHE SUBMERGED. HER LAST KNOWN COURSE WAS 210-DEGS.

2. THE 24-HOUR GUARD WAS REMOVED ONE HOUR EARLIER FROM CHRYSANTHEMUM'S BERTH. MSDF ISSUED NO SAILING ANNOUNCEMENT AS IT USUALLY DOES.

3. REQUEST SOONEST POSSIBLE FLEET DISSEMINATION OF THIS INFORMATION. ALSO REQUEST THAT CHRYSANTHEMUM IS TO BE CONSIDERED HOSTILE XX RPT XX REQUEST THAT CHRYSANTHEMUM BE CONSIDERED HOSTILE.
EOM

That would certainly heat things up, Woodmark thought. The bastards on the other side of the harbor were apparently starting to stretch their muscles. Chrysanthemum was the code name for the MSDF submarine *Samisho* whose captain had been charged with treason. The boat was off and sailing again. This time on a course just west of south . . . directly toward our forces on Okinawa.

"I can't sleep," Kennedy said, slumping into the seat next to McGarvey. "I don't know where the hell we're heading. I no longer have a handle on it, you know what I mean?"

"That's why you came to me in the first place."

McGarvey felt mean around the edges. It was tiredness, in part. And in part because Dominique had followed his suggestion and had gotten out of the city. It was bothersome, however, that she had not confided in him. McGarvey was beginning to have his fill of amateurs.

"It's the crash. It's taken a lot out of us. We lost some damned fine people."

McGarvey thought about Mati who'd died in the Paris Airbus crash. He'd lost some damned fine people in his time too. "I know what you mean."

Kennedy looked at him. "It's different than I thought it would be. You're different."

"I don't build airplanes."

"And I've never killed a person. I have no idea how to relate to you. What to say."

"Are you firing me?"

Kennedy shook his head and looked away momentarily. "We're in too deep now. It's too late. Maybe it was too late even before we came to you, I don't know. But I'm fairly certain that whether Guerin survives or not will depend upon whether or not you succeed."

"Not too late to step away from the plate, David," McGarvey said, giving the airline executive a way out. "You use Rolls-Royce engines. You're going to subcontract wing panels to the Russians. So make a deal with the Japanese. Boeing has had success with them."

"They're murderers."

"You might save lives."

"Never," Kennedy said with feeling. "Not now, not after what they've done to us."

"Do you want me to kill them for you? Fight fire with fire?"

"You told Dominique that your job was saving lives, not taking them. She believes you, and so do I."

McGarvey looked out the window. It would be getting dark in Washington, but they were flying west, chasing the sun, so they would have a few hours reprieve from the night. He'd once asked Phil Carrara if anything they had done in the past ten years had had any effect on how the world had turned out. Carrara's reply had been bothersome. The DDO had told McGarvey that he hoped they'd made a difference, because if he believed for one minute that they had not, it would mean their lives had been terrible wastes. McGarvey had hoped for a little more assurance and a little less sincerity.

"You tell me, Mac. You're the expert. Do we back away from this one? Do we give you severance pay, and then kiss and make up with the Japanese? Do we say fuck those people in '90, and poor goddamned Jeff Soderstrom and the others?"

Kennedy was a good man, McGarvey thought. He had the right stuff. His sense of justice was as clearly defined as the edge on a razor. No mistaking his loyalties.

"Well, I'm not turning my back on them. Neither is Al Vasilanti nor anyone else in this company. What about you? Are you still with us?"

"For the duration," McGarvey said. What other choice did he have?

Newton Kilbourne was the kid born on the wrong side of the tracks who made good. He stood on the engineers' gallery gazing at the P/C2622 on the prototype assembly floor. Building airplanes had been nearly the same as building automobiles, until this one. *Time* magazine said that this airplane was the most sophisticated and most complicated machine ever built. She was on this week's cover, her variable geometry wings fully extended, hanging in space, nose high, the curvature of the earth visible beneath her sonic nose baffles that looked like drooping walrus moustaches. Even on the floor, surrounded by scaffolding and platforms, workers scrambling in, around, and over her like ants at a picnic feast, she looked as if she were flying at supersonic speeds, and Kilbourne was proud. But they were trying to kill her, and it was as if someone were trying to rip out his heart. The pain could have been no worse.

He was a large man, with a thick torso, a massive head set on a twenty-one-inch neck, and huge, rock-hard fists. As a young man he'd been a street scrapper. In the navy, he'd held the fleet boxing championship. Middle age and a desk job had done little to diminish his powers. But this time there was no clear target to hit, no ugly face to smash, no kidneys to punch. Only sneaking around and spying. And sabotaging, he thought sadly. The bastards.

Al Vasilanti came onto the hangar floor, walked around to the front of the futuristic-looking airplane, and stood gazing up at her.

Kilbourne walked to the end of the gallery and took the stairs down. The bulk of the engineering was completed. Only the flight-readiness people were left on the project. The gallery seemed empty.

"When did you get back, Al?" Kilbourne asked as he approached, but he was stopped in his tracks when he got close enough to see what condition Vasilanti was in. The old man looked old. His body seemed to have shrunk inward, and his face had sagged and wrinkled. The sparkle had faded from his eyes.

"She's a beautiful machine, Newt. You've done a magnificent job. The board didn't want me to hire you, but I told them to go to hell." Vasilanti chuckled, the sound dry, like corn stalks rustling in a breeze.

"There's more to be done."

"You'll do it."

"If they'll leave us alone."

Vasilanti tore his eyes away from the airplane and looked bleakly at Kilbourne. His expression was cold, his entire posture changed, as if he were an animal about to strike. "It'll be their mistake if they don't back away."

"Maybe we need help from Washington."

"Fuck them," Vasilanti said. "This airplane will fly, Newton. Any man gets in my way will die. If need be I'll kill him myself."

"Whatever it takes, I'm with you, Al."

"Of course you are," Vasilanti said. "McGarvey will do it for us."

"I don't trust him," Kilbourne said, but Vasilanti turned away and looked up at the airplane again.

"There's never been anything like this. Never."

"No, sir."

"We'll call her 'America,'" Vasilanti said. "And screw all the sonsabitches who'll think that's corny. I want the name painted on both sides of her fuselage, and the flag painted on her tail feathers."

Kilbourne didn't know whether to laugh or cry. "At least it's better than 'Savior.'"

"She'll be that, too," Vasilanti said. "But she's 'America,' and everything that means. Hope, promise for the future, fair play, honesty."

Vasilanti was of another era, Kilbourne thought sadly. But maybe it was time, after all, to bring back a little of the old to mix with the new. *America.* He smiled, the first time in weeks. "I'll have it done by morning, Al."

"See that you do," Vasilanti said.

"By going to Japan I'll be stirring up a hornet's nest," McGarvey said.

"Al Vasilanti did the same thing by showing off the P/C2622," Kennedy replied.

"They'll react. You'll have to handle it."

"I'm not sure that we're up to it. But as I said we don't have the choice."

"More airplanes could fall out of the sky. Maybe it'd be better if you did give up."

"We've covered that, Mac. Now, if you're going to work for me I don't want to hear that kind of shit again. Clear?"

"Clear," McGarvey said, and he felt like a heel for maneuvering the man the way he had.

Technically their patrol should have been on the homeward stretch, Commander Michael Hanrahan told himself. By now the *USS Thorn* should have been heading for the barn at Yokosuka for some much needed R&R, although with the trouble up there he figured he'd have to wrangle transportation for his people to Seoul or maybe even down to Taipei. Yokosuka wasn't safe.

After this one he was due to be rotated stateside for Pentagon duty. Rumor had it that he was being looked at for his eagle, which, considering how little time in grade he had as commander, would put him on the fast track for his first star. Maybe three years, tops four or five. Not bad for a thirty-eight-year-old mick who'd graduated from the Academy at the bottom of the heap. But in the ensuing sixteen years he had busted his hump. Except for flattops, there wasn't a ship or boat in the navy that he didn't know inside and out. From submarines to captain's gigs, Hanrahan had gone to school on design, construction, and operational techniques so that he could recite page and verse from just about every manual in current use. His friends sometimes called him "Professor," and so far as he knew his men liked and trusted him, which in itself wasn't bad in the modern navy.

The only problem was he'd never fired a shot in anger in his career. He'd missed Vietnam, and he'd not participated in the Gulf War. And frankly he didn't know how he would react under fire. Well, he hoped.

You couldn't ask for a better ship under you than the *Thorn,* he assured himself for the tenth time this morning. She was a Spruance-class destroyer laid down in the late seventies and retrofitted with new weapons and electronics systems numerous times in her eighteen-year life. At a little over 560 feet, her four General Electric LM2500 gas turbine engines could push her 7,800 tons through the water at speeds in excess of thirty knots.

In addition to the Sea Sparrow Improved Point Defense Management System (IPDMS) and Harpoon anti-ship missiles, the *Thorn* carried Phalanx Close In Weapons Systems (CIWS) cannons that fired radar-aimed 20 mm Mk 149 depleted-uranium sub-caliber ammunition at burst rates of over four thousand rounds a minute, five-inch deck mounted guns, Mk32 torpedoes, Tomahawk cruise missiles, and the Mk41 Vertical Launch Anti-submarine Rocket System. Some of her ASW rounds were loaded with one kiloton nuclear warheads. Combined with the sophisticated SOS-53C bow sonar system, towed arrays, numerous radars, and a pair of

SH-60F LAMPS III ASW helicopters, no submarine currently operated by any navy in the world was completely safe from the *Thorn* and her crew of two hundred ninety-six men and officers.

The legend over the door to the ship's Combat Information Center below decks was simple and to the point: "Find 'em, shoot 'em, kill 'em."

"Let me see that message again, Red," Hanrahan said. "Maybe we can get out of it after all."

The *Thorn*'s executive officer, Lieutenant Commander Willis Ryder—Red to his friends—handed over the flimsy that comms had sent up less than ten minutes ago. "Looks airtight to me, skipper."

"Nothing's that black and white."

The message from Seventh Fleet Operations was simple and direct. It ordered the *Thorn,* which was 250 nautical miles south of Tokyo Bay, inbound for Yokosuka, to intercept the Yuushio-class MSDF submarine *Samisho,* submerged and possibly heading south. Absolutely no loopholes. But the third, fourth, and fifth paragraphs were the most disturbing to Hanrahan.

3. IT IS BELIEVED THAT THE SAMISHO WAS THE MSDF SUBMARINE INVOLVED IN THE TATAR STRAIT SINKING OF THE RUSSIAN NAVY FRIGATE MENSHINKSKY. THEREFORE THE SAMISHO IS TO BE CONSIDERED POSSIBLY HOSTILE XX RPT XX THE SAMISHO IS TO BE CONSIDERED POSSIBLY HOSTILE.

4. ONCE YOU HAVE INTERCEPTED THE SAMISHO YOU WILL FOLLOW HER UNTIL OTHERWISE DIRECTED.

5. YOU ARE TO MAINTAIN A DEFENSIVE POSTURE AT ALL TIMES. YOU WILL RETURN FIRE ONLY IF FIRST FIRED UPON XX RPT XX YOU ARE AUTHORIZED TO RETURN FIRE ONLY IF FIRST FIRED UPON.

GOOD LUCK MIKE XX TOM SENDS XX

EOM

"I'm not going to get into a shooting match with the Japanese Navy," Hanrahan said.

"Skipper, I don't think anybody wants that."

"You read the brief. Unless Intel screwed up the sequence of events, the *Samisho* tricked the Russians into taking the first shot. That will not happen to us."

"We've got the advantage. The Russians had no idea that he might try something funny. All we have to do is find him and stalk him."

"That's right, Red," Hanrahan said distantly. He was rereading the message.

He and Ryder could have been brothers. Both men were husky, both had red hair—though Ryder's was a thicker, brighter red—both had freckles, and both were very bright. The main difference between them was that Hanrahan was sometimes indecisive while Ryder was sometimes too quick. Together they made a good team.

Hanrahan looked up, a sly grin twisting the corners of his mouth. "If I read this correctly, we're supposed to find the *Samisho* and stick with her wherever she goes until we're relieved. Seventh says she sailed with full stores, which means we could be out here for another ninety days."

"They won't keep us out here that long, Captain."

"Doesn't matter, because I have no intention of chasing that boat all over the Pacific."

"Sir?"

"Red, it's my intention to be back in Yokosuka within forty-eight hours, mission accomplished."

"Captain, I'm one hundred percent behind you. But I will not participate in a sham search. If I'm ordered to find the *Samisho* I'll do everything within my power to do it. Otherwise I'd just be wasting your time, my time, and the time of a damned fine crew."

"That was a pretty speech, X," Hanrahan said frostily. It pissed him off that his executive officer didn't have more trust in him. They'd sailed together long enough.

"I'm sorry, sir. Tell me what you want, and I'll get to it."

"We're going to find the *Samisho*, Red, as rapidly as we can. And then we're going to herd her back to port."

"She might not want to turn tail," Ryder said. "She's a quiet boat. She could try to sneak around us."

"I don't think so," Hanrahan said. He picked up the growler phone, and punched the number for the Combat Information Center. "This is the Commanding Officer. Sonar picking up anything yet on passive?"

"Negative, sir."

"Let me talk to Don."

"Aye, aye, Captain."

Lieutenant Donald Sattler was CIC officer. He was an Annapolis graduate and a fine man. They didn't come much better in Hanrahan's book.

"Good morning, Skipper. Sonar's picked up nothing yet, but we just started."

"I want both choppers up as soon as possible."

"They'll be airborne within five minutes."

"How's it look out there?"

"Surface conditions are good, and there's very little traffic, which means our search pattern won't be cluttered. The sharp thermoclines are below eight hundred feet, so unless that sub-driver has gone deep, or has decided for some reason to run silent, we'll have a pretty good chance of nailing him."

"In passive mode."

"That's right, Captain," Sattler said.

"As soon as the choppers are up and on station I want sonar to go active. I want to find the bastard and I don't want to screw around doing it."

Ryder raised his eyebrows.

"He'll not only know that we're up here, Skipper, he'll know that we're looking for him," the CIC officer said.

"That he will, Don. I want this mission brought to termination as expeditiously as possible. Do I make myself clear?"

"Yes, sir," Sattler replied. "If he's out there, we'll know it real quick."

"Conn, sonar."

Lieutenant Minori answered the comms. "Conn, *hai*."

"I have sonar contact, range fifteen thousand meters

and closing. It's an American war ship. They're pinging us."

"On the way." Minori hit the ship's intercom. "Captain to sonar on the double."

Kiyoda reached sonar just behind Minori, his uniform blouse unbuttoned, his eyes still bleary from sleep.

"What is it?" he asked.

"It's an American Spruance-class destroyer, *kan-cho-dono*," Chief Sonarman Tsutomu Nakayama said. "Bearing zero-five-five, and closing. Under fourteen thousand meters now."

"Still pinging?" Minori asked.

"*Hai.* But I don't think she has us yet."

"What's our depth, Ikuo?" Kiyoda asked.

"Seventy meters. We have a sharp thermocline about two hundred meters under our keel. We could make a try for it."

Kiyoda shook his head. He was watching the display on the screen. "Too late for that. Reduce speed to four knots, turn left to new course one-seven-five."

Minori picked up the growler and relayed the order to the helm. The left turn put them at right angles to the oncoming destroyer, but it would get them out of the way in the minimum time.

"Designate contact as sierra-zero-nine. Sonar conditions good, topsides fairly flat," Nakayama said. "There's a better than even chance he'll find us, *kan-cho*."

This was too close to home waters for Kiyoda's liking. If he instigated another incident now the MSDF would know his location and would send a chopper with a dipping buoy to order him home. They would come after him if he did not comply, but he was not going to run away from a challenge without some response. Finesse, he thought, was everything.

"We're on new course one-seven-five. Recommend we begin a slow dive to three hundred meters," Minori said. "With all that noise they won't hear us blowing our tanks."

"*Matte, kan-cho*," the sonarman said, holding up a

hand for Kiyoda to wait. He jabbed a finger at a spike on the screen.

"They have us, *kan-cho*. His blade count is increasing."

"It's him and he knows we've got a lock," Sattler reported, from CIC.

Within two minutes Able chopper would be directly above the submarine and would drop a dunking sonar, which would make ID and location one-hundred percent certain.

"What's he doing?" Ryder asked.

"He turned beam on and slowed down. Probably trying to sneak off."

"We're bringing in more resources. The skipper wants him boxed in and respectful."

"I hear you," Sattler replied.

"Conn, sonar. They've placed a sonobuoy in the water, range about five hundred meters, bearing one-eight-zero," Nakayama said.

"They will have launched one or both of their LAMPS III helicopters," Minori told Kiyoda. They were forward in the attack center.

"Very well, Ikuo. Bring the boat to battle stations," Kiyoda replied calmly. He buttoned his uniform blouse and accepted a cup of tea from the steward.

Minori relayed the order, and a Klaxon sounded through the sub. Within moments every watertight hatch in the boat was closed and dogged.

"Report battle stations ready," Minori said.

Kiyoda picked up the ship's comms. "Weapons, conn. Load tubes one, two, and three with standard HE torpedoes, and load tube four with a Harpoon."

Weapons Control Officer Lieutenant Shuichiyo Takasaki repeated the order. *"Yo-so-ro."*

Kiyoda turned and smiled. His officers were watching him expectantly.

"Now let's see what the Americans are made of," he said. "Come right nine-zero degrees to new course two-six-five. Make our speed two-five knots. Give me a continuous firing solution on the target."

"Hai, kan-cho," Minori said, his eyes glittering.

Two thousand five hundred feet above the surface, the Lockheed P-3C Orion ASW patrol aircraft was flying a grid pattern at one hundred eighty knots. She'd been in the vicinity at the beginning of her patrol when the *Thorn* asked for help.

"Have you got him yet?" the pilot asked.

"I can count her rivets," the ELINT officer, Ensign Carl Gifford, reported. "We picked her out with the MAD on the first pass. Very clear picture. She's about two hundred feet down, but she's accelerating and turning inboard toward the *Thorn*. Skipper, unless I miss my guess, that sub-driver is setting up for an attack."

MAD was their Magnetic Anomaly Detector, which never missed. It was one of the more powerful ASW tools aboard the Orion.

"Their chopper should have it," the pilot, Lieutenant Fred White, said. He hauled the big plane around for another pass. "Call the *Thorn* and tell them what we're showing. Recommend that they break off until we can get a reading from Fleet."

"Aye, aye, Skipper."

White turned to his co-pilot, Lieutenant j.g. John Littlemore. "Call Operations and lay it in their laps. I for one don't want to get into a shooting match with the Japs. I think that sub-driver is nuts."

Seventh Fleet Northern Patrol Duty Officer Captain Walt Townsend put down his telephone and studied the big board across the room. An electronic map showed an area twelve hundred miles in diameter with Yokosuka at the center and Okinawa at the extreme south. For some reason the crazy bastard conning the *Samisho* wanted to prove a point by heading south. MSDF Submarine Fleet HQ was silent, and the buck had been passed back to Operations.

Was it worth an incident like the one up in the strait

with the Russians, he asked himself? Not likely. Least-ways not just yet.

He called Communications. "Send a flash designated message to Mike Hanrahan aboard the *Thorn*. Tell him to break off immediately. He's to follow the *Samisho* and report her movements. Nothing more."

"Come left to new course two-one-zero. Make our speed ten knots."

"Smart move, Captain," Ryder said after he'd relayed the orders. "He'll know that we no longer want to provoke him but that our intention is to follow him if he wants to continue south."

Hanrahan shook his head in irritation. "Ninety days, Red. That's how long we could be playing cat and mouse with that bastard."

"Never happen."

"You're damned right it won't, because every chance I get I'm going to lean on him."

Ryder started to object, but Hanrahan held him off with a scowl.

"I'll expect your support, X. Completely."

The comment stung, but Ryder nodded tightly. "You've got it, Skipper." He didn't add *You've always had it*.

"He's turning away, and his blade count is coming down."

Minori keyed the comms. "Which way did he turn, Nakayama?"

"*Tori-kaji,*" to port, the sonarman reported. He sounded excited. "Yes, his new course is two-one-zero. I'm estimating he's making turns for ten knots."

Minori turned to Kiyoda. "*Kan-cho,* it looks as if they do not wish to take the bait."

"Very well, secure from battle stations. Make our course two-one-zero, our speed eleven knots."

"I suggest we initiate a shallow-angle dive to three hundred meters," Minori said.

"Negative," Kiyoda replied mildly. "That destroyer

was inbound to Yokosuka. My guess is that her patrol was complete and she was going home. But now she has had a change of orders. She will follow us, and I have no wish to lose her." In one respect Kiyoda was almost sorry that the American warship had broken off the engagement. The Russian frigate had been easy, but a Spruance-class destroyer was a far more sophisticated weapons system. The challenge would have been interesting. And if he had sunk or damaged the American vessel the repercussions *Kamiya-san* had predicted would certainly have come to pass. But much sooner than he thought. So it was better that no shots had been fired. But for more than one reason. This was neither the time nor the place, and the American captain was too fresh, too alert, too much in control. In the right waters, at the right time, and after repeated provocations, the situation would be different.

"Shall we unload the torpedoes from one, two, and three, and the missile from four?"

"No," Kiyoda said. He felt dreamy, as if he could envision everything that would occur over the next thirty-six to forty-eight hours. He felt as if by dreaming the future he could make it so. It was powerful.

"Hai, kan-cho," Minori said.

Kiyoda focused on his executive officer. "The weapons will remain in place."

"Very well."

"We are not finished, Ikuo. We have only just begun."

"I'll need to present a good front when I get to Tokyo," McGarvey said. "I'll have to do my homework."

"The sooner you make your move the sooner they'll react," Kennedy replied tiredly. They were a few minutes from Portland International Airport. Socrates was sound asleep, and McGarvey envied the man for it.

"I'll need a carte blanche from you."

"I think the only thing you don't know about us yet is our bathroom habits."

"I need to know everything there is to know about the 2622."

Kennedy managed to smile. "Maybe you can sell a few for us while you're at it."

Linda went back to wake Socrates so that the engineer could strap in for landing. McGarvey watched her lithe movements. She reminded him of his daughter Elizabeth. Maybe after this was over he would retire.

The world had indeed changed. And, he supposed, in some measure he'd been and continued to be an instrument of that change. The fact was such thoughts did nothing to dispel his bleak mood. What was he looking for, he asked himself? What?

FIFTEEN

L et me introduce you to Arimoto Yamagata."
Kennedy shook hands with the Japanese. "You're with JAL, aren't you?"

"That's right," Yamagata said. "I've spoken with Mr. McGarvey. A very sharp individual. I thought I'd come out here to see Portland for myself."

Their host, Marvin Saunders, was one of the heavy-hitters in real estate development in the Portland-Vancouver area. He'd put up two major downtown office buildings with mostly Japanese money. He'd been involved with the Japanese businessman who'd tried to buy into the San Francisco Giants. And he'd built four separate neighborhoods in and around the city that catered to Guerin middle- and upper-level managers. He'd invited the Kennedys and a dozen others to his palatial Lake Oswego home to meet someone he said was interesting. Given Saunders's connections with the Japanese, McGarvey thought it would be worthwhile for Kennedy to accept, but Yamagata had come as a surprise.

"I wonder if you know that David was one of our top

astronauts before Al Vasilanti lured him out here to build airplanes?" Saunders said.

"Yes, of course." Yamagata smiled. "In addition to baseball cards, Japanese schoolchildren collect astronaut cards. Yours is still a favorite."

"I didn't know that," Kennedy's wife Chance said.

"And this lovely lady is David's wife, Chance Kennedy."

Yamagata turned his complete attention to her, his smile softening. "I'm very pleased to meet you. Your name is rare, isn't it?"

"My mother wasn't supposed to have children. So when I came along my father said I was 'one chance in a million.'"

"Charming," the Japanese said. "Do you work in the industry alongside your husband?"

Chance shook her head. "No." She was a slightly built woman with large round eyes and a lot of blonde hair. She looked unhappy.

"One in the family is enough," Kennedy said.

"Perhaps that's wisest," Yamagata said. "Did Mr. McGarvey come with you?"

"No," Kennedy said.

"Will you be sending him to Tokyo after all?"

The question was startling because of its directness. "Yes, we think so. But it may not be for another day or so. We're a little busy at the moment because of the crash."

"I understand."

"Don't tell me that Guerin is finally going to start selling in Japan," Saunders said. "Move over Boeing."

"Something like that," Yamagata replied before Kennedy could say anything. "Which is why I'm in Portland. I was told to come here and be charming."

Saunders laughed. "He wasn't here fifteen minutes and my wife wanted to run away with him. I'm going to have to watch her like a hawk. But seriously, I think it's a damned good idea that's been on the back burner too long. We're in a global economy whether we like it or not. And with the Japanese offer of a free trade agreement—hell, I don't see any other choice for Guerin except to expand to the east. It'd be a great partnership."

"We think so," Yamagata said. "At least in principle. Of course there would be many obstacles to overcome."

"How do you see that?" Saunders asked.

"It's a matter of trust—on both sides of the Pacific. After the unfortunate incident a few days ago in Yokosuka, and the demonstrations in Tokyo, I'm told that anti-Japanese sentiment is building in America."

"Not in this house," Saunders said heartily. A few of his other guests gathered closer. They nodded their approval. The Kennedys were the only Guerin executives here tonight, but the other guests were influential in Portland's business community.

"The American Northwest has traditionally understood Japan," Yamagata said. "It is why so many Japanese emigrate to this region. But that understanding may not be entirely shared in New York or Washington."

"I think the attitude in the White House will change after the Tokyo Economic Summit next month. This President seems to be committed to working with your government." Saunders turned to Kennedy. "The big surprise is Al Vasilanti's about-face. About time, I'd say."

"It may be premature to talk about any sort of a deal between us," Yamagata cautioned. "We're still in the very early exploratory stage."

"Mr. Yamagata is right," Kennedy said tightly. "It's too early to be making any announcements."

"Not to worry, David. You know the house rules: No journalists allowed within a hundred yards, and absolutely nothing said here gets repeated outside."

"A sensible set of rules," Yamagata said, smiling directly at Chance.

The Faraday cage was completed and in place around the heat monitor/alarm subassembly. No stray electrical or electromagnetic impulses would emanate from the device, nor would any signal from outside penetrate the protective screen. Louis Zerkel had studied the connections for the engine mount for several hours, trying to puzzle out what he was seeing with his own two eyes versus what he knew he should be seeing.

"Something's wrong," he muttered. A second supposedly spare pin on the replacement module in the subassembly was connected through a small amplifying circuit not to one of the engine-frame sensor plugs but to the frame ground. It made no sense. A signal was spit out by the module, its strength amplified, and it led to ground.

"Is something the matter with the unit?" Mueller asked.

"No," Zerkel said, looking up. "I don't know. Something doesn't add up."

"A manufacturing mistake?"

Zerkel interrupted. "Not likely. InterTech doesn't work that sloppy. This was designed this way. But I don't know what they meant by it. Could be crucial, but maybe not. Perhaps if the output signal were modulated maybe the frame itself could turn out to be resonant. But again, for what purpose? Why energize the frame?

"If it were possible to get the frame and harness I could isolate the module and pull it apart to see just what they were aiming for. Either that or run it through the mainframe circuit analyzer. But there's no going back. I haven't looked at the television all day, but I'm pretty sure that my face is plastered over every newscast as a killer and saboteur. The question is are they making the connection between me and the crash right here in our backyard? Because if they are then it's going to get real hot around here." Zerkel looked up at Mueller. "And you know what? If none of that part has hit the news then we're in even bigger trouble than I thought. Because it'll mean that the Japs are looking for me.

"The real problem here is that I don't know diddly squat about Rolls-Royce jet engines. The board says an overheat caused the fan blades to disintegrate, which means they're homing in on Rolls. But in order for me to understand what they're talking about I have to know engines, and that's not possible. So I'm going to come up with another approach.

"The idea is to bring down a bunch of airplanes all at the same time, or near enough the same time so there's no chance the fleet will be grounded before we're done. But if they're guarding the back door as well as the front, and you really don't know what's inside, then there's only one thing left to do, and that's tear the house down. What do you think about that?"

"I don't understand you," Mueller said. "Can you do this thing or not?"

Zerkel grinned, his eyes wild. "Hell, yes, I can do it. But it's going to be crude, nowhere near as sophisticated as I wanted it to be. It's simple lack of data, or even access to data. I could get into the Rolls engineering computer, but I'd have to educate myself on engine design parameters. Not that I couldn't do it, but it would take time. I don't think we've got much time."

"What is it you're going to do?" Mueller asked.

"I'm pretty sure that there's nothing wrong with the jet engines on those airplanes. The triggering device is definitely integral to the heat monitor system. But until I understand completely what's going on, I'm going to back off from trying to trigger it. It's just a feeling, but for now I've got something else to do."

"Distributing the trigger signals?" Mueller prompted.

"Right on." Zerkel keyed up a map of the United States on one of the computer monitors. The areas around most of the major metropolitan centers were shaded in red. "Washington, New York, Atlanta, Chicago, Denver, Los Angeles, they're all designated TCAs—Terminal Control Areas—by the FAA. Any airplane flying under a certain altitude within those TCAs must be equipped with a transponder and an encoding altimeter."

"Continue."

"When an airplane shows up on an Air Traffic Control radar screen, its transponder sends an identifying signal to the ground that tells ATC its exact type and tail number. The encoding altimeter tells the scope dope the airplane's exact altitude."

"Yes, I know this," Mueller said. It was the same in Europe.

"That means ATC computers and airplanes within every Terminal Control Area in this country talk to each other electronically," Zerkel said brightly. "What do you think about that?"

"The signals go both ways?"

"Exactly. When the time comes for us to strike, the triggering signals will be sent out by the Air Traffic Control centers on orders from InterTech's mainframe."

"How?"

"It'll be up to Mr. Reid how many centers you want to hit. But in each Terminal Control Area's ATC facility someone is going to have to install a repeater."

"There'll be risks," Mueller said softly. He didn't like what he was hearing.

"There are risks for all of us, but I'll make it easy. The repeaters that I'll build will be about the size of a package of cigarettes. You won't have to make any electrical connections, or anything like that. Just hide the units behind the computers or radar consoles. When they receive the signals from InterTech, my repeaters will pass them through to the outgoing radar signals. Every airplane within the TCA will get the extra spike, but only Guerin's airplanes will know what to do with it." Zerkel chuckled.

"But this has to be blamed on the Japanese," Mueller said.

Zerkel's grin broadened. "InterTech will send out the trigger pulse on electronic orders from Tokyo Bank's computer center."

"Will he continue to follow us?" Lieutenant Minori asked. He and his captain were hunched over the chart table at the forward end of the cramped attack center.

In the past thirty-six hours since they'd made contact with the American destroyer they had varied their speed from eleven knots to twenty-two knots and their depth from seventy meters to two hundred meters, careful not to show the Americans the *Samisho*'s true best speed submerged nor dip below the thermocline. They wanted to make sure the American skipper would stick with them. But like all submarines they were blind aft when underway. Cavitation noises made by the propeller drowned out all passive sonar sounds behind them. Therefore they had turned inboard twice in the past twenty hours and stopped their motors so they could listen. Both times the destroyer had been behind them on the same course and speed. And both times the American captain had turned inboard and had reduced his speed in response.

"By now he has to know where we're heading," Kiyoda said. He stabbed a blunt finger at a point on the chart just south of Kyushu where the Takara Strait connected the Pacific Ocean to the East China Sea. It was one region of the world's oceans that the MSDF knew much better than the American navy. Once through the strait the advantage would belong to the *Samisho,* something the destroyer's captain had to know. And once in the East China Sea Kiyoda could take his boat to Okinawa's back door.

It would make for some interesting choices on the surface, Kiyoda thought. These were Japanese home waters, but the destroyer captain would know that the submarine he was tracking was the same one that had sunk the Russian frigate. If Seventh Fleet Intelligence was any good it would have informed its ships at sea that the *Samisho* had slipped out of Yokosuka with its captain and full stores aboard.

"He'll have to make his move within the next few hours," Minori said. "Maybe he has called for help."

Kiyoda looked up at his XO. "What is your thinking, Ikuo? What will he do? Shoot?"

Minori studied the chart. "He has superior speed. He might try to block our passage through the strait. The deepest channel is quite narrow."

"It would still put him in a position where he would have to shoot or lose."

"The thermocline is holding at about three hundred meters. We could fool him by heading south, on the outside, and once he took our bait we could dive deep and circle back."

Kiyoda smiled. "Admirable. If I wanted to lose him it is exactly what I would do. But that is not what I wish. We're not here for that purpose."

"If we sink this one our homecoming will not be so benign as it was before."

When—not if—that American warship goes to the bottom in Japanese territorial waters the circle will be complete. Kamiya-san's Morning Star will begin.

"Only if we fire first," Kiyoda said. "Come left to three-one-five."

"*Hai*, turning left to three-one-five degrees," Minori repeated the order.

"Come to all-ahead stop."

"*Yo-so-ro, kan-cho!*"

"Target has turned inboard again and is fading, new course three-one-five," Don Sattler, the *Thorn's* Combat Information Officer said.

"Bridge, aye," Ryder replied. He put down the growler. "He's stopping for another look, skipper. New course three-one-five."

Hanrahan studied the chart. "He'll try for the strait this time. I can feel it."

Ryder joined the captain. "He'd be a fool to go for it out in the open like this. All he has to do is duck below the thermocline where'd we'd lose him, and the option would be his. Wouldn't be a damned thing we could do to stop him. If we hung around the narrows he might continue south and pop inside someplace else. If we took the bait he'd switch back and sneak under us."

"He's not going to do that, Red," Hanrahan said. "Because I'm going to lean on him again."

"Still might force him to duck and run."

Hanrahan looked up. "Then our assets coming from Okinawa will handle it. But it's not going to happen that way. He wants to confront us. Maybe here, maybe farther south. But I'm getting a definite feeling that the crazy sonofabitch wants to have it out with us."

"Seventh will be on our ass."

"I'm not going to shoot unless I'm shot at first," Hanrahan said. "But we're damned well going to be ready for it, and we're going to let him know that we are."

"Let's put the choppers up again, Skipper."

"Do it now, X. And call the Orion back. I want as much help as possible."

"Aye, aye, Skipper."

"Helm, come right to three-one-five," Hanrahan said. "Give me turns for thirty knots."

"Coming right to three-one-five, aye," the helmsman responded. "Engineering answering for speed of thirty knots, aye."

Hanrahan got Sattler on the growler. "Don, I think he's going to try for the strait this time. I'm going to end-run him and try to get at least ten thousand yards out front."

"That'll give him a pretty good firing solution on us if he wants to take it, Skipper."

"I know that. So I want no mistakes here. The choppers are going up again, and I've called for an Orion, so we'll have backup. In the meantime, I want sonar to go active. I want to know exactly what he's doing and how he's doing it."

Sattler lowered his voice. "Mike, that's an MSDF sub out there. We're allies, not enemies. Have you thought this out?"

"All the way, Don. Keep me posted."

"Will do, Captain."

The American destroyer was so close that when her sonar went active everybody aboard the *Samisho* could hear it. Kiyoda watched his attack-center crewmen. All of them, including Minori, looked up as if they could see through the skin of the hull and through eighty meters of water.

"Conn, sonar."

Kiyoda answered the comms. "This is your captain. We hear it, Nakayama." He felt a sense of well-being.

"Hai, kan-cho, but she's making turns for thirty knots, on a new course of three-one-five."

Kiyoda brought the data up on his command console and overlaid a chart outline showing the Takara Strait, Tanegashima and Yaku islands to the north, and the tiny rock, Kuchino, to the south. The target designated sierra-zero-nine was running directly for the entry to the strait, and within minutes she would be well out ahead of the *Samisho.*

"It's what you thought he would do, *kan-cho,"* his XO said.

Kiyoda nodded. "A little sooner than I thought. It would appear that he has concerns about us roaming the East China Sea."

"He has made his intentions very clear to us. Once he's in the strait he'll turn back and confront us bow on."

"Pinging us continuously."

"Hai, kan-cho. He'll want to know exactly what we're doing, and he'll want us to understand his interest. No mistakes."

Kiyoda keyed the comms. "Sonar, conn. What's his range and bearing?"

"Range five thousand meters, and now his bearing is changing. Estimate his new course two-nine-five."

The data was showing up on the command screen. "He's turned twenty degrees inboard," Minori observed.

"Still running around us. But on that course he'll cross our bows." Kiyoda smiled cruelly. It was for this moment, and the subsequent moments of strategy and battle, that he had been born. It was for this task that he'd been selected by *Kamiya-san,* and for which he had picked and trained his fine crew.

"We can help him, *kan-cho,* if it is still your desire to confront that destroyer captain," Minori said.

"Continue."

"I recommend that we come to fifteen knots and turn right seventy degrees—which will place us perpendicular to his port flank—while we make our depth twenty meters."

"Do it now," Kiyoda said, and he turned to his weapons control officer. "Flood tubes one, two, three, and four."

Minori turned back. "With their sonar active they might not catch it."

"I hope they do not," Kiyoda said. "When we are in position and have a firing solution, we need only open our doors and fire. But they will not expect such fast action. They will be waiting for flooding noises, and if need be we shall catch them by surprise."

"Hai, kan-cho, it will catch them by surprise."

The weather over Yokosuka was gray overcast, windy, and chilly, which suited the dark mood of Seventh Fleet Commander-in-Chief Vice Admiral Albert Ryland. He stepped out of his staff car in front of fleet HQ and sniffed the air. It smelled of the sea, and tidal flats, and of other mostly oriental odors: fermenting soya beans perhaps, raw fish, ginger. A foreign place that had always been a mystery to Westerners. Americans no longer belonged here, and yet he told himself a hundred times over that had the U.S. had a bigger presence in Japan in the 1930s maybe Pearl would never have happened. A lot of very intelligent people were predicting an all-out war with the Japanese within the next fifteen years. Ryland for one was a nonbeliever, yet he felt in his military gut that a confrontation between the U.S. and Japan was inevitable. Not an all-out war—the incident would fall far short of such insanity. But people would get killed. Of that he had absolutely no doubt. But was it happening now? Was that MSDF sub-driver getting into position to take the opening shots?

The weather was developing from the south. It meant that for now the tactical advantage lay slightly in favor of the submarine. Surface conditions would make operations aboard the *Thorn* difficult in the narrow strait where seas could build up rapidly. And these were Japanese waters that the MSDF knew a lot better than we did.

"We're supposed to get some rain, Admiral," Ryland's driver said.

"Don't I know it, Chief. Don't bother waiting. This one looks like an all-nighter."

"Yes, sir."

Ryland went in and took the elevator up to Operations on the fifth floor. It was 3:00 P.M. When he'd been recalled to headquarters, he'd been at a meeting with the mayor of Yokosuka about the recent trouble between U.S. Navy personnel and Japanese nationals. The *Samisho* was apparently heading into the East China Sea, the *Thorn* right on her tail. Some hard decisions were going to have to be made, and made soon.

His Operations Officer, Captain Thomas Byrne, was waiting for him. "We're running a three-way link between Mike Hanrahan aboard the *Thorn* and Fred White in one of our Orions. It looks as if that sub-driver wants to force the issue."

Byrne was a big, tall black man who'd played defensive end for Navy and who'd graduated number six in his class. Ryland, who was from Birmingham, Alabama, initially had some difficulty accepting a black man as his Ops officer. But that trouble had lasted only one day. Since that time Byrne was, in the admiral's book, one of the best officers in the navy.

"Nobody's fired any shots yet, I hope."

"No. But Mike is blocking the entrance to the strait, and the *Samisho* is on the way up."

They went down into the pit together where Seventh played its war games, and where search-and-rescue operations were conducted. Byrne had brought in some of his staffers, and by the looks on their faces they were dug in for the duration. The activity was centered on the area south of the Japanese rocket-launching facility on Tanegashima Island. Sensitive waters. But nothing on the display indicated that the MSDF or the Japanese Air Self Defense Force was involved in the unfolding drama. That didn't make sense to Ryland. If somebody were screwing around off Florida's Cape Kennedy, the U.S. Navy, Air Force, and Coast Guard would sure as hell be interested.

"Get me Hanrahan on the phone," Ryland said. He took off his coat and traded it to one of the ratings for a cup of strong, black coffee. Ships at sea ran on nuclear fuel or bunker oil. Admirals ran on coffee.

A half-minute later Byrne handed him the phone.

"Mike, this is Al Ryland. How's it looking down there?"

"Admiral, you know that we've been following *Chrysanthemum,* and now it looks as if she wants to get through the strait. I'm blocking the deep-water passage, and she's on the way up."

"Has she flooded her tubes?"

"We've been pinging her continuously to let her know what we're doing, but my chief sonarman thinks he might have heard flooding noises. Hard to tell for certain, sir."

"If you are fired upon, you can defend yourself, Mike. Do you understand?"

"Yes, sir."

"In the meantime I'm going to see if I can get you some relief down there. But Mike, whatever happens I want you to stick with that sub until you're told otherwise."

"Aye, aye, Admiral."

Ryland looked at the situation board. It just didn't make sense. "Get me Vice Admiral Shimakaze. Tell him it's urgent."

"Yes, sir," Byrne said. Ikuro Shimakaze was CINC of the Japanese Maritime Self Defense Force fleet.

Glen Zerkel stood on the floor of Prototype Assembly Hangar One at Guerin's Gales Creek facility, his mouth open. He was hidden in the shadows beneath a gallery of offices that ran the width of the huge building. Filling the vast hangar was the most fantastic airplane he'd ever seen. The word *America* was painted on her fuselage, and the American flag appeared on both of her two vertical stabilizers that towered a hundred feet off the floor. She was brightly lit by dozens of spotlights from above and below and from all sides. Scaffolding rose around both swept-back wings, where the cowlings had been removed from her engines. Even sitting like that, parts of her missing, parts of her imprisoned inside cages, the hypersonic airliner looked as if she were flying. As if she were climbing straight up into a blue-black sky, stars faintly visible even though it was bright daylight. She was Star Trek's *Enterprise,* only more sexy and fantastic because she was real.

Getting into Guerin's facilities, including this one, had been easy. The company was so vast that tight security was nearly impossible to maintain. It was simply too expensive. The Pantex nuclear assembly plant in Texas, for instance, was much smaller yet spent millions each year on security. Zerkel had penetrated that facility's outer perimeter several years ago but had to get out when he'd stupidly tripped an alarm. This place was much easier. He just didn't want to get careless. Too much was at stake. If he screwed it up he had no doubt that Mueller would kill him.

Zerkel took several photographs of the fantastic airplane. He wanted to show his brother what they were working on out here. He'd already seen Guerin's warehousing and parts distribution system, which included a vast depot that accommodated incoming shipments to Guerin by air, by truck, by rail, and even by sea. Tomorrow he would tackle Guerin's headquarters and main engineering facility at Portland's airport.

"Just who the hell are you?" someone demanded from behind him.

Zerkel pocketed his miniature camera and turned around calmly, although his heart was hammering wildly. He'd been in situations like this one before. Panic and you got busted. The guard was a man in his late forties or early fifties. He was armed with a pistol, but he'd not drawn it.

"I had to come down and sneak a look," Zerkel said. He turned back to the airplane. "She's beautiful."

"She sure is something," the guard agreed. "Now don't tell me that you left your badge upstairs. Let me see some ID."

"I got my wallet," Zerkel said, turning back.

The guard came within arm's reach. "You engineers are all alike . . ."

Zerkel grabbed the man's jacket front in both hands and yanked him sharply forward, driving his forehead into the guard's forehead. The man went limp, and Zerkel eased him to the floor.

It was bad luck. Zerkel hesitated for a second or two before he stomped on the guard's throat with the heel of his shoe, crushing the man's windpipe. He stomped a second time and then a third, the guard's face puffing up and turning purple. After a few moments the guard's body went completely limp. He was dead.

Bad luck, Zerkel told himself. The guard had seen his face.

Karl Schey showed up at the Sterling, Virginia, farmhouse around 10:00 P.M. He'd been picked up from his New York hotel and driven up to the airport at Bridgeport, Connecticut, where he'd been flown by private plane to Washington's National Airport. A *Lamplighter* staffer picked him up and drove him out.

"I approve of the precautions," he told Reid in the stair hall.

Mueller watched from the darkness in the dining room as the two men embraced.

"You look tired, my old friend," Reid said. "The journey must have been long. I assume you took care not to be followed."

"Yes, I am tired. And no, I was not followed. Of that you can rest assured, Edward. But what about you and your fantastic plans? Did Bruno arrive? Have you put him to work?"

"Yes, to your last two questions. And as for my fantastic plans, well, I'm glad that you're here to share them with me, Karl. We'll talk. But would you like to go up to your room to rest? We can talk in the morning."

"I'm too keyed up to sleep now. Perhaps I can have a glass of cognac and we can sit by the fire. It's good to be here."

Reid hung the older man's coat in the hall closet, and they went into the living room where he poured them both a drink. Once they were seated in front of the fireplace, their backs to the door, Mueller slipped out of the dining room and silently searched Schey's coat and his leather bag at the foot of the stairs. There were no weapons, only clothing, toiletries, and an envelope containing several thousand American dollars. If he'd left Germany for good, he'd left light and apparently in a hurry. A man like Schey, however, would certainly have secure access to a considerable amount of money. Enough so that no matter what happened, he could insulate himself from arrest.

Mueller turned and looked up. Louis Zerkel stood at the head of the stairs watching him. He held a batch of computer printouts, and he'd evidently been on his way down to talk to Reid about something. Mueller waved him back. The younger man stood his ground, but finally he turned and disappeared down the hall.

Reid and Schey were talking in low tones when Mueller went to the door. He could just make out what they were saying, but if there was any desperation in Schey's sudden appearance here it was not evident in his voice. He was the Karl Schey that Mueller had always known: strong, certain, and definitely in control.

"It is an ambitious undertaking, my friend," he said. "But will it work, and will you be able to extricate yourself when the time comes?"

"Nothing is foolproof, but just now the Japanese seem to be cooperating with us, and I do have some capable men working for me."

"Bruno is unstable, you know. But he can be useful this one last time. Never again."

"What do you mean?"

"Interpol knows his name and face, and it's possible they know or suspect that he is here in the United States. Which means the FBI has been alerted. Once you are finished with him I would suggest that he be eliminated."

"Thank you for the suggestion."

"We have worked well together for a great many years," Schey said conversationally. "In all that time I have found you to be an engaging, enterprising man. Our little projects have always been interesting, and certainly profitable for both of us."

"Beginning with those pistols."

Schey chuckled, the sound dry in his throat. "Yes, the Lugers. They wound up in Moscow, you know. The Russians paid very well. No telling how many pompous old men showed their subordinates a Luger and told how the pistol was taken from an unwilling Nazi in the Great Patriotic War."

"I think you sold them for more than a hundred dollars each."

Again Schey chuckled. "Of course. I did all the work, took all the risks."

"The Stasi would have bailed you out had you been caught," Reid said evenly.

Schey hesitated for a beat. "How long have you known?" he asked cautiously.

"I've suspected for a long time that you were a double agent. Bruno confirmed it for me."

"Is he here now?"

"I don't know exactly where he is, Karl. He is a difficult man to control. He was concerned that you were in some sort of trouble in Germany, so you were coming here to escape. You've left much behind."

"Is that why you went to such extraordinary lengths to cover my tracks to this place?"

"Yes, it was," Reid admitted. "Are you in trouble in Europe? Are the police searching for you?"

"No one is looking for me, Edward. I swear it. But if they were this would be the last place I would come. At this moment I would be enjoying the summer sun on a certain island where I am well known—by another name of course—and well respected."

Reid looked up as Mueller silently entered the living room and came up behind Schey.

"Maybe you should have gone to your island after all, Karl."

Schey, sensing at the last moment that he might be in mortal danger, started to turn around, but he was too late. Mueller clamped his powerful hands around the old man's throat and squeezed. Schey came half up out of the chair, thrashing and fighting with every ounce of his strength, but it was no use, and in under a minute and a half he was unconscious, and four minutes later his heart stopped.

"You can bury his body in the garbage pit behind the barn," Reid said, shakily.

Louis Zerkel stood in the relative darkness of the stair hall. He'd seen and heard everything, and whatever lingering doubts he might have had about Reid's plans for him and his brother were dispelled. At the end everyone would be eliminated except for Reid.

He backed away, and stopped at the foot of the stairs as he tried to catch his breath, slow his heart. Glen would have to be warned. In the past days working together he had come to appreciate his brother. It was blood. Even though they had different mothers, they shared their father's genes.

There was no safe way for them to get out of this project now, he told himself as he went silently up the stairs. But there could be a way for them to come out on top. To profit by it, while at the same time saving their own lives.

For the first time in many years, he felt as if he did not need Dr. Shepard. He was free.

"What do you think about that?" he muttered.

SIXTEEN

Reid knew that his rationalizing was over. He could put the murders of hundreds or thousands of people in the airliners he would cause to crash in a compartment of his mind where his ideals lived. It was a war he was waging. In war a lot of people got killed. But in war grand issues were at the center of the struggle. Freedom from oppression. The saving of a nation or a religion or a way of life. In this case the saving of the United States from the Japanese. He could also put the murders of Tallerico and Dr. Shepard at the back of his mind because he never really knew either of them. In any event they had been soldiers as well. But the killing of Karl Schey was completely different. He had known and worked with the man for more than fifty years. In a strange way he had trusted the German through all those years, because Schey had it within his power to bring Reid's career crashing down. Now the man was dead, and his body would be buried here. There was no way of rationalizing himself out of that simple fact.

"I'll take his body out now," Mueller said. "You can bring his coat and overnight bag."

"No." Reid stood by the fireplace, looking at Schey's body.

"Why not?"

"We go back too many years together, Karl and I."

"Alive he would have created problems for us. It is better that he is dead. Do you see this?"

Reid nodded. "He should have stayed in Germany, or gone to his southern island to enjoy his retirement. He could have died at peace."

"Do not grieve for this one, Reid. In his long, distinguished service, he was the direct cause of a great many deaths."

"So were you."

Mueller smiled faintly. "It's what I do. What he did."

"Get rid of his body," Reid ordered. "Bury it deep."

"I'll take care of it. But check with the FBI or Interpol. If he was traced here to this country, then we will have to take measures to further mask his coming to this house."

"I'll see what I can do," Reid said.

Mueller gathered up the old man's body as if it were nothing more than a bundle of clothes. "I told you that if I were to be cornered I would take out a lot of people. You included. I'm here to do a job for you. See that you hold up your end of the operation."

Reid said nothing. He felt flushed.

"In the meantime, our strange friend upstairs has something for you, I think. See what he wants."

Reid waited until Mueller was gone and then went upstairs. Zerkel was seated at one of the computer terminals, his fingers flying over the keys, a dense stream of binary figures scrolling in broad columns up the orange-lit screen.

"Do you have something to tell me, Louis?" Reid asked from the doorway.

Zerkel looked up guiltily, then plucked a few sheets of computer printout from the table. "I need these parts for the repeaters."

"Anything difficult?" Reid asked, taking the sheets.

"No," Zerkel said. He typed something else, looked up again at Reid, this time with a sly grin, and hit ENTER, then the print command. The big laser printer began spewing out copy.

Reid watched. Something about Zerkel was different, disturbing. "Is it something more for me?"

"As soon as it finishes printing out," Zerkel said. He nodded toward the door. "Is Bruno burying your friend's body?"

Reid was taken aback. "You saw . . ."

"And heard everything."

"What have you done, you fool?" Reid demanded. He went to the laser printer and pulled the first section of printout from the tray. "What is this?"

"Insurance," Zerkel said. "Names, dates, places, murders, plans . . . everything."

Reid looked up hardly believing what he was reading, what he was being told.

"All of it is buried now inside the FBI's computerized fingerprint records. It'll pop up in the clear all over the place unless I feed it a code word every twelve hours." Zerkel smiled smugly. "What do you think about that?"

"Report tubes one, two, three, and four are flooded," the growler in the *Samisho*'s attack center rattled.

"Confirm visually," Minori ordered.

A few moments later the forward torpedo room watch officer came back. "Visuals of one, two, three, and four confirm weapons in place and tubes flooded."

Captain Kiyoda stood at the periscope ready to raise it the moment they came to depth. He looked across at his weapons control officer, Lieutenant Takasaki. "No mistakes, Shuichiyo. Only on my orders will you open all four doors. And you will do it smartly."

"Hai, kan-cho."

"And only on my orders will there be a weapons launch. Is that clear?"

"Hai," Takasaki replied crisply.

Minori was bringing the boat up slowly, so as not to spook the captain of the American destroyer into doing something rash. If the confrontation were going to come here—which Kiyoda did not think it would—then so be it. But he preferred to push the Americans a little farther if possible. Into the East China Sea, and hopefully to within spitting distance of Okinawa.

After the destroyer was sent to the bottom there would be other American sub-hunters in the vicinity, which would make for interesting targets.

Kiyoda closed his eyes for a moment, and a billion fireflies fluttered in front of him. He had met with

Kamiya-san several years ago at a house in the peaceful mountains outside Tokyo. They'd sat on tatamis on the veranda listening to the gurgle of water and the tinkling of a windchime. It was not Kamiya's house, but, as the old man explained, it was an oasis of peace and hope in a world that had somehow gone terribly mad.

It was then that *Kamiya-san* had assigned Captain Kiyoda a *sensei* to begin his instructions. Since then Kiyoda had barely been able to contain himself waiting for this day. One year ago the fireflies had come to him, and at first he had been disturbed. But his *sensei* explained that what Kiyoda was seeing was in fact a window into the universe. Fireflies or stars, they were of no consequence except that they represented the correct path. They were, in effect, guiding lights.

Kiyoda opened his eyes. His XO was looking at him.

"Our depth is twenty meters, *kan-cho.*"

"Up periscope," Kiyoda ordered. "Stand by weapons control."

"Hai," Takasaki responded eagerly.

Kiyoda squatted to rise with the periscope, and he smiled inwardly. With this boat and this crew he was invincible.

"Port wing lookout has a periscope directly off our quarter," Lieutenant Commander Ryder said.

Captain Hanrahan stepped over to that side of the bridge and raised his binoculars.

"Bridge, sonar. The target has leveled off at six-zero feet, inbound relative bearing two-seven-zero, range two thousand yards." The comms had been put on loudspeaker.

"I have the periscope wake abaft our beam," Hanrahan said. "Secure from active sonar. Listen for tube flooding noises."

"Bridge, sonar, he's opening his doors!" the chief sonarman reported excitedly. "I'm getting four transients. He's definitely opening his doors."

"Stand by to launch ASROC tubes one through four

on my command," Hanrahan ordered calmly. He watched the wake the *Samisho*'s periscope made in the rising seas. "Have the choppers converge and prepare to launch on my command. Tell the Orion driver what we're doing, and get me Seventh HQ on the secure phone."

"Thanks for coming up on the double, Don," Admiral Ryland said. "We're in trouble, and I want your input."

"I'd say we are at that, sir." Captain Donald Moody, Jr., Chief of Seventh Fleet Intelligence, took his place next to Ryland at the situation board. "Mike's going to have to back off, and do it now. We don't want to get into a shooting match, even by mistake, with the MSDF."

"If the sub-driver fires first, Mike will have to defend himself."

"If he gets in the *Samisho*'s way, Admiral," Moody said without hesitation. The intelligence chief had worked for the CIA and National Security Agency as well as naval intelligence. He knew the business backward and forward. Which meant he knew when to tell it exactly like it was no matter the fallout.

"That particular submarine has no business at our back door in the East China Sea. Not after its performance in the Tatar Strait."

"Are you willing to kill that boat in order to stop it from getting past the *Thorn?*"

"You know as well as I do, Don, that it'll come," Ryland said. "Either here and now, or later farther south where he'll be in a position to pose a greater threat. The man is crazy."

"We're talking about our allies, Admiral," Moody said.

"Don't I know it," Ryland admitted darkly. "I'm getting no answer from MSDF Fleet Headquarters. Admiral Shimakaze is not available for my call. The *Samisho* may not be operating under direct MSDF orders, but at least it has tacit approval."

"We'll never be able to prove that. And now's not the

time for us to be taking a stand out here. Christ, Admiral, you know what Washington would do to us. Especially after what happened last week."

"The *Thorn* is my boat, my crew. Means I'm responsible until I'm ordered off the job."

"You're paying me for intelligence estimates and advice. If the *Samisho* wants to bull its way into the East China Sea, let it go. It'll take at least forty-eight hours, maybe longer, for that submarine to get into a position dangerous to us. But that gives us the time to make it an issue with MSDF command and bounce it back to the Pentagon, or at the very least bring up more assets from Okinawa. But goddammit, Admiral, these are Japanese home waters. And they have the right to come and go as they please."

Ryland's XO, Captain Tom Byrne, had been on the phone with MSDF headquarters. He hung up and shook his head. "Admiral Higashi is in conference," he said. Higashi was CINC of the MSDF Submarine Fleet.

"Don thinks Mike Hanrahan should back off," Ryland said.

Byrne eyed the intelligence officer and nodded slowly. "I agree with him, sir. It would give us a little breathing room. Time to press the issue."

"There's always Subic Bay to consider," Moody said.

"I am," Ryland said. "Once they're back on the Philippines and well established we'd have our hands full out here." No matter what the *Thorn* did we were going to come out the losers. If Hanrahan engaged the submarine and sank or damaged it, the Japanese government would be all over the U.S. Navy. These were Japanese home waters. If the *Samisho* got lucky and sent a U.S. destroyer to the bottom, Japan would apologize for another dreadful mistake and offer to make reparations to the families of the victims. And if he ordered Mike Hanrahan to step aside, the MSDF would have won a moral victory over the U.S. Navy, which was coming under increasing pressure to get its bases off Japanese soil and its ships out of Japanese waters.

"Get Hanrahan on the scrambler," Ryland said. "Tell him to back off and allow the *Samisho* through the strait."

"Yes, sir," Byrne said.

"Tell him that I want him to stick on that sub wherever she goes, whatever she does, and I don't care what he has to do to accomplish that mission. Clear?"

"Aye, aye, Admiral," Byrne replied crisply. He picked up the encrypted phone at the same moment Hanrahan's call from the *Thorn* came in.

"Bring me up to date," SUR Director Aleksandr Karyagin said. "Our Tokyo Station cannot be so weak that after all this time nothing has been learned."

"Mintori Assurance is definitely behind the attack on Guerin," General Polunin replied. He'd been called upstairs to have lunch with the director. From the Lubyanka's ninth-floor dining room he could see that this morning's snowstorm had increased in intensity. Coming in from Mar'ina Roshcha traffic had been snarled up, and he'd been late, but not so late he didn't have time to prepare for the director's summons. "There is some question about the Dulles accident, however. From what *Abunai* is giving us, Mintori was just as surprised and shocked as Guerin was."

"The timing seems odd."

"Yes, sir, considering all that has been happening recently. It would have done them no good to engineer such an accident now. They would stand to lose much more than they could gain."

"How does *Abunai* see that?" Karyagin asked. "How do you see it, General?"

Once again the director had put him on the spot. "Basically Mintori, like too many other corporations within that *zaibatsu,* is an information-driven industry whose sole purpose for existence is to make money. It does this by minimizing its risks and exposure. In order to do that, and still get on with the business of manufacturing, or research and development—or in the case of the Kobe banking *zaibatsu,* provide developmental capital—it actively gathers intelligence. As a whole the Japanese have been engaging in industrial espionage since before the Great War," Polunin added. "The entire nation must continue to manufacture at ever-increasing levels or die. Which means they must know what their market competitors are doing and devise strategies to either better them, or destroy them."

"The ultimate capitalists," Karyagin said dryly.

"Every Japanese businessperson who meets with a foreigner is a spy for his country. Whatever information is gathered goes back to the individual companies, which in turn share significant details with their individual *zaibatsus,* which in a final turn share with the government. Specifically the Ministry for International Trade and Industry—MITI. It's as close as we can get to identifying any centralized Japanese intelligence agency, and of course its primary involvement is business."

"I will suffer your lengthy explanations, General, because I am no expert on Japan. But get on with it."

"Simply put, Mr. Director, *Abunai* believes that Mintori does not have enough information to make its final move against Guerin at this time."

Karyagin raised an eyebrow. "*Abunai* is a network of people, or one individual?"

Polunin had anticipated the question. There was no reason for the SUR director not to know that information; it was just that all good intelligence organizations understood the guiding principle of "need to know." There was no reason, until now, for the director to be told the specifics. Polunin took a piece of paper out of his pocket and handed it across the table. The director read what it contained and looked up.

"I see," he said. He handed the slip back and Polunin pocketed it.

"The sinking of the *Menshinsky* shook the Japanese government as much or more than it did us."

"Tell that at the Kremlin."

"It shook the Japanese *government,* Mr. Director,"

Polunin made his point again. "But *Abunai* believes that Mintori—specifically its director, Sokichi Kamiya, and the director of the Kobe Bank *zaibatsu*, Hiroshi Kobayashi—may have had previous contact with the captain of the submarine, the *Samisho*. His name is Seiji Kiyoda, and he comes from a very old, very venerable family. He has apparently fashioned himself and his crew after Yukio Mishima's Shield Society."

"They are using this submarine commander as a tool?"

"A similar incident seems to be developing between this submarine and an American destroyer in the Tokara Strait at the entrance to the East China Sea."

Karyagin sat forward. "Have shots been fired?"

"Not yet. We have a RORSAT due to pass over the region within the hour. If we get a break in the weather we might see something. Short of that, infrared sensors will at least tell us if there has recently been a battle."

"Why, General? If what *Abunai* tells us is valid, if Mintori and Kobe are targeting Guerin, why engineer attacks on our navy and on the Americans? To what end?"

"We cannot answer that yet, Mr. Director. But it's my guess that these naval confrontations may be an effort at misdirection that somehow may help them in their run on Guerin. There is some logic in the idea, especially if it is considered against the Japanese Prime Minister's free trade proposal. But there is another, much darker possibility that would reduce the naval attacks and the bid for Guerin to individual elements of a larger plan."

"What are you thinking?"

"A brief, very intense little war for economic control of the Western Pacific basin. The Japanese desperately need guaranteed supplies of oil and minerals from the region, and a constantly growing market for their manufactured goods. The same things the new American economy is scrambling for."

"Subic Bay comes to mind," Karyagin suggested.

"I'm sure it's foremost in many Americans' minds. As

are the growing anti-American sentiments in Tokyo and Yokosuka—home base to the U.S. Seventh Fleet and home port of the *Samisho*."

"The Japanese are a sophisticated people. It would be suicide for them. They are America's allies. As you said of Mintori's timing, Japan would have everything to lose and nothing to gain."

"A view widely held, Mr. Director," Polunin replied, masking an inward smile. The bastard didn't know his way around as well as he thought he did. "MITI is almost certainly spying on the United States, and *Abunai* believes that a top MITI operative may have been sent to Washington to specifically target Guerin for information."

"Is this surprising?"

"In itself, no, Mr. Director. But this operative was observed meeting with Mr. McGarvey on at least one occasion. Interesting, wouldn't you say, in light of what he told us?"

"Are you saying that Guerin's offer to build an assembly factory here is false?"

"I don't know. In my gut I think the offer is legitimate. But I don't think McGarvey is. In fact it's very likely that he is working on direct orders from the CIA, something Guerin's chief executives might not know. He may even have somehow maneuvered the airplane company into offering us the factory."

"Make your point."

Polunin sat back and rubbed the bridge of his nose between his thumb and forefinger. It was time for caution, very big issues were at stake. Career-breaking or career-making issues. Unlike a lot of people on his staff, Polunin did not pine for the old regime. But he did miss its stability. Russia and the entire world had become politically liquid. It was very much like the Weimar Republic days of Germany. Worldwide, the setup seemed chillingly similar.

"McGarvey offers us a billion dollar factory if we will help him spy in Japan. He's killing two birds with one stone. First he puts us in a position where any retaliation against the Japanese for sinking the *Menshinsky* would be difficult if not impossible, and second gets us to share intelligence data. Something in both cases that Washington may want very desperately. They are in trouble in Japan, and they'll take all the help they can, because if the United States and Japan do go to war over the Western Pacific rim, the United States will lose."

"Preposterous."

"No, Mr. Director, it's likely. Within hours after the first shots are fired, Washington would call an immediate halt to all hostilities. Japan is, after all, its ally and major trading partner. Washington will demand they talk and not shoot. At the end of the . . . peace conference, if you will . . . the Japanese will get what they want. The Western Pacific basin is vital for Japan's survival, but not for America's."

"Keeping us out of it would not help them."

"On the contrary. If we move against Japan, it will give them the legitimate excuse to mobilize, with if not the full approval of the U.S., at least with its understanding."

"Because of one submarine."

"No, Mr. Director, because of two very powerful and important *zaibatsus* that may be maneuvering an unwilling Japanese government into the confrontation."

"Then we must help McGarvey. But you say the man has met with the Japanese spy."

"How better to find out what a government's intentions are than to find out what its spies are up to?"

"Has this information been passed to McGarvey yet?" Karyagin asked.

"No."

"What are you recommending, General?"

"*Abunai* is trying to penetrate Mintori or Kobe or both, but it is very difficult. I recommend that we give Tokyo Station all the support we can. But McGarvey is going to have to be watched very closely. I would like to determine if indeed he is working for the CIA, and what his exact mission might be."

"How would you go about that?"

"By trying to penetrate his cover. If his work for Guerin is legitimate, he'll bleed a little. If not he'll sidestep it."

"But then he won't cooperate with us."

"Yes he will, because he won't know who is after him or why."

"He is an intelligent, capable man, General," Karyagin warned. "Move with care. And do it quickly. The Kremlin is pressing very hard to retaliate for the *Menshinsky.*"

The situation was exactly as Polunin thought it would be. With proper timing and luck, Karyagin would hang at the end of his own rope.

"It wasn't a very smart thing to do. It jeopardizes all of us," Reid told Louis Zerkel.

"It was the only thing he could do," Mueller contradicted.

"What are you talking about? Do you understand the consequences? Our lives are inside the FBI's mainframe. One mistake on Louis's part, one glitch in the system across the river, one careless flick of a key by some bored data-entry clerk, and we're finished."

"It can't happen that way, Mr. Reid," Louis said. He sat at his computer terminal, the screen blank. "I've built in a virus against snoopers. There are only two ways for that information to be accessed. By me, if and when I decide to retrieve it. And also by me, if I don't plug in the proper code twice a day. In that case the entire file will be plastered across nearly every terminal in the headquarters."

"You can get the information from him," Reid said to Mueller.

The German shook his head. "We wouldn't know if he was telling the truth until it was too late."

"You two are forgetting something else," Louis said.

"No," Mueller replied, a slight smile creasing the corners of his mouth. "We need you to build the repeaters, and to test the heat monitor to make sure everything will work. We also need you to somehow generate the signal in Tokyo so that InterTech in San Francisco will send out the firing pulses. I think it will take a genius to figure that out, but I have no doubt that you are up to the task."

"Jesus," Reid said.

Mueller turned to him. "It's life insurance for him. He is afraid that I will kill him the moment his usefulness is at an end."

"Damned right," Zerkel said.

Mueller looked at him. "But you have forgotten something in your haste, Louis. If someone were to go snooping within the FBI's system, your virus would wipe out the material. I think Mr. Reid could come up with someone who would be willing to do a little snooping for us. What do you think about that?"

It dawned on Louis in one fell swoop that the German was absolutely correct. He had been stupid, blinded by his own cleverness. Christ. Christ. It wasn't fair. He turned back to his terminal and brought up the complicated entry system that would get him back into the FBI's system, when the muzzle of a pistol was placed against his temple.

"One keystroke and I will kill you," Mueller said, his voice gentle, as if he were talking to a spooked animal.

Zerkel's fingers were poised over his keyboard as he thought it out. He hardly dared to breathe. "If you kill me now, your plan dies with me," he said very carefully.

"I will kill you only if you attempt to reveal our names and this location."

"I could do it later, while you're out of the room."

"The moment I found out what you'd done, I would kill you, your brother, and Mr. Reid, and make my escape. I am very good at it."

Zerkel took great pains to keep his voice even, as if he were simply discussing the weather. "You'll kill me at the end."

"We'll construct a safeguard against that."

"How?"

"I don't know yet, Louis. But between the three of us we will come to a mutual agreement."

It was always the sly ones, the crafty people who came out on top, not the intellectuals. Most often the men of true genius were left behind, trampled in the dust. It made no sense, nor was it fair. But Louis did understand that it was the way of things in the world. The *usual* way of things. But he wanted to finish this project. Now that he'd come this far, he wanted to see how it turned out. And he wanted to see about it in the journals and periodicals and especially in the analytical newsletters. He wanted to read the studies that would be done. The psychological profiles of the perpetrators, and especially of the genius who had figured out how to beat the system.

He had to survive.

Slowly he brought his hands back from the keyboard and laid them on his lap, then he turned against the pressure of the gun barrel and looked up into Mueller's eyes.

"Yes, *Herr* Mueller, we will construct a safeguard that we all can live with. In the meantime please leave me now. I have to get back to work on my signal system design. It is at a very delicate stage."

Mueller drew back after a beat, safetied the Luger, and headed out of the room. "What do you think about that?" he said as he passed a stunned Reid.

Chance Kennedy spotted Arimoto Yamagata at a window table. She headed across the elegant old Columbia Gorge Hotel dining room aware that it was unlikely anyone here would know her. The hotel was fifty miles east of Portland, and it was frequented mostly by tourists. She'd been here only once, and that had been years ago. Still, she rightly remembered how beautiful the place was with its gardens, stone bridges, and waterfall. But Yamagata's call this morning inviting her to lunch had come out of the blue. Her immediate reaction had been to turn him down. She'd only met the man once, casually, and had barely spoken ten words with him. Although she'd never thought of herself as having sharp prejudices, the man was Japanese. He was of a different race. His skin color was different, and his eyes were not Western.

Too, he was here to do business with Guerin, so by taking the wife of the commercial airplane division's president to lunch he might feel as if he would find an opening. Every company had its secrets. Who better to tell him than a top executive's wife?

But to understand the risks was to be prepared. The Japanese might be using her, but the fact of the matter was that she was bored out of her skull. David was gone most of the time, and the rare moments he was at home he was barricaded in his study reading stacks of arcane reports on everything from the global economy to the stress points of hybrid ceramics.

Besides, she told herself, the game Yamagata was probably playing slid both ways. While he was trying to get information from her, she could be doing the same to him. If she were able to bring some juicy little tidbit of information about the Japanese home with her, David would certainly sit up and take notice for a change.

Yamagata rose as she approached. "Hello again," he said, his voice pleasant, with no trace of an accent. He held out his hand, and Chance shook it.

"Your call this morning came as a surprise," she said. His grip was gentle, his palm warm and dry.

"A pleasant one, I hope."

She looked into his eyes, but there was nothing in them except warmth and a friendly good humor. "Frankly it made me nervous. How'd you ever find this place?"

"The Japanese are inveterate tourists, didn't you know? We go nowhere without a camera and a guidebook."

He helped with her chair, and their waiter came over with menus. Chance ordered a dry vodka martini on the rocks with a twist, and Yamagata ordered another white wine.

"I guess I deserved that," Chance said. She smiled. She felt like a fool.

Yamagata returned her smile. "You were being candid—may I call you Chance?"

"Please do."

"Let me be equally candid. I came to Portland to explore the possibility of doing business with Guerin. But I would like to find out the kinds of things that do not ordinarily show up on an annual report. The sort of things that men sitting across a conference table from one another rarely bring up, or are reluctant to discuss. I felt that you might be able to help me."

Chance could hardly believe what she was hearing. Either the man was a raging idiot or he thought she was. "Like who is sleeping with whom?"

For an instant Yamagata looked startled, but then he threw back his head and laughed, the gesture without guile. He'd heard something funny, and he'd responded.

"My dear lady, what do you take me for?" he asked, when he recovered.

Chance was confused. "I know nothing about you. Nothing at all, except that by your own admission you're some sort of a spy."

"That's exactly what I am. And let me tell you the kind of information I'm looking for. Great corporations, like great nations, often rise and fall not only because of economics but because of an esprit de corps, some inner drive or purpose. If its leaders and its workers are excited then good things usually follow. Strength. Clear-mindedness. Fairness." Yamagata lowered his eyes for a moment. "If the esprit de corps is lost, for whatever reason, the future of a great corporation such as Guerin may not be so clear."

Chance did understand. She nodded. "I know."

"It's hardly a subject I could bring up at a Guerin board meeting, you know. 'Gentlemen, accept my condolences for your recent loss at Dulles Airport, but can you tell me if your mood has been permanently damaged? Are you crying tears of sadness? Has the joy gone out of your soul?'"

Chance could not envision Al Vasilanti shedding tears about anything. She'd attended his wife's funeral four years ago, and the old bastard had sat through the entire ceremony at the church and at the cemetery completely dry-eyed. As if he were attending a stranger's funeral.

"Do you catch my meaning?"

"Yes, I certainly do. But so far as I can tell it's business as usual. It's the new airplane everybody's been talking about. It's the holy grail for all of them—my husband included. And it's the same with every new project. They're in their own little worlds. It's a wonder to a lot of us why the divorce rate among airplane executives isn't higher than it is."

Yamagata shook his head wanly. "Forgive me for saying this, Chance, but if Western men could have the feminine quality of understanding—just that one characteristic—America would be a million times greater than it already is."

"It's called empathy," Chance said, and she felt stupid. The man was obviously using her. It was so flagrant she almost wanted to laugh. And yet there was a quality about him, about his face, the way he held himself, about his eyes, and the set of his mouth, his lips, that was intriguing.

"That's a good word," Yamagata said, studying her face.

She raised her eyes and looked frankly into his. "Do you think so?"

SEVENTEEN

He came through the fence at West Thirteen," Guerin's chief of security William Lisch told the Portland Police detective. "But like I said we didn't catch it until first light this morning."

"Camera troubles out there?" Lieutenant Peter Geiger asked. He was just going through the motions until the feds showed up.

"We maintain sixty-seven miles of fence line, some of it through pretty rough terrain. We always have troubles somewhere. But he was a pro, I can tell you that much. He didn't take any unnecessary chances. The camera was moved a quarter-inch, which gave him about fifteen feet of dead zone to work in, and he shunted the outer fence before cutting a hole in it so nothing showed up on our monitors. When he was done he closed the hole, removed the shunt, and took off. Our first team didn't catch it last night. We had to wait till daybreak."

The Oregon Bureau of Criminal Investigation van had arrived the first thing this morning, along with the medical examiner and a team of forensics experts. It was their responsibility to secure the crime scene, making sure no one inadvertently trampled over some evidence.

"So, he's through the fence. How do you see it from there?" Geiger asked.

"It's about three-quarters of a mile, as the crow flies, from there to Hangar One. I'm guessing he came behind us, across to the operations building, then into One. Would have kept him in the shadows."

"Anything missing? Sabotaged?"

"There's a hundred million dollars worth of parts and equipment lying around here that could be easily sold on the open market. It'll take time to inventory it all."

"He carried it out himself, if he was alone."

"Any one of a half-million sensitive parts would bring that bird down. It's going to take an even longer time to complete that inventory. After Dulles we're all gun-shy."

Geiger looked up, his interest suddenly piqued. "Are you saying that the two incidents are related?"

They stepped into Lisch's office to look at the perimeter map on the wall. The security officer closed the door.

"A lot of strange things have happened around here in the past six months or so, Geiger. You've heard the rumors . . . everyone in Portland has . . . about what the Japanese are trying to do to us. One of our foremen was killed in Portland a few weeks ago. We had the Dulles crash. And now this."

"Anyone have a grudge against your man?"

Lisch shook his head. "So far as I know he was well liked. With us for thirteen years. Wife, three kids. Helped run our softball league. Perfect record."

"Gambling, drinking, another woman?"

"I don't think a jealous husband would have broken in here to kill him."

"Unless it was one of your security people. Could have covered his tracks with the trick in the fence."

"Not a chance. Whoever it was came here looking for something, or looking to do something to us."

"And they were willing to kill for it," Geiger replied. "Who? If you had to guess. The Japanese?"

Lisch's eyebrows narrowed. "That'd be my guess," he said. "But if you claim I told you that, I'll call you a liar to your face."

"The Bureau will ask the same questions."

"Don't I know it," Lisch said heavily.

Special agents Albert McLaren and Phillip Joyce arrived from Washington at six sharp at the Air National Guard hangar, where they were met by the FBI's Portland field office A-S-A-C Edward Judge. The weather had turned mild, but they did not linger on the apron, instead they hurried directly to the waiting automobile and headed into the city. During the twenty-minute drive McLaren and Joyce flipped through the package of material assembled for them.

"Anything new since this was put together?" McLaren asked when he was finished.

"The coroner's report came over just as I was leaving for the airport, but nothing's changed. A broad hematoma at the right temple area might have caused unconsciousness. But what killed him was respiratory failure due to massive injuries to his trachea."

"The perp hit him on the head with something, and when the man was down he stomped him on the throat," Joyce commented dryly. "Nice."

"That's how it looks," Judge said. He was a big man, in his thirties, with wide, serious eyes.

"Anything missing or tampered with?" McLaren asked.

"To this point the Guerin people have found nothing, but it'll take a few days. It's a big place."

"Nobody saw or heard a thing?"

"No. Whoever it was knew his way around."

McLaren looked up at that. "Are you saying it was an inside job? A Guerin employee?"

"Probably not. What I mean to say is that whoever got through the fence and killed the guard was a pro. He had the layout of the place down pat. But that's easy information to come by."

"He did his homework, gained entry to the hangar, for whatever reason, and left," McLaren summed it up. "Killing the guard was happenstance. It wasn't planned."

"No argument," Judge said. "The question is, did he accomplish what he set out to do? Could be the guard interrupted him before he got to it. Might have shaken him enough to make him run."

Joyce shook his head. "If he was on the run he wouldn't have taken the time to put the fence back together. He would have just shagged ass."

"Right," Judge agreed. "So what words of wisdom are you bringing from Washington? Or are you just here to help out?"

"Neither, actually. We're following up a murder investigation in Washington and several more in the San Francisco area that might be related to what happened here."

"Anything to do with the Dulles crash last week?"

"Not so far as we know," McLaren said. "Have you come up with something?"

"The Portland cop who was the investigating officer in charge out there until we showed up said that Guerin's chief of security mentioned the two incidents along with another, apparently an accidental death recently."

"What's the connection?"

"Guerin has been having trouble with a Japanese group gearing up for some sort of a hostile takeover attempt. Off the record the chief of security thinks the Japanese might be involved with the crash, with the accidental death, and with last night's incident."

"That's not the company's official position?"

"No."

"Can we bring this chief of security in for an interview tonight?"

"His name is Bill Lisch, and he'll cooperate to a point. But we're told that he'll deny ever saying anything about the Japanese."

"I think we can get it on the table," McLaren said.

They parked behind the Federal Building and went upstairs. Special Agent in Charge Jack Franson was waiting for them in his office. He was ten years older than Judge and fifty pounds lighter. His hair was already starting to go gray. He looked like a banker, or a college professor.

"Your boss wasn't very specific about what you're looking for, but he asked for my complete cooperation," Franson told them. "You have it."

"Thank you, sir," McLaren replied. "What we need is the short course on Guerin Airplane Company so that when we go out there in the morning we won't be going blind."

"Are you taking over this investigation of last night's murder?"

"No, sir. That's still in your ball park. But we'd like to tag along and maybe point you in some directions you might not have come up with on your own."

"I told them what Geiger told us," Judge said.

"There are a lot of rumors floating around Portland just now," Franson said, clearly not happy with his number two. "That statement might have been made in the heat of the moment. First lesson about Guerin: The company is very big, the biggest thing in Portland. So whatever happens over there affects the entire region. It's just like Boeing up in Seattle."

"Yes, sir, we understand. But last night's incident may have some connection to our investigation."

"I'm listening."

"We've brought a summary file for you, but very briefly we started out on an industrial espionage case involving a man named Benjamin Tallerico. In the middle of our investigation he was murdered. The two men we think did it—they're still at large—are Bruno Mueller, who was, until '89, a colonel in the East German Secret Service, and an environmental terrorist by the name of Glen Zerkel."

"That Idaho ski resort incident—what, five years ago?" Judge said.

"He's on the hit list," McLaren confirmed. "Glen Zerkel's brother, Louis, worked for a company in San Francisco called InterTech, which among other things designs and manufactures electronic subassemblies for Guerin. By the time we got out there to ask him about his brother, he'd skipped. But not before murdering his psychologist and raping her corpse."

"Quite the pair," Franson said. "Are you saying that Louis Zerkel might have sabotaged something InterTech was supplying Guerin?"

"That was our first thought. But as it turns out Zerkel never worked on anything even remotely connected with the devices InterTech built for Guerin."

"I'm assuming that in any event InterTech has been checked out."

"Top to bottom, and they come out clean. Zerkel's behavior is just as big a mystery to them. According to them he might have a grudge against the company. Last week there was a fire in the shipping and receiving area. One of the night watchmen was killed. That same night, Louis Zerkel's supervisor and his wife and children were also killed."

"Anything missing from InterTech?" Judge asked.

"The company says no," McLaren answered.

"If I'm following you the only connection you've come up with between your case and last night's incident is the fact that InterTech is a Guerin subcontractor," Franson said. "That's thin."

"Yes, sir, it is. But the break-in and murder last night do have some similarities with what happened at Inter-Tech. We're just trying to cover all our bases."

Assistant FBI Director Kenneth Wood looked up from his reading when John Whitman showed up at his door. "Come in, John."

"I think I might be getting in over my head," Whitman said. "If you have a minute I'd like to bounce this off you."

"Is it the InterTech case?"

"That's the one. I'm going around in circles, but I keep coming up with the same two names: Kirk McGarvey and Edward R. Reid."

"Close the door, will you, John?" Wood said. He dialed his secretary. "No calls until John and I are finished. And if the director has already left for the day, have Marjorie pencil me in with him for tomorrow, eight sharp."

Whitman sat down across from his boss, his ears still ringing from the conversation he'd had with Colonel Marquand. The man was insistent.

"I'm going to tell you right off that your surveillance request on Reid will be denied," Wood said. "So unless you've come up with something rock solid to nail him with, don't even ask."

"I don't know what I've got, Ken, but it's big. What's the deal with Reid?"

"Is he crucial to your case?"

"He could be."

"Are you talking about the French thing? Has the SDECE been pressing?"

"I talked with Marquand a half-hour ago," Whitman said. "He made his position clear. He says he's talked to the CIA as well."

"Reid has been agitating a lot of people about the Japanese with his newsletter. The State Department asked us to back off for the moment because of the Tokyo Summit. And from what I understand, that has the backing of the White House."

"Back off from what?" Whitman asked. "Who said anything about investigating Reid?"

"I don't know, John. I'm guessing a leak somewhere. Reid knows everyone in Washington, including Director Harding. So unless you've come up with something very big there's nothing I can or will do for you, except put Internal Affairs on it if you want to make waves."

"We'll keep IA out of it for the moment, but without Reid I don't know where I'm at."

Wood leaned forward. "Let me make something perfectly clear, John. I'm saying that if you can come up with probable cause, a strong probability of cause, then we'll go after him no matter what State tells us."

"Four points, not necessarily in any order," Whitman said. "The crash at Dulles last week. That flight was returning from Moscow, where we believe Guerin Airplane Company brass were trying to sell the Russians on some sort of a joint project. Best word I've got is that it involves a significant amount of money that would have to be given to Russia in the form of loan guarantees. The man at the middle is Kirk McGarvey, who Guerin hired to check out a rumor that a Japanese consortium might be trying to buy out Guerin."

"Where'd that come from?"

"An old friend over at Langley. But some of that is guesswork."

"Was the crash an accident?"

"NTSB is still working on it, but there are some similarities to a crash in 1990, same type of Guerin airplane, same type of malfunction. Nothing was found at that time."

"Go on."

"A night watchman was killed last night at Guerin's research and development facility outside Portland. The chief of security for the company thinks the Japanese might have had something to do with it."

"The Japanese again," Wood said.

"The French have asked for help finding Bruno Mueller and Karl Schey, both of whom probably worked for the East German Secret Service. There is a possible connection between them and Reid, and a definite connection between Mueller and McGarvey."

Wood was silent for a moment. "Our initial pass showed Reid was clean."

"Except that he may have been seen having drinks and dinner with Benjamin Tallerico before Tallerico was murdered."

"Where's that connection, John?"

"Tallerico may have been buying industrial secrets from a San Francisco psychologist named Jeanne Shepard, who was the psychologist for an engineer by the name of Louis Zerkel. Zerkel worked for InterTech until he disappeared. Point is InterTech builds some electronic components for Guerin airplanes. The company may have a connection with a Japanese microchip supplier. But Zerkel's psychologist and his immediate supervisor and the man's family were all murdered, and an Inter-Tech facility was broken into, a night watchman killed, and the place set on fire."

"Through Tallerico another possible tie with Reid."

Whitman nodded. "Louis Zerkel's brother, Glen, is an environmental terrorist on our top twenty-five."

"All of it very, very circumstantial," Wood said.

"But there's so much of it," Whitman countered.

"I'll take it up with the director in the morning. But you're going to have to have some help."

"That's for sure, Ken, because besides Reid, I want to go after McGarvey."

"I didn't hear you drive up," Louis Zerkel said.

His brother Glen looked tired and disheveled. "I hitched a ride from town and hiked up from the highway. Where's everybody?"

"The German left right after supper, and Mr. Reid went back to the city a couple of hours ago. Around ten, I think. Are you okay, Glen? Was there any trouble in Portland? Did you find out what Mr. Reid wanted?"

"I found out enough to know that if we go through with this we'd better get it right, because afterward the sky is going to fall in. Guerin Airplane Company is a hell of a lot bigger than I thought it would be. I mean intellectually I knew the figures, but, Louis, you ought to see it. Christ, half the city belongs to them. Half the state."

"What happened out there?" Louis asked.

"I had to take out a night watchman. But that's beside the point. If we take on Guerin like Mr. R. wants us to do, it'll be more than a federal rap. Every agency in the country will be gunning for us. And whether you know it or not there's a lot of fucking good talent out there. This won't be like hitting a ski resort or an open pit mine, this'll be like the Munich Olympics, or the Marine barracks in Beirut, only bigger. Much bigger."

"Did anybody see you?"

"No. I don't think so. And if we're lucky the local cops will handle the case as a break-and-enter. Happens all the time out there. One guy in a bar offered me a job. Told me that's how he made his living. Stealing shit from Guerin. They don't even miss it."

"You said no one saw you."

"Nobody important. The guys I talked to sure as hell won't blow any whistles."

"What guys? How did you find them?"

Glen shrugged. "They're around. You just find them."

Louis needed time to think it out. Circuit design and analysis were easy by comparison. He wished that he could talk it over with Dr. Shepard. She would understand.

"How is your end coming?" Glen asked. "Can we do it without leaving a trail back here?"

"I think so."

"Don't *think* man," Glen shouted. "You'd better be goddamned sure. Our asses are on the line, you understand? Come out of the drift factor, Louis. Can we do it without leading them back to us?"

"When I'm finished no one will be able to electronically trace the signals back here. But we have another problem."

"I know," Glen said. "Mr. R. has no intention of paying us off. He's going to have Mueller kill us. That's why I'm going to kill the bastard before we push the switch. On his own Mr. R. will have to keep his word to us."

"Besides that, I think Mr. Reid may be under investigation by the FBI," Louis blurted.

"Oh, Jesus Christ." Glen pulled a chair over to where Louis sat by one of the terminals and slumped down on it. "Did you get into the Bureau's system?"

"There's nothing in the system, but Mueller thinks it's possible because of that German who called here from Paris."

"Karl Schey? Did he show up here?"

"Yes, and Mueller killed him. He told Mr. Reid that Schey would never have left Germany unless he was in some kind of trouble. If that were the case, Interpol and probably the FBI would be looking for him. The investigation might include Mr. Reid. What do you think about that?"

"We either get the hell out of here now, or we get on with it as fast as possible."

"I've got nowhere to go, Glen."

"We have to get out of the country, that's for damn sure. And to do that takes money. So let's get on with it and hope that Reid has enough connections to stall the feds until we're out of here."

Mueller presented himself at the Visitors Information Bureau at Oakland International Airport a minute before 3:00 P.M. and handed the young woman behind the counter his business card, which identified him as Thomas Reston, a freelance writer for *High Technology Business* and *Aviation Week & Space Technology* magazines.

"Have you an appointment, sir?" the receptionist asked.

"I telephoned the Tower Chief, Mr. Franklin, and he promised someone would be meeting me here."

"Let me call for you."

Mueller had lightened his hair and wore blue contact lenses, which along with a lightweight silk suit, Italian tie, and a butter-soft leather briefcase made him appear successful and at least ten years younger than his actual age.

InterTech was nearby, but he felt no unease returning to the area so soon. Even if someone had seen and identified him last week it was unlikely the police would expect him back, nor would he be recognizable to anyone who didn't know him intimately. He'd had the business cards printed at a Kinko's shop in San Francisco and had done a few hours homework at the periodic-literature section of the public library.

"That's all right, Tammy," a short man with gray hair and a gray beard said, coming across the lobby. His complexion was sallow as if he'd spent most of his life indoors.

"Mr. Franklin?" Mueller asked, stepping away from the counter.

"No. R.C. sent me over. I'm Bill White, chief air traffic control instructor here. Mr. Reston?"

"Yes, that's right." Mueller handed the man a card and they shook hands.

"I'm a little vague on what you'd like to know. Maybe you can fill me in on the way over to the tower. I'm assuming you want to see what we're doing in approach and departure control. But I can tell you right now that our progress since you people were out here last month is bang on."

"That's good to hear. I'm assuming then that your IBM Initial Suite Sector System is up and fully operational."

"It is."

There'd been a lot written about the new air traffic control network in this country. It was called the Advanced Automation System Project and was part of a Washington-driven capital investment plan to spend around thirty billion dollars by the year 2000. IBM had helped design it.

During the five-minute drive across to the tower, White was silent. Before they went up, however, he stopped Mueller. "Just what are you looking for this time? You know the situation out here. We're being squeezed both ways. High tech costs big bucks, and in the middle of it all we need the controller. The human voice talking to human pilots. That hasn't changed and won't."

"The National Airspace Plan . . ."

"That's a worn-out joke, and everybody knows it," White said. "You're dealing with big egos here. Controllers are hotshots, so what's new? But you've got to tell me why you really came out here today. You're after something specific, so you play straight with me, and I'll play straight with you."

"The AAS . . ."

"You've already asked about that, and I told you that we're on track. No problems there. What are you driving at?"

Mueller was at a loss. From his reading he'd gathered that there was a lot of infighting going on between the airline industry, the Federal Aviation Administration, and the management commissions of the various large U.S. airports. But like in most bureaucratic entanglements more was said and written between the lines than was stated openly. His homework had been extensive enough to understand that such a situation existed, but not enough to come up with the answers that a man who claimed to be a technology writer should have. He had stumbled into dangerous territory, with no easy way to escape.

A hint of suspicion was beginning to show in White's eyes. He was waiting for the right answer. But the man had admitted that his own ego was big.

Mueller shrugged. He would have to guess. "I was going to feel you out first, Bill, before I mentioned it. I didn't want you to bite my head off."

"About what?"

"What they're doing at Haren near Brussels International Airport."

"Europe's supposed Central Flow Management Unit plan, is that what you're talking about?" White asked. "Come with me and I'll show you why it's the only way for them to go, but would be totally useless and a damned big waste of money in this country."

Sokichi Kamiya had come to think of himself as a segregationist. There were those who maintained a more accurate description might be isolationist, but they were wrong. Japan could not exist in a vacuum, and he had never preached such a doctrine. International trade and cooperation were facts of life, although that fool Ichiro Enchi had gone completely over the edge with his announced Japan Free World Trade Zone. If the prime minister's plan were somehow to come to pass, Japan would go bankrupt and probably drag the U.S. down with it.

He stood at the floor-to-ceiling windows of the Imperial Hotel's thirtieth-floor suite looking out across the Imperial Gardens. How Western a spot in which to meet, he thought. And yet how Japanese the view. Storm clouds were gathering in more than just a figurative manner. The horizon to the northwest was ominously black. The coming days promised to be bleak.

He was a man who understood that the soul of Japan hung in the balance. There were two hemispheres and two races that mattered. He would see to it that the purity of his remained intact, even if he had to carry on the fight singlehandedly. But the timing was wrong. Other forces were out there, meddling. Everything was coming to a head faster than he thought possible, which left him only two choices: either step aside and let events take their natural course or proceed as planned—much faster than planned. One choice, actually, he told himself.

"We are reasonable men, *Kamiya-san.* Between us we

will find a way," Tadashi Ota said from the buffet across the room.

"Not by giving away our hard-won advantage," Kamiya grumbled. He turned away from the window.

"My dear old friend, if you mean by that our financial position against that of America's, then your concern is as touching as it is misplaced." Ota was twenty years younger than Kamiya, and neither as an old friend nor as Deputy Director General of Defense was he directly involved with the government's finances.

"Then why are you here?"

"To ask for your help, of course, *Kamiya-san.*"

"Who directed you to speak with me?"

Ota smiled wanly. "A delicate situation has arisen that involves a . . . disciple of yours."

Kamiya's left eyebrow rose. He turned back to the window. The trouble had always been that Japan's population was concentrated in a few cities. The nation's international commerce was gathered into definable regions that the military would term primary targets. Japan was an easy mark for destruction. Not a day went by that some event or some comment would not trigger his memories of Hiroshima and Nagasaki. He knew exactly what he'd been doing on those days, at precisely those instants when the bombs had burst. It was the same in America. Depending upon what generation you spoke with, they either remembered the day Pearl Harbor was attacked or the day on which President Kennedy was assassinated. Those events had become national benchmarks. Pearl Harbor had given Americans the resolve to enter the war. Kennedy's assassination had jarringly awakened the nation to a new era. On that day the earth had shrunk by a quantum leap. But the nuclear destruction of Hiroshima and Nagasaki had made Japan a shy nation. It wasn't so much that her people had become peace-loving overnight; it was that they had embraced the attitude of the loser. We cannot win, so let us not fight. It was the very reason that Japan had become so stunningly successful at rebuilding herself in the fifty years since the war, at creating a vibrant economy out of the ashes. Her national energy went from war to commerce. Japan became, in a few short decades, one of the leading economic powers in the world. That, of necessity since the end of the Cold War between the Soviet Union and United States, put Japan on a collision course with America. Like a marriage going bad, the danger existed that the husband would vent his anger at his wife by striking her down. In Kamiya's analogy Japan was the bride at her most vulnerable point. Enchi's offer to create a free trade agreement was the same last-ditch conciliatory gesture a frightened wife might make to her husband in an effort to save the failing marriage. It would not, could not, work.

"I have no disciples," Kamiya contradicted. "What am I being taken for?"

"We have spoken with Yabe Takagi. Actually he was quite open with investigators, I am told."

Kamiya again turned back from the window to face the deputy director general. "He is a teacher, certainly not my student."

"He is *sensei* of that hothead Seijii Kiyoda, a relationship you cannot deny you arranged."

"I know the lieutenant commander and his family very well. His father was a personal friend of mine. But Seijii Kiyoda commands a submarine. He works for you, not me."

"Until a couple of days ago Lieutenant Commander Kiyoda was under arrest for treason."

"House arrest, Minister Ota. Odd for such a serious allegation."

"You are not chief justice of this nation," Ota blurted in vexation.

"Nor are you."

"Kiyoda was responsible for sinking a Russian naval vessel in the Tatar Strait, contrary to standing orders. It was Kiyoda who took the initiative. It was Kiyoda who maneuvered his vessel and his crew into a situation where the Russians had to defend themselves or die."

"He should have been stopped."

"A submarine at sea, submerged, is nearly autonomous."

"Then his arrest should have been handled with greater care."

"You interfered."

"A charge I categorically deny, Deputy Director General," Kamiya asserted. "You arranged our meeting, you selected this place, and you say you have come to ask for my help. 'We are reasonable men. Between us we will find a way.' Your words. Is this meeting official?"

Ota looked at him through narrowed eyes. "Not entirely, *Kamiya-san*. But I am asking for your help not only on behalf of the navy, but on behalf of our country."

"With what?"

"Stopping that hothead Kiyoda from doing irreparable damage. Damage that would put us in grave danger. We need time to bridge the differences between us and the United States. It is time Prime Minister Enchi is buying. It is time Kiyoda is stealing from us by his latest insane adventure."

"Time for what?"

"You read about the young woman's murder in Yokosuka and about the murders of ordinary Japanese tourists in New York and Los Angeles. You read about the gathering in front of the U.S. embassy not far from this very spot. And you have undoubtedly read about the growing anti-Japanese sentiment in the United States. These events and trends are nothing short of alarming. As the Prime Minister said . . ."

"I know what that fool has said," Kamiya interrupted. "But I will ask you again, Deputy Director General, you need time for what? For this so-called free trade nonsense to be put into effect? For the so-called economic summit next month? Is that what you fools honestly expect me to help you with?"

Ota was a diminutive man with sharp features, obsidian eyes, and very thick black hair. He was not unlike many Japanese men. Like rabbits, Kamiya thought. The spirit had been eroded in men such as Ota. No *bushido* here.

"We will uncover the connection between you and the group that calls itself Rising Sun, be assured of that, *Kamiya-san.*"

"That is not possible, because no connection exists."

"Just as we will uncover your direct links with MITI, which has allowed you to use the ministry as your personal tool of aggression."

"Get to the point, you fool."

Ota took a couple of steps closer. "And we shall ultimately discover the true meaning of Morning Star, and stop it before the foul stench of your corruption spreads contagiously out of control."

Kamiya made a supreme effort to keep his emotions in check, to keep his body expression loose, and his voice even. "If there were such a thing as Morning Star, and if I were in some way knowledgeable of it or connected with it you would not leave this room alive, *Ota-san.*"

The Deputy Director General was taken aback. "What is this?"

"Let us talk about treason, *Ota-san.* Fifty years of treason, and I will tell you about my vision for Nippon."

FBI Director John Harding met CIA Director Roland Murphy in the corridor outside the White House cabinet room a few minutes before 9:00 A.M. Justice's breakfast meeting with the President had run over, and Murphy had shown up early for his daily brief.

"Glad you're here, General, if you have a moment I'd like a word with you," Harding said.

"I was just on my way in, but it'll be a few minutes before he's ready for me," Murphy agreed. They went down the corridor and sat on a padded bench against the wall. A number of people nodded their greetings in passing.

"How has the world treated us overnight, Roland? Are you going to give the President heartburn?"

"A few hot spots. But nothing like the old days. How about your shop? Anything new?"

"Frankly we're in the middle of an investigation that seems to be spreading all over the place. My people tell me it might involve one of your former field officers. Could be coincidental, but his name does keep turning up."

"Is it serious?"

"Ken Wood seems to think so. And it might tie into a request that the French made to us initially through your Paris Station."

Murphy gave him a hard look. "This have anything to do with Guerin Airplane Company and Kirk McGarvey?"

"Yes, it does, General. But we've temporarily lost track of him in Portland. We'd like some help with his background."

Steve Nichols came down the hall. "The President will see you now, General."

"On my way," Murphy said, getting up. "I'll send a courier over with McGarvey's file later this morning," he told Harding. "Has this anything to do with even remotely with Japan?"

Harding looked up at the DCI. "There's nothing remote about the connection."

"I see," Murphy replied heavily. "I believe I will be giving the President heartburn after all."

EIGHTEEN

Newton Kilbourne grudgingly admitted that his sister was holed up at his house in Grosse Pointe Shores, an exclusive Detroit suburb on Lake St. Clair. But he cautioned McGarvey against trying to see her. He didn't want her to get hurt again. And riding over from the airport McGarvey couldn't blame the man for trying to protect her. They had nobody except each other; he was the older brother, and she was sometimes impulsive and headstrong.

"She asked about you," Kilbourne had said bleakly. "When I told her that you would be heading for Tokyo, she said 'good,' like she meant something. Like she was trying to tell me something without saying it. Good. What the hell is that supposed to mean?"

"I don't know for sure, but I have an idea," McGarvey told him. "Will she remain in Detroit? Can you make her stay put?"

"I don't think so. She said she wanted to talk to you. I told her you were already gone, but she called me a liar. Told me to get a message to you." Kilbourne shook his head. "Christ, what a mess. I tried to call back, but she won't answer the goddamned phone."

"Is she gone already?"

"She's still there. I hired a detective agency to watch over her. But if she wants to hop a plane and return to Washington, there's nothing I can do to stop her. What's going on?" Kilbourne demanded dangerously.

"Call the detective agency and tell them I'll be showing up."

McGarvey had tried to telephone her from the Northwest flight he'd taken, and again from Detroit Metro without luck. Despite her brother's assurances that the detective agency watching her was among the best in Detroit, he worried that something had gone wrong. A couple of civilians were no match for a team of trained, dedicated professionals. If someone wanted to get to Dominique it would happen.

Kilbourne maintained his Grosse Pointe house because he still had a lot of ties there, and because he would retire on the lake shore. It was home to him and to Dominique.

Pulling up at the gate McGarvey could pick out the house at the end of a long, curving driveway through thick trees, many of them evergreens. All the houses were near the water's edge on lots of an acre or more and were owned by automobile executives. The country club was a half-mile away, and even though it was mid-winter, the streets and sidewalks were devoid of snow and looked freshly scrubbed.

A plain blue Dodge van was parked across the street. A tall man in a dark leather jacket got out of the van and came across the street as McGarvey climbed out of the cab.

"Good afternoon, sir," the man said. He had the cynical expression of a cop or ex-cop.

The driver of the van rolled down his window and watched them. His left arm and hand were in view, but his right was not. He was probably holding a gun. So far as it went they seemed to know what they were doing.

"You're expecting me," McGarvey said.

"Depends on who you are."

"Kirk McGarvey."

"Let's see some ID."

McGarvey reached for his wallet, and the detective's hand went into his jacket. "I'm unarmed."

"Easy."

McGarvey pulled out his wallet and flipped it open for the detective to see. The cabby watched them nervously.

"Miss Kilbourne is expecting you."

"She knows you're down here?" McGarvey asked. "You've talked with her?"

"She made us the second day. Came down and said if we didn't get in her way, she wouldn't get in ours."

"She doesn't answer her phone."

"No."

"She get many calls?"

"A few."

"I'd like to have a list of the backtraces," McGarvey said. "In the meantime do I climb over the fence?"

"Squawk her on the intercom. She'll let you in. Will you be staying long?"

"I have a flight at six."

"I'll have that list for you by then."

McGarvey buzzed the intercom and identified himself. Dominique didn't answer, but after a second the gate swung open and McGarvey took the cab up to the house.

"You a cop or something?" the cabby asked.

"Or something," McGarvey replied. "Can you come back for me at 4:30?"

"I'll be here."

The front door was not locked, and Dominique, dressed in jeans and a sweatshirt, was waiting for him in the large stair hall. Her hair was cut boyishly short, and she wore very little makeup.

"Your brother is worried about you," McGarvey said. "How are you?"

"Newton said you were going to Tokyo. Yamagata went for your proposal?"

"It looks like it. Have you talked to anyone else since you left Washington?"

"My office. There were some things that had to be dealt with. But they won't tell anyone where I am because they don't know."

"There've been a number of calls here."

"Other than you, my brother, and my watchdogs, nobody knows I'm here."

"The calls are being traced. If I want to talk to you, I'll ring three times, hang up, and immediately call again. Have you got that?"

She nodded.

"If I want you to get out of here, I'll ring once, hang up and immediately call again letting it ring only once again. If that happens grab your coat and leave immediately. Go to your brother in Portland."

"You're expecting trouble?"

"I want you to be ready for it."

She wet her lips. "When are you leaving for Tokyo?"

"In a couple of hours."

"Are you flying Guerin equipment?"

"Commercial."

"JAL?"

"No," McGarvey said.

The early afternoon winter light streaming through the cut-glass windows flanking the door and down from the clerestory windows above the landing at the head of the stairs softened the planes and angles of her face. For a brief moment she looked like an innocent, the kind of person totally free of guilt whom McGarvey, in his heart-of-hearts, did not believe existed. It was a fault of his own, a personality defect that did not allow him to see only the good in a person. Lurking around every shadowy corner something hurtful was waiting to pounce. Some word or deed that when uttered or accomplished would destroy him. Nor could he forget. In some ways that was an even greater fault—his inability to forget. He remembered every wrong that had ever been done to him, and every wrong he'd committed. He remembered every harsh word, every slur, every slap in the face, and every death that he had caused either directly or indirectly. God knows the number was legion, balanced only by the one life he had created.

He remembered that as a boy he'd looked up to his parents with a love that bordered on blind adoration. His father was everything that a man should or could be: kind, gentle, intelligent, wise, all-knowing, all-seeing, patient, loving, caring. His mother was the epitome of womanhood: beautiful, strong, loving, intelligent, and caring, just like her husband, only in a different way, in a nurturing way.

When their mangled bodies were pried out of the wreckage of their automobile, McGarvey thought his grasp on the real world, on anything and everything that was good and right, had slipped away and he might never regain it. Especially when the investigating officers thought for a short while that the car might have been tampered with to make it crash. But only afterward, after he'd buried them, and after he'd done his eldest-son duty of straightening out their final affairs did he know for certain that he would never regain his grasp of what was good. At that moment, looking over what he'd inadvertently discovered about his parents and understanding its full meaning, he knew that he would always be able to see the end of his life. He was headed for death, as everyone was, only he would never have the slightest illusion about his own mortality.

It was damned cold being that alone, and he didn't know if he could change. He just knew, looking at Dominique, that for the first time in a long while he wanted to try.

"It's starting, isn't it?"

"Soon."

"I read the newspapers," she said impatiently. "Newton didn't say anything about the murder at Gales Creek. What'd they want?"

"We don't know."

"Was it the Japanese?"

"We just don't know, Dominique."

Color had come to her cheeks and forehead. "At first I thought David was crazy or desperate for dealing with you. But I was wrong."

"I want to save lives."

"You're a killer," she said simply. "It's what you do, and sometimes you're necessary. I can see that now."

She had pulled out his heart, but he couldn't blame her. Not really. "I'm sorry," he said, and he started to turn away.

"Look at this place, look at me. It's a mausoleum, and I'm in hiding."

"You'll be safe here for a little while longer."

"I want to go back to my office in Washington. There are people who depend on me."

"You will, I promise you."

She shook her head. "Now."

"A few days, maybe. Dominique, listen to me."

"I hate you," she said softly.

"Do you want to go to your brother?"

She raised her eyes and looked at him. She was torn by emotion, but beyond that her face was unreadable to McGarvey. She was in pain, and he didn't know what to do to help her.

"Dominique, I'll end it as soon as I can."

"Go, then. Do it," she said. "And leave me alone."

Marine Lieutenant Colonel Robert Blisk was waiting on the ramp at Camp Foster as Captain Don Moody climbed down from the Gulfstream VC-10 on which he'd hitched a ride from Yokosuka. The weather over Okinawa was decidedly better than over the Japanese main island. The sun was shining, and Moody was glad of it.

"I see that you've finally wised up and started to moonlight as a cabby."

"Can't make ends meet on what the Corps pays me."

"Which is a hell of a lot more than you're worth."

Blisk chuckled as they got into his HumVee and headed to headquarters on the other side of the base. As chief of First Marine Air Wing Intelligence on Okinawa he did the same thing for First Wing that Moody did for Seventh Fleet. They'd crossed paths a number of times in their careers and had developed a solid working relationship. They trusted each other's judgment.

"How's life been treating you down here, Bob? You're getting set to rotate back home, aren't you?"

"We'll be back in D.C. in six months. But Keiri's not overly excited about the move. She's in Nagasaki now with her mother, and every damned time she goes they try to talk her into staying."

Moody smiled. "Twenty years and they're still working on her? Tenacious people."

"Yes, they are," Blisk said, glancing at Moody. "You've got your hands full at Yokosuka."

"I think the writing's on the wall, and everybody can see it, but nobody's saying much. We've got a couple more years here before we're eased out."

"Subic Bay sure as hell isn't making anybody happy."

"It's their ocean, Bob. Hell, they're the allies now, and it's up to us to do everything possible to help them. We owe them, remember?"

"You ought to see Keiri's mother when she does her

thing. Pulls off her wig so everyone can see her bald head and wrings her hands and cries about cancer and liver damage and genetic imbalances. Problem is, everyone sympathizes with her even though she was seventy-five miles away from Nagasaki when we dropped the bomb on them."

"And that was over fifty years ago. Like I say, they're a tenacious people."

Of the 34,000 U.S. personnel stationed on Okinawa, two-thirds of them were Marines. Anything happened on the island, Blisk knew about it. Even Air Force Intelligence on adjacent Kadena Air Force Base fed into Blisk's operation. The usual division of labor made no sense out here.

"There's a potentially no-win situation heading your way, and Al Ryland asked me to come down to fill you in," Moody said when they reached Blisk's office.

"You're talking about the MSDF submarine that bulled its way through the Takara Strait."

"Mike Hanrahan's a good man, but there wasn't much he could have done, short of taking a shot."

A sergeant came in with coffee, and Blisk held off making a comment until the aide was gone and the door closed.

"It's that bad?"

"The sub is the *Samisho,* same one that sank the Russian frigate up north. Nobody at the MSDF is talking to us, so Ryland has bounced it back to Washington. In the meantime, Hanrahan is going to stick with it as long as he can."

"The *Samisho* is heading this way?"

"Looks like it."

"At the risk of sounding flippant, so what? It's their ocean, as you say, Okinawa belongs to them, and I'm a ground-pounder, not a sub-hunter. Seems to me if you force that sub-driver into a corner he'll shoot."

"Technically speaking, we're still a force of occupation."

"Bullshit."

Moody had to smile. "That's a good word, Bob. Use it all the time myself. But there's more to the situation than we're publicizing. When's the last time you had this place swept?"

"We're clean. And there are no Japanese nationals on this floor, if that's what you mean."

"I do," Moody said. He took a half-dozen large, oddly tinted photographs from his briefcase and handed them to Blisk. "The first five are computer-enhanced night shots courtesy of the National Reconnaissance Office. They came through this morning. Atsugi, Iwakuni, Komatsujima, Shimofusa, and Hachinowe. All of them naval air installations."

"Tokyo doesn't know we have this capability?"

"We don't think so. Only reason I got these is because of a friend."

Blisk studied the first photographs. "If I didn't know better I'd say they were starting to mobilize and trying to keep it under wraps. This come out of the blue, or did you go fishing?"

"I had a hunch," Moody said. "The sixth shot is of the Air Self Defense Force base on Tanegashima. They're doing the same thing."

Blisk looked at the last photograph. "Readiness drills. They do it all the time."

"This one wasn't published."

"We weren't invited to the show, and someone's getting nervous."

"The *Samisho*'s skipper was under arrest pending an investigation into the incident in the Tatar Strait. MSDF was talking a charge of treason, but they never locked him up. Had him under house arrest, and somehow he managed to get to his fully provisioned, fully armed, and fully crewed boat, which had been under continuous guard, and drive out of the harbor. Nobody tried to stop him. The MSDF didn't scramble its sub-hunters, nor were we notified. And that always happens, Bob. The MSDF moves a ship, and we get the message. SOP. Standard Operating Procedure."

"What are you telling me? That the Japanese military is gearing up for war?"

"There's an outside chance that the Russians might try to pull something in retaliation for their frigate. The entire crew was lost. The Japanese may be gearing up for it."

"That makes more sense to me."

"They didn't tell us."

"They haven't consulted us about Subic Bay either."

"The weather has closed in so it may be a few days before N.R.O. can give us anything further. But why Tanegashima? If the Russians want to start something they'll tie it to the Sakhalin Island issue. If there's any action it'll be up north."

"I see what you mean," Blisk said. "The *Samisho* should be heading north, not south. But if I catch your full meaning, it's still thin."

"I'm not advocating or predicting a thing, Bob. But this is your island. You tell me. Any unusual incidents around here? Increased activity? Accidents that shouldn't have happened. Sabotage. Pilfering. Anything at all?"

Blisk sat back and eyed Moody. "Has Ryland talked to my boss about this?"

"No. So far this is just between us. I'm here to fill you in on the *Samisho*, and to answer any questions you might have."

Major General Marvin Zweibel was commander-in-chief of all the Marines on Okinawa. He was a fair-minded but tough man who had the reputation of cutting his people off at the knees if he thought something was being hidden from him.

"Would you be willing to tell him what you've told me?"

"Say the word."

Again Blisk eyed Moody speculatively. "I might do that, Don, but for the moment let's keep this in our bailiwick. I'm saying that because I can't tell you a thing that might signify anything. Okinawa is doing business as usual. Sorry."

"Don't be, because believe me I hope I'm seeing spooks in the closet."

"You have jeopardized all of us," Reid warned. He'd just come out from the city, and he'd been drinking heavily all day. His eyes were bleary, and he slurred some of his words.

"There wasn't anything else I could do, Mr. R.," Glen Zerkel replied. "You sent me out to gather information, which I did. It was bad luck, that's all. But no one else saw me, so there's no way I can be identified. The only man who did see my face is dead."

"Maybe you can plant a story that a Japanese man was spotted nearby," Louis Zerkel said.

"I've already thought of that. But it'll have to be done with care."

"Especially since you yourself might be under investigation by the FBI because of your involvement with General Schey," Louis took his shot. He had spent the early morning hours redesigning his safeguard system. By eight it was in place within the FBI's mainframe. Mueller's tampering would not destroy it. He and Glen were safe.

"If there ever was a suspicion about me, it has been quashed. And you would be well advised to keep your nose out of places it does not belong. Concentrate on your part of this operation."

"Don't threaten me!" Louis blurted. His face was hot, and he was nauseous. He always felt that way when his anger got out of check.

"Take it easy, Louis," his brother cautioned.

"I don't have to. They can't touch us now. I made sure of that last night. As of this morning there's not a thing they can do. What do you think about that?"

Reid shook his head in irritation. "Then pack your bags and get out of here you prima donna sonofabitch! But leave the way you came, with nothing except some data on a few floppy disks. Leave the computer equipment that I bought for you and go."

The old man walked across the room to one of the terminals and studied the complicated electronic diagram on the screen. He was not an electronics expert so he didn't have the slightest idea what he was looking at, but he knew it was important. His life had finally come down to this moment in time with two men, both of whom could be classified as insane. Where then did the greater fault lie? With the hand that held the gun, or with the man who directed the gunman? Who said that things begin to fall apart at the edges, but as long as the center holds you'll be all right? He couldn't recall, nor was he sure he wasn't mixing metaphors or something. But his plan was beginning to unravel at the edges, and even the center was getting muddled.

His name had apparently come up in some discussion over at the FBI, although exactly in what context he'd not been able to find out. A word to a friend of his at State was filtered to the Bureau through a White House staffer, and he was safe for the moment. But he'd been shaken to the core. Everything was coming apart, but it shouldn't be happening. Not yet.

Reid turned the monitor's brightness control down, and the image on the screen faded. Then he turned the contrast control to zero and the image slowly faded to nothing.

"Gone," he said, looking up at the Zerkels. "And yet not gone. You've done most of the work, Louis, for which I thank you. Now I think I could find perhaps a hundred thousand electronics and computer experts who could finish the job."

"Without me your entire scheme will be plastered over every FBI terminal in Washington."

"Your name is there too."

"I didn't name myself or my brother."

"But I did," Reid said.

"Not in my program . . ."

"In mine, Louis. Shall we talk about your psychiatrist, or about your InterTech supervisor and his family? Or about the murder of the InterTech night watchman and the fire? You're implicated in all of those crimes, of course. And in California they still have the death penalty."

"You're forgetting me, Mr. R.," Glen said. "To this point nobody except us in this room knows I'm involved. I could kill you now, and Louis could find and destroy your program. I don't think it would be hard for him to do."

"And you're forgetting Bruno. I've offered the man one million dollars in gold for his part. What do you think he would do to the people who took that away from him? Or do you think you're a match for him?"

"I think between us we could manage to take him out," Glen said. "He's a man, not a god."

"Why?" Reid asked.

"Why what?" Glen said, his eyes narrowing.

"Go through all of this when we've made so much progress, when we're so near to the finish? You haven't got far to go, have you, Louis?"

Louis shook his head, but then stopped.

"Kill me and walk out of here, and the two of you will be hunted fugitives for the rest of your lives. Stay and finish the job and you'll have enough money to go a very long distance from here, where you'll be able to insulate yourselves from the grubbiness of leading ordinary lives."

"How do we know that Mueller won't kill us when we've done our bit?" Glen asked.

"We've all got our safeguards in place, that's why," Reid answered. "Nobody wants to end up on the run or in jail or, in Louis's case, in the gas chamber. Together we can win. If we separate now, we'll all lose."

"It's you who is the sonofabitch," Louis said.

Reid smiled wanly and nodded. "You are entirely right, my good man, I am indeed a sonofabitch. But right now I'm your rich sonofabitch."

"Goddamned right."

"How soon before you think you'll be ready?"

Louis shrugged. "I don't know. A few days, maybe a little longer."

"Good. Then Glen and I will go over the details of what he learned in Portland. And as soon as Bruno returns with what information he's gathered, the four of us will decide exactly how we'll accomplish our mission with the least amount of risk. Anybody have a problem with that?"

The Zerkels said nothing.

NINETEEN

All right, gentlemen, what have we got so far?" John Whitman asked. It was late, he'd missed dinner, and his stomach was sour from too much coffee and too many cigarettes.

"We have a substantial number of criminal acts, but the connection between them, if one exists, is circumstantial at best," Albert McLaren told his boss.

Phillip Joyce looked up from the file he was studying. "With Reid off limits for the moment, we've got only two choices, John. We either stick with McGarvey, or we take each case on its own merits and pursue the investigations individually."

"McGarvey is one tough sonofabitch, but if I'm reading it right, I think he's in the middle of it all," McLaren said. "Hell, nothing started to come down until he went to work for Guerin."

"Doesn't make him a criminal." Whitman played devil's advocate.

"Maybe not, but I'd sure as hell pick him as a material witness to any one of these incidents, including the Dulles crash."

"If we go after him we're going to have to watch our step," Joyce cautioned. "He's more than a tough sonofabitch. Have you read his file?"

"The man has done some impressive stuff," McLaren said.

"I'll say. Even the CIA treats him with kid gloves. Did your read about that incident with that Los Angeles-class sub? And then the thing in Iran?"

"He's killed some people. He's an assassin . . ."

"Excuse me, Al, but assassins usually take their targets out in a lot more civilized manner. Not usually face to face, and not usually with ten-to-one odds against them. Shit, the Russians respect him! I'm telling you that if we go after him we'd better get some help, and we'd better keep our distance. I don't want to end up in a body bag."

"He's just a man. He can't take on the entire Bureau."

"Take it easy," Whitman interrupted. "Nothing here says the man is directly involved."

"Then why did he accept a job with Guerin Airplane Company?" McLaren shot back.

"You're forgetting the man's file," Joyce said.

"What?"

"I think the real question is why did Guerin hire him. McGarvey's not a businessman, he's not an airplane designer or engineer or electronic technician. He kills people. So what's Guerin doing hiring a killer? What's more, hasn't the CIA always denied—even to us—that it uses assassins? Yet it sent over his file to us. And there can't be any question about what it contains. You tell me what's going on."

"Are we getting caught in the middle of some political game?" McLaren asked.

"Ken Wood seems to think it's a possibility," Whitman admitted.

McLaren groaned and sat back. They met in a small conference room across the hall from Whitman's office so they had more space to spread out their case files. The long table was loaded.

Joyce opened another file. It was a brief case history of McGarvey's last job for the CIA. "You can argue that he harbors some anti-Japanese sentiment."

"Not so uncommon."

"Guerin is worried about a Japanese buyout that maybe the White House is ignoring because of the Tokyo Economic Summit. Somehow Guerin's brass found out that McGarvey has bad feelings about the Japanese, and I assume the Japanese feel the same way about him. They also found out just who and what he is, and that he has the respect of the CIA and presumably even the Russians. Are you following me so far?"

"I'm not sure that I am," Whitman admitted.

"If the Japanese are forced into making a big mistake, maybe the White House would have to sit up and take notice after all."

"The days of the Chrysler bailout are over," McLaren said.

"Right," Joyce replied sardonically. "The first step after they hire McGarvey is to negotiate with the Russians for a factory. Can't be making the Japanese happy. Did Mr. Wood tell you what kind of politics he was talking about?"

"Only concerning Reid. The State Department asked us to back off, and someone at the White House agreed. That's politics."

"But no mention was made about McGarvey?" Joyce asked. "No one has asked us to back off?"

"No."

"The CIA has been extraordinarily cooperative with us, sending over these files. Who'd they come from? Do we have a name?"

"Howard Ryan, the Agency's general counsel," Whitman said.

"What are you getting at?" McLaren asked his partner. "You have the look."

"I'd say we were being *directed* toward Mr. McGarvey."

"By whom?"

"I don't know, and I find that curious, don't you?"

"What's your point?"

"If we investigate each incident—and I think there'll be more—we could get bogged down. But if we go after McGarvey, we might get somewhere."

"Do you think he has his own agenda?" Whitman asked.

"I don't know that either," Joyce answered. "But I do know that Mr. McGarvey booked a business-class ticket from Portland to Detroit . . ."

"What the hell is he doing in Detroit?" McLaren asked.

"That's anybody's guess, but he's already left there on his way, via Seattle, to Tokyo. What do you suppose he's up to this time?"

Technical Sergeant Tony Person removed the last of the six screws holding an electronics panel marked HEAT MONITOR/ALARM, ENGINE, PORT in its rack aboard Air Force One parked in its hangar at Andrews Air Force Base. He pulled the unit out and shunted its connectors through a Tektronix dual-trace scope and spectrum analyzer and back into the twenty-seven-pin receptacle in the rack. It was the eleventh subassembly he'd run diagnostic checks on so far today. There were a lot more to go.

His headset was connected to the aircraft's intercom system. "Jim, I'm ready to power up Hotel Mike slash Alpha, Port."

"Stand by," Staff Sergeant Jim Spallaci radioed. He was on a work scaffold beneath the unbuttoned port engine.

Like the other twenty technicians on the team, he and Person had been going over the President's airplane with a fine-tooth comb for three days. Their NCOIC Chief Master Sergeant Gene Mazorsky was a stickler for details. But so was his boss, Captain Robin Woodhaven. If Mazorsky was a zealot, the captain was a maniac. She had more to prove because she was a woman in a predominantly male career field.

Before and after every flight, Air Force One was thoroughly checked out by Mazorsky's raiders, as they called themselves. And just prior to a long flight—especially a trans-Atlantic, or in this case a trans-Pacific, flight—the preventative maintenance routines were ultra-rigid. But the President's airplane was a Guerin P522, the same type of aircraft that had gone down at Dulles, and this time they were practically pulling the bird apart and rebuilding her.

Each of the five sections on the team had a specific area of responsibility—electrical, structures—including the aircraft's skin, engines, flight controls, and hydraulics systems. But cooperation was orchestrated directly by Mazorsky. They were a well-oiled machine, the best against any standard in any air force or any private sector anywhere in the world.

"Starting on line one, pulse GO-One," Spallaci came back.

GO-One was the interrogative signal that the monitor/alarm subassembly sent to the engine-mounted sensor rack when the system was first powered up. The subassembly said it was ready for action and asked the engine sensors if they were ready.

Person hit the start button on his test set, which simulated the power-up procedure that would be initiated by the crew above in the cockpit. The GO-One pulse showed up on the oscilloscope against the timing grid.

"Shit," Person said half under his breath.

"Looks good," Spallaci radioed.

"Stand by. I'm sending you GO-One again. I had what looked like one-tenth-hertz delay."

"Maybe you were out of phase there, because it looked good on the frame."

Person shut off the power to the subassembly for a moment. "Here it comes." He hit the start button, and again the GO-One pulse showed up very slightly delayed.

"It's good out here," Spallaci radioed.

"I'm still off," Person replied. "Is Sergeant Mazorsky on the floor?"

"Right here," Mazorsky said at the open access hatch in the cockpit floor above. "What's the problem?"

"Jim, he's up here with me," Person radioed. He looked up. "I'm catching a phase delay or shift on the heat monitor/alarm GO-One."

"Let me see the book."

Person handed up the schematic diagram of the subassembly, and Mazorsky studied it for a few seconds. "GO-One is routed through the main CPU chip, but we're using the new sensor frame and harness. Run it again."

"I'm sending you GO-One again," Person radioed. He shut down the subassembly's power, waited a moment, then hit the start button. As before GO-One was slightly delayed on Person's scope.

"Right on," Spallaci said.

Person looked up. "It's good at the engine."

"They probably built a phase delay into the CPU to accommodate the new frame and harness," Mazorsky said. He handed the schematic back down. "It's within parameters, but log it anyway."

"You got it, Sarge."

Bruno Mueller parked his rental car in the lot in front of the low-slung modern Oakland Airport Commission building in the industrial park across the airport from the main terminal. In the distance he could see the control tower rising up across the main east-west runway, and to the north the rotating radar antennae and communications dishes that were used by the tower and by Air Traffic Control. The air smelled of burned kerojet, and as he got out of his car a big jetliner took off with a window-rattling roar.

He was pushing his luck sticking around here this long. Sooner or later someone would think to call the editors at *High Technology Business* or *Aviation Week & Space Technology* magazines to ask about him and find out that no one had heard of Thomas Reston. But he wanted to learn more. As incredible as it seemed, passengers entering the terminal were required to submit to an electronic search of themselves and their luggage, but no such security measures were required of someone entering Air Traffic Control or the tower where a terrorist could do more harm.

Putting Louis Zerkel's repeater somewhere in the Air Traffic Control centers at any airport would present no insurmountable problem (Bill White had assured him that most U.S. airports were similar). But they could only count on keeping them in place undetected for forty-eight hours at most. The real problem was the touchiness of the ATC equipment, which was almost constantly under some maintenance routine. Just about every piece of equipment in a typical Air Traffic Control center was taken apart and cleaned or adjusted every couple of days. The repeater would almost certainly be discovered more quickly than they'd hoped. If that was the route they were going to take, the timing would be tight. Maybe too tight.

For Louis Zerkel's scheme to work, a signal had to be sent to every airplane within a Terminal Control Area, the air space immediately above and around an airport. The firing pulse would be sent to the airplane piggybacked, or superimposed, on a legitimate signal, such as the transmissions Air Traffic Control generated.

But Bill White had given Mueller another idea. Air Traffic Control wasn't the only unit sending electronic signals to incoming and departing airplanes. A lot of electronic traffic went back and forth between jetliners in the air and installations on the ground, among which were the various airport radars, the navigational beacons, and signals from a flight-management-system research project being conducted by the Oakland Airport Commission.

The project manager, Ron Herring, met Mueller in the reception area. He was a compact man in his late thirties with an athletic build, boyish good looks, and a direct up-front manner. His hair was cropped short, and his clothes looked as if they'd just been starched and ironed.

"I'm surprised Bill White even mentioned my name," Herring said, grinning. He and Mueller shook hands.

"I don't think he likes you very much. Seems to think you're wasting your money and his time."

"If we're irritating the feds, it must mean we're doing something right."

Herring led him back to a small suite of offices that were equipped with computer terminals, large-screen monitors, data recorders, and other electronic gear. Three men and one woman were seated at desks or terminals, and they looked up and nodded and smiled. The atmosphere here seemed far less tense than across the field at Air Traffic Control.

"Why the difference of opinion?" Mueller asked.

"Did Bill give you the bit about how air traffic controllers have big egos?"

"He made it a point."

"They're still bitching about what Reagan did to them, but the fact is they're outmoded and downright dangerous. Having a man on the ground watching a radar scope and telling a pilot what to do won't work much longer no matter what kind of new equipment IBM comes up with for them." Herring shrugged. "Did Bill tell you about the incident with the guy and the walkie-talkie last year? A Northwest flight had just taken off, and departure control told the pilot to climb to six thousand and make a turn to a heading of one-two-oh. A second later some joker on the ground, using a Radio Shack VHF walkie-talkie, got on the air and told the pilot to disregard the last instruction and instead climb to five thousand feet and make a left turn to three-zero-zero. If the pilot hadn't been sharp and asked departure control for a repeat, he would have collided with an incoming Quantas flight."

"It's a vulnerable system," Mueller agreed, and after all he'd seen so far he was not surprised.

"You can't imagine how bad it is. But every airplane flying with a glass cockpit, and in a few years that'll be just about every commercial airliner, is equipped with a Flight Management System computer. With the proper ground installation every FMS-equipped airplane can be brought in for a landing or directed on takeoff out of the Terminal Control Area along very precisely defined corridors. And I do mean precise. Every airplane would approach and leave the TCA on a path that would be meters, not kilometers, from a center line."

"No chance for errors? Collisions?"

"Equipment can go down, so we'd provide backup and human supervisors with an override capability," Herring said.

"This system is in place now?" Mueller asked.

"It's not certified yet, but we are running an ongoing test, with electronic cross-talk between us and the FMS-equipped airplanes coming into our TCA."

"From here?"

"The transmitters and some of the recording devices are physically located in the basement, but the controls and data outputs all come to this room."

It was a stroke of good luck.

"Actually all of this started out in Minneapolis where a hotshot friend of mine from MIT—and an Air Guard pilot like me—was working on an airport noise-management system. He wanted to precisely regulate the airport's flight pattern, so he came up with the FMS idea. The feds don't like him any better than the rest of us."

"The rest of us?" Mueller asked as nonchalantly as he could.

"The same study is in place at Los Angeles, at O'Hare, and Minneapolis, of course, at Dulles, and at New York's LaGuardia and JFK. We're working on Miami and Atlanta, but it may be six months or a year before they come on line."

"I understand," Mueller said. "Is there a possibility of seeing the equipment downstairs?"

"Why not?" Herring said.

Tokyo was in the middle of rush hour. All the counters at Narita Airport were jammed. The passport and customs officials were polite as usual, but something was different. At first McGarvey couldn't quite put his finger on it, but the atmosphere in the busy terminal was the same as it had been aboard the flight over. Half the passengers on the jetliner had been Caucasian, while most of the other half were Japanese, or Oriental, and a transparent wall seemed to stand between the two aboard the airplane and here.

"The purpose of your visit, Mr. McGarvey?" the passport officer asked pleasantly.

"I have business with Japan Air Lines."

"What is the nature of this business, Mr. McGarvey?"

"It is financial in nature," McGarvey said evenly.

"What will be the length of your stay in Japan, please?"

"I'm not sure. Perhaps two or three days."

"Do you have hotel reservations?"

"Yes, I do," McGarvey replied. He'd never been asked so many questions coming into Japan. Things were definitely different. It was the growing anti-American sentiment.

"At which hotel do you have reservations, Mr. McGarvey?" the passport officer asked patiently.

"Is there some problem with my passport?"

"At which hotel will you be staying?"

"The Asakusa View. It is in Taito-ku. Is there some trouble?"

The officer stamped McGarvey's passport and handed it back. "Next," he said, smiling pleasantly.

And fuck you too, McGarvey said to himself, taking his passport and following his fellow passengers down the escalators and across to customs. There were a lot of uniformed, armed police stationed throughout the terminal. It was something else he'd never seen before. Japan had prided itself on being a nation with an extremely low crime rate. No need, therefore, for such an open show of force. Things had definitely changed. Narita seemed like an airport geared for trouble.

Mueller had dinner at a Ponderosa Steak House in San Leandro a few miles from the airport, then checked into a Days Inn Motel off Interstate 580 near the Oak Knoll

Naval Medical Center. The evening had turned cool with a sea breeze and thick cloud cover. For its size, America was a very easy place in which to travel. Unlike Europe where every border crossing used to be fraught with danger, here people's credentials were seldom checked. Renting a car required a driver's license and a credit card. But boarding an airplane or train, or driving across state lines, elicited no suspicion or attention. The country was wide open, and it had always amazed him that there weren't more acts of terrorism here. Except for a few incidents such as the car bombing of the World Trade Center towers in New York City, the country had emerged from the Cold War relatively unscathed. Of course all that was about to change. If their project was a success no one in America would ever feel secure again.

At midnight he headed back to the Oakland Airport Commission, traffic much lighter. The last flight was due in at 12:25 A.M., and as he got off the freeway across from the Oakland-Alameda County Coliseum the big jetliner from Honolulu was touching down. It was a Guerin P522, and he thought how lucky the people flying in tonight were. Chances are most of them would not be flying again so soon. For many of them the flight was the termination of a much anticipated midwinter vacation. California was great, but Hawaii was better. They would go back to work a little sunburned, a little weary, but content that they could hold out now until summer. Most of them would not be taking one of the Guerin P522s that would crash at this airport, killing everyone aboard.

There were only two cars in the Oakland Airport Commission's parking lot. Night watchmen. It was one of the additional bits of information he'd needed.

Mueller drove past and put his car behind a long row of trucks and delivery vans at a warehouse identified by a sign in front as Miramax Distributing Company, Ltd. He made his way on foot back to the rear of the OAC building, keeping to the shadows as much as possible. If he were stopped and questioned here, he would have no reasonable answers. He would have to make the kill and get away. Oakland would be out then, but from what he'd learned already there were going to be very few problems bringing down as many jetliners as they wanted to. When it happened, the day would rank right up there with the day Kennedy was assassinated and the day the shuttle *Challenger* exploded. No one would forget. But he needed to know one more thing.

Two vans, one of them windowless, with the Oakland Airport Commission seal on their doors, were parked at a rear entrance. A light over the door illuminated an area fifteen feet from the building. None of the windows showed light.

Mueller examined the situation from where he stood in the darkness beside a pale-gray Dumpster. From his vantage point he spotted the closed-circuit television camera above the door. Someone inside the building would be monitoring the screen. The OAC was security conscious after all.

Asagiri Eto left a message at the front desk that he would come to the hotel at six sharp to meet McGarvey for drinks and dinner. If that was not acceptable he'd left a telephone number. McGarvey had instructed the concierge to direct Eto to the sixth-floor communal *hinoki*—a traditional bathhouse with Japanese cypress hot tubs. Drinks and dinner would come later.

It was just that hour when McGarvey got off the elevator and crossed to the bathhouse that overlooked a beautiful indoor garden. The place was pleasantly warm and humid and smelled of jasmine and teak and cypress woods. Several of the deep tubs were occupied, all of them by Oriental men who glared up at McGarvey when they realized a *Gai Jin* had invaded their territory, and watchful that the barbarian would make mistakes in the bathing ritual that would embarrass them all.

The attendant was a flustered old man who gave McGarvey two large towels and directed him to a changing compartment. He kept bowing and shuffling his feet, almost a parody of how a lot of Americans still thought the Japanese behaved.

McGarvey got undressed and stepped across a narrow corridor to the showers, where he used a lot of soap to scrub himself, including his hair, before rinsing first in hot, then in cold, water. He wrapped one towel around his waist and the other over his shoulders and went back into the tub room.

A slightly built Japanese man dressed in a sharply tailored blue pinstriped business suit was talking with the attendant, his gestures animated as if he were angry. When he spotted McGarvey he hurried over.

"Mr. McGarvey, I am sorry. I thought I misunderstood your message. I was told that you wished to arrange a meeting as soon as possible."

McGarvey glared at the man for several long moments. Everyone in the place was watching them. *"Eto-san,* it has been a tiring trip from the United States. Before I discuss business I would like to sit in a very hot tub, have my back scrubbed, and drink very cold saki. Can you understand this?"

Eto suddenly looked uncomfortable. "I am terribly sorry."

"You may join me, but I caution you we will not talk about business or world affairs."

"Yes, of course."

McGarvey stared at him for several more moments as if he were trying to fix the man's face in his mind. "I am a punctual man, *Eto-san.* The agreed upon time was six. You are late."

Eto's expression sagged even further, and he lowered his eyes. "I am truly sorry, McGarvey-*san.* I only heard at the last minute that you would be arriving, and my instructions were not precise."

"Perhaps I should be meeting with someone else."

"That will not be necessary. If you will give me a moment I will join you."

"Very well."

"And if you will permit me to order the saki, there are a number of varieties you should try."

"I prefer my saki very dry, *Eto-san,*" McGarvey said, and he turned abruptly and went directly to one of the big tubs where he lay his towels aside. Without hesitation, and with no outward indication that the water was so hot it was nearly beyond human endurance, he sat down up to his neck.

For a long time no one in the bathhouse moved or made a sound, until finally a young woman in a snow-white bathing costume got into the tub with McGarvey and began scrubbing his back with a large, rough natural sponge.

One point for the Christians, McGarvey thought. And zero for the lions. He'd taken the opening shot. The next move was theirs.

It was a macabre bit of irony not lost on Mueller that the jetliner taking him back to Washington, D.C., was a Guerin P522. With a crew of seven the airplane could carry three hundred seventy-five passengers nonstop coast to coast. In the past few years most airlines in America had reduced the number of flights made each day in order to get the maximum use out of their equipment, so most U.S. domestic flights were full or nearly full. If ten airplanes went down, at least thirty-five hundred would be killed. That wasn't counting the possible casualties on the ground. The airplanes they were going to knock out of the sky would be approaching for a landing or taking off and climbing out over populated areas. When these huge birds came tumbling down there was no telling what could happen. Mueller made a note to find out which airports maintained approach and departure patterns over schools or hospitals or apartment complexes where population densities would be high.

The flight attendants were getting ready to serve breakfast, and the odors of coffee and food actually smelled good to Mueller. If this was one of the flights they were going to bring down, no breakfast would be served. In fact the first-class passengers would be the only ones to have drinks by then. No time for anyone to get over the take-off nervousness. It gave him a rush thinking about it, and he had to consciously stop himself from grinning like a simpering idiot.

There was little doubt in his mind that Louis Zerkel would come up with the electronic solution to the triggering pulses, and there was little doubt that his brother would hold up his end. Nor, now that he'd seen Oakland's tower, Air Traffic Control, and airport commission facilities, did he have any doubt about bugging the system. But he did have serious reservations about Reid. The man was a drunk, and he was unstable. If the FBI were to approach him he might try to bully his way out, thereby giving everything away. It was a problem, Mueller told himself, that he was going to have to address soon.

Oakland, Los Angeles, Chicago, Minneapolis, New York, and Washington. It would definitely be a day all Americans would never forget.

TWENTY

I don't know if we can be ready in sixteen days," Newton Kilbourne said. He and George Socrates sat with David Kennedy in the first-class section of the P/C2622 in her Gales Creek assembly hangar. The cabin was ninety-five percent complete. The only major work left to be done inside was on the avionics in the cockpit.

"Al Vasilanti wants it. He set the date," Kennedy said.

"We all understand why, and I don't blame him, but it doesn't alter the facts." In actuality, except for the hypersonic engines, the airplane was nearly ready to fly. The FAA's chief regional certification inspector was willing to issue a one-flight airworthiness certificate that would allow Guerin to conduct one test flight over unpopulated areas and for a limited duration. That flight could be conducted tomorrow. The real problem was with unk-unks—unknown problems that couldn't be predicted but always cropped up in the design and manufacture of anything so complex as a modern jetliner. "We've had our share of unk-unks on this project, David. No reason to expect anything has changed."

"I understand what you're saying. But short of the FAA grounding us, or you or George telling us flatly that we can't fly, we're on for Honolulu in sixteen days."

Kilbourne thumped his fist on the armrest of his seat. "It's too soon, goddammit, and you know it."

"I tend to agree with Newton, but not strictly for technical reasons," Socrates said. He'd arrived back from the crash investigation yesterday and had thrown himself into the final pre-test flight preparations and inspections.

"Are you telling me that we can't be ready to fly?" Kennedy asked.

Socrates shook his head. "We can do an initial test flight the day after tomorrow, which would leave us two weeks to fix anything that crops up, and make at least three additional one-certificate runs. If we were trying for hypersonic or even supersonic speeds now, I'd definitely say no."

"But?" Kennedy prompted.

Socrates took off his glasses and wiped the lenses with the end of his tie. "Dulles was very bad, David."

"I know that," Kennedy replied too sharply. "I know."

"There was nothing wrong with our airplane, nor was there anything wrong with the Rolls engines. Sending our AOG teams around the world to switch power plants does nothing but waste money and shake our image."

"Something we don't need just now," Kilbourne put in.

"But our airplane did fall out of the sky," Kennedy said.

"Yes, it did," Socrates agreed solemnly. "We looked for evidence of sabotage, but we didn't find a thing. Sam Varelis says that the Board will probably rule in March that the crash was caused by faulty turbine blades in the port engine. Sir Malcolm wants to disagree, but he's caught in the middle."

"You don't believe it."

"The engine swallowed a blade, but I don't know why."

"We've done a fault-tree analysis," Kennedy said.

"Nothing showed up."

"But you have a gut feeling."

Socrates nodded.

"It shouldn't affect this airplane, George," Kennedy said reasonably. "Completely different engines from the frame out."

"I know. But the break-in and killing here is one more link in what could be a very big and nasty chain. I sat in on some of your meetings with McGarvey. I talked with him, answered his questions, listened to what he had to say. He's a very bright man, David, but he's an alarming man. He's made me think about things I believed were no longer possible. Hitler is dead. Stalin is dead. Hirohito is dead. And the Cold War is over. We won."

"That's exactly why Al wants this flight to go as advertised. Show them that we're not about to cave in." Kennedy shrugged. "There's nothing wrong with this airplane. If some unk-unks crop up we'll fix them."

"There was nothing wrong with our airplane now lying in ugly piles at Dulles."

"It could have been tampered with on the ramp in Moscow by the Russians or by the Japanese, or hell, by someone else with a grudge against Americans. Functioning airplanes don't crash."

"A glitch."

"Yes, and that's something we can't protect against no matter what the circumstances are, George. Just like clear air turbulence and wind shear used to be major problems."

"There would have been an indication," Socrates said. He was tearing himself apart with this. He was an engineer. Effects had causes—it was axiomatic.

"There'll be another big difference between this flight and the one into Dulles."

Socrates looked up. "What's that?"

"We left Moscow after nothing more than a routine pre-flight. Before this airplane leaves for Honolulu it will have been tested from stem to stern a dozen times. You are personally going to oversee that every single system and subsystem aboard is at or above specs."

"What about the engines?" Kilbourne asked.

"I spoke with Sir Malcolm. He's sending a team. In fact they ought to be showing up later today. Put them to work."

"Who'll be crewing?"

"Pete Reiner and John Callahan. Northwest has agreed to loan us fifteen flight attendants."

It took a moment for what Kennedy said to sink in, and when it did Kilbourne and Socrates were stunned.

"What are you talking about?" the engineer demanded.

"We'll carry a full load out to Honolulu and back," Kennedy said evenly. He knew that this was going to be the worst part, especially for Socrates. It's the reason he met them here. The airplane was an impressive piece of machinery.

"Engineers, technicians, monitoring equipment?"

Kennedy shook his head. "Al Vasilanti and his wife. Me and my wife. You two, Fred Taich, Gary Topper, and Larry Cross."

"The Vice President of the United States?"

"Yes. Along with Tom Holder and most of his House Subcommittee on Aviation, a few senators, a couple of representatives from the FAA, the news media, of course, and the Russian ambassador."

"Jesus, Mary, and Joseph," Kilbourne said in awe. "Al has lost his mind."

"We're trying to run an airplane company, Newton," Kennedy flared. "America may be painted on the fuselage, but our name is stamped on the airframe. We've bet the farm on this project, and it either works big or we go under. It's come down to that."

"Somebody wants us to fail," Socrates said.

"That's right," Kennedy agreed. "That's why we hired McGarvey."

"They'll be targeting this flight."

"I have no doubt of it, George," Kennedy said evenly. "Which is why we've got to do it."

"Every passenger and crew member will have to be screened electronically, their baggage searched."

"The Vice President will be aboard so I'm sure the Secret Service will help out."

"Okay. If Reiner and Callahan are available now, I want them to fly all the test flights. The first one goes the day after tomorrow, and I'll schedule four others before the Honolulu flight."

"I'll have them out here tomorrow," Kennedy said. "They might as well be involved with your pre-flights."

Socrates turned to Kilbourne. "I want your people down here along with Fred Taich's shop. We're going on around-the-clock shifts starting now."

"Make it fly, George," Kennedy said.

Socrates looked at him. "That I will. And the day she returns from Honolulu is the day I retire."

"In a few minutes my driver and bodyguard will take me over to the Kremlin where I will be expected to give my recommendation. Do we retaliate against Japan for the sinking of our frigate, and if so, what form shall this retaliation assume?"

General Polunin handed a series of photographs to SUR Director Karyagin. "These are the latest RORSAT shots over the Tokara Strait and East China Sea, including the island of Tanegashima."

Karyagin studied the photos and then put them aside. "There has been no battle between the American destroyer and the Japanese submarine?"

"Not yet. Apparently the *Thorn* received orders from

Seventh Fleet to stand aside and allow the *Samisho* passage through the strait."

"It looks as if the *Thorn* was also ordered to follow the submarine."

"That's what we think, Mr. Director. But look at the Japanese air base on Tanegashima. Photographs six and seven."

Karyagin looked at the two pictures. "A lot of activity."

"Too much activity. The base is on alert, as are the Japanese Air and Maritime Self Defense Forces on Hokkaido in the north."

"It's not unexpected, General. The Japanese are aware that we may make some response."

"Agreed, Mr. Director, which explains their state of readiness on Hokkaido. But why Tanegashima in the south? Those are waters they share with South Korea, not us."

"What are you getting at?" Karyagin asked. He was annoyed by Polunin's continued preoccupation with conspiracy theories.

"I'm suggesting that we proceed with a great deal of caution until we're absolutely certain we have all the facts. There is simply too much going on that we cannot explain. Even *Abunai* is telling us that the situation in Japan is explosive at the moment."

"Apparently he's produced no hard intelligence for us," Karyagin complained sharply.

"That's because of the increased risks he's facing. But I'm told that he is on the verge of gaining access to the Kobe Bank *zaibatsu's* confidential meeting records. Something may turn up soon. But if we accelerate the situation by attacking a Japanese warship or ground installation, there is no predicting what will happen."

"You must know that there is a strong sentiment at the Kremlin to make a show of force."

"At the very least the American government would probably revoke its license for Guerin to export aircraft technology to us, and certainly the loan guarantees would be lifted."

"Which is why, General, I was asked to help devise a plan so that any attack we might make against Japan would seem to be self-defense. The Americans still have the cowboy mentality."

"Have we developed such a plan?"

"The Defense Ministry may have something. What else have you brought to help brighten my day?"

"The FBI has begun its investigation of Kirk McGarvey, as we expected it would, given the information that was made available to it. But it seems possible that the CIA is cooperating with the FBI. If that's true, it may mean that McGarvey is not working for the Agency after all."

"He works for Guerin Airplane Company, as he claims?"

"It seems more likely now than it did before."

"But the CIA is cooperating with McGarvey?"

"He still has friends at Langley, Mr. Director. But the FBI is apparently taking its investigation in a direction that never occurred to us."

"Continue," Karyagin said dourly.

"It may be attempting to tie McGarvey to a series of murders in Washington and California and Oregon centering around Guerin and the company's troubles with the Japanese. The issue that McGarvey asked us to help with."

"Do they actually suspect the man of working for the Japanese?"

"I don't know that yet."

"But it's information that you will get?"

Polunin nodded. He could see that a veil had been lifted from Karyagin's eyes. The director was beginning to understand just how powerful a sword and shield the SUR still wielded.

"Should I know this source, General?"

"Like *Abunai* there is no reason for you *not* to know the name of our penetration network in Washington."

Karyagin shook his head. "And no reason other than my own ego at this moment for me to know."

Polunin was surprised. It was quite an admission for

someone to make, especially a Russian and especially a man in Karyagin's position.

"No, sir."

"But there is something else you have to tell me. I can see it in your eyes."

"We learned that McGarvey spoke with someone from Japan Air Lines in Washington a few days ago and that now he has shown up in Tokyo."

"McGarvey is in Tokyo?" Karyagin sat back. "What is he doing there? Have *Abunai* find out."

"We've sent those instructions, Mr. Director, but it may take a little while to learn anything significant. It is precisely why I think you should warn the Kremlin to slow down."

"General, that puts me in a very difficult position."

"Yes, sir, I know it."

It was the first time the four of them had sat down together to have a meal at the farmhouse. Glen Zerkel stir-fried some thinly sliced beef marinated in soy sauce, along with some julienned vegetables, and served it with cooked rice. He'd also baked bread and made a salad of cucumbers, tomatoes, and onions dressed with lemon juice, yogurt, and garlic. It was quite good, and Reid, who for once wasn't drunk, complimented him on the meal.

"You learn to make do when you live alone," Glen explained.

"I never did," his brother complained. "I think I'll miss this. When we're finished, I mean." He glanced at Mueller.

"It'll be easier than we thought," the German told them. Over the Zerkels' protests he'd waited until Reid came out to tell them what he'd learned. "I'll need seven repeaters—and as it turns out the size isn't as critical as we thought it might be. But I'm going to need a way of shunting a closed-circuit television system so that the monitors won't detect what's been done and will leave no traces when I remove it."

"Seven is a very specific number," Reid said.

"Oakland, Los Angeles, Chicago, Minneapolis, both New York City airports, and Dulles here."

"Potentially that's a lot of airplanes." Reid looked at his plate. "A lot of people will die." He got up and poured himself a stiff shot of Irish whiskey, drank it down, poured another, and came back to the table.

"It's up to you. But Japan will take the blame."

"It might backfire, make Guerin stronger."

"Again, it is up to you, Reid. But if this is done correctly, and we bring down seven or more Guerin airplanes, it will take investigators a long time to figure out how it happened. In the meantime the company's stock will certainly become nearly worthless, and you as a very loyal American who still believes in America for Americans will step in and help save the company. When the signals are finally traced back to the Japanese, you will become twice the hero."

No one said a thing.

Mueller turned to Louis. "Can you do that?"

Louis's head bobbed nervously. "Not this instant. I need more time. A week, maybe two. But I can do anything, including that trick you want with the closed-circuit TVs."

"I'll tell you something else," Mueller said, turning again to a subdued Reid. "When this happens it will have to be nothing less than stunning. Unprecedented. So horrifying that it will be the single worst event in America's history."

"Christ . . ." Reid said softly.

"Isn't it what you want?" Mueller asked. "Isn't that why you gathered us here? Isn't this your invention?"

"I'm still an American."

"Yes?" Mueller smiled. "Then pay us and we shall walk away now."

Reid looked up out of his sudden anguish. "The Japanese would win."

"So what? You're an old man, even if you begin squandering your money immediately you couldn't spend it all before you died. We can walk away from this insanity. Can you?"

Mueller wondered if he could take his fee and turn his back on this project as he'd told Reid he could. He expected it wouldn't be terribly difficult. It wasn't his fight or his cause. He felt no compelling emotions for the plan, although he admitted to himself that he would miss the excitement of causing all those deaths. But it wasn't important to him one way or the other.

The Zerkels were talented sociopaths. Geniuses. But Reid was becoming troublesome because of his drinking, and because he had a conscience. He would self-destruct whether or not they went ahead. He would not live much longer, and he probably knew it.

Mueller smiled. "If you want me to continue, I will give you an account number in a Channel Islands bank. Within twenty-four hours you will deposit one million dollars in that account. It's up to you."

Reid drained the rest of his drink. "I'll take care of it first thing in the morning."

"What do you think about that?" Louis Zerkel said.

TWENTY-ONE

Asagiri Eto refused to discuss exactly who he represented, agreeing that McGarvey needed at least the day and overnight to recover from the effects of jet lag.

"Japan can be a strenuous country for someone new. Please forgive my impatience. Business can wait until morning."

It was midnight when they emerged from the Club Shin-Oki in the Asakusa District a half-dozen blocks from McGarvey's hotel. The evening was cool, but not unpleasantly so, and because of the hour the streets were nearly deserted. This area was Tokyo's oldest section, and unlike the glitzy uptown Ginza area, Asakusa closed down at night. The narrow streets were dark, the arcades, shops, stalls, artist studios, and restaurants shuttered until morning.

"I'll expect you at my hotel at 8:00 sharp," McGarvey said. "I will have had my breakfast, and I'll be ready to conduct my business. Do you understand my English, Mr. Eto?"

"Perfectly, Mr. McGarvey."

"It was my understanding that I would not be meeting with Japan Air Lines, but with another interested party."

"That is the case."

McGarvey stared coldly at the man. "Who will I be meeting?"

"I'm not at liberty to tell you that."

McGarvey stepped in closer so that he clearly made the Japanese uncomfortable. "I'm not here to play fucking games, pal, if you're still catching my English. I came to discuss a business deal that could be worth billions of dollars to your principals."

"Worth the existence of the corporation you work for," Eto said, suddenly matching McGarvey's coldness. His eyes looked reptilian, their lids hooded, their expression unreadable.

"There are other willing trading partners."

"You came to us."

"Yes," McGarvey said. "And Mr. Yamagata was receptive, even though he knows who and what I am. And why I was hired by Guerin Airplane Company. Don't make me an enemy of Japan, *Eto-san.*"

"You already are the enemy."

"All right." McGarvey nodded and stepped back. "So fuck you. I'm withdrawing my offer. No negotiations. I'll book the first flight out."

For a moment Eto was caught flat-footed, but then his face began to fall apart. "No," he said.

"No, what?"

"Mr. McGarvey, I was not sent to antagonize you. Just the opposite. My role is simply to arrange a meeting between you and my principal."

"Who is this man or men?"

"In the morning . . . you will have to trust me."

McGarvey allowed a faint smile to curl the corners of his mouth. "Is that right?"

Again Eto was flustered. "We are interested in a cooperative venture with Guerin Airplane Company. You, acting as its representative, came as a surprise. We were not prepared. We thought it would be someone else. The company's business counsel, or perhaps their chief financial officer."

"Were you expecting Guerin to come to you?"

"No, not exactly."

"Quit jacking me around here. You haven't told me a thing all night, but Yamagata practically dropped his teeth when I showed up in his Washington office. He suggested that I come to Tokyo, and when I stalled him he came out to Portland. My idea was to speak to someone in Washington from JAL, to see if the airline was interested in principle in doing business with us. If it was, we would send a negotiating team over to explore the possibilities. Something like this is not put together overnight."

"You are also dealing with Moscow."

"Your intelligence is not bad," McGarvey said. "The Russians can put together wing panels cheaper than we can, and I'm sure cheaper than you. Besides that, my government is willing to make loan guarantees to the Russians to make the deal work. We can't miss. With you it's a different story."

"Your company is practically bankrupt."

Bingo, McGarvey thought. "I thought you weren't supposed to aggravate me," he said. "In this case your intelligence isn't so good. Guerin may be at its limit, but the company is sound."

"Why did you approach us?"

McGarvey looked at him and smiled. "Is it you I'm supposed to be meeting? Are you Yamagata's principal? Because if that's the case, I damned well will be out of here on the first flight."

Eto's jaws tightened. *"Iie,"* he said. He flagged down a passing cab. "I will drop you at your hotel."

"No, thanks. I'll walk."

"That's not possible, Mr. McGarvey," Eto said as the cab pulled up. "It's too far, and the streets here are very . . . confusing."

"I think I can manage. I'll see you at the hotel in the morning."

"It could be dangerous."

"Are you telling me that the streets of Tokyo are unsafe?"

"There is very little crime in Tokyo compared to New York."

"As a Gai Jin I'm in danger, is that it, *Eto-san?* Or am I specifically in danger because of why I'm here? Which is it?"

Eto looked helplessly at McGarvey. The rear door of the cab was open, and the cabby waited patiently behind the wheel. The cab was spotless. All taxis in Japan were always clean and in very good repair. It was the law.

"I'll walk with you," Eto said.

"I need to be alone. I'll see you in the morning." McGarvey turned and walked down the street, aware that the Japanese was watching him.

McGarvey turned right at the corner and sprinted down a narrow alley twenty yards away, where he pulled up in the shadows of a shuttered stall. Moments later the cab passed on the street, Eto sitting ramrod straight in the back seat.

The confrontation had answered a number of questions, among them just how importantly the Japanese were treating his offer, and just how bad Japanese sentiment toward Americans had become. He'd been treated shabbily at the airport and at his hotel, and Eto seemed to be genuinely frightened for his safety tonight.

McGarvey lit a cigarette as he continued to watch the street. Eto's concern for his safety involved more than a fear of simple street crime. No matter what Japanese group had targeted Guerin, there'd be opposition. Eto and whoever he worked for—which sure as hell wasn't JAL—had enemies. By association they would also be McGarvey's enemies. But they would be a group who, for whatever reasons, opposed the takeover of Guerin. They were one of the reasons he'd come to Japan.

The cab, with Eto still in the back seat, passed on the street again. Even at a distance it was clear that the Japanese was agitated.

"Thanks," McGarvey said. The man had just proved the supposition.

He'd been seen with Eto at the hotel's *hinoki* baths and at the club. From this point two forces would be in motion: that of the principals Eto worked for and that of the opposition. Actually three forces, he corrected himself. If the Russian *Abunai* network got wind that he was in Tokyo—which was likely—the mix would be further changed, perhaps muddied if it believed Guerin was trying to cut a deal with the Japanese.

Working both sides of the fence almost always produced a reaction of one sort or another. And the side that reacted first and with the most force was usually the group with the most to lose.

McGarvey flipped his cigarette away, hunched up his coat collar, and headed toward his hotel.

The Sumidagawa River, which emptied into industrial Tokyo Bay, was somewhere off to his right, beyond Sumida Park. He could smell the odors of oil and creosote wafting up from its banks. A few blocks in the opposite direction was the ancient Sensoji Temple, which had been one of the first things to be rebuilt after the war.

Kelley Fuller had called this place *shitamachi*, the heart and soul of downtown. She'd worked deep cover for the CIA's Tokyo Station, and when McGarvey had come over on an assignment she'd helped out. He remembered her very clearly, and remembered everything she'd told him. By that time she'd been burned out on Japan and on the Company and wanted nothing more than to return home to Hawaii. But it would be nice to have her with him now. Despite her love-hate relationship with the country, she knew the Japanese psyche very well and was able to be objective.

It was difficult for an American to negotiate directly with a Japanese because of the vast cultural and language differences between them. The only saving grace was that if Americans had trouble understanding the Japanese, the Japanese had the same difficulty trying to figure out Americans.

Kelley's perspective had been unique in that she'd been able to clearly see and understand both sides.

McGarvey climbed a broad set of stairs to a long open-air mall, with shops along either side of a brick thoroughfare. Fountains, trees, and park benches were scattered here and there. The only illumination came from a few large globes on short aluminum stanchions. In the early evening with shops open, people strolling or sitting and chatting, the effect would be soothing. Now the mall was in shadows.

McGarvey held up at the head of the stairs and listened to the city sounds, which were far away and faint. The air still smelled of the river, but there were other odors here: spices and flowers and perhaps cooking food. But something was wrong. The hairs at the nape of his neck prickled.

The mall ran roughly east and west for about two blocks, opening at one end on what was probably Nakamise-dori Avenue, which during the day was busy with traffic. The other end of the mall was lost in darkness.

McGarvey had left his pistol in Portland. If he'd been caught trying to bring it through customs he would have been arrested and kicked out. He hadn't come here with any intention of getting into a situation where he might need it, but just now he was sorry he hadn't tried.

A motorcycle engine roared into life, and the bike came slowly up from the dark end of the mall. McGarvey backed up, his left hand trailing on the burnished aluminum stair rail.

The helmeted driver was dressed in black leather, and as he passed, he looked at McGarvey and smiled like a Cheshire cat.

Before he got to the far end of the mall, a second motorcycle started with an angry whine and headed up from the darkness, the driver weaving a path through the benches, trees, and fountains. As he passed McGarvey he looked over and smiled like the first biker.

A third and fourth bike started up and came from the end of the mall, and as McGarvey started to turn back a pair of motorcycles appeared at the bottom of the stairs. The drivers revved the engines, the snarling noises echoing off the storefronts. Two more bikes started up and came from the dark end of the mall as the first four returned.

McGarvey sprinted away from the stairs toward a small tree protected by a low circle of bricks, one of the bikes just missing him as it spun around the fountain a few feet away.

The second bike passed in a roar, something hard smashing into McGarvey's back, driving him to his knees. He looked up in time to see a third and fourth bike heading for him, the drivers swinging what looked like pieces of steel or lead on the ends of three-foot chains.

He'd found the opposition, but they didn't seem inclined to stop and talk.

McGarvey rolled left, away from the first pair of oncoming motorcycles, and they flashed by, the lead weights missing him. He was up on his feet as the two bikes from below burst over the head of the stairs and came directly at him.

He swung around the tree, avoiding the first bike, and then stepped directly toward the second. At the last possible instant he moved aside, like a bullfighter allowing the charging bull to pass. He ducked under the swinging weight, then popped up behind it and grabbed a handful of the biker's leather jacket, dragging the man off his motorcycle and swinging him directly into the path of another charging bike.

The force of the impact spun the downed biker violently around, his left arm catching in the rear wheel's mag struts, taking it off just above the elbow and sending the motorcycle and driver crashing into one of the park benches.

Blood pouring from the open wound sprayed everywhere as the Japanese screamed and tried to get away.

McGarvey snatched the heavily weighted chain that the downed biker had dropped and stepped back.

"This man needs help!" he shouted.

The other bikers circled slowly, well out of range. "Rising Sun is going to get you," one of them taunted.

The Japanese whose arm was torn off lay crumpled in a heap, the flow of blood from his wound slowing. The biker who'd crashed into the bench lay beneath his motorcycle, his head lying at a severe angle.

"I came here to talk to you, not fight, goddammit," McGarvey tried to explain.

"Too bad you're going to die now," one of them shouted.

Two of the bikes cut out of the pack and suddenly roared toward him from opposite directions, the drivers swinging their weighted chains.

"You stupid bastards," McGarvey yelled in frustration. He swung the weighted chain twice over his head and let it fly at the biker to his left, then darted across the path of the other bike, jumped up on the back of a park bench, and leaped at the oncoming driver.

It happened too fast for either biker to get out of the way. McGarvey came over the handlebars and crashed into the Japanese, driving him off the bike, both of them smashing into the bricks.

McGarvey yanked the weighted chain out of the Japanese's hand and, as he scrambled to the left, tossed it at the wheel of one of the other bikes still circling. The chain caught in the mag struts of the front wheel, sending the machine crashing into the bike in front of it.

The bike to his left was down, the driver getting to his feet. The Japanese reached inside his jacket, but then he suddenly looked up and stepped back.

"I want to talk," McGarvey shouted.

The biker McGarvey had knocked down yanked his still idling motorcycle upright, climbed aboard, and roared away, while the Japanese to his left jumped on another bike's pillion as it raced past.

All of the bikes swung around and charged down the stairs at high speed. Only after they were gone did McGarvey hear the police sirens, a lot of them, closing in.

"I've finished with the repeater design, and it won't take me very long to build seven or eight of them," Louis Zerkel said. "But there's another problem."

"With the circuit design?" his brother Glen asked. Louis had been in an odd mood all morning. He was twitchy.

"It's embarrassing."

"What's your problem, Louis? I can't help you if I don't know what it is."

Louis looked down at his hands resting on the terminal keyboard. "In California it was different. I didn't have to ask anyone, not even Dr. Shepard. I knew where to go to get what . . . I needed."

"What?"

Louis looked up, and shrugged. "A woman."

Glen shook his head and grinned. "Shit, man, I can dig it. You're horny. Now that you mention it, so am I."

"Can you do something, Glen?"

"No sweat, brother. I'll talk it over with Mr. R. See what we can come up with. Just hang tight."

"Good," Louis said. "Only thing that's left after the repeaters will be setting up the signal paths from Tokyo and one test of the sensor unit in the Faraday cage."

* * *

There was no use running, McGarvey told himself, because he'd been set up the moment he got off the airplane. If they wanted him they would have no trouble finding him. Besides, cops had the habit of shooting at a moving figure first and a stationary target last. Watching the half-dozen or more squad cars, sirens blaring, lights flashing, race into the mall from Nakamise-dori Avenue, he was glad he'd heeded his first instinct to leave his gun at home. It would not have helped him very much against the bikers, and if he had it now it would definitely start to become a serious problem in about thirty seconds.

He stepped into the pool of light cast by one of the globes and raised his hands over his head, his passport in his left.

The first radio units screeched to a halt in front of him, their headlights making it difficult to see anything. Other units were arriving, and he could hear a lot of activity. Of course there were bodies all over the place, and the police had no real idea what they were walking into.

McGarvey stood perfectly still.

Several uniformed cops, their weapons drawn, fanned out on the double on either side of him. Someone from behind the lights shouted something in Japanese, and a man in civilian clothes slowly approached to within a couple of feet of McGarvey. He glanced at the upraised passport.

"You're an American?"

"Yes. My name is Kirk McGarvey. I'd like to speak with someone from my embassy."

"Are you armed?" the Japanese asked him. His English was very good, but he was dressed in a baggy suit and a rumpled trench coat that made him look like a detective out of a forties movie.

"No."

The plainclothes cop said something in Japanese, and two uniformed cops hurried forward, took McGarvey's passport, then quickly frisked him. When they were done, they pulled his arms behind him and secured his wrists with a plastic wire tie. They were quick and efficient.

"What happened here?" the plainclothes officer asked. He pocketed McGarvey's passport without looking at it.

"They called themselves Rising Sun. Said they were going to kill me."

"This was all of them?"

"There were more of them. Five or six others."

The cop glanced at the crashed motorcycles and the three bodies. A great deal of blood had pooled up around the biker who'd lost his arm. "Who helped you here, Mr. McGarvey?"

"No one. If you won't call my embassy, contact Mr. Asagiri Eto. I have his number. I had dinner with him this evening."

The plainclothes cop studied McGarvey. "What are you doing in Japan?"

"I'm here on business."

Again the Japanese cop studied McGarvey. "I think your business is not possible now," he said. "I am placing you under arrest at this time."

"What am I being charged with?"

The plainclothes cop smiled faintly. "Murder, of course."

"Eight against one?" McGarvey asked. "I call it self-defense."

"I see only three bodies, Mr. McGarvey. And you are a very large, obviously very powerful man. Whereas your victims were nothing but boys. Not a fair fight, if you ask me."

"I'll be damned," Reid said, surprised.

"It's not so much to ask, considering everything he's done so far," Glen Zerkel argued. "Question is, can we get someone out here without putting ourselves in danger?"

"I don't think that would be terribly difficult," Reid answered. "But I don't know if it would be very smart." It was late afternoon by the time he'd come out from the city. He'd put his latest newsletter to bed, and he'd waited until all the copies had been machine-addressed and mailed. This had caught him completely off guard.

"We're not home free yet, Mr. R. We still need him, maybe for another week or two."

"Can't he wait?"

Mueller came into the living room from outside. "Who can't wait for what?" he asked, mildly.

"Young Louis tells us that he wants a whore," Reid said.

Mueller shrugged. "Washington has whores. Get him one."

"We were thinking about the danger."

"When he's finished with the woman I'll kill her and put her body with Karl's. How are his experiments progressing?"

TWENTY-TWO

McGarvey was taken to Metropolitan Police Headquarters downtown on Sakurado-dori Avenue. They removed his wrist restraint, searched him with a metal detector, took everything out of his pockets, and locked him in a small interrogation room furnished only with a steel table and three chairs. It was a half-hour before the plainclothes cop who'd arrested him came in.

"I will ask you some questions, Mr. McGarvey," the cop said, setting up a cassette tape recorder. "It will save time if you tell me only the truth."

"Fine," McGarvey said. "But first I want your name, and I'll want to see some credentials. Then I want a cup of coffee or tea, and my cigarettes and matches."

"There is no smoking."

"In that case you'd better give my embassy a call right now, because I'm not telling you anything until I speak to a consular officer."

"You will answer my questions," the cop said sternly, his expression menacing. "You have no rights here."

"If you want to create an international incident, go ahead and push. Otherwise, fuck you."

The cop managed a faint smirk as he eyed McGarvey speculatively. "You are a murderer, Mr. McGarvey, and just now sentiments are running very high against Americans. I meant it when I said that you have no rights here. So this can be easy for you, or very hard. It is your choice."

"Actually it's your choice," McGarvey said. "Sooner or later the people I came to see will find out what happened and they'll get me out of here. In the meantime we can chat like civilized men, or you can try to force some answers out of me."

"The trouble is that you lied to me from the beginning, so I find it difficult to believe anything you say. You are a murderer *and* liar."

"You cooperate with me, and I'll cooperate with you," McGarvey offered.

The cop's eyes narrowed. "The number you supplied me has no record of this man you mentioned—Asagiri Eto."

McGarvey said nothing.

"How do you explain this discrepancy?"

Still McGarvey maintained his silence.

The cop switched off the cassette recorder, got up, and came around the table to McGarvey's side. "Did this man help you murder those boys?"

McGarvey looked up at him.

"You bastard," the cop said, and he raised his fist.

"If you hit me, I'll take you apart," McGarvey said softly.

The cop's eyes widened.

"Work it out. There were only three bodies down there, but four motorcycles. If your forensics people are on the ball, they should have discovered the tire marks of more than just those four bikes. From what I'm told Asakusa is a traditional family neighborhood. There'll be witnesses, but you'll probably have to go banging on doors to find them. And unless I'm mistaken it was the Rising Sun group that staged the riots in Tokyo last week. I was fair game out there." McGarvey watched the cop. He suspected that there was more to it than that, because of Eto's concern. Problem was he'd blown his chances to ask for the opposition's help.

McGarvey willed the tension out of his muscles and sat back. "I didn't pick the fight, but I sure as hell wasn't going to stand there and take it. They would have killed me. You saw the weapons they carried."

The cop shook his head in amazement. "You would have actually attacked me if I had slapped you?"

"Yes. If the situation were reversed, and this was New York City, wouldn't you have defended yourself?"

"Against a proper authority?" the cop asked, still trying to fathom McGarvey. "No."

"Never come to New York."

"You should not have come to Tokyo, Mr. McGarvey." The cop opened the door, gave somebody some instructions, then came back to the table. He showed McGarvey his gold shield. "My name is Nobuhiku Myamoto, and I am a lieutenant of detectives. Tea is being brought for you. Your cigarettes will be brought as well. It will just take a minute."

"Very well," McGarvey said. "Asagiri Eto works for someone who wants to do business with the company I represent."

"Now we're getting somewhere," Myamoto said. "How was it arranged that you should come to Tokyo and meet with this man?"

"Through a contact at JAL in Washington, D.C."

Myamoto switched on the cassette recorder. "Did Asagiri Eto pick you up at Narita?"

"He came to my hotel, and afterward took me to the Club Shin-Oki."

Myamoto was obviously impressed. "That is a very

exclusive club. I'm surprised that an American was allowed entry."

Someone knocked at the door, and Myamoto jumped up and got it. An older man in civilian clothes said something in rapid-fire Japanese, and Myamoto glanced back at McGarvey, this time a look of wonderment on his face.

"The man is a murderer. How am I supposed to report this?" Police Captain Tsutomu Watanabe demanded.

Hiroshi Ozawa had made his way downtown by helicopter the moment he'd heard that McGarvey had been arrested. "I am very sorry, *Watanabe-san*, to interfere in police business, but if Mr. McGarvey is guilty of murder it was certainly in self-defense. His presence in Tokyo is of extreme importance to us."

"I will not be told why?"

"No," Ozawa said, lowering his eyes politely.

"Mr. Pelham, this is Sam Miller, officer of the day. Sir, I have an amber light for you."

"All right, I'm switching over . . . now," Pelham said after a brief hesitation. He'd been caught by surprise. "I'm secure. What have you got for me?"

The green, circuit-secure light came up on the duty officer's encrypted console. "Mr. McGarvey was arrested a little over an hour ago by Tokyo Metro Police. Apparently he was involved in an altercation of some sort in Asakusa."

"Oh, Christ, that's just great. Have you reached Gates, yet?" Stephen Pelham was the assistant chief of the CIA's Tokyo Station. Cortland Gates was the COS.

"No, sir. He's hunting at the lodge on Hokkaido. But word has been left for him."

"Have the Japanese contacted anyone downstairs on his behalf?"

"There's been no call like that."

"Shit," Pelham said. "All right, it's a little after two now, which puts it noonish in D.C. We'll have to message Langley on this. I can make it in about twenty minutes. Traffic will be light. Thank God for small miracles anyway."

"Yes, sir," Miller said, but the green light on his console winked out. Pelham had already hung up.

The ACOS showed up thirty-five minutes later at the Company's small operations and communications center on the top floor of the U.S. embassy on Akasaka in Minato-ku. Unlike Miller, who was short, dark, and wiry, Pelham was a corpulent man with wispy, almost nonexistent pale blond hair and nearly invisible eyebrows. He looked like an albino.

"What's he been charged with, Sam?"

"Murder, but it's getting more complicated than that."

"Not possible," Pelham said, his acid indigestion rising.

When the bulletin had come from Langley requesting that Tokyo Station be on the lookout for McGarvey, no one had been overly concerned. Such requests were common, and very often bounced downstairs to an embassy officer. Usually it involved visiting businessmen or VIPs whose movements were to be loosely monitored for their own protection. They were to be bailed out of any difficult situation they might put themselves in. But when the follow-up book cable had arrived a couple hours after the first bulletin, filling them in on McGarvey's background, Gates and the entire staff had sat up and taken notice.

"I didn't make the connection until now," the COS told Pelham. "What the hell is *that* McGarvey doing back here? It's a surprise the Japanese even let him in after what he did to them three years ago."

He was a tough man to keep track of, and from the moment he'd slipped out of his hotel with a Japanese national, Pelham had known damned well that something would happen.

"Sir, Mr. McGarvey was released about the same time I was talking to you. The charges have been dropped."

"Jesus. Are you sure?"

"Yes, sir."

"Where is he now?"

"Back at his hotel."

"Has he got company?"

"The same man he left with last night. We don't have an ID on him yet, but apparently he carries some weight. The hotel has provided him with the penthouse suite."

"At this hour?" Pelham asked, rhetorically. "Who're we getting this from, Justine?"

"Yes, sir," Miller said. Justine was the code name of a small network of informants working for the Metro Police. Each person signed on for three years, after which they were brought to the United States, had their eyes Westernized, and were given a new identity and money. They had no trouble recruiting applicants.

"Whoever this Jap is, if he swings enough weight to get McGarvey sprung, we'd better find out who he is."

"It wasn't him, Mr. Pelham," Miller said.

"Goddammit, who was it then?"

"MITI."

Pelham stared at the OD, blankly. "The Ministry for International Trade and Industry? Why? What the hell has that sonofabitch gotten himself into this time?"

"Sir?"

"You were here when the book cable came through. You know what he is, or was. Christ, he's killed people."

"But he's one of us."

"Don't count on it, Sam."

"I don't understand."

"Whenever McGarvey shows up there's trouble."

"Yes, sir."

"I don't like the timing. The President is going to be here is less than a month, and I'd like to know what McGarvey is up to. Exactly what he's up to."

Miller was taken back. "I see what you mean, sir."

"Keep trying to contact Gates. I'll be in my office putting together something for Langley. Who've we got at the hotel?"

"Shapiro and Littell."

"Get Isaacs and Ireland down here too."

"Will do, Mr. Pelham."

In the dawn the air over Tokyo appeared dusty.

"It was an unfortunate incident for which I apologize," Asagiri Eto said.

"One which you tried to warn me about," McGarvey replied. "How did you find out I'd been arrested?" The police offered no explanation why they were releasing him, nor would Lieutenant Myamoto answer his questions. But the cop was clearly shook up. He'd been called out of the interrogation room, and when he came back he was subdued. McGarvey's personal belongings were returned, and after he'd signed an inventory release form printed in English and Japanese he was allowed to leave.

"I waited for you at the hotel, but when you didn't show up I became worried. The police said that you'd been attacked. Frankly, I didn't know what to think."

"Did you arrange to get me out of there?"

Eto looked owlishly at McGarvey. "You are a difficult man. We had hoped to avoid any unpleasantness while you were here, but that's no longer possible. Now we have damage to repair."

"Was it an isolated incident?"

Eto shrugged, a gesture uncharacteristic for a Japanese. "I don't know."

"They were Rising Sun. Enemies of yours?"

Eto took a moment to answer, obviously in some difficulty. "It's not so easy as that. My country is in turmoil, you know. We are coming out of very difficult times. Some people in government think they have the answers but there are . . . factions who believe Nippon will be made to suffer if we continue on our present course."

"Are you talking about a coup?"

"We're a democracy," Eto retorted sharply.

"Who is Rising Sun?"

"A group . . ."

"One of the anti-government factions?"

Eto shook his head. "This is not the West."

"I had to defend myself. Three Rising Sun are in the morgue. Who's got the pull to have the charges against me dropped? Are you one of these anti-government factions?"

Eto looked past McGarvey out the glass wall at the morning over the big city. The distant mountains were completely lost in the air pollution. "If you still wish to pursue your business with us, we'll leave now."

"Will I be returning to this hotel?"

"No."

"Then I'll get my things."

Eto smiled faintly. "Your suitcase is downstairs in the car."

"I told you there'd be trouble with that sonofabitch," CIA General Counsel Howard Ryan said.

"Still just circumstantial, Mr. Ryan," Carrara said, although even he was beginning to have doubts. After listening to what the FBI was working on he knew McGarvey was in the middle of something all right, but after talking with Phillipe Marquand in Paris he didn't know anymore. Maybe McGarvey *had* turned. "He was up front with me about Arimoto Yamagata's connection with JAL, and about Mintori, so he's not masking all movements from us."

"But he didn't tell us that he was going to Tokyo," Ryan said. The former Wall Street attorney had come down to Carrara's office just before quitting time for an update.

"He's not working for us."

"But he asks for our help."

"That's right, and I was told by the general to do just that." Carrara maintained his composure. Ryan's gripe with McGarvey went back several years, and in the DDO'S opinion the general counsel's behavior and attitude were anything but professional. But the man had his point: McGarvey was showing up in too many places at too many times. The Japanese Ministry of International Trade and Industry stepping in to get him out of trouble was problematic, as was the interest in him shown by the FBI and the French Action Service. "What are you telling me, Mr. Ryan? That I should refuse any further contact with him?"

"I'm not saying that," Ryan was quick to correct.

"Well, maybe we should bring him in. Tokyo Station would make contact and pass the message on to him."

"Nobody is calling for that either."

"What then?" *Even if Gates could get to him, there wasn't much chance that Kirk would come running.* "What can I do for you?"

"You're his friend. I understand and appreciate that, so I'm not asking you to stab him in the back." Ryan dismissed the notion with a shake of his head. "In fact, the man has done a lot for us. Accomplished some remarkable feats, actually. But you have to admit that this has become something entirely different. Now he's involving himself directly in international politics."

"He's working for Guerin Airplane Company."

"Spare me," Ryan cut him off. "Practically on the eve of one of the most important summit meetings ever facing this country, the Japanese decide to get into it with the Russians. And who shows up out of the blue in Moscow and then in Tokyo? None other than McGarvey. Of course, whenever McGarvey shows up someplace dead bodies fall like cordwood."

"Mr. Ryan, I repeat, what can I do for you?"

The general counsel looked at him coolly. "Kirk McGarvey is your friend. Find out what he's doing and stop him. For his sake, if not the nation's."

Carrara got slowly to his feet, every muscle in his body bunched into knots. It took everything within his control not to lunge across the desk at the smug bastard. He even managed to nod. "I'll do my best, Mr. Ryan."

"That's all I'm asking, Phil. I'm sure you'll do the right thing."

"Yes, sir."

Heading north out of Tokyo the air cleared and traffic thinned dramatically, so that by the time they were in the foothills, the narrow road was all but deserted. McGarvey and Eto rode in the back seat of the stretched custom Lexus. Their driver was a precise-looking man with wire-rimmed glasses whom Eto said had been a Formula One driver until an accident three years ago.

"Ura Nihon," McGarvey commented, looking out at the terraced fields that led up into the snow-capped mountains.

Eto was startled. "Where did you learn that?"

"A long time ago from an old friend," McGarvey replied absently. He and Kelley Fuller had traveled south together to Nagasaki. The countryside had seemed peaceful and delicate, dollhouse-like, completely different from the bigger-than-life, frenetic pace of Tokyo and Japan's other large cities. *Ura Nihon,* she'd called it. The other Japan. The ancient Japan. Tradition. Honor. Beauty. *Bushido.*

McGarvey glanced at the Japanese. "The old ways are the best. No *kata tataki* out here, no tapping on the shoulder to tell you that you have been voluntarily laid off. That's just for the cities. *Shoganni, Eto-san?* Nothing can be done about it?"

Eto returned his gaze. "You are indeed a troubling man, Mr. McGarvey. If I had my way I would send you back on the very first flight."

"But you don't."

"No."

"Then let's hope for the best, because I sincerely do not want to be your enemy," McGarvey said.

The road climbed higher into the mountains of Nikko National Park, the terraced farm fields giving way grudgingly to forests of tiny trees that seemed to be trimmed, the growth around them carefully cultivated. From a narrow defile the car was passed through a massive wooden gate that swung on a huge arch ornately carved with the figures of fierce dragons. From there a perfectly maintained road of crushed white gravel led up the valley to a broad forested ledge through which a narrow stream bubbled and plunged over the sheer edge. The view from the top was breathtaking. Perched on the far edge was a traditionally styled Japanese house, low to the ground and rambling in every direction. Tiled roofs, rice-paper screens and walls, carved beams, courtyards, broad verandas, gardens, ponds, and ancient statues and figures gave the spot an unreal air, as if it were a setting in a fairy tale.

"Whoever owns this must be a very lucky man," McGarvey said, and again Eto gave him an odd, measuring glance.

At the house their driver let McGarvey out of the car and a young woman in a flowered, pale-pink kimono came across the broad porch to greet him. Eto remained in the car.

"Ohayō go-zai-ma-su, McGarvey-san," Good morning, the young woman said, smiling.

"Ohayō go-zai-ma-su," McGarvey said, bowing slightly. *"Eigo o hanashimasu ka?"*

The young woman tittered and returned his bow. "Yes, of course, I speak English. Please, if you will follow me, tea has been laid out for you. The morning is beautiful, is it not?"

"The morning is brilliant," McGarvey agreed. He removed his shoes and without looking back at Eto followed the young woman into the house, down a wide corridor of highly polished teak, and finally out onto a very broad veranda that overlooked a beautiful garden. Part of the stream had been diverted through the garden, and it splashed gently on the rocks. A windchime hanging in a gnarled old tree tinkled on the pleasant breeze.

At first McGarvey did not notice the old man seated cross-legged like a Buddha in front of a low table at the edge of the veranda. He was dressed in a snow-white kimono and sat absolutely still until the girl led McGarvey across to him. Then he looked up and smiled.

"Please sit down, Mr. McGarvey. You have come a very long way, and you must be weary."

The old man's English was good, his accent British upper class. He looked to McGarvey to be in his seventies, possibly older. His eyes were wise, and from the expression on his face, and the way he held himself erect, sure of himself, McGarvey could guess that he was rich, even wealthy. All of a sudden the light bulb went off in his head.

"Sokichi Kamiya. Mintori Assurance."

Kamiya inclined his round, nearly hairless head, slightly in acknowledgment. "Actually quite clever of you to guess so soon. And to take your quest into the lion's den. Sit down. I'll pour us some tea."

McGarvey stared at the old Japanese for a beat. He'd been finessed, and he suspected that Kamiya was a master at it. But it had been so easy. Like scratching an itch, or swatting a fly. Effortless.

"This is a nice spot," McGarvey said, looking out across the garden.

"It belongs to a young friend of mine."

Another light went off. "Arimoto Yamagata."

"Yes. This place is his solace, although as of late he has not been able to enjoy any peace. But it is war."

McGarvey stared at a lone rock about the size of an irregularly shaped soccer ball. It was placed to one side in the garden. He suspected it had some significance. For the first time since Santiago, what seemed like a thousand years ago, McGarvey felt out of his league, even outclassed. His showing up on Yamagata's doorstep in Washington had come out of the blue, and yet Kamiya's organization was so far reaching and so strong it was able to suck McGarvey in and maneuver him to this place and time. It was tidy.

"Guerin Airplane Company is only part of it, then," McGarvey said.

"A key element, but only that."

"Without Guerin you would fail."

"But we will have Guerin, Mr. McGarvey. There is no question of that. No question whatsoever."

McGarvey sat across from Kamiya. "Maybe I'll kill you."

"You would be dead before you got within striking

range," the old Japanese said. He was supremely confident.

McGarvey had studied the garden for signs that anyone was hiding. Now he studied the facing wall and roofline of the house. No one was in sight, which didn't preclude some kind of remotely operated weapons system. Kamiya would have to be out of the line of fire, but it wouldn't be too difficult a system to engineer. McGarvey could think of several ways of doing it.

"Did you bring me here to kill me?"

"No, merely to neutralize you, Mr. McGarvey," Kamiya said. "You have become a nuisance. A thorn in my side."

McGarvey pushed back away from the table. There was nothing to fight, or to defend against.

"Even as we speak, Mr. McGarvey, a situation is being arranged that will diminish your effectiveness to nearly zero."

"Maybe I'll leave now."

"Then you will die now. You need to remain a little longer."

They came in two teams, leapfrogging out of the city, Isaacs and Ireland in a plain Toyota van and Shapiro and Littell in a four-wheel-drive Subaru. Greg Isaacs got out of the lead car about twenty-five yards from the big gate and immediately started through the thick woods up the mountain. At thirty-eight he was in the best physical shape of the four CIA legmen, so he'd been volunteered for this part of the mission. The others waited on the main road, one car well above the gate, the other retreating to the highway at the bottom of the valley about four miles away. Isaacs carried a powerful pair of binoculars, a sound amplifier with a small parabolic pickup dish, and a walkie-talkie.

The first hundred yards were relatively easy, but then the slope sharply steepened, and until he finally made it to the crest of the defile Isaacs wasn't sure he could do it without mountain-climbing equipment. At the top he found himself at one end of a long ledge, the mountains rising in the back and a sheer cliff plunging five or six hundred feet in the front. A big house was perched at the edge of the dropoff about two hundred yards away. Isaacs raised his binoculars and saw McGarvey seated with another man on a veranda.

Isaacs keyed his walkie-talkie. "I have him."

"You said that this is war. Do you mean a shooting war between Japan and the United States?"

"It may come to that," Kamiya replied calmly. "But not necessarily."

"Not necessarily."

"It depends upon what Russia does in the coming days, and on how your government reacts to certain events that will soon occur."

"I can stop you."

"How?"

"By telling someone in my government what you've said to me. I think I can convince the right people to listen, and to believe enough to at least start an investigation. Tokyo would help."

Kamiya noisily sipped his tea and looked at McGarvey with amusement. "Two days ago you might have had some small chance of success. But not now. By coming here you have damaged your credibility with your government, especially after your performance last night. The authorities in this country are very harsh with murderers, and especially harsh on foreigners. Yet you were released and all the charges against you wiped clean."

"Those things can be explained."

"Not after this morning, Mr. McGarvey. You will be leaving here in about an hour. Afterward you will be of no concern to me."

McGarvey looked again toward the house, then measured the distance across the table to the old man. He would have to keep Kamiya between him and the house.

"Don't forget the garden," Kamiya said, a faint smile curling the corners of his mouth.

"If they miss me, they will hit you."

"No."

"Can you be so certain?"

Kamiya's smile widened. "The system has been tested, Mr. McGarvey. But if you wish to try it, please do so. It might prove to be amusing."

Isaacs steadied his arm on the bole of a small tree as he aimed the parabolic dish directly at McGarvey and the other man. He pressed the headset close against his ear, but there was nothing except what sounded like wind in the trees or a waterfall, but a long way off. The receiver was supposed to be foolproof. Aiming the dish with his left hand, he raised the binoculars with his right and focused on the two men. They were talking. He could make out the Japanese man's lips, but he was getting nothing except the goddamned waterfall in his headset. Shit. He put the dish aside and picked up the walkie-talkie.

"Rover one, copy?"

There was no answer.

"Rover one, this is two, do you copy, over?"

Still there was no answer.

"Your most intelligent observers in Washington are correct in their thinking about one thing," Kamiya said.

"What's that?" McGarvey asked, his frustration mounting.

"These attacks are not directed by my government. They are trying to stop me, though secretly they admire what I am doing. They are frightened."

"I don't blame them," McGarvey said.

The repeaters were finished. There was the possibility that they would be discovered before the operation, so Louis had designed and built them to look like something completely different, so ordinary looking that even if they were spotted they might not be disturbed.

"The technicians will think that the janitors put them out, and the janitors will think that the technicians did it." Louis giggled. "It's not much, but it might give us a little margin of safety. Nobody will want to touch them."

"Roach Motels?" Reid asked in wonderment.

"That's right."

The seven repeaters, each a couple of times bigger than a pack of cigarettes, were covered in simulated-wood brown paper, the Roach Motel logo on the side of each box. Reid picked one up and hefted it.

"It's a little heavier than I would think one of these should be."

"So who's the expert on Roach Motel weights?" Louis asked.

Reid looked through it. "It's hollow, except for the baffles."

Louis giggled again. He was very proud of his handiwork. "The circuitry is on a board sandwiched between the top layers of cardboard. And the ion-exchange battery, which I designed, is sandwiched between the bottom layers. What do you think about that?"

Reid lowered the box and shook his head slowly. "What do I think?" He shook his head again. "I think you're more of a genius than anyone has ever guessed."

"Rover two, this is Rover one. What's going on up there?"

Isaacs keyed his walkie-talkie. "Rover one, this is two, do you copy now?"

"Rover two, negative contact. If you copy, maintain your position. I'm coming up."

"Good luck," Isaacs muttered, laying the walkie-talkie down. Bob Ireland was in no shape to make the climb. He'd be a basket case by the time he got up here. If he made it this far, Isaacs figured he'd end up carrying his partner back down the mountain.

He started to raise the binoculars when someone grabbed him from behind and yanked him away from the tree. He pawed for his weapon, but something smashed into his neck, cutting off his air, a thousand stars bursting in his head.

Isaacs was conscious long enough to understand he was being lifted off the ground by someone very strong, and then he was hurtling over the edge of the cliff and falling toward the rocks five hundred feet below.

TWENTY-THREE

Goddammit, Carrara, the sonofabitch has done it now!"

Phil Carrara had expected Ryan, but not so soon. The book cable from Tokyo Station had come less than an hour ago. "It's too early to draw any conclusions."

"Conclusions, my ass. I warned you about this."

"As you may recall, I asked if you wanted Tokyo Station to bring him in. You said no. Gates is not back from the lodge and Steve Pelham admits his information is preliminary at best."

Ryan's left eyebrow rose. "Your signature was on the return cable . . ."

Carrara flared. "I don't work for you, Ryan."

"Authorizing the operation to contact him. He's left Tokyo. Any word on him?"

"Not yet. All we're doing is following him to see who he meets with. He's done nothing wrong—at least he's broken none of our laws."

"Come off it. He killed at least three people, and now he's disappeared."

"The Japanese police released him. That tells us something."

"He's got powerful friends. He didn't fly over on vacation. Can you say for certain what he's involved with?"

Carrara averted his gaze for a moment. Ryan had

come charging into his office loaded for bear. While the CIA was in the business of intelligence gathering, the politics of influence often was the major factor in an operation. Ryan was the consummate political animal. He had the trust and respect of the director, and he had friends on the Hill and in the current White House administration. He was a dangerous man. "We know he's involved with something we don't understand, Mr. Ryan. I'll admit that much. But what we don't know yet is exactly what that might be."

"Bring him in. Ask him."

"Not so easy a job."

Ryan's lips compressed. "Are you saying that the man is out of control? He's above the law? The bastard can come and go as he pleases?"

"Self-defense . . ." Carrara said, and Ryan cut him short.

"McGarvey is a trained assassin. It was this agency that trained him, and we did a good job of it. Without exception every time he gets involved with something there are fatalities. These three in Tokyo are just the latest. Can you guarantee there won't be more?"

"They'd be justified."

Ryan smirked. "No possibility he's turned?"

"Turned into what?" Carrara demanded. He was tired of Ryan's amateurism. The man was a lawyer and politician, but he was not an intelligence officer, though he liked to think he was. He used sophomoric terminology.

"Into a double by the opposition."

"I don't know what you're talking about."

Ryan came closer to Carrara's desk, his eyes glittering. "The President is concerned that nothing affect his summit meeting in Tokyo."

"I wouldn't know."

"I do. It's my job. The General will want my recommendations. What do I tell him?"

"Operational briefs come from this office."

"My office is responsible for oversight."

"For the legal ramifications of our operations."

"Congressional relations as well. And we all know what that means to this administration."

"Do your job, Counselor, and let me do mine."

Ryan held up his hands in a peace gesture. "Let's not be at odds, Phil, I'm not the enemy. But if I'm to do my job effectively I need the cooperation of all the deputy directors."

"You have mine."

"All I'm saying, Phil, is that I don't trust or like Kirk McGarvey. I think the man is dangerous, not only to this agency, but to the interests of the United States. A view that is shared by a number of important, well-informed people."

"I don't happen to agree."

"I appreciate that. Out of friendship, or whatever, I concede your point that we ought to go slow with McGarvey." Ryan stepped even closer for emphasis. "But let's get with it. The timing is becoming critical. I would like a handle on the situation before it gets out of control. Do you know what I'm saying?"

Carrara nodded. Pissant or not, the Agency counsel was correct in his concerns. The situation with McGarvey was developing into something that promised to become even more deadly. "The follow-up from Tokyo should be coming in soon. When it does I'll put it together with what we've already got and bring it up."

"Fair enough. But I want you to remain objective. Can you do that for us, Phil?"

"Sure."

Ryan took the elevator back up to the seventh floor. The general was expected in a few minutes. In the meantime Deputy Director Lawrence Danielle was free. Carrara, he thought, would have to be eased out. The DDO was very good at what he did, but like a scientist or an engineer the man had developed tunnel vision. He could not see beyond his own office, which in this day and age was not good enough. No longer were our enemies clearly defined. It was a fact that Ryan had tried to get across to Carrara on more than one occasion. Shades of evil existed everywhere, including at home. Even here in this building. But the bastard wouldn't listen to him. In fact Carrara was becoming increasingly difficult. It was as if he thought he *owned* Operations. Just like in Cuba, or Nicaragua, or Chile, Hispanics were basically unstable. It was, he supposed, genetic.

"I thought you were gone for the day," Danielle said from his desk.

"I had a few last-minute items to go over. Have you seen the latest from Tokyo?"

"McGarvey is at it again."

"I think he should be brought in. I'm going to recommend it to the General."

"What's Phil's reading?" the DDCI asked.

"Wait and see. Don't upset the apple cart. Same old same old."

"A view you do not share."

"No," Ryan said. "In fact I think Phil may be in left field on this one. Old friends and all that. I mean, it's understandable, but it does not alter the fact that just now Japan is important to us, and McGarvey's meddling is creating an unlevel playing field."

Danielle gave Ryan an owlish look. "Phil Carrara is a bright, capable man."

"I didn't mean to imply anything different."

"Very well, Howard. But you know as well as I do that McGarvey will come in only of his free will."

"Unless he's charged with something," Ryan suggested slyly.

Danielle's intercom buzzed. "The Director has arrived," his secretary said.

"Tell him that Howard and I have something for him."

"Very well."

Danielle and Ryan walked across to the DCI's office.

"Has something come in from Tokyo Station?" Murphy asked.

"Phil is expecting an update momentarily," Ryan

replied. "But it's possible they'll turn up a blank. Tokyo is a big city, and if McGarvey has help it'll make things doubly difficult."

"Has anyone spoken with Al Vasilanti or David Kennedy in Portland?"

"Not that I'm aware of, General," Ryan admitted.

"Lawrence?" Murphy turned to his DDCI.

"I'd feel better if we had a chance to ask McGarvey a few questions. But he won't come in on his own."

"We charge him with obstruction of justice," Ryan suggested. "The NTSB is considering the outside possibility that Guerin's crash at Dulles may have involved sabotage. McGarvey could be a material witness. At the very least he is withholding potentially important information. Air safety is on everyone's minds these days. Considering Air Force One is a Guerin 522, I think we need to talk to anyone and everyone concerned. With or without their cooperation."

"It's an approach," Danielle agreed.

Murphy nodded after a moment. "Instruct Tokyo Station that McGarvey is to return to Washington immediately."

"He'll certainly object." Ryan's eyes glittered.

"Immediately," Murphy said.

Like their lunch date a few days ago, Chance Kennedy had no intention of accepting Yamagata's dinner invitation, yet at the last minute she had given in. She was fascinated, despite the danger signals. She felt like a foolish schoolgirl, out of her league, but David was wrapped up with the new project, and she was so bored she wanted to scream. Yamagata was after information. But that cut both ways if she could keep her head.

"It was lovely, Arimoto," Chance said over after-dinner drinks.

"Thank you, but it's not over. I have a surprise for you."

Chance smiled wanly. She glanced out the bay windows that looked through the woods toward the resort's cabins, each with its own private path from the main lodge and dining room. "I wondered how you would approach that."

"You accepted my invitation."

"For dinner," Chance said, turning back. His smile was devastating. "But not bed."

"Tea," he said, studying her face.

She looked at him quizzically.

He caressed the rim of his champagne flute with a finger. "You're here for the same reason I am, Chance. Information. I would like to know more about Guerin Airplane Company's will and determination to survive, and you want to know about Japan's interests and intentions." He looked up. "In order for you to succeed you must first understand the Japanese."

"By drinking tea with you?"

"Cha-no-yu. It's a ceremony, but it amounts to us drinking tea together. Two small cups for you, and two for me. Afterward you return to the city if you wish."

"That's it?"

He smiled again and nodded. "I've rented a cha house—actually it's just the living room in one of the cabins—but I've made preparations. It's taken two days."

"Just tea?"

Yamagata helped her with her chair. "Just tea," he assured her.

They got their coats and headed down one of the paths. Chance could scarcely believe that she was going along with him. But whatever Yamagata was, she didn't think he was a rapist. She was a big girl, fascinated but not befuddled. She had a good husband who was simply going through a bad time. She was not going to jeopardize her marriage.

"Humility, cleanliness, and simplicity, these are very important to a Japanese," Yamagata explained. "Everything springs from these three virtues. From these comes beauty, elegance, and the courage to live not only the present but to face the future."

"You're different from us," Chance said foolishly.

Yamagata took her arm as they neared the cabin, which was a chalet-type structure with a sharply sloping roof. The smell of wood smoke drifted on the still night air. Small yellow lights softly illuminated the path, which had been swept clean of snow. "You cannot imagine how different. But after tonight you will understand some things about us for the first time."

A few yards from the chalet's front deck, Chance pulled up short, beginning to wonder if this situation was getting out of control. Not only had the path been cleared, but the snow on either side of the path for as far as she could see into the darkness had been meticulously raked into patterns of gentle swirls and graceful ridges that caught the light from each lantern and reflected it at lovely angles.

"I'm pleased that you notice," Yamagata said, watching her. "Humility springs from simple labors, the results of which are cleanliness and simplicity not only of surroundings but of one's inner self."

"It could have snowed again and covered your work. Or the wind could have destroyed it."

"Then I would have begun again."

Inside, he hung up their coats and had her take off her shoes, which he put with her purse and his shoes out of sight. A small table in the entry hall held a broad earthenware bowl filled with water. To the left were two white cloths and to the right a beautiful arrangement of flowers.

"First we cleanse our fingers," Yamagata said, showing her how to dip her hands into the water, then dry them.

The short carpeted corridor opened to the living room, a fire burning on the grate the only light. Normally the room was furnished with sectional couches, chairs, coffee tables, television and stereo, and a dining-room arrangement. But all of the furniture had been removed. The only items in the big room were a very low table placed in front of the fireplace in the center of a five-by-eight tatami. The table held a cast-iron pot of water simmering on an intricately fashioned charcoal brazier, a porcelain pot, a tiny handleless cup, a bamboo spoon and bamboo whisk, and a small lacquered box.

The wooden floor gleamed richly in the flickering firelight, and the entire room, walls, rafters, ceiling, every single surface was spotlessly clean. The effect was overwhelming. Intimidating on one hand, strangely reassuring, even comforting on the other. Yamagata, or someone he had hired, had gone to a great deal of effort to make everything perfect. But he'd said simple labors made for humility, and that he'd worked two days on the preparations. He did all this, and Chance was impressed. Yet the overall effect was alien. Different. Non-Western.

She stepped back, stumbling into his arms. "Oh." She looked up into his eyes, her heart beginning to pound.

"Cha-no-yu," he said, reassuringly. "I think you are beginning to understand. But wait."

He led her to the low table where she had to hike up her dress to sit on the mat. He gracefully lowered himself across from her. She was mesmerized by him, by the surroundings. Everything within her wanted to get up and leave, but she could not.

"I ask if you would like to take tea, and you reply that it would be a great honor, but I should not go to any trouble."

"It would be a great honor," Chance said. The words wanted to catch in her throat. "But please don't go to any trouble for me."

"It is no trouble. It is my honor."

His voice was soft, his motions slow and precise. She could believe that each movement had been practiced often. He opened the lacquered tea caddy and using the bamboo spoon placed a measure of green tea powder into the cup. Replacing the spoon to its precise position, he poured hot water into the cup, replaced the iron pot on the brazier, and using the whisk delicately mixed the powder and water. Next he added a spoon of cold water from the porcelain pot, stirred the mixture again, and replaced the spoon as before.

He picked up the cup in both hands, bowed to Chance, and offered it to her.

"Return my bow, take the cup, and drink three times. Delicately. Leaving just a little."

She did as she was instructed. The tea was at perfect drinking temperature, but tasted odd. Like flowers, with a hint of some unidentifiable spice or spices, not unpleasant. She looked up.

"Finish it, and return the cup to me."

She did so, languidly as if in a dream, and he repeated the ritual, making a second cup of tea that he again offered to her.

"Refuse. Tell me that I should taste the tea myself," Yamagata said.

She complied, and he studied the contents of the cup for a long moment before he sipped three times, rested for a few seconds, the expression on his face serene, and finished the tea.

He made a third cup in precisely the same fashion as the first two, which Chance took, and a fourth cup, which he drank.

She was floating. The odors of the fireplace, the charcoal brazier, and the tea were distinct and separate in her senses, wonderfully soothing. Sensual. She *was* beginning to understand.

Yamagata helped her away from the table and undressed her, his movements just as slow and precise as they had been making tea.

He was seated naked in front of her, and he brushed rose petals against the erect nipples of her breasts. The effect was hypnotizing. She was seduced into a gently swirling whirlpool. Warmth. Pleasure. Caressing her body, pulling her beyond anything she had ever experienced or dreamed of.

They were sitting, half reclining, side by side, and he was inside her from behind, motionless, yet waves of sexual pleasure coursed through her body. She began to understand that he was increasing and decreasing the size of his penis, rhythmically, and she began to contract the muscles of her vagina in sync with him.

"I love it," she murmured. She did not want to break the spell. She never wanted it to end.

He kissed her neck, increasing her pleasure tenfold.

Then his fingers found her clitoris and in consort with everything else, even with the music that seemed to be playing somewhere, he teased and played with her until she *did* understand. Everything.

She never wanted it to end. "I love it," she said again.

"Talk to me, Chance," Yamagata said into her ear. "I will listen."

Louis Zerkel had become increasingly nervous over the past twenty-four hours. He had diverted his attention from testing the heat monitor subassembly until he'd finished the repeaters and the closed-circuit television shunt Mueller had requested. The Faraday cage had been completed, and the monitor they had stolen from InterTech along with one of the repeaters was safely protected within its electromagnetic confines. Whatever signals were generated by the system would remain within the system. No one wanted an uncontrolled repeat of the Dulles crash.

Louis had not figured out what the extra circuitry in the CPU was used for. All of his diagnostic tests had come up with nothing. He'd hoped that by having the actual unit to test, figuring out what was going on would be easy. But it still made no sense to him, and his inability to accomplish something he thought was little more than basic electronics was frustrating him.

He'd expected to see a modified signal coming from the monitor when the keying pulse was sent, decoded, and processed. A reversal in polarity of some of the critical temperature-monitoring sensors, for example, would cause the engine to rapidly overheat and destroy itself while sending indications to the Flight Management Computer in the cockpit that engine temperatures were well within parameters. But there were no feedback signals into that section of the subassembly.

"How much longer?" Mueller asked.

"I don't know," Louis admitted. "I'll know better after this test. The entire system is on line this time." Louis had set up his Faraday cage and subassembly test breadboard in the basement. Extra lights had been strung up, and some of his test instruments had been brought down along with a computer terminal connected to his mainframe upstairs. Wires snaked across the dirty concrete floor, indicators blinked, the audio-pulse generator connected to the encoding sequencer warbled and beeped, and a white-noise generator that protected the low-frequency sections of the subassembly hissed like a radio tuned off station. But something was missing, Louis thought. Some critical part of the destructive mechanism.

"When will you finish this test?" Mueller asked.

Louis flipped on the computer monitor and watched as the encoding multiplexer homed in on the correct pulse, and seconds later locked on. The heat monitor subassembly was cocked.

"Now," he said.

Mueller stepped aside. Reid was in Washington, and Glen was asleep in one of the upstairs bedrooms. It was just the two of them down here.

Louis adjusted the oscilloscope connected to the input and output sections of the CPU, timing it against the subassembly's GO-One clock, then keyed the walkie-talkie shunted directly to one of the repeaters.

"Boom," he said into the mike. After a short phase delay the CPU delivered a modulated spike to the extra ground wire. Louis stared at the scope. The output signal was less than ten milliseconds duration, but information had been piggybacked onto it. A message had been sent to the engine sensor frame.

"Was that it?" Mueller asked.

Louis continued to stare at the scope.

"Does it work?"

The system was incomplete, Louis thought. One more test. He had to make absolutely certain. He needed to know one more thing for sure. There could be no room for error.

He turned to the German. "You have to go back to San Francisco, or Portland. I need the engine sensor frame and wiring harness."

Mueller's expression was unreadable. "Is this necessary?"

"Yes," Louis said.

"Then I will wake your brother and we'll get it for you."

Louis turned his gaze to the monitor. "What do you think about that?" he mumbled.

"Who do you work for?" McGarvey asked.

"Does it matter?" Eto responded.

They were headed out of the mountains to Narita Airport. McGarvey's bag was in the trunk. His passport had been exit-stamped with today's date. They had thought of everything, their organization spectacularly smooth and extremely effective. It would be no use to fight them here and now. Later, on a battleground of his own choosing, he would even the odds. Whatever Kamiya had arranged to neutralize him would be good. But nothing or no one was impossible to break.

"Out of curiosity—MITI or Mintori Assurance?"

"If I told you, I don't think you would comprehend."

"Try me," McGarvey insisted.

Eto was exasperated. "I am *bushido*—"

McGarvey chuckled. "You're another Mishima fanatic, is that it, *Eto-san?* Have you and your pals formed a Shield Society of your own? Is that what bullshit you people are trying again?"

The chauffeur looked at them in the rearview mirror. McGarvey caught his gaze. The big Japanese was scowling. Throw a rock into a pack of dogs and the one that gets hit yelps.

Eto's lips compressed as he fought for control. "You said that you did not want to be my enemy. But you are.

When I have delivered you to the airport my obligation for your safety will end. Do not return to Tokyo."

"*Wakarimashita,*" I understand, McGarvey said. "But the next time I see *Kamiya-san,* I shall kill him. *O-wakari desu ka?*" Do you understand?

"*Hai,*" Eto said through clenched teeth.

TWENTY-FOUR

Y ou come as something of a surprise, Mr. McGarvey," Sir Malcolm O'Toole said. "Did young Kennedy send you over?"

"I'm here on my own. I wanted to talk to you."

The Rolls-Royce chief design engineer eyed him speculatively. "If this has to do with the crash I don't think it's appropriate at our level."

"Hear me out, and afterward you can do whatever you want. But not here. Let's take a walk."

"Very well," O'Toole said after a heavy silence.

It was a cool, overcast day as they walked along a narrow path away from the company's Barnoldswick, Yorkshire, design and manufacturing facility. A weather front was coming down from the Scottish highlands, and McGarvey hunched up his coat collar against the wind. He was sure he was being followed at Narita, so at the last possible moment he had switched flights from Seattle to London. He'd taken the train directly up here. "Have you sent the engine to the NTSB?"

"Yes, and a pair to Portland. But you must know that we're under increasing pressure to put a hold on *all* engine deliveries."

"Including the hydrogen burner?"

They headed toward a line of trees a few hundred yards distant. A pair of large ravens rose up, cawing raucously. Somewhere a dog was barking. With their backs to the Rolls complex they could have been in any North English countryside.

"Why did you come here, Mr. McGarvey? And why the skullduggery?"

"Because I have something to tell you, and because there is a possibility that your office has been bugged."

Sir Malcolm stopped short. "You mean hidden microphones, and all that rubbish?"

"Yes, sir."

"By whom?"

"The Japanese."

"Good heavens." Sir Malcolm glanced over his shoulder. "Is it the government?"

"I don't think so, but the group involved may have the tacit approval of someone at higher levels. Perhaps the Ministry of International Trade and Industry."

"I really don't think I should be talking to you."

"I'm talking about saving Guerin and Rolls and possibly a lot of lives."

Sir Malcolm looked wan. "Do you believe that our engine failure at Dulles was caused by sabotage?"

"Yes, and the one in '90. A safety-board pathologist found an extra body in that wreckage. The board ruled that the plane fell on the poor bastard."

"Not likely out in the open."

"The doctor was murdered a few months later, and all his crash records destroyed."

"Anything like that at Dulles? I hadn't heard."

"No. But what are the chances of the same type of malfunction occurring?"

"Reasonable, but happening to the engine on the same side of the aircraft—well, it would be fifty-fifty, I suppose. Not a long shot."

"But you've no evidence of sabotage."

"Not to my engine. But then we found nothing to indicate that such a failure should occur either. We've pushed those blades well beyond the most extreme safety parameters, and they've not failed. Not once."

"But two airplanes fell out of the sky for the same apparent nonreason. The first was a test, or maybe an accident in timing. And the second an attempt to stop Guerin from dealing with the Russians."

"I see what you mean," Sir Malcolm said. They started toward the trees again. "It's monstrous if it's true. What would they have to gain by ruining us and Guerin?"

"I've just come from Tokyo. The man I talked to said ruining you and Guerin is just the tip of an iceberg. He seemed pretty sure of himself. He's got the money, the organization, and the connections to make it happen. At the very least, make it damned uncomfortable for us."

"Go to your government with it. I'm told you're well placed in certain circles."

"I was set up. I don't think my word is going to carry much weight just now."

"So you've come to me. Marshalling your forces."

"Something like that. Your engines did not fail of themselves. And it'll happen again, fairly soon, I think. So you'll need to protect yourself."

"How?"

"By being aware of the situation."

"Possible situation," Sir Malcolm corrected. "Why should I believe you? I mean good heavens, sabotage, and hidden microphones, and some nefarious plot by the yellow hordes, what?"

"The Japanese military is the fastest-growing war machine in the world. Submarines are not defensive weapons. And theirs are good."

"Fastest growing perhaps, but still tiny by comparison to yours, ours, or the French, or any number of other nations I could mention."

"You're right. But the Japanese will occupy Subic Bay before long. They have a fully operational rocket launch facility on Tanegashima Island. And they've been rumbling about the development of nuclear capability."

"Because of the threat from North Korea."

"If they go nuclear they'll become a formidable force on that side of the Pacific, whatever the reason."

Sir Malcolm rummaged in his pockets for his pipe and

tobacco. He took his time getting it lit. It was a pipe smoker's gambit to gain thinking time. "Even if they were to start this instant, it would take them six or seven years to develop weapons. Assuming that all your wild speculations are true—and mind you that's exactly what I think you've come here with—where would sabotaging airplane engines come into the scheme?"

"I don't know," McGarvey admitted. "But these are confident people."

"History is filled with confident, and competent, people who've failed," Sir Malcolm said. "You say that your word may no longer carry any weight with your government. Bring me proof that sabotage occurred, or will occur again, and I will take it to my government."

"That's why I'm here."

Sir Malcolm stopped. "You have proof?"

"You're going to find the proof. You've told me how the engine failure could *not* have happened. You're sure of your test results?"

"Absolutely, but as you pointed out, two airplanes have crashed."

"Find out what could have caused those crashes."

"There could be any number of causes."

"Right," McGarvey said, hiding his triumph. He'd known that the Brit would be a hard sell, but once the old man was convinced he would go to the ends of the earth to find the reason for the crashes. He was an engineer. Cause and effect were his *raison d'être*. "Think like a saboteur. You want to bring down Rolls-powered Guerin airplanes in such a way that the best investigators and engineers will not be able to figure out how."

"Could well be an exercise in futility. You cannot imagine how complicated our machines have become."

"No more complicated than human beings," McGarvey said. "I'm asking you to make one assumption—that both crashes were the results of sabotage, whatever the reason. Go from there. Figure out how it could happen."

"A big assumption."

"Not so big, I think, considering the consequences of doing nothing about it."

Sir Malcolm took his pipe out of his mouth and studied McGarvey. "What about you?"

"I'll continue to marshal my forces."

"Gary Topper was here this morning, you just missed him."

"What did he want?"

"Essentially the same thing as you. He's in London. You should get together."

"I'll do that."

"Then what?" the Brit asked.

"My job is to irritate people until they make mistakes."

Sir Malcolm smiled tiredly. "A job at which, I suspect, you are eminently successful."

Louis Zerkel was exhausted. He'd worked around the clock for a solid week, only catching catnaps when he could not continue. Except for the one essential test, which he could not conduct until his brother and the German brought him the engine sensor frame and wiring harness, he was finished with the hardware. All that remained was the signal train. He planned on initiating seven wire transfers of money from the Bank of Tokyo into InterTech's San Francisco account. Before the signals reached InterTech's account, however, they would be shunted through the company's mainframe computer, which would in turn spit out the properly encoded signals to the seven repeaters Mueller would hide at the seven airports around the country. A few milliseconds later the trigger pulse would be sent, and Guerin airplanes would start falling out of the sky.

The date had not been set, but Louis had a definite idea when it would be, and he planned on talking to Mr. Reid about it. He'd been busy working on the circuitry, but not so busy he missed the major television news broadcasts. Especially CNN, which did a special two days ago on Guerin's new hypersonic airplane. The plane was to make its first subsonic test flight, Portland to Honolulu, in two weeks. What Reid and Mueller did not know yet was that the P/C2622 was equipped with the same heat monitor subassembly as the 522s. The Vice President and a lot of other VIPs would be aboard that test flight. The eighth repeater was ready, and eight, rather than seven, wire transfers could be sent from Tokyo. The results, he thought, would be more than impressive.

"What do you think about that?" he muttered.

His computer screens were turned low, and for the first time all the printers were silent. He stood at the bedroom window across the hall looking at the lights of Dulles Airport in the distance, and he felt a terrible surge of loneliness in his gut. He'd been a loner most of his life, but only on rare occasions did he feel lonely for company. He missed his mother, he supposed, but most of all he missed his father. He was glad that his half-brother had found him. Over the past week he had come to appreciate the adage that blood is thicker than water.

"Louis," Glen said from the doorway. "Are you okay?"

Louis turned. "I thought you and Mueller were already gone."

"We're leaving in the morning. Are you finished for the night?"

Louis nodded. "Everything is ready. I just need the frame and harness."

"Then you deserve a break."

"What . . . ?"

"You've done a hell of a job, brother. Mr. R. is very pleased. Even Mueller respects what you've done."

The compliment felt good, and Louis managed a tired smile. "I'm not quite finished yet."

"But you're close, so tonight's yours."

"I don't understand," Louis said.

His brother stepped aside, and a young woman came into the bedroom. She was tall with a decent figure, and a round, wide-eyed face. She wore a halter top, a very short mini-skirt, black fishnet stockings, and spike heels. She smelled of perfume.

"Hi. You must be Louis. I'm Tracy."

"I . . . yes," Louis mumbled.

Her smile was dazzling. "They said you're a genius. How about you teach me some things, and I'll teach you."

Louis's face felt hot.

"I'll see you in the morning before we leave," Glen said, grinning, and he closed the door.

Gary Topper was staying at Claridge's. McGarvey met him in the darkly paneled bar. The lunch crowd was gone, and except for a couple of businessmen at the end of the bar they had the room to themselves.

"You look like shit, McGarvey," the Guerin vice president for sales said.

"Sir Malcolm was kinder."

"I wondered how you tracked me here. Nobody's heard from you, and Kennedy is getting a little tense."

The barman came to them. They ordered martinis, dry. When they got their drinks, McGarvey glanced at the businessmen. They were out of earshot.

"Something's come up?" McGarvey asked.

"You know a guy named Phil Carrara?"

"He's a friend."

"CIA?"

McGarvey nodded.

"According to David your friend is not making friend-noises. They want you in Washington. If you refuse they'll arrest you."

"They don't have the authority."

"Your friend mentioned the FBI. David said he sounded serious."

It was starting faster than McGarvey thought it would. "Did he mention anything specific?"

"David didn't say."

"Did someone from Washington talk to Vasilanti?"

"I don't know," Topper said. His eyes were dark and

serious. Like everyone at Guerin whom McGarvey had met, the VP was consumed not only with making a success of the new airplane, but with keeping Guerin's safety record intact. "You've been to Tokyo. Considering the line you've been touting, that was a pretty gutsy move."

"That's why I was hired."

"Except for pushing us into handing a wing assembly plant to the Russians—which was a nifty bit of business—just what have you done for us?"

"Proved your suspicions. Mintori is trying to take you over, and someone is sabotaging your airplanes."

"Did Sir Malcolm buy into that? He wouldn't listen to me."

"He's agreed to help."

Topper sipped his drink. "The Honolulu flight's a go in about two weeks. Anything happens between now and then, we'll go down the tubes."

"It will."

Topper's expression got hard. "I'm serious, McGarvey. Another one of our airplanes goes down, we'll be fucked. This goddamned administration in Washington doesn't know its ass from a hole in the ground. They're letting the Japanese take the initiative while selling us down the tubes. A couple of Toyota plants in Kentucky or wherever doesn't compare to us. Can't they add and subtract?"

Topper wasn't the idealist that Kennedy was, but he was still relatively naïve. "It's always been that way, Gary. The last President figured the way out of the deficit was raising taxes and tightening belts. This one thinks the way out is in the international marketplace."

"The same thing the Japanese are saying."

McGarvey agreed. "Puts us on a collision course."

"They don't like us very much."

"The feelings are becoming mutual."

"Shit," Topper said into his drink. "Maybe it's time to get out. This isn't fun any more." He looked up. "When I started all I could think about was flying. Making flying machines that wouldn't fall out of the sky. Bigger, faster, better. Everybody respected that. Excellence. Look what Boeing has done. Safety first and profits second."

"Same as you guys."

"So what's happened all of a sudden?"

"The end of the Cold War," McGarvey said.

Topper looked startled. "What are you talking about?"

"When it was just us and the Soviet Union, we were the boss of this hemisphere and they were the boss of theirs. Except for Vietnam and Afghanistan, most of the skirmishes were controlled by us or them. It's different now."

"You can say that again."

"But not so different from the twenties and thirties. Everybody shooting at everybody else. All the old animosities are out in the open again. But this time the weapons are a hell of a lot more plentiful and more sophisticated."

"We won the Cold War."

"Yeah," McGarvey replied tiredly. "Just like we won the First World War."

Topper looked away in frustration. "Are you telling me that it's going to start all over again? Shit, man, if that's the case, we might just as well sandbag our borders and say the hell with everyone else."

"Didn't work then, won't work now."

"War?"

McGarvey shrugged.

"I think you're crazy," Topper said. "Or at least I hope you are."

"Me too," McGarvey said. "Meanwhile there's work to be done."

"Are you returning to Portland?"

"Yes. Then Washington."

"You can fly back with me. I've got a company plane."

"When are you leaving?"

"Now is as good a time as any."

Representative John Davis sat across the table from Reid at the Four Seasons Hotel, a troubled expression on his deeply lined face. It had been thirty-six hours since Reid had asked the Appropriations Subcommittee chairman for help. Like a lot of others in Washington, Davis owed Reid a favor or two. His last campaign, which he'd narrowly won, had been almost entirely financed by Reid, illegally so, a fact that the portly Maryland Republican was acutely aware of. But Washington always had been and always would be a town of special favors and influence. A White House staffer had once commented that lobbyists were to congressmen what television commercials were to the public—a window overlooking a field of possibilities.

"Did you find out something for me?"

"The Bureau wasn't happy. But Harding agreed not to buck my request over to the AG if I promised to keep what I was told strictly confidential."

"Hardly the object of this exercise, John," Reid said. "I've stepped on some toes, that's all. What else is new? But I'm not the enemy."

"The Bureau doesn't think so either. But your name is apparently being linked with some people who are. What I mean to say is that the Bureau is conducting an investigation, and your name has popped up in a couple of places. Might be coincidental, Harding told me. Could even be a case of mistaken identity, but they've taken notice. Especially since someone from State has asked them to back away from you. The White House, by the way, agreed."

"Nice to know I have friends," Reid said. He took a drink to mask his uneasiness.

"You do have friends in this town, Edward," Davis said. "But you've also got some powerful enemies, especially over your stand on the Japanese."

That was an understatement, Reid thought. But once Guerin was brought stumbling to its knees and the crashes blamed on the Japanese, Washington would be like a hornet's nest. "Is that what all this is about? I'm surprised the White House backed me up."

"Only partially, but I didn't get all the details except that it involved the French Action Service. Someone over there is looking for a former East German assassin and a retired West German intelligence officer."

"Where'd my name come into play?" It was all Reid could do to control himself. His hands shook so badly he was afraid to pick up his drink.

"Apparently the West German telephoned someone here in Washington and mentioned the East German's name along with the name Reid."

"I can't imagine who this German could be."

"It wasn't your telephone number, nor did he use your first name. But Harding did mention that you'd been stationed in Germany."

"A long time ago, John."

"Well, both Germans have disappeared, and the French asked for our help in finding them."

"Here in Washington?"

"Apparently."

"What's that got to do with Japan?" Reid asked.

"Harding was even more sketchy about this part, and I had to press him a little. The East German assassin's name is Bruno Mueller. He was a colonel in the Stasi, and when the wall came down he got involved with a group of terrorists that shot down an airliner full of people taking off from Paris."

"So what?"

"One of the passengers was the girlfriend of a former CIA officer who apparently has one hell of a reputation. This guy works for Guerin Airplane Company now and is in the middle of some sort of an operation with the Japanese."

Reid's chest was tight, and he was having trouble catching his breath. Christ, did this idiot have any idea what he was saying? If Mueller were here, Davis would be a dead man. "Where do I come into it?"

Davis looked sharply at him. "You don't directly. Are you okay, Edward?"

"Frankly I'm annoyed. I think this should be sent over to the AG's office. Harding's way off base here."

"Nobody's accusing you of a thing," the congressman said.

"Then where's the connection? Who is the CIA officer?"

"Former officer. Kirk McGarvey. Name mean anything to you?"

"No."

"The only connection, according to Harding, is that Mueller might have come here looking for McGarvey. Since the name Reid was mentioned, and both you and McGarvey are involved with Japan, it got them wondering."

Reid allowed himself to relax a little. Neither Schey nor Mueller had mentioned the CIA or McGarvey. As far as he was concerned that would be a dead end for the Bureau. "I'm not involved with Japan, John. On the contrary, I'm arguing for disinvolvement with them."

"Not a popular view at the White House."

"Then why did someone over there tell Harding to back off when it came to me?"

"Maybe they're giving you enough rope hoping you'll hang yourself." Davis sat forward. "Seriously, Edward, watch your step. These are difficult times."

Yes, they are, Reid thought. But nowhere as difficult as they would become. No matter what happened, the Japanese would have to be dealt with sooner or later. The last time we'd waited too long despite all the warning signs, and the Japanese navy had attacked Pearl Harbor. The same warning signs were back. Japan was flexing its economic and its military muscles, and sooner or later the economic bubble between us and them would burst. The mere fact that the electronic device Louis had discovered aboard the Guerin airplanes had been designed by the Japanese was all the proof that Reid required. The dirty bastards were at it again. This time he wasn't going to let the United States wait for another Pearl Harbor. This time he was going to wake up the White House, and the entire nation before it was too late.

Whoever the hell McGarvey represented—Guerin or not—Reid decided he was no threat to their plans. If need be, when it was over, he would send Mueller out to settle whatever old scores there might be between them. Might even kill two birds with one stone.

No, Reid assured himself, nothing to worry about yet.

On the way across the Atlantic, Topper wanted to call Kennedy on the company frequency to tell him who was aboard, but McGarvey stopped him. Even though the message was scrambled it could be monitored and decoded with the right equipment.

"What about customs?" McGarvey asked.

"Not until Portland, unless you want to leave the plane when we refuel in Detroit."

McGarvey thought about it for a moment. Dominique was there at her brother's house. "Portland will be soon enough."

"Won't be a reception committee if they don't know you're coming."

"That's what I figure," McGarvey said.

TWENTY-FIVE

We wouldn't get away with another fire," Mueller said, looking out the window at the arid countryside.

He rode in a rental van with Glen Zerkel on Interstate 10 southeast of Tucson, the sun setting in a fantastic multicolored swirl behind them. There was nothing like this in Germany. It was as Mueller imagined Africa would be, except that here were strip malls, swimming pools, and the ubiquitous McDonald's. He was still amazed with the vastness of the country. Japan did not have a chance against the United States. None of them ever had.

"That's what I thought. And if we lifted one of the units from Guerin they'd miss it. Wouldn't take them long to figure out what's going on," Zerkel said.

"How did you know about this place?"

"It's pretty much general knowledge. But I read something a while back about what used to be the Strategic Air Command mothballing some of its squadrons when the Soviet Union collapsed. Some of the planes are Guerin 522s. I checked it out at the library."

"They'll be intact?"

"Sealed up but ready to fly. They're too valuable to cannibalize. It's why they mothball them down here. Weather's hot and dry. Nothing will rust. Louis told me how the frame is probably bolted in, and what we're going to have to do to pull it and the wiring harness out. If we do it right nobody will notice the stuff is missing until they recommission the plane."

They'd gone over this on the flight down. "I'll give you the time if you think you can do it."

"I can. But if something goes down it could blow the whole deal."

"Leave that consideration to me," Mueller said calmly.

Zerkel glanced over at him. "I mean it. If we have to fight our way out of there, they'll check to see what's missing."

"Not every component of every airplane."

"That's right . . ."

"Leave no outward traces."

"I see what you mean," Zerkel said. He should never have doubted the German's ability or judgment. Mueller was a professional. It gave Glen pause thinking about going head to head with the man if and when the need arose. But for the moment he was glad to have Mueller on his side.

Commander Hanrahan returned to the bridge after a quick lunch alone in the officers' mess. The sky was covered with a thick overcast, and the wind and seas were beginning to build.

"What's our friend doing, Red?" he asked his exec.

"Same as before. Drift and run."

"Still nothing from Yokosuka?"

"It's only been six hours since our last radio contact."

"Shit," Hanrahan grumbled. He stepped closer to the windows and watched the bow rise and fall on the increasing waves. Meteorology was not predicting any weather more serious than this. Yet he was uneasy. "Same baseline since the strait?"

"He runs in a random zigzag pattern, and when he drifts it's back toward us. But his baseline is still south-southwest."

"Okinawa. What's his SOA?"

"About two knots. Maybe a little less."

"Two weeks, Red, before he crosses Okinawa's inner defense perimeter. Unless he speeds up. In the meantime we babysit."

"Not much we can do about it, Skipper."

Hanrahan faced his XO. "I told you before that I wasn't going to stay out here following that bastard all over the East China Sea indefinitely."

"I hear you. But if he doesn't want to play, there's not much we can do about it. Seventh has set the rules of engagement."

"That they have," Hanrahan picked up the growler phone and called Sattler in CIC. "What are you painting, Don?"

"He's six thousand yards off our starboard bow, making ten knots, course two-seven-zero."

"Straight west this time. What's his depth?"

"Two hundred feet. But when he drifts he comes up about fifty feet. Soon as he goes active we pick him up at about one-fifty. Takes him fifteen minutes to level off at what he's using as a cruise depth."

"We lose him in drift."

"About a half-hour each time."

"He's going to have to come up to recharge his batteries sooner or later."

"That's the point, Skipper. He should've done that by now. He's not a nuke. Whatever he's using for electricity must be damned good. Better than anything I've ever heard of."

"Me too," Hanrahan replied, thinking about it. The days were long gone since the U.S. shared its technology with the Japanese, and even longer since Japan shared with the U.S. The *Samisho* was state of the art. He wondered how good her weapons were.

"When's he due to drop off our scopes again?"

"About an hour from now."

"Half-hour duration each time?"

"That's been the pattern so far, Skipper."

"Next time he shuts down I want to continuously ping him. Set up a firing solution for a pair of harpoons, and we'll close the range to a guaranteed no miss."

"That'll get his attention. How long do we keep it up?"

"Until he makes a move, or until he comes out of the drift mode."

"Half-hour of that racket will drive him nuts. You know how he reacted last time."

Hanrahan chuckled. "That's the idea, Don. We'll go to battle stations each time. Give the crew some practice—"

"Wait!" Sattler interrupted. "Skipper, we have two incoming jet aircraft from the northeast about three miles out, just subsonic! Altitude four hundred feet! Right on the deck!"

Hanrahan put it on the speaker. The targets were showing up on the bridge radar. "What type of aircraft?"

"Looks like fighter/interceptors. F/A-18 Hornets. I think they're Japanese out of Tanegashima. We're being lit by their radars."

"Switch our after Phalanx to automatic," Hanrahan ordered.

"Mike, these are not enemy aircraft," Ryder objected.

"Then they better stay the hell out of my envelope," Hanrahan turned on his XO. "Do it now!"

"Aye, aye," Ryder replied, and he gave the order.

Moments later the jets responded to the threat, climbing sharply out of the limited range of the *Thorn*'s

Phalanx system radar, one left and the other right. Then they passed directly overhead, standing on their tails, the noise from their engines aimed directly at the bridge.

"Bastards," Hanrahan shouted. The bridge radar showed their tracks converging as they swung back to the northeast. He got back on the growler to Sattler. "What'd they get from us, Don?"

"They covered every frequency range we monitor, including infrared. Probably took pictures too. We did."

"We're showing them out of here."

"Us too, but they're dropping back to the deck, so they'll be over our radar horizon in about a minute and a half. Should we send up a chopper to see where they're headed?"

"We couldn't see any markings. Were they definitely Japanese Air Self Defense jets?"

"We got a good look up their tails. Definitely F/A-18JDs. Only country in the world has that class of Hornet is Japan."

"No need for the chopper. We know where they're going. What about *Chrysanthemum?*"

"Still ten knots on two-seven-zero."

"Did he launch a comms buoy by any chance?" Hanrahan asked.

"If he did we missed it, Skipper."

"Any chance of that?"

"Not at this range."

"Keep a sharp eye, Don. I think they just sent us a message."

"What's going on?" Ryder asked.

Hanrahan smiled knowingly. "Someone just told us that the *Samisho's* skipper is probably not a rogue after all. They're starting to pay attention in Yokosuka."

"Maybe in Tokyo too."

Hanrahan ignored the comment. "Message Seventh. I think the rules have changed."

They parked the van behind a small school off Valencia Road a half-mile from the Pima Air Museum on the extreme south edge of Davis Monthan Air Force Base. To the northwest the lights of Tucson were bright in the night sky, and directly north, the tower beacon rotated white and green. Here, however, they were in darkness. The school could have been abandoned. Shutters covered the windows. In any case no one was likely to come around until morning.

In addition to the 9 mm silenced Beretta, Mueller carried a long, razor-sharp stiletto in a sheath across his chest. Zerkel carried his tools, including insulated wire cutters and a set of battery jumper cables, as well as a sling to carry the sensor frame and harness.

They headed across the desert, keeping well away from the road that went up to the museum. They had to cross a concrete-lined drainage ditch and then the Southern Pacific railroad tracks to reach the tall, electrified fence that marked the air force base boundary.

Mueller dropped down behind some low bushes and motioned for Zerkel to do the same. They were less than twenty-five yards from the fence. Directly north they could see the end of the main runway, but in the distance to the east Mueller could see row after row of vague shapes that could have been buildings in a darkened town.

"Is that it?" he asked.

"Just the edge of it, I think," Zerkel whispered. "There's ten thousand airplanes parked here."

Mueller looked sharply at him, trying to gauge from the expression on his face whether he was joking. But he was serious. "That's a significant portion of your air force."

"Some of those planes are World War II vintage."

"Why haven't they been scrapped?"

"The article didn't say."

"But they're guarded."

"Probably," Zerkel said.

"Incredible. There must be tens of millions of dollars worth of equipment out there."

"Yeah. Impressive, ain't it?"

Mueller didn't reply, turning inward to what he'd learned since joining Reid. Even in the early days of the Cold War he'd been enough of a realist to know that the Soviet Union's military strength was being exaggerated in the West. They'd all assumed that Soviet estimates of NATO's strength were similarly overestimated. That was not the case.

At 11:30 P.M., the lights of a vehicle worked its way up and down the rows of mothballed aircraft. It turned back to the north a half-hour later.

"Might be another before dawn," Zerkel said.

"We'll watch for it."

At the fence Zerkel connected the jumper cables across a five-foot section, and carefully cut it away with the insulated wire cutters. If there were security alarms on the fence the break would not show up. And they were far enough away from the nearest road that the opening likely would not be spotted by a passing patrol.

They headed in a brisk pace across the desert to the nearest rows of parked airplanes, keeping a wary eye for approaching lights from the north. The night was utterly still. Even the light breeze earlier had died to nothing.

Airplanes of all sizes, shapes, and vintages were parked in orderly ranks and files for as far as the eye could see. Some had their engines removed, others were propped up on cradles, their landing gear missing, but most were intact.

It was after 1:00 A.M. before they chanced upon a row of twenty-seven Guerin 522s, which the Air Force had designated C-7C Globelifters. The engines were in place, but sealed, as were the windshields and windows along the sides.

"Keep your eyes open," Zerkel whispered. "If someone comes, knock twice on the hull. I'll hear it."

"Four hours," Mueller warned. "If you're not finished by then we'll return tomorrow."

"Right," Zerkel said, and he scrambled up onto the nose wheel and disappeared into the landing-gear well.

Mueller moved back into the shadows and took up

position behind the main gear on port side of the big jetliner. From where he stood he could see the road, but he would be practically invisible from anyone passing in a vehicle.

There was the sound of metal scraping against metal from inside the airplane, and then a muffled thump. Mueller waited for more noise, or for Zerkel to call out for help, but there was nothing.

When these planes started falling out of the sky it would be the most devastating single day in the history of the United States. Mueller knew that he would probably spend the next several years on the run, and that he would be lucky to survive. The authorities would not soon give up the chase, unless they were misdirected from the start.

He turned that thought over. If Reid and the Zerkels were found dead, the search would be concentrated on one man. Their murderer. But if they were found dead by suicide or by accident, and if his name were to be removed from Louis's computer programs, he might have a head start.

Mueller had no illusions about the FBI or the CIA. They had the money, the expertise and, after the button was pushed, they would have the motivation. As did the French.

Over the past few years the SDECE had become more aggressive, emboldened by the end of the Cold War. Yet he thought the French would have been more cautious because of the reunited Germanies.

It was a different world. And it would be made even more different by what Reid had set them to do.

That was the other thing. After this was over he was going to have to retire. Reid had made good on his promise by depositing one million dollars in Mueller's account. The question was where could he go? The Caribbean? The South Pacific? Perhaps South America? Wherever, he needed to begin making his arrangements.

Zerkel climbed down from the wheel well a half-hour later.

Mueller moved out of the shadows. "Something wrong?"

"No. Help me up on the wing, and then watch for company, I've got to open the engine cowling."

Mueller boosted him up onto the wing, then tossed the tools up. "Did you get the harness?"

"Just the plug. There's nothing between the panel and the frame except wire."

"Are you sure?"

Zerkel looked down at him. "I think so."

"Do it correctly, Glen. I don't wish to return here."

"I'll do what I can. But to get the entire harness out I'd have to tear the wing apart. Watch for the patrol."

Zerkel undid a dozen fasteners and lifted a section of engine cowling up on its hinges.

Mueller saw the problem at once. "How long are you going to be up there with the engine open?"

"I don't know." Zerkel shined a dim red light inside the cowling. "An hour, maybe less if I'm lucky."

"Hurry," Mueller said, and he headed down the road in the direction from which the patrol had come. At the first intersection he looked back. Just as he thought, the upraised cowling broke the orderly line of silhouettes. It was out of place and would be noticed even at a distance if another patrol came by.

From the number of airplanes and the size of the area, Mueller doubted that more than three patrols would be mounted each night: one at dusk, one in the middle of the night, and one at dawn. With luck they'd be okay here for several more hours.

He settled down to wait in the shadows of a Boeing 727 from where he would see an approaching patrol before it reached the airplane Glen was working on. If one did come he would have no time to warn Zerkel. He would have to flag them down, kill however many guards there were—one or two, he suspected—and move their bodies to another area of the mothballed fleet. He thought about this without any emotion, only a detached interest in the technical difficulties of such an action.

Looking back again the cowling still jutted above the wing. But an hour later it was gone, and Mueller trotted back to the jetliner.

"Where the hell were you?" Zerkel whispered urgently.

"Making sure you were not disturbed. Are you finished?"

"Yes." Zerkel handed down a stamped metal frame in the shape of a capital A about three feet long, and two feet wide at the base. Several dozen single wires, plus a thick bundle tied in a harness, dangled from the sensor frame. It was lighter than Mueller thought it should be if it were made out of aluminum. Titanium, possibly.

Zerkel tossed down his tools, and then eased himself off the wing. "Let's get out of here. I've got a bad feeling."

"Are you finished up there, and inside?" Mueller asked calmly.

"I said I was—"

"You left no outward traces? Nothing that a casual inspection would uncover?"

"Christ."

"Think about it."

Zerkel started to say something, but then he looked up at the engine cowling, and back to the nose gear well, and nodded. "It's cool, man. They'd have to tear this plane down to find out what happened. I even tucked the loose wires out of sight."

"Then it's time to go."

"What about the hole in the fence?"

Mueller smiled. "As you say, they'd have to tear this aircraft apart to find out what you did. I don't think they'll do ten thousand."

Air Force One, the Presidential seal on her tail and the American flag on her fuselage, was trundled out of her hangar at Andrews Air Force Base. At two hundred eighteen feet in length, she was nearly as large as Boeing's 747, and in her various configurations could carry up to four hundred passengers. Except for the two accidents in seven years, the 522's safety record was perfect. The engines had been replaced by a Guerin AOG team three days ago, and no one this morning expected any trouble. Yet everyone on the maintenance team and flight crew was nervous.

The pilot, Lieutenant Colonel Bob Wheeler, went through the extensive pre-flight checklist one meticulous step at a time with his co-pilot, Major Larry Marthaller. On this flight the maintenance crew aboard would backstop every move that was made on the flight deck. Test equipment monitored every electrical, hydraulic, mechanical, and electronic function of the jetliner's 3.7 million parts. A crew on the ground would monitor everything from their vantage point. As the saying went, the President was a hundred times safer aboard Air Force One than he was riding out to the base on his chopper, and ten times safer than in his limousine.

"That line of thunder bumpers to the southeast isn't breaking up as fast as we thought it would," Chief Master Sergeant Mazorsky said.

Wheeler looked up from the checklist. "What'd meteorology say?"

"They'll hang around a couple of hours. You might swing that way. Tops at less than forty thousand."

Wheeler shrugged. "We've got the time if you've got the stomach, Chief."

"I hate these goddamned things, Captain, but I want to see what shakes loose. We'll tear the airframe apart when we get back."

"Scuttlebutt is that we might fly in two weeks. President may be moving his Tokyo trip up."

"We've got plenty of time. I just want to make sure."

Major Marthaller had been talking to ground control. He looked up. "You know something we don't, Chief?"

"Not a thing."

"But?"

Mazorsky hesitated a moment. "After the incident at Dulles I want to make sure about this bird."

"Has anything turned up?"

"Nada. I just want to make sure about her."

"So do we, Chief," Wheeler said. "One thunderstorm coming up."

Getting off the base was no problem. By ten in the morning they had driven the one hundred twenty miles to Phoenix where they rented a Ford Taurus at the airport. They transferred the frame and harness plugs to the car, and turned the van in where they'd rented it at the Hertz counter downtown. By lunch they were headed north on Interstate 17.

"It'll be a long haul back to the East Coast," Zerkel said. He drove.

"It's too risky to take that thing on a plane." Mueller laid his head back. "When you get tired I'll drive."

"It'll be awhile. I'm too keyed up. But we did it."

"What do you think about that?" Mueller mumbled, and he fell asleep.

TWENTY-SIX

Have you talked to your friends in Washington?" Kennedy asked on the way down the hall to Vasilanti's office.

"I wanted to update you first. You're going to have to make another hard decision," McGarvey said. "What did Carrara tell you?"

"They want you in Washington. Has something to do with your trip to Tokyo, but he wouldn't be more specific."

"Did he warn you off?"

"Wouldn't have been very politic. They recommended you."

"Things have changed again, David. Maybe now you won't want me on the payroll."

"Thank God that's not a decision I'm going to have to make alone," Kennedy replied. "But for what it's worth, I still have confidence in you. It's the situation that has me worried. It may be out of our hands. Out of your hands."

"You may be right," McGarvey said, and Kennedy gave him a strange, penetrating look.

McGarvey had met with Guerin's chairman of the board and chief executive officer only once since the Dulles crash, so he wasn't prepared for the drastic change in the man. Where before Vasilanti had been a tough old buzzard with an acerbic tongue, now he appeared subdued, even withdrawn. His eyes darted around the room to his executives as if he were looking for their approval. Or, McGarvey thought, their sympathy. Besides Gary Topper, George Socrates, and Newt Kilbourne, who glared at McGarvey, Kennedy introduced Tony Glick, who had taken over as Guerin's general legal counsel, and Maggie Drewd, who'd taken over as chief financial officer. No one seemed happy. Their conversation died when McGarvey came into the room, and no one said much when Kennedy made the introductions.

They were expecting more bad news. One thing he had learned about airplane people was that they were an emotional breed. Much more so than the intelligence community. They were boys and girls playing with toys, and when something went wrong they pouted. He knew that wasn't exactly right, but it seemed that way. Especially now.

"Mr. McGarvey has just returned from Tokyo. He's warned me that we're going to have to make some tough decisions," Kennedy said.

No one responded.

"The Dulles crash and the American Airlines crash in 1990 were both acts of sabotage," McGarvey said. "By the Japanese in an effort to bring this company down."

"Christ," Vasilanti said softly.

"Rolls-Royce is under intense pressure to stop engine deliveries to you—including the hydrogen engine—until we get this business straightened out."

"Sir Malcolm tell you that?" Socrates asked.

"Yes."

"He told me the same thing," Topper interjected.

"That's it then," the design vice president said in resignation. "I don't build gliders."

"But he's agreed to try to figure out how his engines are being sabotaged," McGarvey told them. "In the meantime Rolls will keep to its delivery schedules."

"Wait a minute," Vasilanti said looking up. "You mean to say that Malcolm O'Toole wouldn't listen to Gary, but he would you?"

"That's right. I told him that I had proof that the Japanese sabotaged his engines, that I just didn't know how they did it. I asked him to figure it out."

"Do you have this proof?" Tony Glick asked. He was a blond, blue-eyed California lawyer who'd been Howard Siegel's assistant.

"Sokichi Kamiya, the head of Mintori Assurance, admitted it."

"Extraordinary," the company lawyer said excitedly. "No witnesses, of course. Just you?"

"Just me."

"So it's your word against his. Lay it on your friends in Washington. The State Department is slavering at the bit about anything having to do with the Japanese. Somebody will listen."

"It won't be that easy," McGarvey warned. "I was set up over there, so I don't think my word is going to carry much weight. At least not until I can get the hard evidence."

"You're saying there's nothing we can do about it?" Kennedy demanded.

"Not that at all. But it's going to get a lot tougher from here on out. I'm going to get a lot more unpopular than I already am. Might even become a fugitive. And there'll almost certainly be some more deaths."

Vasilanti sat up. "Another crash?"

"Possibly," McGarvey said. "I'm going to stir things up, and Kamiya's people will probably come after me. Or at least I hope they will. Maybe we'll get lucky, maybe they'll make a mistake."

Maggie Drewd shuddered. "Jeff wasn't very keen on hiring you," she said. "I guess I can see why. Is there any other way out for us? Short of this violence, I mean?"

"Stop building airplanes, stop flying."

"What about your pals the Russians?" Kilbourne asked.

Kennedy said that Dominique had returned to her job in Washington, and that she and her brother were not talking. The new product development vice president blamed McGarvey.

"They pointed us in the right direction. Knowing who we're fighting helps."

"What good is it if no one will believe you?" Kilbourne looked at the others. "I don't know if I do."

"Then fire me, and go about your business."

Kilbourne flared. "I'd just as soon see you in jail—"

"For what? Upsetting your sister?"

The airplane executive half rose from his seat. "For taking advantage of her. You're sleeping with her . . ." Socrates waved him off.

"We build airplanes, Newton. Mr. McGarvey catches spies," the designer said. "Let's all of us get on with it." He turned to McGarvey. "Nine days from now— Sunday, February ninth—*America* flies. Portland to Honolulu. I think you have that much time to help us. After that it will be too late. Once our airplane flies, we will have won. Nothing will hurt us."

"I'll do what I can. But it'll get ugly. Guaranteed."

McGarvey walked down the hall to Kennedy's office where he tried to call Carrara, first at Langley and then at the DDO's home without luck. His old friend was either not in, or he wasn't taking calls.

Next he tried to get through to Danielle or the General, but neither of them was accepting his calls either. Which was odd, he thought, if they wanted him in Washington.

Kennedy came from Vasilanti's office a minute later. "When are you leaving for Washington?"

"Not just yet. Is Yamagata still here in Portland?"

Kennedy looked startled. "Has he got something to do with this?"

"He's connected with Mintori."

"He's here. At least I think he still is."

"What's wrong, David?"

Kennedy shook his head miserably. "Tit for tat, I guess. Only if it's true he's using her."

"What are you talking about?"

"My wife and Yamagata. I think they're having an affair."

"He's made four calls here," Carrara told the DCI. "One to my office, one to my home, one to Larry's office, and finally one to you, General."

"From Portland?" Howard Ryan interjected. He was practically licking his chops.

"David Kennedy's office at Guerin's headquarters. We lost him at Narita, and this is the first we've heard from him."

"That's been more than twenty-four hours, Phil. He could have gotten into a lot of mischief in that time," Ryan suggested.

"Doesn't mean he did."

"Greg Isaacs was a good man, from what I'm told. His body was broken up by the long drop onto the rocks."

"I don't have to listen to your fucking histrionics, Mr. Ryan," Carrara sparked. "He was my field officer. I read the reports. I talked to Cort Gates and Steve Pelham."

"All right, Phil," Director Murphy said placatingly.

"No, sir, it's not all right. Kirk McGarvey deserves at least the benefit of the doubt from us, considering everything he's done for this country. Some fucking New York corporate attorney—"

"That will be enough!" Murphy roared.

Ryan was grinning behind his teeth. "Phil, for God's sake, we're all on the same side here. If I've said it once, I've said it a thousand times: just because McGarvey and I have a personality conflict doesn't mean I don't respect what the man has done for this Company. And I appreciate your friendship with him. And understand it, too. All I'm saying is that this time there have been too many coincidences surrounding him to ignore. I say we turn this over to the FBI and let them handle it as a counterespionage investigation."

"As a criminal investigation," Carrara countered.

Ryan raised his hands in defeat. "Okay, Phil, we'll do it your way. But let's get the investigation—whatever sort you recommend—out of the realm of emotions. Considering everything that's at stake I think it's terribly important."

"That's fair," Murphy acceded.

"If he's found innocent, we back off," Ryan said.

"You're forgetting something, Mr. Ryan," Carrara reminded the attorney coldly. "That surprises me, especially coming from a man of your training and background."

"Yes?" Ryan asked languidly. "What's that?"

"In this country a man is still considered innocent until proven guilty. Don't forget it. I won't."

Carrara went back to his bailiwick on the third floor and instructed his secretary that he was not to be disturbed for the next half-hour. He poured a stiff measure of brandy from a bottle in a sideboard and set the glass on his desk. He looked at it for a long moment, then turned away to stare out the window. He had been a sober alcoholic for the past eleven years. Whenever he was in crisis he poured a drink as a test of willpower—his, over whatever problem he was facing. He had beat the booze. He could beat anything else in his path.

McGarvey had been placed on at least two occasions in the company of a Japanese national by the name of Arimoto Yamagata.

He had made inquiries about the man.

He'd met an unidentified Japanese man at his hotel in Tokyo. They'd had dinner and drinks together at an exclusive club, and that evening McGarvey had been involved in a street brawl in which at least three Japanese were killed.

He'd been arrested and released within hours, and had shown up at Yamagata's home outside of Tokyo, to meet with a so far unidentified Japanese.

Isaacs was dead.

McGarvey had shaken their leg men at Tokyo's airport, and now he was back in Portland trying to call in as if nothing had happened.

Yamagata was presently in Portland.

What was going on? Was Mac finally around the bend? Had he finally snapped? Gone freelance, in the parlance? Or was there some other explanation?

If there was, Carrara thought, it would be ominous. He shivered. He'd not felt this bad for a very long time. It was time to look a little deeper into McGarvey's background. A lot deeper, as a matter of fact.

The sensor frame was clamped to the bench in the basement workshop at the Sterling farmhouse. Mueller and Reid watched from the foot of the stairs as Louis hooked test equipment to the several dozen wires connected to various parts of it. For the moment he ignored the main wiring harness, which would have to be reconstructed from the connector plugs that Glen had snipped from the frame and from the heat monitor unit in the airplane's electronics bay. It would have to be tested as part of the entire assembly, including his decoding and triggering circuits.

"Each of these has a diode on the frame side," Louis said to his brother who was helping.

"What does that mean?" Glen asked. "Does it tell you something?"

Louis looked up, a wide-eyed expression on his face. "You clipped the ends of all these smaller wires because they were connected to self-locking plugs on various parts of the engine. Right?"

"We didn't have much time."

"No sweat. What I mean is that each of these wires comes *from* the engine. Information is coming down these wires, across the frame, and out the main harness."

"I still don't understand."

"A diode lets a signal move in only one direction. In this case *from* the engine to the wiring harness and heat monitor's CPU. The only reason you'd design a diode into this circuit is if there were stray signals floating around the frame that might accidently find their way back into the engine. Probably burn up the thermocouples that measure the heat output at various sections of the engine."

"Is that how they fuck with the engines?" Glen asked. "By sending an overriding signal to burn out the diodes and then the thermocouples?"

Louis looked at his brother with new respect. "Nice idea, and it'd work, but I don't think that's going to happen here. The sensor wires are also electrically isolated from the frame. In fact they've gone to a lot of trouble to completely isolate the frame."

"Go on."

"Think about it. Every electrical circuit needs a two-way path. The hot side and a common ground. The frame, in this case, should be the common ground. But it's not. It's electrically isolated for some reason."

"Why?"

"I don't know," Louis admitted. "But I'm going to find out as soon as I finish running down the rest of these connections."

"How long before you will be ready?" Reid asked from the stairs.

"Few hours," Louis said, glancing over.

"I mean with everything. With the entire detonating setup."

"Depends on what I find out when I test the frame with the monitor and my circuits. I'll probably do that later today, maybe tonight." Zerkel grinned. "Don't worry, Mr. Reid. Won't be long now and you'll get what you want. More than you want."

"Very well," Reid said, and he and Mueller went back upstairs.

"No use in putting the repeaters in place until he's ready," Mueller said.

"I agree." Reid poured a drink of Irish whiskey at the sideboard in the living room. "The chances of discovery would be too great if we had to wait long." He took a deep drink. "February ninth is the day we go. Guerin is sending its new airplane on a flight from Portland to Honolulu. A lot of VIPs will be aboard, including the Vice President of the United States."

"That will create a lot of attention."

Reid smiled. "Indeed it will, my friend. Indeed it will."

"What's going on with Ed Reid?" U.S. Representative John Davis asked on the phone. He'd become increasingly worried about his own vulnerability since speaking with the former deputy undersecretary of state.

"You've got to see Harding on that one," Dwight Coster said. He was legal counsel for the Bureau, and a friend of Davis's.

"Ed's damned worried about what's going on over there. Someone put the bug in his ear that it had to do with his stand on the Japanese. Either State or the White House is trying to sit on him."

"Come on, you know I can't discuss an ongoing investigation with anyone outside the shop. Not even you."

"Then you're saying it's true that Reid is under investigation? What the hell's he done?"

"Nothing, so far as I know. His name just popped out of nowhere in another investigation."

"What kind of an investigation? Does it have anything to do with the Japanese? Because if it does it's going to look damned suspicious when the dust settles that someone was out to put the ax to Reid."

"I wouldn't answer that even if I could, John. All I can say is what I've already told you."

"This is counterespionage, right?"

The line was silent for a long time. Davis almost thought he had lost the Bureau lawyer. But when Coster came back his voice was guarded. "Where'd you get that?"

"Does the name Kirk McGarvey mean anything to you? Former CIA spook on contract to Guerin Airplane Company. Does a deal Guerin's cutting with the Russians have anything to do with it? Or a French Action Service inquiry into the whereabouts of a couple of former East German spies?" It was all the stuff Harding had given him in confidence, but Davis figured Coster didn't need to know his source.

"I'm not going to talk about this on the phone."

"Fine. Name a time and place."

"Ten minutes. The atrium bar at the Grand Hyatt Washington Center. It's public enough that nobody'll notice."

"Ten minutes." Davis took a cab over to the hotel and arrived just as Coster was sitting down at a table near the front where everybody could see that they had nothing to hide.

"I could get my ass in a major jam here," Coster said.

"When we signed on the dotted line for this town we took that responsibility. Nixon found out the hard way. You don't beat the system, you just play the odds."

When their drinks came, Coster eyed his old friend speculatively. "Is that what this is all about, John? Odds? You owe Ed Reid a favor?"

"Sort of. But I also want to cover my own ass. If he's in trouble I want to know about it."

"Where'd you get all that information?"

"Harding. Said it was confidential."

"Why the hell don't you go back to him?"

"Because I figure he's already given me as much as he's going to give. And two calls in one week will start him wondering."

"And I'm the boy who's got to play ball with you and lie to his own director."

"We're friends."

"Yeah," Coster said. "In this town that's more expensive than a mistress. McGarvey is under investigation for industrial espionage, selling or trading secrets to the enemy, and murder. That's just for starters. The CIA called today to turn up the heat. They want him burned. Somebody over there has a grudge."

"What's Reid's involvement?"

"Nobody knows, but he's on the top of the hit list because of State's queries, the White House's interest—and by rights I should throw your name onto the list."

"That's his only connection?"

"One more. When Reid was stationed in Germany in the sixties he knew Karl Schey, who was a deep-cover East German intelligence agent working for the West German Secret Service."

"Did Reid know that he was a double agent?"

"I don't know. But Schey is one of the East Germans who is missing."

Davis sat back with his drink. "Shit," he said softly. Knowingly or not, Reid was up to his elbows in this one. The question was what to do about it?

CIA Director Roland Murphy rode his limousine to the White House. The President had agreed to see him immediately. He wasn't going to like what Murphy was bringing over, not so soon before the Tokyo Summit. But that's what being President was all about: making the tough decisions when no matter what you did was wrong. This one, Murphy thought, was doing a better job than most.

There was trouble enough without McGarvey's meddling, which was on a much larger scale than ever before. Despite the fact that Howard Ryan could be an asshole at times, he was essentially correct in his fears about McGarvey screwing up the works. Negotiations with the Japanese were at a critical stage. A wrong move on our part could push the United States one step closer to bankruptcy. Not in any real sense, but in the sense that

trying to pay down the national debt would cut even
further into such basic services as health care, entitle-
ment programs, and aid to states.

Murphy was damned glad that he wasn't President. In
fact he thought any man who aspired to the job had to be
certifiably nuts.

"Go right in," the President's Appointments Secretary, Steve Nichols, said.

"Ask Harold Secor to join us," Murphy said.

"He's already inside."

"Good." Murphy entered the Oval Office. The President and his National Security Adviser were hunched
over a series of documents spread out on the desk. They
looked up.

"Hello, Roland."

"Good afternoon, Mr. President. Harold."

"What crisis are we facing this afternoon?"

"The situation with the Japanese military. It looks as
if it's beginning to heat up."

The President exchanged glances with Secor. "What
have you got for me this time?"

"National Reconnaissance Offfice satellite photographs, along with the latest batch from our own KH-
15."

Secor moved the documents he and the President had
been studying.

Murphy opened his briefcase and spread out a dozen
high-resolution photos on the desk. "These are Japanese
Air Self Defense and Maritime Self Defense bases.
Atsugi, Iwakuni, Komatsujima, Shimofusa, Hachinowe,
and Tanegashima."

"What am I looking at here?" the President asked.

"It would appear that there's a lot of activity," Secor
suggested. "An exercise?"

"That's right," Murphy replied. "Every base we've
looked at is on alert, only no one is calling it that."

"What do you mean?" the President asked.

"When the Japanese military stages an exercise it
always informs us well in advance. More often than not

we're invited to participate, or at the very least, observe. Not this time. Seventh Fleet Intelligence at Yokosuka spotted this for us."

"All right, Roland, spell it out for me."

Murphy took another series of photographs out of his briefcase and laid them on top of the first. "Russian naval and air force bases at Korsakov, Kholmsk, and Yuzhno-Sakhalinsk on Sakhalin Island. Svetlaya, Sovetskaya-Gavan, and Vladivostok on the mainland. And Kurilsk on Iturup Island in the Kurils. All on alert, all gearing up for an exercise."

The President was stunned. "You mean to say that they're going to shoot at each other over the Tatar Strait thing? The Russian ambassador sat in this room last week, and there was no mistake that he understood perfectly what I told him."

"I don't know if it'll come to that, Mr. President, but something else has caught our attention."

"What?"

"Half the Japanese bases that are on alert are in the south and east. Nowhere near the Russian threat."

"What's that supposed to indicate?" Secor asked.

"The same submarine that sank the Russian frigate in the strait is now heading toward Okinawa in the East China Sea. One of our ships is shadowing it, but we were overflown by a pair of fighter/interceptors from Tanegashima."

"What do the Japanese have to say about it?" Secor demanded.

"Nothing."

"Let's put a different spin on this, Roland," the President said. "The Japanese and Russians have apologized to each other for the incident in the strait. But we've upgraded Seventh's readiness status to a DEFCON FOUR. Perhaps the Japanese forces are simply following suit, which has made the Russians wary. We've heard nothing from Moscow?" the President asked Secor.

"Not a word."

"Are any of their other bases on alert?"

"We've had no indications of that," Murphy said.

The President nodded. "As far as the submarine is concerned, the East China Sea is its home waters. It's got every right to send a patrol down there. Isn't that correct?"

"Yes, sir. But this time is different. We ought to keep an eye on it."

"I agree," Secor said.

"Very well. We need to hold the status quo for another nine days, that's all."

"Sir?" Murphy said.

"I'm going to Tokyo several days before the summit is scheduled to begin. Prime Minister Enchi and I have several things to work out between us before we get started. I'll discuss this with him."

"We won't make an announcement until the last minute," Secor said. "Sunday, February ninth."

"The conspirators appear before me."

"Do not be so certain in your judgment, or so quick to make it," Sokichi Kamiya said. He and Hiroshi Kobayashi, who'd come from Kobe for the meeting, sat across the low table from Hideyoshi Nobunaga, the director of the Ministry of International Trade and Industry, and Tadashi Ota, the Deputy Director General of Defense. They met in a private room at Fukudaya, Tokyo's premier *rotei* restaurant.

Nobunaga, a short thin man with a deep bass voice, took a thick envelope from his coat pocket and tossed it imperiously on the table in front of Kamiya. The rude gesture was an insult. "Your connection to Rising Sun and what we have managed to gather so far about your project Morning Star is there."

Kamiya did not even look at the envelope. "Shall we meet with the Prime Minister, *Nobunaga-san?* Or debate before the Diet?"

"I forbid this insanity."

"Amusing, coming from a man who directs spy efforts against the United States and every other Western industrialized nation. Your efforts would be better spent against China and North Korea. Leave the real work to those of us who have the intelligence and the stomach for it."

Their attendant, a beautiful young woman in an immaculate flowered kimono, entered the room on her knees to serve them tiny lacquered trays of artfully arranged seafood and vegetables. She poured each of them saki in Imari porcelain cups and then gracefully withdrew. She glanced up at the hanging scroll in the alcove before she closed the rice-paper door.

"He prospers who values another's life." The Deputy Director General of Defense motioned toward the printing on the scroll. "Fifty years is not such a long memory for a man of your . . . wisdom, *Kamiya-san.*"

"I have not forgotten, but you were a snot-nosed kid. You can't remember."

"Whatever you think of me, I am a student of history. Perhaps I can see the past better for not having been prejudiced by living through it. These are not such simple times."

"I disagree. These are the 1920s and 1930s all over again. *Dai Nihon* is again faced with terrible choices for her survival. If you do not understand, then come with me to the stock exchange and I will explain the facts of our life to you, Deputy Director General!"

Ota wanted to argue, but Nobunaga gestured for him to be still.

"We are working toward the same ends, *Kamiya-san,*" the MITI director said. "Many of our methods are similar. But yours will surely end in catastrophe."

"Think what you are saying."

"I have. But you must think what you are doing. Your misadventures are ego-driven. The last acts of an old man."

Kamiya smiled. "Then why are you here?"

"Because you and your foolish friends are powerful men."

"Patriots," Kobayashi spoke for the first time.

"Misguided."

"No. I remember as well."

"Do you fools want to start that all over again?" Ota blurted. "Don't you remember the privations? The humiliations? The patronizings?"

Kamiya leaned forward and stabbed a blunt finger in Ota's direction. "Tell me who we share Yokosuka with? Tell me who we defer to on Okinawa? Tell me whose television, and blue jeans, and pop culture our young people are being force fed?"

Nobunaga leaned forward, his palms on the table. "And tell me who buys more manufactured goods from us than any other nation on this earth? Tell me who provides jobs? Tell me who has become friend from enemy?"

"Then why are you spying on them?" Kamiya asked.

"It is business. It is war. But not your kind of war."

"We'll see." Kamiya and Kobayashi got up and made to leave.

"Don't forget your envelope," Ota said. "If you look inside perhaps you will gain some respect for loyalty."

"We will stop you," Nobunaga warned sternly.

Kamiya looked down at him. "I would not suggest you try to arrest us. It would tear the country apart. We have many more friends than you can possibly imagine."

McGarvey spent the afternoon with Socrates and the team of crash engineers that had been assembled after Dulles. Every system on the airplane had worked to its design parameters up to the moment of the crash. The only possible conclusion was that somehow the engine's composite turbine blades had failed.

"But I don't like it," the chief engineer said.

"Maybe Sir Malcolm will come up with something for us," McGarvey replied.

"I'm glad you talked to him, and made him see our point. Hell, we're all grateful. But everything is so bollixed up around here that nobody can think straight."

"Maybe you people should think about postponing the Honolulu flight."

"Believe me, that's the only thing keeping us going."

It was almost five when McGarvey went up to Kennedy's office, but his secretary said he would be in conference for at least another two hours, after which he, Mr. Vasilanti, and Mr. Kilbourne would be having dinner in the executive dining room.

"If it's urgent, I can break in on him."

"Tell him I'll see him tomorrow."

"Yes, sir."

From his own temporary office downstairs next to security he tried again to call Carrara without luck. The Deputy Director of Operations was away from his desk.

Next he telephoned Dominique's office, but they would tell him nothing. Her secretary was even hesitant to take a message. Nor was Dominique's answering machine switched on at her apartment. He could understand why she was avoiding him. It was probably for the best. But he wished she had remained in Detroit. In Washington she was impossible to protect.

Before he went out there, however, there were a few things he wanted to take care of here.

Guerin supplied him with a Buick Riviera. He drove south to the affluent suburb of Lake Oswego and was just pulling into the Kennedys' driveway when the garage door opened and Chance Kennedy backed out in a metallic green Mercedes 560SEL.

She stopped when she saw him and powered down her window.

McGarvey got out of his car and went over to her. "Can I have a couple minutes of your time, Mrs. Kennedy?"

"David's not home."

"I know. I came out to see you. I'd like to ask you a couple of questions."

She eyed him with mistrust. "You're the spook they hired. What do you want with me? Shouldn't you be chasing bad guys?"

"I am."

"Peachy. But I have to run now. Maybe if you can

corner my husband long enough to sit down for dinner you can come back Sunday." She hit the garage-door switch.

"Arimoto Yamagata."

An abject look of terror crossed her face, and was gone.

"Are you going to see him now?"

She shivered. "What are you talking about?"

"You're having an affair with him, Mrs. Kennedy. But I have to warn you that he represents the people who want to bring Guerin Airplane Company to its knees. His people sabotaged that airplane that went down at Dulles. Some good people were killed. Even more may die."

"I don't believe it," she said, regaining some of her composure. "Why'd you come here?"

"To warn you. And to find out how much you've already told him."

"I don't know where the hell you got the idea that I was having an affair. Jesus, Mary, and Joseph—"

"Your husband told me."

For just a moment Chance looked up, but then her face sagged, and she averted her eyes. "He wouldn't have told you something like that, even if he believed it was true. Not my four-square David."

"What have you told him?"

"David's a forty-three-year-old Boy Scout. True blue, loyal to the platoon, or corps, or whatever." She looked up again. "But not to me. Can you understand that?"

McGarvey felt sorry for her. But then, he thought, he wasn't such a hot judge of women. He'd never been able to sustain a relationship. *The job comes first.* Hadn't that always been the line?

"Yamagata is a dangerous man."

"Somebody give me at least a little credit," she said, once more in control. "I've not told the man a thing that he couldn't get out of a newspaper or an aerospace magazine. But he will tell me what I want to know. What David wants to know."

"Stay away from him, for your own sake."

She laughed. "Even if I were having an affair with him, it wouldn't be any of your business."

"I'll follow you if need be."

She laughed even louder now. "Go ahead. I'm having drinks downtown with the girls. But you're welcome to tag along." She powered up her window and backed out of the driveway.

When she was gone, McGarvey glanced up at the house. Nine days, he thought. He wondered where they'd all be on the day after.

TWENTY-SEVEN

The sensor frame was set up in the wine storage room forty feet from the heat monitor unit. Louis had rewired the connector plugs. The thick cable snaked across the basement floor from the workbench.

"This probably seems like a waste of time, but it isn't," Louis said, adjusting a signal generator's output. "I'm not sure about that first incident. Could have been a fluke. Could have been a real accident, not caused by me."

"Is that possible?" his brother Glen asked.

Louis looked up. He stank of stale sweat, garlic, beer, and perfume from the whore he'd been with. He hadn't taken a shower in days. "Anything's possible. This is a lot more complicated than you think."

"I know."

"No you don't," Louis said sharply. "It's complicated in a different way. This circuit is designed to look like one thing so that even an expert would be fooled. Really it's something else. And I've got most of it decoded. *Most* of it, Glen. We're not there yet."

"It'd be a hell of a coincidence."

Louis smiled grimly. "Would you bet your life on it?"

Glen held his silence for a long moment, but then he shook his head. "Let's get on with it. What do you want me to do?"

"There's a hundred thirty-two leads coming out of the monitor. Almost all of them are interrogators. Asking the frame to ask the engine thermocouples what the temperatures are. The CPU processes the data, and sends it up to the cockpit. I want to check each of those wires, one at a time, for any surprises."

"You say almost every lead checks temperatures?"

"One should be the common ground to the frame."

"But it isn't?"

"It comes from the modified CPU in the monitor, but there's a signal on the line when my encoder keys the circuit."

"To shut down the thermocouples?"

"I thought that. Or to burn out the diodes, like you suggested. But it's not that. The goddamned signal is modulated."

"What do you mean?"

"I mean when I key the encoder, a tone is sent from the CPU to the sensor frame. When I say hello or boom, or when I send an audio frequency signal, the CPU sends out a stream of information. The monitor talks to the sensor frame. It tells it something."

"Like what?"

Louis shrugged. "I don't know. If I put it up on a speaker the signal sounds like a bunch of monkeys in a zoo all getting pissed off at once. Gibberish."

"Then what?"

"That's what we're going to find out tonight, just as soon as we finish with the first hundred thirty-one interrogators." He was being overly cautious, but he didn't want to admit that he was totally at a loss. Whoever had designed this circuitry was cunning as well as intelligent. Alien, the notion popped into his head. It was the Japanese. They thought differently from us.

Their culture and background were vastly different from ours, so their engineering would be different too.

"I don't understand, Louis."

"I was hoping to find something on the frame. Something that would explain how it works. Something that would make it clear. But I can't see a fucking thing. Wires, diodes, and metal. Aluminum, magnesium. I don't even know that. I'm no metallurgist."

"If anybody can do it you can," Glen told him.

Louis flashed a hard, angry look at his brother.

"Don't let it get to you. Take it a step at a time. You're smarter than they are. You've already proved that."

"If I can't figure it out it becomes a moot point. We won't have anyplace to go."

Glen lowered his voice. "You worry about the circuit and let me take care of getting us out of here. Just do it, Louis."

"Nothing," Louis said.

One hundred thirty-one tones, one hundred thirty-one zeroes. Each of the leads from the monitor to the frame came out exactly as they should if they were doing the legitimate work of keeping an eye on conditions in the engine. Nothing in the circuitry would bring down an airplane.

"Maybe we should wait until morning to finish up." It was midnight, and Glen looked haggard. His eyes were bloodshot.

"All that's left is the modulated ground wire. We'll do it now."

"Same drill?"

"Yes."

They had tested all but the ground lead three times. The first with a signal from the monitor, down the harness to the plug before it was connected to the frame. A second time with the harness plugged in. And a third with a signal generated, wire by wire from the engine side of the diodes back to the monitor. Each time Glen watched an oscilloscope attached to the leads for a spike, a tone, or a modulated signal, which on the scope looked like the odd shapes the old lava lamps made.

Louis clipped the O-scope's leads to four different spots on the frame. If there was any response to the modulated signal sent from the monitor it would show up here. He adjusted the four traces, each at a different potential, from a few millivolts to 1.5 volts, the same as from an ordinary flashlight battery. Glen, his hand resting on the frame, watched intently.

"Don't touch the frame," Louis ordered. "Might screw up the results."

Glen did as he was told and Louis walked back to the workbench on the other side of the basement. "Watch the scope."

"Right," Glen called back.

Louis keyed the decoder, got the trigger pulse, and a few milliseconds later the audio frequency tone went out.

An intense white light suddenly bloomed in the wine storage room, and an instant later Glen screamed, the inhuman sound torn out of his throat. Louis had to fall back behind his equipment, because the heat blasting across the basement was so intense. He knew what was happening! He knew how it worked!

Glen's screams died as abruptly as they'd begun, and the brilliant light faded.

Saturday morning after breakfast, McGarvey decided to drive back out to Gales Creek to talk with Socrates and Kilbourne about the 2622. Since the Honolulu flight was only eight days away he figured they'd be out there. He wanted to know if the 2622 shared any parts with the 522. Especially engine components that had anything even remotely to do with heat management systems. It would be the perfect plane to knock out of the sky on its first VIP flight. Whatever was sabotaged could already be built into the jetliner, and all their searching on the day of the flight would be for nothing. He suspected that line of thinking would be a dead end because Kilbourne had made the point that the hypersonic jetliner was a brand-new design from the wheel struts up. Nonetheless he wanted to make sure.

Guerin had put him up in an executive turnkey apartment downtown. Within two blocks after leaving the underground parking garage he realized that he had picked up a tail, a black windowless van alternating with a brown Chevy Caprice. He'd tried again this morning to reach Carrara without luck, but there were automatic traces on all lines to CIA headquarters and to its top deputy directors, so his location had been pinpointed. But it was extreme, even for the General, to cut off all contact and then have him followed. Besides, these guys weren't very good.

Instead of heading west out of the city, he stayed in the downtown area between the Hawthorne and Burnside bridges on the west side of the river. When the Chevy was behind him, he slowed enough to be caught by a red light on Salmon Street a few blocks from the World Trade Center. The van was already through the intersection and had to continue with traffic.

McGarvey got out of his car and walked back to the Caprice. The driver hesitated, then lowered his window. He and the passenger wore dark suits, their overcoats tossed in the backseat. Neither of them looked happy that they'd been made.

"You're too obvious to be Company. What are you, Bureau or local cops?"

"What the hell are you talking about?" the driver said.

McGarvey stared at him.

The passenger pulled out his ID and showed his badge. "We're FBI, Mr. McGarvey. Could you tell us where you're headed?"

"Your office," McGarvey answered. "Call your S-A-C and tell him to meet us there."

It took a half-hour for the FBI's Portland Special Agent in Charge, Jack Franson, to get downtown. When he came through the door he motioned McGarvey to come into his office, but for the others to remain where they were.

"I understand you gave my agents a hard time this morning," the older man said. He wore a USC jogging suit. He took off his jacket and tossed it on the couch, then motioned for McGarvey to have a seat in front of his desk.

"I don't like being followed."

"Nobody does," Franson said. He picked up his telephone. "Roger, see if we can borrow Kathy or one of the other stenos from downstairs. Have her come up on the double, please."

"Am I being charged with something?"

"Not at this time, Mr. McGarvey."

"Are you investigating me in connection with some crime?"

"Sorry, I can't tell you that."

"Then this conversation ends now," McGarvey said, coolly. "Before the steno arrives."

"Where were you going this morning?"

"The next time somebody comes up behind me, I'm going to break their legs just below the knees. Then I'll disarm them. When I find their IDs, I'll apologize. But the streets aren't safe these days, and a man has got to protect himself."

Franson was unimpressed. "We'll keep that in mind."

"Do that. In the meantime you obviously know who I am, and you know that I'm working for Guerin and what I'm doing for them. So where's the problem?"

"I'm not going to discuss that with you."

"Somebody in Washington is pulling your chain. Probably John Whitman, unless I miss my guess. He has pals at Langley, the people who are most interested in me. They must have told you something, S-A-C. Warned you. Told you I was dangerous."

"Will you answer a few questions?"

"No. But I will exchange information with you."

"It doesn't work that way."

"Your call," McGarvey said getting to his feet. "But if

you want something from me, all you have to do is tell me what you're working on. I'll be happy to give you whatever help I can."

"Don't screw with us, McGarvey," Franson warned.

"Tell them in Washington that I'm available anytime for a trade of information. In the meantime I've got work to do, so stay out of my way."

McGarvey left the S-A-C's office just as a young woman pushing a court reporter's typewriter got off the elevator. No one tried to stop him.

Chance Kennedy had been asleep last night when David finally came home, and waking now she could hear him in the shower. She didn't know what to say to him, but they could not go on like this much longer.

Any pretense she might have had about getting information from Yamagata had been dashed by Kirk McGarvey yesterday afternoon. As incredible as it seemed, David somehow knew or suspected she was having an affair. What she couldn't fathom, however, is why he had told someone. And how many other people had he discussed her with? How could she look any of them in the eye?

She felt like public property. Like a common tramp. A slut.

The shower stopped, and a couple of minutes later David came out of the bathroom. Chance feigned sleep. She heard him cross to the closet, get something, then go back. She opened her eyes. He was looking at her from the bathroom door.

"Did I wake you?" he asked.

She glanced at the clock. It was after nine. "It's time to get up. Where are you going?"

"I have to get back to the office."

She sat up and propped the pillows behind her back. "Stay home. Let's do something today. Maybe take a drive."

"Sorry, Chance, I can't. Not this close to the flight. But it'll slow down afterward. We'll take a vacation. Europe maybe. How's that sound?"

"When?"

"In the spring."

"What about the hydrogen engines?" she asked sarcastically. "Someone will have to keep on top of Rolls, won't they? You'll have to make the decision whether to start production. You could end up like Boeing with dozens of planes on the ramp waiting for engines. Remember the problems they had with the 747? And you've got a big job ahead of you on the sell-through. What's your break-even point this time? A hundred airplanes? Two hundred? Three? Lots of travel, David. Meetings. Conferences. Arm twisting. Not to mention keeping the Russians on the straight and narrow. And the Japanese out of your hair."

"It's what I do. It's my job."

Chance could feel tears well up in her eyes. But she didn't want to cry in front of David. "What about our marriage?"

"What about it?" he asked.

"You're never home!" she snapped, her voice brittle.

"If I did come home, would I find you here?" he demanded.

For a second she was speechless. She hadn't thought he'd bring it up so fast. It wasn't his style. She figured there would be days or weeks of hints and arguments about every subject but that one. David was something of a prude, and naïve. Only once in their marriage had he strayed, and he had been so miserable for so long that Chance had ended up comforting him when it should have been the other way around.

He stormed into the bathroom.

Chance threw back the covers and went after him. "What do you mean by that?" she screeched.

David refused to turn toward her. Instead he faced her reflection in the mirrors above the sink. "Arimoto Yamagata."

"I've had lunch with the man twice, and dinner with him once. For you and the company."

"What the hell are you talking about?"

"He's here spying on us. He told me that the people he

works for back in Tokyo want to buy Guerin and build an airplane factory in Japan. He wants to know everything about us. Especially about you, and about McGarvey. But that's a laugh."

David turned. "What?"

"McGarvey was here. Warned me away from Arimoto. He's trying to protect his friend. Did you know that?"

"When was McGarvey here? What'd he want?"

"You told him I was having an affair. If you want to discuss our marriage, David, discuss it with me. Not the people who work for you."

"Are you?"

"Am I what?" Chance asked, her voice disdainful. But she was frightened that he was willing to take this so far.

"Sleeping with Yamagata?"

Her breath caught in her throat. She raised a hand to her mouth. "Why do you think that?"

"I saw the way you reacted to him at Saunders' party. I know the signs."

"Like what? Have you had me followed?"

"No need for it. Somebody mentioned to me on Thursday that they'd seen you in Holbrook. You and Yamagata."

"I told you I met him."

"Lunch and dinner. Not overnight. Are you sleeping with him to get back at me? Is that what this is all about? Tit for tat?"

"What if it's true?" Chance blurted, surprising herself. "Is it?"

"Are you going back to that bitch Dominique Kilbourne?"

David shook his head sadly. "That was a mistake that I'll never live down. But I didn't love her then, and I don't love her now. I love you."

"You love airplanes and jet engines and rockets more than you love me!"

"That's not true."

"I'm trying to help!"

"Don't. I mean it. Stay away from Yamagata. These

people are out to hurt us, and they'll do whatever it takes to win. Including using you."

"Then stop him!" Chance cried.

"We're trying."

Stop me, she wanted to say, but he looked away, and after a moment she went back into the bedroom.

Chance Kennedy got to the newly opened Hyatt Regency Hotel downtown on the riverfront about noon and took a seat in the bar overlooking the water. Her emotions were badly bruised. She wanted to hide in a dark corner somewhere until everything worked itself out. Maybe they would take a vacation in the spring after all. If she could hold out that long.

David was right, of course. She was out of her league trying to deal with Yamagata. Yet being with him was like nothing she'd ever experienced or even imagined. He was so different. So caring. So knowledgeable. No fumbling, no hesitation, he knew exactly what pleased her.

She ordered a glass of champagne, and when it came she had to force herself to sip it and not gulp the whole thing down at once. She was being an absolute fool to think that she could outwit the man. The first time she'd laid eyes on him she'd been captivated. And since the tea ceremony she'd not been able to stop thinking about him.

David was respectful of him, and even McGarvey had warned her away. Which meant he probably had the key to their problems. Break him and they'd have the answers. Sex, after all, was a powerful persuader. She was no slouch. Her breasts were small, and though she often went without a bra, they were still firm. Her tummy was reasonably flat, her ass wasn't sagging, and her legs were in great shape because of tennis. He wouldn't get so aroused if she were unappealing. The trick would be to make herself alluring to him. There wasn't a man she knew who couldn't be brought around by sex, or the promise of a lack thereof. And when it was over she would make David understand what she had done and why she had done it. Hadn't he said that he'd never loved Dominique? Well, she certainly didn't love Yamagata. That was ridiculous.

When they came out here to see about a position with Guerin, Al Vasilanti had told them that working for an airplane company was more than just a job. Because of the complexity of the product, and because of the religious commitment to safety, building airplanes was a way of life that involved the entire family. Chance would have to be like a doctor's wife: on call with her husband twenty-four hours a day. At first she thought it was a bunch of macho bullshit, but now she was starting to think that maybe the old fool had something after all.

Chance paid for her drink and took the elevator up to the twenty-first-floor penthouse with the key Yamagata had given her. The suite had already been cleaned, but he wasn't there.

She stood in the middle of the big living room, her heart beating rapidly, torn by two emotions. She was sorry she'd missed him, and yet she was glad he wasn't here. She was frightened of him. And of herself.

His clean, sandalwood scent was in the air. She could almost feel his touch, his caress.

She needed help, but there was no one to turn to. This time she was on her own.

It was for David, she told herself. Otherwise she would not be here. For David and for the company.

"The certificate is ready for my signature?"

"It will be by this afternoon," the FAA's Flight Standards Service Director Archie Darden said. "Are you going to stop down, Jay?"

"Monday morning will be soon enough."

"The Renton, Washington, regional office gave the bird a clean bill of health."

"This one's got to be right for them," Federal Aviation Administration Administrator Jay Hansen said from his house. "And for us too."

"Nothing more we can do with this budget. Every time one goes down they scream for our blood. But in the interim they cut our funds so we can't do the job they expect of us."

"That's called politics. Nothing we can do about it. But if our Northwest office says Guerin's plane is ready to fly, then I'll sign off on their recommendation."

"Yes, sir," Darden said. He was in shirt-sleeves, his thick red hair tousled. A 24x30 color photograph of the P/C2622, *America* painted across her fuselage, was propped up on a chair across the room. She was stunning.

"It's my own neck as well."

"You flying to Honolulu on Sunday?"

"That's right, Archie. So I've got a vested interest to watch."

"Well, we've done our job." He looked at the photo. "I can tell you that I wish it was me instead of you on that flight."

Lieutenant Sattler watched over the radarman's shoulder as the slow-moving target passed across the very top of the screen. The aircraft was an Orion P-3D on a parallel track just under one hundred miles south-southwest of the Thorn's position.

"Fifteen thousand feet at two hundred twenty knots, he's mushing along up there," the radar operator said. "He's not one of ours, L-T."

"Japanese?"

"Not Chinese or North Korean out here. I'd say ASDF. I can try their patrol frequencies."

"Go ahead. Ask them if they've lost something," Sattler ordered. He turned to the ECM's console. "Is he looking at us?"

"His radar just went active," the rating said. "He has us. Shall we jam?"

"Negative."

"There's his IFF. We've been interrogated. He wants to know who we are."

"As if he didn't already know," Sattler said.

The radar operator looked up. "Negative response on the regular channels. Want me to keep trying?"

"Stand by," Sattler said. He called the bridge on the growler phone.

"Hanrahan."

"We've just detected what appears to be an ASDF Orion one hundred miles south of us. We've been illuminated and interrogated, but we're getting no response on any of their patrol frequencies."

"Is he one of ours out of Okinawa, Don?"

"Negative. We can jam his radar."

"He knows we're here, and he knows what we're doing. Keep an eye on him."

"Will do, Skipper."

"What about the *Samisho?*"

"Same as before."

"This might get interesting after all," Hanrahan said. "Keep me posted."

"We have to talk," Reid said from the doorway. "We've just eight days to get everything into place."

Louis Zerkel sat at the bedroom window watching the lights of Dulles Airport in the distance. "Ending up buried in a fucking garbage dump isn't right. He deserved better than that."

"There wasn't much else we could do. I'm sorry, Louis."

"I owed him."

"Do you believe in God?" Mueller asked.

Louis turned away from the window. The German leaned against a work table, a hint of compassion in his expression that was probably fake. "Of course not."

"Then it doesn't matter where his body ended up. Your brother is dead, and you killed him."

"Jesus," Reid said softly.

"It was an accident," Louis blurted.

"Glen knew that a bullet in the head from some cop somewhere was always a possibility. It's better than spending the rest of your life cooped up in a prison, being fucked up the asshole."

Louis wanted to throw up. He had nobody to rely on now that both Dr. Shepard and Glen were gone. He had no idea where he could go, or what he could do. He was lost.

"Question is, are you capable of finishing the project?" Mueller asked. "If the tables were reversed do you think Glen would give up?"

"No. He'd rather die than quit." Louis stopped. "Christ." He couldn't get the sight of Glen's horribly charred body out of his mind's eye. The heat had been so intense that there'd been very little left that could have been identified as human.

"That's right, Louis. So now it's up to us to finish the job. Otherwise his life would have been in vain."

Louis wanted to tell Mueller to shut his lousy lying mouth. But if they quit now all the work would go to waste. The Japanese would continue to threaten us, and no one would do a thing about it. Worst of all the devious ones, the devils, the power-mad money brokers of the world would have won.

"Eight days."

"That's the day of Guerin's VIP flight to Honolulu," Reid explained.

"I built an extra repeater for Portland."

"You're a very strong man," Mueller said. "I'm impressed."

Louis looked at the German to see if he was kidding. But Mueller was deadly serious. Reid had brought him over from Europe, and even Glen respected him. Something in the set of the man's jaw, in the confidence of his manner, was frightening and yet comforting in an odd sort of way. Louis could see that Mueller had something that neither Dr. Shepard nor Glen had. Experience in the real world of international struggles.

Mueller knew the score. He'd been a soldier for practically all his life. He wasn't afraid to kill or be killed. He was a force unto himself.

He'd been an East German intelligence officer. But

when the Wall came down and East Germany ceased to exist, Mueller hadn't quit. He'd taken the fight elsewhere.

Mueller was a soldier.

"My life for yours," Louis mumbled, a part of him afraid that he would be rejected.

"What do you think about that?" Mueller smiled, warmly.

TWENTY-EIGHT

I 'm here unofficially, Mr. Kennedy," Jack Franson said.

"Right now that sounds ominous."

"I can't say there's no problem, but it's something I think we can handle here in Portland without taking it any further. At least for the moment. But I have to tell you up front that Washington is taking an interest in Mr. McGarvey. A serious interest. It's just that they don't have as full an appreciation for Guerin as we do here."

"Then maybe you can answer a few questions for me," Kennedy said on the way into the board room.

"That's what I'm here for, sir. But I've got a few of my own. I just want to head off any repercussions for you. Right now especially."

Kennedy motioned the FBI agent to a seat at the long table. Nancy had brought in coffee for them. It was Sunday, but Guerin was fully staffed and would be until *America* flew to Honolulu and safely returned. "I appreciate your concern."

"Like I said, this is an unofficial visit. But McGarvey is going to become a problem for you. Some of the things I'm hearing are just incredible. Yesterday he actually threatened me. He sat right in my office and told me that if we continued to follow him, he'd retaliate. My boss didn't take it lightly." Franson hesitated a moment. "I want you to be clear on one thing, Mr. Kennedy. We take this very seriously. Mr. McGarvey is presumed innocent until he's proven guilty."

"I wasn't aware he was under investigation. What is he being charged with?"

"His case file hasn't been sent out yet, but he is under investigation. Washington has asked that we keep an eye on him."

"What can I do for you?" Kennedy asked. His stomach was tied in knots.

"Do you know about his background? I mean before you hired him, did you do a background investigation?"

"We know that he worked for the CIA. It's the main reason we hired him to deal with our . . . special security concerns. Internationally."

"How did his name come to your attention? This kind of guy doesn't advertise in the positions-wanted column. Did he approach you? Or what?"

"He was recommended to us by someone in Washington, as a matter of fact. It was a personal friend of Mr. Vasilanti."

"May I ask who that was?"

"Roland Murphy. The director of the CIA."

"I see," Franson said. If he was affected by Murphy's name, he didn't show it. "May I also ask what those special security concerns are? I mean I can imagine some of the problems a company this size has gotta face. But McGarvey is something more than just a night watchman or cop. His talents are, shall we say, unique?"

Kennedy studied the FBI agent. "I don't know if I should discuss this with you, on an unofficial basis. We're in an extremely competitive situation just now, especially in light of the dollar's position against certain foreign currencies."

Franson held up his hands. "I understand, completely, Mr. Kennedy. But I'm talking about a criminal investigation of one of your employees."

"On what charge?"

"I'm not at liberty to say at this time."

"In that case I'm afraid I can't be of much help. But if you could be more specific."

"McGarvey is a bad apple."

"Should we fire him?"

"Let's just say that despite his talents I wouldn't want him working for me."

Good advice or bad, Kennedy asked himself. But considering the problem they faced, McGarvey might be the *only* one who made any sense for the job. Fight fire with fire.

Kennedy got up. "Thanks for coming out."

"One thing, Mr. Kennedy," Franson said, rising. "I'd appreciate it if you didn't mention our talk to Mr. McGarvey."

"I'll keep that in mind," Kennedy replied. "And I'd appreciate being kept informed."

"Sure," the FBI agent said, and he left.

Kennedy sat down. If the Bureau had something on McGarvey, it would have arrested him instead of coming out here with vague innuendoes and warnings. It would have been more of a surprise, however, if Washington had not been interested. McGarvey stepped on toes. He irritated people. His own admission, because irritated people made mistakes. But that wasn't what building airplanes was all about. Nobody was happy about hiring McGarvey. It had simply come down to dealing with what they all perceived as a necessary evil.

It came down to survival.

As long as McGarvey wasn't being formally charged with any crime he would stay on the payroll. If Franson told him what McGarvey was being investigated for, and what evidence the FBI had, he might make a different decision. As it was, no matter how uneasy the man made them feel, he was making progress, Kennedy hoped.

"Are you okay there?" Phil Carrara asked.

"Probably not," McGarvey answered, and he hung up.

Carrara was calling from the untraceable number at his home, or he wouldn't have asked if McGarvey's phone was clean. It meant he finally had something to say and he didn't want anyone else to know about it.

A dark-blue Chevy sedan followed McGarvey at a discreet distance from his apartment to Union Station just off Fareless Square where he used a pay phone in the arrivals hall to return his old friend's call. No one approached him.

"The Bureau is taking an interest in me these days," he said. "Your doing?"

"Ryan's got the General convinced that you've finally sold out."

"That's why nobody's been in for me? Maybe I have, Phil."

"Don't fuck with me. One of my people bought it outside Tokyo a few days ago," Carrara said, a sudden hard edge in his voice. "Found his body, what was left of it, at the bottom of a cliff. You were placed at the scene."

It was Kamiya's doing, which meant the Japanese probably had an informant at the CIA's Tokyo Station. "That's not my style, Phil. Was I being followed?"

"We just got word that you threatened the Portland S-A-C."

"That's bullshit, and you know it. I was set up in Tokyo, which means your operation there is rotten."

"Leaks like a sieve," Carrara admitted. "But your name keeps popping up all over the place. Like you're pulling in all your chips. Like you're getting back at everyone who ever crossed you. One minute you're in Moscow dealing with the old KGB at the same time their navy is involved in a shootout with the Japanese. Then your name comes up in connection with a couple of former East German spies who could be involved with Ed Reid, at the same time he's shouting about a war with the Japanese. And finally you get yourself involved in the deaths of three Japanese nationals. Talk to me, Kirk. Japanese cops don't take hard crimes lightly. Especially not now, and especially not involving an American. Yet someone in the government over there had you sprung and the charges dropped, and a few hours later one of my people is murdered. Ryan is going nuts. What the hell is going on, *compar?"*

"Sokichi Kamiya. He's the power behind something called Mintori Assurance. They're the ones targeting Guerin. The East German thing is a coincidence."

"Why kill one of my people? What's he gain by taking such a big risk?"

"To shut me up."

"It would have been easier to have you killed."

"Would have started you thinking that maybe I was right after all. This way instead of getting help, I'm being investigated for murder and counter-espionage."

"You took the offer to Tokyo. It wasn't the other way around."

"I was trying to push them into making a mistake, which they did. We fly next week, and Kamiya is going to do everything in his power to stop us."

Carrara was silent.

"Think about it, Phil. What the hell would I have to gain after all these years?"

"The President is going to Tokyo early. We just got that word this morning. The official announcement won't come for a few days yet. But we were asked about you."

"When is he leaving?"

"Sunday."

McGarvey tried to think it out. The coincidence of *America's* flight to Honolulu with the Vice President aboard on the same day the President was leaving for Tokyo was ominous.

"If I'm the chief suspect why tell me?"

It took Carrara a moment to answer. "Because I think Ryan is wrong. But you're being set up in an even more sophisticated way than you can imagine."

"Let me come to Washington to talk to Murphy."

"He won't listen to you now."

"Goddammit, Phil. Whatever's coming down will happen next Sunday. I think they're going to try to knock Guerin out of the sky."

"Then you'll have to stop them, but we can't help you."

"Air Force One is a Guerin 522."

"Oh, Christ," Carrara whispered. "It never occurred to me."

"Murphy's got to convince him to wait until Monday."

"Nobody will listen to you now, Kirk. It's too late."

"What are you talking about?"

"Ryan's got the headhunters after you."

"That's Internal Affairs. What's my past got to do with this?"

"It's your deep background, Kirk." Carrara's voice was distant. "I pulled your initial background investigation, and they picked up on it. They're just about back to the forties. When they get to the Manhattan Project . . . shit, there's no hard evidence, but there'll be enough for Ryan."

McGarvey had been hit in the gut with a battering ram. All these years he had managed to keep a lid on it, hoping against hope that it would pass, as all things do, but never really believing he'd ever be safe until he was dead. Now they were going to use his past against him.

A father's sins after all did pass to the son.

He hung up.

"We've got a problem."

Al Vasilanti looked up tiredly from the spreadsheets on his desk. His skin was pale, his eyes watery. "So what else is new, David? Is it Rolls?"

"The FBI was just here about McGarvey."

"Are they going to help us?"

"He's under criminal investigation," Kennedy said. "I was all but told to fire him or we'd find ourselves in trouble. They're coming at us from all directions. It's getting crazy."

"What are you suggesting?"

"I think we should postpone the Honolulu flight."

"Not a chance."

Kennedy shrugged. "Then it beats me what I'm supposed to do."

Vasilanti eyed him coldly. "Lead, follow, or get out of the way. The Commercial Airplane Division is yours as long as you think you can handle it. Can you?"

"Yes."

"We design and build airplanes. Safe airplanes. If there's a problem with that, we fix it. Now talk to me. Is there a problem getting *America* ready to fly?"

Kennedy remembered the aftermath of the shuttle *Challenger* disaster. He'd been on the investigating team. "Technically no. But after Dulles it's hard to be sure what to do."

"A different airplane, David. One that either flies or breaks us. What have they got on McGarvey?"

"Franson wouldn't say."

"Do you trust McGarvey?"

"Not any farther than I could throw this building. But he knows what he's talking about. He set up the deal for us with the Russians. He identified our enemies in Japan. And he turned Sir Malcolm around. But it's like there's a dark halo over his head. He's a dangerous man."

"That's what we were told before we hired him. But he came highly recommended. Do you think he can do the job?"

"If anyone can," Kennedy admitted.

"Then support him anyway you can, or cut him loose and we'll do this on our own. It's your decision, David. But make it, and then stick with it. We fly on Sunday."

"Then that'll be my decision too, Al."

Vasilanti's eyes narrowed. "Don't cross me."

"So long as I'm president I'll decide whether we go or stay. In the end if you want it any different, you'll have to fire me. But for now, I'm in charge."

"Make it work."

"One way or another, I will."

Louis Zerkel powered up the encoding circuitry and then the triggering interface. The first five repeaters ready to be tested were stacked up on the workbench waiting for their fresh batteries. He'd held off installing the batteries until he was sure of the mission date. They only had a useful life of thirty days, and he wanted a safety factor of at least three. He'd have at least that because Reid had confirmed that they were a definite go for next Sunday. Seven days. Mueller was leaving for the West Coast sometime tonight.

He slit the seam at the bottom of the first repeater with a razor knife and carefully peeled the paper back, exposing the plain cardboard. Clipping the paper aside with a clothespin, he slit the glue joint at the top edge and lifted the cardboard top away from the old battery, which looked like a black plastic credit card with no markings except for a gold stripe at each end. Holding the cardboard aside, he lifted the battery away from its bed with a pair of tweezers and inserted a fresh battery in its place. Reversing his steps he reglued the cardboard top and refastened the paper covering. Next he switched on a field-strength meter, which he placed next to the repeater, and then keyed the encoder and trigger generator. A few milliseconds later, an audio tone went out, and the repeater kicked out a duplicate of the signal, but piggybacked on the same VHF-FM frequency that the seven airport noise-reduction research units they'd targeted were using.

He looked up. Mueller and Reid had come down again to watch. "It works."

"How long before you're finished?" Mueller asked.

"With this batch a couple hours. I'll do the rest later."

"What about the closed-circuit camera shunt?"

"It's ready," Louis said. "I'll show you how it works as soon as I'm done with these. Now get out of here."

"No mistakes."

"None. Leave me alone."

Reid and Mueller went back upstairs.

"His brother's death hasn't affected him as much as I thought it would," Reid said when they got to the living room.

"In California he depended on his psychologist. Here

on his brother. But now he's transferred his trust to me."

Reid poured an Irish whiskey. "He's unstable."

Mueller watched Reid toss the liquor back. "But brilliant. Without him we'd have nothing."

"He's to be eliminated when he's finished. His safeguards need to be neutralized."

"I don't think that will be a problem. But it'll have to be soon. Before Sunday. Because afterward we may have to move very quickly."

Reid poured another drink, his hand shaking slightly. "You'll have to be very careful placing the repeaters."

"I'll leave tonight. Oakland first because I know it, Los Angeles, and Portland. On the way back, Chicago and Minneapolis."

"How long will it take you?"

"Three days. Still gives us plenty of time for La Guardia and JFK in New York."

"Dulles?"

"I'll do that last. Security there must still be very strict."

"The blame must fall on the Japanese," Reid said. "Not so much as a hint of any of this can come back to me. Not if my ultimate plan is to succeed."

Mueller looked at him. "All those Guerin airplanes have been sabotaged to be destroyed. Have you given thought to that? Someone has come before us. Someone else has the same plan as you do."

"The Japanese."

"I don't think it's the government."

Reid shook his head. "Neither do I, but someone has gone to the trouble. And whatever their thinking is, it's definitely long range."

"To embroil the U.S. and Japan in a war?"

"It's possible. But there's no way of knowing."

"Still time to walk away from this, Reid. Let the others do your work for you. Now that you know that every Guerin airplane flying with that device can be knocked out of the sky, you have the advantage."

"No," Reid said, girding himself. "It's too uncertain. It could be years."

"Which you don't have?" Mueller suggested.

"Which I'm not willing to give," Reid responded sharply. "You hold up your end of the plan, and I'll take care of mine. I'm returning to the city tonight."

Mueller glanced toward the basement door. "Do you think it's wise to leave him here alone?"

"There's no choice." Reid finished his drink. "You have work to do, and so do I. My part in this does not end on Sunday. It just begins."

Newton Kilbourne showed up in Kennedy's office at four. "Tell me we're postponing the Honolulu flight, and you'll make me a happy man."

"I wish I could, Newt, but I want to talk to you about something."

"Sir Malcolm talked to George, said he might have come up with a couple of possibilities. But we're torn both ways at the Creek."

Socrates had split his engineering staff into two teams: one studying the Dulles crash and the other working around the clock in an effort to make sure *America* would be ready to fly on Sunday. The strain was showing on all of them, including Kilbourne.

"This is about McGarvey. Has he been told about Sir Malcolm's call?"

Kilbourne's jaw tightened. "I haven't seen him all day. But he's no engineer. When he's out there he gets in everybody's way. I don't know what he said to Sir Malcolm, but frankly, David, I don't give a shit."

If you had your way, you'd take him out back and settle your differences with fists, Kennedy thought. Or at least try. "Will we be ready to fly Sunday?"

"Unless some more unk-unks show up, or unless you can talk some sense into the old man."

"If the plane is ready to fly, we go. But this is about McGarvey. You and he have a problem. I want to know what it is."

"You know."

"Tell me."

"He's in bed with my sister, and he's got her head so messed up she's become afraid of her own shadow. No matter what I say to her, or try to do, she tells me to mind my own fucking business."

"He didn't want her involved in the project in the first place. It was my decision, and hers."

"That's right, she's a grown-up woman doing a damned fine job for us in Washington. Who she sleeps with is none of my business. When it was you, I didn't approve, but I understood. With McGarvey it's a whole different ball game."

Kennedy held himself in check. He'd never known that Dominique's brother knew about their relationship.

"Ah, shit, I'm sorry, David. I was way out of line. But McGarvey is a spook, for Christ's sake. He's killed people. Not like a soldier on a battlefield, but like some stinking weasel in the night. Dominique's no match for him. She's already been mentally hurt. I'm scared shitless that one of McGarvey's enemies will try to hurt her physically."

"She can't be protected against her will." Kennedy's heart was aching. Twice in two days he had been hit with his affair.

"Bullshit. Before McGarvey went to Tokyo he saw Dominique at my place in Grosse Pointe. Convinced her to return to Washington because she wasn't doing anybody any good hiding out. He doesn't give a flying fuck about her. She's nothing more than insurance against your firing him. And probably cannon fodder against anybody gunning for him. She needs to be pulled off the firing line, and right now. And we need to get rid of McGarvey—by any means, fair or foul."

"What about the Japanese?"

Kilbourne shook his head. "Maybe Dulles was nothing more than an accident after all. Sir Malcolm admitted that he's running around in circles. Finding out *how* an airplane could be sabotaged doesn't mean someone actually did it."

"Do you believe that?" Kennedy asked gently.

Kilbourne started to make a quick reply, but bit it off. It was clear he was deeply troubled. "I don't know what I believe anymore, David. All I know is that we seem to be headed hell bent for leather down the toilet. I've got this bad feeling that it's all coming apart at the edges, and I don't know how long we can hold out."

Paraphrased Yeats, Kennedy thought. Just as disturbing then as it was now. "McGarvey warned us."

"We shouldn't have hired him. Greg and the others might still be alive."

"He's helped already."

"How?"

"By identifying our enemies. At least we know who we're fighting. Maybe he'll finish it for us."

Kilbourne said nothing.

"Do you have any confidence in him?"

"No," Kilbourne said. "Do you?"

McGarvey telephoned Viktor Yemlin from a phone booth a few blocks from his apartment. It was the blind number the Russian had given him. "Has *Abunai* given you anything new?"

"I'm glad you called, Kirk. I'll be pulling out of Washington in a few days."

"What's happened, Viktor Pavlovich?"

"Are you aware that the FBI is investigating you for the murder of a CIA operative in Tokyo? And presumably for having some dealings with a former Stasi assassin?"

"I just spoke with Phil Carrara."

"One of our operatives was murdered in Tokyo last night. If you'd still been in Japan we would have suspected you."

"Was he working for *Abunai?*"

"I'm told he was one of the best. He'd managed to get inside Mintori. His death was made to look like a suicide."

"Was he Japanese?"

"Yes. His double cover was as a MITI operative. But listen very carefully to me, Kirk. In his last drop he said he was getting proof that Mintori was behind the crash of the American Airlines flight in 1990. But he was just as certain that Mintori knew nothing about the Dulles crash."

"That means someone else is involved. Another Japanese *zaibatsu?*"

"Mintori is just as confused as we are. No one knew anything, except that the Japanese seemed to be getting ready to go to war. Against us. All of their military installations are on alert status."

"What about Russian bases along your far eastern coast?"

"They've been on alert since the incident in the strait. But, Kirk, this goes beyond any agreement between my government and Guerin Airplane Company. I'm sorry, but I do not know how much longer I can help you, or even if I should be helping you now."

"What about *Abunai?* Has it been shut down?"

"I don't know. But something very strange is about to happen that has us all worried. My suggestion to you is to convince Guerin to ground its fleet. Now; before it's too late. God only knows what will happen if more of your airplanes fall out of the sky. Are you listening to me, Kirk?"

"I need more information, Viktor Pavlovich. Before you leave Washington."

"I don't know."

"The Japanese must have some idea who was responsible for the Dulles crash. Even a suspicion, a hint. Anything. Find out."

"I'll try," Yemlin said. "It's all I can promise."

Mueller had three new sets of identification. Whatever problems Reid was facing he still had very good connections. So far as Mueller could tell the driver's licenses and Social Security and voter registration cards were authentic. He'd been assured that they were not on any hot sheet. Even the credit cards were valid and had substantial balances. He packed lightly, and this time since he would be doing most of his travel by air, he took no gun. No real need, he told himself, packing a straight razor with his shaving things. If he was caught with it he would have no recourse except to run. He had a substantial amount of money now, enough for his retirement. But he wanted to see this job to its end. And he wanted to eliminate Louis, and of course Reid, so that he would not have to spend the rest of his life looking over his shoulder because they talked.

He took his bag down to the front hall and listened to the silence of the house for a few seconds. The high-pitched whine of computer printers that they'd lived with for the past week or so was gone. Irritating, he thought. A noise he would never have to put up with again. He was old-fashioned. It was his East German upbringing. Time now to step away from a world that had become entirely too modern.

Downstairs Zerkel was seated at the workbench, drinking a Coke. "I'm finished," he said.

"Good. I'm ready to leave." Mueller walked over.

"What are you going to carry these in?" The five repeaters were stacked next to a Sony Walkman and earphones.

"My overnight bag. Will there be a problem with airport security equipment?"

"Lead foil baffles. They'll show up hollow. And the radio will look like a radio." Zerkel picked up the Walkman and switched it on. It was tuned to a country-and-western station. "Switch it to tape play anywhere within a ten- or twelve-foot radius of a closed-circuit television camera and the monitor will freeze on its last image."

"How does it work?"

"This picks the image off the camera tube, digitalizes it, and sends it right back, blocking out whatever's happening in real time. Seamless."

"Wonderful."

Zerkel grinned. "What do you think about that?"

Zerkel finished the last three repeaters a few minutes after midnight. Before he continued he searched the entire house room by room to make sure he was alone. Back in the basement workshop he took a ninth repeater, which he'd built in secret, out of its hiding place, installed a fresh battery, and tested it.

Sooner or later the President would fly Air Force One to Tokyo for the economic summit. Somehow, against all logic and wisdom, he'd been convinced by traitors in the White House that the Japanese were our friends. The situation was impossible.

The President's plane would depart from Andrews Air Force Base southeast of the city. If Dulles were to be shut down after the air disasters, Air Force One would still fly, controlled by the Air Force at Andrews. Louis was not going to let that happen.

He got up and went to the wine storage room, the walls deeply charred. They'd had a hell of a time stopping the fire from spreading to the rest of the house. It would have been a total disaster.

"Sorry, brother," he said. "I didn't know."

TWENTY-NINE

Mueller took the red-eye flight from Baltimore, arriving in Oakland at midnight. An hour later he retrieved his bag, rented a Chevy Lumina from Budget, and drove across the airport to the industrial park. He left the car behind the Mirimax Distributing Company's warehouse, took one of the Roach Motels, the Walkman, and a small set of tools from his bag, and made his way in the darkness to the rear of the Oakland Airport Commission building. The closed-circuit television camera was stationary, focused on a spot in front of the door, so Mueller was able to approach it from the side without being seen. He activated the Walkman, set it down beneath the camera, and went to work on the security-card door lock. Within a minute and a half he had the cover off and the code reader shunted. The door lock clicked, and he let himself in.

He went directly to the equipment room in the basement, defeated the security-card door lock, and placed the Roach Motel behind one of the electronic bays, pushing it as far back as he could reach.

Retracing his steps, he relocked the equipment-room door, and outside relocked the back door, switched off the Walkman, and hurried back to his car.

By 2:00 A.M. he was on the San Jose Freeway heading south.

Louis Zerkel presented himself to the Andrews Air Force Base public-affairs office a couple of minutes before eight in the morning. He had telephoned a few days ago about base tours. Nine other people were there, one of them a reporter for a small Midwestern newspaper who kept flashing his press card around and asking if it would be okay to take pictures for his readers. Their young WAF sergeant tour guide gave them packets containing brochures on the base's history, maps, charts, an Air Force recruiting poster, and a visitor badge. This was the base that protected Washington, and from this base presidents flew to and from the world's capitals on the "business of democracy." By 9:30 they had toured the operations center, meteorology, a fighter/interceptor hangar, and then headed to the top of the control tower for a view of the base. Louis held back so that he was the last one up the stairs into the glass-enclosed observation center. There was a moment when the reporter was posing the operators for a picture when no one was looking toward the door. Louis slipped the Roach Motel out of his coat pocket and slipped it behind one of the consoles, pushing it way out of sight with his foot. He didn't think it was likely that the repeater would be found anytime soon. He'd had a brief look behind the console and had seen at least an inch of dust.

* * *

Mueller got a few hours of sleep at a Holiday Inn outside of Oxnard, then drove into Los Angeles to the public library a few blocks from Pershing Square. He went up to the information desk on the second floor in the non-fiction collection and asked one of the librarians about a history of Los Angeles International Airport.

"LAX," the pleasant young black woman said. "Quite a colorful past, what with movie stars and all."

"So I'm told," Mueller replied diffidently, slipping into a thicker German accent. "I'm doing a freelance piece for *Die Stern.*"

"I get it." The woman grinned. "We see a lot of German tourists here. Is there a specific era or subject you might be interested in?"

"The present-day facility. The terminal, the traffic, the electronic controls, all the safety aspects, you know."

"They're just about done with the renovation. We have some material, but you really should talk to someone at the airport commission. I'm sure they'd be happy to help."

"I wanted to stop here first for the preliminary background. I don't know so much about the airport yet. I'm just beginning."

"I'm with you. You don't wanna look like a fool asking the wrong questions."

"Something like that," Mueller said.

"Well, you just come along with me, and we'll see what we can find." The woman jumped up and hurried off.

Mueller thought she was shaped like a pear, small on top and large on the bottom. Her skin was very black. Most Germans were just as prejudiced against *Schwartzers* as was the average rural Mississippian. But this one seemed reasonable.

She found several files of brochures, pamphlets, maps, photographs, and magazine and newspaper clippings, which she laid out for Mueller on a table. Then she came up with a thick sheaf of blueprints and a bundle of aerial photos.

"Before and after," she said. "I brought you both sets, in case you wanted to compare."

She stood, smiling shyly, as if she were a waitress waiting for a tip.

Mueller returned her smile. "You have been very helpful. I can't tell you how much."

She beamed. "You need anything else, you come see me."

"I'll do that," Mueller said. When the woman was gone he started working his way through the mound of material she had brought to him. It was incredible. No matter how long he was in this country, he never ceased to be amazed at its openness. The material he'd been so freely given would have been highly classified in any Eastern European country less than ten years ago, and still on a restricted list in almost every other country in the world. Now the problem wasn't so much one of access but one of volume. There was so much information available that espionage had become an endeavor for the computer expert.

Within the hour, Mueller had what he needed, and he checked into a Hyatt near the airport, after booking a ticket on United to Portland leaving LAX at 11:30 P.M. Los Angeles, tonight, would be a near carbon copy of Oakland, and he was getting the feeling that the others would be just as easy.

George Socrates felt his sixty-seven years. Working around the clock on two projects at the same time was taking its toll not only on him, but on both of his crews. Tired engineers made mistakes. And in this business mistakes sometimes cost lives, a fact he was reminded of every time he looked at a 522. But it was the safest airplane in the history of aviation. He had designed it that way, and it had been built that way. The learning curve had been very shallow. Before the assembly plant had gotten up to full speed, eighty of the jetliners had gone out the door. At every stage of the manufacture and assembly, Socrates had demanded and gotten perfection. Now Sir Malcolm was telling him there could be flaws in the engine and in the way the engine was installed.

"Only two possibilities," McGarvey cautioned. "Sir Malcolm said nothing about probabilities." Engineering had told him that Socrates was in the research hangar where a 522 was being disassembled one nut and bolt at a time.

Socrates said nothing as the port engine was lowered out of the wing onto a maintenance stand. It was a little smaller than a military fighter/interceptor engine. About fourteen feet long and four feet in diameter at the widest, it weighed nearly forty-five hundred pounds dry. But it was a hot engine, producing seventy-five percent more thrust than the old-style jet engines. There were only two stages, instead of the normal four, in the turbine section: a high-pressure blisk and a low-pressure blisk that counter-rotated against each other. It had been a major breakthrough for Rolls in design efficiency.

When the engine was secured the technicians removed the exhaust nozzle and then the inspection plates around the turbines and, just forward of them, the ceramic combustor. Next they removed some of the plumbing and sensors blocking a cowling that covered a section of bypass ducting.

"The NTSB should be doing this," Socrates grumbled.

"If you find something we'll pass it on to them," McGarvey said.

The engineer looked at him. "We shouldn't be doing any of this. There should have been no crash."

"But there was. Quit now and they win."

I don't care, Socrates wanted to say, but he bit it off. He did care. In 1990 when the American Airlines 522 had gone down, it was as if his child had been killed. And when their own equipment went down at Dulles someone had ripped his beating heart out of his chest. The bastards!

The first of Sir Malcolm's suggestions was that someone had tampered with the bypass duct air-flow channels. High-pressure air and fuel were mixed in the combustor to create a controlled explosion, the mixture burning as high as thirty-eight hundred degrees Fahrenheit. This was too high a temperature for the ceramic turbine blisks, so more air was ducted to the combustion gas to reduce its temperature. If this airflow were to be interrupted the engine would overheat, swallow its blisks, and disintegrate. Literally blow itself to pieces.

The technicians blocked the duct intake forward of the low-pressure compressors, placed a pressure gauge just aft of the combustor, and powered up the test rig that Sir Malcolm had outlined. It took a few seconds for the system to fully pressurize.

"It's normal," one of the technicians reported, looking up. "Air flow is well within specs."

"Double the pressure," Socrates ordered.

"It'll pop our seals."

"Or something else."

The technicians did as they were told, slowly adding more pressure to the system until at one hundred eighty-five percent the pressure seal they'd used to block the forward intake ruptured with a bang.

"Followed us all the way up, Mr. Socrates," the technician said. "Nothing wrong with the airflow on this engine."

"Could it be the material that the walls of the bypass duct are made of?" McGarvey asked. He'd taken a crash course on engine design, manufacture, and operation before he'd gone to Tokyo, and then to England to see Sir Malcolm, so he knew something about what he was watching.

"We tested this particular engine on a static stand at full thrust and didn't find a thing," Socrates said patiently.

"But that's different than in actual operation. No vibrations from the wheels against the pavement. No landing shocks. No air turbulence."

"There's better than seven hundred 522s flying. That's fourteen hundred engines. We've only had trouble with two."

"Were there enough pieces found of both of those

engines that sections of the bypass duct could be identified?"

"I imagine there were."

"What if something was wrong with the metal? If the
bypass duct were to fail the engine would blow."

"Sensors would shut it down first."

"Not if the failure were catastrophic. Not if the entire
bypass duct disintegrated because it was designed and
built that way. Was the bypass duct wall on either engine
magnafluxed to see if it was good?"

Socrates looked startled. "I don't know," he said,
thoughtfully. "But I'm going to find out."

"It could be nothing."

"We'll check everything." Socrates stepped away from
the noise of the compressor and made a call on his
cellular telephone.

McGarvey walked over to one of the technicians. "Are
you going to run the same test on the other engine?"

"Probably. We'll tear this one down first. Rolls wants
us to check the thermocouples. If they're bad it could
send faulty readings to the on-board monitor."

"Any of them critical?"

The technician looked at him. "A few."

"What about the bypass duct on this engine? Any way
of magnafluxing the walls?"

"Not without pulling the engine completely down.
Which we'll probably end up doing."

"These are different engines from those on the 2622?"

"Totally," the technician said.

"I see," McGarvey said. He walked around to the
boarding ladder and climbed up to the open hatch just
aft of the cockpit. All the seats had been removed from
the main cabin and the floor pulled up so they could
inspect the hydraulics and wiring. Even the two seats on
the flight deck had been pulled out and the deck removed. Much of the control panel had been dismantled
as well, many of the electronic instruments removed and
hanging free, connected only by their cables.

McGarvey peered down into the electronics bay beneath the cockpit. A trouble light was on, casting harsh

shadows. He climbed down the ladder. The cramped space smelled of electronics, hydraulic fluid, and kerojet.

Something was here, he thought. Something had been done to the American Airlines flight in 1990 and the Dulles flight last week to bring them down. Someone knew, and someone was still stalking them. Someone besides the Japanese.

There had to be a connection between those incidents, this airplane, and the 2622 that would fly to Honolulu next week. He could feel it just as thick on the air as the strange smells down here.

Something was coming. Some malevolent beast was raising its ugly head, threatening to devour them all.

President James Lindsay met with Edward Reid in the Oval Office. It was an impressive room, and everyone who came here was moved. But Reid did not delude himself into believing that the President had agreed to see him because he was a former State Department official, or because he was any friend of the administration. Steve Nichols, the President's Appointments Secretary, had been very specific about it. "He'll give you fifteen minutes if you're prepared to leave your newsletter histrionics at home and give him some straight talk. Japan is very important to him at this point."

"And to me, Steve."

The President was behind his desk. "You're looking fit, Edward. How do you do it?"

"Clean living, Mr. President. That and a fifth of good Irish a day." They shook hands.

The President motioned for him to have a seat and then picked up the telephone. "Harold, why don't you come over now? Ed Reid is here." He hung up. "Harold might be able to lend some insight."

"By all means, Mr. President," Reid said, not surprised. Lindsay and his National Security Adviser were nearly inseparable.

Harold Secor came in and shook hands with Reid. "It's been a while since we've talked, Ed. Things are going well for you?"

"Can't complain. I have a lot of happy readers."

"So we've been hearing—from State, among others. Carter said you and he had a little chat a couple of weeks ago."

Reid forced a smile. He was on very dangerous ground. He could not afford the scrutiny of a full-scale Bureau investigation. This was his last chance to stop it. "Which is why I'm here. Somehow what I've been writing lately has gotten distorted. I want to clear the air."

"I read your stuff. Frankly, it's got me concerned," the President said.

"I'm flattered. But I *want* my readers to be concerned."

"You're advocating something we could not do, even if we wanted to. I've had my fill of Japan bashing, and I won't tolerate it. They're our major trading partners, and right now they're touchy as hell. Can't say as I blame them."

"Then, respectfully, Mr. President, I'm being misread. I am anything but a Japan basher. By the way, that's a term invented by the Japanese, before the Second World War."

"What's your point, Ed?" the President asked, coolly.

"The Japanese are having their own financial troubles. They're getting themselves into a position where they'll either have to start calling in their notes, all of them, or start an aggressive round of expansion. South Korea, the Malaysian peninsula, the Philippines, Borneo, maybe even Australia."

"You heard Prime Minister Enchi's free trade announcement," Secor said.

"He can't possibly make that happen," Reid replied. "In the first place the Diet would never go along with it. There are enough hotheads in Tokyo to block him. But for the sake of argument, if he somehow got it passed, Japan would face bankruptcy. Either that or it would have to take over a significant percentage of the same markets we're trying to develop in the region."

"I didn't just get off the banana boat," the President

retorted angrily. "I understand what he's trying to do, and I understand what's at stake for us. It's one of the things we'll discuss at the summit. But we can hardly block them from Subic Bay. That's what you're calling for."

"You're right, Mr. President, and I was wrong. They're a peaceful sovereign state, and we can no more stop them from developing a defensive military force than we can block Germany from doing the same."

"Then you admit you were wrong?" Secor asked suspiciously.

"In that, yes," Reid said earnestly. "I'm an old man, and I tend to get carried away in the past." He sat forward for emphasis. "But I don't believe I'm wrong in warning about the potentially dangerous climate that's developing in Japan. We have our Japan bashers, as you so rightly point out, Mr. President, but the Japanese have a growing anti-American sentiment that could get out of hand."

"Tokyo is aware of that. It doesn't change anything."

"Potentially no. Providing there are cool heads at the tiller. And providing we all understand the differences between protectionism and simple common sense."

"Jesus Christ—" Secor said, but the President held him off.

"What the hell are you telling me?"

"Half this country thinks that you're going to give away the farm in Tokyo. That when you're finished, our balance of trade deficit will at least double. America is for sale, and you are going to broker it. Just like Truman did with our nuclear advantage. Like Kennedy did with Cuba after the Bay of Pigs. Nixon did with Vietnam. Carter did with the Panama Canal. The list isn't endless, but it's sufficiently long and harmful that we can't afford another addition."

The President and his NSA exchanged glances.

"You're not doing such a hot job clearing the air, Ed," Secor said. "From where I sit you're digging yourself a pretty deep hole. Would you mind explaining just what the hell you're doing here this afternoon?"

"I've come to offer my support and assistance. I think you need it."

"You may be old by your own admission, but you're a gutsy SOB," the President commented wryly. "I'm listening."

Reid's stomach was beginning to cramp, and he wanted a drink more than anything else. But from the start he'd known that the path he'd chosen was a dangerous one. "I'm not in the timid business," he'd told his wife, years ago. Her counsel was that if he truly believed in what he was doing, then he should never hold back. Admiral Farragut.

"Mr. President, as you know the readership of my newsletter is international. Politicians, financiers, scientists, journalists. People in the know. Men and women of varying interests—and agendas. I depend upon them for feedback. For information. For news tips. Two months ago I received a warning that a Japanese terrorist organization was responsible for the 1990 crash of an American Airlines flight out of Chicago and that there was more to come."

"Did you tell the FBI?" Secor asked.

"I didn't take it seriously. The NTSB said the crash was an accident. But considering what's happening in Japan now, I started to wonder. A few of my readers are Japanese. Businessmen. All of them opposed to Prime Minister Enchi."

"They can't be your friends," the President said.

"No, sir. But they are my subscribers, and they do provide me an insight that I would like to offer to you."

"I'll be damned."

"I don't want to be an enemy of this administration, Mr. President. I'm here to serve."

"How?" Secor asked.

"Prime Minister Enchi needs to be made aware of the nature of his opposition. Coming from you, he'll owe you one. And so will my grateful readership. Take me with you to Tokyo. If nothing else, my presence just might polarize Enchi's enemies so they will be easier to spot and deal with."

"You've got a deal," the President said, before Secor could comment.

"You won't regret it, sir. I'll be ready in a couple of weeks."

"Sunday."

Reid looked blankly. "Mr. President?"

"The announcement will be made in a couple of days. But we're going over early. I leave on Sunday from Andrews. Are you with me?"

Reid was flabbergasted. "Yes, Mr. President," he mumbled. It was all he could say.

Mueller arrived in Portland a little past 1:30 A.M. Instead of waiting until morning to do his research at the public library downtown, he looked up the Portland Airport Commission's address in the telephone book and located it on the map at the head of the *Yellow Pages*. Like at Oakland and Los Angeles, the commission was housed in a modern building across the airport from the terminal. He rented a car from Hertz and drove directly over, parking in back of an office building a block away. In the distance he could see a huge complex all lit up. It was Guerin Airplane Company's worldwide headquarters. Glen had told them how big the place was, and Mueller decided he hadn't been exaggerating. The facility was awesome. There was no television camera on the rear entrance to the Airport Commission building, but there was one just inside the corridor that Mueller almost missed. When he spotted it he stepped back into the shadows, waited several moments for an alarm, and when nothing happened he switched on the Walkman. He made his way down to the basement, and after searching four rooms he found the noise-management project transmitters and placed the repeater. He was away from the airport by 2:30 and checked into a nearby hotel by 3:00. The first flight to Chicago left at 6:45 A.M.

America was bathed in strong lights, her muslin shroud removed. She crawled with people, inside and out. Scaffolding surrounded her, and many of her cowlings and inspection plates were off. Heavy cables snaked across the floor to her from dozens of test and diagnostic stands, and her starboard subsonic engine had been removed and lay naked on a test stand beneath her delta wing. Newton Kilbourne and George Socrates stood to one side talking with Kirk McGarvey. None of them seemed happy, but they were not interfering with the work in progress. Even as Socrates' engineering team was checking every single system aboard the hypersonic jetliner from the bottom up, interior decorators were feverishly racing to finish the coach and first-class cabins and heads. An FAA-designated inspection team worked around the clock alongside Guerin's prep crew. Most of them were Guerin engineers. The FAA could not afford to field its own inspection teams, so it relied on the commercial airplane industry to check itself. As odd as the system was, it worked. And as stripped as *America* was at that moment, she still looked as if she were flying Mach five at the edge of space.

Kennedy stood in the shadows on the balcony in front of Engineering looking down at the activity on the assembly floor. Nothing was the same, nothing could ever be the same, since they'd hired McGarvey. No longer were they simply in the business of designing, manufacturing, and selling airplanes. Now they were in the business of survival. What a terrible price they were paying just to keep the company alive, or more accurately, just to keep the company here in America. It would have been so much easier if in the beginning they had worked in cooperation with the Japanese like Boeing. But of course they were beyond that now. Way beyond that.

McGarvey turned and looked up. Kennedy stepped farther back into the shadows although there was no possible way that he could be seen from below. They'd been warned that while McGarvey always got the job done, no one connected with him would come out unscathed. Kennedy hadn't really believed that until now. The entire company had been affected by the man's presence. Yet Kennedy couldn't think of any other way out for them. He shook his head. "Christ," he said, under his breath, and he headed through Engineering to the back stairs and his waiting car. Time to go home. After a few hours sleep the situation would look different. He hoped.

Loneliness was a familiar feeling to McGarvey. One that he'd figured he had control of. It had begun in Kansas after his parents' funeral when he'd returned to the ranch to straighten out their affairs. From that day forward he'd carried a secret with him that was so heavy at times he thought he would stumble and fall. But it wasn't until Carrara's admission that Internal Affairs would probably find out, that the real loneliness hit him like the weight Atlas had to bear. Crushing.

He stood, smoking a cigarette at the window of his eleventh-floor apartment, looking toward the river and the sparse early morning traffic on the Burnside Bridge. During the day the city was pretty, the views toward the mountains spectacular. But at night Portland was like any other city with its shadows and secrets, most of its people safely locked away against harm.

But there really were monsters in the world. Creatures that could hurt you even if you were securely hidden.

He knew about them. He'd been dealing with them for most of his adult life. But had he made any difference, he wondered? Most of the time he thought he had. But on nights like these he wasn't so sure. McGarvey got the cordless phone from the kitchenette and entered Dominique Kilbourne's Washington number as he walked back to the living room window. As it started to ring he lit another cigarette.

For instance, was the world any safer for people like Dominique because of him? He thought not. In fact because of him the sanctity of her apartment had been violated, and she would carry that fear with her for the rest of her life. In Detroit she'd looked haunted, angry.

"Hello?" she answered, her voice thick with sleep.

"It's me."

"Are you here in Washington?"

"Portland," McGarvey said. "How are you?"

The line was silent.

"Dominique?"

"Leave me alone," she said, her voice strangled. "Just do your job and keep me out of it. I've spoken to David, and he agrees."

"I'm sorry. I wish it were different. But I'm worried about you."

Again the line was silent.

"Dominique?"

She didn't answer, and a second later he had a dial tone.

It would be morning soon, and he would have to make a decision. Stay or go. Maybe, he thought, he'd finally gotten involved with something beyond his abilities.

The telephone rang, and he answered it. "Yes?"

"This is David Kennedy."

McGarvey looked toward the river. "Good morning."

"We're terminating your services."

"Has something happened?"

"Too much," Kennedy said, his voice strange and distant. "We'll send a check to you care of the college at Milford. I'm sorry it didn't . . . work out."

"David?"

"What?"

"Be careful," McGarvey said. "And good luck."

THIRTY

The winds and seas had risen all afternoon and into the evening from the northwest, so that by 10:00 P.M. the *Fair Winds,* her rail buried, was making six knots on a long tack to the northeast. They'd left their anchorage off the Island of Yoron at midmorning hoping to make the one hundred twenty miles to the city of Naze on Amami-O-Shima by the next morning, but what the locals called the Kuroshio—Black Current—had set them farther to the south than Stan Liskey had expected and had sharply reduced their speed of advance. All he was hoping for now was to make the lee of Okinerabu Island, barely thirty miles from their morning anchorage, and take shelter from the storm.

The companionway hatch banged open, and Carol Moss, dressed in yellow foul-weather gear, deftly hoisted herself up on deck. She slammed the hatch shut and clipped her safety harness to the jack line that ran from the cockpit forward to the bow, before slumping down next to Liskey on the low side. "Some show," she shouted over the shrieking wind.

"What's the SatNav say?"

Carol glanced at the compass. "Three miles on this course and we'll be home free. Okinawa weather predicts the winds will top forty-five sustained, with gusts above that."

The Aires windvane was still managing to hold the boat on course, so despite the noise, and the violent motion, which made life below decks nearly impossible, they were in no immediate danger. And within a half-hour, if the Magellan GPS satellite navigation unit was doing its job, they would be in the island's wind shadow. By midnight they would be anchored safely out of the building storm.

"How are you doing, kid?" He studied her eyes. She looked nervous but not frightened.

She grinned. "I'd feel safer walking on Times Square. But what the hey, a girl only lives once."

Howard Ryan was on a witch hunt, but he'd been strangely aloof for the past two days. Phil Carrara was getting concerned. He knew the Agency's counsel well enough to understand that when the noise from the seventh floor stopped, something big was on the wind.

As Deputy Director of Operations he figured it was his business to know what was going on. There was no other way he could do his job. Rumor was that Internal Affairs had come up with a phone intercept involving McGarvey. He called upstairs to Ryan's secretary who said he was with the General, but that he'd be back at his desk in a couple of minutes. It was a very busy day, though, she warned.

He was always busy. The question this afternoon was busy with what? Ryan was in his office when Carrara came up. He didn't look happy to see the DDO.

"A minute of your time, Howard," Carrara said.

"Can whatever you have wait until later?" Ryan asked. "I'm simply stacked to my ears here."

"No, it can't wait. But I'll make it short." Carrara closed the door.

Ryan eyed him coldly for a second or two, then withdrew a file from his drawer and handed it across. "You want to see this?"

It was the Internal Affairs telephone transcript of a conversation between McGarvey, who'd called from Portland, and Viktor Yemlin at his blind number here in Washington. It was brief and to the point.

"Confirms what we're getting from the satellites," Carrara said.

"I'll tell you what it confirms, mister. It confirms our suspicions that McGarvey has become a wild card and he's waging a one-man war on Japan. He's got the goddamned Russians so riled up they don't know whether to shit or go blind. He's got Guerin convinced they're under attack. And he's got the Japanese government screaming for blood. They don't even know what's going on in their own backyard, and they've got their fingers on the triggers of a whole bunch of military hardware. I'd say he's done a pretty fair job of screwing us. Don't you agree?"

"That's not the way I read this," Carrara said, keeping his voice even.

"I didn't expect you would."

"Tokyo is my operation."

"True, but this is an Internal Affairs investigation in cooperation with the FBI's Counterespionage Division."

"We'll see what the DCI has to say."

"The General is on his way to the White House. If you want to wait for him, that's your prerogative. But as of this moment you are to consider yourself on administrative leave. And that, Mr. Carrara, comes directly from the man. Dick Adkins will take over your duties for the moment."

"Puta," Carrara said softly, every muscle in his body screaming to leap across the desk and beat the sonofabitch to a pulp.

"What does that mean?" Ryan shouted, but Carrara turned on his heel and left.

Downstairs in his office he telephoned John Whitman at FBI headquarters. It took a minute for the call to go through. Internal Affairs probably had a monitor on his phone, but he didn't give a shit.

"I just hung up with Howard Ryan. He said you'd probably be calling," Whitman said. He and Carrara went back a few years.

"What's going on?"

"I can't really talk about this with you, Phil. But McGarvey is heading for a big fall this time."

"He's been set up."

"That's not how we're seeing it," the FBI special investigator said.

"Come on. He wouldn't have been involved in the first place if Guerin hadn't come to him. He didn't go looking for this."

"Well, that's a moot point. Guerin fired him this morning. So now he's on his own."

Mueller arrived at Chicago's O'Hare Airport a few minutes after one in the afternoon. After he retrieved his bag, he went upstairs to the main floor of the terminal to book his late-night flight to Minneapolis and from Minneapolis back to Washington first thing in the morning. As he headed across the main concourse to the Northwest ticket counters he passed a large display showing the proposed new airport expansion for completion in 2010. "Chicago Metropolitan Airports Commission working for you." Alongside the display were maps and photographs showing a history of the airport, including the present-day layout. The Airport Commission was located near the terminal, on this side of the airport. But something else caught his eye. The commission was to be headquartered in a new building when the expansion was completed. Color-coded tags corresponded with the functions that the commission was responsible for. A yellow tag, representing the noise-management program, wasn't on this side of the airport with the commission's other offices. Mueller searched for it on the present-day map, finding it in a building adjacent to the control tower. Security would be more difficult here than it had been at Oakland, Los Angeles, and Portland. But not impossible, he decided.

He rode a shuttle over to the Airport Marriott Hotel, where he took a shower and tried to get some sleep. But another thought intruded, and after a while he got dressed and called the Sterling farmhouse from a pay phone in the Holiday Inn lobby a quarter-mile away. He was worried about Zerkel.

Reid answered out of breath. "Get back here as soon as possible," he said. "We've got a problem."

Carrara had a drink alone in town at the Grand Hyatt. He telephoned his wife to say that he would be late and then phoned David Kennedy at Guerin Airplane Company in Portland. He got Kennedy's secretary, who after Carrara identified himself said that her boss was in Washington at the Hay Adams. He called the hotel, but although Mr. Kennedy had checked in an hour before, he did not answer his phone. Next he telephoned Dominique Kilbourne's office, but her secretary said that Ms. Kilbourne had gone home. Back at the bar he tried to work out his feelings. All his life he had fought to control his Hispanic temper. He sparked easily, and he hoped that Ryan would never know how close he had come to physical harm this afternoon. Now Carrara's anger had lost its edge, but it had deepened. It was his overblown sense of justice. Ryan and Murphy were dead wrong about McGarvey. They all were. And Carrara found that wrapped like a poisonous snake around his anger was fear. He'd never known his old friend to exaggerate. Never. If McGarvey was concerned, he told himself, then they all should be concerned. He drove over to the Watergate complex, parked in one of the visitor's slots, and took the elevator up to Dominique's apartment. She answered her door only after Carrara held his CIA photo ID up to the camera lens.

"If he's left Portland, I don't know where he is," Dominique said. "You people are going to have to find him on your own, and leave me out of it."

"If you're talking about Kirk McGarvey, Ms. Kilbourne, I'll find him. Right now I'm trying to catch up with David Kennedy."

"What makes you think he's here?" she flared. "Why don't you leave me alone?"

"Kirk told me that you and Mr. Kennedy often worked together. He's here in the city, and I thought you might know where he was. I'd like to talk to him about Kirk."

"David fired him. So he's no longer our concern."

"You're wrong about him," Carrara said, reading the hurt in Dominique's eyes.

"Don't tell me," she snapped. "He's a goddamned saint."

Carrara couldn't suppress a grin. "He's anything but that. But he's not a traitor. And he genuinely wants to help Guerin."

"You're not trying to arrest him?"

"No, but the Bureau might try to bring him in. If that happens someone might get hurt."

"So what?"

"He needs friends, Ms. Kilbourne. More than just me.

He can't fight the whole world alone. But he'll try. I'll guarantee it. He's done it before and almost gotten himself killed."

"I don't want to hear it," Dominique said, turning away in anguish.

"Just tell me how to get in touch with David Kennedy and I'll leave you alone."

The door opened the rest of the way, and David Kennedy, in shirt sleeves, his tie loose, stood there. "You'd better come in. This can't get any worse."

"I'm afraid it can, Mr. Kennedy."

Carrara followed them into the living room, where drinks were laid out on the coffee table in front of the long white couch. They offered him nothing. Dominique sat alone at one end of the couch, Kennedy at the other end, Carrara in a thick leather chair across from them. He could see the deepening afternoon sky out the big windows. The Watergate was an expensive address, but the airplane business involved very big money—so big that many governments couldn't afford to maintain viable airlines. The stakes were high, but Carrara reminded himself that for the most part it was ordinary men and women who operated the world's institutions; from the President in the White House to the janitors in the Kremlin, all were born, lived their lives the best they knew how, and then died.

"I've talked to you on the phone," Dominique said. "Just who are you?"

"I'm the Deputy Director of Operations for the CIA. I've known Kirk McGarvey for a long time. He's a good man. He's done a lot for this country."

"Why are you here, Mr. Carrara?" Kennedy asked. "What do you want from me? It was you people who recommended McGarvey to us, and now I'm finding out that the FBI has him under investigation. What the hell do you want?"

"I have a pretty fair idea why you hired him. He talked to me about it. As a matter of fact he asked for my help. But why did you fire him?"

"Unless you're here officially, which I doubt, that's company business."

"No doubt someone from the Bureau talked to you, but is that the only reason, Mr. Kennedy?"

"Why is the FBI investigating him?" Kennedy asked.

"Kirk has his enemies at the Bureau and at Langley. Especially at Langley. People he's crossed before, and who'll believe what they want to believe."

"Murphy?"

"No," Carrara answered, which wasn't quite accurate. "But it's someone who has access to him. The point is that whatever evidence they think they have against him, will never hold up in court. All that'll happen is they'll pull him away from what he's working on until it's too late."

Kennedy shook his head. "It may already be too late. If McGarvey is right they're going to hit us again on Sunday."

"What are you talking about?"

"He's convinced that the American Airlines crash in 1990 and our crash last week at Dulles were engineered by a Japanese consortium of businesses working under the banner of Mintori Assurance."

"The American Airlines crash was probably engineered by Mintori, but not Dulles. That was either an accident, or caused by someone else trying to bring you down."

"Where did you get that?"

"Kirk got it from his Russian contact."

"He never told me."

"Not until he had the proof, Mr. Kennedy. The Russians are working on it."

"But not us?" Dominique asked. "Not the CIA?"

"No." Carrara turned back to Kennedy. "What's this about Sunday? Are you talking about the Honolulu flight?"

"That's right. McGarvey thinks that whatever is going to happen, will happen then."

"Like bringing that flight down?"

"And maybe some others. Enough to wipe us off the map." Kennedy sat forward. "But Dulles was no accident. McGarvey is convinced of it, and so am I. We just can't find out how it happened."

"Ground the fleet. The FAA could be convinced to issue the order. At least our carriers would have to comply."

"The net effect would be the same," Kennedy said tiredly. He was strung out. "And I don't know what I would tell the FAA, not to mention my board of directors and stockholders. All that, providing McGarvey is right. He could be wrong. Hell, even my own government doesn't believe it."

"I do," Carrara said quietly. "Why'd you fire him?"

"There was a lot of dissension because of him, which we don't need. But McGarvey's a dangerous man. He's an assassin. We build airplanes, not sniper rifles."

"Excuse me for saying that firing McGarvey because he's dangerous is like pulling the lightning rods off the barn because they attract lightning. If anybody is going to find out who's after you, it's him."

"Our real troubles didn't start until after we hired him."

"You're wrong. Otherwise why'd Al Vasilanti ask the General for help? And why'd you hire Mac in the first place? You understood what you were getting into. You were told about him, about what he does, and how he goes about his business. You must also have been told that he doesn't give up so easily."

"We hired him, we can fire him," Kennedy said doggedly. "He's caused us no end of trouble. One of our airplanes went down for Christ's sake. We lost some very good people at Dulles. There's no end to it."

"Not the way you want to go at it."

"I'm here in Washington to officially ask the FBI for help. Hiring some maverick sharpshooter was a bad idea at best. It should never have happened. Whether or not he's guilty of anything, the man is bad business."

"Why didn't you go to the Bureau for help in the first

place?" Carrara asked, although he already knew the answer.

Kennedy seemed a little uncomfortable. "Without evidence there was nothing they could do for us."

"Do you have the evidence now?"

"Yes, we do."

"Where did you get it, Mr. Kennedy? Who supplied it to your company? Because if you tell the Bureau that McGarvey came up with it, I don't think they'll be very impressed. After all, they think he's a bad apple."

"He's innocent until proven guilty."

"The Bureau doesn't investigate people they believe are innocent. And I don't suspect you fire them."

"I didn't fire McGarvey because I thought he was guilty of any crime. I fired him because I can no longer justify keeping a murderer on the payroll. My job is to build and sell safe airplanes, nothing more. I don't need someone like McGarvey to fuck us up."

"Someone like McGarvey," Carrara repeated. "I don't think either of you has any idea who he is, what he's gone through."

"He's a loser," Dominique said angrily. "The CIA fired him!"

"Yes. And since then we've given him assignments that our people simply couldn't manage. Without exception he's come through for us, because . . . he loves his country. He's one of the best men I know. Even his ex-wife will defend him."

"Then why's she his ex?"

"Because she couldn't stand seeing what the job was doing to him. She had a hard time living with a man who has the habit of putting his life on the line for nothing more than an ideal while the people around him—supposedly his friends—have the habit of stabbing him in the back."

"You're taking a big risk coming here like this," Kennedy said.

"Yes, I am," Carrara admitted. "But before you write McGarvey off—which I think would be the biggest mistake you've ever made—I want you to hear me out. The Bureau knows that you fired him, which is a strike against him. And they know that he spoke to his Russian contact on Guerin's behalf, which is another strike against him. When the CIA's Internal Affairs Division finishes with its witch hunt, it'll be all over unless he can find out who's after you and stop them."

"He's got a dark secret . . ."

"That's right, and it's all crap, but they'll use it against him. When it comes time to corner him he'll fight back, and he'll lose. They'll kill him. I can guarantee it."

"Does he know?" Dominique asked.

"Yes, he does. I told him."

"When?" Kennedy asked.

"Before you fired him."

"God," Dominique said softly.

"Don and Elsie McGarvey, Kirk's parents, were graduate students of engineering at the University of Chicago. They worked with Enrico Fermi on the first atomic pile, and then went down to Los Alamos during the war to help develop the atomic bomb. They weren't outstanding, but they were bright enough to stick around for Teller's hydrogen bomb program. That was the big deal back then, and they stuck it out. Saved their money, and when Kirk's sister was born they headed north and bought a big cattle ranch in western Kansas. Did okay for themselves.

"Funny thing about them. They were friends with Oppenheimer. And Don McGarvey was an avid student of Russian history and the Russian language. It was in their security clearance files. But at the time no one took much of an interest. They were just engineers, not scientists. When Oppenheimer fell, and when Klaus Fuchs was arrested, nothing ever happened to the McGarveys. Nobody thought much about them."

"Are you telling us that Kirk's parents were spies for the Russians?" Dominique demanded.

"Kirk and his sister were raised on the ranch, and all they ever knew about their parents was that they were a loving, very intelligent couple who doted on their children and who had a deep interest in Russia.

"They were killed in a car accident in the sixties. Left their money to their daughter, who by then was married and had a family of her own, and the ranch to Kirk. But a few days after their funeral, he put the place up for sale, and took the first offer."

"He found out they were Russian spies?"

"He was working for us by then, and since he spoke pretty good Russian, and he understood them, he was on a debriefing of a KGB defector. The man was one of the bankers for North American operations. He brought out a list of agents, identified only by code names, and what and when they had been paid. One of the names on the list matched something he found going through his parents' files and records. Some of them, I guess, were hidden on the ranch. But he found out."

"He didn't tell anybody?"

"No," Carrara said. "That was the first time someone he loved and trusted betrayed him. There were others. Still are. There was also some evidence that his parents had been assassinated, to keep them quiet."

"By the Russians?"

"It pointed that way."

"So he became a super-spy not only to atone for what his parents did but to get back at the Russians."

"That's right. He's taken a lot of hits since then. Damned near died several times. Lost just about everything he ever had. His first wife died of alcohol poisoning. His second wife and daughter were almost killed by someone trying to get to him. A woman he lived with in Switzerland for five years was killed by the East Germans. And one of his best friends, a man named John Lyman Trotter, who was his control officer, turned out to be a double agent for the Russians."

Dominique glanced at Kennedy. "Now us."

"It's even worse than that. Could be the Russians didn't kill his parents after all. Might have been us. A lot of crazy shit happened in those days."

"Does he know?"

Carrara shook his head. "There's no proof. And I don't think I'd care to be in the same room with him when he was told."

"What do you want?" Kennedy asked Carrara. "I don't know what to do anymore. Where to turn. Should I rehire him?"

"No," Carrara said. "Just don't write him off."

"I was wrong . . ."

"*We* were wrong, David," Dominique interrupted. "What happens next, Mr. Carrara?"

"I'm going to help out. But we don't have much time, so I'm going to need your cooperation."

"You've got it," Kennedy said.

Dominique nodded. She had started to cry, but she cut it off. "What can we do?"

"Mac cares about you, and they probably know it. Makes you a target. So you're going to have to disappear for a while."

She wanted to protest, but she didn't.

"I'll talk to him first, and then arrange something. In the meantime both of you should go back to what you were doing."

"Should I go to the Bureau for help?" Kennedy asked.

"Definitely, and then return to Portland."

"It's going to be difficult—" Dominique was shivering.

Carrara felt genuinely sorry for her, but she was one tough woman. "Welcome to the club," he said, not unkindly.

Arimoto Yamagata was sitting cross-legged on the floor in the middle of the Hyatt Regency penthouse when Chance Kennedy let herself in. The afternoon sun slanting through the windows gave his skin a golden glow. God-like, the thought popped into her head, and she shivered despite her resolve that she would be objective. She didn't want him to leave, but if he stayed she was convinced that he would get hurt. They were talking about a multibillion dollar business that Al Vasilanti would do anything to save. He'd hired McGarvey, some ex-paramilitary thug. God only knew who else was out there ready to pounce.

She watched him from the entry hall. He was doing something to the branches of a very small tree, his movements precise, very liquid. It was the same each time they made love. He made it an experience. Something more than sex. Something almost transcendental. She knew that she was gushing like a teenager, but she couldn't help herself.

"The bonsai tree is a horribly mutilated, terribly misshapen dwarf that lives in particular agony for many years," Yamagata said without turning. "But look closely, and you will see that all of its parts—its stems, its leaves, its flowers—are in perfect proportion. It glories in its perfection."

"You have to leave Portland," Chance said.

"Only through patience can come perfection. In the doing, one receives tranquility and beauty as a reward."

"Did you hear me?" Chance asked, coming into the living room. "My husband knows about us. And Guerin has hired a CIA agent or something to come after you. He knows about us too. He warned me about you."

"Are you distressed?"

The question caught her off guard. "For God's sake, Ari, aren't you listening to me?"

Yamagata got smoothly to his feet and turned to her. He wore a black kimono with a red rose embroidered over his left breast. "The feeling of distress is the root of benevolence. This is very important in my society, Chance." He brushed her cheek with his fingertips.

The intimacy of his touch was staggering. She opened her mouth to speak, but the words caught in her throat.

He pushed her coat off her shoulders, and she let it fall to the floor with her purse. Next he unbuttoned her blouse.

"This man's name is Kirk Collough McGarvey, is this correct?"

She nodded. Her entire body was humming, as if she'd been plugged into a high-tension circuit.

He removed her bra and brushed his fingers so lightly against the nipples that she could barely feel it. Her knees were weak. She wanted to sink to the floor with him and make love now.

"He knows that I am your lover?" Yamagata asked, his voice distant, dreamy.

"David told him."

"Has David spoken to you about this?"

"He can't do a thing until after Sunday, except send McGarvey after you." Chance's breath caught in her throat as Yamagata touched her just above the waistband of her skirt. She was more than ready for him.

"What did Mr. McGarvey tell you about me?"

"You're here to hurt Guerin, and you'll use anything or anyone."

Yamagata slowly unzipped her skirt and eased it off her hips. He steadied her as she stepped out of it.

"Do you believe him, Chance?"

"Business is war."

"Yes, I know that you learn well. But do you believe the man?"

It was difficult for her to concentrate. He slid her pantyhose and panties down together, and she held his shoulder as she lifted one foot at a time so that he could pull them all the way off. "I don't know," she murmured. "I mean, I'm not sure . . ."

He was kneeling in front of her, looking up, his eyes smiling. She took his head in her hands and gently pulled him forward until his lips found her vagina, and she arched her back and sighed with pleasure, all other thoughts gone from her head.

"Do you know who this is?"

The voice was muffled, and McGarvey could hear traffic noise in the background, but he knew it was Carrara. "I'm not at a secure number."

"Doesn't matter. Have you made any progress out there since you were fired?"

"I have a couple of leads," McGarvey said, not

surprised that Carrara had found out. "They're good people, but they're running scared. Sunday's a big day. Do you know about it?"

"More than I did yesterday. But you may be better off out of Portland, unless your leads are solid. I spoke with some of the . . . principals. They're behind you now, one hundred percent. Understand?"

"Might be too little too late. What about your end?"

"Nothing officially, but I'm told Guerin is going to ask the Bureau for help."

"Will they get it?"

"No. Can you get out of there clean?"

"Sure."

"I'll meet you where you met Viktor. Tomorrow, 8:00."

"Take care," McGarvey said.

"You too."

Reid picked Mueller up at Dulles, but neither of them said much until they were safely in the car heading away from the airport. Reid was extremely tense, and he kept searching in the rearview mirror as if he suspected they were being followed. His actions were as unsettling as his telephone message.

"Is the Sterling house still safe for us?" Mueller asked.

"Yes, of course it is," Reid answered sharply. But then he backed off. "I think it's as safe as it's always been. Nobody's been out there snooping around."

"Then what's the problem? Is it our young friend, Louis?"

"You can say that again. He built an extra repeater, and he placed it at Andrews Air Force Base. I didn't know about it until yesterday."

"Andrews . . ." Mueller was drawing a blank, but then suddenly he had it. "The President's airplane, Air Force One, operates from there. It's a Guerin 522."

"That's right. The sonofabitch is gunning for the President."

Mueller shrugged. "It fits your plans."

"No!"

"You are willing to kill the Vice President."

"Larry Cross is a twit. Lindsay is different. He can be predicted. Besides, I'm scheduled to be on that flight. I'm going with the President to Tokyo."

"When?"

"Sunday."

Mueller could barely suppress a laugh. In addition to being a sociopath, he had no sense of humor. But the irony of Reid's predicament was too rich to ignore. "Make your excuses."

"Don't you see that by jumping on Lindsay's bandwagon the Bureau will have to drop its investigation of me."

"Didn't help your President Nixon."

"That was different. Wasn't the FBI brought him down. It was the media. Thank God they're not after me."

Mueller thought it over, looking for the advantage. "We could convince Louis to exclude Andrews on his program."

"We can't trust him. He could bury the command in his computer somewhere. We'd never know for sure."

"*You'd* never know," Mueller corrected. "I'll kill him before Sunday."

"Still couldn't be sure. His programs could be automatic."

"How did he find out that Air Force One would be flying on Sunday?" Mueller asked.

"I don't know. But you'll have to go out to Andrews to retrieve the repeater."

"It might be difficult to find. It could be anywhere or nowhere. Maybe he is lying."

"I don't think so," Reid said.

"Did he say why he did it?"

"Just that if we were going to do a job, then let's do it all the way."

"He's right," Mueller replied, but Reid said nothing else.

A light in the kitchen of the farmhouse spilled out into

the hallway, and one in an upstairs room partially lit the second-floor corridor. There was a fire on the grate in the living room that gave the place a comfortable, homey feel. It struck even Mueller odd that from such a setting mass murder was being arranged.

Louis was drinking a glass of white wine in front of the fire. An empty bottle, and one half full, were on the floor next to the couch. He was drunk. He looked up bleary-eyed. "Are you done already?"

"Just the West Coast." Mueller perched on the arm of the couch. "Mr. Reid thought I should come back and have a chat with you."

"I don't know what the big fucking deal is. He wants to stick it to the Japs. Let's do it."

"Killing the President may be a bit extreme."

"Bullshit." Louis slurred the word. "We're all fucked anyway. What difference one murder or a thousand? The sonofabitch is in bed with the Japs anyway."

Mueller glanced at Reid but the older man wouldn't meet his eyes.

"We'd like you to tell us where you placed the repeater, Louis," Mueller said patiently. "I'll go out tomorrow and get it."

"Not a chance. On Sunday Air Force One is a dead duck. Boom."

"Mr. Reid may be on that flight with the President."

Louis giggled. "It wasn't on the White House program."

"We need your help."

Zerkel looked up, his eyes flashing. "You've got my help! You finish placing the repeaters, and on Sunday airplanes will fall out of the sky on signals that will definitely be traceable back to Japan!"

Mueller waited a moment, then nodded. "Fair enough," he said evenly. "Is the signal train in place?"

"Just about."

"You'll show me how to work it?"

Again Louis's eyes flashed. "Why? So you can kill me?"

"You have your safeguard in place. It would be stupid

of me to harm you. I value my freedom as much as you do yours. When we're finished Sunday I want to be well away from this place. I want to know how the system works in case you are incapacitated, or for some reason cannot get to your computers."

"What are you talking about?"

"If this farmhouse were to be stormed, let's say, and we had to get out. If we were separated I would want to make sure the signals were sent."

Louis was breathing through his mouth, his complexion pale. He looked as if he were about to be sick. "All right," he said. "I'll show you."

"In the morning," Mueller said.

"What about me?" Reid asked.

Mueller looked at him. "You'll make all the preparations you need for Tokyo on Sunday with the President. Unfortunately on the way out to the airport you will have an automobile accident that will be investigated by the Highway Patrol. You will have a perfect excuse, and a solid alibi."

"What do you think about that?" Zerkel said.

McGarvey stood on the engineering gallery looking down at *America*. This was a favorite haunt of everyone in the company with enough rank to get in. His security badges had not been yanked. That would probably happen by tomorrow morning, so he'd been able to drive in without subterfuge. He wanted to see the airplane one last time before he headed out.

"You're not supposed to be up here, Mr. McGarvey," Saul Edwards, the Gales Creek operations manager, said.

"I know, I just had to see it again."

"She's a beauty," Edwards agreed. He was a short, swarthy man with thick dark hair and wide dark eyes. Like the others he'd been working around the clock and looked it.

"Tighten up your security. Even without a pass I could have gotten in here easily."

"I'll see what I can do."

"At least until Sunday."

"For what it's worth, Mr. McGarvey, I think you have been a real gentleman around here. I don't know why you got the ax, but if we have a problem it's not going to disappear when you're gone. You know what I mean?"

McGarvey nodded. "I'll do what I can, Saul. Just watch your security until Sunday."

"Will do," Edwards said. "Good luck."

"Thanks. You too."

THIRTY-ONE

McGarvey showed up at Kennedy's tomb in Arlington National Cemetery at 8:00 sharp. Phil Carrara, wearing a light gray jacket and dark flannel trousers, was waiting for him, head bowed as if he were praying. The morning was gray, and damp, the wind off the Potomac raw. Very few visitors were in the cemetery at this hour.

"Working spooks are supposed to be dressed in suits and ties on weekdays," McGarvey said, coming up to him. "How's your field work?"

"I'm clean, if that's what you mean." Carrara looked up. "But I'm no longer an employed spook. I've been placed on administrative leave."

"Internal Affairs?"

"They're not that far yet. It was Ryan. He convinced the General that I no longer have the spirit of my position firmly in mind."

"You have questionable friends."

"That too," Carrara answered, staring at the flame.

"How long have you known about my parents?"

"Couple of days. I went digging and came up with a few things."

"They were murdered."

"No proof of that, *compar.*"

McGarvey faced his friend. "They spied for the Russians. What made you dig that far back, Phil? Those were OSS days. Ancient history. Was it a case of nerves?"

"I had to be sure about you. There are a lot of accusations flying around. Lots of coincidences, dead bodies here in Washington, out on the West Coast, and in Japan. All the time you were in and out, talking with your Russian . . . friend."

"Control officer."

"That's right. But you came up clean."

"You so sure the son hasn't followed in the father's footsteps?"

"You came up clean."

"Are you sure enough about that to risk your career?"

Carrara's face fell a little. "I already have, *compar.* I'm here."

"Ah, shit." McGarvey looked away for a moment. He felt like hell. "You didn't deserve that. Sorry."

"You don't deserve the treatment you're getting either. But Ryan is right about one thing: you are a dinosaur. Things aren't done your way these days. Maybe that's good, maybe that's bad, I don't know. What I do know is that no matter what happens this time, when the dust finally settles you'll be cut completely adrift from the Company. No more assignments, no more favors, no bending the rules."

"Are you telling me to retire?"

"Compar, I'm calling in all my markers, and I'm going to get some of my old friends to do the same. All out this time, but it'll be the last time. *Comprendes?"*

"Let's go for a walk," McGarvey said. They headed away from Kennedy's grave as McGarvey lit a cigarette, the smoke whipped away by the wind. The trees were bare, and there was still snow on the ground. The place seemed desolate.

"I explained the situation to David Kennedy, and I think he understands," Carrara said.

"Is he here in Washington?"

"He's going to ask the Bureau for help this morning. I don't think he's going to get very far, but he'll try. Business as usual. In the meantime he'll do whatever you want, short of grounding the fleet or canceling Sunday's flight."

"Then that's the timetable," McGarvey said. He didn't like it, but only a major disaster would stop Guerin now, which was exactly what it was heading for. "You're going to have to help me get Dominique out of the firing line."

"Already done. I took her to one of our safe houses in Falls Church last night."

"She's agreed to keep her head down?"

"Until Sunday night. I talked to her and Kennedy at the same time. She understands the situation just as well, if not better, than he does." Carrara managed a slight grin. "She's something else."

"She's that, all right," McGarvey agreed. "Anybody watching her?"

"The manpower would be missed. But the place is secure. No leaks from our end. As long as she doesn't do something foolish, she'll be okay. It's only a few days." Carrara gave him the location.

"No chance you were followed?"

"Even Ryan wouldn't dare. She's safe for the moment. The ball's in our court now. You said you had a couple of leads in Portland."

"Arimoto Yamagata. He works for Mintori's Sokichi Kamiya, the man I was maneuvered into meeting with outside Tokyo."

"What'd he say to you?"

"Not much that made a lot of sense. But he said that destroying Guerin was only part of some grand plan."

"Is the government involved?"

"He said it wasn't, and at this point there's no reason to disbelieve him."

"Except that the submarine that sank the Russian destroyer in the Tatar Strait is on the loose in the East China Sea. Apparently with the same skipper and crew."

"Where are they headed?"

"Okinawa."

"Any connection between Kamiya and the navy?"

"None that I could pin down. But, Mac, he's in tight with practically everyone in their government. Hell, half of them owe him big favors. He's got the power base to do whatever he wants."

"If he were to be taken out it might slow them down," McGarvey speculated.

"What about *Abunai?* Do you trust Yemlin?"

McGarvey was startled. "Did someone get to Viktor's blind number?"

"Ryan's got the transcript, but everybody upstairs is discounting the Russians. But if *Abunai* is right, then we've got another problem on our hands. Who brought down the plane at Dulles and why? The Russians?"

"They'd be shooting themselves in the foot. Without Guerin they'd lose a billion-dollar assembly plant."

"How about a separate Japanese group—assuming that Mintori was responsible for the crash in '90?"

"Kamiya is too powerful for that to happen. He'd know about it. But it's one of the things I'm going to ask Yamagata."

"Why did you wait?"

McGarvey looked at his old friend and smiled wryly. "Still a few doubts?"

Carrara held his silence.

"Yamagata is having an affair with David Kennedy's wife."

"Christ," Carrara said. "Does he know about it?"

McGarvey nodded. "I wanted to give him a shot at getting her out of there. Could get ugly."

"Still leaves Dulles. Whoever engineered it wants Guerin to take the fall."

"Either that or blame the Japanese for it," McGarvey said. "If it was a second group that caused the Dulles crash why did they go through the trouble of making it happen exactly the same as the American Airlines crash?"

"I don't know, but if the two groups never worked together it could mean that more than one Guerin airplane was fixed at some point for the engine to fail. Maybe all of them.''

"If that's the case they're smarter than all of Guerin's and Rolls-Royce's engineers put together. Those planes have been pulled apart piece by piece, and no one has come up with a thing.''

"Hide the thimble,'' Carrara muttered.

McGarvey looked at him.

"It's a game we played when we were kids. You take an ordinary object, like a sewing thimble, and while everyone is out of the room you hide it. The trick is to put the thimble out in the open, someplace so obvious that everyone who searches for it will see it but won't see it. Or won't recognize it. Might fool the best of them.''

"Did you tell that to Kennedy?''

"No, it just occurred to me. Maybe Guerin's engineers are looking in the right places, they're just looking too hard.''

"Knowing something's there in the open and finding it are two different things,'' McGarvey said. "In the meantime what else do you have for me?''

"A long shot, but maybe it's worth something. Do you remember the Action Service query we got on Bruno Mueller?''

"The Stasi hit man.''

"There might be a connection between him and Edward Reid. It's thin, like I say. But Mueller was pals with a former West German intelligence officer by the name of Karl Schey. Schey and Mueller are both missing, but before the Bureau backed away from investigating Reid they found out he had some connection with Schey.''

"Why'd they back off?''

"State told them to, and the White House agreed,'' Carrara said. "But the interesting thing is that Reid is rabidly anti-Japanese. Thinks that we're going to be at war with them any day now.''

"Would he have the connections to hear about Mintori Assurance?''

"Possibly.''

"If he somehow found out how Mintori brought down the American Airlines flight in '90, he might be planning on bringing down a bunch more and blaming them. It'd be a long time before Japan recovered."

"Not only that, *compar*. Reid is very rich. Maybe he wants more. If Guerin planes go down, so does its stock. But if the Japanese take the blame, Guerin will recover. Someone who knew what was going on could make a bundle."

"And come out the hero," McGarvey said. "You're right. It's a long shot, but anything's possible. Can you get the FBI file on him?"

"I can try. In the meantime, where are you staying?"

"The Watergate. I lifted a spare key from Dominique's purse."

Carrara managed a thin smile. "Sure is interesting back in the field."

"That it is," McGarvey agreed.

"The timetable has been set, but for the moment there is no need for you to know the exact day and hour," Russian Defense Minister Vyacheslav Solovyev said.

"Shall I be told the target?" SUR Director Karyagin had been summoned to the Defense Ministry in the evening. It was one of the stunts the military liked to pull on civilians.

"The Air Self Defense Force radar installation at Wakkanai."

"I am not familiar with this place."

Minister Solovyev handed him a sketch map of the Japanese north island of Hokkaido. Wakkanai was a small town on the island's extreme north end, at Cape Soya.

"That base is responsible for monitoring all traffic into the strait, a capability that we will deny them."

Karyagin looked up. Solovyev was one of the new breed who'd been too young for the Great Patriotic War but who had proved himself as a tactical commander in Afghanistan. He had a firm grasp of Russia's military strengths and weaknesses, but in Karyagin's estimation he was naïve about almost everything else.

"Have you read my reports on Japan's military readiness?"

"It's why I called you here, Aleksandr Semenovich. I need an update, and I want your current assessment of the situation."

"I'm not a military man." Karyagin shrugged to mask his excitement. The Defense Minister's request was nothing short of extraordinary. It meant the military was sticking its neck out and wanted civilian endorsement.

"I mean the political situation."

"Between us and Japan?"

"Yes," Solovyev said. "And between us and the United States. What reaction will Washington have beside bluster?"

"That is very difficult to predict, Minister Solovyev. Nevertheless, I think that if we put our heads together we will come up with something. But first I will need more information. We cannot work blind."

Carrara had lunch with the new acting Deputy Director of Operations, Dick Adkins, at a Denny's restaurant in Bethesda. Dick was a short, husky man with pale skin and wavy hair. He'd always looked up to Carrara. Now he was nervous. Ryan had him on a short leash, so he had to be very careful.

"You're my only shot at staying on top of this," Carrara said. It wasn't quite true, but he wanted to keep the need-to-know list small and compartmentalized. "Ryan is wrong and unless I can work independently he's going to maneuver us into making a colossal mistake."

"He's got a one-track mind when it comes to McGarvey, all right. And you're on his short list too. He wants you out. Permanently."

"I know. In the meantime I need your help. Arimoto Yamagata, Sokichi Kamiya, and Edward R. Reid. I want all three of their files. You'll have to talk to someone over at the Bureau—anyone but John Whitman."

"I can tell you right now that Reid's file is totally off limits."

"Why?" Carrara asked.

"It came after you left. Reid's on the President's Tokyo Summit team. He'll be on Air Force One on Sunday. Makes him an untouchable unless the Attorney General gives her nod, which I'm told she won't."

David was in Washington again, probably with that bitch Dominique, so Chance had not bothered to go home. After their long talk last night Arimoto had not wanted her to stay. She'd seen it in his eyes. But he'd finally given in, and they'd made love several more times, her way, with some old Kenny G on the disc player.

She'd slept late, and waking with the sun streaming through the penthouse bedroom windows she had a few moments of luxury before the terrible guilt returned. The fact is she was a failure as a spy. When she was with Arimoto, when they were talking and making love, she had no control. Even last night, when she'd taken charge, her focus had remained on the sex, not on what she'd set out to do.

Lying in bed, her mind racing, she knew that McGarvey was right to warn her about Arimoto. At some point last night, despite her self-indulgence, it came to her that Arimoto was no businessman. He was not here to negotiate a deal with Guerin. In fact he was here to spy on the company and do whatever it took to bring it down.

She turned those thoughts over. So what? When Guerin fell, David would be free. One airplane company more or less would not have that much of an effect on the international balance of trade. Portland would be devastated, but as a whole the country would be just fine. After all, the Japanese already owned most of Hawaii, half of California, and a bunch of buildings in Manhattan.

Chance got out of bed and used the bathroom. Putting on a white silk kimono, she went into the living room just as Yamagata was seeing a man to the door. They stopped and exchanged bows, Yamagata's back to her. But his guest spotted her and said something.

Yamagata turned and smiled. "I hope we did not disturb you."

"Not at all," Chance said. "I didn't mean to interrupt."

"Run the bath, and I'll order us breakfast."

"Okay," Chance said. She went back into the bedroom and closed the door, her heart beginning to race. The man was Japanese, and Arimoto's bow had been slightly deeper than his. Etiquette was very important, he'd taught her. It marked the difference between civilization and chaos. Respect for one's superiors was at the very top of the list. His bow had been deeper.

What the hell had she gotten herself into here?

The *FF Cook* and *FF Barbey* pulled out of Yokosuka at 3:00 A.M. with no fanfare. They headed down Tokyo Bay past the rest of Seventh Fleet in port, pouring on speed as soon as possible. Even before they passed the sea buoy and turned to the southwest, both Knox-class anti-submarine warfare frigates were making in excess of thirty knots. The wind and seas continued to rise and it promised to be a rough eighteen hours until they rendezvoused with the *DD Thorn*, which was still well north of Takara Jima Island.

The *Cook's* skipper called the *Barbey's* skipper on the encrypted radiotelephone. "How's it going back there, Jim?" The night was black.

"Tough to keep coffee in a cup, but we're right on your tail," Lieutenant Commander James Otter replied.

"We're painting two supertankers southbound eighty miles out."

"Got 'em. Did you catch the illumination on the way out?"

Lieutenant Commander Adam Zimmerman glanced at his XO and grinned. "Sure did. No guesswork where we're headed, so keep a sharp watch. *Chrysanthemum* may not be their only asset out here."

"Won't happen until after the strait."

"You're probably right. But we'll keep on top of this one."

"Tanegashima," Otter warned.

"They're not going to put anything into the air in this weather."

"They'll be telling us something if they do."

"That's for sure," Zimmerman said. "Keep your eyes open."

Japanese Self Defense Force destroyer *DD118 Murakumo* was on full alert at her Yokosuka berth. The entire fleet was being held at the state of readiness because of the deteriorating situation with the Russians. Even in port, however, the Escort Fleet Headquarters flagship maintained an around-the-clock vigilance. Pearl Harbor had taught them that lesson in reverse. No place was truly safe, not even home port. When the two American frigates were finally out of radar range, the Murakumo's skipper, Commander Noburo Shirokita, and his XO, Lieutenant Commander Yashusi Morita, left the bridge for the skipper's battle cabin. This was how wars began, one confusing situation developing into another, like cherry blossoms suddenly popping out after a sharp change in the weather. Only long afterward, when the survivors picked through the rubble, could any sense be made of the situation, especially the first days. But what was happening now seemed especially senseless to Shirokita, whose father had survived the war as a young lieutenant and helped reestablish the navy under pressure from the Americans to do so in the fifties and sixties. They were supposed to be the first line of defense against a Soviet breakout into the Pacific. Just like West Germany had been the first line of defense against Soviet land forces moving in from the east. But those threats no longer existed.

"Unless we receive orders to follow them, there is little

else we can do this morning, *Kan-cho.*" Morita poured their tea.

"I'm told the air force will handle it from Tanegashima. We have no business running after them."

"Pardon me, sir, but they know that we are on alert, and they know that we are monitoring their progress and their transmissions. Won't an Air Force fly-over be perceived as a threat?"

"Certainly, but a threat to whom?" Shirokita asked. "The Americans or that bastard Kiyoda?" Nobody was claiming responsibility for allowing that fool to regain his command and actually sail out of here. But sooner or later heads would roll.

Bruno Mueller arrived back at Chicago's O'Hare Airport a few minutes after six and went down to retrieve his single overnight bag from the carousel. The flight from Washington's National where he'd left his car had been less than half full, so the luggage came out quickly. He'd had a lot to think about on the way out, and he was still preoccupied as he turned to leave. Louis had run into trouble with the signal train out of Tokyo. At first he'd been annoyed, and he'd thrown one of his tantrums. But when he'd finally calmed down, he discovered that the Bank of Tokyo had installed what he called an "antivirus" program in its computer system. "Designed," Louis explained, "to stop the kind of shit we're trying to pull."

"Do they know we're tampering with their system?" Mueller asked.

"No. It's just a precaution. Means they're nervous."

"Can you get around it?"

Louis had a wild look in his eyes. He was losing it. "There isn't a program I can't defeat," he said. He studied his computer screen. "Twenty-four hours, man. The bastards won't know they've been raped. What do you think about that?"

The operation was disintegrating. With Glen gone there was no one to control Louis, whose devotion to Mueller had been short-lived. Reid was falling apart and was about ready to crack. And Mueller was beginning to believe that he should kill them both and get out.

But Reid's plan was charming. One last strike at the West. One final act of terrorism that would go down in the books as a day of infamy in America's history. Not that anyone but an Islamic fundamentalist would care.

"Reston," someone called. "Tom Reston."

Mueller was instantly alert. There were only a few people who knew him by that work name. None of them would do him any good here. He stopped as a short, gray-haired man with a neatly trimmed beard came over from a United carousel where he was waiting for his bags to come up. Mueller put a name to the face immediately.

"Bill White. Air Traffic Control, Oakland."

"That's right. Nice to see you again." They shook hands. "How's the article coming?"

"Slow but steady."

"If you're working your way east, O'Hare is a good stop," White said. "Damned fine crew. Earl Heintz, the chief controller, is one of the best in the country."

"What brings you so far from home?" Mueller asked. If this one discovered that no one at *High Technology Business* or *Aviation Week & Space Technology* magazines had ever heard of Thomas Reston, the operation would definitely be in jeopardy.

"Union meeting."

"Here at the airport, tonight?"

"Holiday Inn. Starts tomorrow, but some of the guys will be drifting in tonight. You might want to drop by, if you have the time. I'll introduce you around. For background."

"That's a coincidence. I'm staying at the Holiday Inn. You can ride over with me, I'm going to rent a car."

White glanced back at the still empty carousel. "I have to wait for my suitcase."

"I'll get the car and meet you out front. There're a couple of questions I'd like to ask you on the way over."

"Sounds good," White agreed.

Mueller hurried to the Budget counter where he rented a Chrysler LeBaron for dropoff in Minneapolis, using his Howard Ellefson identification and credit card. White was waiting in front when Mueller drove up. He tossed his small suitcase in the back seat.

"I hate those damned shuttle buses, but they're a lot cheaper than cabbing it," White said. "How come you had to rent a car?"

"I want to get over to Meigs Field tomorrow sometime."

"There's nothing much worth seeing there. Not for your article anyway."

"I thought I'd take a couple of days off. See some friends. It's been a long time since I've been back here."

"I know what you mean," White said. "But except for O'Hare, you can have Chicago. Too big, too dirty, too much crime."

"Oh?"

"It's getting as bad as L.A. Too dangerous to be anywhere near downtown at night."

"How about this far out?" Mueller asked.

White shrugged. "Who knows? There's no place really safe these days."

It only took a few minutes to get over to the Holiday Inn from the terminal, and Mueller pulled around to the side of the hotel and parked in front of some bushes next to the building.

"Hope you don't mind the extra walk, Bill. But I didn't want to register first and then have to move the car."

"No problem," the air traffic controller said.

Mueller got around to the passenger side of the car just as White was pulling his suitcase out of the back seat. The parking lot was nearly full, but for the moment no one was around.

"Here, let me help you." Mueller took White's arm with his left hand and pulled him around. With his right, he plunged the nine-inch stiletto into the man's chest just below his left breast.

White was surprised. He looked down at the stiletto in his chest and then up at Mueller. "Why—?" he asked, then he collapsed. Moments later he was dead.

Making sure that no one was coming, Mueller removed the stiletto from the dead man's chest, wiped the blade off, and then took the man's wallet and money from his pockets before hiding the body behind the bushes.

He drove immediately to the rear of the hotel, where he rifled through White's suitcase and tossed everything into a garbage dumpster, along with the wallet after he'd taken the credit cards and a hundred dollar bill stuck behind the photograph of two small girls hugging Mickey Mouse.

It would be hours before White's body was discovered. Possibly not until morning.

An unfortunate happenstance that would, however, not slow him down, he told himself leaving the Holiday Inn parking lot. He would find a good steakhouse for dinner, place the repeater in the Commission's Noise Management Program office, and then drive immediately to Minneapolis. With luck he would be finished well before the morning shift arrived.

Carrara telephoned McGarvey at Dominique's Watergate apartment. "Are you clean?"

"For the moment."

"No file on Reid. The Attorney General's office has quashed that part of the investigation for the moment on another strong recommendation from the White House. But listen to this, *compar,* Reid has switched sides. He's going to Tokyo on Sunday with the President. It changes everything."

"I thought he was anti-Japanese."

"He is. Which means he's probably covering his ass in case everything's worked out at the summit. But he can't be involved with this plot to bring down Guerin, or else Air Force One won't be a target. He wouldn't risk his own life."

"Unless he comes up with a last-minute excuse not to go Sunday," McGarvey said.

"I never thought of that," Carrara replied after a moment.

"You know Reid's background better than I do. How likely is it that he's had a legitimate change of heart?"

"Not very likely, Mac. He's been too long at it, and too vocal to switch sides overnight. He has a lot of supporters who read his newsletter. But the President evidently bought it."

"He's worth a quick pass before I go back out to Portland and lean on Yamagata."

"It'll have to be quick, if you're right about their timetable," Carrara cautioned. He sounded worried.

"Is there any way of getting through to the President?"

"The General, but he won't listen to either of us."

"Do you think Ryan might be a part of it?"

"No."

"Neither do I," McGarvey said, although it would have given him a certain amount of pleasure to attend the Agency counsel's fall from grace. "Does Reid live here in Washington?"

"Georgetown." Carrara gave McGarvey the address on R Street. "His newsletter is the *Lamplighter*. Offices in the Grand Hyatt Washington. Do you want me to go with you?"

"Not this time, but I might need some help from Technical Services. You got anyone over there who owes you a favor?"

"A couple of guys."

"Good. In the meantime, I want you to try to get to Murphy one last time. Set up a meeting for the three of us. Anytime, anyplace, so long as Ryan isn't there."

"I'll see what I can do. But watch yourself. If Reid is involved, and Mueller or Schey is nearby, they'll be tough. I saw their files."

"I hope they are," McGarvey said.

"Watch yourself," Carrara repeated.

"Will do."

McGarvey found a parking place across the street and down the block from the driveway to Reid's Georgetown place. The house, set back in the trees, was visible from the road. A few windows were lit inside, and the yard floods were on, indicating that someone was home. But to do a proper job of monitoring the man's movements, Carrara's Technical Services friends would have to be called out.

He had no gut feelings this time, but he was running out of options. Short of returning to Japan and taking Kamiya out, there wasn't much for him to do. One by one his moves were being sidestepped by the Japanese, by Guerin, and by his own government.

If Reid were involved with Schey and Mueller, however, whatever they were up to would be big. The Germans had their backs to the wall. There were very few places left for them to run. But it did not mean that they were involved in the plot to bring Guerin down. There were no solid connections. Everything was different this time. Less precisely defined. The blacks and whites had turned to shades of gray.

Time to get out for good. Time to quit chasing demons that hadn't been catchable in any event. Like a donkey with a carrot dangling in front of its nose, he'd made the moves but he'd never really accomplished anything.

Headlights came on at the end of the driveway, and moments later a slate-gray Mercedes sedan emerged, Reid behind the wheel, and headed east on R Street.

McGarvey had to wait for a break in traffic before he could make a U-turn and catch up, but Reid was apparently in no hurry, nor was it likely from the way he was driving that he suspected he was being followed. Either he was a pro, or he had nothing to hide tonight.

The man had good connections in this town. The very best. It was likely that he would hear about any investigation in which he was involved, and either cooperate if he were innocent or take steps to have the Bureau sidelined if he weren't. Such as signing on with the President. It wouldn't stop them for long, but Sunday was only five days away.

Reid turned on Pennsylvania Avenue toward the White House, McGarvey two cars behind him in moderately heavy traffic.

* * *

Up to this point the American had been extremely difficult to follow. His moves, apparently erratic, were those of a highly experienced intelligence officer. Yozo Hamagachi and Toshiki Korekiyo had been allowed to see a portion of McGarvey's file, and they were impressed.

"Be very careful of this man," Yamagata had warned them. "Under no circumstances must you underestimate him. If you are discovered he will not hesitate to kill you."

"There are two of us," Hamagachi had suggested.

"Pardon me, but although your abilities are impressive, McGarvey would nevertheless kill you."

They had their doubts, but they did as they were told, taking extra care with their tradecraft. McGarvey showing up at Edward Reid's house, however, had been a surprise.

Korekiyo telephoned Yamagata in Portland on the scrambler. "Target Red is following Teardrop."

"Teardrop," Yamagata repeated. "Are you certain?"

Korekiyo had brought Reid's file up on his laptop after getting his name from the address listing in the Washington-area reverse telephone directory. He'd been assigned the codename because of his recent anti-Japanese writings. *"Hai."*

"Follow them to their destination and report to me."

"They've arrived," Korekiyo said.

"Where?"

"The Department of State."

"At this hour?" Yamagata demanded.

"Hai, Yamagata-san. The building is busy. Many windows show lights."

"Remain with them."

"Which one?"

"McGarvey," Yamagata ordered.

Except for the glow from the computer terminals the upstairs rooms were in darkness. Louis Zerkel was chugging white wine from a bottle, his feet up on the desk, watching the streams of data crossing the screens.

He knew that he was slowly sinking toward some point of deep insanity, a place from where he would no longer be able to reason rationally, but he could do nothing to stop the disintegration.

He'd found Reid's extensive wine cellar in the basement, and had picked the dustiest bottles at the top of the racks. This one had a French label with a 1928 date. It gave him heartburn.

Tokyo Bank's anti-theft virus was like a germ that attacked any unauthorized entry into the system. The entry would get sick, and when it returned to its source, the hacker's computer program would catch the disease and die.

It was really quite simple, Zerkel told himself. He took another pull at the bottle. To beat the germ you played doctor and invented a magic bullet, such as penicillin, administering it to yourself first so that your system would become immune. The next part was trickier. Injecting penicillin directly into Tokyo Bank's system, thus killing their anti-theft germ, would almost certainly set off alarm signals. Instead, Louis had designed a penicillin-impregnated sheath, or condom, around his entry signal, so that only the germs that came in direct contact with him would die.

"Like fucking a diseased whore," he muttered. He had to giggle. He was around the bend, but not stupid. Who'd they think they were screwing with? The stupid bastards hadn't learned a thing from Pearl Harbor. Well, they were going to get another Hiroshima and Nagasaki.

He had not found the magic bullet yet, but the same multiplexed program he'd used to defeat the heat-sensor triggering code was working on this problem. It would only be a matter of time before the Japanese system would be breached.

He giggled again.

Mueller reached the Twin Cities shortly after 4:30 in the morning. He looked up the Metropolitan Airports Commission address in the telephone book at a roadside phone booth, located it on a map, and got over there a little after 5:00 A.M. The layout was similar to Oakland and Los Angeles, and by 6:00 he had returned his rental car and was heading back to the Northwest Airlines check-in counter for his early flight to Washington.

THIRTY-TWO

Carrara telephoned Murphy from his car first thing in the morning, and the General reluctantly agreed to see him at home. The guards at the gate leading up to the DCI's house behind Gallaudet College were expecting him. They passed him directly through.

"Good morning, General," Carrara said at the door. "Thanks for letting me have my say."

Murphy was a good director, and although he was tough he was usually fair. Over the past couple of years, however, he'd drifted away from his military style of leadership to that of a politician. A lot of Agency officers, Carrara included, did not like the change.

"I'm leaving for my office shortly, so you've only got a few minutes."

"Fair enough."

"We'll do this in my study." The DCI led Carrara back and closed the door. "All right, Phil, I'm listening."

"General, I think you should talk the President out of leaving for Tokyo on Sunday. Air Force One is a Guerin 522, the same type of airplane that crashed last week at Dulles and in '90 out of O'Hare. The first accident may have been engineered by Mintori Assurance, but the Dulles incident could have been caused by another group. Someone who'd stand to profit if Guerin were to be hurt and it could be blamed on the Japanese. Right now Sunday seems to make a lot of sense on those terms, because Guerin is also flying its new bird out to Honolulu. If it were to go down, along with the President's plane, Guerin's stock would take a nosedive. And considering the fact that all of Japan's military installations are on alert the situation out there would become explosive. There's a lot of tension between our countries. This could be the incident that sparks a bigger disaster."

"Are you talking about a shooting war between us and Japan?" Murphy asked. It was clear he wasn't impressed by what he was hearing.

"If the President were to be killed aboard Air Force One, and the Vice President aboard the new Guerin airplane, and if we thought Japan was to blame . . . yes, sir, I think a shooting war would be possible."

"How?"

"Blocking Tokyo Bay would be easy enough, which would lock most of the Seventh Fleet in port. And if, let's say, a supertanker were to accidentally explode in the Panama Canal, destroying one of the locks, it would slow sending reinforcements out of the Atlantic. The Japanese would own the western Pacific."

"You're forgetting the Air Force."

"Look how long it took us to get enough personnel and equipment over to Saudi Arabia in '91 to go up against Iraq."

"Okinawa is well equipped," Murphy pointed out. "And unless the Japanese sank the Seventh Fleet at the dock, there'd be nothing stopping us from heading back up Tokyo Bay right into the city. Have you considered that?"

"No. But I'm sure someone has."

"The crash in '90 and the one last week involved Guerin 522s, the same type of airplane as Air Force One. Where's the connection between them and their hypersonic plane?"

"I don't know, General."

"Has the Federal Aviation Administration made any suggestions about grounding Guerin airplanes?"

"No."

"Has Guerin thought about recalling its own airplanes?"

"I think they've discussed it," Carrara replied.

"But they're going ahead with Sunday's flight, isn't that right?"

"Yes, sir."

"So in effect, what you're saying to me is that you think McGarvey is getting the shaft from us. Which means that you've been in contact with him."

"That's right, General."

"Which is why I placed you on administrative leave. Nothing I've heard this morning makes me regret that decision." Murphy's attitude hardened. "McGarvey's going to take the fall this time. Watch out that you don't go down with him. I'm sure that you've already broken a few laws."

"You won't speak to the President?"

"No."

"And you won't let McGarvey come here to explain what he's doing?"

"You're a good man, Phil. Back away from this now, while there's still the chance."

It was about what Carrara had expected. The Murphy of a few years ago would have listened. "Thanks for your time, General. I think we'll talk again on Monday."

Murphy's eyes narrowed. "Yes, I believe we will."

Sam Varelis compared the findings from the 1990 American Airlines crash with the Dulles crash last week, for the fourth time in as many days, amazed that he had been so blind. That everyone else on his staff at the NTSB was so blind.

Both crashes were apparently caused by the same set of physical circumstances. In both crashes the same section of the port engines received the same heat damage, causing the same catastrophic failures. Exactly the same. In both crashes. But that was a statistical improbability, if not impossibility.

Mueller arrived back at the Sterling farmhouse before noon. All that was left to do was plant the remaining three repeaters at JFK, La Guardia, and Dulles. There was plenty of time for that. In fact everything was on schedule.

He parked in the garage and went in through the kitchen. The house was quiet. Although someone had done the dishes the place stank of food odors mingled with an electronic smell, the acrid stench from the fire, and something else that smelled like wine. A few more days and he would be away from here.

"Louis?" he called from the stair hall.

"Up here."

Mueller left his bag downstairs and went up to the front bedroom where Zerkel was stretched out with a pillow on the floor. Several empty wine bottles were lined up in front of the window. "Are you celebrating?"

"Damned straight. The deed is done. What do you think about that?"

"You found a way to get into Tokyo Bank's computer?"

"It was a snap." Zerkel sat up and got unsteadily to his feet. "Mr. Reid has got a horseshit wine cellar, I'm here to tell you." He rubbed his temples. "Headache. But I fixed his ass. Now he'll have to start his collection all over. I busted every fucking bottle down there."

"I'm sure he'll be grateful to you," Mueller said. "Is he here?"

"I haven't seen him since yesterday," Zerkel replied. "What about the repeaters?"

"Three to go, which I'll do tomorrow. Are you certain that everything will work?"

"You can do it from a pay phone, man. I'll give you the Tokyo number and access code. Soon as their tone comes on line, whistle and it'll happen." Zerkel gave a short whistle. "Like that."

"Brilliant," Mueller said, and he sincerely meant it. The man was a genius. It was a shame he had to be killed. Mueller could think of any number of uses for him. "Get some rest now. You've earned it."

"I want out of here."

Mueller looked mildly at him. "When?"

"I don't care. Just as long as it's before Sunday."

"Where will you go?"

"Buenos Aires," Zerkel said firmly. "And I want a million dollars in cash."

"All right."

Zerkel was surprised. It showed on his face. "Just like that?"

"You've kept your end of the bargain. I'm sure Reid will keep his. After all, he's going to make a lot of money. A million is very reasonable."

"Will you talk to him?"

"Soon as I clean up and get something to eat. You might even be able to leave tonight. Or certainly first thing in the morning."

"Christ."

Mueller smiled. "What do you think about that?"

Carrara parked behind the Georgetown Holiday Inn, locked his car, and walked back to the gray windowless van parked two rows away. He got in the passenger side. Roy Ulland, an operative from the Agency's Technical Services Division, was behind the wheel. He was a slightly built man with fair skin, blond hair, and huge, drooping moustaches. They headed out immediately.

"Hello, boss. You're late."

"I put JoAnn on a plane for Montpelier, and it was late taking off," Carrara explained. He was sending his wife to Vermont to be with her sister through the weekend. "Did you run into any trouble?"

"No. He has three incoming lines. One for his fax machine, one that didn't answer this morning, and a third that transfers calls to the *Lamplighter* offices at the Hyatt."

Carrara studied the younger man. "If this goes bad I won't be able to do much for you. Still time to back off, Roy."

Ulland grinned. "You've bailed me out before. I figure it's payback time. Besides, this is my job, remember?" He was, in addition to being a good second-story man, a barroom brawler. Carrara had taken a liking to him because of his expertise, his easy manner, and his loyalty, and had gone to bat for him more than once with the D.C. police and with Personnel.

"Just so you know. Okay?"

"Piece of cake, boss."

They pulled up on 29th Street around the corner from Reid's house. From where they were parked they could see anyone entering or leaving the driveway. Daylight operations like this made Carrara nervous. But if McGarvey's timetable was correct, they were running out of time, and they would have to take chances.

"How do you want to work this?" Ulland asked.

"Let's establish where he is first. If I can stall him on the phone while he's away from the house, it'll give you a chance to get inside, plant a few bugs, and make a quick pass for anything on Japan, Guerin, or the two Germans."

"What are you going to say to him?"

"I'll think of something."

"It'll sure as hell shake him up."

"That's the idea, Roy," Carrara agreed. "Let's try his house number first."

Ulland swiveled his driver's seat aft, handed Carrara a handset, then flipped a switch on a console that brought up a dial tone on a speaker, and entered Reid's number on a keypad. It rang five times. "He's still not home."

"Try the rollover number. He's probably at his office."

"Right." Ulland broke the connection, but before he could enter the second number it rang. "He's got an incoming."

"Trace it."

"Just a minute. There's a privacy screen on it," Ulland said.

The call rolled over on the second ring and was answered on the fourth. "Good afternoon," a woman said. "Thank you for calling the *Lamplighter*. How may I direct your call?"

"Out of state," Ulland whispered, as the number came up on a display. "Sterling, Virginia. Just across the river."

"Let me speak with Mr. Reid," the caller said.

"Who may I say is calling, sir?"

"Tom Reston."

"One moment while I connect you."

"German accent?" Carrara asked.

"Maybe," Ulland replied. "Okay, it's rural. Billing is to a P.O. box here in Washington. But the line location shows a fire number. I'll bring up a map."

Reid came on the line. "Are you back?"

"Yes. Our friend is finished. He wants his money and the means to get out."

Reid was silent for a moment. When he came back his tone was guarded. "Can you . . . take care of it."

"You need to talk to him. He still has his safety procedures in place. He'll need to be convinced of your sincerity."

"I'll come out within the hour."

"With care," the caller cautioned, and he hung up.

"Got 'em," Ulland said. He'd brought up a map on a computer console. It pinpointed the house. "South of Sterling, and east of Highway 28. Just off Highway 7. Looks remote. Maybe a farm."

Carrara studied the map, a sudden chill playing up his spine. "Less than five miles as the crow flies from Dulles. Line of sight."

"Maybe we'd better take a look," Ulland suggested.

"Good idea."

From where McGarvey was seated in the Grand Hyatt's lobby he could watch the elevators. Shortly before one, Reid came down in an obvious hurry. The man had spent much of the evening at the State Department and then had come directly here to his offices. McGarvey had booked a room and kept watch from the stairs on the *Lamplighter*'s floor until this morning. He got up and headed across the lobby.

Ryan switched off the tape recorder. "He can be charged under the Secrets Act. Trial in camera."

"He's the Deputy Director of Operations, Howard. I can definitely see his point of view, even though I think he's wrong. But he and McGarvey have both served this Agency well," Murphy said. He suddenly wondered if it was such a hot idea taping his conversation with Carrara and sharing it with Ryan.

"Well, you warned him."

"Yes, I did. I've trusted Phil's good judgment for a number of years, and he's never let me down. He knows the score. And he knows the limitations imposed on him because of his position. But we're not going to take any action against him unless and until he steps over the line."

"I think you're wrong, General."

"As always, I appreciate your candor. But this time I'm going to overrule you. I've relieved him from active duty for the time being, which cuts him out of the mainstream."

"He's got plenty of friends here. I'm sure he's still plugged in to everything that's happening."

Murphy didn't like the petulant note in Ryan's voice. "Nonetheless, he's still a top-level administrator with this agency. And he'll continue to have our trust and support. I expect that I've made myself clear."

John Whitman was summoned to the FBI director's office after lunch. His people had worked hard on the Guerin case (as it had come to be known) for the past ten days, but they were still stymied by a lack of hard evidence. The State Department and White House had warned them away from Edward Reid, and now the CIA was dragging its feet about Kirk McGarvey. He was going to talk to the director to approach the Attorney General again for a little slack. Without some leeway they simply could not do their jobs. It was aggravating, he thought, and he was tired of giving his people excuses when they needed answers. The director's secretary passed him inside immediately.

"I know that look on your face," FBI Director John

Harding said. "But this time you don't have to say a thing. The CIA has agreed to cooperate."

"That's good news."

"The A.G.'s office is preparing a warrant for McGarvey's arrest on obstruction of justice and industrial espionage. But you're going to have to take it easy, John. All we've got is circumstantial evidence for the most part, and you've seen his file. I don't want anyone hurt."

"I understand." Whitman could hardly contain himself. McGarvey might not have all the answers, but he'd be a start.

"Get your people ready, and I'll let you know when we have the paperwork in hand."

Phil Carrara and Roy Ulland headed out of Washington through Arlington toward the rural Sterling address that had come up on the computer-generated map. They'd tried to contact McGarvey at Dominique's Watergate number without success, which bothered Carrara, especially after his talk with the General this morning. If Mac were taken out, Carrara thought, they'd lose. Simple as that. He didn't carry a weapon and neither did Ulland. But he didn't really think they'd need to be armed. They were just going to take a look. If they needed reinforcements they'd call for them.

McGarvey watched in his rearview mirror as the white Toyota van with darkly tinted windows came up the ramp to the Washington Memorial Parkway behind him. He thought it was the same car that had followed him from the Hyatt over to Reid's Georgetown house. He'd not slept in the past thirty-six hours, and he knew that his judgment was affected.

Reid's gray Mercedes was three cars ahead, and following him was easy. His trail could be picked up at anytime either from his house or from the Hyatt. But whoever was in the Toyota was a different story. McGarvey was betting that they were Japanese. But who were they following, him or Reid? If it was Reid, it meant that the former State Department official was somehow involved with the Dulles crash. Or at least the Japanese thought he was and were investigating him. If not, it meant they were Kamiya's people sent to finish the job that had been started in Tokyo. If that were true it could mean that he was getting close, which led again back to Reid. The arguments were circular, and therefore worthless.

A few miles north, Reid turned off the parkway and headed west on State Highway 123 toward the back entrance to the CIA. For a brief moment McGarvey had the wild notion that Reid was working with the Agency and that all this was some sort of gigantic setup engineered by the General and Howard Ryan. But the Mercedes passed the access road without slowing and a couple of miles later turned east, toward the airport, on the Dulles Airport Access Road.

It was possible that he had gone home to pack a suitcase and was booked on a flight somewhere. If he were involved with the Dulles crash, and with whatever was going to happen on Sunday, he would want to get out of Washington or even the country until the dust settled. But that wasn't right. If Reid were going to end up the Monday-morning hero he would have to stick around.

Perhaps he was going to the airport to meet someone, or perhaps he wasn't going to the airport at all. There were several other exits from the access highway before Dulles.

McGarvey drove past the ramp Reid had taken, crossed under the highway, and turned up the westbound ramp, back toward the city.

He looked in his rearview mirror. The Toyota passed the east ramp, and as he merged with traffic on the highway, it was two cars behind him.

One question was answered.

"I think I was followed part of the way out here," Reid said. He was agitated.

"But not here to the house?" Mueller asked. They watched the highway from one of the front bedrooms. No one had come up the driveway.

"It was a blue Saturn. Followed me from the Hyatt to Georgetown, then as far as the Dulles highway. But it turned off."

"Coincidence?"

"Maybe," Reid said uncertainly. "I only got close enough once to see that there was only the driver. And it was a rental car. The Bureau doesn't operate that way."

"Are you sure?"

"I'm not sure of anything," Reid snapped. "But if I am being followed, and it's not the Bureau, then who? The CIA?"

"It doesn't matter. If someone shows up out here, we'll be ready for them."

"I'm getting out of here tonight," Zerkel said from the doorway. "Did you bring my money?"

"As a matter of fact I did," Reid said, turning away from the window. "But first we're going to discuss your safeguards. They'll have to be neutralized."

"What guarantees will I have—?"

"You'll have a million dollars in cash, and my word, Louis. Isn't that enough?"

Zerkel teetered on the brink of insanity. His eyes were wild, and his lower lip twitched. He nodded finally. "I want to see it first."

"Very well," Reid said. "The money is downstairs."

"Kan-cho on the bridge," the XO announced.

"As you were," Seiji Kiyoda said. All his best officers were present, he noted with satisfaction. He glanced at the clock. It was 0300 local. A steward handed him a cup of tea.

"We're ready," Minori said.

"Very well," Kiyoda answered. He stepped back into the sonar room. "How's it look on the surface?"

"Pretty rough, sir." Chief Sonarman Tsutomu Nakayama brought up one of the displays. "Lots of surface clutter. I'd say they're sailing into forty-knot winds or more, six- to seven-meter seas. But it's hard to hold any target."

The crewmen aboard the American destroyer would be fatigued fighting the storm, and their important officers would probably be asleep at this hour. The *Samisho,* on the other hand, cruised in comfort seventy meters beneath the surface, and her important officers had been ordered to rest for the last twelve hours.

"How far back are they?"

"Twenty-five thousand meters. Same course and speed."

"They remain in passive mode?"

"Yes, *Kan-cho.* They go active only when we shut down."

Kiyoda studied the displays. "Anything else out there?"

Nakayama brought up another display. Barely visible in the waterfall were a series of straight-line dots. "I think it's an oil tanker. One hundred thousand meters plus, to the south-southwest. She'll be out of our range within the next couple of hours. No designation."

"Then it's just us and Sierra-Zero-Nine. Keep a sharp eye for anything else coming up behind him. They may have called for help."

"Aye, aye, *Kan-cho.*"

Kiyoda returned to the control room, and brought their present course, speed, and depth up on his command console, then overlaid that data on a chartlet of their operational area. Their speed-of-advance had steadied to ten knots on a course just west of south that would allow them to clear Amami-O-Shima Island and the off-lying reefs and islets. The waters here were treacherous, alternating between very deep and very shallow. Even experienced sailors could come to grief here because of the many uncharted shoals and dangerous currents.

But these were Japanese waters.

He looked up at his XO and officers and gave them a faint smile. Good men, he thought. Expert, dedicated, and loyal. No captain could ask for more. Sad that this would be the last time they'd sail together.

"Sound battle stations."

"Hai, Kan-cho." Minori rang the Klaxon.

"Come right to two-six-zero, dive to six hundred fifty meters."

"Yo-so-ro, turning *omo-kaji* to two-six-zero degrees, down angle on the planes eighteen degrees."

"Very well," Kiyoda said. His boat was coming alive. "Report when battle stations are manned and ready. Report when at course and depth. And prepare for silent running."

"Aye, aye, *Kan-cho,"* Minori said, his eyes bright.

Carrara steadied his shoulder against the bole of a tree as he studied the sprawling farmhouse and outbuildings one hundred yards across a clearing. The fire number at the entrance to the long driveway off the highway matched the one from the trace. Whoever had telephoned Reid had done so from here less than two hours ago.

They'd confirmed the location and then had discovered the dirt track through the woods east of the house. So far as they could tell no one had used the road for a long time. The snow was undisturbed except for animal tracks.

Someone was in residence. Smoke curled from the chimney, and Carrara could make out the rear bumper of what looked like Reid's Mercedes on the other side of the garage at the rear.

He brought the glasses around to the south. The end of Dulles's main runway was five miles away. A five-hundred-yard-long blackened scar was plowed through the woods on the other side of the airport. Bits and pieces of glass, plastic, and metal debris from the crash still sparkled in the distance.

"We can wait for darkness, if you want. But I think I can get to the house, put a bug on the phone line, and get back without detection," Ulland said.

Carrara looked up. Ulland was studying the open field through his binoculars.

"The grass is tall enough so that if I keep down nobody in the house will spot me." The TS operative grinned. "Might be able to put a pickup on one of the downstairs windows."

Carrara studied the approach across the field through his binoculars. The grass was tall enough. "I'll cover you from here. Anything goes wrong, I want you out of there on the double."

"Gotcha," Ulland said. He went back to the van for his equipment.

Takako Kunihiro and Masao Yakota, driving a white Toyota van with dark windows and identical to the one that was following McGarvey, made a second cautious pass by the driveway to the farmhouse Edward Reid had come to. Beside the fact that Reid was rabidly anti-Japanese, they were only interested in him because McGarvey was. They'd had a difficult moment when McGarvey had broken off tailing Reid and had headed back into the city. It was obvious that he knew he was being followed, so Hamagachi and Korekiyo, driving the lead unit designated Sand Dollar, had kept with him. They now knew that they were of more interest to McGarvey than Reid was. It told them something.

"Nothing," Yakota said.

"I agree. Find out where Sand Dollar is, and if they need our help we'll join them, or we will return to the embassy," Kunihiro instructed.

For the first time Carrara wished he had a weapon. From where he stood within the woods he could see where Ulland had entered the tall grass, but he could not spot him now. If Reid were involved with the Dulles crash, and if he were somehow involved with the former East German intelligence service, they would not take kindly to being spied upon. Especially if Colonel Mueller were here. The man was an assassin and would be armed.

Ulland popped up at the far edge of the clearing, about ten yards from the back of the house, and keeping low hurried the rest of the way to where the phone line came in.

Carrara studied the back of the house through the binoculars. Because of the angle of the sun there was nothing to be seen in any of the windows, either downstairs or upstairs. Nor was there any movement anywhere on the property that he could see.

Ulland removed the cover from the telephone junction box on the side of the house, did something to the wires inside, and replaced the cover. Next he reached up and attached something to one of the windows and then melted out of sight back into the tall grass.

The entire operation at the back of the house had taken less than sixty seconds, and Carrara breathed a sigh of relief.

Mueller stood perfectly still ten yards behind and to the left of the man watching the back of the house through binoculars. The second man had probably placed a bug on the phone line and possibly a sensitive microphone on the dining room window and had started back across the field.

Their van had made two passes on the highway and then had not come back. This was the only vulnerable approach, and Mueller had come up to wait for them. He did not think they were FBI. The Bureau conducted operations on a much larger scale. And except for the white Toyota van that had also made a couple of passes, no other vehicles of any interest had gone by. If they were CIA, however, they were working out of their charter, which made this a rogue action. Reid must have been mistaken about the Saturn.

He'd gotten two clear looks at both men, and he was satisfied that neither of them were Kirk McGarvey, the only man he had any cause to fear.

He raised up to sniff the air. A confrontation was coming between them. He didn't know how he knew it, but he felt that somehow they would meet, that their destinies were intertwined. Melodrama, he thought. But the feeling was strong, and growing stronger.

"This is David Kennedy."

"Sam Varelis, National Transportation Safety Board. I'm calling from Washington for Kirk McGarvey."

"Mr. McGarvey is not here."

"I'm trying to reach him. Can you help?"

Kennedy hesitated. "Mr. McGarvey is no longer in our employ. Has this anything to do with the accident last week?"

Varelis wanted to talk to Mac, but Kennedy was the ultimate responsible party. "This is an unofficial call, Mr. Kennedy. Can you tell me what happened with McGarvey? Have you been pressured by someone here in Washington?"

"If this isn't an official call, then what do you want?"

"I'm trying to save lives."

Again Kennedy hesitated. "So am I."

"Where is he?"

"You're a friend?"

"Yes, he's a friend, so far as I'd trust him with my life. Or anyone else's."

"I don't know where he is. But the Attorney General is going to issue a warrant for his arrest."

"On what charge?"

"Industrial espionage and obstruction of justice. I just received the call."

"That's bullshit," Varelis blurted.

"I agree," Kennedy said. "Have you come up with something?"

"I think there's a possibility that your Dulles crash, and the accident in '90, were not accidents."

"What have you found?"

"Both crashes were caused by port engine failures. The exact same failures, which caused the same structural damage to the wings. That's nearly impossible."

"Can you be more specific?"

"I'm faxing you the material. But Mac has to be informed."

"I'll see what I can do. How can I reach you?"

Varelis gave him a number. "Be quick about it, Mr. Kennedy."

"I will, believe me," Kennedy assured him.

The snow muffled Mueller's footsteps as he came up directly behind the man waiting next to the tree. At the last moment Carrara turned.

Mueller pushed him back against the tree and drove the stiletto through his throat hard enough to sever his spinal cord at the base of his skull and penetrate the tree trunk, pinning him like a bug on a specimen card.

Carrara tried desperately to fight back, but Mueller held him in place until his body finally went limp, then propped his legs under him so that the knife through his throat would temporarily hold him upright.

The second man suddenly rose up from the grass at the edge of the clearing twenty feet away and charged like a bull in an arena.

Mueller languidly turned toward him and raised his left arm as if to ward off a blow. At the last possible moment he reached up with his right and yanked the stiletto out of Carrara's throat. He stepped quickly to the left, inside Ulland's guard, and plunged the blade into the man's chest, just below his left breast.

THIRTY-THREE

Reid was shaken to the core. "I know this one." Mueller had brought both IDs down to the house. "Phillip Carrara, was he someone important?"

"He was Deputy Director of Operations. The third most important man at Langley."

"What about the other one?"

"I don't know. Probably a technician from the Technical Services Division. But you know what this means. There's going to be an all-out manhunt."

Mueller shook his head. "I don't think so."

"What the fuck are you talking about? Weren't you listening? We're done! Everything is down the tubes. My life . . . everything. It's all over!"

"Not unless you fall apart. They weren't here officially."

"How can you be so sure?"

"Think about it, Reid. Does the CIA work this way? You said they didn't. If you were under investigation the FBI would have brought a team out here, not the CIA. These two were freelancing for somebody. McGarvey."

"They'll be missed."

"Yes, they will," Mueller said mildly. "But I'll take care of it."

Reid wanted to believe everything was okay. But like Zerkel he was on the verge of a breakdown. "How?"

"Leave it to me. In the meantime I want you to get ready to get out of here. You're going to go home to resume your normal activities until Sunday."

"Normal activities?" Reid looked at the German as if he were crazy.

"That's what you want, isn't it?"

Reid opened his mouth, then closed it.

"I'll be back in an hour. Be here."

Mueller donned a pair of thin leather gloves, pocketed the wallets, and went outside. From the back porch he studied the woods across the clearing. There was no sign that anything had happened, nor, from where he stood, could he see the van parked at the end of the dirt track. The forecast was for more snow sometime this evening and tomorrow morning. If it was heavy enough the van's tracks would be covered. He removed the bug from the telephone junction box at the side of the house, and the pickup from the dining room window, then crossed the field on the same path Ulland had used to sneak down from the woods.

The gray windowless Dodge van was equipped with sensitive electronic eavesdropping equipment, some of it low-lux cameras and infrared-sensitive recording devices used for nighttime surveillance operations. One rack contained telephone-tap receivers, tape recorders, and tracing apparatuses. Another contained two-way communications radios, at least two of which were high-speed burst encryption devices designed to maintain up- and down-links with satellites. Still another contained sophisticated computer equipment that could be patched into any number of bases. Mueller had seen or heard of a lot of this. His KGB training had been the best, and during his six months in the States he had gleaned information about such equipment then in the developmental stage at the National Security Agency. One of the tape recorders had been used. He switched it on.

"Thank you for calling the *Lamplighter*. How may I direct your call?" a woman said. "Let me speak with Mr. Reid," Mueller's own voice answered.

He rewound the entire message and erased it. They'd probably had a tap on Reid's Georgetown house this morning. There'd been a two-ring delay before the call had been rolled over to the *Lamplighter* office. Next he went searching for the trace to the Sterling farmhouse, finding it without problem, and erasing any evidence of it from the computer memory. He could find no indication that anything had been sent back to Langley.

He drove the van to the end of the dirt track and loaded the two bodies in back. Then he covered what blood had splashed on the snow and the drag marks from the bodies. By morning all traces of what happened would be hidden until a meltoff and then would be washed away. Mueller got behind the wheel of the van, drove it around to the garage behind the farmhouse, and went back inside.

"How is Louis doing with removing his safeguards?" he asked Reid.

"He says he's working on it. I saw you put the van in the garage. It can't stay there. Sooner or later it'll be discovered."

"That's right. When we leave I'll take it up to Baltimore and dump it."

"If you're stopped, or if someone sees you, it'll be all over."

"That's what you're paying me for. Before Sunday I want an additional two million dollars deposited into my Channel Islands account. Will this be a problem?"

Reid looked at him sharply, but then shook his head.

"I'll take the cash you brought for Louis as well."

"I understand. What about the last three repeaters?"

"I'll take care of them tomorrow." Mueller stepped closer. "You understand what I am capable of, Reid. If something happens and the authorities come after me, nothing on this earth will stop me from getting to you."

"I'd be a fool to breathe a word—"

"Believe me," Mueller said softly.

Reid's eyes widened. He nodded. "I do," he said.

"Bridge, CIC."

"CIC, aye," the *FF Cook*'s second officer answered.

"I've got two airborne incoming, bearing one-seven-zero, twenty-seven miles out, speed five hundred knots."

"Can you say type of aircraft and altitude?"

"Sir, they look like F/A-18 Hornets, at two thousand feet. They've illuminated us."

"Ours?"

"I don't think so, Mr. Boyle. They're coming from the northeast. I'd guess Tanegashima."

"Stand by."

"Aye, aye."

Ensign Tim Boyle called the captain on the growler phone. "This is Boyle, Captain. We have a pair of incoming aircraft that CIC thinks is Japanese."

"Have the *Barbey* and *Thorn* been notified?"

"Not yet, sir."

"Do it. I'm on my way."

"Aye, aye, Captain." Boyle hung up and called their

sister ship, the *FF Barbey,* first. They too were painting the incoming fighter/interceptors, and they'd already informed the *DD Thorn,* thirteen thousand yards southwest.

Captain Zimmerman showed up on the bridge a minute later, his utility blues rumpled as if he'd slept in them. "Get me Jim Otter on the *Barbey,*" he told Boyle. He called CIC on the growler. "This is the captain. How far out are they?"

"A little under twelve miles, sir. Should be overhead in ninety seconds. But they've dropped to below five hundred feet."

"Any chance they're ours?"

"Negative, Captain. ELINT has intercepted a transmission to the aircraft from Tanegashima."

"What'd they say?"

"It's encrypted. We're working on it."

Zimmerman hung up the growler phone and accepted a handset from Boyle. "Jim, we'd better stand by battle stations."

"It'll be provocative."

"Overflying us in the early morning without first establishing a comms link is aggressive enough for me. Especially now. Mike Hanrahan's got his hands full."

"Has anyone tried talking to them, or to Tanegashima?" Lieutenant Commander Otter asked.

"ELINT picked up a transmission from their base. As soon as it's decrypted and translated we'll have a better idea."

"Could take awhile, Adam."

"We're here to escort the *Thorn*. We're not going to act like sitting ducks."

"You're the boss," Otter said at the same moment the two Japanese Air Self Defense Force fighter/interceptors screamed overhead and CIC called back.

As soon as the Japanese submarine had gone deep and faded from sonar detection, the *Thorn* had gone to battle stations. The arrival of the two Japanese fighter/interceptors had not improved anyone's disposition.

"They just passed over the *Barbey,* ten thousand yards and closing," Sattler in CIC reported.

"Same drill as before," Hanrahan told his XO. "If they want to get close enough to trigger our guns, then so be it."

Ryder didn't argue. He gave the order.

Forty seconds later the ASDF Hornets passed port and starboard of the *Thorn* just outside the Phalanx's Vulcan cannon aiming and firing radar envelope.

"They're making wide turns. Looks like they'll come back for another pass," Sattler said.

"Did they drop anything into the water?" Hanrahan asked.

"Negative."

"Anything from sonar yet?"

"Nothing, Captain. We lost them at fifteen hundred feet, and nothing's showed up since. But he's not supposed to be able to dive that deep."

"No breakup noises?"

"Negative."

"Well, we're getting another lesson in Japanese technology," Hanrahan said. "We'll stay on this course and speed. Sooner or later he's going to have to come up for air."

"Meteorology says the winds might be diminishing for the next few hours. We might be able to send the choppers up."

"Good idea. Meantime, anything else out there?"

"Not a thing."

"Keep a sharp eye. If I'm right they'll send out another Orion for station keeping."

"What's going on, Skipper?" Sattler asked.

"Don, I wish the hell I knew," Hanrahan replied.

McGarvey pulled up across the street from the CIA safe house in Falls Church where Carrara had placed Dominique. The neighborhood was well maintained, each large house set back on a half-acre of carefully tended lawns and trees. According to Phil this place had been owned by a drug lord and had been acquired by the Bureau of

Alcohol, Tobacco, and Firearms when the man took his fall. It had been transferred to the CIA's inventory five years ago.

There was little traffic, and nothing seemed out of the ordinary here, yet McGarvey hesitated. He was so tired his hands shook when he lit a cigarette. At times he saw spots in front of his eyes. He glanced in the rearview mirror.

At one point he'd realized there were two identical white Toyota vans leapfrogging behind him as he drove around Washington. But when he'd tried to double back, they disappeared. Although he'd managed to get them off his tail, they'd also shaken him. It was his fault, but such sloppiness could get him killed. Whatever else happened he desperately needed a few hours sleep. Someplace safe.

On the way out here he'd stopped at a gas station to telephone Carrara. But there'd been no answer at his house. Not even the answering machine was on. It was troubling.

He rolled down the window and tossed out the cigarette before he drove across the street and up the driveway to the house, parking in front. Dominique, dressed in UCLA sweatpants and shirt, met him at the door. She looked concerned.

"Has something happened, Kirk?" she asked.

"I need some rest."

Dominique took him by the arm and led him inside. "Are you hungry?"

"Yeah."

She smiled. "Bacon and eggs okay?"

"Sure."

She sat him at the kitchen counter and poured him a cognac, then started the food. "I've been going crazy not knowing what's going on."

"Have you seen Phil Carrara?"

"Not since he brought me out here."

"I'm surprised you agreed. Have you talked to David, or to your brother?"

"Nobody," she said, her voice suddenly husky. "Phil

told us about your past. Everything. What you've done for everybody, and how you've been treated."

"I'll live," McGarvey replied. He no longer had the strength, or the stomach, to fight her. In many respects she was like his ex-wife Kathleen. Certain of herself and where she fit. Certain of the difference between right and wrong, between what was fair and what was unjust. Certain that he was something to avoid if at all possible. The septic tank pump-out man was a necessity, but you didn't invite him to dinner, especially if it was impossible for him to change out of his workclothes. They were right.

"He told us about your parents—"

"Leave it," McGarvey ordered harshly.

Dominique drew a sharp breath. "I'm sorry."

"Phil had no business telling you any of that. I have a job to do, and when it's finished, however it turns out, I'll leave and you can get on with your life."

Dominique shook her head.

"Your brother is right. All of you are. David should never have come to me."

"Where would we be if he hadn't?" Dominique flared.

"Not hiding from your job and your friends, afraid for your life."

"We'd probably be dead."

"No," McGarvey disagreed.

Dominique turned to him. "Do you honestly believe that everything would have turned out okay, Kirk? Can you sit there and tell me that people wouldn't die?"

"Nothing I've ever done has made the slightest difference."

"Oh no, you're wrong," Dominique blurted. "Just because you've had friends betray you all of your life doesn't mean you were at fault. The CIA wouldn't have kept coming back for your help."

"You don't know what you're talking about."

"Yes I do. Or at least now I know how badly we treated you."

McGarvey got unsteadily to his feet. "Stay here until

Monday morning. Don't call anybody. Don't show yourself." He started for the door.

Dominique came after him. "Goddamn you, Kirk. You're not going to walk out on me! I won't allow it!"

"Stay away from me."

"I can't," she cried. "Goddamn you, goddamn you to hell, can't you understand what I'm saying? I love you."

She'd caught him totally off guard. For a moment he basked in a warm glow, but then his past came rushing in like a load of bricks. "That'd be the biggest mistake you've ever made."

"I'll deal with my mistakes. You handle your own," she said pragmatically. "As you say, you have a job to do, and you'll do it. But afterward you'll have to deal with me."

"You don't know what the hell you're talking about."

"Yes I do. And when I want something I usually get it. Right now you're going to sit down and eat something, and then get some sleep. You're doing nobody any good in the shape you're in."

"I've got a lousy track record. Did Phil tell you that?"

"Your first wife was an alcoholic who drank herself to death. And your second wife loved you but couldn't stand living with someone in your profession."

"Could you?"

"I don't know," Dominique said honestly. "But I'm going to try."

"Did he tell you about Marta?"

"They weren't after her. She was in the wrong place at the wrong time. It can happen to anybody."

"It was no accident what happened to my wife and daughter."

"Nor was it your fault, Kirk," Dominique insisted. "Stop beating yourself to death with it. Ever since you found out about your parents you've been driving yourself."

"Stop," he warned.

"No, I won't. What your parents did wasn't your fault either."

McGarvey had to get out of there. He couldn't take much more of it. A thousand demons rose up inside his gut, threatening to blot out his sanity. A hundred voices pleading for help rang in his ears. And in his mind's eye he could see the faces of every one of his kills.

"Grow up, for God's sake," Dominique said. "Deal with it!"

"I'm an assassin. Is that what you want?"

"You're a soldier, and you're on the front line. If you have nightmares about the people you've killed, do you have pleasant dreams about all the lives you've saved?"

He stepped back. "I don't want you hurt," he whispered.

"Then don't leave me, Kirk. Please." She came into his arms. For a long moment he did nothing, but then he held her, and she let out a pent-up sigh. "I can help, if you'll let me," she said.

"It's bad."

"I know."

"Worse than you can imagine."

She looked up at him. "Then you'll need all your strength. First something to eat, and afterward sleep."

"I'll call David."

"After you get some rest," Dominique insisted. She made him sit down again, and she went back to the stove.

He finished his drink as he watched her cook. He was frightened for her safety. She was naïve. No matter how bad she believed the situation was, she could not imagine the savagery rampant in the world. He was also afraid of his own growing feelings. Afraid that he was falling in love with her, and what it would do to both of them.

Dominique came into the bedroom to wake him up. She brought a cigarette and a cup of strong coffee laced with brandy. He only vaguely remembered eating the breakfast she'd prepared for him and then allowing himself to be led upstairs to one of the bedrooms where he'd fallen asleep. At one point he'd awakened, and she'd been in the room, watching him. He fell back asleep to her smile.

"What time is it?" he asked.

"Five. You only got a few hours, but David phoned and he says he's got something important."

McGarvey sat up and took the coffee and smoke from her. "What's happened?"

"I don't know." She handed him the phone.

"Are you feeling any better?" Kennedy asked.

"A little. Are you back in Portland?"

"Until Sunday. But Sam Varelis called. He's looking for you. He thinks you might be right after all about the Dulles accident and the American Airlines incident in '90. Socrates is looking over the material he sent."

"Sabotage?"

"That's the implication, but there's nothing definite other than the coincidence that both accidents happened in precisely the same manner. With precisely the same damage."

"What's Sir Malcolm have to say?"

"He tends to agree with you and Varelis, but we're still coming up empty-handed. There was nothing wrong with either of those engines. Nothing wrong with any engine we've tested. Absolutely nothing."

"But it's there."

"Yes," Kennedy said. "But we don't have a thing to take to the FAA or the airlines. And we're still scheduled for Sunday."

"Your AOG teams have found nothing?"

"That's right. We're back at square one, except for you. We got word that the Attorney General's office has issued a warrant for your arrest. The FBI called, wanted to know where you were."

"We expected that, David. What'd you tell them?"

"That you no longer worked for us."

"They refused to help?"

"Nothing they can do," Kennedy said bitterly. "When you look at it from their viewpoint, they're right. We don't have a single shred of evidence that anyone is gunning for us. At least not to the extent of sabotaging our airplanes."

"Al agrees?"

"He's changed since Dulles." Kennedy was guarded. "The accident took a lot out of him. I think that no matter what happens or doesn't happen on Sunday he'll get out of the business. George is quitting too. Everything is different. Maybe we should have cooperated with the Japanese after all, like Boeing did. There'd be no reason for them to come after us."

"If it is the Japanese. Might be someone else."

"The possibilities are endless," Kennedy said resignedly. "Everything is going to hell."

"What is it?" McGarvey asked.

"Chance is gone."

"What do you mean gone? Has she left you?"

"No note, if that's what you mean. She's just gone. She didn't come home last night."

"Did she pack a bag?"

"None of her things are missing so far as I can tell."

"Have you tried to reach Yamagata today?" McGarvey asked.

"He checked out of the Hyatt. Nobody has heard from him," Kennedy said. "Do you think . . . she's run off with him?"

"I think he's kidnapped her."

"Why?" Kennedy demanded.

"He wants your cooperation."

"I haven't heard a thing."

"Either that or she heard something or saw something she wasn't supposed to hear or see. Call the Bureau. Tell them she's missing."

"They'll think it's a put-up job."

"Doesn't matter. Call them anyway," McGarvey said. "It'll put them on record. Whatever they think they'll at least have to go through the motions."

Kennedy hesitated. "I don't know if I believe it myself."

"Get a hold of yourself, David. Your wife didn't run off with Yamagata. She would have confronted you with it if your marriage is that bad. She would have hurt you with it."

"I don't know . . ."

"I do," McGarvey said bitterly. "I've been there."

"What the hell are we supposed to do?"

"If there's anything wrong with those engines, Sir Malcolm and Socrates will find out about it. In the meantime save me a seat on Sunday's flight."

"You'll never get past security."

"Leave that up to me."

"Yeah," Kennedy said dispiritedly.

McGarvey broke the connection and tried Carrara's house again. Dominique was watching him, wide-eyed. There was no answer. Next he called Sam Varelis at the NTSB.

"I just talked with David Kennedy. Any chance of grounding the fleet?"

"The FAA wouldn't go along with it, because we don't have anything solid to give them. Do you know the Bureau is looking for you?"

"I've heard," McGarvey said dryly. "I need a favor, Sam."

"Name it."

"Phil Carrara was placed on administrative leave because he was helping me. Now he's disappeared. Can you make a few discreet inquiries?"

"Will do," Varelis said. "Where can I reach you?"

"You can't, Sam. I'll call you at home tonight."

"Make it here at the office. I have a feeling the next few days are going to be long ones."

Captain Kiyoda and his XO stood behind the chief sonarman watching the displays on his console. Because of their extreme depth, targets on the surface were hard to pick up and even more difficult to identify with any certainty. But their equipment was better than that of any navy's, and Nakayama was the best of the best.

"Here's the first dipping buoy, sir." Nakayama pointed to the display on the right. "Eighteen thousand meters out. From a LAMPS III, I think. Below the seasonal thermocline, but still well above the permanent layer. Broad-band processing, I'd guess, which means he's still searching for us."

"The second?" Kiyoda asked.

"We had it briefly, now it's gone, *Kan-cho*. But look here, there are two other surface targets. Very hard to analyze."

"Try."

The display on the left side of the sonar console showed the measured and predicted sound transmission paths based on the salinity, temperature, and currents at various levels above them. The display on the right made corrections for the conditions. What remained were the theoretical contacts. Under ideal conditions the targets would paint as distinct points, or a series of dots, from which the operator-assisted electronic equipment could process real-time intelligence: the type of ship, its speed, and bearing. Now the display looked like a swiftly flowing waterfall through which they had to look.

"Definitely surface ships, sir, not just noise." Nakayama circled one of the possible contacts with a grease pencil. "Sierra-One-Four. Same course and speed as Sierra-Zero-Nine. Much smaller. A lot less noise. Maybe a frigate."

"American?" Kiyoda asked.

"I think so, sir. The other is much weaker, but it seems to be the same type of ship, on the same course and speed."

"Seventh Fleet sent out reinforcements," Minori suggested.

"It would appear so," Kiyoda replied. "Have you designated the second target?"

"Sierra-One-Five." Nakayama circled the second indistinct target. "They're looking for us, *Kan-cho.*"

"Will they be successful?"

"Not unless they get lucky, or we make a mistake," Nakayama said, and he stiffened.

Kiyoda smiled at Nakayama's sudden embarrassment for questioning his captain's judgment and ability. "On this boat, *Nakayama-san,* we are dedicated only to the truth. Do you understand why?"

"Hai, Kan-cho," the sonarman replied without looking up.

"What are the surface conditions?"

"Still rough, sir. Judging from the noise I'd say they're dealing with seven-meter waves, maybe bigger. Can't be very comfortable when their search pattern brings them abeam the seas."

"Can't be easy on the helicopter pilots either," Minori said.

"There may have been a break in the weather. The surface noises were starting to die down a couple hours ago."

"They'll recall the helicopters," Kiyoda said. He walked across to control and brought the surface ships' plots up on his command console display.

Minori came with him. "They're keeping to the same baseline," he pointed out.

"They've made the assumption that we're heading for Okinawa. As long as they continue the pattern, their speed of advance will be slow." Kiyoda keyed the numbers into his computer, getting his answer immediately. "Less than eight knots."

"If we're careful not to exceed twelve knots there is a very good chance we will not be detected," Minori said.

"They will abandon the search at some point."

"Hai, Kan-cho, but if we have a few hours' head start we could get well south of them, placing us between them and Okinawa."

"And then, Ikuo?" Kiyoda asked.

"That is for you to decide, but it would give us the superior position."

"For a shooting solution?"

"Hai."

"Or to ascend suddenly to seventy meters, thus announcing our presence?"

Minori grinned. *"Hai, Kan-cho.* In that case they might be induced to attack us."

"Indeed," Kiyoda agreed. "Come left to two-zero-zero degrees. Make your speed eleven knots."

"Yo-so-ro. Helm, come left to new course two-zero-zero. Make your speed eleven knots," Minori ordered.

"Aye, coming left to new course two-zero-zero degrees. Engineering answering eleven knots."

"Very well," Kiyoda said. He went back into sonar.

"The second dipping buoy has disappeared, *Kan-cho,"* Nakayama reported.

"As we thought it might. How do you feel?"

The sonarman looked up, surprised. "Sir?"

"The next eight or ten hours might be critical. Are you rested enough to remain alert for that long?"

"Of course."

"The truth now, remember?" Kiyoda reminded gently.

"Hai, Kan-cho, in truth I am well rested."

"Very well. We are changing course and speed to slip away from our pursuers. If we are going to make a mistake, it will come in the next few hours. It is up to you not to lose them. Especially not Sierra-Zero-Nine. And it is up to you to alert us of any change in their search pattern."

Nakayama nodded. "I will do my best, *Kan-cho."*

"That is all anyone can ask," Kiyoda replied.

Mueller stood at the head of the stairs listening to the vagrant sounds of the house. Now that the computer equipment no longer ran twenty-four hours a day, he'd come to appreciate the quiet. To each operation that would succeed there came a point at which a symmetry became obvious. Like now, he thought. Coming here from Europe had been the left side. Accomplishing Reid's task and leaving would be the right. They were at the pivot point.

Louis came to the bedroom door. "Are we ready to leave?" he asked.

"First I need to make certain that you removed your safeguard."

"It's already done. I told Mr. Reid."

"Show me."

"It's okay with me if you guys want to make a big production out of this," Louis said. "I just don't want to miss my plane, man."

"You won't," Mueller assured him.

Louis switched on one of the terminals, brought up a phone line, and got into the FBI's mainframe, his fingers flying over the keyboard. "I had the program on a coded timer," he explained, pulling up a block of fingerprint records from the Identification Division. "At the beginning of each six-hour period, plus or minus five minutes, had the recognition code not been entered, this is what would have happened." He hit a key, and suddenly the screen went red, with the word WARNING flashing on and off.

"This is not happening now?" Mueller asked.

"Just here because I pulled the program, like I said." Louis chuckled.

The red screen was replaced with photographs of Reid and Mueller, with a complete narrative description of everything they'd done, and what they'd planned.

"Your program has been erased?" Mueller asked.

"Yeah," Louis said. "Watch." He brought the FBI's logo back up on screen, hit a series of keys, and this time he was denied access.

"IMPROPER ACCESS CODE."

"Very good," Mueller said, and he plunged the blade of the stiletto to the hilt in the back of Zerkel's neck, at the base of his skull, severing his spinal cord.

Zerkel flopped forward, his head hitting the computer screen, and within a few seconds his body stopped shivering.

Mueller withdrew the blade and carefully wiped it clean on the back of Zerkel's sweat-stained shirt. "What do you think about that?" he said.

A messenger came down from the FBI director's office and handed John Whitman the warrant. "Mr. Harding asks that you proceed with caution."

"Will do," Whitman said.

The District of Columbia police had agreed to cooperate. Every hotel and motel within its jurisdiction would be canvassed. The CIA had sent over a recent file photograph of McGarvey. If he was a registered guest anywhere within the district, under whatever name, he would be found. Every Bureau office around the country would get copies of the warrant, and the photograph would coordinate their efforts with local and state police units. The Portland office was especially on the alert, and Guerin Airplane Company would be the subject of a massive, but very quiet, surveillance operation. Outside the country, the CIA would conduct its own search. It would only be a matter of time before he was picked up, with or without his cooperation, Whitman assured himself.

They left at dark. Mueller went first with the van and headed up to Baltimore to get rid of the bodies. From there he planned on flying to New York where he would place repeaters at La Guardia and JFK airports before returning to Washington. Sometime Saturday he would place the final repeater at Dulles. Reid left a half-hour later, closing down the house. Zerkel's body was buried in the garbage pit in back, and within twenty-four hours a crew would remove the computer equipment and dispose of it. Mueller thought it was a weak link, although he agreed that Reid knew what he was doing and that the step was necessary. Sunday was the day that the United States would wake up to what the world was really all about.

John Whitman called Howard Ryan at the CIA. "We're trying to locate Mr. Phillip Carrara. We'd like to speak with him about Mr. McGarvey."

"Have you tried his home?"

"There appears to be nobody there. I thought you might be able to help."

"Just a moment," Ryan said. He came back on the

line several seconds later. "You understand that he is presently on administrative leave."

"Yes."

"He may have left the city. Nobody has heard from him since this morning. In any event I don't know if he would be terribly cooperative. He and McGarvey are friends."

"Yes, Mr. Ryan, it's one of the reasons we'd like to interview him."

"I'll see what I can do. But I think that such an interview would have to be conducted here. We'd have to monitor it. Could be that questions of national security would arise."

"I agree. You'll let me know?"

"As soon as," Ryan said.

What a pompous ass, Whitman thought.

"He's gone," Sam Varelis told McGarvey.

"Gone where?"

"No one knows, Mac. He's just gone. His wife is up in Montpelier, and the FBI and CIA are looking for him. Should I dig deeper?"

"If you can without making waves," McGarvey replied, but he was worried.

THIRTY-FOUR

The ocean sounded as if it were just outside the bedroom window. At any other time the pounding surf would have been soothing. But not tonight. Now it sounded ominous, the big waves coming as they did from some distant storm. Maybe even as far away as Japan. Chance's head felt as if it was about to split open, and she was frightened. They'd given her some drug in Portland, and she couldn't remember much after that, except that what had begun as some sort of crazy adventure had turned into a nightmare.

"How are you feeling?" Yamagata asked from the doorway.

Chance turned. "Where are we?" Her voice sounded slurred to her.

"Someplace safe. And now you're going to have to help us." He sat down beside her on the edge of the bed. "Actually, it's your husband you can help. If you still want to."

"I don't understand. Who are you?"

"A businessman—"

"No, damn you," Chance cried. She rose up and tried to strike him, but he grabbed her arms and eased her back.

"I was sent here to make a deal for Guerin. We want to merge with them."

"Businessmen don't take advantage of women."

Yamagata laughed. "I think it was you who tried to take advantage of me."

"You used drugs on me."

"The effects will pass, and in a few hours you'll feel better. But you must believe me when I tell you that I am here to save lives. That is very important, Chance. Nothing else matters for the moment. It's something you're going to have to help us accomplish. Are you listening to me?"

"They'll stop you."

"Who will stop us?"

"McGarvey. He warned me."

"Yes, I know. But why did your husband hire him? What is the company afraid of?"

Chance turned away. Her head was pounding. "The accidents. Somebody is doing it."

"Who?"

"I don't know. David's afraid. They all are. Even the old man."

"You'll talk to your husband," Yamagata said, his voice a long way off. "We'll change it."

The weather had been spotty throughout the day and late afternoon, with the sun breaking through the clouds for as much as an hour at a time. In the lee of Okinerabu's east shore, the *Fair Winds* was protected from the brunt of the winds and seas rolling across the East China Sea. But as soon as they'd cleared the island's northern tip for Tokuno thirty miles to the northeast they were hit by the full force.

Her full-keeled displacement hull bit into the steep seas, her rail forced well into the water by the forty-knot-plus winds, her stubby, over-stayed mast supporting the three sails of the cutter rig with brute strength. For a full minute or two Stan Liskey reveled in the storm, ten tons of boat straining against the thick tiller in his hand. But then he glanced at Carol.

"How're you doing, kid?" he shouted.

"Make that Harlem at night. Times Square would be too easy," she answered. Her face was strained, and her knuckles were white from a death grip on a stanchion.

A heavier gust hit them, beam on, driving the lee rail even deeper, the mast visibly bending. She stayed over for a long time. Liskey, on the windward side, was standing almost upright, his feet braced against the lee cockpit well, the pressure on the tiller very pronounced. But then the wind eased and *Fair Winds'* rail came up, water streaming off her decks.

"Time to pull in some sails?" Carol shouted hopefully over the wind screaming in the rigging.

"The boat can take it."

"Good! But I don't think I can, Stan. What's there to prove?"

She was right, of course. This weather would only last another few days at most. But when it cleared he wanted to be much closer to the Japanese south island of Kyushu. If they turned back now, to hide again behind Okinerabu, they'd be stuck there. On the other hand, if they could make it to Tokuno by tonight or early morning, and Amami-O-Shima tomorrow afternoon, they'd be in striking distance of a lot more interesting cruising grounds.

The seas were running above twenty-footers, but they were not breaking yet, and they were on the beam, not the nose. He studied the strait ahead of them. On a clear day Tokuno would be visible from here, he expected. But not now. There was too much spray and mist in the air. Too much haze.

He glanced at the compass. They were on course. When he engaged the windvane it would keep them there. And the Magellan GPS would unfailingly tell them where they were. If not the GPS, then they'd dead reckon. They were in no danger, just discomfort.

They shook off a smaller gust, water flying everywhere, and the boat shuddered.

"I'm going below," Carol shouted.

"Wait, I need you here," Liskey told her. "I'm going to pull the headsail the rest of the way in, then put a reef in the staysail and another in the main."

"Are we going to turn back?"

"We'll see how we handle the weather once I reduce sail. But I'd like to make Tokuno sometime tonight." He studied her anxious expression. "Unless you'd feel more comfortable back at anchor."

She didn't answer at first. Instead she looked out toward the weather, watching the big seas marching in toward them. Each wave would rise up on the port beam, as if it would engulf them, but then the boat lifted up, almost as if she were a woman lifting her skirts, and the wave would pass beneath them, leaving a huge trough over which they seemed to teeter.

"Hell yes, I'd rather be at anchor," she shouted, turning back to him. "But you tell me, Stan, are we all right out here like this?"

"If we were racing . . ."

"We're not, are we?"

Liskey shook his head. "Something might break, but

we're okay." He grinned, a sudden overwhelming wave of love for her washing through him. "It'll be a lot more comfortable when I get the sails reefed."

"Will it make much difference in our speed?"

"Not much," Liskey assured her. He moved forward so that she could slip in beside him and take the tiller. "I'll signal when I'm ready. Then turn her into the wind so I can get the sails in."

"Thanks," she said.

"I love you," Liskey shouted.

"Yeah, that too," she replied wryly. "But thanks."

Kirk McGarvey was a deeply troubled man, Dominique thought, watching him as he came awake. Different from most other men she'd ever known. In some respects like her brother: strong, self-assured, with a bit of a chip on his shoulder.

"It's morning," he said, opening his eyes. Gray light came through the windows.

"I didn't want to wake you."

"Did you get any sleep? Or did you stand guard all night?"

"All I've done out here is sleep," she said. "Do you know that you dreamed?"

"Yes."

"Was it about your work?"

"That, and other things. But mostly about the people I've been . . . involved with. Some of them didn't seem too bad afterward. Just people trying to live their lives," McGarvey said distantly. "When the rules change it's hard to know what's right. There's never any easy answers. No black and white. It's not what you think."

"I don't know if I can believe that," Dominique said. "Whoever brought down the airplane at Dulles is evil."

"Maybe they were soldiers like you say I am."

"Not like you. I can't believe that you've killed innocent people."

McGarvey smiled wanly. "Tell that to the Russians," he said. He reached over and kissed her. "I have to go."

She stayed in bed while he showered and dressed. He kissed her again before he left. At the window she watched him drive away, and when his car was gone, she placed a telephone call to a Washington number. Last night he'd told her everything, because there was no reason for her not to know, and because she'd promised to stay put.

"Good morning," a woman said. "Thank you for calling the *Lamplighter*. How may I direct your call?"

"I'd like to speak to Mr. Reid, please. Tell him it's Dominique Kilbourne, from the Airplane Manufacturers and Airline Association."

Reid, a guarded note in his voice, came on a moment later.

"Good morning, Ms. Kilbourne. What can I do for you?"

"You can buy me lunch today."

"Lunch?"

"Yes, Mr. Reid. I happen to agree with you about the Japanese. I've been reading your newsletter lately, and there's something I'd like to ask you. Something the people I represent are concerned about. Very concerned."

"Sounds intriguing. Would you care to give me a hint?"

"Noon," Dominique said. "Shall we say the Rive Gauche?"

"Very well," Reid replied, but it didn't sound as if he was happy about it.

McGarvey left a message at the Russian embassy for Viktor Yemlin. The former Washington *rezident* met him at the coffee shop in the Washington Plaza Hotel a couple of blocks away on Thomas Circle.

"Guerin will not ground the fleet," McGarvey said. "And the President leaves for Tokyo on Sunday, aboard a Guerin 522."

"My hands are tied, Kirk. Believe me. In fact I have orders to return to Moscow."

"Two days, Viktor Pavlovich. Goddammit, I'm trying to avert a disaster here."

Yemlin spread his hands. "What do you want from us?" he asked in frustration. *"Abunai* has been shut down. I'm no longer your case officer, and for all I know the Guerin deal has already been written off."

"If airplanes start crashing your hands won't be clean."

"What's that supposed to mean?"

"The President won't cancel his trip. If Air Force One were to go down, the CIA would turn to the Japanese. But it'd also want to know what part the SUR played. Exactly what *Abunai* did to . . . create the situation in Tokyo."

"We did nothing—"

"When I turn myself in and tell them about Mintori Assurance's part in the 1990 crash, they'll see it differently. You know goddamned well they will, Viktor. I suggest you tell Moscow exactly that."

Yemlin shook his head.

"You people are in this up to your necks, just like we are."

"I'll see what I can do, Kirk." Yemlin sighed. "Call me at my blind number this afternoon."

"The FBI is monitoring that line. We'll meet at Arlington."

General Polunin had a terrific case of heartburn, and nothing that Colonel Lyalin was telling him helped. This time it wouldn't be so easy to pass the buck to Karyagin.

"What's the upshot?" he asked his First Department chief.

"It's lucky for us that Viktor Pavlovich decided to delay his departure from Washington. Otherwise we would be in the dark. There is no basis for any guesswork. We no longer have the assets." Lyalin spread his hands.

"Spare me the economic complaints. What does McGarvey want?"

"Help with their situation. We're reasonably certain that Mintori was involved in the American Airlines crash in 1990, but not the recent accident at Dulles. But both crashes were apparently caused by the same malfunction, which would appear to be a statistical long shot. Someone else has become involved."

"Who?"

"Unknown at this point, and with network *Abunai* inoperative for the moment we're getting no fresh intelligence from Tokyo. That is assuming the second party is also Japanese."

"But we're not certain of even that much," Polunin said. "The fucking fools are willing to sacrifice a billion-dollar aircraft factory because they want to save face."

"We may get lucky. There might not be a connection," Lyalin replied hopefully. "The problem is that Air Force One is a Guerin 522, which President Lindsay will be flying to Tokyo on Sunday. If it goes down we could conceivably be implicated."

"How?"

"McGarvey says he will tell the CIA about *Abunai*'s help identifying Mintori. Langley will want to know why, if we suspected the President's plane was sabotaged, we didn't warn them."

"Why don't we?" Polunin asked.

"I think it's too late, General. We have no other way out except by helping McGarvey. Providing the Kremlin won't change its mind about a retaliatory strike on Japan."

Polunin shook his head. "Even you are not supposed to know about that."

"Everyone knows."

"Can we send *Abunai* to Washington without trouble?"

"I think so."

"Then do it, Colonel. The sooner he talks to McGarvey, the better I'll feel. In the meantime I'll light another fire under Tokyo Station's ass. Its political section is busy, but its field officers aren't."

* * *

Carol Moss slid open the hatch from below and handed Stan Liskey two big mugs of hot beef noodle soup. The weather had closed in, covering the moon, blotting out anything beyond the ship's running lights. Any movement, especially below, was nearly impossible. The fact she'd somehow managed to heat some soup was practically miraculous.

"No need for you to be up here," Liskey shouted. "Stay below out of the wind."

"Unless you want barf all over the cabin sole, I need fresh air," she shouted back. She waited until a wave passed under them, then levered herself over the hatchboards into the cockpit and deftly slammed the hatch.

"How's our track holding up?"

"We'll be out of this soon. From what I could tell on the chart there's at least one good anchorage along Tokuno's south coast in the bight, and a bunch around the hump to the east."

As soon as she hooked on with her safety harness and braced herself against the bulkhead beneath the spray dodger, Liskey handed her a cup of soup. "We'll go for the bight. If the wind shifts it'll give us an easier choice, east or west."

"We're good on this course then." She took a ham and cheese sandwich wrapped in a paper towel from a pocket in her foul-weather gear for him. "Mustard okay?"

"You're amazing."

Carol laughed. "Just don't forget it when the sun is shining and we're on dry land and I burn your toast."

"Never happen."

"Count on it," she said. She started on her soup.

Liskey checked the lines on the Aires windvane that automatically steered the boat, then drank his soup. It was very hot and very good. Despite the increasing wind and waves, and the steadily decreasing temperature, he felt a sense of well-being. He was on his boat with a woman he loved in a time and place of his own choosing, doing exactly what he wanted to be doing. They were in no real danger, although there was always the possibility that a weakened swage on one of the shrouds or stays could fail and the mast would fall down. Or the wind-vane could break, forcing them to hand steer to their anchorage, which was a difficult and very tiring job under these conditions. Or they could hit something tossed off a passing freighter or tanker that was big enough to hole them beneath the waterline. It wasn't an uncommon experience. There'd been cases in which small boats had been sunk in as little as ninety seconds. But even that thought did little to dampen his spirits. They had an automatically inflating life raft well equipped for just such an occurrence. They even carried an emergency position indicating radio beacon—an EPIRB—that would automatically send out a mayday signal to other boats and to high-flying commercial airplanes.

Nothing was foolproof, Liskey told himself. But then neither was life itself. He smiled to himself. A philosopher he wasn't, but out here like this he felt a very strong sense of his own life force in sync with the ebb and flow of life in, on, and above the sea.

"What's so funny?" Carol shouted.

"You'll have me certified and put away if I tell you."

"Let me guess. You love this."

"We're alive." Liskey glanced at the compass and knotlog. They were sailing just east of due north and making better than five knots even under severely reefed sails. He studied their phosphorescent wake aft. The Aires steered an S pattern. "I don't know if I can explain it any better, Carol."

"I think I know what you mean," she replied after a moment or two. "But it's so goddamned macho I don't know if I understand."

"It's easy."

"If you mean that you have to put your life in danger in order to feel alive, you know, like a bungee jumper or something, then I guess you should be committed. Except if that were the criterion our asylums would be crammed to the rafters with men, leaving none of them on the outside. A situation I, for one, wouldn't like."

"Vive la différence."

"Something like that," Carol said. "But I'm not just a passenger on this sailboat. I chose to be here just as you did." She swept an arm toward the darkness around them. "My blood is pumping too, Stan. But it doesn't mean I have to like this part of it. For me sailing across a quiet lagoon with ten knots of wind kicking up nothing more than a ripple is pretty exciting. Gets my blood racing thinking I'd be there with you."

"There aren't many people who could do this."

"Or would," Carol said. "Doesn't make them all bad, just different. And when we drop the hook you let out as big a sigh of relief as the next person."

"A sense of accomplishment."

"Yes, but for me that's a better part than this."

"You can't have that part without first doing this."

She laughed out loud. "What a load of crap, Stan. But here I am." Again she swept an arm toward the darkness beyond. "Even if they were forty-footers, and you chose to be out here, I'd be with you."

Liskey opened his mouth but didn't know what to say.

"Not a particularly nineties thing for me to admit. And Gloria Steinem would probably spit up if she heard me. Fact is, I love you. Nothing's going to change that."

"You never said that before."

She laughed again. "Death-bed confession."

He couldn't take his eyes off her. He wanted to drink her in great draughts. He wanted to absorb her entire body and personality into his. "I love you," he shouted. He raised his head. "I love you," he shouted into the wind. "I love you!"

Yemlin was waiting for McGarvey at Kennedy's tomb in Arlington Cemetery. "A meeting has been arranged."

"With whom?" McGarvey asked. They headed away from the eternal flame. The weather was once again overcast and cold. It looked like more snow.

"Somebody who might be able to help. But listen to me, my old friend. There is no guarantee that he will know anything of value to you. He has been instructed to cooperate. But don't shoot the messenger."

"SUR?"

Yemlin shrugged. "He is *Abunai.*"

"What's his position in the network?"

"No, Mac, he *is Abunai.* The network, except for a few field officers—a very few field officers—is only one man. He has agreed to come from Tokyo to talk with you."

"When, Viktor Pavlovich?"

"He'll be here tonight."

McGarvey stopped the Russian. "That doesn't make sense. There's no way he could get here from Tokyo in such a short time."

"He's coming from Honolulu."

"Are you going to tell me what the hell he's doing there, or am I going to have to wait?"

"You'll have to wait, because I don't know."

"Ms. Kilbourne, you look radiant," Edward R. Reid said.

"That's what I like about mature men. They don't get tongue-tied when they pay a woman a compliment."

"The nineties do seem to have gotten away from us. But the good side is that women like you are doing well, although it puts some of us men at a disadvantage."

"We do our best," Dominique said as she and Reid followed the maître d' to their table. The restaurant was full, as usual for a weekday. People at a couple of tables waved to Reid, but she didn't see any familiar faces. One thing she had caught, though, was Reid's nervousness. Something was bothering him. "How's the *Lamplighter* doing now that you've taken on the Japanese?"

"Circulation is up, as a matter of fact." Reid eyed her speculatively. "Is that what you wanted to talk about?"

"Some of the people I represent are worried. About the Japanese."

"And well they should be," Reid said as they sat down. "Although Boeing seems to be doing well working with them. Problem is there's no telling how long Japan can remain stable. It's been on the brink of bankruptcy since the early nineties. Of course so have we, although we have a depth of resources that they do not."

"You're talking about natural resources?"

"Exactly. Especially oil, which it desperately needs from the Middle East. It's completely dependent on the sea lanes. If its supplies were to be cut for even a short time, it'd suffer."

"There are no threats now that the Soviet Union has broken apart," Dominique said.

The waiter came, and they ordered drinks.

"Haven't you been watching television, or reading newspapers?"

"It's a localized problem. Or do you see it differently, Mr. Reid? Do you think the Russians will retaliate?"

"It could happen. Which would further destabilize the political situation out there." Reid looked across the room as if he were suddenly unsure of himself. As if he were worried that someone was watching them.

"We have a problem."

"With the Japanese?" Reid asked. Two men followed the maître d' across the dining room to a nearby table. They looked like cops.

"One of my companies thinks the Japanese are after them. It's Guerin. They're worried about the accident at Dulles last week. They think it could have been sabotage. And there's been a move by a Japanese consortium to force an unfriendly takeover, which would be easy if Guerin's stocks went down the drain."

Reid moistened his lips. "I've heard the takeover rumors, but nothing about the accident. Is the company sure about the sabotage? The National Transportation Safety Board hasn't made a ruling yet, has it?"

Dominique shook her head. "It's more complicated than that, Mr. Reid. Which is why I decided to ask for your help."

"Please call me Edward. But are you saying that you've come to me on your own initiative, without telling anyone?"

"Not Guerin . . . Edward. I don't want to raise any false hopes. But they're really in trouble." Dominique glanced across the room for effect. "All this is in strict confidence."

"Of course. How can I help?"

"They're so desperate that they've hired an ex-CIA spy. But he's got them so confused that they're starting to believe everyone is after them. There was that American Airlines crash in '90 that McGarvey—he's the spy they hired—thinks was engineered by the Japanese. But the one last week, according to him, was caused by someone right here in this country."

Reid visibly blanched.

"It's stupid, but he's convinced the FBI and probably even the CIA to take a look. But it has to be Japan, don't you think? They're the only ones who have anything to gain if Guerin goes bankrupt."

Their drinks came and they ordered lunch, but Reid was obviously distracted.

"Have you talked to him, this fellow Kirk McGarvey?"

"Of course. He's here in Washington now, as a matter of fact."

"Where's he staying?"

"I don't know. Thing is, Edward, I need your help to convince him and Guerin that it's the Japanese consortium that's after them. Not somebody here. Will you do it?"

For a moment it didn't seem as if Reid would answer her. But then he nodded. "It'll have to wait until after the weekend."

"Oh?"

"I'm flying with the President on Sunday to Tokyo. When I come back I'll be happy to lend a hand."

Ryutaro Teramura looked like a college student, McGarvey thought, not the head of a Russian intelligence-gathering network. His effectiveness stemmed, Yemlin explained, from the fact that he was the number-two most powerful man in the Japanese Socialist Party. They met in an apartment in Arlington.

"I've heard about you," *Abunai* said. "I thought you were inactive."

"Except for this assignment, I am. Now I need your help."

Teramura glanced at Yemlin. "Was it explained why I was in Honolulu when the call came?"

"No," the Russian said.

"It's ironic, but my party sent me to Hawaii to meet the Guerin airplane *America* on Sunday. It's to be a goodwill gesture to show that the government does not back Kamiya's plans."

"Morning Star?" McGarvey asked.

"Yes. The fool wants to somehow embroil Japan in a war with the U.S. Evidently for ultimate economic control of the western Pacific rim."

"Is it possible without Tokyo's cooperation?"

"Sokichi Kamiya is a powerful man. A lot depends on how your government reacts."

"To what?" McGarvey asked.

Teramura peered at him through rimless glasses. "I don't know. But whatever it is will happen very soon."

"Sunday?"

"Possibly, Mr. McGarvey. But I think the issue with Guerin may be separate, and possibly just as troubling to Kamiya as it is to you. Are you aware that Mintori Assurance has a connection with one of Guerin's subcontractors here in the States?"

"What's the name of this company?"

"I haven't been able to find out. One of my people was assassinated, and now our lines of communication have been severed." *Abunai* took a cigarette from Yemlin. "It may be impossible for you to do anything to avert his plans."

"What if Kamiya were to be killed?" McGarvey asked.

Teramura considered the suggestion. "His death might be of some value. But if you are concerned that some catastrophe will happen on Sunday, you are already too late. You do not have the time to get to him."

"What about the network?"

Teramura shrugged. "My part was to pass intelligence to Moscow in order to help avoid conflict between our countries. That may be a moot point finally." He smiled wanly. "We are at a difficult juncture. Nothing is the same, yet everything is the same."

"As what?" McGarvey asked.

"The late twenties and early thirties, of course."

John F. Kennedy Airport is located on Jamaica Bay at the southern edge of Queens, and La Guardia is on Flushing Bay at the northern edge of the borough. Traffic to and from both airports is almost always heavy. But security, or the lack of it, is no different from any other major airport in the country. No one seems to notice or care who comes and goes, as long as there are no snarls.

Apparently it was all the authorities could manage, Mueller thought, watching a Delta Airlines Guerin 522 come in for a landing at JFK. Why there hadn't been more terrorist attacks in the United States was an incredible mystery to him. From what he'd read in the magazines and newspapers, it was just as big a mystery to Americans. Yet no one was doing anything about it.

He turned in his rental car at the Budget counter and took the bus over to the American Airlines terminal. The last flight to Washington's National Airport left at 11:01 P.M. He checked in a half-hour early, got a cup of tea, and sat down with a *Newsweek* magazine in the boarding area.

Tomorrow he would do Dulles and on Sunday at 3:00—when Air Force One was scheduled to depart from Andrews and *America* from Portland—he would send the signal.

Something stirred in his gut, and he looked up for a moment. One of the gate agents, a pretty woman in an American Airlines uniform, was looking at him. He smiled, and she smiled back.

* * *

The afternoon was gray, the wind outside the bight of Tokuno Island still blew hard, kicking up big seas. *Fair Winds* rode easy at her protected anchorage. Nevertheless Liskey had gotten up several times to make sure they were holding. Standing now at the half-open hatch, drinking a cup of coffee he'd brewed, he studied the rockbound shoreline a hundred yards away. If the weather were better it would be interesting to take the dinghy ashore to look around. But for now he wanted to head farther north.

"A penny for your thoughts," Carol said, emerging from the vee-berth forward.

"I was thinking about a Japanese fishing village where the food is good and the saki is cheap."

She poured a cup of coffee. "How about warm weather?"

"If not that, how about warm saki?"

"Ugh. Tastes like snot to me."

He shook his head and laughed. "You've definitely got a way with words, toots."

"How about coming back to bed, in that case. I'm cold."

Liskey ducked back inside and put his cup aside. "See what I mean," he said.

THIRTY-FIVE

Dominique was gone. McGarvey stood in the middle of the kitchen, listening to the sounds of the house, her note in one hand, his gun in the other. She said that she was in town having lunch with Edward Reid. But that was impossible. He'd told her the situation. She understood that these people were desperate and that killing one more person would be totally meaningless to them. So what was she trying to do? Christ, the stupidity, he thought.

A car pulled up in the driveway. McGarvey raced down the corridor to the stair hall in time to see Dominique getting out of her Corvette, and then he hurried upstairs to a front window from where he could see the street. He half expected to see a white Toyota van, but there was no traffic. He stepped back away from the window, lowering his gun, allowing a measure of relief to pass through him. She hadn't been kidnapped, nor had she been followed back here. The note was legitimate.

Dominique let herself in as McGarvey came down the stairs, and her eyes went from the note in his hand to the expression on his face. "Before you say anything, hear me out," she said.

"There'll be nothing to say when you're dead," he told her mildly. "They'll kill you if you get too close."

"Reid's in this up to his ears. When I mentioned your name he practically fell down. But he knows you. I only used your last name, but he knew your first."

"What'd you say to him?"

"I told him that Guerin hired you because it was worried about the Japanese, but now you're convinced someone else caused the Dulles accident."

"If he knows me, it means somebody is feeding him information. He has help. But he has a lot of contacts."

"When I told him that you'd convinced the FBI and the CIA to investigate I thought he was going to have a heart attack."

"Did he say anything about Sunday?"

"That's the only part that didn't make any sense to me, Kirk. When I asked him for help convincing you that the Japanese were behind the Dulles crash, he said it'd have to wait until after the weekend. He's flying to Tokyo with the President."

"I know."

"Do you think he's involved?"

"Phil Carrara thought it was possible."

An odd expression crossed her face. "Where is he?"
"I don't know."

"The brakes are fried," the Delta Airlines chief mechanic on duty at Dulles International Airport said.

"We really had to lean on them to slow down," senior pilot Robert Rodwell replied. They were hunched over the main landing truck on the port side. A lot of black debris and metal shavings had collected from the brake rotors.

"Same on the other side, Captain. This bird'll have to go into the shop tonight."

"She's not scheduled to fly until morning. Can you get it done by then?"

"We're down to a weekend crew. Company won't budge on that with the overtime pay and all." The mechanic, Ted Neidlinger, shined his flashlight on the huge brake rotors. "Could be these are already turned to tolerance, which means we'll have to bring spares up from Atlanta. Something I know we don't have in shop." He shrugged. "Your call, Captain."

"Without calling in an extra crew, what are we looking at for time?"

"Twenty-four, maybe thirty-six hours."

"They're not going to like it," Rodwell said. He'd have to have Operations bring another aircraft up from Atlanta to make the morning La Guardia round-trip. It would probably be one of the older birds, like an L1011 or DC-10, and not the more modern and more comfortable Guerin 522. There'd be a lot of bitching.

"I don't break 'em, Captain. I just fix 'em."

It was a shitty remark, but it was late, and besides, he was right. "Are we going to have it for Sunday morning's La Guardia?"

"No. But I'm pretty sure we can have it for the seven-five-six."

"That's when I fly next," Rodwell said. "Fix it good."

"I hear you."

The pilot took the stairs up to the jetway and went

back into the airplane to get his brain bag. His co-pilot was already gone, but Mary White the chief stew was still aboard, finishing her flight log.

"How's it look?" she asked.

"This bird is down until Sunday. You flying tomorrow?"

She nodded tiredly. "Not until three. What'll they send up for us?"

"Nothing good. How about Sunday?"

"Yup, then too."

"Busy weekend."

"Not so bad," she said. "I have a four-day layover in L.A., and I've got a ton of things to do in my apartment. How about you?"

"Not until Sunday. I've got seven-five-six, O'Hare direct, then L.A." He glanced at the panel clock. It was a few minutes after midnight. "Still time to grab a couple of drinks and a bite to eat."

"Where are you staying?"

"The Drake."

"They put us across town at the Tudor. It'd be too late by the time I got back. I've got to get some sleep."

"My room has a king-size bed."

Her eyes widened slightly.

"Ah, shit, sorry," Rodwell apologized. "I didn't mean anything. It's late and I'm tired . . ."

She smiled. "You don't snore, do you, Captain?"

Project supervisor Scott Hale came up to *America*'s cockpit where Socrates and Kilbourne were watching the last of the diagnostic tests on the flight management system computers.

"We're ready to re-cowl the engines," he told them. "Do you want to sign off?"

Socrates took the clipboard Hale brought up and ran through the checklist. "Do the thermocouple interfaces again," he said tiredly. It was well after midnight. His throat hurt, and his eyes burned.

"That'll take at least three hours on each engine," the

engineer replied. He was frustrated. They all were because of the long hours.

"I know. And before we move over to Portland Sunday morning we'll do them again from the forward electronic bay."

"Well, you're going to have to settle the argument between Rolls and InterTech, Mr. Socrates. They're at it again."

"What's their beef this time?" Kilbourne growled.

"They're still showing a phase delay on one of the sensor ready pulses. Sudursky came up from San Francisco yesterday to look it over. He says it's well within tolerances, but Danson can't find it on the schematics."

"Have we seen anything like that from this end?" Socrates asked the technician.

"Are they talking about GO-One?"

"I think so."

"We've seen it. The problem is with the schematics, not the subassembly. It was a minor redesign that hasn't shown up in the manuals."

Something about that didn't quite set right with Socrates, but he couldn't put his finger on it. "Let's test from here."

"The phase delay involves the thermocouple circuitry. Do you still want the main tests run?"

"Yes," Socrates replied tiredly. "As soon as this question is settled. Then you can re-cowl."

There was no security at Dulles other than a night watchman at the Airport Commission building. Mueller stood in the darkness of a basement corridor for several seconds, waiting for the uniformed but unarmed man to finish his rounds and return to his office upstairs.

In Europe after any crash, whether caused by accident or terrorist attack, airports were closed up as tight as prisons. In addition to the usual security people, the military or in some cases anti-terrorist police, heavily armed with automatic weapons, swarmed over every square meter. From food service to baggage handling, and from ticketing to passport control, electronic sensing equipment and police sniffer dogs were on duty twenty-four hours per day.

A couple of weeks ago an airplane had crashed here, but the only security Mueller had encountered was one old man unarmed except for a walkie-talkie and a set of keys.

Incredible.

He went upstairs, hesitated at the end of the corridor to make sure the guard was gone, then walked across to the exit and let himself out. Keeping close to the building, out of camera range, he removed the Walkman and disappeared into the night.

"America is still at Gales Creek," Kennedy said from his secure line in Portland.

"When are you moving it to Portland?" McGarvey asked.

"Not until Sunday morning, a few hours before the Honolulu flight. How is everything there in Washington? Are you with Dominique?"

"Yes. But listen to me, David. I don't know how much good I'm doing here. Have you found anything?"

"Nothing."

"I'll be aboard that flight."

"You'll never get through security."

"Yes, I will," McGarvey promised. "Have you heard from your wife?"

"No," Kennedy said, his voice choked.

"Did you call the police?"

"Yes. But until I get a call or a note or something, there's nothing they can do. She doesn't have anything to do with this, Mac. What the hell do they want?"

"I don't know, David, but Yamagata is in the middle of it," McGarvey answered. "I'll be there tonight. Hang on."

Roland Murphy came to the White House first thing in the morning. President Lindsay and his NSA Harold Secor were waiting for him in the Oval Office. Except for last-minute details, this would be the President's final regular intelligence briefing before he took off for Tokyo tomorrow.

"I've spoken with President Yeltsin and Prime Minister Enchi, who assure me that their military movements are nothing more than exercises," the President said. "Does this square with your shop?"

"If you want my gut reaction, Mr. President, I'd say both of them were lying through their teeth."

President Lindsay grinned. "Put a military man in charge of an agency, and you'll get straight answers. Not always the ones you want to hear, but straightforward. What do you have for us this morning, General?"

Murphy handed the President the leather-bound folder that contained the in-depth national intelligence estimates that ran to more than twenty thousand words this morning, twice as long as normal.

"Three main points, sir. The first involves the military standoff in the region. As of last night, every Japanese Self Defense Force base, installation, and ship was on alert. All leaves are canceled."

"Prime Minister Enchi called it a 'national exercise,' to test the entire system. He says their weapons are unarmed."

"Yes, sir, under federal command. Their system is similar to our nuclear weapons release codes plan. But only in theory."

President Lindsay was troubled. "You're saying that their local commanders have launch autonomy?"

"More than we've been led to believe, Mr. President."

The President exchanged glances with his National Security Adviser. "I see. Go on, General."

"Russian naval and air force bases all along their far eastern zones of defense—which extend for three hundred miles inland from the Seas of Okhotsk and Japan—have gone to a similar state of readiness. Some specialist troops have also been moved out from Moscow. We're not quite sure of the numbers, or all the units involved, but they seem to be commandoes and first-strike troops."

"What is your confidence in these reports?" Secor asked.

"Very high, Harold. Except for the incident in the Tatar Strait, no shots have been fired. But both sides are ready."

"And apparently lying about it," the President said. "What else?"

"The submarine *Samisho,* which caused the trouble in the first place, has disappeared."

"What do you mean?"

"One of our destroyers was tailing the sub south in the general direction of Okinawa, when it went to a silent-running mode and dove very deep—apparently well beyond the range of our sonar equipment. Seventh Fleet sent out two frigates to help in the search, and they're being continuously overflown by surveillance aircraft as well as all-weather fighter/interceptors."

"What the hell is going on?" the President demanded.

"Routine exercises, Mr. President. Except in the case of the *Samisho,* which Escort Fleet Command at Yokosuka claims it is trying to contact for recall."

"Are we sending more assets into the region?" the President asked.

"It's not recommended at this time, sir."

"What are we waiting for?" Secor asked.

"For someone to start shooting. Nothing else we can do," Murphy replied. "Which brings me to the third point—the civil situation in Tokyo and Yokosuka. The riots are continuing to grow, Mr. President."

"Who's behind it?"

"An organization calling itself Rising Sun," Murphy said. "There is an addendum report on the group in your briefing folder. It appears to be an offshoot of the old Red Army faction. I think it would be a good idea to discuss it with Prime Minister Enchi tomorrow."

"I'm turning it over to the Vice President."

"Sir?"

"I've decided to send Larry tomorrow. I'll go over Wednesday as previously scheduled."

"Is there anything I should know about, Mr. President?" Murphy asked.

"No. But keep your eyes open, General. I want briefings from you personally every day until then."

"Yes, sir."

"I want you to go over this material with Larry. Can you do that this morning?"

"Will do, Mr. President."

On schedule, Mueller called Reid, who was waiting at a public telephone in the Grand Hyatt at Washington Center. He phoned from Lafayette Square across Pennsylvania Avenue from the White House. "Everything is ready."

"You've disposed of the big trouble?" Reid asked.

"Yes, and the three small packages. It happens tomorrow at three. In the meantime I am still waiting for the second deposit to my account."

"It's on its way. Don't be impatient."

"Very well."

"If we push the button now I won't have to invent any excuse for tomorrow . . ." Reid said.

Mueller hung up without responding.

Chief Investigating Officer John Whitman had known that finding a man of McGarvey's caliber and experience would be difficult. But apparently he'd been tipped off and had gone to ground. Despite their best efforts the man had not turned up. Guerin was no longer cooperating, although secretly Whitman couldn't blame anyone. The Bureau had turned down its request for help. The police in Portland and in D.C. were coming up empty-handed, and the college where he'd taught until a few weeks ago hadn't heard from him either. His apartment in Milford was staked out, although Whitman personally thought it was a waste of time and manpower. Even if McGarvey did return there he would almost certainly spot the surveillance team, and they'd have trouble on their hands. That was another problem. When they did finally find him, making an arrest would not be easy. If McGarvey chose not to cooperate or, as Carrara had warned, if he were taken by surprise, there would be casualties. Whitman had read parts of McGarvey's amazing file, made all the more stunning by what had been left out. Every page had major deletions—*For considerations of National Security.* Yet what remained was nothing short of deadly. First they had to find him. Special Agents Joyce and McLaren were in Portland and would remain there for the time being. They were banking on the probability that McGarvey would eventually show up at Guerin. Whitman thought it would happen tomorrow. Despite the tight security around the VIP flight on the new airplane, McGarvey would make a try to get aboard. Overall, though, the case made less and less sense each day. They were missing something. But what?

Special Agent in Charge Charles Colberg called from San Francisco. "We might have something for you on the Guerin case. Apparently Bruno Mueller surfaced in Oakland ten days ago, and possibly Chicago just this last week. We're still looking for connections, aren't we, John?"

"At this point we'll take everything. What'd he do?"

"Killed an air traffic control instructor. It's got us running around in circles out here. Something's going on that we can't figure out. But since his name came up in connection with Guerin, who's flying its new bird out to Honolulu tomorrow, we're getting nervous. Anything on McGarvey yet?"

"Nothing, Chuck. But you're not the only one puzzled and nervous."

"We got a call from Ron Herring who runs the noise-abatement research program for the Oakland Airport Commission. A couple of weeks ago a guy who identified himself as Thomas Reston showed up at the airport and asked a bunch of questions. Took the grand tour of Herring's project and the tower. Said he was a reporter for *High Technology Business* and *Aviation Week & Space Technology* magazines. Herring said the guy looked good and sounded good so nobody got suspicious until last week."

"Does Herring check out?" Whitman asked.

"He's clean. After Reston was finished at Herring's project, he took a tour of the tower with Dick White, the chief ATC instructor. Last week White's body was found outside his motel in Chicago. Whoever did him used a stiletto. Single thrust to the heart."

"It was either a lucky hit, or the killer was an expert."

"I checked with the French. The stiletto is one of Mueller's weapons of choice."

"How'd Herring get on to it?" Whitman asked. To his cop's instincts, the connection had a ring of truth.

"He knew that Reston talked to Dick White in Oakland, and he wanted to make sure the guy knew what had happened. But nobody at either magazine had ever heard of him. So he called us. Soon as I saw the IdentaKit drawing, we showed Herring the Mueller photo and he made a positive ID, although he said Reston had different color eyes and hair. We dusted the business card that Reston gave to Herring. Except for Herring's prints it was clean. The guy is a pro."

"Did you talk to Paul Granger in Chicago?" Whitman asked. Granger was the S-A-C there.

"Yes. Reston rented a car at the airport the night of Dick White's murder. Question is, why did he follow an air traffic control instructor out to Chicago and then kill him? John, if it's Mueller—and I believe it is—what the hell am I missing?"

Whitman tried to work it out. "Is there any connection, no matter how remote, between Dick White and Guerin?"

"None that we can come up with. But Mueller took his time. Herring said he had the technical patter down pat. He knew the system, where it had been, and where it was going."

"What was White doing in Chicago?"

"A union meeting. Could be that Mueller was there to interview somebody else, and White's bumping into him was just a coincidence."

"That, or for some reason he was stalking White," Whitman said, then he stopped. "Anybody except for the car rental people in Chicago see Mueller? At the airport?"

"Paul didn't say."

"Where and when was the rental car returned?"

"Minneapolis the next morning."

"All right, assuming there is a connection between Mueller and the Guerin case, what was he doing at those three airports? And which other airports has he visited in the past week or two?"

"Jesus," Colberg said. "I'll check Oakland and San Francisco International."

"Right," Whitman said. "I'll send a bulletin to all our field offices. If you find anything, Chuck, anything at all no matter how seemingly insignificant or disconnected, call me."

"Will do."

"Larry, did Murphy get a chance to go over everything with you?" the President asked.

"I talked to him when he dropped off the briefing book."

"Are you finished with it?"

"I will be by morning, and there'll be plenty of time on the flight over for a second look." Vice President Larry Cross was a ruggedly built Oklahoman who preferred cowboy boots and blue jeans to suits and ties. He was a fast but thoughtful study, and a competent VP.

"Well, no decisions will be made."

"Then what's the purpose of sending me tomorrow, and not waiting until Wednesday?" Cross asked. They were in the President's study on the second floor. The afternoon light coming through the bowed windows was gray.

"They'll probably hit you with the Russian thing."

"Why not call the Russian and Japanese ambassadors over here this afternoon and hash it out?"

"Wouldn't accomplish a thing," President Lindsay replied as he filled his cup from the coffee service. "The trouble is they're not ready to talk yet. Not to us, not to each other. The step from where you are to where I sit is a hell of a lot bigger than you'd think. George Bush found out that eight years of being vice president did nothing to prepare him for his own presidency."

"I don't have the same ambition, Jim," Cross said, and he sincerely meant it. He hadn't told Lindsay yet, but he was considering not running for re-election. He wanted to get back to his law practice in Oklahoma City and to his ranch.

"That's not the point. When Enchi talks to you in Tokyo everybody will accept that whatever is said won't be final in the sense that no decisions will be expected. What they'll do is float a few trial balloons past you, see what your reactions are so that when the actual talks begin on Thursday they'll have had time to fine tune their positions. Statecraft."

"It was Enchi's suggestion that you delay your arrival, wasn't it?"

"Yes, it was."

"Maybe he's stalling for time."

"That's exactly what he's doing, Larry. It's the CIA's guess that Enchi is not in complete control of the situation with the street demonstrations, or even his own military. Puts him and his trade agreement in a dangerous position."

"Puts us all in a dangerous position. Those are our ships shadowing that submarine."

"That's correct."

"While most of the Seventh Fleet is at the dock in Yokosuka. Pull them out of there."

"Not unless we have to," President Lindsay said. "Any further ship movements by us are going to be looked upon with a lot of suspicion."

"Some of our ships in port are carrying nuclear weapons. If that were to come out, we'd be in a lot more trouble."

The President smiled faintly. "You're catching on, Larry."

* * *

Dominique finally agreed that no matter what happened she would stay put at least until Monday morning. McGarvey was driving down to Richmond, where he would catch a flight to Eugene and rent a car from there to Gales Creek.

The Bureau had a warrant for his arrest, but it simply did not have the manpower to check every single passenger on every single flight from every single airport in the country. With care he didn't think he would encounter trouble until he got out to Portland, where the Bureau's efforts would be focused.

Once he was out of Washington, heading south on I-95, and certain he wasn't being followed, he pulled in at a truck stop and telephoned Phil Carrara's wife at her sister's in Montpelier.

"He told me to stay up here until Monday," she said.

"Have you heard from him since Thursday, JoAnn?"

"No. Is something wrong, Mac?"

"Not that I know of, honestly. But when he calls tell him I've headed west. He'll understand."

"This is between you and him."

"Something like that. We'll all have dinner next week, and I'll tell you about it."

"Yeah, right," she said.

He telephoned Carrara's house, but there was still no answer, so he phoned Dick Adkins at home. Carrara and Adkins were friends. He hoped it would count for something.

"Dick, this is Kirk McGarvey. I'm glad I caught you at home."

"Jesus H. Christ. The Bureau is turning the country upside down looking for you. Where the hell are you?"

"I'm trying to find Phil Carrara. I need your help."

"You're the black plague. There's not a thing I can or will do for you."

"He's on administrative leave. He sent his wife to Montpelier, and he was trying to do something for me. Now he's disappeared. Do you know where he is?"

The line was silent for a few seconds. It was possible

that Adkins was tracing the call, but McGarvey wasn't going to stick around much longer.

"Are you turning yourself in?"

"No."

"Okay," Adkins said, and he sounded very nervous. "I'm going way the hell out on a limb, but Phil trusted you, so I guess I'll have to go along. Nobody knows where he is. But one of our Technical Services guys and a surveillance van are missing too."

"Does it have to do with Ed Reid?" McGarvey asked.

"Maybe. Phil asked for the files on Reid and on two Japanese—Sokichi Kamiya and Arimoto Yamagata. But he never called back."

McGarvey watched the traffic on the highway. A big eighteen-wheeler pulled in and headed toward the diesel pumps. Kamiya was presumably in Japan, and Yamagata was out West.

"They probably went after Reid, but they may have run into trouble. There may be a connection between Reid and a former East German assassin."

"Bruno Mueller. The French are looking for him."

"That's right, Dick. I want you to convince the Bureau to take a look right now. But there's something else. Yesterday I followed Reid part of the way out of town, toward Dulles, but I had to break it off because I was being followed by a pair of white Toyota vans. D.C. plates. Possibly Japanese MITI. When I doubled back I lost them."

"There's big trouble brewing over there. Riots in Tokyo and Yokosuka, and there's a Japanese submarine heading toward Okinawa right now."

"What are the Russians doing?"

"Their entire Far Eastern Command is on alert. It's probable they're going to start something because of the Tatar Strait incident. Everybody thinks you've got some of the answers."

"I wish I did. Just convince the Bureau to check out Reid as soon as possible."

"I'll see what I can do."

"Have them issue an APB on Phil and your Technical Services guy."

"What about you?"

"Depending on what goes down tomorrow, I'll come in on Monday. You can tell that to the General if you want."

"Listen, Mac, if you're heading out to Portland, they've got the place closed up tighter than a gnat's ass. Something is going on. Ryan was talking with someone over at the Bureau as late as this morning. It's got them shook up, but I haven't been put in the loop."

"Because you're friends with Phil."

"Probably."

"Convince them to go after Reid," McGarvey said. "In the meantime keep your eyes open."

"Good luck, Mac," Adkins said.

McGarvey telephoned Yemlin. "We have to meet now, at the same place."

"Twenty minutes," the Russian agreed. He sounded shook up.

"I'm going home," Reid said when Mueller called the *Lamplighter* office to check on him.

"Why?"

"Everything is closing in on me. I'm a wreck. I don't know how I'm going to manage. Christ, do it now!"

"No. Are you ready for tomorrow? Do you know what to do?"

"I can't . . ."

"Do you know what to do tomorrow?"

"Yes," Reid said, his voice barely above a whisper.

"Very good. I want you to arrange to meet with some friends this evening for dinner. You will tell them how much you are looking forward to going to Tokyo with the President. How you expect to accomplish great things. Maybe even avert armed conflict."

"I don't know."

"Be convincing," Mueller said. "Your life depends on it."

* * *

Portland had become the center of activity. With less than twenty-four hours to go before *America*'s VIP flight to Honolulu, San Francisco S-A-C Charles Colberg was surprised that it had not been canceled. There was a former East German Stasi assassin running around visiting airports and killing people, so something important was going on. Possibly connected with San Francisco's own troubles over the past weeks with the fire and deaths at InterTech—which supplied subassemblies to Guerin—and the brutal murder and rape of the psychologist aboard her Sausalito houseboat. Louis Zerkel had still not turned up, nor were there any leads in the murders of Zerkel's supervisor, his wife, and children. He'd been a cop long enough not to ignore the itchy feeling between his shoulders.

He telephoned Portland S-A-C Jack Franson. "Got your hands full, Jack?"

"I could use a few extra troops, Chuck. It's become a goddamned international media circus up here."

"I'll send you half a dozen men. You've seen John Whitman's query about Colonel Mueller. Any early leads?"

"I saw it, but we haven't come up with a thing. If Mueller were here, nobody who saw him has come forward yet. But we're beating the bushes for him and for McGarvey."

"Do you want me to come up there?" Colberg asked.

"No need. It'll be history by this time tomorrow."

"Right." Colberg sat back in his chair and looked out the window toward Market Street. He was missing something. They all were. Something between McGarvey and Colonel Mueller. There was a connection between the two of them in that they were enemies. Or at least they'd once been on opposite sides of the fence. But what if that were no longer true? Or were they tilting at windmills by trying to manufacture facts out of possible relationships instead of sticking with what they already knew? Basic police work. Jack Franson had his hands full in Portland, which left Colberg on his own in San Francisco. What exactly did they have, he asked himself?

Mueller had come to Oakland for some definite purpose that was important enough for him to kill Dick White later. The second element was InterTech and the brutal murders involving Louis Zerkel. Colberg decided he had plenty to keep his field office busy without envying Franson. S-A-Cs of productive offices were first on the promotions list.

"We're having dinner with Jim and Amanda at the White House tonight," the Vice President told his wife.

"Will it be a pep talk, or will it be last-minute instructions?" Sally Cross asked.

"Probably a little of both. Are you packed?"

"Nearly," she said. "I read the news like everyone else, Larry. Are we being sent over as sacrificial lambs?"

"Politics aren't that tough, sweetheart."

"I have a bad feeling, that's all," she explained. "Women's intuition."

The Vice President forced a laugh. "Well, this time you're wrong."

"I'm leaving for Moscow soon, Kirk. I will not be returning. Do you understand what this means?"

"Beyond the fact I won't have a control officer, no, I don't understand. What are you trying to tell me, Viktor Pavlovich?"

"The trouble between my country and Japan is very nearly at the breaking point. I can say nothing beyond that."

"What about the contract with Guerin?"

Yemlin shook his head. He looked as if he'd aged ten years in the last couple of weeks. His skin was mottled from the cold, and his pale eyes were watery. "I don't know." He stared at the flickering flames on Kennedy's tomb. "The world changed after that day, Kirk. Especially for Americans. Your age of innocence ended. After tomorrow I think there will be another very big change for you. For all of us."

"All your military installations in the region are on

alert. Will Russia make a retaliatory strike? Is that what you're telling me?"

"They provoked us, Kirk. Just as they are provoking your navy even as we speak. We can make no sense of it."

"Has *Abunai* said anything else?"

Yemlin continued to stare at the flame as if he hadn't heard the question.

"It's very important, Viktor, that I know the name of the Guerin subcontractor that Mintori controls. Many lives are at stake."

Yemlin looked at him. "Will you go to Portland for the flight?"

"Yes."

"If I learn something, anything at all, I will get the information to you, Kirk. I swear it."

"What we have here is a cascade. One problem causing another," Delta Chief Mechanic Ted Neidlinger said, inspecting the 522's carbon-type rotors. There were five in each set of brakes, and they were shot.

"It's the anti-lock computer," the crew chief, Henry Verbeke, agreed. "Both the main and backup failed at the same time. Ate the brakes. Unusual."

"I'll say." Neidlinger had hung around long enough to make sure that his weekend crew was on top of the problem. They'd pulled the wheels off the mains and disassembled the brakes, then had run the diagnostic tests on the electronics. "Atlanta give us an ETA on the parts?"

"Midnight," Verbeke said. "We'll get it done in time for seven-five-six."

"I'll stop by in the morning to see how it's coming."

McGarvey drove down to Richmond, where he returned his rental car to the agency and checked on flights to Eugene. There were none direct, but a Delta flight was leaving for Des Moines within the hour, with connections via Denver to Eugene. The ticket clerk assured him that the layover in Denver was very short. He would not have to get off the plane.

"I need to get some sleep," McGarvey explained. "We partied pretty late last night, and I've got back-to-back meetings this evening."

"I know what you mean, Mr. Lyman. After Des Moines you should be okay."

"Sounds good." McGarvey handed her his credit card, and the clerk booked him on the flight.

"I gave you a window bulkhead seat," she said, stuffing his ticket into a folder.

"What kind of a plane am I getting?"

She glanced at her computer. "A 737 to Des Moines, and it looks like a 522 out to Eugene."

McGarvey took his single bag through the terminal to the boarding gate. The airport was busy. He wondered what it would be like tomorrow. What airport terminals around the world would be like tomorrow.

"Far as I can see we might have a bigger problem than I thought," John Whitman said. "And if I'm right, we have less than twenty-four hours to do something about it."

"What have you come up with?" Assistant FBI Director Ken Wood asked.

"Bruno Mueller was at the Oakland Airport two weeks ago, and it's strongly possible that he murdered an air traffic control instructor in Chicago last week. We can also place him in Minneapolis, and we have a possible at La Guardia. We're not sure about New York, but Colonel Mueller is definitely here, and he's definitely up to something involving our air traffic system. People in Oakland who spoke with him said he seemed to know what he was talking about."

"Where'd you get the timetable?"

"We're still looking at a connection between Mueller and Guerin. It flies its new plane tomorrow."

"Let me get this straight," Wood said after a moment's hesitation. "Are you saying that Mueller is working for the Japanese?"

"Through Ed Reid."

"Reid will be on Air Force Two tomorrow, headed for Tokyo. It'd be like jumping into the lion's den if he were somehow involved."

"Goddammit . . ."

"I'm not saying you're wrong," Wood told him. "But there may be other possibilities that you're overlooking. McGarvey, for instance. What's the word on him?"

"Nothing yet. But he'll have some of the answers."

"Undoubtedly. What are you doing to find him?"

"He's damned good, but we expected that. We think he'll try to make it to Portland for tomorrow's flight, so we've set up a team to watch for him. I won't guarantee he'll be stopped, but if he somehow manages to get through he's even better than we thought."

"What about Mueller?"

"We're watching every major airport, but that's about the limit of our personnel. As it is we're stretched thin."

"Okay, John, you came up here with something specific in mind. Let's have it."

"If Guerin is the target—I mean beyond the maiden flight tomorrow of *America*—then it could mean that all its airplanes are in danger. So ground the fleet."

"Impossible."

"All I'm asking is twenty-four hours, Ken."

"Then what?" Wood demanded. "Unless you come up with McGarvey or Mueller, we'd be back to square one on Monday. Even if I thought Harding would go along with us, and that he could convince the FAA, which I don't think would happen, what you're suggesting simply wouldn't work."

"It'd be better than nothing," Whitman said bitterly.

"Find McGarvey and Mueller. Whatever else happens, find them!"

"Any word on Phil Carrara yet?" John Whitman asked.

"We were about to make a formal request of the Bureau," Howard Ryan said. He was in his office at Langley.

"He's definitely missing?"

"Along with one of our Technical Services people and some equipment. A surveillance van, actually. I'll fax you the material immediately."

"Thank you, Mr. Ryan. We'll do what we can."

"It is almost time for Morning Star." Sokichi Kamiya's voice was recognizable but hollow because of the encryption device.

"I understand," Yamagata replied nervously. When the signal was up-linked to the U.S. GeoPositioning Satellite constellation, a spike would be sent to every satellite navigation set in use on the North American continent. Every airplane using the system would receive an eleven-millisecond modulated pulse, but only Guerin airplanes equipped with the InterTech heat monitor/alarm subassembly and explosive thermocouple frame would be affected. Then airplanes would fall out of the sky like "starlit raindrops on a barren plain." Kamiya's words. For as long as the up-link remained open the pulse would be sent. The destruction, the confusion, the anguish would be awesome. Far worse than Pearl Harbor.

"What progress have you made?"

"The woman refuses to cooperate. Now Portland and Gales Creek are untenable because of the upcoming flight. Their security measures are extensive. Will the signal be sent tomorrow?"

"No," Kamiya replied, his tone sharp. "In a few days, perhaps. First your situation must be resolved, *Yamagata-san*. In this you may not fail."

"I will not."

"You *must* not. There are other considerations, other situations developing at this moment, that are crucial to our mission. Everything has been foreseen. But everything must be perfectly in place to guarantee our success."

The dark thought that Kamiya was insane passed through Yamagata's thoughts, but he pushed it aside. If the master were mad, what then of his disciples?

"*Hai, Kamiya-san*. It will be as you wish." Yamagata hung up, walked out of the study, and went upstairs to the bedroom where they were keeping Chance Kennedy.

The others were in the city. For the next few hours he would be alone with her. He stood at the end of the bed watching her sleep. They'd tapered off her drugs so she would be coming out of her stupor soon.

Such a naïve woman, Yamagata thought. Little girl, actually, as most Western women he'd met were. Prudish beyond belief. Yet they all wanted adventure, and they all thought that a small bit of anatomy gave them nearly absolute control over every man.

He drew back the covers from her body and gently removed her nightshirt. The problem was they needed her *undrugged* cooperation. They needed her to telephone her husband and convince him to cooperate. They needed information. Who did the company think was coming after it? Why had it hired Kirk McGarvey, and where was he?

Yamagata tied Chance's wrists and ankles to the bedposts with rubber straps, leaving her spread-eagle and vulnerable. Her eyes began to flutter. The room was cool. Already she had goose bumps and her nipples were inverted.

The Western mind did not understand pain. In America, especially, people looked for instant gratification. Comfort. Pleasure. Absence of confrontation.

He plugged an electrical cord into an outlet at the head of the bed and carefully placed the bare probes of the wires on the sheet between Chance's legs. Moist tissue conducted electricity better than dry tissue. The junction between pain and pleasure could be infinitesimal.

"Chance," he said softly. "It is time to wake up. Time to talk."

The airport terminal at Eugene's Mahlon Sweet Field was nearly deserted at midnight. The twenty people who deplaned with McGarvey shuffled tiredly downstairs to get their bags. As soon as the jetliner was unloaded it would continue to Portland where it would stay the night, not flying until morning back to Des Moines via Eugene.

McGarvey rented a Ford Probe from Hertz and twenty minutes later was heading north on State Highway 99W, which paralleled Interstate 5. Security surrounding Portland would of necessity be concentrated on the main routes, including the interstate highways. The FBI and local cops did not have the manpower to effectively watch every state and county road.

Kennedy said that *America* would remain in Gales Creek until just before the Honolulu flight, when it would be moved the twenty-five miles to Portland for the ceremonies and to board the VIP passengers. It was a weak spot in the security measures.

McGarvey stopped at an all-night diner north of Corvallis, and while he waited for his bacon and eggs to come he studied a highway map, working out the route to Guerin's prototype assembly facility that would least likely be patrolled tonight.

Whatever was going to happen would affect *America*, and he was going to be aboard to stop it.

David Kennedy stood at the tall windows in the darkened living room, watching the lights across Lake Oswego as he held the telephone to his ear.

Dominique had called him from the East Coast. "Have you heard anything from the police?"

"Not a thing. They're not even sure that she was kidnapped. I guess they talked to some of the neighbors and some of Chance's friends. They told them about the troubles we've been having. So the Bureau thinks she may have just run off. I don't believe it."

"What does Mac say?"

Kennedy closed his eyes. "He thinks the Japanese took her. But I haven't heard a thing. No one has called."

"Jeez, will you look at all this shit," Baltimore Police Sergeant of Detectives Frank Gentilli said, peering at the electronic equipment jammed in the back of the van.

The coroner's people had bagged the two bodies and had taken them to the morgue. One had a knife wound through his throat, front to back, probably severing his spinal cord. The other man had been killed by a narrow chest wound, probably a thin-bladed knife, which most likely pierced his heart. Gentilli's partner, Jerry Kozlowski, found the two wallets stuffed between the front seats. He removed them and stepped out into the light to examine the IDs. He almost dropped them.

"What the hell?" he said, half to himself.

"Government-issue plates," Gentilli said, coming around to the front.

The van had been left in an airport self-storage garage just off Poplar Avenue. It might not have been discovered for months except that two juveniles had been caught breaking into the storage units. The one with the van was the last they'd jimmied.

"Frank, keep everyone the hell out of here. I gotta call this one in," Kozlowski said.

"What've you got?"

Kozlowski showed him Carrara's CIA identification card. "I want to talk to those two punks who broke in, and I want the manager down here on the double. Somebody paid for the rental, and it wasn't very long ago."

John Whitman got the call at home from the night watch commander. It took him several seconds to come fully awake. "Say that again?"

"Sir, we have a flag on that Langley VIP—Phillip Carrara. Baltimore police found him and another CIA officer both dead, stuffed in the back of what appeared to be a surveillance van, parked in a self-storage garage by the airport."

It was as if someone had injected a liter of ice water into his gut. "How long have they been dead?"

"Not more than two days. The coroner has the bodies now."

"How were they killed. Did Baltimore say?"

"Yes, Sir. Mr. Carrara was killed by a knife wound to his neck. Mr. Ulland, by a puncture wound to his heart."

"The van was found near the airport?" Whitman asked, getting out of bed and taking the phone into the bathroom.

"Yes, sir."

"Okay, this is important. I want the crime site secured. Get our forensics people up there within the hour. I want the place down pat. And send someone up with Colonel Mueller's photograph. Hit the manager, and the airport staff." They had canvassed Dulles without luck, but so far as Whitman knew no one had thought to include Baltimore.

"Shall we inform someone at Langley?"

"I'll take care of that."

"Yes, sir."

"I'll be at my desk within the hour. Whatever you get, send it up to me."

McGarvey left his car in a thicket of trees off the highway a couple of miles southwest of Guerin Test Facility One's western perimeter fence at five in the morning. The sun had not come up yet, and the sky was darkly overcast, a bitterly cold wind slicing through the valley. Some snow had fallen in the night and more threatened.

He checked the action of his pistol, then reholstered it at the small of his back and headed northeast away from the highway through the woods. It was very quiet. From time to time he could hear the wind in the treetops, but nothing else.

He walked for nearly forty-five minutes before he came to the tall, chain-link fence. A clearing had been cut for a perimeter road, and there were fresh tire tracks in the snow. Saul Edwards had taken him seriously when he'd told them to beef up their security here.

Beyond the fence was a sloping field of tall grass that led to the end of the fifteen-thousand-foot runway. In the distance the hangars and assembly halls were lit up. The ILS system towers were off to the right, and to the left the fence followed a rock-strewn hill that rose a couple of hundred feet.

Keeping back well into the woods he worked his way up the ridge line parallel to the fence. Near the top he found what he was looking for.

They'd had trouble maintaining some sections of the sixty-seven miles of perimeter fence because of water runoff during the fall rains and the spring meltoff. Drainage ditches had been dug, and where they crossed under the fence, concrete drainpipes had been installed and blocked with wire mesh. But in several such spots, because of the rugged terrain, the perimeter road was thirty or forty yards away from the fence. He crouched behind a boulder directly across from one of the pipes.

From his vantage point, McGarvey could look down across the runway toward the complex of brightly spot-lighted buildings, the biggest of which housed *America*. There was a lot of activity over there.

Twenty minutes later his patience was rewarded when a four-wheel-drive Jimmy passed below on the perimeter road.

When it was gone he scrambled down to the drainage pipe and, using a large rock, hammered the wire mesh away and crawled through to the other side.

He walked back down the hill toward the end of the runway, keeping as low as possible in the tall grass, and watching for other headlights moving along the perimeter road. Sooner or later another patrol would pass by. He wanted to be in place before that happened.

"Are we ready to fly?" Air Force Two Pilot Lieutenant Colonel Bob Wheeler asked.

"We're running the final diagnostics now," Chief Master Sergeant Mazorsky replied.

The food service people and stewards had not been allowed aboard, and their liftoff time was less than four hours away. But nobody messed with Mazorsky's Raiders. When the chief said the bird was ready to fly, they flew. Not until then.

"We're ready to button it up," Delta Crew Chief Henry Verbeke said. "And we've got time to spare."

"Run a ground test, and then I'll sign off," Neidlinger instructed. "I want to make sure the anti-lock works this time."

The White House was like a magnet to Mueller. He had come often to Lafayette Square across Pennsylvania Avenue to stare at the building and grounds. If the city were ancient Rome, a place of grand monuments and institutions from which emanated political, economic, and military power, then the White House was Caesar's palace.

If America were to fall, it would have to decay from within. No foreign enemy would ever defeat the country. And now, after more than two weeks in the U.S., he did not believe the nation would decay, or would in any lasting way be hurt by what Reid had set in motion.

"It's wonderful," a woman standing beside him said.

Mueller looked at her. She was plainly dressed, possibly in her mid- to late fifties, with the smile of a Sunday-school teacher. "Yes, isn't it?" he said, and he turned and went looking for a restaurant to wait in until it was time.

It was 6:30 by the time McGarvey reached the new airplane development complex. Most of the activity seemed to be concentrated toward the front of the prototype assembly hangar.

The sun was due to rise in forty-eight minutes, and it was essential that he be inside before then. Without the proper lapel badges he wouldn't get far in daylight.

He ran to the back of the assembly hall and looked around the corner. A Mercedes station wagon with two people inside headed across to security. A service vehicle, its bed on scissor jacks, came around the corner and backed into a service bay at the rear of the prototype hangar. The driver got out and went inside.

McGarvey walked to the far end of the assembly hall and held up long enough to make certain that no one was coming. Then he sprinted across the twenty or thirty yards between buildings, concealing himself behind the truck.

The VIPs would not be boarding the airplane until it was moved to Portland in a few hours. With any luck the FBI would be concentrating its security there. But the advantage was theirs. Under the proper circumstances they would not hesitate to shoot him, whereas no matter what happened he could not return fire.

But he had to be aboard that airplane.

He went around to the back of the truck and flattened himself against the wall next to the service door. He could hear the sounds of machinery and power tools, and somebody's voice raised in anger or frustration.

McGarvey eased around the corner and looked inside. The rear of the hangar was in darkness. Out in the open bay *America* was bathed in strong lights and was still crawling with technicians and engineers getting her ready for her flight. The truck driver stood about thirty feet away, talking with a man dressed in white coveralls. Their backs were to the door.

McGarvey slipped inside the building and, keeping to the shadows, reached the back stairs to the engineering galley above and hurried up. At the head of the stairs he turned the corner just as George Socrates and Saul Edwards came out of the drafting offices.

"Good Lord Almighty," Socrates said.

McGarvey forced himself not to overreact. To remain calm. Both men looked worn out, to the point of collapse. In their state there was no telling what they would do. "David is expecting me."

"How did you get in here?" Edwards asked, keeping his voice low. "The place is crawling with cops."

"That doesn't matter. I've got to get aboard, and the crew has to be alerted to what's going on."

Socrates glanced over the rail to the big hypersonic

jetliner on the floor. "We can get you aboard, but I can't guarantee Portland. They might turn the airplane inside out before they let any of the VIPs board."

"I'll have to hide somewhere, and the crew will have to keep them away from me."

"Have you found something?"

"Maybe. The Japanese company that's been targeting you controls one of your subcontractors."

"That's it," Socrates said. "Which company?"

"I don't know yet."

"There're hundreds of them," Socrates said. "Impossible to check."

"I have someone in Washington trying to find out for us. Can you cancel the flight? A last-minute technical problem?"

"No," Socrates said, tiredly. "It's still all just speculation."

"Where's David?"

"Portland. He'll meet us there," Edwards said.

"That's it then?" Socrates asked. "It's come down to the wire, and despite what the authorities say, you still believe that we're in danger?"

"I hope I'm wrong, George."

Socrates shook his head and glanced again at *America* rising like a *Star Wars* model from the hangar floor. "Why are they doing it? They want us to build them an airplane, we'll be happy to. Then they can take it apart and improve on our technology. That's how it's done."

"There may be more at stake than Guerin."

Socrates looked at McGarvey. "Get him a security pass and a set of coveralls," he told Edwards. "We'll wait in engineering."

Nancy Nebel took the call. At first she had trouble understanding what the obviously troubled woman was trying to say. But then she realized it was Chance Kennedy, and for a moment she froze.

Security had installed the Caller-ID system on their phones. She switched it on. "Mrs. Kennedy, do you wish to speak with your husband?"

"Yes, yes, please," Chance mumbled.

Kennedy came to the office door.

"It's your wife," Nancy said.

Kennedy came out of his office and snatched the phone from her. "Chance? Chance, where are you?"

"David, it's Yamagata. They're planning something, but they're worried that someone else is . . ."

The phone line went dead.

"I'll call the FBI," Nancy said. "I got the number."

"No," Kennedy told her. "I'll make the call."

America's pilot, Pete Reiner, wasn't happy about McGarvey's presence aboard, but when everything was explained to him he accepted it. "Cancel the flight."

"Can't," Socrates said.

McGarvey had ridden with the crew up from Gales Creek, and now he watched from a cockpit window as the ceremonies began in front of a terminal at Portland International Airport. Security would not be as strict because the Vice President had canceled at the last minute, sending instead the assistant director of the Federal Aviation Administration. There were media everywhere, their remote satellite up-link trucks parked along the apron to the west, their cameras trained on *America* and on the grandstand where the VIPs and a substantial crowd of onlookers had gathered to hear remarks by the governor and others, including Al Vasilanti. McGarvey was unable to pick Kennedy out of the crowd, however.

Making sure the flight-deck door was latched, he plugged into the aircraft's public correspondence communications system and called Yemlin's Washington number. It was answered on the tenth ring.

"InterTech," Yemlin said, and the connection was immediately broken.

A few minutes after 2:30, Vice President Cross, his wife Sally, his advisers, his secretary, his Secret Service contingent, a White House photographer, and a dozen White House correspondents arrived at Andrews Air

Force Base and boarded Air Force Two. The plane would return to Washington within twenty-four hours so it could be redesignated Air Force One and be made ready for the President's Wednesday flight to Tokyo. The weather was overcast, but the winds were light.

"Ground control, this is Delta seven-five-six, we're ready with Baker to push away from the gate at this time," Delta Senior Pilot Bob Rodwell radioed.

"Roger, Delta seven-five-six. Hold up at eight-left for an incoming American Airlines. You'll be . . . ah, number four behind a Northwest seven-four-seven. Report to the tower on one-two-one-point-niner when you're in position."

"Roger, ground control," Rodwell said, and he gave the ground crew below the thumbs up. Immediately the big jetliner trundled away from the gate, pushed by a tractor on her nose gear.

In Baltimore Special Agent Clifford Wiener walked back to his car and telephoned John Whitman at FBI headquarters. The manager of the self-storage facility where the bodies of the two CIA spooks had been found had positively identified Bruno Mueller from the photographs. Wiener had sent his partner, Stan Tarnowski, over to the airport to interview the chief of security about the photos they'd distributed several hours ago. He'd not heard back yet, but it was clear that Colonel Mueller had killed the spooks less than forty-eight hours ago.

Aboard Air Force Two they were late starting up because a courier came with a last-minute dispatch for the Vice President from the White House. Edward Reid, who was to have flown with them, had a car accident on the way out of the city. He would not be able to make this flight. He'd fly on Wednesday with the President.

It was nearly three by the time Lieutenant Colonel Wheeler ordered the starboard engine to be motored to speed. When the RPMS came up into the green, the fuel and ignition were switched on. Immediately the exhaust gas temperature came up, indicating that the engine had lit. Fuel and hydraulic pressures were in the green as well, and the start-up procedure was initiated on the port engine.

Delta 756 moved up to the intersection as a Northwest Airlines Boeing 747 rolled out onto the main runway and majestically turned into take-off position. Captain Rodwell noted the time on the panel clock as 2:58. He keyed the aircraft's intercom phone so that he could talk to the passengers. They were carrying a full load, only one seat in first class a no-show.

"This is the captain. We're next for take-off in just a minute or two, which will put us in the air at exactly three o'clock. Thanks again for flying the on-time airline. If there's anything I or my crew can do for you during this flight, don't hesitate to ask. Now just sit back and relax."

Lieutenant Colonel Wheeler picked up the intercom phone. "Are you all set back there, Mr. Vice President?" he asked.

"We're ready any time you are, Colonel," Larry Cross answered.

McGarvey had to hide in the electronics bay beneath the flight deck while the FBI and Guerin security checked the hypersonic jetliner's main cabin, galleys, and heads before allowing the VIPs to board. Socrates came for him as they taxied away from the grandstands, out toward the active runway.

"InterTech," McGarvey said scrambling up from bay.

"Are you sure about this?" Socrates asked.

"It comes from the Russian spy network in Japan. They've got too much to lose to lie."

Socrates was working it out in his engineer's mind. "It makes sense. But we never caught it."

"Do you know which units they manufacture? Can we get to them from here?"

"You were standing right in front of them," Socrates said, blinking.

"What the hell is going on?" Captain Reiner demanded. "Do we fly or don't we, George?"

"If McGarvey is right, I think I know what the problem is." Socrates yanked open the hatch to the electronics bay. "I'm going to pull the heat monitor/alarm panels. You'll have to go to the override if the temperatures get critical."

"We might get a shutdown," Reiner said. "Christ, we'll be out over the water without engines."

"Just the port engine," McGarvey said. "But stop the flight now, George."

"What if you're wrong?"

"Then I'm wrong, and you'll fly later."

"We'd be right back where we started from," Socrates said, and he climbed down into the equipment bay.

"Keep everybody out of here," McGarvey told the pilots. "No matter what happens."

THIRTY-SIX

Bruno Mueller got back to Lafayette Square across from the White House a minute before three, and he placed a long-distance call to Tokyo Bank from a phone booth.

It took fifty seconds for the call to go through, and a computerized voice, speaking Japanese, answered, giving the options for the system.

Mueller entered three-four-eight, and in three seconds he was connected with the bank's electronic international funds transfer system. A warbling tone indicated the program Louis had secretly installed was ready to accept an input.

A tour bus rumbled past, and he waited for it before

whistling a single-pitched note. The warbling was replaced by a high-pitched screech, and he hung up, his job finished.

Everything else that happened took only two seconds.

First the bank's computer prepared a funds-available query from a special foreign account in the amount ¥ 2,707,750,000. The account verified that such an amount was indeed available, and Louis's program made the electronic funds-transfer order, payable to InterTech Corporation of San Francisco, California, U.S.A. At the current exchange rate of ¥ 108.31 to the U.S. dollar, the order was automatically converted to $25,000,000 and sent via satellite to InterTech's account at Wells Fargo.

InterTech's bank automatically relayed the information to the company's mainframe computer in Alameda, and the second stage of Louis's precisely crafted program kicked in.

At 3:00:00 P.M. Washington time the encoded signal was simultaneously sent, via InterTech's own communications satellite in geosynchronous orbit 22,500 miles over the equator to nine airports around the country.

Portland, where Guerin's *America* had just taken off.

Oakland, where United Flight 425 was taking off.

Los Angeles, where Delta's 558 was just rotating.

Chicago's O'Hare, where American 228 was on the ground next for take-off.

Minneapolis, where Northwest 142 was landing, Northwest 342 was eight miles out on final, and Northwest 1020 was on the ground waiting for a clear runway.

La Guardia, where United's 310 was on the ground waiting for Northwest 165, which had just taken off, and Lufthansa's Flight 009 from Frankfurt was eleven miles out.

JFK, where United's 280 was on the ground, American 138 had just taken off, and British Airways 111 was nine miles out.

Dulles, where Delta 756 had just taken off, and U.S. Air's 1211 was stacked twenty-one miles southwest.

Andrews, where Air Force Two, which had been late getting away from the apron, was just starting its takeoff roll.

All the airplanes were Guerin 522s, equipped with the InterTech heat monitor/alarm subassembly and special wiring harness on the port engines.

THIRTY-SEVEN

C aptain Bob Rodwell initiated a gentle climbing turn to the left, which would take them out of the pattern, while at the same time he reduced power because of noise-abatement regulations. There wasn't an ATR pilot who didn't grumble about the inherently unsafe procedure.

The signal from the Dulles repeater reached the Inter-Tech heat monitor/alarm subassembly as Delta 756 passed through 2,500 feet twelve degrees nose high. There were no indications on any of the cockpit instruments, nor did the jetliner's sophisticated computer that monitored the performance levels of every system notice anything was wrong. But within the first ten milliseconds the fate of the airplane and her crew and passengers was irrevocably sealed.

First to occur was the blockage of heat information from the port engine's thermocouples, which caused internal temperatures to soar several times beyond design limits almost immediately. The Mintori Assurance engineers who had designed the method of sabotage correctly reasoned that in order to mask evidence of an explosion when the sensor frame ignited, there would have to be massive and legitimate heat damage to the engine. Three times out of ten the blocked thermocouples would have created sufficient overheating to cause the engine to disintegrate on its own. But thirty percent was not good enough odds.

The internal structure of the Rolls-Royce turbine blades began to change. In this instance several of them would have disintegrated on their own within four minutes. As it was the engine would be destroyed much sooner than that.

The overheat also began to affect the fuel nozzles that metered heated kerojet into the combustion chamber. Much of the plumbing was already beginning to deteriorate. Soon the metal walls would be breached and a catastrophic amount of fuel would be dumped into the chamber, causing a massive explosion that in itself would seven times out of ten take not only the engine but the entire wing.

Still there were no indications on any of the cockpit instruments. Nor were the designers satisfied with seventy-percent odds.

Next out of the InterTech CPU was a modulated pulse that delayed GO-One by less than a quarter wave shift. At the end of the wiring harness the complicated signal spread resonantly across the engine-mounted harness frame, which erupted in a fireball as if an uncontrolled fuel flow had suddenly occurred, which it did a few hundredths of a second later.

Now the cockpit crew knew that something very bad had happened. Alarms flashed and buzzed all over the panel as the Guerin 522 began its fatal roll to port.

Captain Rodwell was the first to understand that what was happening was the same as the accident at Dulles. When the flight recorders, including the cockpit voice recorder, were recovered, the investigators' first indication that something had gone wrong, was the single expletive from the captain: "Fuck!"

Rodwell immediately powered back on the starboard engine in what he knew was a futile effort to bring the jetliner back to level flight.

"Mayday, mayday, mayday," his first officer, Carol Gerrard, radioed, her voice in reasonable control. "This is Delta seven-five-six, out of Dulles, calling mayday. We have lost our port engine and most of the wing. We are going down approximately four miles southwest of the airport."

They could hear the passengers screaming in abject terror as the airplane plunged toward a wooded knoll.

Air Force Two accelerated down the runway past one hundred knots to V1, the point of no return at which the aircraft was committed to taking off. Everything in the cockpit showed normal. Lieutenant Colonel Bob Wheeler anticipated V Rotate and a smooth liftoff. He figured they would be on top of the overcast in just a few minutes, when they would turn northwest on the great circle route to their refueling rendezvous out in the Aleutians. Delta's mayday call came over 121.5 and 243 MHz simultaneously. An instant later a huge fireball engulfed Air Force Two aft on the left. For just a moment Wheeler thought that the Delta flight had somehow collided with them, but that was impossible. Air Force Two lurched sharply to port and began to slide, helped in part because the starboard engine was still developing full thrust. Wheeler started to pull all power when he correctly guessed that they had completely lost their port engine. Instead he hit the starboard engine's thrust reversal immediately slowing their rate of skid to the left, and averting a cartwheel, which would have been a much greater disaster. The airplane began to shudder, and the rate of slide again increased. Wheeler realized that his co-pilot, Major Larry Marthaller, was applying brakes, or they had locked. In either case it was exactly the wrong thing to do to avoid rolling. Their center of gravity needed to be reduced now. Barely thinking, most of his actions reflexive, Wheeler yanked the landing-gear retract control, and the jetliner sank onto its belly, its rate of slide still impressive, but definitely slowing. He cut all power, and then braced himself. There was nothing left for him to do except listen to his co-pilot's mayday call override Delta's.

* * *

Viktor Yemlin had spent the morning packing the remaining books from his apartment. He was finally leaving for Moscow at eight this evening, and he'd already made the last of his courtesy calls on his American friends. He'd been in the U.S. for four years under the cover of cultural attaché, and he was going to miss a lot about the country. Not the high prices and the incredibly high murder rate, but he would never forget the quality of things.

Through the morning he'd thought about what Kirk McGarvey was suggesting, and what *Abunai* seemed to confirm. It was insane. If it had been anyone other than McGarvey he would not have given the notion a second thought. As it was he drifted from his apartment down to the communications center in the embassy on 16th Street around 3:00. It was Sunday and eleven in the evening in Moscow. Except for emergencies most of the offices in the Lubyanka and the Kremlin were closed, so there were only three clerks on duty. But the new SUR *rezident* was probably still in the embassy.

In addition to maintaining a communications link with Moscow, the center was a sensitive listening post. Its efforts were concentrated on intercepting transmissions from the White House, the State Department, and the FBI, in addition to police, fire, ambulance, and airport traffic. Pentagon communications were handled by military intelligence from a different location, although all information came back to the embassy for collation and analysis before being sent on to Moscow.

One of the scanners stopped on the aircraft emergency frequency.

"Mayday, mayday, mayday. This is Delta seven-five-six, out of Dulles, calling mayday."

"What the hell . . ." Yemlin said half to himself. He went across the room to the bank of radio receivers.

"We have lost our port engine and most of the wing. We are going down approximately four miles southwest of the airport—"

"Get this on a recorder," Yemlin ordered one of the clerks.

"It's being done, sir."

The Delta transmission was overridden by another aircraft calling mayday, and for a second Yemlin did not want to believe what he was hearing. It was more than impossible, it was unthinkable.

". . . Air Force Two, on the ground at Andrews. We have lost our port engine and wing, and are on fire. Eagle Two is on board. Repeat, Eagle Two is on board."

Yemlin grabbed a phone and called the SUR *rezident*'s emergency number. Whatever the man's current location was he would be found.

"Mayday, mayday, mayday, this is U.S. Air twelve-eleven. We're going down, we're going down!"

Yemlin stared at the scanner radio. What the fuck was happening?

The scanner erupted in a babble of voices that lasted for several seconds, until the Delta transmission ceased. A moment later the Air Force Two transmission also stopped.

Yemlin held the phone tightly against his ear, waiting for the *rezident* to come on the line.

"Mayday, mayday, mayday, this is U.S. Air twelve-eleven! We've lost our port engine and wing! We're going down . . . ! Twenty-one miles ah . . . southwest of Dulles! Haymarket intersection!"

"U.S. Air twelve-eleven, say again nature of your problem?"

"We've lost our port engine . . ." The transmission abruptly ended.

The *rezident* came on the line. "This is Soroshkin."

"Stanislas Ivanovich, this is Viktor Yemlin, this is an emergency."

"What is the nature of this emergency?"

"Air Force Two has apparently crashed on takeoff with the Vice President aboard. You should come down to Communications."

"Is this the McGarvey operation?"

"Yes, Mr. *Rezident.* Two other airplanes have also crashed. There may be others."

"I'm on my way."

Amanda Lindsay poured her husband a glass of iced tea and passed it across the small table to him. They were having late lunch in the family dining room. It was a Sunday ritual that Mrs. Lindsay insisted on whenever matters of state did not interfere. It was the only time they had alone together. Whenever possible they dismissed their personal staff so that she could serve and sometimes cook for her husband. It was a homey tradition that suited everybody, and one which was never interrupted except for the most extreme emergencies. After lunch he would go to his office to catch up on his reading until five, when he would prepare for his "Sundays at Six" half-hour radio broadcast over the NPR network. It was something FDR had started, and Reagan and Clinton had picked up. Since he had been scheduled to be enroute to Tokyo this evening, he'd taped his talk three days ago. But before it aired he wanted to review it again. There were a number of new points he wanted to bring up, among them the increasing civil unrest in Japan and what effects that would have on his upcoming talks in Tokyo. There was a commotion out in the corridor, and Lindsay turned as Justin Owen, chief of the Secret Service weekend detail, came in, a look of troubled concern on his face.

"Mr. President, Air Force Two has crashed on takeoff, and there's no word on survivors yet."

"My God," Lindsay said, his hand shaking as he put his tea down.

"Apparently one of the engines exploded during their takeoff roll. The rescue crews are on site now."

"Is there fire?"

"Yes, sir, but there's more. At least two other airliners both out of Dulles have crashed. Right now it looks like they had the same problem. Could be sabotage."

The color drained from Amanda Lindsay's face. "You were supposed to be on that flight today," she said.

Operations for Air Force One and Two and other governmental VIP flights were conducted out of Andrews Air Force Base by the 89th Military Airlift Wing. Emergencies were handled by the Air Wing's Search and Rescue squadron. Even before Air Force Two broadcast its mayday, the tower had notified SAR that the airplane was in serious trouble, and the crash teams were scrambled. Each GO truck was manned by seven SARTECH personnel in hot suits.

In the first seconds of the crises, Captain Thomas Moore, 89th SAR commander, thought the U.S. was under attack. Moments before the Vice President went down, they'd monitored Delta 756's mayday. Then came U.S. Air's 1211. Airplanes all over the place were falling out of the sky.

Air Force Two lay tilted to port off the end of the runway. Flames and greasy black smoke rose from where the engine and wing had been torn off. Debris from the wreckage was spread for five thousand feet along the runway. Moore watched the television monitors as the first crash team neared the site. It didn't look good.

"Any comms from the aircraft?" he asked one of his Mission Communications System specialists.

"Negative. They're off the air on all bands, except for their EPIRB."

"Cockpit's intact." Moore picked up the red phone direct to the Air Wing Commander's locator. It only took a few seconds. "Sir, this is SAR. We have Air Force Two down at the end of the runway with Eagle Two aboard. Our units are rolling."

"I just heard," Lieutenant Colonel Brian Skeggs replied. "How does it look, Tom?"

"Not good."

"What about backup?"

"The Secret Service is scrambling a VH-3 chopper, and a second is coming down from Bethesda Medical with the ER team. ETA about seven minutes."

"Fire?"

"Some, but if we can get to it before it spreads we'll have a chance." Moore watched the television monitors. The first crash team had arrived on site and was spraying fire retardant foam from its main nozzles. "But Colonel, something else is going on. Air Force Two lost a port engine. It exploded. In the last ninety seconds two other aircraft have gone down out of Dulles with exactly the same problem. Delta seven-five-six, and U.S. Air twelve-eleven."

"Have you talked to intelligence?"

"Not yet."

"Do it now."

"Yes, sir."

The Marine helicopter carrying the Secret Service personnel touched down near the end of the runway and six agents, wearing flak jackets and armed with assault rifles disembarked and took up defensive positions.

Smoke was everywhere. Emergency lighting aboard the downed Air Force Two cast a pale orange glow through the jumbled main cabin. People moaned, others cried for help. Outside, sirens seemed to be converging on them, and something that sounded like a waterfall was striking the side of the fuselage. Vice President Larry Cross, his left arm, hip, and legs crushed, lay wedged beneath one of the desks and two aircraft seats. They'd crashed. He knew that much, but he was having trouble focusing his thinking.

"Larry?" a woman cried weakly.

Cross knew the voice. He managed to turn his head toward the sound. His wife, blood spurting from a huge gash in her right side, the sweater she'd been wearing torn off her body, lay beneath one of the communications consoles that had somehow been thrown aft from near the front of the airplane.

"Sally," he called, and he tried to reach out for her, but his arms were pinned.

Her cries stopped, although her eyes remained open.

* * *

A half-dozen Secret Service agents surrounded the President as he was hustled to the situation room beneath the White House. His wife was escorted in a different direction.

"Your chopper is ready, Mr. President," Owen said. "Recommend that you leave for White Mountain immediately."

"Not till we see what's going on," Lindsay replied curtly. He stepped off the bombproof elevator. Already much of the weekend duty staff had arrived, and his NSA Harold Secor had just entered the building.

"Mr. President, two more civilian airliners have gone down," the situation room operations officer said. "Both in New York, out of JFK. A British Airways nine miles out, and an American Airlines on takeoff."

"What's the word on Larry?"

"Nothing yet," Owen said. He wore an ear piece. "They've got the fire out. There's a good chance there'll be survivors."

At Secret Service headquarters in the Treasury Building across from the White House, special investigator Don Huberty telephoned his boss Burt Anderson, Assistant Director of Investigations, at his home in Bethesda and explained the developing situation.

"Where is Eagle One?" Anderson demanded.

"In the White House situation room. He wants to stay there for the moment."

"Any word on Eagle Two? Have we got him out of the plane yet?"

"Not yet."

"All right, listen up, this is important," Anderson said. "If Air Force Two was sabotaged, they might try again. Eagle One was supposed to be on that plane. I want as many of our people out there as possible. In the meantime I'll call the director and see if we can't get Eagle One over to White Mountain."

* * *

"Are you calling to tell me that you have finally located Mr. McGarvey?" Arimoto Yamagata asked, careful to keep his voice free of fear and anger.

"No, but another situation has arisen," Yozo Hamagachi reported from the secure telephone in the Japanese embassy in Washington.

"Is it about the air crash in Oakland? The United Airlines crash? We know about that."

"Iie, Yamagata-san, that makes seven crashes so far."

"What are you talking about?"

"A Lufthansa flight coming into La Guardia Airport in New York City crashed just moments ago eleven miles from the runway. Four other civilian airlines have gone down within the past two minutes. Plus, Air Force Two, carrying the Vice President, crashed on takeoff from Andrews Air Force Base. *Yamagata-san,* he was on his way to Tokyo *in place of* the President. What is happening?"

"I do not know," Yamagata admitted. "But it is very important that you locate McGarvey. Do you have any leads?"

"None."

"What about the other man, Edward Reid? Has he disappeared as well?"

"We concentrated our efforts on McGarvey."

"Follow Reid. See where he goes, what he does, who he meets with. Find out everything you can about him. He may be a key to finding McGarvey before it's too late. This must be contained."

"It may already be too late. The Ambassador's staff has sent a flash-designated message to Tokyo. They are preparing more messages."

"Stop them," Yamagata said, fighting to maintain control.

"We will try."

Yamagata broke the connection, a sour taste in his mouth. He called Kamiya in Tokyo.

"Hai," the old man himself answered.

"Are you hearing about the airplane crashes?"

"Yes," Kamiya hissed the single word. "You have gone ahead with Morning Star without my authorization."

"I have not, *Kamiya-san*. I thought it was you."

"You lie!"

"Iie, there is no reason for me to lie. Someone has found out about the computer chips and is using them."

"Why?"

"I do not know at this time, *Kamiya-san*. But I believe McGarvey is behind this."

"What would he have to gain?" Kamiya paused. "Unless it was to help the Russians. He is working with them. He was in Moscow. The world makes strange bedfellows, *Yamagata-san."*

"There is another problem. Our embassy is sending traffic to Tokyo about this incident. It may be monitored."

"I will take care of that. Find Mr. McGarvey and kill him. Immediately."

"Hai," Yamagata promised, not quite sure how he was going to do either.

Japanese Prime Minister Ichiro Enchi, an early riser, was seated in his private study watching CNN when the first bulletin about the crash of Air Force Two, with the Vice President aboard, came on the screen. He watched in stunned disbelief for a full minute before he reached for his telephone. It was a few minutes after five in the morning in Tokyo. It rang before he could pick it up. His Deputy Director General of Defense Tadashi Ota was on the line.

"Mr. Prime Minister, apparently it has begun."

"I'm watching CNN now. Is it that fool Kamiya and his Morning Star?"

"It's possible."

"But why kill the Vice President?" Enchi asked confused.

"There's more, Prime Minister. So far seven airplanes have crashed. There may be others."

"Arrest Kamiya and Kobayashi. Immediately!"

* * *

America's take-off roll and lift-off were beautiful and went without a hitch. Dominique was relieved that McGarvey was wrong. "Thank God," she murmured. It had all been a nightmare, nothing more.

She went into the kitchen to fix a sandwich and make a cup of tea when an announcer broke in on the CNBC live broadcast from Portland with a news bulletin. Air Force Two, carrying the Vice President, had crashed on takeoff from Andrews Air Force Base. Seven and possibly more civilian airliners had gone down in what was already being described as the worst air disaster in history.

She stood in the kitchen doorway, a hand to her mouth, as she watched the first reports.

McGarvey and Socrates had braced themselves as best they could in the cramped electronics bay beneath the cockpit during the take-off and initial climbout. Their official departure time was 11:58 A.M. PST, two minutes earlier than scheduled.

The InterTech heat monitor/alarm subassembly lay in Socrates' lap. He'd left the input cable connected, but had disconnected the output jack.

"It seems to be functioning as normal," he said. "If it were in the loop it'd be working within parameters." He looked up. "I don't see anything wrong here, McGarvey."

"Nothing that would cause an engine overheat?"

"This is the computer that could do the damage. But we've checked it a dozen times, a hundred times . . ." the engineer hesitated.

"What?"

"I don't know," Socrates muttered. He took a screwdriver out of his pocket and quickly undid the fasteners holding the unit's top cover in place. He set it aside, switched on a penlight, and studied the circuit boards and components.

"How's it going down there?" Their pilot, Pete Reiner, called from topsides through the open hatch.

"Fine," Socrates answered absently. "How are the port engine temperatures holding up?"

"In the green for now."

"I know this," Socrates said slowly. He looked at McGarvey again. He was frightened. "I don't do the hands-on engineering anymore, otherwise I might have seen it." He shook his head in wonderment. "This is exactly the same subassembly that's in every 522 flying. But it should be different."

"That's it," McGarvey said.

"But nothing's wrong with it, Mac. Nothing."

"Jesus H. Christ," Reiner said.

"Is it the engine temperatures?" McGarvey started up the ladder.

"A United flight out of Oakland just went down! It's one of ours!"

"Wait," John Callahan, the co-pilot, overrode him. "Air Force Two is down. What the hell?"

At the National Security Agency's tightly secured eleven-acre Fort Meade, Maryland, headquarters, Marvin Amundson, chief analyst on duty, picked up his secure telephone from North American Intercept Section. NSA, in cooperation with Britain's Government Communications Headquarters, known as GCHQ, was capable of monitoring virtually every form of electronic communications anywhere in the world. Radio, telex, teletype, microwave, satellite, as well as private telephone calls by the military, diplomatic, and commercial sectors, were automatically intercepted, tested for value of information, and either dumped, recorded for later analysis, or brought to human attention.

"We have a partial decryption and translation of the Japanese embassy burst to Tokyo," the intercept intelligence officer reported.

Amundson brought it up on his computer display. Data streamed across the screen as their computers continued to decode the material. But the substance of the text was already becoming obvious.

"They're definitely involved with the downing of Air Force Two," the intelligence officer said.

"I concur," Amundson replied. "Looks as if they know something about the other crashes too. We show the total now at nine, with Delta 558 at Los Angeles International and Northwest 342 inbound to Minneapolis International."

"Sir, what the hell is going on?"

"Don't know yet," Amundson broke the connection, and switched consoles, entering a FLASH-designated message for the White House, Pentagon, Central Intelligence Agency, Federal Bureau of Investigation, and the Federal Aviation Administration. Then he picked up the phone to call a friend of his at Andrews.

Amundson's call caught 89th Air Wing Commander Lieutenant Colonel Brian Skeggs in his car on the way to Andrews. "The Japanese are behind this?" the Air Force officer demanded. It was hard to believe. What were they thinking?

Navy Captain Tom Eddington was the senior duty officer at the Pentagon's Crisis Management Command Center when the flash arrived from NSA. He was eating a sandwich and drinking a Coke at his console. It took him several moments to realize that it wasn't a test message, nor was it one of the practice alert scenarios. The authenticator codes were for real this time.

He glanced at the locator board. CINCPAC Rear Admiral Warren Talbot was the flag officer on duty. This would be right up his alley since it involved the Japanese. He hit a button on the secure phone and got Talbot upstairs just as the admiral was leaving his office.

"This is Eddington in the Crisis Management Command Center."

"I heard," Talbot answered sharply. "I'm raising the Pacific Fleet to DEFCON THREE. Prepare a message to that effect."

"Aye, aye, sir," Eddington hung up and switched to

another console. The Pacific Fleet had been raised to DEFCON FOUR last week because of the trouble between the Japanese and Russians. Admiral Talbot's order would considerably increase tensions over there. Anything beyond THREE was tantamount to war. Only the President could take that step.

Sam Varelis was home in Chevy Chase when the first bulletins started coming over CNN. At least six civilian jetliners were down in addition to Air Force Two. But no one seemed to be making the connection that every one of those airplanes were Guerin 522s. McGarvey was right after all, but it didn't give him any satisfaction.

He didn't bother calling NTSB operations in the Department of Transportation building on Independence Avenue until he was in his car and heading downtown. He got John Hom, the duty officer.

"This is Varelis, I'm on the way in. Has the FAA issued the grounding order yet?"

"Nobody knows what's going on, Mr. Varelis, but all hell is breaking loose. The count is up to twelve with the latest three."

"What aircraft? Where?"

"A United exploded on the ground, and a Northwest went down on takeoff at La Guardia. And another United over at JFK exploded on the ground."

Varelis was having trouble keeping a grip on it. "What kind of equipment were those three?"

"Sir?"

"What kind of airplanes were they, goddammit?"

The line was silent a moment. When Hom came back he was subdued. "Sonofabitch. They were all Guerin 522s. Mr. Varelis, what's happening?"

"That's what we're going to find out."

Most of the fire was out, but SARTECH team leader Technical Sergeant Roy Halvorson, covered in foam, was so hot inside his suit that he could barely think straight. He'd gone directly into the fire before it was completely extinguished so that he could set up his cutting equipment to get inside the twisted wreckage. He knew it would take several minutes before the heat he'd absorbed would bleed off. He would just have to endure it. Eagle Two was inside.

His SawsAll cut through the aluminum pressure hull of the Guerin 522 like a hot knife through soft butter. His partner, Staff Sergeant Mike Salo, was beside him with the big pry bar, and together they wedged out a door-sized section of hull aft and above where the port wing had connected. Dense smoke billowed out of the opening. But the emergency lights were still on. The interior of the aircraft was a mess. About as bad as Halvorson had seen.

"Going in," he said into his helmet mike.

Captain Don Moody, Jr., Chief 7th Fleet Navy Intelligence, was having a nightmare in which he was stumbling along a hot jungle road. All around him were American POWs, many of them half dead. It was World War Two on Luzon's Bataan Peninsula. In spite of the dream he wasn't surprised when he was awakened by his beside telephone.

"Captain, this is McCarty. We've been ordered to DEFCON THREE." Lieutenant, j.g., Michael McCarty was Intelligence Staff OD.

Moody glanced at his nightstand clock. It was a few minutes after 5:00 A.M., Tokyo time. "I'll be over there in five minutes. Has Admiral Ryland been notified?"

"In the process, sir. We've sent the twixt out to the fleet."

Moody was completely awake now, as if someone had stuck an electric probe up his ass.

FAA Administrator Jay Hansen refused to make the decision to ground all air traffic within the continental U.S. until he got to his office and could personally assess the situation. "Cool heads will prevail," was his motto.

"The number stands at thirteen now, sir," Byron Swanson, his associate administrator for operations said. "American Airlines Flight 228 exploded on the ground at O'Hare just two minutes ago."

THIRTY-EIGHT

The storm continued to grow into the night and early morning hours. For the first time Stan Liskey feared for his and Carol's lives. Problems had started to pile up within hours after they'd rounded the southwestern tip of Tokuno Island. The weather, which had cleared Saturday morning, had closed in on them that afternoon, the wind shifting viciously out of the northeast. It made the rock-strewn west coast of the island a dangerous lee shore. Their Magellan satellite navigator had developed a problem and was no longer reliable. The LORAN chain, operated by the Japanese, had mysteriously stopped transmitting. The roller-furling gear on their headsail had jammed, forcing him to cut the sail away, leaving them with a double-reefed main and staysail. It was a good running rig, but having no way to accurately determine their position, they were sailing blind. Their only option was to stand farther out into the East China Sea, to windward, to gain as much sea room as possible. If they crashed into the island, or onto the off-lying rocks, they would not survive. Thank God the Aires windvane was still working. If they had to hand steer in these conditions he didn't think they would make it. They would wear down before the storm was over, and they would be driven back onto the island, or they would be broached and sink.

It was a few minutes after five in the morning. He'd sent Carol below a couple of hours ago to get some sleep, and to get her out of the way so that she would not see his concern. The hatch slid open, and she scrambled up into the cockpit. Her eyes were wide, her face white, and she was panting. Liskey helped her attach her safety harness.

"What are you doing up here?" he shouted.

"I can't handle it, Stan. I want to be with you."

"You need your rest. You might have to take over."

"If we're going to die, I don't want to drown locked inside the boat!"

"We're not going to die. Don't be stupid."

The *Fair Winds'* rail was buried again, the motion tremendous. They could not see the waves in the darkness, but from the way they were being tossed around, Liskey figured they had to be twenty footers or bigger. They were not breaking yet, he was thankful for that much. If one of those monsters dumped on top of them, they would go to the bottom without a chance of getting aboard the life raft lashed on deck. But if the storm continued another twelve hours or more, the seas would build to a point where they would have to break. Then they would be in trouble. Liskey's best guess was that the storm would last much longer than that. The barometer was down farther than he'd ever seen it, except in a hurricane. And the last he'd looked it was continuing to fall.

"Can we get behind one of the islands?" she shouted. "Can we go back?"

"It's too risky."

"Why?"

"We'd pile up on the rocks."

"How about launching the life raft? We could key the EPIRB. Somebody would find us in the morning. We'd be a lot better off."

"No we wouldn't."

"Goddammit, Stan, I'm scared out of my head!"

"So am I," Liskey admitted. "But listen to me, Carol. This is a strong boat. As long as we don't do anything stupid we'll ride this out. We'll be okay. The life raft is just a last-ditch stand. Remember Fastnet in the eighties? Most of the guys who got killed drowned trying to get into their rafts. The next day their boats were found, battered, the floorboards awash, but still floating. We'll launch the life raft only when this boat sinks out from under us. In the meantime we've got a lot of work to do."

"All right, all right," she said breathlessly. "We've got work to do. What can I do?"

"Get some sleep."

"I'm done with that. What else?"

"Then hang on here. I'll go below and check the bilges."

"I did it just before I came up. It only took ten strokes."

"Then we're okay for now."

Carol pulled a package of Marlboros and a Bic lighter out of her pocket. "I brought these along just in case. Want one?"

"Why not, if you can get it lit."

"Lieutenant, we have a target," the helmsman said.

The *DD Thorn*'s senior officer on the bridge, Lieutenant, j.g., Roger Boberg, stepped across to the radar screen, bracing himself against the console. They were painting a small boat on the eighteen-hundred-yard ring, on what definitely was a collision course.

"I make our rate of closure about twenty knots, sir. Which means he's doing about five. The sub?"

"I don't know," Boberg said. "Come left to one-six-zero."

"Aye, coming left to one-six-zero."

Boberg rang engineering to reduce speed to ten knots, which barely gave them steerage way in these winds and seas. He was about to pick up the growler phone to call the captain when the communications officer came onto the bridge with a message flimsy.

"This just came, Lieutenant. It's not a drill. We're at DEFCON THREE."

"Holy shit." Boberg read the brief message from Seventh, then snatched the growler phone and called the captain. "This is Boberg on the bridge. You'd better get in here on the double, sir. We're tracking an unidentified object on the surface at eighteen hundred yards, and Seventh just took us to DEFCON THREE."

"On my way," Hanrahan said. "Sound general quarters, and pass it on to the *Cook* and *Barbey.*"

"Aye, sir." Boberg hit the ship's intercom. "Now hear this, now hear this. General quarters, general quarters, all hands man your battle stations." He switched on the Klaxon, then radioed the two frigates.

The skipper was the first on the bridge. He took the message from Boberg, quickly scanned it, then checked the radar. They were no longer on a collision course with the surface target, but they were slowly closing.

"Good work, Rog," he told his second officer. He called sonar. "This is the captain, what's the status on *Chrysanthemum?*"

"Sir, we were picking up what might have been hull popping noises a couple of hours ago, but weren't sure. Still no contact. This surface noise is killing us."

"Radar is showing what could be just the sail, sixteen hundred yards on a relative bearing of zero-two-five. Could it be our boy?"

"Captain, anything is possible in these conditions."

"All right, listen up. I want to know if he floods his tubes and opens his doors."

"We'll do the best we can."

Lieutenant Commander Willis Ryder came on the bridge. "What's up?"

Hanrahan showed his XO the Seventh Fleet message. "Authenticated?"

"Looks like it, but we haven't received a follow-up yet, so it's anybody's guess what's going on," Hanrahan said. "We've got a surface contact to the south, under sixteen hundred yards now. Could be the sub."

Ryder studied the radar screen. "Looks more like a small boat radar reflector than a steel hull."

"Could be we're just catching the sail. Sonar had what they thought was hull popping noises."

"But we don't have a hot contact?"

Hanrahan shrugged. "Conditions aren't good. We'll close for a visual. In the meantime contact Seventh and see what the hell is going on."

"Aye, aye," Ryder said.

"Bridge, CIC, we have a contact in the air."

Hanrahan keyed the phone. "What is it?"

"Looks like an Orion, Skipper. I'd say Japanese . . . definitely Japanese. He's just lit his downward-looking radar."

"Contact the *Cook* and *Barbey* again," Hanrahan told Boberg. "Tell them we're going in for a look."

"Could be four contacts up there now, *Kan-cho,*" the sonarman said.

Lieutenant Commander Kiyoda stood braced in the doorway to the sonar compartment. They'd slowly come up to thirty meters over the past few hours. The storm on the surface, which was ruining their passive sonar capabilities, was also moving the submarine around.

"Sierra-Zero-Four and Sierra-Zero-Five fade in and out. They're about twenty thousand meters at zero-six-zero and closing slowly, I think. But I'm losing Sierra-Zero-Nine. Sometimes it sounds like it has split apart. It's very hard to tell. No identifiable screw noises now. I just can't be sure."

"They could have launched a life raft," Lieutenant Minori suggested.

Kiyoda turned to his XO. "Do you think they are in trouble?"

"It's possible, sir."

"Then why aren't the other two ships hurrying to the rescue?" Kiyoda asked thoughtfully. "Maybe it's a trick."

"No way of knowing for certain until the conditions ease."

"We'll go up for a look." Kiyoda smiled. "Who knows what reaction we might provoke."

"Kan-cho, we're very close to Sierra-Zero-Nine," the sonarman warned. "I cannot guarantee their exact position."

"We'll take it slow," Kiyoda said. He went back to the control room with Minori. "Come to periscope depth."

"Recommend plus two meters to compensate for the waves."

"Make it so."

"Diving officer, make your depth one-eight meters," Minori said. "Five degrees on the fairwater planes. We'll do this slowly."

"Sound general quarters," Kiyoda ordered, and he turned to his weapons control officer, Lieutenant Takasaki. "Look sharp. If we get a clear target I'll want a continuous firing solution. There's no telling what they're up to."

"Hai, Kan-cho."

Kiyoda watched the depth indicator on his CRT command display countdown toward eighteen meters. He started for the periscope when the sonar operator suddenly shouted.

"Contact closing! Contact closing!"

A tremendous crash slammed into the optical and electronic arrays on top of the sail, slewing the *Samisho* almost ninety degrees onto her starboard side. Lights in the control room flickered and died, and water rushed in on them from a dozen places on the overhead.

"That was a major event," Ensign Masao Osanai radioed from ELINT in the back of the Lockheed/Kawasaki P-3C ASW aircraft.

"What happened?" the pilot, Lieutenant Fumiko Miyake, asked. He was fighting the aircraft's controls. The winds were boiling at this low altitude, making level flight difficult. His co-pilot flew the yoke and rudder pedals with him.

"A collision, I think. We were painting the *Samisho* on the MAD as it started to surface. It just merged with the American destroyer."

"What are you seeing now?"

"The *Samisho* is going down. She's trailing bubbles."

"Comms," Miyake radioed.

"Hai, Kan-cho."

"Get that off to base. Ask for instructions."

Since the brutal murders of the young Japanese woman and the policemen two weeks ago, officials in Yokosuka had become timid. It was a few minutes after five in the morning before anyone challenged the crowd that had been growing along the waterfront all evening. Americans were a violent people from a violent land. The only lesson they understood was violence. If Tokyo could not see this then Prime Minister Enchi's government would fail. The people would be heeded. It was time to embrace the old values of respect and of *bu-shi,* Takushiro Hatoyama thought. Now the MSDF had to share the port with the American navy. Both sides of the harbor were busy this morning, lights and movement everywhere, as if both bases were on alert. It was disturbing because it was unexpected. The crowd stopped in front of a line of Japanese policemen in riot gear stretched two deep across the road a half-block from Seventh Fleet's main gate. Hatoyama went across to them.

"We are Rising Sun," he shouted. The police line stiffened. "We are here in the name of the people to arrest Rear Admiral Albert Ryland for crimes against the state of Nippon."

A police lieutenant near the middle of the line raised a bullhorn. "You are engaged in an illegal activity," he shouted. "You are ordered to disperse at once or face arrest."

"There are ten thousand of us here, Lieutenant. More are continuously arriving. You cannot arrest us all. Stand aside."

"By order of the government, return to your homes immediately."

"Do not be a traitor to your own homeland," Hatoyama shouted. "Contrary to international agreement many ships of the Seventh Fleet are equipped with nuclear weapons. Admiral Ryland is a criminal."

A pair of armored personnel carriers came up the road

from the navy base and stopped in front of the gate. A dozen Marines in battle fatigues scrambled out of each and took up defensive positions, their weapons at the ready. It was extraordinary. Nothing like this had ever happened before.

"Disperse at once," the police lieutenant's amplified voice carried over the crowd.

"Look at what is happening behind you!" Hatoyama pointed to the Marines. "Will you let a foreign military power fire on innocent civilians?"

A few of the policemen glanced nervously over their shoulders.

"My fellow countrymen, listen to me! Japan must be cleansed of all foreign military! How long must we remain an occupied country?"

Shotoro Ashia came up from the mob and pulled Hatoyama back a few feet. He had been talking to someone on a cellular phone. "Something is happening."

"What is it?" Hatoyama asked. He kept his eyes on the police line and the Marines blocking the gate behind them.

"The American Vice President's airplane crashed on take-off just minutes ago. And there are other crashes. All over America."

Hatoyama's breath caught in his throat. "Has it started?"

"I don't know. I cannot get through to Kobe. But Takushiro, all American forces have gone to DEFCON THREE. That's why they are guarding this base so well. They will fire on us."

"Do they want war?" Hatoyama asked, stunned.

"No one knows."

Hatoyama looked at the police line. "Perhaps it will start here. Perhaps this is our destiny. Our *giri*, for the *Yamato Damashi* of Nippon."

"At least six airplanes are down, maybe more," Captain Reiner said excitedly. "I'm turning back."

"Hold on," McGarvey shouted. He and Socrates scrambled up from the electronics bay. They would cross the coast in another minute or so, the Pacific Ocean stretched to the horizon ahead of them. *America* was still climbing to a cruise altitude of sixty-six thousand feet, but already the party had started. They could hear music and people talking and laughing. The panel clock showed 12:05:00 PST. Callahan was on the radio with Guerin's operations center at Gales Creek.

"Where'd Air Force Two go down?" McGarvey asked.

"On take-off at Andrews."

"What about the others? You said Oakland. Where else?"

"Dulles, Minneapolis, New York. All over the fucking country."

"What kind of equipment?" McGarvey asked, but he already knew. It was starting just as he'd feared it would.

"I don't know," Reiner admitted.

"All 522s, Mr. McGarvey," Callahan said. "Ops says the number is up to thirteen."

"Jesus H. Christ, that's fucking impossible!" Reiner blurted.

"What happened to them?"

Callahan's eyes were round. "Six of them lost port engines. They're not sure about the others. What the hell is going on?"

"It's the heat monitor," Socrates muttered. "The new CPU. The modification came up from InterTech in '90. Right after the American Airlines crash."

"The same one you just pulled?" McGarvey asked.

Socrates looked down into the electronics bay where the heat monitor lay on the deck, connected only by its input cable. "Has to be something on the engines themselves. The port engines. Something that has a left and right. Mirror images."

"The engines aren't interchangeable, port and starboard?"

"Yes, but there are some differences," Socrates said. Then he had it, and his breath caught in his throat. "The heat monitor is connected to the thermocouple frame. One's for port, the other's for starboard. My God, it's as simple as that, but we never saw it."

"Call the FAA and ground the fleet, now," McGarvey told the engineer. "Wait. How would it work? Would it be on a timer? An outside signal. What?"

"Probably a triggering signal from somewhere. Maybe through the VOR system. Maybe even via satellite—the GPS system. Could be anything."

"Any way of blocking it?"

"Pull the heat monitor, just like we did," Socrates said.

"Call the FAA and tell them to get that message out to every 522 whose engines are turning. Do it right now."

Callahan relayed that to Guerin Ops. "Mr. Socrates, the company wants a clarification."

"No time." The engineer plugged a spare headset into the phone system.

"Do we turn back or keep going?" Reiner asked. He scanned his instruments almost continuously.

"Get us out of the mainland air traffic control system as quickly as possible," McGarvey said. "In the meantime try to find out which airports have been affected. Maybe it's not the entire system."

"Right," Reiner replied.

McGarvey unlocked the flight-deck door and stepped out into the forward galley. Two flight attendants were opening champagne. They looked up, startled.

"Oh," one of them cried out. She dropped the open bottle on the deck. It didn't break, but champagne squirted all over the place.

"Is David Kennedy on board?" McGarvey asked. He kept his voice and manner nonthreatening.

"No," the other stew said.

Several people at the front of the main cabin saw what was going on and sensed that something was wrong. They stopped talking in mid-sentence. Two men rushed up the aisle from the back of the plane, drawing their pistols.

McGarvey stepped back half a pace and spread his hands away from his body. The flight attendants moved out of the way.

"FBI, Mr. McGarvey," the lead man said. "You're under arrest." He stepped to the left to give his partner a clear firing path.

"That'll have to wait," McGarvey said, keeping his voice low. "We've got a problem."

Mangled bodies and blood were nothing new to Technical Sergeant Halvorson. He'd been on SARTECH teams in the Philippines, Labrador, and Greenland and had personally participated in five accident rescues and cleanups. Some of them had been a lot worse than Air Force Two. But this time the Vice President was involved.

A total of thirty-seven persons were aboard, including Eagle Two and his wife, the flight-deck crew, the communications staff, the stewards, the Secret Service, the Veep's personal staff, and the media. At first glance he estimated more than half of them were dead or critically injured.

At least they didn't have to contend with fire for the moment. But with a heavy aircraft down, that was always a potential problem.

Halvorson could hear screams and cries for help even through his thick helmet. His partner, Staff Sergeant Salo, was right behind him as they carefully climbed through the jumbled wreckage.

"Okay, we've got many survivors in here," Halvorson radioed. "Let's go, let's go."

"Over there, Roy." Salo pointed toward the front of the crumpled main cabin where the VP was wedged beneath a desk and two aircraft seats.

"We see Eagle Two," Halvorson said.

Cross was struggling, trying to reach his wife, who was several feet away from him. She was obviously dead.

"Able Leader One, say his condition," the SARTECH coordinator radioed.

"He's alive but badly injured. We need a backboard in here."

Halvorson and Salo eased the aircraft seats away from the desk and set them aside. They could see that the VP's left side had been badly mangled when the desk had slammed into him in the crash. Another few inches and his head would have been crushed. It was one bit of luck at least.

Two other openings were being cut into the aircraft's hull, and a pair of SARTECH personnel joined Halvorson and Salo with a backboard. The VP would have to be stabilized before they moved him.

Still others were starting to administer first aid to some of the accident victims, but their primary consideration was the Vice President. Until he was clear no one else would be moved.

Between the four of them they managed to lever the heavy desk off the VP. Three of them held it away, so that Halvorson could ease the man out from under. Immediately blood began spurting from two major wounds.

"We've got two bleeders here," Salo radioed. One of the SARTECHs pulled a big pressure bandage out of his First Response kit and handed it down.

The first was the femoral artery on the VP's left thigh. It took Halvorson several moments to put the pad in place and get enough pressure to slow the blood flow to a trickle. Next, he positioned an inflatable tourniquet bandage on the VP's left leg below the knee, which had been badly crushed, and quickly pumped it up.

The Vice President screamed and his eyes fluttered. His complexion turned pasty white. His breathing became shallow and rapid.

"He's going shocky," Halvorson said, maintaining his calm. He cut the VP's coat and shirt sleeves away from his right arm, as the SARTECH behind him ripped the seals off a plasma administration kit.

He pulled off his hot-suit gloves. A SARTECH handed him an alcohol pad that he used to swab the VP's arm above the elbow. Then he found a vein and eased the plasma needle into the skin and through the tough venal wall, taped it into place, and released the clamp to start the flow.

"Sally," the Vice President called weakly.

Halvorson pulled off his helmet. "It's all right, sir. She'll be fine. Do you understand?" He moved forward so that they could get the backboard into place beside the VP. "We're going to move you now onto the stretcher. Just hang in there, sir."

While Salo held the plasma bag up, Halvorson and the two other SARTECHs eased the Vice President onto the board.

"Easy now, Mr. Vice President, you'll be okay," Halvorson said.

Padded wedges were placed on either side of the VP's neck before they strapped his head down so that it could not move. They placed a strap across his shoulders, one across his hips, and wedged his legs, strapping his ankles.

"All right, we're coming out with Eagle Two," Halvorson radioed.

The streets of Tokyo were practically empty at this hour. Prime Minister Ichiro Enchi rode in his limousine to Government House while speaking on the telephone with his Director General of Defense, Shin Hironaka.

"What is the situation with Vice President Cross?"

"Mr. Prime Minister, we have had no further word in the past two or three minutes. But already thirteen airplanes have gone down in the U.S. And there is another situation developing. Have you called your entire cabinet?"

"Yes," Enchi said, trying to grasp the enormity of what he was being told. "What situation?"

"Admiral Shimakaze called me from Yokosuka. Rising Sun has gathered a mob at Seventh Fleet Headquarters. They are threatening to arrest Admiral Ryland because nuclear weapons have been brought here aboard his ships."

Enchi closed his eyes. "Have you spoken with Admiral Ryland?"

"No, Mr. Prime Minister," Hironaka said. "The Seventh Fleet has been raised to a Defense Condition Three. The same order was apparently transmitted to the American Marine and Air Force installations on Okinawa."

"What are you telling me?"

"The timing makes it seem likely that the Americans believe we are responsible for the attack on their air fleet."

"Kamiya and Kobayashi are to be arrested."

"I understand, Mr. Prime Minister. But that may take too much time. Considering the situation in Yokosuka, as well as the continuing threat that the Russians may make a retaliatory strike at any moment, I suggest that we raise our readiness level to Defense Condition Two."

"That's tantamount to a declaration of war."

"We may have no other choice."

"I will call President Lindsay," Enchi said.

"First let me give the order, Mr. Prime Minister. We must not be caught unprepared. We must be ready."

"Very well," Enchi said. "Do they want war?"

CIA Director Murphy got into his limousine and, before it rolled down the driveway, he was speaking to his Deputy Director of Intelligence, Doyle. "What's NSA's best estimate?"

"There's continuing flash traffic from the embassy to Tokyo. I've seen the partial decryptions and translations, General. They're definitely involved."

"Sonofabitch." He motioned for his bodyguard to give him a cigarette. "Any word on Cross?"

"He's hurt but alive. The number's at thirteen now. Should have word from the FAA any minute to ground the system."

"I hope so. Where's the President?"

"White House Situation Room."

"What the hell do they want?" Murphy asked. "War?"

* * *

"Mr. President, the general is on his way," Tommy Doyle said. He was on a conference call between the White House and the National Security Agency.

"Am I to understand that the Japanese military readiness has been raised to DEFCON TWO?" President Lindsay asked. His gut was sour. This wasn't supposed to happen.

"That's correct, sir," Amundson said from Fort Meade. "It gibes with the increased communications we're intercepting, not only between Tokyo and its embassy here, but between all its military units."

The President exchanged glances with his National Security Adviser and the others who had arrived. The call was on the speakerphone. "What does the CIA have for us?"

"I don't know if it's a coincidence, sir, but Rising Sun is rioting in Yokosuka again. They want to arrest Admiral Ryland for allowing the Seventh Fleet to bring nuclear weapons to Japan."

"How the hell do they know that?" Lindsay asked.

"We don't know, Mr. President. As I say it may be a coincidence."

"I don't believe in coincidences," Lindsay said. "What else?"

"The number of downed airplanes stands at thirteen. We're expecting the FAA to shut down the system at any moment."

"What about Larry?" the President asked.

"Mr. President, he is alive," one of the communications specialists said from his console at the back of the room. "They're pulling him out of Air Force Two now."

"The FAA refuses to act until Jay Hansen shows up," Socrates reported bitterly. "I don't understand."

"Where the hell is he?" McGarvey demanded.

"Apparently on the way to his office."

Special agents McLaren and Joyce were crowded into the galley behind McGarvey at the open flight-deck door.

"Call the White House," McGarvey said. "The fleet has to be grounded."

Callahan turned around. He was still talking with Guerin Ops and he was shook up. "Eight airports. La Guardia, JFK, Dulles, O'Hare, Minneapolis International, LAX, Oakland, and . . . Portland plus Andrews."

Reiner's hand shook on the arm rest. "The sonsabitches had us targeted."

Marine Major David Ross, chief of security at Seventh's Yokosuka Base, rode in a HumVee toward the trouble at the main gate. The wind blew from that direction so he could hear the amplified voices from bullhorns and the deep-throated rumble of a large, angry crowd. They'd been expecting a major event of this sort for the past two weeks, but this morning of all mornings made it spooky. All they knew at this point was that a mob of at least ten thousand Japanese nationals was threatening base security at the same time CINCPAC had raised Seventh to DEFCON THREE. Already engines on half the ships in port had been lit in preparation for emergency departure, their crews called to general quarters. The Marines, who would be the last off, had been scrambled for a Stage One perimeter defense. No unauthorized personnel were to be allowed anywhere near the base or the ships. Don Moody had asked Ross to personally try to defuse the situation at the main gate.

"At least buy us the time to get the hell out of here, Dave."

"Begging your pardon, Captain, but I'm not going to order my men to fire on civilians," Ross had said.

"Not unless they threaten lives or sensitive materials," the chief of Seventh Fleet Intelligence replied, and Ross knew what he was talking about. "If it comes to that, the Admiral himself will give the order."

"I hear you, Captain."

He parked just inside the main gate and hurried the rest of the way on foot to the defensive position Baker platoon had established. Lieutenant Otis Green, the unit leader, came over and saluted.

"How's it look, Green?"

"Not good, sir. The police have tear gas and riot guns, but I don't think they'd last long. It'd leave us holding the bag. You got orders, sir?"

"You're to hold your position, Marine. But no one fires into the crowd except on the Admiral's orders." Ross looked down the road at the police line and the mob. The noise was starting to get ugly.

"Aye, aye, Major."

"We won't leave you hanging." Ross unstrapped his holstered sidearm and handed it to Green. "I'll talk to them."

"Watch yourself, sir."

"Okay, talk to me," Captain Don Moody said.

"The DEFCON THREE has been authenticated, and the fleet has been notified. Admiral Ryland ordered all of our assets to make ready for sea as soon as possible," Lieutenant, j.g., McCarty said. "But all hell is breaking loose."

Moody looked sharply at the young OD. McCarty had been in the command less than six months, but in that time he'd proven to be a good officer who never exaggerated.

"Has the Admiral arrived yet?"

"He's expected any minute. But Captain Byrne is already upstairs."

"All right, Mike, they're going to have some tough questions for me. I've already got Major Ross on track. Bring me up to speed."

McCarty handed him a sheaf of message flimsies. "These are in the order we received them. Read them as soon as possible because you're sure as hell not going to believe me, Captain."

"One at a time."

"Air Force Two, with the Vice President aboard, crashed on take-off from Andrews. In the past several minutes at least thirteen commercial jetliners have gone down across the CONUS, most of them apparently because of the same problem. NSA has been monitoring a lot of flash traffic between the Japanese embassy in Washington and its Department of State in Tokyo. It's the reason for the DEFCON THREE."

Moody was stunned. "What else?"

"All Japanese self-defense forces have gone to DEFCON TWO in the past couple of minutes, and Flotillas One and Four are getting ready to leave Yokosuka."

"Are they sharing their mission orders?"

"No, sir," McCarty replied. "You know about the mob at the main gate. They want to arrest Admiral Ryland and charge him with war crimes for bringing nuclear weapons into Japanese waters. What you can't know is that Mike Hanrahan has finally gotten into it with the *Samisho*."

A phone rang and one of the communications techs answered it. "Captain Moody, the Admiral has arrived. He wants you in Ops on the double."

"On my way," Moody replied, a troubling ache in his gut. What in God's name was happening?

The green Ford Probe rental car crossed the Key Bridge and headed northwest out of the city. Mueller drove with the flow of traffic, careful not to be too slow or too fast. His bag was packed and lying on the back seat. The money he'd taken from Zerkel was in the bag. Before he crossed the Canadian border at Detroit sometime in the night or early morning, he would tape the cash to his body. He expected no trouble from Canadian customs, he simply wanted to minimize the risks. It was happening now, he knew. Although he had very little curiosity at this point he tuned the radio to a station that was broadcasting the first bulletins about what the announcer was calling the "worst air disaster in the history of aviation." He sat back, totally relaxed, to listen and enjoy.

"In what may be the most bizarre twist to this disaster, federal authorities are looking for a former East German spy, Bruno Mueller, in connection with the thirteen crashes."

Another voice came on with an accurate description of Mueller, and of the Thomas Reston persona he'd used at Oakland and Chicago.

Mueller slowed down as he searched for an exit that would take him back into the city.

"Is the FAA cooperating?" McGarvey asked.

"I can't get through to them or to the White House," Socrates said. He was pale. "But there's been nothing for the past several minutes. It might have been a one-time pulse, not an ongoing signal."

"Either that or there's no 522s left near those eight airports," McGarvey warned. "They could have been diverted."

"That's possible," Reiner said. "But we have equipment all over the place. Every airline flies our aircraft."

They were out over the Pacific Ocean at their subsonic cruising altitude five miles up. The West Coast was well behind them. The music had been shut off, and the party had been stopped, but there was angry conversation, the passengers demanding to know what was happening.

"What I don't get is why just the port engines on 522s?" Callahan said.

"They're targeting Guerin, and they want everyone to know what's happening is no coincidence," McGarvey said.

"The Japanese?"

"I'm not so sure."

"Who else?" Reiner demanded. "I'm trying to fly this airplane. I wish somebody would tell me what the hell is going on. If it's just a corporate takeover, give it to the bastards. No company's worth all this."

"I agree," McGarvey said. "But this may be the start of something a hell of a lot bigger." He turned to the FBI agents. "Is there anyone from the FAA aboard?"

"I think there's someone back there from Washington," McLaren said.

"Explain the situation to him and see if he can get to his boss."

McLaren hesitated.

"You can arrest me when we land," McGarvey said. "In the meantime, there's not much chance of me going anywhere."

"Right," McLaren said, and left.

"I'll try my boss," Joyce said. "He's got a real hard-on for you, Mr. McGarvey. I think I'll his attention."

"How about Al Vasilanti?" McGarvey asked.

"He's back there, but he won't do any good," Socrates replied. "He was in bad enough shape after Dulles. Now? It's anyone's guess."

"Kennedy's not aboard?"

"No," Socrates said puzzled. "I didn't see him in the confusion."

"Try to get through to him. See why he stayed behind. And see if he can get through to the White House." McGarvey turned to Callahan. "Get back with Gales Creek and find out for sure that it was the port engines on all those crashes, and have them stand by to let us know if anything else happens."

"What about you?" Socrates asked.

"I'll try the CIA. Maybe they'll listen now."

"Okay, stand by," Reiner cut in. He flipped a couple of switches on an overhead panel. "Number two is overheating. We have about a minute before it shuts itself down."

Socrates studied the readouts on one of the CRT monitors. "Increase the air flow to the combustion chamber."

"Already at maximum."

"Ops says everything is quiet for now," Callahan reported.

"We need the port monitor," Reiner said urgently.

"No other way around it?" McGarvey asked.

"No," Socrates said. "We'll lose the engine otherwise."

"Do it," McGarvey ordered. "Callahan will stay with Gales Creek. If there's another crash you can pull the plug. In the meantime we head to the nearest airstrip. If you can get the engine cooled down before we get into Portland's air traffic control range, you can yank the monitor again so that we can land."

"I hope the hell you know what you're doing," Reiner said as Socrates scrambled down into the electronics bay.

"I'm not an engineer," McGarvey replied.

"No, but you've got balls, I'll say that much for you."

The sharply flaring bows of a huge gray ship suddenly appeared out of the darkness directly overhead. Obviously in trouble, it wallowed at an oblique angle to the seas. The acrid stench of diesel oil was thick on the wind. Stan Liskey, his adrenaline pumping, fumbled with the lines connecting the Aires windvane, slipped them off, and hauled the tiller hard over to port.

They couldn't have been more than forty or fifty feet from the monster. For several agonizing moments Liskey was sure they would be sucked in by the bow wave. But *Fair Winds* clawed herself away, the gray wall slipping farther and farther aft.

"What was it?" Carol screamed over the shriek of the wind.

Liskey had caught a glimpse of the bow numbers, 988. He didn't know the name of the ship, but he knew it was Seventh Fleet out of Yokosuka.

"I think it's a destroyer. One of ours."

"What's it doing here?"

"I don't know, but it's in trouble."

The *Fair Winds* caught the wind and charged east in the direction of the islands. Liskey let the boat have her own way for a full minute to give his heart a chance to slow down. He glanced up at the port shrouds where the radar reflector was still in place. The destroyer had seen them. There was no doubt about it. So they were in trouble and could not maneuver for some reason. The near collision was just bad luck. What kind of trouble?

"We've got to get the sails down," he shouted. "I want to lie ahull until dawn so we can see what's going on.

Soon as we're set I'm going to try to raise them on the radio, see what's happening."

"Are you crazy?" Carol screamed. "It's a warship. Their lifeboats are bigger than us. I say we have our own problems. Let's go."

"Are you going to help me, or not?"

She opened her mouth to say something, but changed her mind. She nodded. "I'll take the tiller. As soon as we're settled down we can bring the handheld up here and try to raise them on sixteen."

"Whatever it was ate our starboard prop and partially jammed the rudder," the chief engineer reported. "No way of bringing that turbine back on line. It'd pull the shaft right out of the ship. I can answer the helm from down here, but it'll be slow. And I do mean slow."

Hanrahan and the others were braced against anything they could grab. The *Thorn* was nearly broadside to the wind and seas, rolling past twenty-five degrees each time a crest hit.

"Lee, we need to come eighty degrees left as soon as you can manage it. Otherwise we stand a good chance of capsizing."

"I'm on it," Lieutenant Commander Leland Rapp replied, and he hung up.

"It was the sub," Ryder said.

"Goddamned right it was, Red," Hanrahan agreed. He keyed the phone. "CIC, bridge."

"CIC, aye."

"What's our friend doing, Don?"

"He's making a hell of a racket, blowing lots of bubbles. I'd say we clipped his antennas and masts, periscopes too. Might even have taken a bit out of his sail. He's probably blind, or nearly so."

"Got him with our starboard prop and rudder."

"Then he's in big trouble."

"Set up a firing solution."

"He got our towed arrays, Mike. Both of them."

"Use the fifty-three on the bow, goddammit."

"Seventh says hold on."

"That's an order, Lieutenant. Find that submarine and give me a firing solution."

"Aye, Skipper."

"Message the *Barbey* and *Cook*," Hanrahan told his XO. "Tell them we're going sub hunting."

"What about the sailboat? Could be Japanese out here to set us up."

"A trap?"

"Wasn't for them we might not have hit the sub."

"I see what you mean, X," Hanrahan said, grim lipped. "First things first. We'll deal with the sailboat later."

"We can send up the comms buoy and ask for help, *Kan-cho*," Minori suggested. They were taking on water, but the pumps were keeping ahead of it. Lights and power had been restored to the boat, and although their ability to maneuver had not been affected by the collision, they were blind except for sonar. Their observation and attack periscopes had been jammed in their wells, and the ELINT and communications arrays on top of the sail had been damaged or sheared off.

"In any event we'll have to surface within ten or twelve hours to recharge our batteries," Chief Engineer Lieutenant Kiichi Owada warned.

Even the *Samisho*'s advanced battery and electric motor designs had their limits. When their available electrical power dropped to a certain level, limiting relays automatically tripped, cutting nonessential systems one by one. Eventually only the life-support systems would have power, at which time they would cease being a warship.

Kiyoda keyed the phone. "Sonar, conn. What is Sierra-Zero-Nine doing?"

"It's hard to say, *Kan-cho*. But I think she has lost one of her props and maybe damaged her rudder. She is turning very slowly to port."

"What about Sierra-Zero-Four and Zero-Five?"

"Definitely incoming, but judging by the surface noises I'd say it's getting worse up there."

"Do you still have the fourth target?"

"It fades in and out. Could be some kind of a decoy buoy. A trap."

Kiyoda turned back to his chief engineer. *"Owada-san,* at full maneuvering power, using all of our sonar and weapons launch capabilities, how long before we must surface?"

"A few hours, *Kan-cho,* maybe four."

"Give me four."

"Hai, Kan-cho."

"What do you mean to do?" Minori asked.

Kiyoda looked at him. "Kill all four of those targets. What did you think, Ikuo?"

Twenty-five miles southeast of Minneapolis International Airport, Northwest Flight 1020, with two hundred seventeen passengers and crew, came within range of the repeater. The port Rolls-Royce engine erupted in a burst of flames and metal parts, shearing off much of the wing and tearing a hole four feet tall and twenty-three feet long out of the side of the fuselage. First officer Rick Pearson's mayday was the fourteenth broadcast in less than ten minutes. The FAA system had not reacted fast enough to save them.

THIRTY-NINE

Federal Aviation Administration Chief Administrator Jay Hansen arrived downtown fifteen minutes after the first crash. Although it was Sunday, and the system was in crisis, he was dressed in a three-piece blue pinstriped suit, his tie correctly knotted. He was a man driven to precision, and he ran his agency the same way he conducted his life: by the book.

"Number fourteen went down a couple of minutes ago," Byron Swanson reported, meeting him at the elevator. "Northwest 1020 inbound to Minneapolis."

"Any word on the Vice President?" Hansen asked, crossing the corridor to his office.

"Hurt but alive. We've narrowed the problem to nine airports, including Andrews. We're running checks on the entire system. So far there've been no accidents at any other airport. But we're talking all Guerin equipment. Port engine failures. Just like at Dulles two weeks ago, and the O'Hare incident in '90."

"Sabotage?"

"Anything is possible. Guerin is asking the Bureau and the CIA for help, whatever that means. But we've got to shut down the system right now."

"I agree," Hansen said. "Close those eight civilian airports and advise Andrews. Divert any incomings to the nearest availables. Is Russ Neil here yet?"

"On his way. In the meantime Archie Darden is holding on line one for you."

"He's aboard *America,* isn't he?"

"Right," Swanson said. He used the phone in the outer office to relay the closure order to the air traffic control system, as Hansen went inside and picked up his phone.

"Archie, this is Jay Hansen. Where are you?"

"About eighty miles inbound to Portland. We think we've got the problem pinpointed."

"I'm closing Portland and seven others. Looks like something's wrong with the 522 fleet. I'm going to ground them all."

"Good. We'll divert to Gales Creek. The problem is in a heat-sensing subsystem supplied by a subcontractor in San Francisco."

"Does it affect you?"

"George Socrates thinks so. Call the President. Tell him what we're facing."

"That's exactly what I'll do, as soon as I find out. But we're not going off half-cocked."

The Ministry of International Trade and Industry is by far the most powerful governmental agency in Japan. Its operations are directed by an elite group of men drawn from industry and finance. The nation's industrial policies are created and conducted by the ministry, as are business practices through the *Keidanren*—a sort of super chamber of commerce. Japan's foreign investments, and therefore her foreign policies, are managed by MITI. And more importantly, all defense requests must be approved by the ministry, which in effect means that MITI controls Japan's military budget. MITI got its start before the war as the Ministry of Munitions, so its control of the Self Defense Forces is fitting.

In 1953 a law was passed giving MITI the power to control the development and manufacture of all aircraft and weapons, including any civilian technology that might be of use. In the past few years, for example, the ministry funded a number of ongoing projects: superconductors, artificial computer intelligence, advanced optical fiber systems, fuel cell power generators, laser and ion beam processing systems, satellites and launching facilities, high-tech aerospace materials, and since 1990, the development of hypersonic aircraft engines.

In order to do all of that effectively MITI has the full cooperation of every segment of Japan's government and industry. Information flows into the ministry twenty-four hours per day from all over the world. From captains of international conglomerates to lowly cipher clerks, MITI gathers data, some of it electronic (such as that collected by the National Security Agency's Fort Meade headquarters) but most of it HUMINT—human intelligence.

Hideyoshi Nobunaga, MITI director, rode in a Kawasaki AH-7C turbojet helicopter into the city from his palatial home near Chiba on Tokyo Bay's eastern shore. Before he'd taken over the ministry he'd been CEO of

Mitsubishi Heavy Industries, and he knew how to handle a crisis. He'd been having premonitions for the past two weeks, so he'd not been surprised when he'd been awakened. He would have to advise Prime Minister Enchi when he had all the facts. But talking with Sokichi Kamiya over encrypted telephone, he wasn't so sure how long that might take.

"I have no reason to lie to you, *Nobunaga-san,*" Kamiya said from a secret location near Kobe. "This is not Morning Star."

"Is it some hothead?"

"Arimoto Yamagata assures me not. Somehow the preparations we so carefully made were discovered and put to use. It's possible we will be able to lift something from the ashes. But for now we should not overreact. The American forces here and on Okinawa have been moved to Defense Condition Three. Our own forces are at the second level."

"There are other developing situations that you might not be aware of," Nobunaga cautioned. "We may be facing a threat from the north."

"The Russians?"

"Yes. It's possible they'll be moving soon. It would confuse an already dangerous situation."

"What are you saying to me?"

"Proceed with extreme caution," Nobunaga warned. "The man seen rooting about in the ashes might not be understood."

Kamiya laughed. "You don't wear the Western stereotype of the traditional Japanese very well. We can make the situation ours if you will help."

Nobunaga smiled to himself in the darkness as he looked out at the vast spread of Tokyo. "I will not stand in your way now, *Kamiya-san.* But neither will I stand behind you."

Kiyoda wanted to pull young Nakayama out of his seat in front of the primary sonar console and do the work himself. But his chief sonar operator was the best in the entire MSDF, and he certainly knew the equipment better than his captain did. But it was hard to wait. A billion pinpricks of light flashed in Kiyoda's head. Stars. There was a god, and it was the universe.

"Sierra-Zero-Nine has definitely turned, *Kan-cho*. But it was slow. I'm seeing turns on only one screw. I definitely have rudder damage."

"What about the other two warships?"

"Incoming. They're making a lot of noise. The conditions are very bad up there." Nakayama used a grease pencil to mark the positions of the three ships on the sonar screen.

"What about the decoy?"

"It may be a small boat after all. Non-metallic hull—wood or maybe fiberglass. No machinery noises."

"A threat?"

"Unknown, *Kan-cho*."

Kiyoda took the grease pencil and plotted the courses and speeds of the three warships, as well as the position of the fourth target. He drew a small circle where they converged. "We will wait here," he said.

"I spoke with Nobunaga a few minutes ago," Kamiya told the director general of defense via encrypted telephone.

"Enchi has called an emergency meeting of his cabinet," Hironaka said. "The moment Nobunaga arrives we will begin, so I have very little time. Did he accuse you of instituting Morning Star?"

"Yes. But I assured him that what is happening is not of our doing."

"But it is of your devising."

"Someone else stumbled onto the devices. We're still trying to find out how they were triggered. But Nobunaga said the Russians may be getting ready to retaliate. Perhaps now is the time to go ahead after all."

"We will take care of the Russians, *Kamiya-san*. In the meantime, are you absolutely certain that there have been no leaks or defections from your organization?"

"There've been none."

"Could this be an accident?"

Kamiya hesitated. "My engineers tell me that it's theoretically possible, but unlikely. MITI will not help us, but Nobunaga assures me that he will no longer oppose us."

"Don't be a fool. He never blocked you. Young Arimoto Yamagata should be proof enough. In 1990 he looked aside, and he will now if he is given half a chance. What do I tell the Cabinet?"

"That will depend entirely on how you read their mood, *Hironaka-san*. If they are for us in sufficient numbers, then Morning Star should be ordered. If not, we will simply wait until the opportunity arises again."

Hironaka started to speak, but Kamiya held him off.

"If we need to deny knowledge of what is happening we will do so . . . convincingly. But everything we have worked toward is coming together. The air disasters, the Russians, our young friend, Lieutenant Commander Kiyoda. Even the Prime Minister's proposed trade agreement—which no one can possibly believe is valid—has helped set the stage."

"The Americans may believe we are behind the crashes no matter how strongly we deny it."

"But they will not go to war over it, *Hironaka-san*. We are their major trading partners. We are their allies. Their friends. Shots will be fired, perhaps. And the blame for the air disasters will fall on young hotheads. But the United States government will step back from the brink. When they do, the western rim will be ours."

The Minegumo-class destroyer *DD118 Murakumo*'s six Mitsubishi diesels had been fired up, her crew called to general quarters, and one by one the other ships of Flotillas One and Four reported they were up and ready for action.

Communications patched a secure call to the bridge for the captain. It was Vice Admiral Ikuru Shimikaze, CINC Maritime Self Defense Forces. "Good morning,

Commander Shirokita. Is your command ready for sea?"

"Hai, Vice Admiral. Am I to be told what has happened? Is it the Russians?"

"In part, yes. We are expecting a strike somewhere in the north very soon. But there is more, *Shirokita-san.* We know that you will comport yourself well."

"Against whom?"

"Any and all enemies of Japan, whoever they may be, and wherever they may strike."

Shirokita had known the Admiral for twenty years, ever since the Maritime Self Defense Force Academy. Not once had he ever heard the Admiral cover himself like he was doing now. It was deeply disturbing and ominous.

"Your orders are to lead Escort Flotilla One, including the 41st, 43rd and 61st Destroyer Divisions, to the mouth of Tokyo Bay, where you will protect the city."

"Again I must ask you, Admiral, defend the city against whom?"

"Any forces who might attack."

"Will I have those orders in writing, Admiral?"

"Do you wish that?" Admiral Shimikaze asked coldly.

"Under the circumstances, I do."

Crash trucks and ambulances were still arriving on site when the call from Washington on the FAA hot line came through. Oakland's on-duty chief tower operator Vance Weiser studied the activity across the field through binoculars, and it was clear to him that there would be no survivors. The jetliner's port wing had come off in midair three miles north of the airport. He'd watched it disintegrate, pieces flying everywhere as the big plane went straight down. The only thing they could be grateful for was that it happened when it did. Another thirty seconds and the aircraft would have been over the heavily populated town of Alameda, and a lot more people would have lost their lives. First Bill White had been murdered in Chicago, and now this. Weiser was beginning to wonder if there was some sort of conspiracy against them.

"This is Byron Swanson. Who am I speaking to?"

"Vance Weiser, senior tower operator on duty. Sir, we're on top of rescue operations, but it doesn't look good. We've temporarily closed Three-Left until we make sure there's no debris on the runway."

"We're shutting Oakland down until further notice. Nothing in or out."

"I understand your concern, but ATC is holding eight inbounds at Santa Rosa intersection. And we expect the NTSB to be here within a couple of hours."

"I've already spoken with the chief controller. Your inbounds are being rerouted. If you have any aircraft on taxiways or at gates with engines running, they are to be shut down immediately. Right where they are, do you understand?"

"No, sir. What the hell is going on?"

"We're not sure, but it looks like sabotage might be involved."

An off-duty controller rushed up the stairs. "The goddamned system has crashed! Fourteen planes down! It's on television!"

Weiser turned, his mouth dropping open.

"It's true," Swanson shouted. "Shut everything down now, Vance."

"What's going on?" Weiser demanded, pulling himself together.

"I wish I knew," Swanson replied. The connection was broken.

Weiser slammed the phone down. "Shut the fuck up," he told the still shouting controller, and he started closing down his airport, one eye toward the smoking wreckage of United 425. What the hell *was* going on?

Major General Marvin Zwiebel, CINC of Marine forces on Okinawa, arrived at Camp Foster operations less than ten minutes after the alert message had been received. Most of his staff had already arrived.

"We've been ordered to DEFCON THREE, that's confirmed," his chief of staff, Colonel Howard Stromgren said. "But so far nobody is giving us any reasons."

Zwiebel removed his uniform blouse and took a cup of coffee from a sergeant. "What's our readiness status?"

"We'll be fully operational in another five minutes. But we've got no mission orders. All we can do is close and secure the base."

"Where's Blisk?"

"On his way over from communications," the chief of staff said. "He's been here all night."

"Were we expecting this?"

"Nobody said anything to me, Marvin."

"Okay, set up a unit commanders meeting for 0525. That gives them ten minutes. By then this base had better be closed tighter than a gnat's ass."

"Let's get Seventh on the horn," Stromgren suggested. "I'd like to know what the hell we're facing."

"First set up the meeting, and then get me Hagedorn at Kadena."

"Will do." Stromgren went to the phone on his desk.

Lieutenant Colonel Robert Blisk, Chief First Marine Air Wing Intelligence, came in, carrying a leather folder. He looked worried. "You're not going to like this very much, General."

Zwiebel motioned him into the glass-enclosed briefing room. "Spell it out," he said when the door was closed.

"There's no particular order to this, so you're going to have to take it in one big bite. At this point the DEFCON THREE we're under applies only to this theater. Everyone else stays at FOUR at least for now. Mission orders for all of Seventh Fleet, including us plus Kadena, are to hold our ground but not to fire unless fired upon."

"By whom?"

"By anyone. The Japanese have increased their readiness to DEFCON TWO, which means they'll shoot anyone they take to be a threat to their homeland or their assets. Anywhere. The entire MSDF has been ordered to sea, fully twenty-five percent of their ASW, observer, and remote-command post aircraft are already in the air, and their ground defense and missile services have been scrambled. Seventh has sent another Orion to back up our destroyer north of here. Looks as if we're getting into it with that submarine."

"More?"

" 'Fraid so, General. The Russians may be getting ready to make their retaliatory strike somewhere on Hokkaido's north coast, which ostensibly is the reason for Tokyo's jumpiness. But our DEFCON THREE is not just a knee-jerk response. Something else is going on that mystifies the shit out of me." Blisk opened the leather folder and handed the general a half-dozen intercept and message flimsies. "Some of that we got from CNN. The confirmations are from Washington through Don Moody's office in Yokosuka. So far a total of fourteen Guerin 522 jetliners have crashed stateside, all within a ten-minute period. Among them was Air Force Two, which was bringing the Vice President to Tokyo. General, it's believed that those airplanes were sabotaged. Possibly by the Japanese."

The general leaned back against the conference table. "Has everyone gone nuts?"

"I can't think of any other explanation," Blisk replied.

Now that *DD Thorn* had turned into the wind and seas she rode much easier. The *Barbey* and *Cook* were fighting their way downwind. It would take them another twenty minutes to make the rendezvous, but they would be in firing position sooner. Seventh was advising caution, still not sure what had happened, but that made no difference to Hanrahan. Despite the surface noise and the damage to *Thorn*'s towed sonar arrays, they'd gotten a good position on the *Samisho.* Besides the turbulence caused by her mangled sail, the boat was leaking air, which at times sounded like a whistling tea kettle.

"We lost him, Captain," Sattler reported from CIC. "No screw noises, no air leaks."

"What's your best estimated position?"

"Five thousand yards, bearing three-two-zero, depth one hundred feet."

Hanrahan walked over to the chart table where Ryder plotted the submarine's possible location. It was clear what the submarine driver was trying to do.

"The sonofabitch is waiting for us," Ryder said. "In all the racket he could have loaded and flooded his tubes without us hearing it."

"They're our allies, remember?" Hanrahan said.

His XO looked up. "Nobody's fault he ran into us."

"It'll be our fault if they sink us." Hanrahan called CIC. "Ping them once for range and bearing, and a second time for confirmation."

"Aye, aye," Sattler replied. "But, Skipper, that unidentified target we were painting on radar is hailing us."

"Ident?"

"She says she's a U.S.-documented sailboat out of Okinawa. Wants to know if they can be of any assistance."

"A trick?"

"Unknown."

"We'll find out when we're done with the sub."

"Stand by. *Thorn* is going after *Chrysanthemum*," *FF Cook*'s second officer, Ensign Tim Boyle, told his skipper. "They'll send us a position."

"What about the surface target?"

"Could be a bogey."

"The MSDF duty officer sends his regrets, but Admiral Shimikaze is still in conference and unable to take your call," Captain Byrne said.

"Recommendations?" Admiral Ryland asked his staff tersely.

"I think you should move your flag out to the *George Washington*. She's three hundred twenty miles southeast, about halfway between here and the Bonin Islands," Don Moody suggested.

"Makes sense to me, Admiral," Byrne agreed. "It's your call at this point, but if we go to DEFCON TWO you might not have the time."

The Seventh Fleet was composed of three carrier battle groups, forty-five ships and submarines in all, assigned to defend the western Pacific rim. Now that the Soviet Union was not a threat, Seventh Fleet duties had been reduced to showing the flag and providing operational readiness for local or regional conflicts. In the old days the Third Fleet, based at Pearl, mingled freely with ships of the Seventh. The middle of the Pacific was their playground. These days, however, Third kept east of Midway, and Seventh patrolled from the Japanese home waters down to the Philippines. The Pacific was a very big patch of ocean, but since the commissioning of the *CVN 73 George Washington,* an improved Nimitz-class carrier with superior nuclear reactors, state-of-the-art technology, and augmented air wing, co-mingling of the fleets was no longer considered vital. At best flank speed Third was one hundred hours from reinforcing Seventh. Not a comforting thought. In any initial trouble, Seventh was on its own.

"There's the matter of the rioters at the main gates," Moody cautioned. "The crowd is growing, and we may be faced with shooting at them, or allowing them to overrun the base. The Japanese military is unwilling to help, and the local police force is inadequate."

The last combat Ryland had seen was the Gulf War more than six years ago. In his wildest dreams he never imagined something like this.

"Gentlemen, I'm transferring my flag to the *George Washington* right now. Get Tony Benson on the horn, tell him we're on our way."

"Shall we inform the MSDF?" Byrne asked.

Ryland didn't have to think about it. "After we're aboard," he said.

In the old days Captain First Rank Anatoli Anishchenko would not have been so nervous. He stood on the bridge of the 512-foot destroyer *Sovremennyy,* name ship of the class, and tried to pick out the lights of their target to the south. They were heading almost due west through the Soya Strait separating Japan's north island of Hokkaido from Russia's Sakhalin Island. These were disputed waters, but by agreement Russian vessels were allowed unhindered access to the open Pacific. All that, Anishchenko thought, was about to change.

Before Gorbachev and the Kremlin Coup that toppled him from power, the military chain of command was made of iron links. Now it was made of papier-mâché. Moscow was in shambles and so was the officer corps. Yet field commanders were expected to show initiative with nothing to back them up if something went wrong. Three days ago Anishchenko had received detailed verbal orders via encrypted laser-beam transmission from CINC Pacific Fleet, Vladivostok. He was told to ignore all further ordinary telex transmissions that were not secure. The written messages would be a disinformation ploy. Twelve hours ago the *Sovremennyy* was ordered to return to her home port of Vladivostok at all possible speed via the strait of Soya. The message had come by telex transmission, which meant their primary orders to attack and destroy the Japanese Air Self Defense Force radar installation at Wakkanai were still valid.

Anishchenko was willing and able to carry out the attack, but if something went wrong he would have nothing in writing to back him up. It weighed heavily on his mind.

"Sound general quarters," he told his executive officer, Captain Lieutenant Gennadi Roskov. "Battle stations missile."

"Aye, Captain, sounding general quarters, battle stations missile," Roskov replied crisply.

"Turn left to new heading two-three-zero degrees," Anishchenko told the helmsman. The new course would clear Cape Soya and Rebun Island to the west, but it brought them closer to Wakkanai, which was less than one hour away at flank speed, and already within weapons range.

* * *

Thirty-two miles down the coast from the Wakkanai radar installation, the Air Self Defense Force Eighth Intercept Squadron at Embetsu was at full alert in response to the DEFCON TWO. Northern Air Defense Command at Misawa had been warning them for the past six days about a possible attack by the Russians in retaliation for the Tatar Strait incident, so everyone was on their toes. Squadron Commander Major Yumiko Osani, who'd been bunking on a cot behind the ready room, came in, buttoning up his tunic.

"It's Crimson-Three, Major," his operations officer Captain Tokako Kotoda said. Crimson-Three was the call sign for Wakkanai radar.

"Anything other than that destroyer they were tracking?" Osani asked. He took a cup of tea from an orderly.

"Iie. But they've turned south. Looks as if they could be targeting Wakkanai itself."

"Are we going to get any help from the MSDF?"

"The nearest surface ship is at least three hours away. But that destroyer is in firing range right now."

"Anything else on the threat board?"

"Not in our sector, Major," Kotoda said.

"Is anybody up?" Osani asked. He picked up the direct-line phone to Misawa.

"Kaifu and Tatewaki. Six others on the line and two in the alert hangar."

"Have Wakkanai give vectors out to the ship, but make sure they stay out of that destroyer's Close-in-Weapons-Systems envelope. When they get an ID, scramble the squadron." Osani held his hand over the phone. "I am not giving them authorization for weapons release at this time, unless they are fired on first."

"We're at DEFCON TWO."

"I am well aware of our alert status, *Kotoda-san.* But I want a positive visual on that ship first."

Lieutenants Hisayuki Kaifu and Keisaku Tatewaki reached their crusing altitude of twenty-five thousand feet above the Sea of Japan southwest of the base within three minutes after take-off. Their F/A-18JD Hornets were equipped with the modified AAS-38 Forward Looking InfraRed pod, which used thermal imagery to display high-definition pictures of ground or sea objects on their Master Monitor Displays. The optic head of the FLIR pod automatically followed either a pre-set search pattern or a designated target. If anything was down there they'd see it, day or night. And if anything was emitting, their surveillance radars would detect it. Each Hornet was armed with a pair of Harpoon anti-ship missiles, one Sparrow and two smaller Sidewinder air-to-air missiles, as well as Vulcan 20 mm cannons.

"Falcon-Eight, this is Seven-Seven-Charlie and Four-Three-Delta on station," Kaifu radioed. "Looks clean." Falcon-Eight was Embetsu's call sign.

"Roger, stand by for vectors from Crimson-Three," their mission control officer instructed.

"Air or surface?" Kaifu asked.

"Surface contact in Soya Strait. Stand by."

Kaifu switched to his encrypted inter-aircraft channel. "Look sharp, Keisaku, this might be it."

"Hai. I hope the bastards try something."

He and Kaifu, who were second cousins, had gone through the defense academy and flight school together. They were both engaged to be married to each other's cousins. It was a small, close-knit family.

"Seven-Seven-Charlie, this is Crimson-Three. We have an unidentified surface object incoming at approximately thirty knots. Bearing zero-four-eight, eight-zero miles from your position."

"Single bogie?" Kaifu asked. He hauled his Hornet in a five-G turn to starboard and kicked in his afterburners, accelerating smoothly toward Mach two.

"Roger, Seven-Seven-Charlie. We're presuming it's a Russian destroyer, so watch yourself. We need a positive visual ID."

"Copy," Kaifu radioed. At Mach two their time to target was under four minutes.

* * *

"Report all weapons systems armed and ready," *Sovremennyy's* weapons control officer Lieutenant Nikolai Burov announced.

"Very well," Anishchenko acknowledged. He glanced at his exec, then picked up the growler phone. "CIC, bridge."

"CIC, aye," Combat Information Center officer Lieutenant Grigori Kalmykov responded.

"What are our threat receivers picking up?"

"Other than Wakkanai, nothing, Captain. But there have been radio transmissions between Wakkanai and the Eighth Intercept Squadron at Embetsu, and between a pair of patrol aircraft to the southwest. They are turning toward us now."

"They've picked us up?"

"Yes, but there's no reason for them to attack until we fire. They've only sent two aircraft, and we'll be ready for them. The moment they light their combat radar systems we'll shoot them out of the sky."

"Could they be preauthorized?"

"I don't think so, Captain. We detected a brief transmission between Embetsu and Northern Air Defense Command at Misawa. The transmission was encrypted, so we were unable to read it. But it's my guess the squadron commander asked for instructions."

"Which were?"

"Wait and see what we do, then act accordingly. But there'll almost certainly be a delay on their part."

"We won't wait for their radars. The moment they pass overhead and present their tail fins to us, we will open fire on them and the radar station at the same moment."

"They'll be overhead in less than ninety seconds, Captain."

"Very well," Anishchenko said.

"That's definitely a Russian destroyer," Tatewaki said on the inter-aircraft channel. "No mistake."

They were eighteen miles out. They'd dropped down

to five hundred feet above the surface and had eased back to subsonic. Kaifu's recognition program pinged when it had the silhouette identified. "I agree." He keyed his radio. "Falcon-Eight, this is Seven-Seven-Charlie."

"Falcon-Eight," their mission control officer answered.

"Sir, we have a positive identification on that surface target. She's a *Sovremennyy*-class destroyer. Looks as if she'll clear the cape. Probably on her way home."

"Stand by."

The ghostly thermal image of the destroyer grew larger and more detailed on their Master Monitor Display CRTs as they closed. The Russians knew that they were incoming, but nothing showed on the Hornets' threat receivers. By all outward appearances a Russian military vessel was clearing the Soya Strait and a pair of Japanese ASDF fighter/interceptors had come for a look. Routine.

"Seven-Seven-Charlie, kill the target. Say again, kill the target. You have weapons release authorization."

"*Yo-so-ro*," Kaifu replied, his heart in the back of his throat. He switched to inter-aircraft. "Launch all four Harpoons at her starboard side on the count of five. Break off, come around, and if need be we'll go for the bridge with Sidewinders."

"Let's sink the bastard!" Tatewaki agreed.

Kaifu dialed up the AGM-109 anti-ship missiles with his weapons selector switch on his stick, and entered the distance-to-target radar program into the strap-down inertial system. When launched the Harpoon would drop to the deck and skim low over the water. At the programmed distance-off the missile's radar went active and when it found its mark it locked on. At the last moment, the Harpoon pulled up and dove into its target. There was almost no defense against it.

"Five-four-three-two-one-launch," Kaifu radioed. He hit the fire switch once, and then a second time.

Anishchenko went to the windows and looked outside. The morning was pitch black, there was nothing to see other than the forward twin-mount 130 mm gun, and the bows crashing through the seas. In a matter of seconds the two ASDF patrol aircraft would pass overhead and he would order the attack. Four SS-N-22 SSM anti-surface missiles would be launched against Wakkanai, and a pair of SA-N-7 air-defense missiles would be sent against the fighter/interceptors.

From that point he could only assume that help would be nearby. His orders were to shoot, then turn and run for the protection of Kuznetsova thirty miles north on Sakhalin Island. But that was at least an hour away. Long before they reached safety, the Japanese would respond.

The time for self-doubts and recriminations was gone. He was a military commander, and Russia was trying to become a nation that lived by the rule of law, which meant civilians controlled the military. He would follow his orders. Someone had to know what was going on.

"Bridge, CIC."

Anishchenko walked back to the phone. "This is the captain."

"Captain, the bogies have turned away! They are no longer in formation!"

"Are they returning to base?" Anishchenko demanded.

"Nyet, nyet! I think they've fired their missiles. Recommend we commence our attack now."

"I concur," Anishchenko said without hesitation. "Launch the twenty-twos. Get a re-lock on the bogies, and fire at will!"

Almost instantly two anti-surface missiles were fired from a launcher on either side of the ship just forward of the bridge. The flash of their rocket motors temporarily filled the bridge.

"Many weapons radars . . ." CIC shouted, when something crashed in on them from overhead, and a tremendous yellow light filled the air.

The Harpoon came straight through the overhead into the bridge before exploding. Anishchenko and the others never knew what hit them. One moment lights were flashing, and in the next they ceased to exist as sentient beings.

Technical Sergeant Halvorson hesitated a moment at the open door of the Marine VH-3 helicopter. The emergency response team from Bethesda worked frantically on the Vice President, while the Secret Service detail watched, their guns at the ready. Everything that could be done to save Eagle Two's life was being done. In the meantime, there were thirty-six other people aboard Air Force Two, many of them still alive. He headed back to the downed aircraft.

"Eagle Two is transferred," he radioed SARTECH control. "We're going back in, but we're going to need more help."

"Roger, able leader one. Can you say condition of Sea Gull Two." It was Sally Cross's code name.

"Deceased," Halvorson replied tersely. Sometimes he hated this job.

Behind him the chopper's engines came to life, and it lifted off, swinging toward the northeast beneath a lowering overcast.

James Lindsay had wanted to be President of the United States all of his life. As a schoolboy he wrote essays about it. In the Air Force his fellow officers kidded him about his ambition, telling him he should have joined the Navy so he could have gotten a PT boat command like Jack Kennedy. And in his first years as a state senator and then a U.S. congressman, he'd been ignored. But by the time he became Senate Minority Leader he didn't have to talk about his dream; everyone else told him.

All of his life he'd studied and prepared for the job, had become an expert on every facet of every agency of government, had read the writings of every president including his predecessor, with whom he'd vehemently disagreed, and had himself written a book called *Crisis Management—Preparations Before the Storm*. But he'd not expected this. In order to manage a crisis, Lindsay told himself, he needed an enemy. A Russian, not a Japanese, adversary.

"The number is holding at fourteen, Mr. President," Jay Hansen said on the speakerphone. "It looks as if eight airports plus Andrews were affected. I've ordered them closed until we get this straightened out."

"Any word on casualties?" Lindsay asked.

"Not yet. It'll be high, but the worst should be over. We never expected this. There was no way to prepare."

"No one ever does. You're doing a good job, Jay. I'll let you get back to it."

"Can you tell me what's going on, Mr. President?"

"Not yet." Lindsay broke the connection and picked up the conference call to the CIA and NSA. "Has General Murphy arrived yet?"

"He's on the Parkway, Mr. President. Should be here within the next couple of minutes," Tommy Doyle answered.

"Has CIA come up with anything new?"

"Sir, we're getting information from all over the place, but none of it is conclusive. We can tell you that the Yokosuka riot has spread to Tokyo and several other cities. It started as a Rising Sun demonstration, but we think they've lost control of it."

"You are aware that fourteen airplanes have gone down, including Air Force Two, and that the Japanese may be involved in some way?" the President's National Security Adviser Harold Secor said.

"The traffic between their embassy here and Tokyo remains heavy," Amundson replied from Fort Meade. "But we're monitoring another incident in the Soya Strait. That's the water passage between the Japanese north island of Hokkaido and the Russian island of Sakhalin. The Japanese Air Force may have gotten into it with another Russian destroyer. The latest satellite infrareds show the heat signatures of multiple explosions consistent with air-launched missiles."

"How do you know it was a destroyer?" the President asked.

"We copied traffic between the ship—she's the *Sovremennyy*—and Pacific Fleet at Vladivostok."

"What does the CIA know about this?"

"We're reading the same satellite data as NSA," Doyle said. "But the attack is not unexpected. The Japanese self-defense forces are at DEFCON TWO. Under the rules of engagement they would view any near incursion into their waters as a hostile act. By whomever."

"We have American people dead on American soil. Where's the connection?" the President demanded. "Who is doing it? Can somebody give me a straight answer?"

"The airplanes were sabotaged. There's no question about that," Doyle said. "And the Japanese may be involved, but we're in the middle of another developing situation. One that we just don't understand yet, Mr. President. But it may have some bearing on what's going on."

"What do you mean?"

"Mr. Carrara, our deputy director of operations, has been working with one of our former case officers on the idea that a former East German Stasi assassin may somehow be involved. There has been a series of murders involving Guerin Airplane Company and our air traffic control system that the FBI is investigating. It's possible that another group is responsible for the sabotage and for some reason wants the blame to fall on the Japanese."

"The Russians?"

"It's possible, Mr. President, but not likely."

"Let me speak with Carrara."

"Sir, he's dead. His body was found last night in Baltimore."

None of this was making any sense to Lindsay. "It could be the Russians after all."

"Yes, sir. Or the Japanese, or a third group. We just don't have enough information to say for certain."

"Fine," the President said.

One of the Marine communications specialists turned from his console at the far end of the room. "Mr.

President, you have an incoming call. It's Prime Minister Enchi."

"Just a moment," the President said. "Who is this former case officer of yours?" he asked Doyle.

"Kirk McGarvey."

"Isn't there a warrant for his arrest over this business?"

"Yes, Mr. President."

"Did he kill Carrara?"

"It's not likely."

"In other words, you have nothing conclusive."

"No, sir," Doyle admitted.

The President broke the connection, and looked at his advisers. "Now what the hell do I say to Enchi that'll make any sense?"

McGarvey stood in the forward galley, the telephone to his ear wondering what he was going to tell JoAnn Carrara when he faced her. "Was it Mueller?"

"We think so, Mac," Dick Adkins said. "But it's crazy here. No one knows what's going on, and everyone's afraid to make a decision until the General arrives."

"Has the system been shut down?"

"Just the eight airports. There haven't been crashes anywhere else, and nothing in the past few minutes. Everybody is holding their breath. But the Japanese and Russians have gotten into it again, and our Seventh Fleet has been ordered to DEFCON THREE. The White House is about to start a war."

"Have the Japanese made any moves against us?"

"The submarine north of Okinawa . . ."

"Besides that."

"There are riots all over Japan."

"Goddammit, Dick, has the government of Japan made any official move against us? Any military move? Has our fleet been bottled up in Tokyo Bay? Has Seventh's flag been moved off shore?"

"I don't know."

"Find out," McGarvey said.

"Doyle went to bat for you, but the President wouldn't

listen. Are you so goddamned sure it isn't the Japanese? They need facts up there now, not speculation. NSA is reading heavy traffic from the Japanese embassy here to its Ministry of State in Tokyo. Some of it has to do with the crashes."

"I'll be on the ground in a few minutes. Have the General convince the President to hold off for as long as possible."

"Where are you landing?"

"Gales Creek."

"That's within Portland's air traffic control area, isn't it?"

McGarvey was caught off guard momentarily. "You said the eight airports have been shut down. What do you mean by that?"

"Just what I said: shut down. It was your suggestion. No traffic in or out, especially no Guerin 522s."

McGarvey pushed his way past McLaren to the flight deck where Socrates was on another phone. The engineer looked up, sensing more trouble.

"Pull the heat monitor, George," McGarvey said calmly. "Now."

Socrates' gaze turned toward the windshield for a moment. They had closed the coast, and in the distance to the northeast they could make out a hint of Portland, snow-covered Mount Hood rising behind it. "Right," he said. He put the telephone aside and climbed down into the electronics bay, Reiner and Callahan watching him.

"You'll have to go manual," McGarvey told them.

"Too late, Portland ATC has us," Callahan announced.

"It's disconnected," Socrates called up.

McGarvey held his breath for a long moment, waiting for their port engine to explode, but it never happened. He looked down at Socrates, who was grinning weakly.

The Vice President was slipping away from them. Excessive blood loss, early untreated shock, and severe trauma to the left side of his brain, which was swelling inside the cranial cavity, and to his heart, which was not responding to their treatment. Navy doctor Captain David Scorse, primary ER physician working on Cross, had suspected they were too late when he'd first started his examination and treatment. Now he was certain.

"What's our ETA?" he asked without looking up.

"Five minutes," someone said.

"We need to relieve the cranial pressure before then," Scorse said, knowing they were just going through the motions. But the man was Vice President.

FORTY

Prime Minister Ichiro Enchi stared at his cabinet around the long table as he waited for President Lindsay to come on line. His advisers were suggesting one thing while his heart was telling him something else. If the attack against the Vice President and the airplane crashes were not a result of Morning Star, either the Americans themselves were doing it or somehow the Russians were involved. They'd just learned about the attack on Wakkanai. Combined with Seventh Fleet's increased alert status, the unthinkable was suddenly becoming plausible. It made a terrible sense. Yet he could not believe, would not believe, that a battle between Japan and the United States was imminent.

The telephone chimed, and Enchi picked it up. "Mr. President, we are monitoring news reports on CNN of terrible disasters at several of your airports. And our observers in Washington have notified us of the developing situation. It is my understanding that Vice President Cross was on his way to Tokyo when his airplane crashed. May I offer my condolences for him and his wife, and for the crew and other passengers aboard Air Force Two."

"Mr. Prime Minister, thank you for your concern. At this point it looks as if Larry Cross will be all right. But at least thirteen passenger airplanes have crashed in the past twenty minutes with a great loss of life. My security advisers believe that the crashes may have resulted from acts of sabotage by an as yet unknown group . . . or government."

The call was on the speakerphone. President Lindsay's voice was kept at a lower volume so that the voice of the simultaneous translator could be more easily heard and understood. The delay caused by this arrangement was negligible. But the inflection in the President's voice was unmistakable.

Hironaka, seated at the end of the table, bridled, but Enchi did not wait for him to speak.

"If your advisers are correct, and if this attack was made by terrorists or by a government-sponsored terrorist group, then it could be considered an act of war."

"That is how we view the situation. We believe we have it under control for the moment, but the economic summit between our countries will have to be delayed until our investigation has been completed."

Enchi touched the mute button. "Can they know about Morning Star? Should I say something?"

"It's possible but not likely," Nubunaga said. "They do know about our military readiness, however."

Enchi released the mute button. "I agree that we should delay the summit, Mr. President. As you may know by now, a Russian destroyer attacked one of our radar installations on the north coast of Hokkaido. We had to take action to protect ourselves. Since we cannot rule out the possibility of further attacks I have placed our military forces at DEFCON TWO."

"We are aware of the attack, and of your response, Mr. Prime Minister. I have advised the Russian government against such an action, and I shall do so again. Because of the attack against us, I have placed our military forces at DEFCON THREE. But this must not be taken as provocative except by our enemies. We are merely taking a stronger defensive position."

Again Enchi pressed the mute button. "Have all their forces gone to DEFCON THREE?"

"Only the Seventh Fleet and the Marine and Air Force installations on Okinawa," Hironaka said. "It's obvious whom they consider their enemy to be."

"It could simply be a response to our increased alert status."

"They were ordered to DEFCON THREE *after* the attack on their air traffic system."

Enchi released the mute button. "Your actions are understandable, as I hope ours are to you. I advise caution. Both of us face difficult situations that must first be resolved before we can go on."

"I agree," President Lindsay replied.

"May we keep this line of communications between us open, Mr. President?" Enchi asked.

"By all means. Let there be absolutely no misunderstanding between us. We have been friends for too long to act otherwise."

Enchi cut the connection. "What can we do?"

"Defend ourselves," Hironaka said. "There is no other consideration."

"The number's up to fourteen if you count Air Force Two," NTSB duty officer John Hom said.

"I heard some of that on the way in," Sam Varelis replied, heading for his office. He was having a hard time accepting it. "Has the FAA issued any orders?"

"Yes, sir. You were right about them all being Guerin 522s. So far it looks as if eight airports, plus Andrews, were involved. The FAA has shut them all down. Nothing in or out." Hom handed him the list.

"That's a start." Varelis dialed the FBI's counterespionage number. "We're going to have to dig deep to come up with that many teams. Have our regional offices been notified?"

"New York, Chicago, Seattle, and Los Angeles. We'll have to handle Dulles from here. But our last team is still in town. The 89th Air Wing is covering Air Force Two."

"Any word on Cross?"

"He's still alive. They're taking him to Bethesda."

"Get Sweedler on the phone. I'll talk to him next." Alan Sweedler was President Lindsay's appointment as chairman of the NTSB. As a Washington insider, he had the connections to cut through the red tape.

The FBI's duty officer answered. "Three-nine-three seven-one hundred."

"This is Sam Varelis, National Transportation Safety Board. I'd like to speak with John Whitman."

"Sir, Mr. Whitman is not available."

"Tell him this concerns Kirk McGarvey. I'll hold."

Dominique drove east on Interstate 66. Her numbness after seeing the news bulletins about the air crashes had given way to anger. Kirk had been right all along, and she felt like a fool for not believing him. They'd all been fools. Even David hadn't believed what McGarvey had come up with. And now this. They'd have to live with their mistake for the rest of their lives. It wasn't just the Japanese, as the news media was suggesting. There was more, and she was going to do something about it. She phoned a Georgetown number. It was answered on the fourth ring.

"Hello?"

"Thank God it's you, Edward. When I saw the news about the Vice President . . . I had to call to make sure."

Reid hesitated. "Who is this?"

"It's me. Dominique. We had lunch together at the Rive Gauche."

"Ms. Kilbourne?"

"You were right, Edward. McGarvey was dead wrong. It is the Japanese. We have to convince Guerin, and the FAA."

It seemed as if Reid suddenly came back from a long distance. "Do you know where Mr. McGarvey is?"

"He's working with the FBI, I think. But I need your help, Edward. You're the only person who makes any sense."

"Where are you?"

"I'm coming across the river from Arlington. I could be at your house in ten minutes. Please, will you see me? Before it's too late?"

"I don't know if that's such a good idea."

"There's nowhere else for me to go. Nobody will listen to me alone. But together we can convince them. Dear God, you must help me!"

"Do you know where I live?"

"Yes."

"How do you know where I live, Ms. Kilbourne?"

"I just do, Edward. I'm not stupid. It's my job to know people in this town. Powerful people."

Reid hesitated again. "Very well. In ten minutes, then."

"You won't regret it, Edward," Dominique said. She hung up and concentrated on her driving, her rage solidifying. The fact that Reid was safely at home, not aboard Air Force Two as he was supposed to be, was one final check of Kirk's warning. Whatever lingering doubts she may have had were shattered the moment Reid answered his phone. Somehow he was involved with the destruction of fourteen airplanes and the deaths of hundreds of people.

She reached in her purse on the passenger seat and touched the reassuring bulk of the 9 mm Bernadelli automatic pistol. Reid would talk to her. There was no doubt about it.

David Kennedy parked his Range Rover on the beach at Cape Meares seventy-five miles west of Portland, unable for the moment to drive. It was happening just as McGarvey warned it would. Fourteen airplanes down now. All of them Guerin. All of them because of port engine failures. It looked as if the Vice President would survive. But hundreds of others would not. Aboard the other thirteen airliners there had to have been two thousand passengers and crew. Many of them dead, blown out of the sky. Others dying, trapped in piles of burning wreckage of what had minutes ago been the most sophisticated jetliners to fly anywhere in the world.

He closed his eyes as he listened to the radio. By now *America* was well out over the Pacific on its way to Honolulu. The flight crew would be hearing the news. But there was nothing they could do about it. Even McGarvey, for all his skills, was powerless to stop what had already happened, what was happening. They had not listened to him.

"Okay," he said, looking across the beach at the big waves rolling in from Japan. Vietnam had proved that we were vulnerable. That we could lose. Granada, Panama, and the Gulf War had not done as much to erase that image as the explosion of the space shuttle *Challenger* had done to prove our technology was flawed. But if this was another Pearl Harbor, they'd badly underestimated the American will again. As a nation, we'd screwed up the post-Cold War, just as he had failed Guerin and his marriage. But that was about to change, he thought. The bastards would be sorry they ever started something.

The caller-ID system on Nancy's phone provided the number Chance had called from. And one of the data crunchers downstairs in Processing had hacked the telephone company's reverse directory to come up with an address. It was a place on the beach between the towns of Cape Meares and Oceanside listed under the name East View, which was a Marvin Saunders company. It was at the developer's Oswego home that he and Chance had been introduced to Yamagata. The bastard had taken them all in.

Kennedy pulled out of the scenic overlook parking lot and swung back onto the coast road heading south. There was no other traffic in either direction. When he'd driven through Cape Meares the town had seemed all but deserted. These were primarily summer places, isolated in the winter.

The mailbox marking East View was a mile south on the right. A chain stretched between two thick wooden posts blocked a paved driveway that led through a thick stand of trees down toward the beach. Kennedy parked off the road. Hunching up his coat collar against the sharp wind, he got out and walked down to the driveway. The chain was secured with a padlock. There was no way to drive around the posts. The roofline of what appeared to be a large house was just visible through the trees. Kennedy thought he could smell wood smoke. Chance had called from here less than two hours ago, in trouble.

He went back to the Rover and got the tire iron from the back, then stepped over the chain and started down the driveway. It had snowed last night, but there were no tire tracks or footprints on the driveway, which meant Yamagata had brought Chance out here sometime yesterday. The thought of what might have gone on during the past twenty-four hours hardened his already strong resolve to take it back to the sonofabitch. He could envision breaking the man's arms and legs with the tire iron, and then starting on the rest of his bones, one at a time.

The low, expansive house was perched on a jumble of boulders fifty feet above the water. A gray Lexus sedan and a green Toyota van were parked in front. Kennedy hid behind a tree and watched. Nothing moved except for the smoke from the chimney and the tree branches in the breeze.

Kennedy tightened his grip on the tire iron and started toward the north side of the house. He hoped to find an unlocked door or window so he could get inside without raising an alarm. If he could surprise Yamagata and whoever was with him, he'd have a chance of overpowering them. At least he'd give it a good shot.

He reached a wooden walkway that led around the boulders to the front of the house. A small window was cranked open a couple of inches. He could hear music playing softly.

A slightly built oriental man armed with a large handgun came around the corner from the front of the house. "Mr. Kennedy, please throw your weapon to the side."

Kennedy stepped back. "I came for my wife."

"Yes, we know. If you will please disarm yourself I will take you to her."

Kennedy hesitated.

"Mr. Kennedy, I do not wish to shoot you, but I will," the Japanese said calmly.

Everything in Kennedy's soul wanted to rush forward and beat the crap out of the bastard. But he wouldn't get two steps, and he knew it. He tossed the tire iron over the rail, and it clattered down onto the rocks. "If you've hurt my wife, I swear to God I'll kill you."

Edward Reid sometimes thought he lived in a vacuum, and when someone or something intruded on his life he was surprised, though he knew he shouldn't be. He'd purposely run his car off the highway on the way out to Andrews. By the time he'd informed the White House he wouldn't be flying to Tokyo, had AAA pull him out of the ditch, and had gotten home, he'd been exhausted. He'd been watching the frantic news bulletins on CNN, knowing he should be doing something, when Dominique Kilbourne's call had come out of left field.

He stood at the window of his second-floor bedroom looking down at the street. He was conscious of his beating heart, of the breaths he drew, of the fact he'd not had a drink yet today.

They'd done it. They'd actually pulled it off. But it was happening faster than he'd thought it would. Now it was up to him to deal with the aftermath. It was something, he supposed, that he hadn't considered as carefully as he should have. Secretly he never believed it would happen. Or he hoped that it wouldn't happen. But the young woman's call had brought him back to reality. Through her, he'd somehow have to deal with McGarvey. And before the night was out he would have to write the first of his *Lamplighter* bulletins. Try to pull something out of the ashes.

Reid was more frightened than he'd ever been of

anything in his life. As long as he could keep his wits about him, however, he knew he could pull it off.

Takushiro Hatoyama stood facing Major David Ross in the twenty yards of no-man's land between the crowd and the police line, a dozen other protesters with him. The marine, Hatoyama noticed, was unarmed, though he was dressed in battle fatigues. When he'd come out from behind the armored personnel carriers, an uneasy hush had fallen over the crowd. But it'd taken time to spread to the rear. People were pouring in from all over the city. Similar gatherings were occurring across the country. It was time for Japan to take her rightful place among the family of nations unoccupied by foreign forces.

First they would have to deal with this base. Make it so uncomfortable, so dangerous for the authorities that they would have to fire into the crowd. There would be many casualties, but they would serve the cause well. They would become martyrs.

At thirty-two, Hatoyama was a full professor of history at Tokyo University. He had a wife and two children, and every morning when he kissed them goodbye a deep shame filled his chest. *To bear what you think you cannot bear is really to bear. Honor. Patience and forgiveness.* It was *bu-shi.* But the *kamikaze* was blowing across the land, and his shame would be assuaged.

Two large ships had already left the docks. He could see their superstructures, bristling with antennae and radar dishes moving away. The entire fleet would probably head to sea because of the DEFCON THREE. Hatoyama was going to see to it that they had no base to come back to.

"My name is David Ross. I'm chief of security here. Do you speak English?"

"Yes I do, Major," Hatoyama replied. "It is required in Japanese schools. Do you speak Japanese?"

"Nihongo o amari hanashimasen." I don't speak very much Japanese, Ross said. "It's possible that we can

come to some agreement if you will tell me why you have come here."

Hatoyama smiled politely. "We have come to arrest Admiral Ryland for crimes against Nippon."

"What crimes?"

"He has brought nuclear weapons to Japan."

"That's not true."

"It is," Hatoyama said.

Ross glanced over his shoulder at the line of Japanese police. They looked very nervous. "It would appear that your government doesn't agree."

Hatoyama drew a pistol. "Then it is up to you and me to convince them." He fired a single shot, hitting Ross in the chest, just above his flak jacket.

The protestors surrounded the Marine's body before it hit the ground.

McGarvey watched from *America*'s cockpit as they came to a halt in front of the prototype hangars. Dozens of emergency vehicles were on the field. Several buses were parked along the ramp to whisk the VIP passengers back to Portland. Four Guerin LX-17B turbojet transport helicopters had also been brought out.

Callahan had been on the radio to company operations, who said that Kennedy should have been aboard the flight. In the confusion no one had missed him.

The problem would be sidestepping the FBI long enough to find out where Kennedy had gone. For the moment the FAA was doing the correct thing by closing the eight airports. If everyone did their jobs, there would, hopefully, be no more crashes.

He could not get through to the CIA again, which by now would be on an emergency footing. Even if he talked to Adkins or to Doyle, he didn't think they would listen to him. From the news reports they were monitoring, the media was convinced that the Japanese government was responsible for the crashes. It was going to take time for him to prove otherwise. Yamagata was one of the keys, and it was a fair bet that Kennedy had gone after him. But that was over an hour ago.

"No trouble, Mr. McGarvey?" McLaren asked hopefully.

Boarding ramps had been trundled up to the three exits, and the passengers were already streaming off the airplane.

"Save the handcuffs until we get out of here."

"Do I have your word?"

McGarvey glanced at Socrates and nodded. "Have a car pick us up at the forward boarding ramp. I don't want to be paraded across the field."

McLaren motioned for his partner to arrange it. "Are you armed?"

"If I was, you'd try to take it away from me and someone would get hurt. Let's just say for now that I'll cooperate."

The FBI special agent didn't like it, but he'd read McGarvey's file. "I guess I'll live with that. But I hope you understand there's a lot of twitchy people out there."

"Are you taking me to Portland?"

"For now. But I'm sure they're going to want you in Washington, ASAP."

"I'll get the word out to the fleet," Socrates said. He looked pale.

"Watch yourself around anyone from InterTech," McGarvey warned. "It's going to take me a few hours to make them listen."

"Have to prove it first."

Joyce came back. "The car is here."

McLaren checked McGarvey's jacket and gave it to him. "We'll do this nice and easy," he said. "No sudden moves."

There hadn't been enough time to bring up a prisoner transport van so Portland S-A-C Jack Franson, who'd started back to the city after *America* had taken off, returned with a brown Chevy Caprice sedan. "I told you not to screw with us," he said when McGarvey climbed into the back seat with McLaren.

Joyce got in front, and Franson headed away from the ramp.

"I guess you were right, sir," McGarvey said, when they'd cleared the Guerin facility. He twisted around to look out the back window.

McLaren grabbed for him, but McGarvey managed to pull the Walther out and cock the hammer as he swiveled back to the front. He jammed the muzzle of the gun into the base of Franson's skull. The S-A-C almost ran off the road before he straightened the car out.

"Goddammit," McLaren swore, reaching for his own pistol.

"Back down!" McGarvey ordered. "McLaren, hands on the back of the front seat! Joyce, hands on the dash!" McGarvey jabbed the pistol hard against Franson's neck.

"Shit," Franson said.

"Now!" McGarvey said, jabbing the pistol into Franson's neck again.

The two special agents did as they were told, and although Franson had slowed down, his driving was no longer erratic.

"Every cop in the country will be on your case if you kill us, you sonofabitch," Franson promised.

"I'm not going to kill you. I need your help."

"What are you talking about?"

"I'll explain on the way. For now you're going to have to do as I tell you."

"I swear to Christ, I'm going to nail your ass."

"I need to talk to Kennedy's secretary. Try his office first."

Franson's grip tightened on the steering wheel, his knuckles turning white, but he motioned for Joyce to make the call.

"Easy," McGarvey warned.

Joyce made the call. When he had her on the line, he put it on the speakerphone.

"Nancy, this is Kirk McGarvey. I want you to listen very carefully because this is important. Chance Kennedy has been kidnapped, and I think David knows where she's being held. If he's gone after her, he's put himself in a great deal of danger. Did he say anything to you this morning? Do you know where he went?"

"Dear God," the woman said. "He wasn't aboard *America?*"

"No."

"I was afraid of that. Mrs. Kennedy called here this morning. She sounded like she was in trouble. We got the number from the caller-ID system. Mr. Kennedy doesn't know that I know, but he used that to get the address from someone downstairs in Processing. It's called East Wind, on the coast highway between Cape Meares and Oceanside."

"Does he have a gun?"

"I don't know," Nancy said breathlessly. "What's going on, Mr. McGarvey? We're watching the news. Is it the Japanese?"

"We're trying to find out. I want you to stay there. If David calls, tell him not to go near Yamagata. No matter what he thinks is happening, tell him to come back to Guerin."

"I'm frightened."

"I know," McGarvey said. He nodded for Joyce to end the call. "Do you know where this place is?" he asked Franson.

"I can find it," the S-A-C replied, puzzled.

"I think you'd better call for backup. We might need it."

The police line was moving forward into the roiling curtains of tear gas to merge with the crowd. So far, except for the one pistol shot, the mob had not fired back, but the noise was getting ugly, out of control. People continued to stream down to the waterfront, most of them armed with shovels and rakes and kendo-staves. But a lot of them had guns, which in Japan were almost impossible to get. The entire city was coming alive. Whatever was going to happen was on the verge of happening. From the Marine position behind the armored personnel carriers in front of the main gate it was hard to tell what was going on, except that it appeared as if the police were being absorbed into the crowd. As each one disappeared, a cry of triumph went up. Lieutenant Green was worried that he could no longer see Ross. The major had been unarmed. If the Japanese wanted to take him, they'd do it easily. And if the police line disintegrated, as it was starting to do, there'd be nothing stopping them from overrunning the base except for one augmented platoon of definitely nervous jarheads.

"All right people, look sharp," Green told the line. Unlike the police his men were not equipped for riot control. Their job was security, which meant keeping unauthorized people out.

"Are you going to give the order to fire on Japanese nationals, L-T?" his platoon sergeant, Ingrid Wentz, asked.

Green still wasn't used to working with women in combat units, but he had to admit that Wentz knew her job. He would put her up against any man in the unit and bet even money on the outcome.

"Ross said the admiral would give the order," Green replied, studying the situation through binoculars.

"The major isn't here," Wentz said.

"Jones, raise base ops," Green shouted.

"Yo," the radioman responded.

"We either try to hold them or step aside," he told Wentz.

"Big decision either way."

"Yeah," Green said.

"L-T, it's Captain Byrne." Jones handed him the handset.

"Captain, this is Lieutenant Otis Green, baker platoon at the main gate. Looks like Major Ross is down, and the Japanese police line is folding. In about two minutes we're going to have ten thousand Japanese nationals coming at us. What do we do, sir, stand and fire, or get out of the way?"

"Give us five minutes, Lieutenant, and then get your ass out of there."

"To where?"

"We're heading off shore. We'll get choppers back for you. Call them in when you've secured an L-Z."

"Aye, aye, Captain, we'll do our best."

"I have sounds of breakup," *SSGN Strelka*'s chief sonarman, Lieutenant Mikhail Abrashkin said. "Hull compressions now. Machinery breaking loose."

Captain First Rank Vadim Lestov listened on a spare headset. He agreed. It was the *Sovremennyy* going down. She'd probably been attacked by the Japanese Air Self Defense Forces based on Hokkaido. Maybe Misawa. Their sonar sweeps over the past couple of hours showed no MSDF warships in the near vicinity. But had the *Sovremennyy* managed to let her missiles fly against Wakkanai before she was destroyed?

Lestov took off the headset and walked back to the control room. "Come to periscope depth, I want to take a look," he told his executive officer, Lieutenant Commander Viktor Savin.

"Aye, Captain. Officer of the Boat, make your depth one-eight meters."

"Aye, one-eight meters," the starpom repeated. Lestov called his ELINT officer, Lieutenant Vladimir Bychkov. "We're coming to periscope depth. Put up your snoopheads. I want to know what's up there. Look sharp."

"Aye, Captain."

Lestov hung up. "Prepare for emergency dive on my orders," he told his XO. The *Strelka* was a Sierra-class attack submarine equipped with nuclear weapons. Just her presence in these waters was tantamount to a declaration of war. However, sinking a destroyer was one thing, while killing a cruise-missile submarine was something completely different. The radar station at Wakkanai would be destroyed. He would make sure of it.

"Is it your opinion that the attack on Wakkanai was diversionary in nature?" Prime Minister Enchi asked his Director General of Defense.

"It's certainly worth considering," Hironaka said.

"The radar station was heavily damaged and there will probably be some loss of lives. The first reports are sketchy." He'd taken the call from Misawa a minute ago.

"In retaliation for our attack in the Tatar Strait."

"But it keeps our attention to the north," Hironaka argued. "Combined with the riots and the movement of the Seventh Fleet offshore, it gives one pause for thought, Mr. Prime Minister. We are vulnerable."

"Has there been any word about Kamiya and Kobayashi?" Enchi asked Nobunaga.

"Nothing yet," the MITI chief said. "They're probably in hiding."

"Traitors."

Nobunaga started to reply, but Hironaka motioned him off.

"We should give thought to blocking the Seventh Fleet."

"What are you talking about?"

"The Forty-First Destroyer Division will be in place at Point Miura slightly ahead of the Seventh's lead escort ships. We could hold them in Tokyo Bay."

This was developing into a nightmare from which Enchi wished he could awaken. "To what end?"

"To allow us time to regain control of the tactical situation," Hironaka said. "We could declare an emergency aboard one or more of our ships, and ask for help. It would not be refused."

"Have you spoken with Admiral Ryland?" Enchi asked.

Hironaka shook his head. "He is unavailable to our repeated queries."

"Try again," Enchi ordered.

"We must defend ourselves, Mr. Prime Minister."

"Yes, we will defend ourselves, *Hironaka-san*. But we will initiate no action. Do you object to that?"

"No," Hironaka said.

"Try again to reach Admiral Ryland."

"Larry Cross is dead," Secor said, putting down the phone. "That was Bethesda. They lost him aboard the chopper enroute from Andrews. Massive injuries to his head and to the left side of his torso. His heart was badly damaged."

President Lindsay was stunned. Cross had been his Rock of Gibraltar. No matter the situation, he kept his head. His counsel was always calm.

"What about Sally and the others?"

"Sally is dead. There'll be some survivors. Not as many as the rescue teams first thought, but there'll be some." Secor looked away momentarily. "The bastards killed them." His voice was filled with emotion. "Jim, it's murder, no matter how you slice it."

Part of Mueller's tradecraft was instinct and an almost preternatural attention to detail. Those inborn skills had kept him alive in situations where other men of his profession would have been killed. He parked the Probe two blocks from Reid's house on R Street, locked his bag in the trunk, and went the rest of the way on foot. Reid was the weak link, and Mueller had a hunch that the FBI had come to the same conclusion. He stopped at the window of a gift shop on the corner and watched the street for a full minute. Something was familiar. It nagged at the back of his head, a detail he'd seen before.

Volta Place. Tallerico's house not far from here. When he and Zerkel had come out of the house they'd walked past a GMC conversion van with smoked-glass windows. The plates were SMP—something. The same van was parked across the street a half-block from Reid's house.

Associated Press Tokyo Bureau Chief Sam Norita held the telephone in the crook of his neck as he furiously made notes on his computer. He could scarcely believe what he was hearing. Heidinori Inoguchi, who was a top aide to the director general of defense, was practically making a declaration of war.

"We will defend ourselves. You have to see that in order to understand what is happening," the aide said.

"Besides the riots at this moment, the defense forces

are engaged in two battles, as you say—one with the Russian navy north of Hokkaido. What about the other?"

"Forget the riots. They don't mean a thing. In hours they will be over. What's really happening is that the U.S. Seventh Fleet is making for sea and there's a strong possibility that we will have to stop them at the mouth of Tokyo Bay."

Norita looked up and frantically motioned for the overnight editor, Ben Brown, to listen in on the call. "What do you mean?"

"The second battle is in the south, near Okinawa, between one of our maritime defense ships and a U.S. destroyer and two frigates."

Brown picked up the phone.

"Are you saying shots have been fired between our forces?" Norita asked. He'd been born in Honolulu and was a U.S. citizen. But he'd been raised by his grandparents and spoke perfect Japanese. Inoguchi, who was a good source, always spoke to him in Japanese and treated him as if he were Japanese.

"Yes. But it is very confusing here because of the American attitude over the air crashes. We are being blamed, but it is not Morning Star. It is not us."

"I don't know what you're talking about. What is Morning Star?"

"I've already said too much. If you can reach Sokichi Kamiya in Kobe he will tell you more. But if there is war between Nippon and the United States we will fight for our home waters. Let no one make that mistake."

Inoguchi broke the connection, and Norita brought up an A-wire direct circuit to AP headquarters in New York City.

"Sokichi Kamiya is the big dog at Mintori Assurance. See if you can get to him and find out what the hell Morning Star is supposed to mean," he told Brown.

His circuit came up.

A0023 FLASH
TOKYO—JAPANESE MILITARY FORCES BATTLE

U.S. NAVY.
EOM 1720 GMT

Normally such an important story would not be filed
unless two independent sources had offered corrobora-
tion. But Inoguchi had never given him false information before, and this was too stunning to sit on.

He started his follow-up to the flash.

A0024 BULLETIN DRAFT
TOKYO (AP)—A reliable source in the Japanese government early Monday morning said that a ship of the Maritime Self Defense Force was engaged in a sea battle with a
U.S. Navy destroyer and two U.S. Navy frigates somewhere
near the island of Okinawa south of the Japanese home
islands.

The Japanese police were all dead, their bodies hacked
to pieces and trampled by a mob that was completely out
of control. The American Marines had pulled back
through the main gates and blocked the road with the
two APCs and Major Ross's HumVee. They had fired
their weapons, and at first Hatoyama and the others in
front had fallen back, thinking they were under attack.
But when they realized that no one was being hit, that
the Marines were firing into the air, they surged forward.
The noise they made was something special. It was raw
and powerful. Animalistic. Like a dinosaur on the ram-
page. Nothing could stand up to them, Hatoyama
thought.

"Kamiya-san, pardon this intrusion, but there is another
telephone call for you," his secretary said at the open
shoji screen.

Kamiya was watching CNN at his secret home in the
hills overlooking Kobe and the harbor. "I will take it
here," he said.

"Pardon me, but it is not *Kobayashi-san, Nobunaga-
san,* or *Hironaka-san.*"

Kamiya looked up in surprise. Those were supposedly

the only three men of any importance in Japan who knew he was here.

"It is an American journalist with the Associated Press in Tokyo who wishes to speak to you. About Morning Star."

A callused hand closed around his heart. *Chi* and *jin*, but above all, *yu*—courage. He who shows no sign of joy or anger is the true stoic. He has true self-control. Kamiya composed himself.

"Tell this man that I am not here."

"Hai, Kamiya-san," his secretary said.

"Then telephone Kobayashi and the others that Morning Star should go ahead as planned. When that is finished, call my helicopter crew. I wish to go to *Yamagata-san*'s home, where I will await the outcome."

"Hai," his secretary said, withdrawing, and leaving Kamiya to his thoughts.

"Fall back," Green ordered. "Jones, call in the choppers. We'll give them the coordinates as soon as we have them."

"If we leave the APCs here, it might slow them down long enough for us to make the parking lot in front of base HQ," Wentz suggested.

Green didn't think they would make it either way, but her idea was as good as anything he was coming up with. He gave the order, and they headed away from the gates as fast as they could run, encumbered by combat gear.

"Choppers are eight minutes out, L-T," the radio operator reported.

"Tell them to pick us up in front of HQ. And pour on the fucking gas."

The Marines had left the keys in the ignitions of the APCs and the HumVee. It was a mistake. Hatoyama and a couple of the others quickly moved the vehicles out of the way. A cry went up from the crowd as it poured through the gates and caught sight of the fleeing Americans.

"They have called for helicopters to rescue them," Ashia told Hatoyama on the run. He carried a walkie-talkie. "But it will take them eight minutes to get here."

"Where will they land?"

"Base headquarters."

"Kill them!" Hatoyama shouted into the bullhorn. His amplified voice boomed and rebounded off the buildings. "Kill!"

The mob spread across the road, some of the people racing down side streets when they realized where the Marines were headed. The noise seemed to double and re-double every few seconds. All sanity was gone. A blood lust was on them. They had a common enemy, and a fifty-two-year-old frustration that had come down to this place now. Their collective anger had coalesced on the soldiers running from them. They were like warriors on the battlefield, adrenalin transforming them into samurai on a righteous quest.

The Marines would not fire back until it was too late for them. They were too disciplined. They'd proven that when they'd abandoned the main gate and called for the evacuation. Americans had become soft. Too soft.

Three minutes after they'd stormed the gates, the first volleys of gunfire erupted from the mob, and at least two Marines went down in sight of the base headquarters parking lot. Almost immediately thousands of rounds poured into the platoon as the first helicopters, their searchlights sweeping the ground ahead of them, appeared in the distance.

They'd won, Hatoyama thought triumphantly. Nothing would stop them now.

Franson pulled the car across the road a hundred yards from Kennedy's dark gray Range Rover. The overcast had deepened, yet the wind had picked up, blowing snow in ragged plumes from the woods. "In fifteen minutes this place is going to be crawling with federal agents. Are you going to tell us what's going on?"

"Kennedy and his wife have been kidnapped by a man named Arimoto Yamagata," McGarvey said. "He's probably going to try to use them as hostages so he can get out of here."

"Wait a minute," McLaren interrupted. "Are you saying now that you think it was the Japanese who attacked us?"

"They might have planned something, but I think someone else got involved. Maybe by accident, I don't know. Yamagata should have some of the answers."

"Are you talking about Bruno Mueller?"

"I think Mueller killed Phil Carrara and another guy from the CIA because they were getting too close. They've been targeting Guerin and a company called InterTech, which I think is a link back to the Japanese."

"What the hell are you talking about?" Franson demanded.

"A lot of people have already been killed. I'm trying to stop it from escalating."

"Okay, so we wait here until we get some backup, and then we go in and take them," McLaren suggested.

"If he takes a hit he won't do us any good," McGarvey argued. "He's probably got help, and they'll fight back if they're cornered."

"You thinking about taking them one on one?"

"I'd have a better chance alone."

"I'll go with you," McLaren said.

"Bullshit!" Franson started to turn, but Joyce grabbed his arm.

"Sorry, Mr. Franson, but you and I will wait here for the others."

"Sonofabitch!"

McGarvey withdrew the pistol from Franson's neck, eased the hammer down, and climbed out of the car. He started down the road. McLaren caught up with him as he screwed the silencer on the end of the Walther's barrel, then pulled the ejector slide back, jacking a round into the empty firing chamber.

The FBI agent laughed. "Don't tell Franson you wouldn't have shot him. He'd probably kill you with his bare hands."

* * *

FBI Special Agents Kris Wentworth and Brian Strong had been on surveillance duty since six in the morning, and they were bored.

"How about some music?" Strong suggested.

"I don't care," Wentworth said, lighting a cigarette. They'd not listened to the radio all morning.

Reid had been re-scheduled to fly on Air Force Two, and they would have had the rest of the day off. Sundays were slow unless they were on special assignment like now. But the dumb sonofabitch had driven his car off the Suitland Parkway five miles short of Andrews. By the time the tow truck had come to pull him out of the ditch he was too late to catch the flight. They'd monitored his two cellular calls from the car: one to the AAA and the other to the White House. But it hadn't seemed right to Wentworth. He'd bet anything that Reid had deliberately missed the flight.

"Hang on," Strong said from the rear observation position.

Wentworth looked up from the viewfinder of the powerful telephoto camera lens as a yellow Corvette came down the street, turned up the driveway, and parked next to Reid's house. A young, good-looking woman got out of the car and went to the door.

"Who is she?" Strong asked.

"I don't know. Run a trace on the plates." Wentworth studied her through the lens. She rang the bell, and a few moments later Reid came to the door and let her in. It was odd the way she'd clutched her purse, as if she was afraid she'd drop it, as if she were carrying something important.

"Dominique Kilbourne, Watergate Apartments," Strong read from the computer screen. "No warrants."

Kilbourne, Wentworth thought. The name was vaguely familiar, but he couldn't dredge it up. "See if we have anything on her."

"Shall we call it in?"

"Not yet. Maybe she's just a call girl, and the old boy is getting it on."

"Here it comes again," Strong said.

A white Toyota van had passed Reid's house a minute ago. It came back from the opposite direction and parked at the corner.

The angle was wrong for Wentworth to get a clear camera shot—the van was fifty yards away on the other side of the street. "I can't make the plates."

"Stand by," Strong said excitedly. He flipped a couple of switches on a bank of sensitive receivers. "That was really fast. VHF band, but high-speed burst. Encrypted, I think."

"From the Toyota?"

"Yeah, they just sent a message to somebody. It's not one of ours."

"Amundson."

"Sir, this is North American Intercept. We've got that back trace. It's Bank of Tokyo. No doubt about it now. Started out as an international funds transfer to Inter-Tech Corporation's Alameda mainframe. But the funny thing is there wasn't any transfer of funds. The signal is being automatically up-linked to the company's geosync satellite, which is relaying a two-thousand-cycle tone modulated onto its microwave carrier."

"Is InterTech processing the signal?"

"No way to tell for sure. But there's no appreciable delay, so I'd say it's automatic. Could be InterTech doesn't know what's going on."

"Is it still running?"

"Yes, sir."

Amundson sent the FLASH-designated message to the Pentagon, CIA, FBI, and FAA, then picked up the telephone and called the White House Situation Room direct.

* * *

"Gentlemen, there's no longer any doubt who's behind this attack on us," President Lindsay said after the NSA call. "It means Enchi is lying."

"He might be in the dark just like we are," Secor suggested. "Could be some faction other than his government. He's had trouble with the Democratic Socialist Party since the beginning."

"He would not have placed his military at DEFCON TWO."

"Mr. President, the FBI is sending someone to InterTech. I think we should wait to see what they come up with."

"In the meantime, how much more damage will be done to us? How many more lives will be lost?" the President demanded. "I want all Japanese Self Defense Forces held to their home waters and air space."

"Considering what's going on north of Hokkaido, they might not back down," Secretary of Defense Paul Landry cautioned.

"I'll call Enchi and tell him what we're doing and why. If he's not part of whatever the hell is going on, he'll take steps to stop it. If he is part of it, he'll understand that I mean business."

Mueller had no doubt that the GMC was an FBI surveillance unit. But he couldn't think who was in the Toyota, except they were interested in Reid or perhaps the young woman who'd shown up in the Corvette.

He screwed the can silencer on the end of the Beretta. He could not afford to walk away, but neither could he afford to attract any attention. Holding the pistol out of sight at his side, he stepped around the corner and headed for the Toyota. Most people would be at home, glued to their television sets, watching the unfolding drama of America's greatest air disaster. The chances that someone would be looking out a window were slim, but present. This would have to be done quickly.

For the first moments the advantage would be his. Most cops on stakeouts had tunnel vision. They were focused on the object of their surveillance. It made them vulnerable. In addition, most of the cops he'd ever met had little or no imagination. The unexpected froze them. They saw what they expected to see.

As he approached he could see that no one was behind the wheel. The driver had crawled into the back. It confirmed his suspicion that it was a surveillance unit. Their attention would be directed elsewhere.

Reaching the van, he opened the passenger door and climbed inside. Two slightly built men were in the back. One of them wore a headset, the other was looking out the rear window through a pair of binoculars. They turned in surprise.

Mueller shot them both in the face, driving their bodies backward, blood splattering the banks of electronic equipment.

They were Japanese. But it didn't surprise him. America's intelligence services leaked like everybody else's. No doubt there was a pipeline back to Tokyo from the CIA and the FBI's counterespionage division. The only thing that bothered Mueller was the extent of their knowledge. He did not want to spend the rest of his life running from them as well as the Americans. In many respects the Japanese were a more efficient, more patient people than Americans.

He eased the Beretta's hammer down and stuffed the gun in his belt as he checked the GMC in the rearview mirror. Even if they'd been watching, they could not have seen what had gone on inside the van. But he did not want to give them time to think about it.

He got out of the Toyota, waited for a cab to pass, then walked across the street and down the block. As he approached the GMC, he held his open wallet up as if he were a cop showing his ID.

Someone powered the passenger door window down, and Mueller lowered his wallet. "I need to use your radio."

"What the hell are you talking about?" the FBI agent asked suspiciously.

"I've got two men down in the Toyota, and I need a Technical Services unit from Langley over here pronto. Will you guys call it in for me? I'm Tom Rheinberger, Operations. Tell them it's Scarlet Ribbon."

"What's going on, Kris?" someone asked from in back.

"A guy says he's CIA."

"Look, I don't want to blow your operation, pal, but if Reid happens to look out his window and see us having a powwow we might as well all pack it in. Either call Langley for me, or let me do it. But make up your mind."

"I don't know if we've got your frequency," Wentworth said.

"You gotta have it," Mueller said, opening the door. "I'll show you."

"Just a sec," Wentworth said. He turned to the back.

Mueller pulled out his pistol and climbed in behind him, pushing him down. The second FBI agent reared back as Mueller shot him point-blank in the face. Then, as Wentworth tried to get free, Mueller shot him in the back of the head just behind his left ear.

"What do you think about that?" he said to himself.

McGarvey waited below the wooden walkway for McLaren to come down the driveway. Kennedy's footprints crossed the parking area to the walk where they were joined by another set. There were no signs of a struggle, nor was there any blood. They'd seen him coming, and they'd taken him. Simple. He didn't think they would shoot another lone man, apparently unarmed, approaching the house on foot. But they'd sure as hell come out to challenge him.

Coming through the woods from the highway, McGarvey had spotted one of the closed-circuit television cameras trained on the driveway and had sent the FBI agent back.

"Are you wearing a vest?"

"Yeah, but it hurts like hell to get shot," McLaren said. "If it comes to that, don't miss."

"I won't."

"No, I don't expect you would."

McLaren, his coat buttoned and his hands in plain sight at his sides, came into view at the end of the driveway. He stopped a moment, as if he were studying the house, and then followed the footprints toward the walkway around the side.

A Toyota van and a gray Lexus were parked in front of the house. They'd not been moved since the last snow. Unless Yamagata and whoever he had with him had another way out of here, they were still inside.

McGarvey lay still and watched as McLaren climbed the steps to the walkway and again hesitated a moment before starting toward the front of the house. Before he got halfway, a Japanese man dressed in a Cal Tech track suit, armed with a Glock-17 automatic, came around the corner.

"Who are you?" the Japanese asked.

McLaren stopped, his hands out. "Hey, take it easy. I'm looking for Dave Kennedy. I was told he was here."

"You're mistaken."

McGarvey eased the Walther's hammer back and switched the safety catch off as he rose from his hiding place. "Lower your weapon now, or I will shoot you."

The man's eyes flicked to McGarvey, but his aim never wavered from McLaren. "We wish you no harm, Mr. McGarvey. In fact, we were expecting you."

"Is Yamagata here?"

"Yes."

"Then put your gun on the railing and step back."

"It's not what you think."

"Hayai," quick, McGarvey said.

The man's eyes widened slightly in surprise.

"Ima!" Now!

The Japanese intelligence officer carefully placed the big handgun on the snow-covered railing and stepped back a pace.

McLaren pulled out his pistol and pointed it at the Japanese. McGarvey climbed up on the walkway and retrieved the man's weapon.

"How many others besides Yamagata are inside?"

"One," the Japanese responded.

"If you're lying, I'll kill you, and there'll be no honor in it."

"One," the man said. "But they are seeing and hearing everything that is happening here. So be very careful. No one wishes to kill or be killed."

"I hope you're sincere, because I am in a very bad mood."

"Hai," the Japanese said.

McGarvey and McLaren followed him around the corner to a broad veranda that ran the length of the house. A sliding glass door was open. They went inside to a huge living room with a central fireplace.

Yamagata was seated on the arm of a long couch, Chance Kennedy next to him. David was seated near the fireplace, another Japanese intelligence officer behind him, pointing a gun at his head.

"I'm glad you're here, Mr. McGarvey," Yamagata said seriously. "We have a lot to discuss this afternoon if we are to avert a horrible tragedy between our countries."

"It's already happened."

"It is not our doing."

"But your design," McGarvey countered sharply.

McLaren moved to the left so that he had a clear shot at Yamagata, who was unarmed.

"We can discuss that later," Yamagata said, eyeing the FBI agent. "For now you must tell me who you suspect, and together we will prove it to our governments. Believe me, Mr. McGarvey, I do not wish a war between our countries."

"Are you all right, David?" McGarvey interrupted.

"I'm okay, but the bastards did something to Chance. Drugs, I think."

"Nothing more than a mild sedative," Yamagata said. "I assure you we mean no harm."

"They tortured me," Chance cried, her voice strangled.

"You sonofabitch!" Kennedy roared.

"Wait!" Yamagata shouted.

McGarvey motioned for Kennedy to back down. "Listen to me, David. I want you to take Chance back to the highway. There are some FBI agents up there waiting for you."

"We won't hesitate to kill you, assassin," Yamagata warned. "There are considerations at stake here that are beyond your comprehension. Put your guns down now, or we will start the killing."

McGarvey switched aim and fired one shot, hitting the Japanese behind Kennedy in the forehead just above his left eye, killing him instantly.

The other Japanese grabbed McLaren's gun hand and swung him around toward McGarvey. But he was too late. McGarvey stepped inside his guard, and reaching over the FBI agent's shoulder, fired point-blank into the Japanese intelligence officer's face.

Yamagata jumped up, dragging Chance to her feet. He held her head in a vise grip. "I'll break her neck!"

"Then I'll kill you," McGarvey replied stepping to the right.

McLaren disentangled himself from the dead Japanese. He was shook up.

Yamagata looked at them. "It's not Morning Star. I swear it."

McGarvey inclined his head very slightly, and Yamagata's eyes narrowed. He'd caught the gesture. "Step away from the woman. McLaren can take her and David back up to the highway."

"No fucking way," McLaren burst out.

"Give me ten minutes," McGarvey said, watching Yamagata. He was struggling to keep his anger in check.

"Goddammit, McGarvey."

"You owe me."

"You know what the fuck is going on! You know what they've done to us!"

"Ten minutes," McGarvey said evenly. "Then you can bring Franson and the others down here. The Bureau will take the credit."

McLaren looked at him in amazement. "You cock-sucker."

"Do it!"

Yamagata released Chance and moved aside. He held his hands away from his body so that there would be no mistake that he was reaching for a weapon.

Kennedy got to his wife before she could collapse.

"Get them out of here," McGarvey ordered.

McLaren hesitated several moments longer, but then he lowered his gun and backed off. "No shit, McGarvey. Ten minutes and we'll be back for some explanations. A lot of fucking explanations."

McGarvey waited until they were gone, and then he lowered his gun and eased the hammer down. "Did you torture her?"

"I needed to get her husband here, and through him you," Yamagata said. "It was the only way."

McGarvey almost raised his gun and shot the man. But he continued to hold his anger in check. "How were you planning on getting out of here?"

"Helicopter. It's parked under a covering on the other side of the house. But you knew that."

"Who's the pilot?"

"I am."

"Then we have ten minutes to make our escape. You can tell me about Morning Star on the way. Maybe we can avert a war after all."

"Delta 142, this is Oakland Approach Control. I repeat, we are closed to all traffic including emergencies. Suggest you divert to San Francisco International, immediately."

Captain Mark Quade had been in some tough spots in his flying career, especially as a young pilot at the end of Vietnam, but never anything like this. "I understand, but we have unknown damage to our hydraulic system and backups affecting our ailerons and rudder. I need a straight in. We're fifteen miles south of you over Dumbarton Bridge, requesting an emergency landing on three-three-left."

"We are closed. Divert to San Francisco International."

"I can't turn this fucking airplane around. I either land at Oakland, or I put it in the bay."

"Stand by."

The Delta flight was a Guerin 522, and it was in trouble. Ron Herring was picking up transmissions on the VHF walkie-talkie on his hip. He was checking one of the satellite dishes on the roof of the Oakland Airport Commission building with a field-strength meter. When the FAA's warning had come through, he'd started looking for anomalies in their own equipment. Something, anything that might help. He couldn't get the picture of Tom Reston's eyes out of his head. The man was a killer. He should have been able to see it.

They were picking up a low-frequency spike from somewhere. It was showing up on their equipment downstairs. But it wasn't a fault in one of the dishes, or in the on-site amplifiers up here.

Which meant what?

Since he'd talked to the FBI he'd become a driven man. Reston had murdered Bill White in cold blood. But he'd been here, looking the place over, and for the past three days Herring had tried to find out if he'd done anything to sabotage them.

The signal was coming from somewhere. If not up here, and not in the equipment in the office, the only place left was the basement.

Herring got up. He'd shown Reston the equipment down there! Shit!

"Oakland Approach Control, this is Delta 142. Have you got that runway clear for us?"

"Roger, Delta. We have emergency equipment standing by. Suggest that you shut down your port engine."

"Negative. We're having enough trouble steering as it is."

"Roger that. Good luck."

* * *

Herring pounded downstairs to the basement and fumbled with his security card to get the door open. He switched on the lights and stood for a moment looking at the racks of monitoring equipment.

The only place they saw the signal was in the equipment upstairs that monitored transmissions between ATC and aircraft. But the tower had come up totally clean.

Which meant that the signal had to be coming from here, but not from within their own equipment.

He switched on the field-strength meter and immediately picked up the spike. He walked forward slowly, the signal strength increasing . . . but not from the front of the racks. He raised the meter toward the ceiling, and the signal strength decreased.

To the left. Behind the equipment.

He crouched in the dim light behind the rack and for a moment he wasn't sure what he was seeing. It looked so ordinary. A trap to catch cockroaches, and maybe other bugs. A small brown cardboard container.

Herring pointed the meter at it, and the indicator went to maximum.

"Sonofabitch." As soon as he picked up the Roach Motel he knew what it was. The damned thing was far too heavy.

His walkie-talkie hissed. "Delta one-four-two reporting ten miles out. I have the runway in sight."

Herring ripped the brown paper covering off the small, open-ended box to reveal a small circuit board. Again he was stopped by the simplicity, and genius, of it.

"Roger," approach control radioed.

Herring pulled the circuit board away from the box, and yanked it free of its connecting wires. He checked the field-strength meter, but the spike was gone. Then he sat back on his heels to listen to his walkie-talkie until the Delta flight was safely on the ground.

FORTY-ONE

I n five minutes I'll call the President," Roland Murphy said. "What do I tell him?"

"I don't think there's any doubt in light of NSA's intercept from Tokyo Bank," Ryan answered.

They met in the conference room adjacent to the DCI's office. Besides Murphy and Ryan, Danielle had come from down the hall, and Tommy Doyle and Adkins had come from downstairs.

"Circumstantially we can build a pretty good case against some Japanese group, but anyone could have initiated that signal train from Tokyo," Adkins cautioned.

"Oh, for Christ's sake, Dick," the Company's counsel said. "The evidence is overwhelming. The bastards are overrunning Seventh's headquarters in Yokosuka. Admiral Ryland is transferring his flag to the *George Washington.*" He turned back to Murphy. "It's probably not Enchi's government. He's lost control. But their actions are definitely directed."

"Tommy?" Murphy asked his deputy director of intelligence.

"It looks bad, but I think Dick has got a point. The Russians have their *Abunai* network in Tokyo. It's conceivable that they could have gotten into Tokyo Bank's computer system. Hell, my fourteen year old says he can get into just about any computer anywhere with his PC, and I believe him."

"Those airplanes were sabotaged in this country," Ryan argued. "That takes resources and long-term planning."

"Agreed," Doyle said. "I'm just saying that we don't know all the facts yet."

"Lawrence?" Murphy turned to his deputy DCI.

"We might have the damage contained for the moment . . ." Danielle said, and Ryan interrupted.

"The death toll will top two thousand, including the Vice President, who, need I remind you, was en route to Tokyo."

"If the Russians hadn't made their move at the same time by attacking the Japanese, I might agree without reservations," Danielle said patiently.

"Which means?" Murphy asked.

Danielle shrugged. "Kirk McGarvey may have something after all."

"Please!" Ryan said.

"If Bruno Mueller is involved, as the FBI thinks he is, it could implicate the Russians. He was trained by them."

Murphy held Ryan off. "What's your point?"

"Tell the President to go slow until we have more facts. Could be a Japanese faction. Could be a Russian plot to embroil us in a shooting war with the Japanese."

"For what reason?" Ryan shot back.

"I don't know, but both possibilities are, I think, worth considering. As is a third—that another independent organization is behind this. Every airplane that crashed was a Guerin 522. That means something. As does Phil Carrara's murder. He was working with McGarvey, and McGarvey is—or was—working for Guerin."

"He went to Japan."

"Yes, and to Russia," Danielle answered, tiredly. "Whatever your problems with him are, Mr. Ryan, I have known Kirk since he first started for us. He is a good man."

"Did you know his parents well?" Ryan countered.

"I don't want bickering," Murphy said finally. "Where is McGarvey?"

"Portland. The FBI has him," Ryan said.

"Have him brought here as soon as possible."

"We'll try. But it seems that every time we make a

decision, he finds out about it faster than I can write a memo."

"Mr. President, it's my understanding that you have ordered a blockade against the Japanese navy leaving its home waters," Murphy said. "That may not be the best course of action."

President Lindsay could hear the hesitation in his DCI's voice. It was uncharacteristic, and unsettling. "We don't have many options, General. I assume you've seen the latest NSA intercept."

"Yes, sir. But there's a possibility—it's remote but still possible—that something else is going on here. We just don't have all the facts yet. It's too soon."

"What other possibility?" Lindsay asked, looking down the table at his advisers. They listened on the speakerphone.

"A former East German intelligence officer could have something to do with the crashes."

"Mr. Doyle mentioned the possibility."

"He was trained by the Russians, Mr. President. And it seems too coincidental that the Russians have picked this moment to attack the Japanese."

"They attacked because of the Tatar Strait incident."

"Yes, sir. But isn't it odd that a Russian frigate was blown out of the water so easily?"

"Are you saying that the Russians sacrificed that ship?"

"No, Mr. President. I'm saying that it is one of many possibilities that we must consider. The Japanese are our allies."

"Somebody brought down those airplanes for a specific reason, General. It was no act of random violence."

"I agree," Murphy said. "Could be a group in Japan. Could be a Russian group. Or it could be a third, as yet, unknown organization with an unknown motive."

"That's no help to me, Roland," the President said firmly. "Based on all the available information to this point, can you say it's not the Japanese?"

"No, sir. But I can't say it's not the Russians."

"Then I have to go with that until you can bring me some additional information." The President sat forward in his chair. "Nobody is going to war with anybody, Roland. I merely want the situation contained long enough to find out what's going on, who is behind it, and why."

"I'll get back to you, Mr. President," Murphy said.

"Do that, General."

Ryan walked into Dick Adkins' office on the third floor and set a portable cassette player on his desk. "We're placing you under arrest at this time, Mr. Adkins. As an attorney, I can advise you that you have the right to remain silent. Security is waiting in the corridor."

"What's the charge?" Adkins asked calmly, as if he had expected this.

"Violations of the National Secrets Act." Ryan switched on the tape recorder. The first voice was Adkins'.

"*. . . NSA is reading heavy traffic from the Japanese embassy here to their Ministry of State in Tokyo. Some of it has to do with the crashes.*"

"*I'll be on the ground in a few minutes,*" McGarvey said. "*Have the general convince the President to hold off for as long as possible.*"

Ryan switched the tape recorder off.

"I see," Adkins said. "Who's going to run Operations?"

"I am," Ryan replied smugly.

The MSDF naval and naval air station at Otaru in Hokkaido's western bight had been on continuous alert for seventy-two hours. During that time ninety percent of its ASW ships and planes were at sea or in the air. Lockheed/Kawasaki P-3C sub-killer, tail number 4417, was given vectors to the Soya Strait where the Russian destroyer *Sovremennyy* had been sunk.

"Looks like they've sent a submarine," the pilot told his weapons officer. "The bastards."

"We'd better call for more assets. Where there's one, there's probably another."

"The *Aukumo* and *Akiqumo* are en route from the 23rd. We just need to buy them some time." The two ships were destroyers.

"At least the American Third Air Force at Misawa is staying out of it."

"For the moment," the pilot said, a fierce expression on his face. "This is our country. Our fight."

The seas were rough in the Soya Strait. Nevertheless, Captain First Rank Lestov figured he would be able to spot the orange distress markers sent by survivors of the *Sovremennyy*. But nothing showed up in the scope after two sweeps. *"Nyee-cheh-vaw nyet,"* he said. Nothing.

"Conn, ELINT. Wakkanai is still sending on at least one of her arrays. The others are apparently down."

"We'll see about that," Lestov said.

The Russian's Pacific Fleet Far Eastern Reconnaissance Center at Vladivostok was fully staffed. Lieutenant Arkadi Papyrin watched the thermal imaging down-link terminal from the RORSAT satellite currently making a pass over the Japanese north island of Hokkaido and the Soya Strait.

He keyed his comms. "Major, I have an update at Zebra-Two."

Major Ivan Isakov walked over from his command console. "Have the Americans at Misawa responded?"

Papyrin enhanced the region from Otaru north. "No, but there is a new image in the air in addition to the two MSDF jets. Looks like a P-3C ASW aircraft. Almost over the *Strelka*. But look there, just south of Rishiri. Two destroyers, maybe an hour out."

"The *Strelka* is still near the surface?"

"Da. He's probably looking for survivors."

"Send it to them," Isakov ordered. "But in case he misses the message, we'll send it out on ELF as well."

"I have him on the MAD."

P-3C 4417 pilot Lieutenant Togame Muto corrected his course to the right and reduced throttle to bring them closer to the surface. The night was black. "How deep is he?"

"Kan-cho, he's just below the surface," the ELINT officer reported. "Stand by. Radar is picking up his periscope and snoophead."

"Is he looking for survivors?"

"Maybe, but his radar is lit. He's headed toward Wakkanai."

"Do we drop a fish on him?" the weapons officer asked excitedly.

"Prep a pair of Mark-50s," Muto said. "And get that off to base and to the *Aukumo* and *Akiqumo.*"

The message from Pacific Fleet came at the same moment the *Strelka*'s own sensors detected the presence of the Orion ASW aircraft.

"Presents us with an interesting problem, Viktor," Captain Lestov told his XO. He lowered the periscope. "Do we wait to see if they attack, or do we dive now and launch a sub-sea missile on Wakkanai, which would pinpoint our position, or submerge and wait to see what other assets they bring up, which would tell us how serious they are?"

"I think there is no question of their seriousness, Captain," Savin replied.

Lestov smiled sadly. "We have no business being here."

"No, sir. But we have our orders."

"Indeed." Lestov looked at his crew. Good men and true. "Mr. Savin, crash dive the boat. Make your depth three hundred meters. Sound battle stations missile."

* * *

"The target is diving," the ELINT officer reported. The P-3C 4417 was on her outbound pass, the Russian submarine behind them.

Muto hauled the big four-engined airplane in a tight turn to the left. "Do we have a weapons release authorization?"

"Stand by," his comms officer said.

"Weapons, do you have a positive lock?"

"Hai, Kan-cho."

"Launch on my mark," Muto said, fighting the low-altitude turbulence.

"We have weapons release authorization alpha."

"Stand by," Muto said. The nose of the Orion came around to one-hundred-eight degrees. "Weapons lock?"

"Hai!"

"Fire one and two!"

The moment the two torpedoes—each weighing in excess of three thousand pounds—were released, the P-3C's nose came up sharply. Muto compensated.

"One and two away."

"Time to impact?"

"Estimate nine-five seconds," the weapons officer reported.

"Prep torpedoes three and four. Launch sonobuoys on my mark," Muto said. They crossed over the submarine's submerged position, and he banked the P-3C hard to the right to bring them around for a second pass.

"I have sounds of bubble making," the ELINT officer reported excitedly. "Many decoy buoys in the water."

"Time to impact?"

"Four-zero seconds."

Out of the corner of his eye Muto could see fires burning at Wakkanai ten miles to the south. It made his blood boil. Almost certainly there were dead comrades down there. The shame of it was almost impossible to bear.

"Stand by," the weapons officer said. "Time to impact, now."

What the P-3C made up for in endurance and stability, it lost in speed. The nose seemed to take forever to come around.

"Negative ten seconds from impact."

Muto looked at his co-pilot.

"*Kan-cho,* I show a miss with both torpedoes," the weapons officer reported.

"Launch the sonobuoys now," Muto ordered, his stomach sour. "What does the MAD show?"

"We've lost him, *Kan-cho,*" the ELINT officer said.

"Not for long," Muto replied. "We've just started."

Mueller stood at the head of the stairs listening to Reid and the young woman argue. She had come to kill him, but first she wanted answers. Hundreds of people dead, and she wanted to know why. What did he hope to gain? How could he live with his conscience? She wanted to batter him with her anger and her guilt. She was to blame, as they all were, for not listening to McGarvey. He was the only one who knew what really happened, but they wanted to arrest him.

There it was again: McGarvey. He could hear what in the woman's voice when she spoke the name? Love?

Mueller had two considerations if he was going to remain at large for any length of time, hunted by every legitimate law enforcement agency in the world. He would need Reid's money and he would have to kill McGarvey.

Reid could transfer funds electronically once they got clear of this place, but McGarvey was a different story. Sooner or later the FBI and Interpol would give up. New issues would arise, and this case would drop off the most active file. But McGarvey would never give up. He'd read McGarvey's Stasi and KGB files, and he had a great deal of respect for the man. If he was going to meet McGarvey head to head, he would need an advantage.

He eased the Beretta's safety off and walked down the hall to the open sitting-room door.

The young woman, her back to the door, stood facing Reid. She held an automatic pistol at arm's length. If it went off she'd break her wrist. She was an amateur.

Reid stood next to a wingback chair near the window. His face lit up.

Dominique started to turn. Mueller stepped into the room, and reaching over her shoulder snatched the gun from her grasp.

"No," she cried. But any thought she had about trying to fight ended when she looked into his eyes. She lowered her arms.

"Who are you?" Mueller asked.

"Her name is Dominique Kilbourne," Reid said. "She's a lobbyist for the airlines."

"Let her answer," Mueller said mildly, pocketing her gun. "Are you a friend of McGarvey?"

"You're Colonel Mueller," she replied in wonderment. But her eyes betrayed her. She was more than just a friend to McGarvey.

"Yes."

She shuddered. "You're an assassin."

"The same as McGarvey." Mueller turned to Reid. "Are you capable of driving?"

"Yes."

Mueller tossed Reid the car keys. "Pack a bag and leave it in the downstairs hall. Then get my car. It's a green Ford Probe on the upper side of R Street two blocks from here. Across from a woman's boutique."

"I can't leave."

"Two FBI agents were out front watching your house. I killed them."

Reid stepped back as if he'd been slapped.

"They were gathering evidence against you, I suspect. They'll send others, so hurry."

"But . . ."

"It very nearly worked as you planned, *Herr* Reid, but not quite. Stay here and you will be imprisoned. Come with me and you will have a chance of continued freedom."

"Where are we going?"

"The Canadian border at Buffalo."

"And then?" Reid asked.

Mueller watched Dominique. "We'll see. Mr. McGarvey will come for her, as he has all of his women."

"He'll kill you," Dominique said softly.

"That is a possibility." Mueller smiled pleasantly. "It will be most interesting to see how it turns out."

"I'll get the car," Reid said.

"In the meantime, I'll get acquainted with Ms. Kilbourne."

The chopper that had tried to land on the roof of Seventh headquarters burned furiously where it crashed in the parking lot. Platoon Sergeant Ingrid Wentz figured they had five minutes before the mob reached the upper floors where she and Jones, who were the only survivors from Baker Platoon, had retreated. They'd rounded up seventeen other HQ personnel who'd gotten left behind in the bugout and herded them upstairs. They were admin types and wouldn't be able to offer much help in a knockdown dragout. But they were military personnel, and most of them carried sidearms. She raced down to the fifth-floor corridor from the roof where the others were covering the elevator and two stairwells.

"Lima and Kilo companies are pinned down across base at 26th," Jones reported. "And I can't raise security ops."

"An air evac is out unless they can control the small arms fire," Wentz said. She was so frightened that her voice wanted to catch in her throat. But she wouldn't let it happen. She was a Marine.

"Search-and-rescue is standing by three minutes out."

"Didn't you hear me, goddammit? The fucking chopper is down."

Jones just looked at her. He knew the helicopter had crashed.

"Okay, let me talk to them."

The power suddenly went out, and the emergency lights at each end of the corridor automatically switched on.

"Fuck!" someone shouted.

"Belay that!" Wentz ordered. "It means they can't use the elevator. Kill those lights, and double up on the stairwells."

"SAR One," Jones said.

"Anything comes through those doors, kill it." Wentz took the handset as the emergency lights went off, plunging the corridor into darkness. "SAR One, Baker Platoon Sergeant Wentz."

"What's your situation, Sarge?"

"I'm set up on the fifth floor with fifty well-armed personnel. But I don't want to hurt any civilians unless I'm forced into it."

"What about Charlie-Seventeen?"

"No survivors, SAR One. We need some help right now!"

"Roger that. The Japanese authorities are en route."

"We need an air evac. Can you lay down enough tear gas to come in? I really don't want to use my grenade launchers or LAWS. A lot of people will get hurt." She hoped to Christ they knew that communications weren't secure, and that she was bluffing. The platoon hadn't been equipped with anything heavier than M16s.

Something crashed on the floor below them, and there were many sounds of breaking glass, twisting metal, and splintering wood. The mob was destroying the building.

"Ten minutes."

"We don't have ten minutes, SAR One. Suggest you get serious or we're dead meat."

"There weren't fifty people left in the building," Don Moody said. "Admiral, if we don't do something there's going to be a lot more casualties on both sides."

"Don't I know it," Admiral Ryland said. "Nothing from the Japanese authorities?"

"Not a thing," Captain Byrne said.

The morning outside the windows of the Boeing Sea Knight helicopter was still pitch black. To the east it was impossible to pick out where the sky met the sea. Only behind them could they see the loom of Tokyo on the horizon.

"Do we have any tear gas aboard those choppers?"

"No, sir. They're search-and-rescue, not crowd control."

"I've got an idea," Moody said. "It's a long shot, but I don't see any other options."

"Go ahead."

"Assuming the Japanese are going to send someone down there to clear out the base, we have to buy some time. But no matter what happens there'll be casualties. We need to minimize them by keeping the crowd away from our people."

"I'm listening," the Admiral said.

"The mob has reached the fourth floor. If we move our people up to the roof, the fifth floor will be empty long enough to bring in some choppers."

"What the hell are you talking about, Don?" Byrne asked.

"Covering fire. We shoot through the windows on all four sides of the building. Make the fifth floor a no-man's land."

"You're talking about the Iroquois and Super Cobra assault helicopters," Byrne pointed out. "The nearest birds are at least an hour away."

"Christ," Moody said.

"Get 'em started, Tom," Admiral Ryland ordered. "In the meantime we'll put more pressure on the Japanese, and I'll call Washington."

"What about Sergeant Wentz?"

"She'll just have to hold on."

The television monitors in the White House situation room were tuned to the three commercial networks and CNN, covering the carnage at and around the eight airports. They were all reporting death tolls in the plus-two-thousand range. Every major highway into those airports was jammed with traffic, and the nation's long-distance telephone system was so overloaded that it had finally broken down. Almost no calls were getting through anywhere. It was as if the entire country had gone into gridlock.

An aide came in with the AP bulletin from Tokyo. Secretary of Defense Landry took it.

"What is it now?" Lindsay asked.

"The Associated Press is quoting an unnamed Japanese government source about a battle between three of our warships and the MSDF submarine north of Okinawa." Landry passed the wire copy down the table.

"Has Seventh said anything about this?" the President asked.

"There's something going on down there all right, but no one knows for sure exactly what. The curious thing is that someone in the government is willing to talk about it."

Lindsay read the brief report. "Have shots been exchanged?"

"I don't know."

"Find out, Paul."

"Yes, sir." Landry picked up one of the phones.

"If it's true, it changes everything," Secor said.

"Depends who in Tokyo told the AP," Lindsay said. "Call Westin and find out who the hell his people talked to." Bert Westin was the general manager of the AP.

"Mr. President, we have reached Prime Minister Enchi," a technician said.

"The question is whether or not Enchi is in control over there," Secor said.

"I'm about to find that out."

"There are at least four Russian nuclear submarines in the vicinity of Soya Strait," Director General of Defense Hironaka said.

A light flashed on Enchi's console. He stared at it hypnotically. The Japanese had had no war crisis-management practice in more than fifty years. He was a politician, a friend of big business, not of the military. "Is that confirmed?"

"One of our ASW aircraft spotted the first submarine near where the Russian destroyer went down. It dropped a pair of torpedoes, but then lost the sub when it went deep."

"You said there were four of them."

"That one is confirmed, Mr. Prime Minister. The others are probables. Based on best estimates from available data."

"Then we don't know this for sure?"

"Where there is smoke there is fire."

Enchi slapped his open palm on the table. "I deal with facts, not speculation, *Hironaka-san.*"

"The Russians have attacked Wakkanai, *Enchi-san.* That is a fact. As is the presence of a Russian nuclear submarine ten miles off our coast. If you wait until you have *all* the facts the entire north island may be nothing but smoking cinders!"

Enchi composed himself for a moment, then viciously jabbed the button on his console. "Mr. President, I have learned the unfortunate news about Vice President Cross."

"He was just one of more than two thousand," President Lindsay cut in. The anger in his voice was unmistakable. "I have heard about a battle between several of our navy vessels and one of your submarines in the East China Sea north of Okinawa. What is going on?"

"We are trying to recall that submarine. But I assure you that we are engaged in no incident with your navy."

"Someone in your government thinks so. They leaked the information to the Associated Press there in Tokyo. It has hit all of our media."

Enchi looked down the table at his advisers, but they were just as nonplussed as he was.

"My country is under attack," President Lindsay said abruptly.

"So is mine," Enchi replied in English before the translator could catch up.

"I have evidence that our air traffic control system was sabotaged. We've traced the triggering signal that brought down those airplanes to a source in Tokyo."

Enchi was suddenly cold. "Impossible," he replied. It

was Morning Star. He'd been warned, but he'd not believed it was possible.

"Nevertheless it is so," President Lindsay said. "If you are not in control of the situation, I will offer my assistance."

Enchi could scarcely believe his ears. Hironaka jumped to his feet.

"It is my understanding that all of your naval and air forces are on the move. Recall them to their bases and home ports immediately. I have instructed the Seventh Fleet to help you with this."

"What are you saying?"

"I am telling you to order your forces to stand down before it is too late."

"But we are under attack, Mr. President. We must defend ourselves."

"We are not attacking Japan!"

"Not you," Enchi replied sharply. "It is the Russians. They are threatening Hokkaido with a force of nuclear submarines. We are facing another Hiroshima and Nagasaki!"

The translators were silent.

"Mr. President, I am formally asking the United States for help thwarting an almost certain nuclear attack on us by the government of Russia."

President Lindsay punched the mute button on his console. "Can we confirm this?" He was stunned.

"We're working on it," Landry said. "But so far we can't even get a clear update on the Okinawa situation. One of our ships, the *Thorn,* has been damaged, but it may have been because of a collision. No one is willing to say yet whether or not shots are being exchanged."

"Could be a rogue submarine skipper after all," Secor cautioned.

"This is too much," Lindsay said. "Get me the CIA again, and then Yeltsin on the Moscow hotline." The President released the mute. "Prime Minister, you will have to give us a few minutes to confirm what is happening. In the meantime I suggest that you make absolutely certain that your military forces are clear on who the enemy is."

"Yes, Mr. President, they are crystal clear who our enemies are. But do not take too much time. The situation is becoming critical."

Lindsay cut the connection. "What the hell did he mean, 'our enemies'? Plural." His call to Langley came in. "Did you get that, Roland?" The CIA was monitoring hotline calls and messages in and out of the White House situation room.

"National Reconnaissance is on it, Mr. President. There's definitely a military buildup in the region, both Japanese and Russian. But we're waiting for word about submarine assets up there."

"What's the current situation in Moscow?"

"The attack on the Japanese radar installation didn't come as a surprise. But there's been no word that the Russians are willing to escalate the situation."

"How reliable is that information?"

"We don't have a direct source, if that's what you mean, Mr. President. What I'm giving you is a best estimate based on available data."

"Thanks, General," the President said. "Stay on the line."

"Yes, sir."

The hotline phone to Moscow blinked. Lindsay picked it up. "President Yeltsin, forgive me for calling you so late in the evening." It was after midnight at the Kremlin.

"I know why you are calling, Mr. President, but the situation in the Soya Strait will be resolved soon."

"Prime Minister Enchi believes that his country is under threat of imminent nuclear attack by your forces."

"Nonsense."

"Please withdraw your warships from the area. I believe any differences can be worked out peacefully."

"The order has already been given, Mr. President. But you might consider who the real enemy is. Your country is under attack on several fronts. Take care that you are not misdirected."

"Is there some information you can offer me?"

"No, Mr. President. But I wish you luck."

Lindsay broke the connection. "Was he lying?"

"We'll know after the next satellite pass," Murphy responded, and Landry nodded his agreement.

The air traffic control system had ground to a halt, and the only good thing about that, Michael Schaeffer thought, was that no more airplanes would crash. There'd been no mistaking Herring's urgency when he'd finally gotten through from Oakland, but it had taken Schaeffer the better part of an hour to make it out to O'Hare Airport from his home in nearby Mount Prospect. Herring was talking about a sophisticated system of sabotage that was affecting at least eight airports. Except for what he'd been watching on television, Schaeffer would never have believed it. As it was he didn't know what to think. He'd grabbed a field-strength meter from the lab, and the moment he'd switched it on, he started receiving the signal Herring had warned about. But it wasn't coming from the roof, or from first-floor offices. It was coming from the basement. Schaeffer was an engineer, not a cop, so he felt faintly ridiculous crawling around in the dark behind the equipment racks looking for clues. There was dust everywhere. It was months since the janitors had cleaned up.

For a moment Schaeffer had trouble accepting that what he was seeing was a threat. The field-strength meter pegged. It was exactly as Herring said it would be. But even if someone had spotted the thing they wouldn't have known what it really was.

He put the meter down and picked up the Roach Motel. It was heavier than he expected it would be. Slitting the paper cover with his thumbnail, he peeled it back to expose the circuit board. The work was not exceptional, that of a competent amateur, but the design was intriguing. In the dim light Schaeffer tried to trace the intricate circuit for several seconds until he realized that he had become mesmerized. Whatever this was, however it worked, it killed people.

Schaeffer pried the small circuit board from the cardboard box and ripped the wires away from where they connected with the battery on the bottom.

The field-strength meter went to zero.

With the way the telephone system was across the country, Schaeffer hoped to God that Herring had managed to get word to the FAA and the other six airports. But at least here they could start getting back to normal.

"It's legal, Mr. Zussman," InterTech's attorney Freemont Perry said. He handed the search warrant back to Charles Colberg.

"What are you looking for?" the company's vice president, Milton Zussman, asked. He'd been notified at home of the pending FBI search. He'd shown up with Perry and InterTech's chief of security Neil Hood. They met with a half-dozen FBI special agents in the parking lot of the company's Alameda Research and Development Facility.

"We'll start at your mainframe," Colberg said.

"No," Zussman replied. He was a corpulent man, a full head taller than Colberg, and he was angry. "Half the projects we're presently working on are under top-secret government contract. You don't have the clearance."

Colberg held his own anger in check. "With or without your cooperation, sir."

"It's going to take more than a local judge's order."

Colberg shoved the executive up against the FBI van, pulled his hands behind him and cuffed them. "You are under arrest at this time for obstruction of justice. You have the right to remain silent . . ."

"Just hold on there," Perry warned.

"The charge is obstruction of justice," Colberg said, and he finished reading Zussman his rights. "InterTech has been implicated in at least fourteen acts of sabotage to our Air Traffic Control system. Does your client understand his rights as I've explained them?"

"You sonofabitch, you'll fucking well take the fall for this," Zussman shouted.

"Put this bag of shit in the van," Colberg instructed one of his agents.

"This is preposterous," the attorney argued.

"As I said, Mr. Perry, with or without your cooperation," Colberg warned. "This is a national emergency." He was from the East Coast, and he hated California. He didn't think he'd be staying in San Francisco much longer. Especially if he played his cards right and they found something.

"You're making a terrible mistake, but we won't stand in your way."

"Are there any engineers or technicians on duty today?" Colberg asked. "I don't see any cars in the parking lot."

"Only security personnel," Hood said. The company attorney looked sharply at him.

"Is this place normally staffed on the weekend?"

"It depends on what projects we're working on," Perry answered, clearly flustered.

Hood said something into a walkie-talkie, then took them inside to the vast mainframe complex in the sprawling facility's east wing. The lights were on, and half the monitor screens were up and running. Colberg got the impression that the place was deserted. One moment it had been filled with technicians, and the next it was empty. As if they'd simply gotten up from their consoles and walked off. He could see that Perry was having the same reaction.

"Won't do you much good unless you know the passwords," the chief of security cautioned.

Kevin Winter, a special agent who'd recently graduated from Cal Tech, sat down at one of the terminals, and within a half-minute brought up the company's financial file.

"What the hell?" Perry said softly.

"Can you get in?" Colberg asked.

"There's no lock on the incoming cash transfers," Winter said, his fingers flying over the keyboard.

Whitman had relayed the information that NSA had supplied. "It's a long shot, Chuck. But we're running out of options."

"Okay," Winter said. He hit several other keys, and two files came up on the split screen. "At noon today there was a wire transfer for twenty-five million dollars from the Bank of Tokyo, but it's not showing up on any of InterTech's Wells Fargo accounts."

"Where'd it go?" Colberg asked.

"Never was any money, sir." Winter hit another set of keys. "Here it is. The wire transfer was shunted to their comms satellite, which keyed some kind of a down-link program. Microwave, with a couple-of-kilohertz tone piggybacked." He looked up. "It's still on line."

"Can you explain that?" Colberg asked Perry.

"No." The attorney shook his head. "I'm not aware of any such financial transaction."

"Can you shut it off, Kevin?"

Winter hit another set of keys. "It's down."

Yamagata had to fight the wind shears through the Coast Range mountains. The helicopter was an old Augusta-Bell 206A Jet Ranger, past its prime, but he was a good pilot. He kept looking over at McGarvey.

"You and I are the same . . ."

"Shut your fucking mouth," McGarvey said. He dialed up Guerin's company frequency on the radio and called the operations center at Gales Creek. "This is Bell Ranger Nancy-Zero-Zero-Four-Seven-Echo. Let me speak to Gary Topper."

"You are operating on a restricted frequency."

"This is McGarvey."

"Ah . . . stand by."

They hit a sharp updraft, and Yamagata adjusted the controls. "I don't know what you think is going on, but you can't imagine the truth. You're going to have to help me calm your government down."

"You work for Sokichi Kamiya, don't you?"

"That's beside the point," Yamagata dismissed the question.

"Bell Ranger Four-Seven-Echo," Gary Topper radioed. "That you, Mac?"

"Are there any FBI still there?"

"They got out of here in a big hurry. Something's going on over in Oceanside. Where the hell are you?"

"About fifteen miles out. Listen, Gary, can you fly me to Washington?"

"I can take one of our TransStar biz jets."

"How fast can you get it ready?"

"Ten minutes."

"Good. Taxi to the end of the runway, and we'll set down there."

"What about David?"

"He's okay. Can you do this for me?"

"It's not over yet, is it?" Topper said.

"Not quite."

"I'll have to file a flight plan. They'll be waiting for us unless we divert."

"It doesn't matter."

"Ten minutes," Topper said. "But I hope the hell you know what you're doing, Mac. There's a lot of people pissed off at you."

"I've been there before," McGarvey said.

The moment the helicopter lifted off from the clearing south of the beach house, Franson got on the radio to his Portland office and was patched through to Washington on one of the direct links. Even with priorities, it took several minutes because of the overloaded telephone lines.

"Where is he going?" John Whitman demanded.

"I don't know. But he's got at least one Japanese national with him. A man named Arimoto Yamagata."

"They're going to try to make it back to Washington," McLaren interrupted.

Franson ignored him. "The sonofabitch won't get far.

The chopper doesn't have much of a range. I'm putting out an APB from Vancouver to L.A."

"Goddammit, they're headed to Gales Creek," McLaren tried to break in. "They can get an airplane there. Tell Whitman to watch for incomings."

"Hang on a second, Mr. Whitman," Franson said. He motioned for McLaren to back off. "I've had all I'm going to take from you, Mister."

McLaren snatched the phone from the S-A-C and bodily shoved the man away. "This is McLaren. McGarvey is heading to Washington. He'll probably get an airplane at Gales Creek. Have ATC monitor all their outgoings. If Dulles is closed, they'll try for Baltimore."

"How did you guys lose him?" Whitman demanded.

"It's a long story. Just cover Dulles and Baltimore. Phil and I will make it as fast as we can."

"I'll notify Portland National Guard. What the hell is he trying to do?"

"According to him, prevent World War Three."

FBI Headquarters in the J. Edgar Hoover Building on Pennsylvania Avenue between Ninth and Tenth streets was on full emergency footing. All of official Washington was. Whitman was too impatient to wait for the busy elevator, so he ran up three flights of stairs to the director's office. John Harding's personal secretary was expecting him.

"They're waiting inside for you, Mr. Whitman," she said. She was upset. The television in the corner was tuned to CNN, showing an aerial view of the carnage at Los Angeles International.

Harding and his assistant director Ken Wood were watching another bank of television sets all reporting on the disaster. They looked up.

"Word from the West Coast?" Harding asked.

"Looks like we're getting a handle on at least part of this," Whitman said. "The signal was definitely being shunted through InterTech's computer system from Tokyo Bank out to one of its satellites. We managed to shut it down. Colberg's people are starting to round up the company's officers, but it looks like a lot of them left the country."

"That nails it," Wood said.

"Not quite, Ken. InterTech might not have known about the signal relay."

"You said its people are leaving the country."

"Could be they headed out at the last minute when they realized what was happening. Means that it came as just as big a surprise to them as it did to us. But that's not all."

"Go ahead," Harding prompted.

"The signal was downloaded from the satellite to devices that were hidden at the eight airports, plus Andrews. Thing is, those repeaters were definitely not made by the Japanese. At least that's the opinion of two engineers who've seen the things."

"Russian?" Wood asked.

Whitman spread his hands. "They just said not Japanese."

"Could Colonel Mueller have been behind the attack on InterTech?"

"It's possible, Mr. Director. It has a lot of his earmarks, although if it was him, it beats the hell out of me why."

"What about McGarvey?" Wood asked. "Is Franson bringing him in?"

"Not quite," Whitman said. "But he's on his way here."

"What do you mean?"

"He managed to get away from our people and commandeer a jet and Guerin pilot from Gales Creek. They've filed a flight plan for Dulles, if it opens by the time they get here, or Baltimore as an alternate."

"Then we'll have him finally," Wood said.

Whitman nodded. "Sure will, Ken. Along with a man by the name of Arimoto Yamagata, who's probably a spy for Japan."

The phone system was still jammed. McGarvey tried twice to get through to Dominique's office and apartment and to Reid's Georgetown home and *Lamplighter* office, without luck.

"It would appear that we are incommunicado for the next few hours," Yamagata said. He'd found the liquor locker and calmly sipped a glass of white wine.

McGarvey stood just aft of the open flight-deck door. "What's our ETA?"

"Seven our time, ten Eastern," Topper said. "They'll know you're aboard."

"Will we have to refuel?"

"If the winds hold out of the west we'll make it."

McGarvey glanced back at Yamagata, his muscles bunching up. He handed his pistol, and the one he'd taken from the Japanese intelligence officer, to Topper. "I'm going to have a talk with our friend."

Topper grinned viciously. "If you close the door, I probably won't hear a thing."

An odd expression came over Yamagata's face. He put down his glass.

"Okay." McGarvey closed the flight-deck door.

Platoon Sergeant Wentz knew that they would run out of time before help arrived. She had never quite understood why American troops were still stationed on Japanese soil, especially since the Soviet Union was no longer a threat. But she was a Marine, and she knew how to follow orders. She also knew how to fight.

She'd sent Jones and ten of the admin types to the roof while she and the remaining seven navy personnel covered the two stairwells. If their fifth-floor position was overrun, which she figured it would be in a couple of minutes, Jones and the others would be able to hold out a while longer.

It was a delaying action until the choppers arrived, or until the Japanese authorities managed to get through.

"They're civilians," one of the desk jockeys said, nervously. "What the hell are we supposed to do?"

"Defend ourselves," Wentz said.

There was a tremendous racket from below.

"Here they come!" someone shouted.

Both stairwell doors crashed open, and the first of the mob poured into the corridor. For a long second nobody fired. Some of the Japanese were women, many of them dressed in kimonos.

"Fire! Fire!" Sergeant Wentz shouted, and she opened fire with her M16 on full automatic, spraying the west corridor and stairwell door.

People in the mob began firing back.

Sergeant Wentz took two hits to her chest, her flak jacket saving her life, but the force of the blows spun her sideways, her arms flying out. She took a hit to her armpit, and two to her legs, before a round caught her in the neck just below her helmet's chin strap, the bullet angling up through her throat into the base of her brain.

Director General of Defense Hironaka telephoned the communications supervisor downstairs. *"Takefumi-san,* do you recognize my voice?"

"Hai."

"We are experiencing difficulty on the direct circuit to the White House in Washington, D.C."

"What is the nature of this difficulty?"

"We believe that the circuit is no longer secure. An impostor has someow broken in. The information we are receiving can no longer be considered valid."

"That is a grave situation."

"Cut the circuit for now, until we can determine who is doing this to us."

"Hai."

"Why hasn't the White House responded?" Prime Minister Enchi demanded.

"They asked for time to confirm what we've told them," Nobunaga cautioned. "They may not have a satellite in position."

"Or they're stalling," Hironaka said, coming in and sitting down. "We must consider all possibilities and act accordingly."

"By attacking the Seventh Fleet?" Enchi said angrily. "That's suicide."

"Without honor."

"We're not discussing honor here. We're talking about lives."

"Then we must do something, Mr. Prime Minister. Surely you can see that."

"But what?"

"Show them that we are willing to defend ourselves, of course."

"Could the Japanese have built these repeating devices in such a way as to disguise who built them?" Lindsay asked.

"Anything is possible, Mr. President," Murphy admitted. He'd listened to the call from the FBI. "But there's no reason for it. Everything else points their way."

"Too much."

"Sir?"

"Everything they've supposedly done to this point has been highly sophisticated. But now I'm being told that these devices were probably constructed by an amateur. It doesn't fit. We're missing something."

"I'm afraid I have more bad news for you," Murphy said. "National Reconnaissance confirms that there are at least three Russian submarines in the Soya Strait. All of them are within Japanese territorial waters."

"This is insanity," Lindsay said heatedly. "Get Enchi on the phone."

"Sir, that circuit is down," one of the technicians said. "Their relay people say they are having some sort of technical difficulties."

Lieutenant Fred White steadied the P-3C ASW patrol aircraft against the low altitude wind gusts as they searched for the *Samisho*. The *Barbey* and *Cook* were slowly closing on the crippled *Thorn*'s position, and White had the feeling that the Japanese submarine was lying in wait for them. The sonofabitch was crazy. There could be no other explanation.

"Skipper, we're going to have company," their ELINT officer, Ensign Carl Gifford, radioed.

"What have you got?"

"We're being lit by many radars. The Doppler shift on two of them is really moving out. Looks like fighter/interceptors. Incoming."

"Roger. Get that off to Flag and to Foster."

Admiral Ryland's helicopter was on final vectors for the *CVN George Washington*. The call from the White House was patched through the carrier's communications center while they were still twenty miles out. It came on the heels of the update from the Orion on station above the *Thorn* and from the SAR units off Yokosuka who reported that they'd lost contact with the Marines cornered in base headquarters.

"Admiral, you have a difficult situation coming your way," Lindsay said. "And there's not much we're going to be able to do for you from here."

"We're all in the dark here, Mr. President. Can you tell me what's going on?"

"Prime Minister Enchi has formally asked for our military help against a Russian attack in the north."

"It's a retaliatory strike, sir. The Russians won't take it any further. We have no assets up there. But if need be the Air Force at Misawa should be able to help out, though I'd advise against it."

"It may develop into something more, Admiral. They've brought at least three nuclear submarines into Japanese territorial waters already. We're waiting for updates, but we've already seen increased activity throughout the Pacific Fleet."

"What can I do, Mr. President?" Ryland's stomach was sour.

"How much of your fleet is still within Tokyo Bay?"

"Sixty percent."

"The Japanese may try to blockade them from breaking out."

"Yes, sir, that's what my people tell me."

"You're not to force your way out, unless you get personal word from me. Is that perfectly clear?"

"Yes, Mr. President."

"If the situation warrants action I won't hesitate. Are you clear on that as well?"

"Yes, sir." Ryland was beginning to wonder if he ever knew anything about military or political strategy.

"Very well. How soon can you have your carrier battle group in striking distance of Soya Strait?"

"With mid-air refueling we can go now. Give me eight hours and we can do a more accurate job."

"I'm not going to tell you how to do your job, Admiral. But time is critical. Eight hours may be too late."

"I understand, Mr. President."

"Godspeed, Admiral."

"Thank you, Mr. President. You too."

"It belongs to the Bureau," District of Columbia cop Luis Vasquez said, looking up from the squad car's computer.

"So it was a crank call. These guys can take care of themselves." Vasquez's partner, Steve Shockley, looked across the street at the van. "Wonder what they're doing here?"

"Maybe I'll ask, just in case it wasn't a fruitcake." The precinct had received a tip from an anonymous caller that there'd been a shooting off R Street near the Oak Hill Cemetery involving a GMC van.

"If they're on surveillance, they'll tear you a new asshole."

"What else is new?" Vasquez asked. He got out of the squad car and walked across the street to the driver's side of the GMC. No one was in front. He opened the door.

"Yo, anybody home?"

He cautiously stuck his head inside and recoiled at the sight of all the blood. "Shit!"

FORTY-TWO

The *Samisho* had eleven hours of battery power remaining before she had to surface. Less if she pressed the attack. Captain Kiyoda walked back to his compartment, locked his door, and then opened the door of a small cabinet beside his bunk. It was his Shinto shrine. He bowed before it, and thought about *kami,* nature, and what it meant to his life. He asked for benevolent treatment and protection for his boat and all who sailed in her, and for all who would fight and might soon die.

To bear what you think you cannot bear is truly to bear.

He thought about his *sensei* whose idea it was to place the rock, "future" and "hope," in *Yamagata-san*'s garden. A haven for the body as well as the spirit.

Your primary duty will be loyalty. Obedience to the call of duty. The sacrifice of everything for the emperor. For the laws and the state.

A veil descended over Kiyoda's eyes, and in the darkness a billion stars passed overhead, surrounded him, penetrated his body to the farthest corners of his soul. He smiled cruelly, his thin lips pulled into a grimace.

Two years ago there'd been an incident at *kendo* in which he'd been carried away by the match and had nearly beaten his opponent to death before his comrades had pulled him away. Afterward he'd questioned his own sanity.

Not to mar the pleasure or serenity of another by expressions of our own sorrow or pain is self-control. He shows no sign of joy or anger. This is stoicism.

His opponent had understood this and had said nothing about the incident. A few days later Kiyoda had put it out of his mind.

Chi, jin, yu. Wisdom, benevolence, courage.

Someone knocked at his door. Kiyoda slowly withdrew from his reverie. *"Hai."*

Minori came in. "Pardon me for interrupting you, *Kan-cho.*"

"What is it?"

"We are experiencing difficulties with one of our battery banks. Lieutenant Owada recommends that we shut down that cell and isolate the entire compartment."

"How will it affect our endurance?"

"If the cell remains on line, power from the other batteries will be dissipated very rapidly. Perhaps two hours. If we follow Owada's suggestion he can give us eight hours."

"Less if we attack?"

"Hai, Kan-cho."

"More if we shut down every non-essential system, except for passive sonar, and reduce our life-support systems to fifty percent."

"We can operate with a skeleton crew, and the others can stay in their bunks. That will give us additional time. But at some point the CO_2 levels will impair our abilities."

Kiyoda thought about it for a moment. A picture of his wife, Moriko, came into his mind's eye, and he smiled again, this time gently.

"Break out the emergency re-breathers from the escape trunks and issue them to all duty personnel."

Minori's eyes widened slightly. *"Hai, Kan-cho."*

"The crew will understand."

"Shall I instruct Owada to isolate the bad cell?"

"Yes."

"Very well." Minori started to withdraw.

"Matte," Kiyoda said. Wait.

"Kan-cho?"

The veil was completely lifted from Kiyoda's eyes. He buttoned his tunic. "What is happening on the surface?"

"Sierra-Zero-Four and -Five have slowed their speed of advance, and Sierra-Zero-Nine has begun to circle again."

"What of the fourth target?"

"It is dead in the water. Drifting downwind."

A threat or not, Kiyoda wondered? Or an innocent vessel caught in the middle of a . . . storm? "What of the circling action?"

"They are still wary of us."

"But we have not been discovered by their sonar?"

"No, *Kan-cho.* Sierra-Zero-Nine is ten thousand meters out, the other two much farther. They have not found us. But they know that we are damaged. They may be waiting until we have to surface."

"Or until they find us."

"Hai," Minori replied.

"Other than the batteries, how is damage control coming along?"

"The flooding has been stopped, and we still have weapons systems integrity."

"Then we are still a fighting ship."

"Hai."

"Then that is what we shall do, Ikuo," Kiyoda said. "Return to your duties. I will join you in the conn momentarily."

"What do you mean, technical difficulties?" Enchi demanded. "I have personally asked President Lindsay for help, and now you say that the direct circuit to the White House is inoperative? Who is at fault?"

"I cannot say, Mr. Prime Minister," Hironaka admitted. "Our technicians are working to resolve the problem, if indeed it is one of a technical nature."

Enchi ignored the innuendo. The full Security Council had finally arrived. In addition to his cabinet, which included Hironaka and Nobunaga, also present were the ministers of foreign affairs and of finance, the chairman of the public safety commission, and the director general of the Economic Planning Agency. Businessmen, like himself. None of them had ever been involved in the planning or execution of an actual war, and yet the fate of Japan rested on their shoulders.

"Has there been any response from the U.S. Third Air Force at Misawa?"

"No," Hironaka said. "Nor has there been any word from Admiral Ryland. It's believed that he is no longer at his headquarters in Yokosuka. He's probably already aboard the aircraft carrier *George Washington,* well off shore."

"The American naval base has been overrun," the public safety commissioner said.

"By rioters?" Enchi asked. "Why hasn't something been done?"

"The crowd is very large, possibly more than twenty-five thousand people, and already there have been many deaths. We can only hope to contain them. In the dark, there is too much confusion."

"For the moment we cannot assume that President Lindsay will offer any assistance, other than his offer to *help* us recall our forces," Hironaka said slyly.

"I can at least partially understand their position," the Foreign Minister said. "The United States is under attack by terrorists."

"Not us," Hironaka responded angrily.

The foreign minister shrugged. "We have not heard from Kamiya or Kobayashi. This could have been engineered by them. I think there is little doubt in this room about that."

"What information are we receiving from our intelligence operations in the United States?"

"Beyond the fact of the crashes and the high death toll, very little that is of any use to us at the moment," Nobunaga said.

Enchi looked down at the table for a response from his other advisers. Besides MITI there were a dozen or more specialized intelligence-gathering agencies in Japan. Among them were the Public Security Agency; the Police Guard Division and Agency Research Association; the Cabinet Investigation Board; the Defense Agency's First and Second Research Intelligence Divisions; the Security Bureau's Research and Foreign Affairs Divisions; the Ministry of Justice's Public Security Investigation Agency (which dealt primarily with subversion); the Foreign Ministry's Intelligence and Research Organization; and the Self Defense Forces individual military intelligence units. But there was no intelligence-data clearinghouse such as America's Central Intelligence Agency.

"There were no legitimate advance warnings," the Foreign Minister explained delicately. "With time . . ."

"We do not have time," Enchi interrupted impolitely. "The Russians would not have done this, nor did the Americans do it to themselves. That is unthinkable. Which leaves Kamiya and his *Zaibatsu,* or an as yet unknown organization whose purpose we can only guess."

"Pardon me, Mr. Prime Minister, but we are still left with two intolerable situations," Hironaka warned. "We are under attack in the north, and despite your formal request to President Lindsay, the Americans have not responded. In fact the Seventh Fleet is making a run for the open sea."

"Can we hold the majority of the fleet to the bay without firing shots?"

"A diversion can be arranged. Say an emergency between one or more of our ships." Hironaka sat forward. "But if the Americans chose not to respond, our commanders would have to be given clear orders."

"When the time comes I will consider those orders," Enchi said. "I will call President Yeltsin."

"He will lie."

"I will tell him that we mean to defend Hokkaido with everything in our power. In the meantime we will continue our efforts to reach President Lindsay and Admiral Ryland."

"For now it's a waiting game," Nobunaga mused. "Who will blink first?"

Marvin Amundson called from Fort Meade.

"Mr. President, NSA has another update from our

Japanese Intercept Division. Two separate orders have been issued from their C-and-C, presumably under Prime Minister Enchi's authority. The first was to their Forty-first Destroyer Division at Cape Mirua—that's the mouth of Tokyo Bay—to do whatever is necessary to hold the majority of the Seventh Fleet from breaking out."

"Hold on," Lindsay said. "Have they been ordered to shoot at our ships?"

"That's not clear, Mr. President. We only have a partial decryption and translation. But it was a flash-designated message, which means they're serious. They want to box Seventh inside the bay."

"All right. What's the second message?"

"Their military forces in the north have been ordered to Defense Condition One, which gives their local commanders unlimited weapons release authorization. That means they will shoot anything within their national boundaries."

"That includes all of Soya Strait?"

"Yes, sir. Presumably this is a clear message to the Russians to back off."

The President looked down the table at his advisers.

"That means us as well when Ryland sends help up there, or if Third Air Force responds from Misawa," Secretary of Defense Landry said.

"What about our telephone circuit to Enchi?"

"There is no technical trouble at our end, Mr. President," Amundson said. "But we're still working on it."

"Goddammit, are you sure?" John Whitman swore. "What the hell were those guys thinking about?"

"I don't know, but they were shot to death in the back of the van. Looks like maybe Kris put up a fight, but neither of them pulled their weapons."

"I don't believe this. What about Reid? Have you got the sonofabitch?"

"He's gone," Special Agent Irving Newton said. "But there's more, Mr. Whitman. Whoever did our people also did a couple of guys parked across the street. White Toyota van, registered to an invalid address in Rockville. They're Japanese. The van is equipped with some sophisticated surveillance gear. But it was the same deal. They didn't put up any resistance. Might have known who it was."

Whitman was numb. This just wasn't happening. "Any witnesses?"

"We're working the neighborhood. But we got a name on the yellow Vette parked in front of Reid's. Belongs to Dominique Kilbourne. Address in the Watergate."

"Any sign of her?"

"No, sir. But if you want a quick turnaround here, we're going to need some help."

"Nobody left," Whitman said. "Use the D.C. cops."

"President Yeltsin, I am told that your submarines are still in the vicinity of the Soya Strait, well within Japanese territorial waters."

"These things take time, President Lindsay. I assure you that the situation in the strait is being resolved. Since our submarines are submerged, we can only communicate via ELF. It is very slow. But the Japanese fired the first shot."

So far NSA had intercepted no such message from the Russian's Pacific Fleet headquarters in Vladivostok. But the system was not one-hundred percent accurate, nor did Lindsay wish to reveal that capability to Yeltsin.

"Japanese military forces in the region have gone to Defense Condition One. Your ships are in their territorial waters!"

"I am aware of this. We are taking every precaution. But we will defend our withdrawal. I have told Prime Minister Enchi this."

"You spoke with him?" Lindsay asked, surprised. It was the first ray of hope.

"Two minutes ago. But he seems, how shall I put it, agitated. I don't know if he completely understands the situation that we are facing. That all of us are facing."

"I appreciate your candidness, Mr. President. Let me be equally candid. Since we are still not sure who attacked us, I am sending some aircraft to inspect the situation in the strait. I want no misunderstanding between us. We merely want to monitor what is going on."

"Then allow me to repeat myself, President Lindsay. Our warships will be instructed to defend their withdrawal."

"We will shoot only in self-defense."

"So will we, President Lindsay," Yeltsin said.

"What the hell does the sonofabitch mean?" Secor demanded when the connection was broken. "His forces have already exchanged shots with the Japanese."

McGarvey poured a brandy from the airplane's liquor locker and sat down. Yamagata had recovered much of his poise, that much was clear from his expression, and from the way he sat back in his seat. But there was something else hidden behind his eyes. Wariness. An Oriental cunning.

"By now the situation is becoming serious," McGarvey said.

"I'm glad that you understand," Yamagata replied mildly. "Kennedy did not."

"Fourteen airplanes are down. That's a lot of dead people. Countries have gone to war over a lot less. Is that what you want?"

"It wasn't us."

"Funny you should say that, when everything points to Kamiya and Mintori Assurance." McGarvey tossed back the drink and set the glass aside. "When I asked him about trying to ruin Guerin, he said it was only part of a much larger operation called Morning Star. Does this mean anything to you?"

"Yes, it does. But over the past few days I've come to the realization that Sokichi Kamiya is insane. His plan was brilliant, and actually would have worked, I think, had it not been for a happenstance."

McGarvey said nothing. He'd always had trouble dealing with misplaced arrogance.

"Business is war, and unless Japan acts soon, it is a war we will lose."

A muscle in McGarvey's left leg began to jump.

"You Americans are innovators. You have the ability to see things differently than we do. You are individualists. It's what you do best. While we Japanese are manufacturers. We can take your innovations, improve on them, and then produce them for a profit. As partners we could be unstoppable. No country on earth, not Russia with her resources, not China with her population, could compete. Do you understand this much?" A note of sarcasm had crept into Yamagata's voice.

McGarvey focused on keeping his temper in check. He'd seen the defeated look in Chance Kennedy's eyes, the anguish in her voice.

"The original idea was to engineer a small war between our countries. But only after we were established at Subic Bay, and after your military installations were removed from our soil. Then, once the shooting had begun, an immediate cease-fire would have been called. We are trading partners. Supposedly equal partners. It is something Americans cannot see yet. You are guilty of the worst kind of racial prejudice. Against the blacks as well as us. In your mind we are an inferior race."

McGarvey thought about how Korean and Vietnamese immigrants were still treated in Japan. It was an issue that the Japanese government had sidestepped for years. As it had sidestepped the treatment of the Chinese during the war, and of our own prisoners in the Pacific.

"We were going to destroy Guerin. It was to be another indication to the world that American technology and manufacturing were flawed. No one would want to fly in a Guerin airplane. They would be unsafe."

"Bringing fourteen airplanes down at once was extreme."

"It wasn't us," Yamagata said, vexed. "Our plan was to create a series of accidents throughout the world over a period of several years. To slowly destroy confidence in the company."

"InterTech was yours?"

Yamagata smiled. "It was clever of you to figure out at least that much."

"The entire fleet has been sabotaged?"

"Yes."

"What about the crash in 1990? Was it a mistake?"

"It was a test."

"But one of your people was killed."

"I gave him that honor," Yamagata said matter of factly.

"You had a remote-control device?"

"Yes. I waited on the ground south of the city until the plane was overhead."

"What about the Dulles crash?"

Yamagata's expression darkened. "It wasn't us. Someone else has discovered what we've done and has taken advantage."

McGarvey almost went across the aisle, but he willed himself to remain in his seat.

"It's too soon, but between us we'll find out who it is and stop them. We'll share information. A partnership."

"What about the war?"

"We were going to create a number of incidents that would increase the tension between us and Russia, as well as America. A new Cold War, if you will, in which the Russians would finally launch an attack against us. It would give us a reason to rapidly build up our military without Washington forcing us to back down. Sooner or later tempers would run high, and the war would erupt. We would be defending ourselves, nothing more."

"To what end?" McGarvey asked.

"Either take us seriously as full and equal business partners, or get out of our way in the western Pacific so that we can develop our own markets." Yamagata pointed a finger at McGarvey for emphasis. "Faced with the same choices Japan is faced with—continue to expand or starve—the United States would do the same thing. And has done the same thing in the past. Any nation would to ensure its survival."

"Chance Kennedy?"

"I needed her to get to her husband and then to you. But she'll live. In fact her marriage will probably be all the better for her experience."

"You made a mistake by not running when you had the chance," McGarvey said dreamily.

"It wasn't us. We think a man named Edward Reid may be involved."

"Yes, I know."

"I want to make a deal," Yamagata said.

"Do you?" McGarvey asked.

"Yes. I'll cooperate with your government to put a stop to this nonsense, and your government—or you personally if Washington won't or can't help—will give me Mintori Assurance."

"I'll need to know everything. All the details, including names."

Yamagata grinned. "You won't believe the names I'll give you. Do we have a deal?"

"Sure," McGarvey said. "I'll give you a deal."

"Tell me more about your Mr. McGarvey. He sounds like an interesting fellow," Mueller said conversationally.

Dominique had to pretend that she was not too frightened to drive, even though she wanted to curl up into a ball and retreat within herself. Reid, lost in his own thoughts, sat in the Probe's passenger seat. He'd been drinking from a whiskey bottle since they'd left Georgetown. The German was in the back seat. They were heading toward the Pennsylvania state border on Interstate 83 north of Baltimore. The afternoon had become cold and gray.

"I don't know very much about him," Dominique answered, trying to keep her voice even. She'd had fifteen minutes alone with Mueller, and it had seemed like an eternity in hell. He'd been so perceptive, so reasonable and rational that she'd nearly fallen under his spell. It was like being in the presence of a mass murderer and kidding yourself into believing that at heart he was a good person. Kirk had warned them about people like Mueller, but she hadn't believed him until now.

"Don't be coy. I think that you have fallen in love with him."

Dominique glanced at Mueller's reflection in the rearview mirror. His eyes locked into hers, and she shuddered. "Do you have a wife?" she asked.

"Oh, dear me," Mueller laughed pleasantly. "No, I have no wife. But do you believe that Mr. McGarvey will ask you to marry him?"

No one could possibly know where she was. Even if they found her car in front of Reid's it wouldn't give them a clue. She figured her only chance of survival was to attract some attention. The only way which she could do that, without making the German or Reid suspicious, was by driving too fast. Since Baltimore she'd slowly increased her speed. Maryland was tough on speeders.

"I don't know how to answer that."

"With the truth, of course. Isn't it every little American girl's dream to marry a strong, handsome boy?"

They passed an eighteen-wheeler, and Mueller leaned forward so that he could look over Dominique's shoulder. A half-mile later they passed a fifty-five-miles-per-hour speed-limit sign. "You are driving too fast. Please slow down to sixty."

"The speed limit will change to sixty-five any minute now," Dominique said.

"Slow down."

Dominique glanced into the rearview mirror again in time to see a police car, its lights flashing, catching up to them. She increased their speed.

Mueller looked out the rear window. "I admire your courage, Ms. Kilbourne. But if you wish to survive the next few minutes, you will do exactly as I tell you. Believe me, I will not hesitate to kill you and the police officer."

"You'll never get away," Dominique told him, and her threat sounded dumb even to her.

"We're discussing your survival now."

There was no way out. She was so stupid. "What if he wants us to get out of the car?"

"You'll convince him that's not necessary."

Reid turned ponderously to look back. His eyes were bloodshot, and he reeked of alcohol. "We're not going to get out of this one."

"Hide the bottle and keep your mouth shut," Mueller ordered. "Slow down, Ms. Kilbourne. There is no reason for you to throw away your life so soon."

"You bastard," Dominique swore. "I swear to God I'll see you dead if I have to do it with my own two hands."

The patrol car was nearly on them when Dominique slowed down and pulled off to the side of the highway. The cop pulled in behind them.

"Take your driver's license out of your purse, and lower your window. Smile, Ms. Kilbourne. Your life depends on it."

She did as she was told. She could see the Maryland Highway Patrol car in the door mirror. The trooper got out, put on his campaign hat, checked the traffic behind him, and came forward. He was alert, but not on his guard. Dominique wanted to warn him, but her insides were churning.

"Good afternoon, ma'am. May I see your driver's license and vehicle registration?"

They hadn't thought about the registration. "It's not my car," Dominique said, flustered.

Something was wrong. The trooper's attention had switched to Mueller in the back seat, recognition and fear dawning on his face. He stepped back as he fumbled for his service revolver.

Dominique started to turn around as Mueller powered down the rear window. "No!" she screamed.

The trooper had his gun out and was bringing it up, when Mueller fired two shots, both of them catching the cop in the chest, driving him off his feet onto the highway.

"Drive, Ms. Kilbourne," Mueller ordered calmly. "At the speed limit, please."

Dominique dropped her driver's license out the window, slammed the car in gear, and pulled away without bothering to check for oncoming traffic.

In nearly twenty years of service Trooper Douglas Schultz had never been shot. But his luck had finally run out. He felt weak, his insides loose and watery, as if he had a serious case of diarrhea, but he marveled that there was no pain. He almost laughed out loud.

From where he lay on his back, his head turned to the side, he could see that he was on the highway with traffic coming his way. It'd be a hell of a note, he thought, to survive being shot only to be run over.

Holding his chest and gut with his right arm, he managed to turn onto his side and lever himself up to his knees.

The Probe was speeding away, too far to shoot even if he could aim. It was a bitch. He'd catch hell from the lieutenant for not wearing his vest, but the damned thing was uncomfortable. And Peggy was going to get on his case big time to quit the force.

"First things first, Doug," he told himself, getting shakily to his feet. The entire world was spinning around, and the overcast seemed to have deepened in the past sixty seconds. At least traffic was slowing down.

He stumbled back to his patrol car, his legs impossibly long, his feet clumsy. He slumped against the side of the car and reached inside the open window for the microphone. "This is Three-Alpha-Seven, on eight-three north just past the Heresford exit. I need assistance. I've been shot."

"Three-Alpha-Seven, roger, help is rolling."

"It was the German the FBI is looking for. Bruno Mueller. He's in a ninety-seven green Ford Probe, Virginia six-niner-zero-Zulu-Mike-Tango, northbound on eight-three. Woman is driving, thirty to thirty-five, short dark hair, dark eyes, wearing a black leather coat, a light color sweater or blouse beneath. Front-seat passenger is a man, late sixties, maybe seventy, large build, white hair, red complexion. He may be drunk."

Schultz realized he was sitting on the pavement, his forehead resting against the side of his car. He felt a fluttering in his chest, but he was too tired to think anything about it. A little sleep was all he needed until help arrived.

"Mr. President, we've finally intercepted an ELF message from Vladivostok," Amundson said from Fort Meade. "The decryption just came up. They are not calling for a withdrawal of forces."

"What was the message?" Lindsay asked.

"Four code groups, sir. Directed specifically to the *SSN Strelka*. She's a Sierra-class attack submarine. They warned her that the MSDF is bringing assets into the strait."

"Yeltsin was lying," Secor said.

"It would appear so," Lindsay replied. "Have any shots been fired since the initial attack on the radar base and the sinking of the destroyer?"

"There may have been a torpedo launch from one of their ASW aircraft. But we're still waiting for confirmation."

"None of the Russian submarines has been withdrawn?"

"Not so far as we've been able to determine, sir."

"Keep me informed," Lindsay said.

"Is our ETA holding?" McGarvey asked.

"So far, so good," Topper said. "Did you get anything from our guest?"

"He's admitted that every 522 flying has been sabotaged. He brought down the American flight in '90. They wanted to test the system."

"Sonofabitch," Topper swore softly. He looked over his shoulder at McGarvey in the doorway. "Why? Just to get control of an airplane company? We would have sold them all they wanted. Al Vasilanti was right all along. They haven't changed since Bataan."

"It's not that easy, Gary. Someone else got in the middle."

"What are we going to do with him?"

"I want you to try to get through to the FBI. Talk to a man by the name of John Whitman. Tell him who we're bringing in. He might have to talk to Adkins at Langley, but have them meet us when we touch down. And make sure the fleet is grounded. Worldwide, Gary."

"Will do."

"Is there a cassette recorder aboard?"

"There might be one in the locker aft of the head," Topper said. "Do you suppose he's telling the truth?"

"I'll ask him."

McGarvey started to turn when something hard smashed into the side of his neck just behind his right ear, the force of the blow driving him to his knees.

"Amerikajin," Yamagata snarled. He grabbed McGarvey by the throat and dragged him to his feet. "I would have given you everything." He shoved McGarvey back against the bulkhead and drove a knee into his groin.

It was a mistake. McGarvey had been momentarily stunned by the first blow, and his air supply was cut off so that he was seeing spots, but the sudden excruciating pain was like a shot of adrenalin. He tore Yamagata's hand away from his throat and smashed his forehead into the Japanese's face, just above the bridge of his nose, driving him backward.

Yamagata recovered quickly enough to sidestep McGarvey's charge, smashing a rock-hard fist into McGarvey's side, breaking three ribs, before he danced away.

"Mac! Here!" Topper shouted. He held out the Walther.

McGarvey glanced at the gun, then turned back to Yamagata, who had dropped into a karate stance, and was watching warily. A trickle of blood came from his nose.

"Just fly, Gary." McGarvey closed the flight-deck door.

"It's still possible to make a deal," Yamagata said. "You can't know what's at stake."

"Tell me again about Chance Kennedy," McGarvey said, feinting left.

Yamagata threw his right hand over his defensive left, but instead of fighting by the rules and trying to deflect the strike, McGarvey reached up and caught the Japanese's fist in mid-air, pulling the man off-balance against the seats.

Once again Yamagata recovered fast enough to pull away, expecting McGarvey to hesitate for just a split second, as most fighters would. Time enough to reverse direction and get inside the opponent's reach.

Yamagata turned back at the same instant McGarvey's roundhouse blow hit him squarely on the chin, breaking his jaw and knocking him nearly off his feet.

Still he had no real idea what he was up against. He managed to bat McGarvey's left jab away and tried to kick for the kneecap, when McGarvey smashed a karate blow to the bridge of his nose, shattering the bone and tearing the cartilage loose.

"Tie!" Yamagata screamed, blood and bits of teeth expelling from his mouth.

"I don't like bullies," McGarvey growled, and he smashed the heel of his right hand upward against the bottom of Yamagata's nose, driving the broken bones and cartilage into the Japanese's brain, killing him instantly.

"The advantage could turn out to be ours," SUR Director Karyagin told President Yeltsin. "But the situation is extremely fluid."

They were alone for a moment in an antechamber outside the Kremlin's situation room. Karyagin, who'd just arrived, was agitated.

"This was not the response we expected," Yeltsin said. He'd approved the attack on Wakkanai against his better judgment because he'd seen the military logic of the situation. The Japanese were at long last starting to flex their considerable military muscle. Each success would spur them to greater adventures. Each failure would give them pause. For more reasons than anyone could count, the Russian Pacific Fleet was a shadow of its former self. There was much at stake including national honor and prestige.

"Because we didn't have all the facts, Mr. President."

"What have you learned?"

"The Japanese want war with the United States."

"Nonsense!"

"On the contrary, Mr. President. In fact, it has already started under the code name Morning Star, and we have played a vital role toward ensuring Japan's success."

Yeltsin tried to find the advantage Karyagin was seeking with such a preposterous lie. But he couldn't. "What do you mean?"

"Our Tokyo asset *Abunai* figured out that the attack against the American air traffic control system was just one element of a much larger plan. President Lindsay and his advisers believe the Japanese did it, but they have no hard proof. It enables Prime Minister Enchi to deny any involvement."

"But the Americans will suspect he is lying."

"For the moment," Karyagin said. "But as soon as any serious fighting erupts between them, the Americans will call it off. They still have guilty consciences over Hiroshima and Nagasaki. And President Lindsay is a moderate."

"You're not making sense. The Japanese could not possibly win."

"But they can and will, Mr. President. All they want is a concession from the United States to leave the western Pacific to Japanese business, and the Japanese navy. Not such a big price to pay for peace. Lindsay will agree."

"What part are we playing in this scenario of yours, Aleksandr Semonovich?"

"The Japanese forced us into attacking them so that they would have an excuse to mobilize their defense forces."

"What do you recommend?"

"Press the attack against Japan."

"What are you talking about?"

"We've served Japan's purpose by striking against one of its radar stations. Now we're supposed to back off. I think we should attack in force."

"Then the Americans will help them."

Karyagin shook his head. "I would agree with you, Mr. President, except for one overriding consideration. The Japanese navy has been ordered to contain the U.S. Seventh Fleet within Tokyo Bay. It is a clear act of aggression."

"But why would Enchi give such an order?"

"Because he does not know who his enemies are. He is simply defending his country to the best of his abilities."

"It is confusing."

"Yes, Mr. President. And the confusion can be turned to our advantage. If Japan is forced to relinquish her plans for expansion, it will give us at least twenty years of breathing room in which to consolidate and strengthen the commonwealth."

"You recommend that we attack Japan," Yeltsin said.

"Yes, Mr. President. While the advantage is still ours."

The P-3C ASW patrol aircraft climbed out of five thousand feet over the East China Sea so that it would be well above the surface clutter that might confuse a targeting radar. They wanted the oncoming Japanese fighter/interceptors out of Tanegashima to be crystal clear that they were heading away from the area.

They were running low on fuel, so it was about time to turn back to Foster anyway. But Fred White felt odd about ducking a fight, even if it involved an ally. Something screwy was going on. One of their ships was in trouble on the surface, but all Seventh ordered up was a single sub-killer with no backup.

"They're turning away," the ELINT officer said.

"Did you establish comms?" White asked.

"Skipper, we tried, but they didn't answer on any of their tactical frequencies."

"Okay. Keep a sharp eye."

"What the hell is going on?" White's co-pilot, Lieutenant, j.g., John Littlemore, asked.

"Beats me. I'd just like to see us start kicking some ass."

"Yeah, right. Against the Japanese."

Tony Benson, skipper of the *George Washington,* and his XO, Lieutenant Commander Paul Horvat, were waiting in the captain's ready room when Admiral Ryland and his chief of operations, Tom Byrne, arrived. The nuclear aircraft carrier had turned into the wind, ready to launch her aircraft when the order was given.

"We're at minimums, but the weather is supposed to hold or improve slightly over the next six hours, so we should be okay," Benson said. He was a slightly built wire-haired terrier of a man.

"What's the latest from Mike Hanrahan?" Ryland asked. Horvat handed him a cup of coffee.

"He's been damaged, but he says he's still operational. Can you tell me what the hell is going on, Al? The ASDF scrambled at least four Hornets out of Tanegashima and chased one of our Orions off station. Gene Hagedorn is waiting for word. He wants to put up a squadron of sixteens. It'd been screening for Okinawa. Can't say as I blame him."

"We're not going to war with the Japanese," Ryland said. "But we are going to defend ourselves."

"The MSDF on Hokkaido has been ordered to DEF-CON ONE."

"What about their air force?"

"Intel couldn't say, but I'm assuming the order included all their northern commands."

"Makes sense if they're expecting further attacks from the Russians," Horvak suggested.

"Any answer from Admiral Shimikaze?"

"No," Benson said. "But in about fifteen minutes the

majority of our fleet is going to come head to head with the Forty-first. What do we tell them?"

"They're to proceed unless challenged, in which case they're to stand by."

Benson raised his eyebrows.

"We're going to stabilize that situation first, before we do anything else, Tony," Ryland said. "In the meantime I want you to make best speed possible to the north. In a few hours we can be in position to carry on operations from Tokyo Bay all the way north to the Soya Strait."

"Like I said, Al, what's going on?" Benson said.

"I don't know yet. I don't think anybody does. So we're going to wait until we find out. In the meantime, I want another Orion on station over the *Thorn,* and tell Hagedorn he can scramble one squadron, but I want them to keep station fifteen minutes out from the *Thorn.*"

Horvak lifted the phone on the desk and issued the orders.

"How about some breakfast?" Benson asked. "We won't be needed on the bridge for several hours."

"Just coffee," Ryland said. "I talked to the President."

"How'd he sound?"

"Confused, but in control."

Benson managed a slight grin. "That's something anyway." He got serious. "I heard you lost some people at HQ."

"Tony, that's the part I understand the least. I think that no matter what happens it's time for us to get out of Japan."

"I hope it doesn't become a moot point, Al."

"Bridge, sonar, we have a positive contact," the *Thorn*'s chief sonar operator Ed Zwicka said. "Depth two hundred feet, bearing zero-eight-five. I have hull popping noises . . . she's on the way up. Turning now inboard . . . bearing changing to zero-eight-zero . . . speed six knots."

"Roger," Hanrahan said. "CIC, bridge. Don, how's it look to the north?"

"The bogies are gone, but so is the Orion. Seventh advises us to stand by."

"Is the admiral aboard the *George Washington?*"

"Last word I got, he was en route."

"Means we're on our own out here for the time being." Hanrahan glanced over at his XO braced against the plotting board. They had a job to do, and he was going to do it. "Prepare to launch ASROC one and two on my signal."

"Goddammit, Mike, are you sure about this?" Sattler demanded.

"Give me a firing solution, Don, or relieve yourself of duty."

Ryder and the others on the bridge were looking at Hanrahan. The growler phone was silent. Sattler finally answered.

"Aye, aye, Skipper. Recommend we turn right to new course one-niner-zero."

"Kan-cho, we have Target Motion Analysis on Zero-Nine," the *Samisho*'s weapons control officer, Lieutenant Shuichiyo Takasaki, said.

A great serenity had come over Kiyoda. His crew could see it, and they were at ease. They understood.

"Open doors one and two."

"Yo-so-ro, opening doors one and two," Minori answered.

"Check weapons visually."

"Yo-so-ro."

They would be firing on the way up from a depth of under thirty meters. Since the *Samisho*'s mast-mounted sensors and periscopes were inoperative they would rely on the SQS-36 attack sonar for final range and bearing to target. The data would be entered automatically into the Japanese-designed GRX-2(2) torpedoes' guidance systems.

"Weapons in place and armed," Minori reported.

"Very well. Ping once for range and bearing, and a

second time for verification, then launch. No further authority necessary," Kiyoda said, his gut tightening despite his resolve.

The sonar went active for two pings.

"Target data entered," Takasaki said. "Launch one. Launch two."

The *Samisho* shuddered as the two torpedoes were launched.

"Bridge, sonar, two torpedoes incoming," Zwicka shouted. "GRX."

"Give me a bearing," Hanrahan replied.

"On our port bow, low, on the way up!"

"Helmsman, make your rudder amidships."

"Aye, rudder amidships."

"Ring for all ahead slow."

The Japanese torpedo was very fast and accurate, but its warhead was small, less than one hundred fifty pounds of high explosive. With a hit on the *Thorn*'s heavily plated bow they stood a good chance of surviving. The torp had one other weakness: it was guided by its own sonar.

"Launch sound-producing canisters aft," Hanrahan ordered. "Bridge, sonar. Go active with the bow unit. Hit them with everything we've got."

"Sonar, aye," Zwicka responded. "Time to impact ten seconds."

"Brace yourselves," Hanrahan shouted. "Prepare to launch ASROC one and two on my order."

"If we lose our bow sonar we'll be blind," Sattler warned.

"Time to impact, seven seconds."

"The *Barbey* and *Cook* can give us targeting data," Hanrahan said.

"We're bow on," Zwicka reported. "One of the torps is turning away . . . it's definitely taking the bait! Now four seconds to impact on two."

Hanrahan wedged himself against the radar console. The explosion hammered them, shoving their bows fifteen feet to starboard and momentarily stopping them dead in the water

"Damage reports," Hanrahan shouted.

"Detonation on number two," the *Samisho*'s chief sonarman Tsutomu Nakayama reported unnecessarily. They'd all heard the explosion. "Number one is a definite miss!"

"Come right to two-seven-zero degrees," Kiyoda ordered. "Crash dive the boat. Make your depth six hundred meters."

"The thermocline is at three hundred meters, *Kan-cho*," Minori pointed out. "In our condition I do not think we can survive beyond that depth. Recommend we level off at three hundred fifty meters."

Kiyoda walked back to sonar. "Was it a good hit?"

"On the bow, *Kan-cho*," Nakayama said. "But I don't hear any breakup noises."

"Are they searching for us?"

"Their sonar is silent, but Sierra-Zero-Four and -Five have us."

"We have target acquisition from *Barbey*," Sattler reported. "*Cook* confirms. Skipper, she's diving fast."

"Can we fire on their data?" Hanrahan asked.

"Aye."

Ryder came across the bridge and pulled Hanrahan aside. "Mike, we've got a hole in our bow, and we've taken casualties. We need to break off and turn downwind, or we're in danger of sinking."

"The sonofabitch attacked us."

"If he shoots again we might not be so lucky!"

"We're a U.S. warship, and we will defend ourselves. That's from Seventh."

"Goddammit . . ."

"Either you're with me or against me, X!" Hanrahan shouted angrily. "Which is it?"

Ryder backed off. "You're the boss."

Hanrahan keyed the growler phone. "Fire ASROC one, fire ASROC two."

The eight-tube anti-submarine rocket launcher was on the deck just forward of the bridge. The weapons launched one after the other on long trails of fire and smoke. At a pre-set distance from two thousand to eleven thousand yards out, the Mark 46 acoustic homing torpedo would detach itself from the rocket and splash down.

"Bridge, CIC. Estimate we'll lose the target in ninety seconds if she continues to dive."

Too late, Hanrahan said to himself. They'd waited too long. "Follow it down," he told Sattler. "Maybe we'll get lucky."

"If we miss, he'll run," Ryder said. "He's hurt. He won't come back against three-to-one odds."

"Yes, he will," Hanrahan replied. "And we'll be waiting for him."

"Two torpedoes in the water, eight thousand meters to starboard and fading," Nakayama reported.

The *Samisho* was sharply down at the bow. Everyone in the conn was holding on to something for support.

"Have they found us?"

"Iie, Kan-cho."

"We are passing beneath the thermocline," the diving officer said.

Kiyoda looked across at Minori. "Level off at six hundred meters, then shut down all non-essential systems. Bring life support to forty percent."

"We could make the run around Okinerabu and surface for repairs," Minori suggested.

"No," Kiyoda replied, and he turned and headed back to his compartment.

The *Fair Winds* lay ahull. Stripped of sails, her tiller lashed hard to starboard, her bows were held forty-five degrees off the wind so that she slowly skidded down the waves, making a half knot to leeward.

Liskey steadied himself against the boom gallows as he scanned the horizon to the west through binoculars. He and Carol had been below to get some rest when they'd heard the explosion. They'd scrambled topside in time to see what looked like a pair of rockets taking off.

Now there was nothing but blackness to the west, although the eastern horizon was gray.

"What was it?" Carol shouted.

"I'm not sure. Maybe cruise missiles."

"That was one of our ships. Are we fighting the Japanese?"

"Damned if I know, Carol. But it sure as hell isn't an exercise in this weather."

Carol glanced at the apparent wind indicator. "The wind is dropping. Let's put up the trysail and storm jib and get out of here."

"Not yet. I want to see what happens."

"Downwind."

"The islands are downwind," Liskey said.

"A beam reach, then. Back to Okinawa."

"We don't know what's out there. We're okay here for the time being."

"Okay?" she cried.

"Easy," Liskey said. "Whatever it was, the shooting has stopped, and we're drifting away from it. We'll be okay here, trust me."

Carol looked into his eyes. "I do," she said, shakily.

It was late. John Whitman was alone in his office for the moment, watching CNN, one part of his mind tying to figure out what had gone wrong. The mistakes he'd made over the past couple of weeks were enough to fill a hard disk drive. Trouble was none of them had ever understood what they were facing. And the call from Gary Topper, the Guerin pilot, had done nothing but muddy the waters. Adkins was apparently no longer running operations at Langley, and Howard Ryan was unavailable, but Whitman left a message for him. Nothing made sense.

One of his clerks came in with a message from Dulles.

The Guerin TransStar had just touched down. Two of Whitman's people, Special Agents Mark Lusk and Don Harrington, were standing by with a half-dozen D.C. cops to take McGarvey into custody. "Even if you have to bring him in a body bag, do it," he'd told them.

Whitman called upstairs to the assistant director's office. "They just touched down."

"Did you call the FAA?" Wood asked.

"Yes, sir. The fleet is being grounded."

"Call me when they get here," Wood said.

"Will do."

A call came in. "Mr. Whitman, this is Special Agent Newton, I'm in Hereford, Maryland. It's Mueller again. He offed a Maryland Highway Patrol cop a few miles from here."

"Tell me you have him."

"No, sir. Pennsylvania Highway Patrol thought it spotted him, but we just got word from New York that he's been seen north of Elmira. They're setting up roadblocks."

"How'd he get that far?"

"Well that's the problem, Mr. Whitman. The shooting took place a little before six."

"That was four hours ago, for Christ's sake," Whitman swore.

"I just found out about it. Maryland H.P. wanted to handle this on their own, since it was one of their people who bought it. But I convinced them otherwise."

Whitman patted his shirt pocket for a pack of cigarettes. He'd quit five years ago, but he still felt the urge when he was under stress. "You say New York Highway Patrol is setting up roadblocks?"

"Yes, sir."

"Has he got Reid and the Kilbourne woman with him?"

"Looks like it."

"Don't try to force the issue, Newton. Make damned sure New York H.P. understands that they're dealing with a professional. You make damned sure you understand."

"I hear you, sir. Nobody is going to take a chance."

Whitman's other line rang. It was Special Agent Mark Lusk.

"We're just leaving the airport."

"Any trouble?"

"McGarvey's cooperating for now."

"What about the Japanese?" Whitman asked.

"He's dead."

The ride from Dulles seemed to take forever. It had begun to snow and the roads were slippery, but there wasn't much traffic, so they made good time, Lusk driving and McGarvey and Harrington in the back seat. They were bracketed front and back by D.C. cops, lights flashing and sirens wailing. Lusk pulled up at the Tenth Street entrance to the J. Edgar Hoover Building, and McGarvey was hustled upstairs to a fifth-floor conference room, where Whitman waited with Kenneth Wood and a steno. The guard at the door was armed.

"At long last, Mr. McGarvey," Whitman said.

"Are you John Whitman?"

"That's right . . ."

"Have your people picked up Edward Reid or Bruno Mueller yet?"

"I think we'll ask the questions here," Wood said, motioning for the steno to begin, and for McGarvey to take a seat.

"Unless I miss my guess the President is in the White House situation room trying to figure out why the Japanese attacked us, and how to avoid an all-out war."

"We'll get to that in due time."

"If you don't listen to me right now, it'll be the biggest fucking mistake of your life. The Japanese didn't bring down our airplanes this time. Reid and Mueller did it through a company called InterTech."

"Sonofabitch," Whitman said. He looked at Wood.

"What do you have?" McGarvey asked.

"We think all of Guerin's 522s have been sabotaged. We got that from you. But the triggering signals were sent through InterTech to a series of devices that were planted at the eight airports, plus Andrews. The signals were generated in Tokyo, we know that for sure, but the repeaters were not Japanese-made."

"A computer hacker could have set up the signal transfer to make it look like it came from Tokyo."

"It was confirmed from NSA."

"For Christ's sake, John," Wood warned.

"What do you have on Reid and Mueller?"

"Even if they are involved, they're working for the Japanese," Wood said.

"A Japanese *zaibatsu* called Mintori Assurance sabotaged the fleet. They brought the American Airlines flight down in '90, and they were going to bring down a few others over the next couple of years. But not this time."

"This is crazy," Wood shouted angrily. "You've been directly linked to I don't know how many murders. You've had meetings with Japanese spies and Russian spies, and the CIA thinks you should be shot on sight."

"You've seen my file."

"You're damned right we have!"

"Then what would I have to gain?"

"Frankly I don't know, yet. That's why you were arrested."

"I called you, remember?" McGarvey said. "Unless you want a lot more people killed, you'd better cooperate with me."

"Jesus Christ!" Wood swore.

"If it was Reid and Mueller, how did they do it, and why?" Whitman asked.

"I don't know. But Reid has the answers, if we can get to him in time, and convince the President."

"Put him downstairs, and get an interrogation team in here. Maybe they can get the truth out of him," Wood ordered.

"Just a minute, sir," Whitman cautioned. "What if he's right?"

"He's a murderer. Even the CIA cut him loose."

"But what if he's right? Can we afford to take the chance now?"

Wood was fuming, but he said nothing.

Whitman turned back to McGarvey. "Reid and Mueller are in upstate New York right now. They're probably going to try for the Canadian border."

"How many people has Mueller already killed?"

Whitman hesitated. "A pair of our agents in front of Reid's place, two Japanese nationals in what appeared to be a surveillance van, and a Maryland Highway Patrol cop. New York H.P. is setting up roadblocks, but they're taking it easy because of the woman."

McGarvey went cold. "Dominique Kilbourne?"

"Yes."

McGarvey looked away for the moment. Mueller would know that Reid was under suspicion by the FBI as well as the Japanese, but he would protect his benefactor because running and hiding took money. But why take Dominique?

"Would Reid know that I was involved in the investigation?" McGarvey asked.

"It's possible."

He should have killed her. She was excess baggage. She would slow him down. Almost impossible to get across a border with a hostage. Too many things could go wrong.

"What is it?"

"He knows that he's lost, so he's willing to exchange Reid and the woman for me."

"Do you know him?"

"He's one of the ones who killed an old friend of mine in Paris a few years ago. He'll think I want to settle an old score."

Wood shook his head. "What the hell are you talking about?"

"There's no place for him to go. Has he switched cars since he killed the highway patrol officer?"

"Presumably not," Whitman said, understanding dawning in his eyes.

"You're talking about some high-noon standoff," Wood said. "You're crazy."

McGarvey thought about it. Compared to the Kennedys and Socrates and Kilbournes of the world he probably was.

"Have the local cops isolate them until you can fly me up there."

Wood was speechless.

"You want answers that only Reid can give you. But you'd better make up your mind, before it's too late."

After a few hours sleep on Okinawa while his Orion P-3C was refueled, Fred White's eyes were gritty, but he was alert. So was his entire crew. Shots had been exchanged between the *Thorn* and the *Samisho,* and Seventh was taking the situation very seriously. The Japanese sub-driver was probably crazy, and it had everyone worried.

Kadena had sent out a squadron of F-16/91As, designated Charlie-Seven, which were on station keeping, in relays, one hundred miles south. They were seriously crowding the fifteen-minute separation order—in fact at Mach two they could be overhead in a little more than four minutes—but nobody was complaining.

They'd found nothing on MAD in a dozen sweeps over a grid ten miles on a side, so White had dropped to within two hundred feet of the surface and throttled back to deploy dipping sonobuoys. Either the sub had bugged out, or it was hiding beneath the seasonal thermocline, which around here was at about nine hundred feet.

"We've got company," Ensign Gifford said. "Two bogies in the air, bearing zero-one-zero. They have us on radar."

"Tanegashima?" White asked.

"Definitely F/A-18s, estimated closure speed above Mach one-point-five."

"Sonar, have you got contact yet?"

"Negative, the buoy is still deploying."

"I have a definite weapons radar lock," Gifford reported excitedly. "Skipper, they have us."

"Get that off to Charlie-Seven."

"Aye, aye," Lieutenant Littlemore said.

"How far out are they?"

"Forty miles . . . Skipper, they've launched missiles! Two missiles incoming, same bearing!"

"Deploy ECMs!" White shouted.

"Home Plate, this is Charlie-Seven leader."

"Charlie-Seven leader, Home Plate, we've monitored the transmission. You are authorized to engage. Splash them."

"Roger," Lieutenant Todd Kraus said. "Let's go, Gene," he radioed his wingman.

Kraus hauled his aircraft left in a seven G turn, hit the afterburners, then set the weapons selector on his stick to the new Hughes AIM-140 air-to-air missile. He activated his target-detection radar, but they were still too far out for a positive lock. The Orion was probably as good as dead, but the two bogies wouldn't survive either.

"I have a positive contact," the Orion's sonarman reported. "Depth two thousand feet . . . sounds quiet . . . she's just lying there."

"Get that off to the *Thorn*," White ordered. He slammed the throttles full forward and forced the nose of the big four-engine ASW aircraft down. Their only chance of survival was to fly so low to the waves that the incoming missiles' targeting radar would be confused by the surface clutter. It was a long shot.

"Oh, shit . . ." Gifford shouted. A split second later the Orion exploded in a ball of flames.

"The Orion is splashed," Sattler reported excitedly from CIC. "Charlie-Seven has orders to engage!"

"Have we got the targeting data on *Chrysanthemum?*" Hanrahan demanded. His blood was singing.

"Roger that."

"Program two Captors for zero delay at two thousand feet and launch immediately." The Captor, or Encapsulated Torpedo, consisted of a Mark 46 Mod 4 torpedo housed in a tube. It was designed to sit on the ocean floor and, using its passive sonar, watch for traffic. When a submarine was identified the sonar system went active and the torpedo was launched.

"The data is entered," Sattler reported moments later.

"Launch one, launch two!"

"Shit, the Orion is a definite kill," Kraus's wingman, Gene Levitt, said.

"Range is forty-four thousand yards. I have target acquisition on bogie one," Kraus replied calmly, although his heart was pounding.

"I have a lock on two," Levitt reported. "But they're starting to turn away."

The pipper on Kraus's head-up display was correct. He hit the trigger once, and then a second time. Both AIM-140 missiles streaked away, accelerating to better than Mach four.

A second later Levitt launched his pair of missiles.

"Kan-cho to the conn!" The battle stations Klaxon sounded throughout the *Samisho*.

Kiyoda felt sluggish because of the high CO_2 content in the air. He stumbled to the attack center without bothering to button his tunic. Sweat poured from his forehead.

"Sonar reports two objects passing through the thermocline, but we can't make them out," Minori reported, his voice hoarse. "No sounds of torpedo screws."

Kiyoda tried to think it out. He stepped back to the sonar compartment.

Nakayama, his head cocked, was intently listening to something in his headset. He looked up and shook his head.

"ASROC?" Kiyoda asked. He had to think. His boat and crew were in jeopardy.

"Iie, Kan-cho."

"Captor," Kiyoda said, suddenly making the connection. He raced back to the attack center. "Launch all weapons! *Ima! Ima!"* Now! Now!

"What range and bearing?" Minori shouted.

"Extrapolate from their last known position!" Kiyoda screamed. "Emergency surface the boat. Launch the SOS buoys! *Ima!*"

The distance was too great for Kraus to see the flash of the explosions, but both enemy radars went off the air within moments of each other, and his targeting radar showed a clear sky.

"Home Plate, Charlie-Seven-Leader. Splash two bogies."

"Many targets incoming!" Levitt radioed.

Kraus switched his APG-88 to search mode, which expanded his look-up radar range to one hundred miles. At least six targets were just entering their sensor envelope.

"Say again, Charlie-Seven," Kadena demanded.

"Many targets incoming from the north," Kraus responded. "We need help!"

"We've lost the Captors below the thermocline," Zwicka reported.

"We had good targeting data," Hanrahan said triumphantly. "The sonofabitch won't get away this time."

A tremendous explosion hammered the *Samisho* somewhere aft, increasing the already severe upward angle they'd assumed to emergency surface the boat. Still the submarine's extremely tough double hull withstood the hit.

Kiyoda was violently thrown against the attack periscope, breaking his shoulder. He tried to straighten up when the second Captor torpedo struck them just below the attack center. The last conscious thought he had was that they'd not had time to launch their weapons when the tremendous pressure of the ocean at this depth crushed the hull like an eggshell.

"Charlie-Seven, Home Plate. Disengage! Repeat, disengage!"

"Roger, returning to station," Kraus radioed. "Gene let's get out of here."

"That's a kill!" Zwicka shouted.

"One down, one to go," Hanrahan said grimly. "Give me a range and bearing on the surface target."

Sattler was on the growler phone. "Skipper, that target could be just what she claims to be. A sailboat out of Okinawa."

"What's she doing out here, Don? Doesn't make any sense."

"Let's give them the benefit of the doubt."

"Range and bearing to the target," Hanrahan over-rode his CIC officer.

FORTY-THREE

Yeltsin looked coldly down the table at his advis-ers. It seemed to him that the higher one went in any organization the less access he had to the truth. He wondered if President Lindsay had the same problem.

"We are not going to war with the Japanese," he said.

"Judging from the thermal images we're receiving from our satellite over the East China Sea it would appear that the Americans are," Minister of Defense Solovyev said.

"Nonsense. It was an unfortunate accident. You said yourself that the MSDF had trouble with the skipper of that submarine. The same captain, need I remind you, who was responsible for sinking the *Menshinsky*."

"Yet the captain was allowed to leave Yokosuka with his boat and crew, presumably reprovisioned."

"That has nothing to do with what is happening at this moment in the Soya Strait," Yeltsin replied angrily.

"Morning Star," Karyagin interjected.

Yeltsin glared at his Secret Service director. "In my estimation there is no directed effort on the part of the Japanese government to foment a war either between the United States or us. It would be folly for them."

"Begging your pardon, Mr. President, but I cannot agree with you," Karyagin pressed his point. "The sinking of the *Sovremennyy* and the high state of readiness of all Japanese forces would suggest otherwise. As has the attack on the American air traffic control system. That was no act of terrorism. It was a highly sophisticated and very *directed* operation."

"Has the order been sent to our ships in the Soya Strait to withdraw?"

"There has been some difficulty with the transmitting equipment," Solovyev admitted.

"The American National Security Agency has the ability to monitor our ELF messages," Yeltsin said.

"That has not been confirmed," Karyagin cautioned.

"Assuming they can, President Lindsay now believes that I am lying."

No one said a thing.

Yeltsin lifted the telephone. "This is Boris Yeltsin. I wish to speak to Admiral Aladko at his headquarters in Vladivostok."

Aladko was CINC of the Pacific Fleet. He came on the line a few seconds later.

"Good morning, Mr. President."

"Listen to me very carefully, Stefan Mikhailovich. I want you to send a message immediately, by any and all means at your disposal, to all your warships in or near the Soya Strait, or near any Japanese national waters and airspace, to unilaterally withdraw. As of this moment I am revoking their authorization to fire their weapons. Have I made myself clear?"

"Yes, Mr. President. But what if my ships are attacked as they withdraw? Are you taking away their ability to defend themselves?"

"Of course not," Yeltsin shot back. "But we will launch no further first strikes."

"I understand, Mr. President. And I agree with you."

"It's good that you do, Admiral," Yeltsin replied coolly.

Admiral Aladko gazed out of his office window, which overlooked the busy navy base and, beyond it, the breakwaters to the Golden Horn Bay. Japan was less than four hundred miles to the east across the treacherous Sea of Japan. In this day of modern weapons and delivery systems, it was an impossibly small distance. Now Japan was beginning to flex her muscles. This day, he suspected, would come again.

He wrote out the disengage order and called for an aide to hand deliver it immediately to the communications center.

These were the twenties and thirties all over again. At fifty-three he fully expected to be a part of the next war, though he did not look forward to it. No rational professional soldier would.

"Takefumi-san, we are faced with another grave problem," Director General of Defense Hironaka said.

"How may I be of assistance, Director General?"

"A telephone call has been monitored between Moscow and Vladivostok."

"Hai, I saw to the translation myself."

"I admire your efficiency. But we have learned that President Yeltsin was speaking in a carefully crafted code."

"Sir?"

"The actual order for the Russian Pacific Fleet is to press the attack against the North Island."

"This is very serious."

"I want you to establish a communications link with Seventh Fleet Commander-in-Chief Admiral Albert Ryland, who is currently aboard his flagship, the *George Washington,* off shore to our east. Tell him, in my name, about the Russian intent. We need his help."

"Hai," Takefumi, who was a devotee of Mishima, replied without hesitation.

"Your patriotism does not go unnoticed, *Takefumi-san*."

"Sir, this is Morrison from Security. A Mr. Ryan and two other gentlemen from the CIA are here to see you. They say it's urgent."

Whitman put his hand over the mouthpiece of the telephone. "Howard Ryan is downstairs."

"It's your choice," McGarvey told Assistant Director Wood. "Reid has the answers, but in order to get to him we're going to have to take Mueller."

"We'll discuss this with the CIA," Wood said. "Have Mr. Ryan brought up."

"We don't have the time. As it is it'll take a couple of hours to get me up there. Ryan will insist I return to Langley. He's probably brought muscle."

"He's right," Whitman said. "I can get a chopper over here from Anacostia within a few minutes."

"You're playing into his hand!"

"I'll go with him," Whitman argued. "Ken, we've got too much to lose."

Wood shook his head in irritation. "Have Ryan escorted to my office. I can stall him for at least ten minutes."

Whitman gave the order to the security guard downstairs.

Wood eyed McGarvey. "If you're fucking with us, I'll probably shoot you myself."

Director General of Defense Hironaka walked back across the hall and was admitted by the security guard into the situation room. In the seven minutes he'd been absent the atmosphere in the room had changed dramatically.

Prime Minister Enchi barely seemed able to control his anger. The others around the long polished teak conference table seemed stunned.

"Is it the Russians?" he asked, the first warning signals going off in his head.

Enchi held up two pieces of paper, without a word.

Hironaka went stiffly around the table and took them. One was a transcript of the telephone intercept between Yeltsin and Admiral Aladko. The other was a transcript of the burst telex that had just been sent from the Ministry of Defense Communications Center downstairs to Admiral Ryland aboard the aircraft carrier off shore. His hand shook.

"Can you explain the discrepancy?" Enchi demanded.

Hironaka looked up defiantly as he gathered himself. "It is time for Nippon to take her rightful place in the world."

"By going to war?"

"It was you who asked for American help defending against a Russian attack."

"President Yeltsin has recalled his ships."

"He may have given the order to the Pacific Fleet, but they have not complied. The submarines remain within the Soya Strait. We are still under attack."

"We will deal with the United States on the basis of truth."

"Mr. Prime Minister, the Americans no longer belong on Japanese soil. If you seize this opportunity, you can drive them out. All the way back across the Pacific."

"Have you such a short memory?"

"Not as short as yours."

"Has the past fifty-two years meant nothing?"

"On the contrary, Mr. Prime Minister, the years since Hiroshima and Nagasaki have meant everything. They have reopened our eyes. We rebuilt ourselves from the ashes, rebuilt our cities, our factories, our ships and airplanes, and our economy. We no longer need to be a dependent nation."

"Perhaps you are correct."

Hironaka was momentarily speechless.

"But you cannot believe that we are ready for such an adventure. Perhaps in twenty years. Perhaps fifty."

"If you believe that, Prime Minister, and yet you are still against us . . . it makes you a traitor to Japan."

"No, Hironaka. It is you who are the traitor to Japan." Enchi lifted the telephone. *"Ima."*

Hironaka looked to the others for support, but they avoided his eyes.

"You are relieved of your duties," Enchi told him.

"It's not over."

"I will try to see that it is."

Two uniformed civilian police officers came in.

"The Director General of Defense is to be placed under close arrest for treason," Enchi said. "See that no harm comes to him until his trial."

Secretary of Defense Landry put down the telephone. "I'll be damned if I know what that meant."

"What is it, Paul?" the President asked. They'd been at it for more than eight hours, and his eyes were bloodshot.

"The Japanese are talking to Al Ryland."

"Did he establish contact with the SDF?"

"Not two-way. But Director General of Defense Shin Hironaka sent him a transcript of a telephone call between Yeltsin and Russian Pacific Fleet Commander Admiral Aladko. Naval Operations Pacific is faxing us a copy. According to the Japanese, Yeltsin has ordered Aladko to press the attack on Hokkaido."

Lindsay lifted the phone and punched the button for NSA. "Amundson, this is the President. The Japanese are sending us the transcript of a telephone call between Boris Yeltsin and Admiral Aladko in Vladivostok. Presumably this call was made within the past half-hour or less. Can NSA help? We would like a confirmation."

"Mr. President, we probably monitored that call. But it'll be in our computer system. I'll have to dig it out."

"Do that. In the meantime have we monitored any further ELF traffic from Vladivostok?"

"No, sir."

"Very well." Lindsay hung up. How the hell was he supposed to make informed decisions when the information he was receiving was contradictory and confusing?

Dulles Airport was in chaos. It took Sam Varelis the better part of an hour to make his way from the wooded field south of the active runway where Delta 756 had gone down, to the hangar where the NTSB had set up shop next to the hangar where the remains of the Guerin company jet that had gone down two weeks ago were still being studied. All crash sites were nightmares, but this time it was something out of hell. The bodies they were still prying out of the wreckage here represented only one-fourteenth of the total nationwide.

The reports he'd gotten from the other teams were sketchy because of the overloaded long-distance telephone system, which made calls almost impossible. But it definitely pointed to the InterTech-designed heat monitor subassembly. His technicians had removed one of them from an American Airlines Guerin 522 that was down for maintenance, and they were analyzing the circuitry.

Varelis parked his car near one of the service doors, and, an unlit cigar clamped in his mouth, went inside where a test stand had been set up in back.

"The problem is the thermocouple frame attached to the engine," NTSB technician Mason Dillard said. "We didn't pick it up before because nobody was looking for it. The frame is explosive. Semtex blended with a magnesium alloy. A CPU in the monitor triggered it."

"Japanese?" Varelis asked.

Dillard looked up from his test equipment. "Well, that's the problem, Sam. The monitor and CPU are Japanese design. But the Semtex-magnesium frame is called P-4. It was being experimented with about ten years ago. By the Russians."

"Holy shit." Varelis took the cigar out of his mouth. "No mistake?"

"I don't think so."

"NTSB, John Hom."

"The monitor is definitely Japanese, but what brought the airplanes down was an explosive thermocouple frame on the engines. Russian."

"Sam, are you sure?"

"Dillard pulled a unit out of an American Airlines

bird in the hangar. He's sure. Stuff called P-4, Semtex and magnesium. Get that over to the FBI, CIA, and FAA."

"What about you?" Hom asked.

Varelis looked back to the growing pile of Delta wreckage being brought in. "I guess I'll stay here and help out. It's a goddamned mess."

"Yeah."

Acting Deputy Director of Operations Howard Ryan was in love with the CIA and even more in love with his new title. Lawyers had to make the best spies because by training they had more practical sense than just about everyone else. This time he was going to nail McGarvey, who'd not only outlived his usefulness in the new world order, but who had become so dangerous he could no longer be allowed to remain at large anywhere in the world. He'd obviously cut some sort of a deal with Bruno Mueller, and he'd managed to convince the FBI that he was a knight in shining armor. Ryan was going to catch him in the act. It was the only way anyone would listen.

The Marine VH-3 helicopter, the same model that the President used, touched down in a clearing in the Ellipse eight blocks from the J. Edgar Hoover Building. Ryan and the two bodyguards he'd drawn from the Domestic Operations Division, Brian Pratt and Warren Hughes, climbed aboard.

"Where are we going, Mr. Ryan?" the pilot called back.

"Upstate New York. Southeast of Buffalo. I'll have an exact destination for you when we get close."

Ryan grinned to himself. Two could play McGarvey's game. He too had been convincing. Wood had agreed to keep him up to date on Whitman's progress. This was easy.

Amundson read the transcript of the NSA intercept of the telephone conversation between Yeltsin and Admiral Aladko.

"That's the opposite of what the Japanese told us," President Lindsay said.

"Sir, the Russians know that we monitor at least some of their sensitive telephone circuits, so it's a safe bet that President Yeltsin figured we might be listening. What's not clear is whether the Russians believe the Japanese have the same capability."

"So you're saying that Yeltsin may have said what he did for our benefit?"

"Either that or they spoke in a code," Amundson said. "I think it's a possibility."

"Still no ELF from Vladivostok?"

"No, sir."

Russian Ambassador Yanis Zagorsky was in conference with SUR Washington *rezident* Stanilas Soroshkin when Yemlin was summoned upstairs. He was admitted immediately.

"It's unbelievable, but nobody is listening," Soroshkin said.

Zagorsky looked up as if it were an effort. "Our patriotic navy has attacked a radar squadron on the north coast of Hokkaido, and now the fools cannot be recalled. The Japanese fear that we mean to invade them, and Prime Minister Enchi has asked for U.S. military assistance against us."

Yemlin knew something was coming, yet he was stunned by how far it had gone. "How are the Americans reacting . . . especially with everything they're facing?"

"Not good, Viktor Pavlovich. I spoke with President Yeltsin who believes that President Lindsay thinks he is lying. Shots are being exchanged not only between our navy and the Japanese, but between the American navy and the Japanese. The situation is very confusing. Very dangerous."

Yemlin sat down. "The catalyst is the attack on the American air traffic control system. That was a Japanese operation, not Russian. Surely Lindsay's advisers know this."

"That's why we called you," Soroshkin said. "The ambassador believes that you should convince Mr. McGarvey to somehow get a message to the President about Mintori Assurance and everything else that *Abunai* supplied him."

"I can't."

"You cannot simply turn your back and walk away!" Zagorsky shouted.

"No, Mr. Ambassador. I mean that I don't know where Mr. McGarvey is, nor would I know how to find him."

Zagorsky looked at Soroshkin with despair.

"I think that you should go to the President and tell him everything," Yemlin suggested. "Perhaps more can be accomplished in person."

"He's right," Soroshkin agreed. "In any event we have nothing to lose."

"I'll call the White House immediately," the ambassador said. "Gather whatever materials you may need for your presentation, Viktor Pavlovich, and meet me downstairs in five minutes."

"Mr. Ambassador?"

"You'll brief the President, naturally. You know more about this than anyone else."

Lindsay, Secor, Landry, and Murphy met with the Russian ambassador and Viktor Yemlin in the Oval Office.

"We are dealing with a difficult situation, so I will give you only a few minutes," Lindsay said coldly.

"I appreciate the difficulties you are facing," Zagorsky said. "But we have some important intelligence that was gathered for us in Tokyo."

"We're listening."

"Mr. President, my name is Viktor Yemlin. Until recently I acted as SUR *rezident* here in Washington. Several weeks ago Kirk McGarvey came to me for help with a situation he felt was becoming dangerous for the United States. Do you know this man?"

"Go on."

"Mr. McGarvey uncovered a plot by a Japanese group to sabotage Guerin airplanes in such a way that public confidence in the company would be seriously eroded. When that happened the Japanese group would attempt an unfriendly takeover. Our . . . sources in Tokyo found out that such a plot indeed existed and was being directed by a group of powerful corporations called Mintori Assurance, led by Sokichi Kamiya."

"Get to the point," Lindsay warned.

Yemlin was confused. "Mr. President, the attack on your nation's air traffic system was conducted by the Japanese, not us. Russia has no desire to damage the good relations we have with the United States."

"Your warships are at this moment attacking Japan. President Yeltsin has promised to withdraw his forces, but so far that has not happened. Can you tell me why?"

"Mr. President, it is my understanding that the Pacific Fleet has been ordered to stop all activities in the region—" Zagorsky said. Lindsay cut him off.

"We will consider any further acts of aggression against Japan an act of war to which we will have to respond. Have I made myself clear?"

"Yes, Mr. President, you have," Zagorsky replied.

"Let us all act with care."

"They were telling half-truths," Secor said on the way back down to the situation room. "But the effect is the same as an outright lie. They're obviously stalling for time."

"We have to base our judgments on the facts alone," Murphy advised.

"I tend to agree with you," Lindsay said.

A message from Naval Operations Pacific was waiting for them. Landry took the call. When he was finished he was ashen.

"That was about the *Thorn* in the East China Sea. The Japanese submarine has been destroyed."

"Were there casualties on our side?" Lindsay asked.

"One of our Orions was shot down. No survivors. Our fighters out of Kadena shot the two Japanese jets out of the sky."

"I want it stopped now!" Lindsay roared.

"The Japanese have backed off, and so have we."

"Make sure," the President ordered.

"Mr. President, we are monitoring a lot of encrypted traffic between the Russian Embassy here in Washington and the Kremlin," Amundson said.

"Do you have a decryption?" Lindsay asked.

"Not yet. They're using new equipment. But we think the messages are being directed to the Kremlin's Situation Room."

"Any ELF traffic out of Vladivostok yet?"

"No, sir. And the latest satellite pass still shows Russian warships approaching the Soya Strait."

"Keep me informed."

"Mr. Director, this is Tommy Doyle. We just got a message from the NTSB."

"Where's Ryan?" Murphy demanded.

"I don't know, General. He's not in the building, so this was bounced over to me."

"What do you have?"

"NTSB says that what brought down the planes was an explosive thermocouple frame on the engines. One of their engineers at Dulles figured it out. The frames are Russian built. Stuff is called P-4, Semtex and magnesium."

"Sonofabitch!" Murphy swore. "No mistakes?"

"I talked to their chief investigator out there, Sam Varelis. He says they're real sure about it. Thing is the triggering signal came from a Japanese-designed unit. And the repeating transmitters that were placed at the eight airports were of an unknown design. Could have come from anywhere."

Lindsay was looking at Murphy.

"I'll tell the President," the DCI said. "In the meantime find out what the hell happened to Howard."

"Will do," Doyle said. "General?"

"Yes?"

"Good luck, sir."

"I think there can no longer be any doubt," Lindsay said.

"Just a minute, Mr. President, anyone could have purchased the material from the Russians," Murphy cautioned.

"Isn't it also possible that the Russians copied the design for the triggering mechanism from the Japanese?"

"Yes, sir."

"We'll deal with facts," Lindsay asserted. "Fact is the incident in the East China Sea happened because of a rogue submarine captain. But the situation in the Soya Strait is definitely by design."

Murphy closed his eyes. He was bone weary. They all were. And tired men under stress made mistakes. There was too much that was confusing here. For the first time since this all began, he found that he was actually wishing McGarvey were here. He was a sonofabitch. But he was usually right.

"Mr. President, the circuit to Tokyo has been reestablished," a technician said. "Prime Minister Enchi is calling."

"Good. Now we're getting somewhere." Lindsay put the call on the speakerphone. "Mr. Prime Minister, I have just learned something that has clarified the situation between our countries."

"That is why I am calling, Mr. President, to explain the message that my director general of defense sent to Admiral Ryland."

"We understand the mixup. We also monitored the telephone call that President Yeltsin made to Admiral Aladko. We know that the Russians mean to follow up their initial attack on your Hokkaido radar station."

The circuit was quiet for several long beats. Lindsay figured Enchi was waiting for the translators to catch up.

"The Russian submarines have not withdrawn from the strait?" Enchi asked cautiously.

"Not at this time. I have ordered Admiral Ryland to send forces to monitor the situation."

"Have you spoken with President Yeltsin?"

"Yes, I have. He understands that it is our intention to repel any further attacks against you."

Again there was an odd pause on the circuit.

"I will inform my local commanders," Enchi said. "Now, about the incident north of Okinawa."

"An unfortunate misunderstanding, Mr. Prime Minister. Let us deal with first things first."

"I have a solution on the target," Sattler reported. "Range forty-seven thousand yards, bearing zero-niner-seven."

"Prepare to launch TASM Tomahawk on my mark," Hanrahan said. The surface-to-surface missile carried nearly a half-ton of high explosives to its target at more than five hundred miles per hour.

"Skipper?"

"On my mark," Hanrahan repeated.

Ryder slammed down the phone he was using. "Belay that order!" he shouted.

Hanrahan turned on him. "You're relieved of duty right now, XO!"

"Skipper, we've been ordered to disengage immediately. Comes direct from Seventh. What do you want me to tell them?"

Hanrahan was shaking. "Goddammit!"

Ryder came across the bridge. "For Christ's sake, Mike, it's just a sailboat. We got confirmation from Foster on Okinawa. Belongs to a jarhead lieutenant."

"What the hell is he doing out here?"

"Trying to survive," Ryder said. "Just like us."

Z100417ZFEB

TOP SECRET

TO: CINC 7TH FLEET

FM: CINCPAC

1. EVIDENCE CONTINUES TO MOUNT THAT RUSSIAN NAVAL FORCES INTEND TO CONTINUE THEIR ATTACK ON THE NORTH AND EAST COASTS OF HOKKAIDO XXX RPTD WARNINGS TO WITHDRAW HAVE BEEN IGNORED.

2. PROCEED AT BEST POSSIBLE SPEED TO A POSITION FROM WHICH AIR OPERATIONS CAN BE CONDUCTED IN THE SOYA STRAIT.

3. USE ALL MEANS AT YOUR DISPOSAL TO WARN RUSSIAN NAVAL FORCES OUT OF THE REGION XXX IF THAT FAILS YOU WILL ENGAGE THE ENEMY WITHOUT RESTRICTION.

4. YOU MAY ACT INDEPENDENTLY OF LOCAL JAPANESE FORCES.

XXX

EOM

GOOD LUCK, AL.

Admiral Ryland and Captain Benson stepped off the *George Washington*'s bridge into the admiral's ready room.

"We can't stall any longer," Benson said.

"Was that what we were doing, Tony?" Ryland asked. The Japanese were withdrawing their blockade from the mouth of Tokyo Bay, and after a brief but deadly skirmish in the East China Sea, the ASDF had also withdrawn to Tanegashima. He'd truly believed that the Russians would step back from the brink as well.

"You wanted the situation to stabilize. Well, it's gone about as far as it's going to go."

"What can they be thinking? There has to be a mistake."

Benson didn't ask who the admiral was referring to, the Russians or Washington. "We have our orders, Al."

Ryland reread the message. It was tantamount to a declaration of war on Russia. "I want a confirmation, ASAP. We'll hold until then."

"Very well."

Since they'd crossed the state line into New York, Mueller suspected that they were being followed. When they'd stopped for gas outside Corning, Reid had come back from paying certain that the clerk had recognized him. A highway patrol car had followed them for about ten miles north of the rest stop, and then had dropped back, only to be replaced by another for a dozen miles. Either the Maryland Highway Patrol trooper he'd shot had survived to radio their description or eyewitnesses had provided a description of the Probe. Whatever the case, the authorities were showing what he thought to be remarkable restraint. They were wary. But they were too wary, which meant someone had told them who they were dealing with. McGarvey?

The roads had become slippery from the snow, which had increased in intensity throughout the evening.

"If you lose control and slide off the road, I will kill you," he'd told Dominique, and she'd taken care with her driving.

Mueller studied a map which showed I-390 curved to the north toward Rochester in the next few miles. South of the city, I-90 branched off to the west to Buffalo and the Canadian border.

He looked up. Although it was dark and heavily snowing he could see that the countryside they were passing through was hilly and thickly wooded. A couple of miles to the west was a state park that would be closed at this time of the year, although he suspected there might be a park ranger on duty. In Europe park rangers lived through the winter seasons with their families in cabins. He couldn't think why it would be any different here.

He was faced with a difficult decision. The authorities might stand off for now, but they would never allow him to cross the Canadian border. Even if they did, he wouldn't get far with Reid and the woman. Either he would have to cut Reid loose and continue with Dominique as a hostage, or he would have to kill them both and make his own escape. In either event he needed to get off the main highways so that he could buy some time.

He was still faced with the problem of McGarvey, who would never stop coming after him.

He sat forward. "Take the next exit to the west. It will be marked Mount Morris. About five miles."

Dominique glanced in the rearview mirror at him. She was terrified.

"What's wrong?" Reid asked.

"We are being followed, so we need to get another car," Mueller replied.

Dominique glanced in the mirror again.

"If you do exactly as you are told, Ms. Kilbourne, no harm will come to you," Mueller said reasonably.

"Yeah, right."

The navy pilot expertly set the ponderous Sikorsky SH-3D/L Sea King helicopter down in the median strip within twenty-five yards of the roadblock. The ceiling was low, and in the darkness and blowing snow they would have missed the landing spot except for the flashing lights from the dozen highway patrol cars.

"I'm damned if I know why we're going along with you, except I don't see any other choice," Whitman said. He handed McGarvey his Walther, the two extra magazines of ammunition, and the thick silencer tube.

"I'll owe you a drink when this is over," McGarvey replied, pocketing the ammo and silencer and holstering his pistol at the small of his back. He'd worried about Dominique all the way up. It was *déjà vu*. He'd been here before.

"If you're right, it'll be us owing you."

They jumped down from the chopper and made their way up to the roadblock, where they were directed to the New York Highway Patrol officer in charge, Lieutenant Earl Lawton.

Whitman clipped his FBI badge to the zipper flap of his coat. "What's the situation?"

Lawton, a tall, slender man with drooping moustache, eyed McGarvey uncomfortably. "They should be coming up the road in about five minutes. Green Ford Probe. Bad guy is in the back seat. Woman driving. A second man in the passenger seat."

"How do you know they'll be here in five minutes?" McGarvey asked.

"We've been following them so they can't double back."

"Show me on a map."

Lawton pulled a map out of his car. "We're here, at the Lakeville exit. They've already passed Sonyea, about fifteen miles south."

"What's this?" McGarvey demanded.

"Mount Morris. Letchworth State Park."

"Closed?"

Lawton nodded.

"Anybody living in or near the park?"

"There's Mount Morris, and I think there's probably a ranger on duty," Lawton said. "What are you driving at? If they're trying to make I-90, and then the border at Buffalo, there'd be no reason for them to turn off."

McGarvey looked down the highway. "Don't count on it."

"Al, your orders are confirmed," CINCPAC Admiral Billy Floricher said.

"I'm going strong on the warnings before I start shooting," Ryland replied. "They're stupid, not crazy."

"The President has cleared it with Prime Minister Enchi. The Russians are telling us one thing while they're doing another."

"There's a lot of that going around."

"Good luck, Al."

Captain Lestov met with his officers in the *Strelka*'s wardroom. They'd hovered in silence just below the thermocline at four hundred meters into the morning hours. Although they knew that other Russian submarines were somewhere in the vicinity, their passive sonar had picked up nothing in the past six hours. Nor had they received any ELF traffic from Vladivostok. For all intents and purposes they were utterly alone at the bottom of the sea.

"I think it is safe to say that although the Japanese

suspect we're down here, they cannot know our exact position," Lestov said. Within an hour after they'd gone deep, he'd stood them down from battle stations missile. His officers were tense, as well they should be, but they were rested.

"When we launch a missile they'll know how to find us," his XO, Lieutenant Commander Savin, said.

"This close to shore would put us in a difficult position, with little room to maneuver."

"We have our orders."

"Da, Viktor Abramovich. We have carried them out, have we not?"

"We did not completely destroy Wakkanai."

"You suggest we press the attack?"

"Unless we receive orders to the contrary." Savin was becoming uncomfortable, as were the other officers. It was a captain's duty to lead by decision, not by committee.

"I agree. But we also have a responsibility to our fine boat and crew. We've not been ordered to recklessly endanger our lives."

Savin nervously fingered his cigarette. "Captain, I am confused. What are you telling us?"

"I am simply trying to gauge the mood and determination of my officers."

"Captain, we are with you!"

"Even if my orders are to slink away like a coward in the night? Before a fight two men are boasting; afterward only one. Do you remember that proverb?"

Savin looked around the table at the other officers. He nodded. *"Da.* If that is your order."

"If I turn the boat to the south and order full speed ahead so that we would be driven onto the beach?"

"That too, Captain."

Lestov closed his eyes for a moment. God help him, but he did understand Moscow's orders, as he did their silence now. The Japanese had to be contained, even if it took a sacrifice of good men and ships.

"We will obey our orders," he said. "First let's determine if Wakkanai is still transmitting. If it is, we shall finish our attack. Afterward we will go home . . . defending our retreat with every resource at our command."

Savin nodded grimly.

President Lindsay recalled the Russian ambassador to the White House. This time Zagorsky came alone.

"I'll come directly to the point, Mr. Ambassador. I have ordered the Seventh Fleet to the Soya Strait to assist Japanese forces in defending the island of Hokkaido and their territorial waters."

"We are not attacking Japan," Zagorsky said, keeping his voice as even as possible.

"At least three Russian submarines remain within a threatening position in the Soya Strait. No communications have been detected from Pacific Fleet Headquarters in Vladivostok ordering the withdrawal of those warships, despite President Yeltsin's promise to do so."

"There are technical difficulties at the ELF transmitter."

"Inform your government that a continued refusal to withdraw your forces will be considered an act of aggression against Japan, and, as our allies, against us."

"Mr. President . . ."

"That's all," Lindsay said coldly.

"They should have been here by now," McGarvey said, looking at his watch.

Lawton got in his squad car to use the radio. "Two-Seven-Baker, this is Lawton. Where are you?"

"We're coming up on the Mount Morris exit. Have they reached you?"

"No," Lawton said.

"They turned off," McGarvey said. "Get your people on the other side of the park and block those roads. In the meantime I need to borrow one of your cars."

"We'll do this my way—"

"If you crowd him a lot of your people are going to get hurt. This guy is a professional."

"Who the hell do you think you are?" Lawton demanded angrily.

"You don't want to know," Whitman said. "Give us a car and a driver who knows the area."

"Is the FBI taking over this case?"

"We're here to assist," Whitman said. "We want to take Mueller and the others alive. How about a car? We don't have a lot of time."

"Goddammit," Lawton swore. He got out of the car. "Alger," he shouted.

One of the highway patrol cops came back. "Lieutenant?"

"Take these guys down to Mount Morris," Lawton said.

"Block the roads out," Whitman advised.

"You've got one shot, then I'm sending my people in," Lawton warned.

The Marine VH-3 helicopter landed a few yards from the Sikorsky parked in the median strip. Ryan and his two domestic operations officers hurried over to where Lawton was radioing orders to his people.

"You in charge here?" Ryan interrupted.

"Now who the hell are you guys?" Lawton demanded.

Ryan showed him his CIA identification. "Where's McGarvey?"

"Mount Morris," the cop said. "Would you mind telling me what's going on?"

"We'll need a car and driver."

"Of course."

"Mr. President, I think you should call Yeltsin and explain to him what we're doing," Secor suggested.

"He knows what we're doing," Lindsay replied. "When an ELF message is sent from Vladivostok ordering their warships out of the strait, and when they actually leave, we will stand down. Not until then."

"Captain, you have permission to launch," Admiral Ryland said from his chair on the bridge.

Benson relayed the order, and within fifteen seconds the first of the six Lockheed S-3C Viking ASW jet aircraft lifted off the deck of the carrier. The Vikings would be followed by eight F/A-18L fighter/interceptors from the Peregrine Squadron. Their job would be to maintain air superiority over the strait so that the Vikings could find the submarines and kill them if necessary. Twenty minutes ago they had launched an E-2C Hawkeye early-warning aircraft, designated Sugar Hill, to provide over-the-horizon contact information. It would take up station at thirty thousand feet fifty miles out.

The *George Washington*'s diminished battle group consisted of one Aegis cruiser, two guided missile destroyers, and two ASW frigates. The rest of the fleet was playing catch-up out of Tokyo Bay and deployed with the *Thorn* in the East China Sea north of Okinawa. They were too spread out to be an effective force, but Ryland hoped he wouldn't need the entire fleet. If that were the case a lot of people would be killed, and peace would be a long time coming. It would not be another hundred-hour war like they had pushing Iraq out of Kuwait.

They were a little under three hundred miles from the strait. The F/A-18s would make that in less than fifteen minutes, but it would take the much slower Vikings thirty minutes to get on target.

It seemed like an eternity to Ryland. Like all rational fighting men he abhorred battle. But when one was imminent he wanted to get it over as soon as possible.

"I have contact," the *Strelka*'s ELINT officer Lieutenant Bychokov reported. "Wakkanai is still on the air."

They'd slowly risen to one hundred meters from where they'd sent up an extremely low-profile intelligence-gathering buoy capable of receiving on a broad band of frequencies. Connected to the sub by a long wire, the device was practically undetectable by surface ships or aircraft.

"Anything from Pacific Fleet?" Lestov asked.

"Nyet."

"Very well. Cut the buoy loose and come left to three-zero-zero degrees. Make your speed fifteen knots."

"Aye, aye, coming left to three-zero-zero degrees, make my speed fifteen knots," Savin acknowledged the order. "The buoy is away."

"Sound battle stations missile."

A Klaxon sounded throughout the boat, and one by one the watertight doors were closed and dogged. Lestov's plan was to gain as much sea room as possible before turning and firing.

"Sonar, conn. Anything ahead of us?"

"Two contacts, bearing two-one-five degrees . . . range fifteen thousand meters and slowly closing. Type signature looks like a pair of Yamagumo-class destroyers. Designate Sierra-Thirteen and Fourteen."

"Have they got us?" Lestov asked.

"Nyet."

"Keep a close eye on them, Vladi. They're in a position to cut us off."

"Aye, aye, Captain."

They spotted the green Ford Probe abandoned in front of a metal barrier gate on the park road a hundred yards from Highway 408. The highway patrol cop slammed on the brakes, slewing them sideways half into the ditch.

McGarvey leaped out of the car and drew his gun as he raced the rest of the way on foot, keeping to the trees at the side of the road in case Mueller had set a trap for them.

Three sets of footprints in the freshly fallen snow disappeared in the darkness down the road into the park.

Whitman, his gun drawn, joined him. "Are they gone?"

McGarvey held up his hand for silence. He cocked his head to listen. In the distance someone was shouting, or crying something. A woman's voice.

"He'll know we're coming, so watch yourself," McGarvey said.

"He might suspect . . ."

"He'll know."

Whitman nodded.

"You take the left side of the road, I'll take the right. Whatever it takes, I want Reid and the woman alive."

"I want to take Mueller in too."

"It'll never happen," McGarvey said. "Don't underestimate him. He's the best the Stasi ever fielded. If you see him, shoot him immediately. If you hesitate he'll kill you."

"Hold up, you guys. Help is on the way!" the cop shouted.

"Christ," McGarvey swore softly. "Tell him okay."

"Okay, we'll wait," Whitman called to the cop. When he turned back, McGarvey was gone.

Ryan rushed over to the squad car half in the ditch. "Where the hell are they?" he shouted, holding up his CIA identification.

"I tried to stop them, sir," the flustered highway patrol officer explained. "They went into the park on foot."

"Let's go," Ryan told his two bodyguards.

"Mr. Ryan, I don't think that's such a good idea," Hughes warned. "We stumble around back there in the dark somebody could get shot."

"You wait here then," Ryan instructed. "Give me your gun."

"Sir, he's right. You shouldn't go after them. New York H.P. is right behind us," Pratt said.

"I'll watch myself. Give me a gun."

Hughes took out his Colt 10 mm automatic. "Safety's on the left side."

"Right," Ryan said. He snatched the gun and raced down the road into the park.

Lieutenant Paul O'Neil's Peregrine Able Flight lined up with the four Hornets of Lieutenant Bill Gifford's Baker Flight, and they hit their afterburners rapidly accelerating to Mach two, passing above the much slower Vikings already on their way to the strait.

Their flight path would take them along the northeast

coast of Hokkaido, over Japanese air space, which under normal conditions would be no cause for concern. But everyone was on their toes this morning. The ASDF was at DEFCON ONE, which meant a lot of nervous fingers were on a lot of cocked triggers.

For this mission the F/A-18s were armed with two AGM-84 Harpoon anti-ship missiles with a range above seventy nautical miles; four air-to-air AIM-9/L Sidewinders, which used the Argon-cooled Indium Antimonide Sensor that was extremely sensitive to infrared emissions of a hot jet exhaust; as well as the 20 mm Vulcan cannon, capable of shooting one hundred rounds per second.

If the Russians decided to send MiG-31 Foxhounds from their bases on Sakhalin Island, or the Sukhoi-27s from Khabarovsk on the mainland, they would be in for a nasty fight. There was little doubt in anyone's mind who would hold air superiority over the strait.

O'Neil's threat receiver pinged. He was being illuminated by several ground radars. "They've got us, Bill," he radioed Baker Wing leader. "Squawking eight-seven-seven-seven." The 8777 transponder signal identified them as friendlies to Japanese ground radar.

They crossed the coast at Akkeshi, but nothing rose from the ASDF base at Misawa seventy miles away, and O'Neil allowed himself to relax a little. They'd passed the first hurdle. For sure he didn't want to get into it with the Japanese like the *Thorn* had. Their orders were very clear. If they were illuminated by Japanese aircraft weapons radar and were warned off, they were to bug out immediately. The Russians were their targets.

"Conn, sonar. I have a possible submarine contact, bearing three-five-five degrees, approximately twenty thousand meters, and below us."

"Is it one of ours?" Lestov looked across the attack center at his XO. So far as they knew, no American submarines should be in these waters.

"Hard to tell, Captain. It's very quiet. I think it just went into drift mode. . . wait. *Da.* I have it now. She's one of ours. Definite Sierra class. She just turned right, speed under ten knots, and she's on her way up."

"It seems as if we're not alone after all," Lestov observed. "What about Sierra-Thirteen and -Fourteen?"

"Twelve thousand yards now, same course and speed, bearing two-six-five degrees."

"Our other sub must be hearing them," Savin suggested.

"Providing our comrades know where we are and what we're up to, we'll be okay."

"Conn, weapons. Report tubes one and two loaded and ready to fire."

"Aye," Lestov replied. He walked over to the plotting board. "If the Japanese destroyers continue on their same course and speed, they'll find our submarine."

"It looks like it," Savin said.

"Then let's be quick about this."

"Sugar Hill, Able and Baker Wings on station," O'Neil radioed. The clouds toward the Siberian coast were thick, but above the strait the skies were clear. Hokkaido was off his left wing, and the Russian-held Sakhalin Island rose ruggedly on his right. He was being illuminated by many ground radars, including the one array at Wakkanai that was still transmitting. He could see smoke rising from the installation twenty miles away.

"We show contacts to your south. One commercial transponder heading away, the others look like MSDF Orions from Otaru."

"Paul, ten o'clock low," his wingman radioed. "Two on the surface."

"Stand by Sugar Hill," O'Neil told the Hawkeye controller. He turned his Hornet into a shallow diving turn to the left. His look-down-shoot-down radar picked up the targets almost immediately.

"I got 'em," Bill Gifford radioed. "Japanese destroyers, just coming around the cape."

Moments later O'Neil's AAS-38 FLIR—Forward-Looking-InfraRed pod—produced a clear image on the Master Monitor Display on his panel.

"Sugar Hill, this is Able Leader, we have two Japanese destroyers making for the strait around Cape Soya."

"They're hunting. Stand by."

"I have two additional submarine contacts, both definitely ours . . . Sierra class. Bearings zero-one-five and zero-nine-zero degrees . . . range on both targets is above thirty thousand meters."

"Course and speed?" Lestov demanded.

"They're both making forty knots, course two-seven-zero."

It was immediately obvious that both submarines were closing on the two destroyers. But they were making so much noise that their presence would be detected.

"The destroyers have gone active," Bychkov reported excitedly. "They're turning toward our submarines."

The *Strelka*'s tubes one and two were fitted with the conventional high-explosives version of the SS-NX-21 cruise missile. Once they were launched, however, and until they struck their targets, they would be indistinguishable from the nuclear-tipped version. It was a very dangerous game they were playing by trying to teach the Japanese a lesson in vulnerability and humility.

"Open doors one and two. Prepare to launch on my order," Lestov said.

"Able and Baker leaders, this is Sugar Hill. The friendlies are in acquisition of two submerged targets. Spread out at flight level twenty-five to provide air cover. Eliminator Squadron will be on station momentarily."

"Roger," O'Neil responded. "Bill, go north, we'll take this end."

"Roger."

Eliminator Squadron had the six Viking ASW aircraft. If the Japanese missed, they wouldn't.

Mueller had lost his sense of urgency. Escape was becoming increasingly unlikely, especially dragging Reid and the woman with him. They stood in the darkness just outside the pool of light cast from a window in the house adjacent to the park's visitors and information center. Parked beneath a carport was a four-wheel-drive Jimmy.

"I can't go any farther," Reid wheezed. He slumped down into the snow.

Dominique, her eyes wide, stepped back.

"You'll spend the rest of your life in prison," Mueller said mildly.

"I don't have much life left," Reid looked up, and shook his head. "The Japanese will be blamed. I've accomplished at least that much."

"They'll know it was you."

"The equipment was of Japanese design. The message is clear enough."

Mueller shifted his gaze to Dominique, and she flinched. He'd always had to fight this detachment in himself, the feeling that he'd rather stand back and watch events unfold than take action. It was a sense of inevitability in him that had increased since the collapse of the Soviet Union and the dismantling of the GDR. And the walls came tumbling down, the line crossed his thoughts. America was Joshua's seven trumpet-blowing priests. Her time in history had come.

"Remain here. I'll get us a car," he told Reid.

"You're going to kill the park ranger," Dominique said.

Mueller shrugged.

"For God's sake stop!" Dominique cried. "Hasn't there been enough killing?"

Mueller smiled despite himself. "My dear little girl, hasn't your Mr. McGarvey told you that the killing never stops? It's our nature."

"You're not human!" Dominique started for him.

Mueller raised his pistol. "No, I'm not."

Dominique stopped.

"If you cry out, I shall come back and kill you," Mueller said matter of factly. "Do you believe this?"

"Yes."

Mueller turned and crossed the road to the ranger's house without looking back. He knocked at the door, and moments later a man dressed in a sweater opened it and Mueller went inside with him.

A muffled pistol shot came from somewhere ahead, and moments later Dominique came running up the road.

"Don't shoot!" McGarvey shouted to Whitman, who was in the woods across the road.

"Mac?" Dominique screamed.

McGarvey rushed out to her and pulled her back into the safety of the woods. She was all over him, crying and babbling incoherently.

"Where's Mueller?" McGarvey shouted her down.

"Back there! He's killed the ranger, and he's going to steal the car! Reid's back there too!"

Whitman came across the road in a dead run. "What's going on?" he demanded.

"McGarvey!" someone shouted from behind them.

"Jesus Christ, it's Howard Ryan," McGarvey said. "Stay here with Dominique," he told Whitman. "And try to stop Ryan. He's going to get himself killed."

"No," Dominique cried, but McGarvey pulled away from her and moved off.

He kept to the side of the road. Just now it was snowing much harder, which reduced visibility to thirty yards. Mueller had made very few mistakes to this point. Nor had he made a mistake allowing Dominique to escape. He had created a diversion, hoping to slow them down. Or he had sent a specific message, targeted to one man. It would explain why he'd taken Dominique in the first place, and not killed her at Reid's. The thought was chilling.

The woods ended abruptly at a wide clearing across which was a large log building, and beside it a low ranch-style house, lights in the windows.

McGarvey stopped at a picnic table. He could just make out what appeared to be a figure of a man sitting in the snow at the side of the road. He switched the Walther's safety off and raised the gun.

Someone was coming up the road behind him. "McGarvey!" Ryan shouted.

The hunched figure turned at the same time the engine of a car started. A second later its headlights came on, illuminating Reid, and the Jimmy roared out of the carport, sliding on the slippery road as it turned left, toward the lake.

McGarvey raced up the road and fired five shots at the retreating Jimmy, the last one hitting its gas tank just before it reached the woods. The rear of the car exploded, a fireball lighting up the entire clearing.

Ryan fired from behind, the single shot catching McGarvey in his side, just above his right hip, knocking him to the ground.

"You bastard, you're under arrest," Ryan shouted triumphantly.

McGarvey rolled over as Ryan came up holding his gun in shaking hands, a wild look on his face.

"You're under arrest, you sonofabitch! You're under arrest."

Two shots were fired from the direction of the burning Jimmy.

McGarvey leaped up and shoved Ryan down, the third shot catching the CIA lawyer in the side of his face just below his jaw.

Whitman fired toward the Jimmy as McGarvey disentangled himself from Ryan.

"He's down! He's down!" Whitman shouted.

McGarvey scrambled painfully to his feet and trained his gun on what appeared to be Mueller's body lying at the edge of the road twenty feet from the furiously burning Jimmy.

Ryan, hurt but still alive, was fumbling for his gun, which he'd lost in the snow. In the distance they could hear sirens.

"Stay with him," McGarvey said, and he limped down the road before Whitman could object.

Mueller lay on his back, his arms outstretched, his eyes open. He still had his gun in his right hand. "McGarvey," he said, and he started to rise.

"You lose," McGarvey said, lanquidly raising his own pistol. He waited a moment, then fired one shot, hitting the German in the middle of the forehead above the bridge of his nose.

FORTY-FOUR

Many active sonobuoys in the water!"

"Range and bearings," Lestov demanded. The destroyers had probably deployed LAMPS ASW helicopters. But he would have thought they'd be too busy with the other two submarines to venture this far out.

"Captain, they're all around us. Must be eight, maybe ten of them."

"Do they have us?"

"I don't think so . . . but it won't be long."

"Has Reid said anything?" McGarvey asked hoarsely.

"He insists on talking only to you," Whitman said. "But it'll have to wait. We'll get what we need from him once we're back in Washington."

"It can't wait, and you know it. We'll take the chopper back. Have it brought here."

"Listen, pal, you're not going anywhere except to a hospital," the paramedic bandaging McGarvey's wound told him. They sat in the back of one of the ambulances Lawton had sent up. "You're mostly one lucky bastard, but I think there may be some internal bleeding."

"I need a couple of hours, so do the best you can." His entire body was on fire, and he didn't think that he could walk ten yards without help. But the crisis wasn't over. More than ever they needed to get to the President.

"The chopper's going to try for it," Whitman said.

"But in this weather the best he can do is follow the interstate."

McGarvey closed his eyes. He'd refused any pain medication, but he blocked that out of his mind. They still didn't have all the answers. More than two thousand people were dead, and they could only guess why.

"Ms. Kilbourne is shook up, but she's okay. We'll take her back with us," Whitman said.

"What about Ryan?"

"On the way to the hospital. He'll live."

"They won't listen to me, John, so it'll be up to you to convince them."

"Convince them of what? What the hell happened?"

McGarvey shook his head. "That's what Reid's going to tell us."

"You hope."

McGarvey managed a grim smile. "You're learning, John."

"Conn, sonar. They've dropped a DLC buoy," Bychkov said excitedly.

"Are they sending us a message?" Lestov asked. The DLC was a down-link communications buoy used by aircraft or surface ships to communicate with submerged submarines.

"Aye, Captain. But it's in Russian!"

"Conn, Elint. It's not one of our buoys, but they have the proper codes."

Lestov tried to work it out. It was thought that the Americans had their ELF codes, but they could have shared them with the Japanese.

"They're sending three groups. Are you ready to copy, Captain?"

"Go ahead, Mikhail."

Х Д К	П С б
Disengage immediately	Come to Periscope Depth

Ж З И
Prepare for Further Xmssn

"What do we do, Captain?" Savin asked.

"I don't know," Lestov admitted.

From where they were parked at the side of the road in the hills above Yokosuka, they could see the entire city as well as the harbor and naval bases, which were nearly empty of warships. With the morning, the riot had begun to collapse of its own accord. They'd accomplished what they'd set out to accomplish, and the people had begun to drift away. For the most part the police had done nothing, but fifteen minutes ago a half-dozen troop transport trucks had pulled to the gates, and a hundred Ground Self Defense Force soldiers were helping the remaining U.S. Marines clear out the base. Dozens of ambulances and police cars came and went from the Seventh Fleet's headquarters building, while several American helicopters hovered overhead like a swarm of angry, but ineffectual, bees. Considering the size of the demonstration, and the resistance they'd met, there'd been surprisingly few Japanese casualties.

"Rising Sun has won this battle, *Ashia-san,*" Takushiro Hatoyama said. "Now it is up to our navy and air force."

"It worries me that we cannot reach Kamiya. Is Morning Star taking place?"

"If not now, the day will come."

"We are not ready."

Hatoyama smiled. "No matter the outcome, from this day forward the United States will treat us differently."

"Hai."

"Isn't that what we wanted, *Ashia-san?*"

Ashia nodded uncertainly.

"Let's return to Tokyo. I'm hungry. I'd like to have a steak and some beer. We'll celebrate."

"I hope it's a celebration," Ashia said.

They rode in two highway patrol cars back to the interstate highway where the Sikorsky Sea King helicopter waited for them. The snow was still heavy, but the navy pilot said they could get over the low clouds with no real problem. Already it was beginning to show signs of breaking up to the south.

Dominique was strangely aloof from McGarvey as Whitman and a cop helped him aboard the helicopter and strapped him in. She sat in the rear, leaving McGarvey and Whitman to sit with a very subdued Reid, who looked like he was on the verge of collapse.

As soon as they were airborne and headed south, McGarvey lit a cigarette and Whitman bummed one from him. The smoke made him lightheaded for a few moments. Reid did not look like a monster, just like a tired old man. "You wanted to talk to me?"

"I saw them taking Colonel Mueller away in a body bag. Did you kill him?"

McGarvey nodded. "I'm surprised he didn't kill you and Dominique."

"He wanted a diversion. Something to slow you down. But it didn't."

"How did you discover that the Japanese had sabotaged Guerin airplanes?" McGarvey changed subjects.

"It was a stroke of luck. A company in California by the name of InterTech designed an electronic subassembly for Guerin under a secret contract with a Japanese company." Reid stopped. "But then you know most of that, otherwise you wouldn't have come this far."

"Was it the engineer who killed Jeanne Shepard?" Whitman asked.

Reid glanced at him. "His name was Louis Zerkel. He figured it out and designed a triggering mechanism that they hid at eight airports, plus Andrews."

"Where is he?"

"Dead, like the others. Colonel Mueller buried them in the garbage pit behind my country house in Sterling."

"How about Phil Carrara?" McGarvey asked.

"There were two of them. Mueller took them up to Baltimore somewhere."

"Your house in Sterling, is it near the airport?" Whitman asked.

"We can see the runways from the upstairs windows."

"Did you cause the crash two weeks ago?"

"Zerkel was conducting an experiment. But it came as a surprise to all of us."

"Were you working with the Japanese?" McGarvey asked.

"On the contrary," Reid replied. "I wanted them to be blamed for the crashes. I wanted Americans to see what they were still capable of, and do something about it before we're faced with another Pearl Harbor. You can't believe how politically naïve we, as a people, have become. It's going to happen all over again unless we do something about it."

"More than two thousand innocent people were killed," Whitman said.

"The number will probably go higher. Remember the Japanese killed more than twenty-six hundred Americans in their attack on Pearl Harbor. They're willing."

"But they didn't do it. You did."

"It doesn't make any difference. The effect will be the same. America awakened today."

"Okay," McGarvey told Whitman. "Call your boss and tell him what we've got. He'll have to convince the DCI, who's probably in the White House situation room."

"It's that simple?" Whitman asked.

"Does it surprise you?" McGarvey asked tiredly.

"I don't know."

"You'd better hustle, John."

"Didn't it bother you thinking about all the people you were going to kill?" McGarvey asked Reid.

"It was a lot less than would be killed in a war with Japan," Reid replied. "You're too young to remember the last war. Three hundred thousand Americans lost their lives. But worldwide the number killed was over twenty-five million. The horror of it is beyond imagination."

"You were going to make a profit, weren't you?" McGarvey accused. "When Guerin failed, you were going to buy its stock for next to nothing, bolstering the company. It would have made you a hero."

"Actually we would have bought their bonds for ten or

fifteen cents on the dollar," Reid said smugly. "Stocks don't mean much. He who owns a company's bonds is the one who owns the company. You see, we need Guerin, so I was willing to do whatever it took to save it."

McGarvey sighed to relieve the pressure in his chest. It would be easy, even in his condition, to reach across and kill the man. But it would serve no purpose. There'd been too much killing. The pain and suffering would continue for a very long time. This was like Pearl Harbor, Kennedy's assassination, and the shuttle disaster all wrapped into one. It was a watershed for the United States. Now they would have to end it, to make sure the killing stopped.

"I know what you're thinking," Reid said. "But even if we do step back from a war with Japan, it'll come in the not too distant future, for the same reason it came in 1941. The same pressures are building, now that the Cold War is over. With Japanese bases in the Philippines, and a Japanese nuclear weapons program because of the threat of North Korea, the next war won't be so easily won."

"Shut up," McGarvey said. "Just shut the fuck up."

It took fifteen minutes to convince Ken Wood and FBI Director John Harding that McGarvey had something. They patched the call through to Roland Murphy at the White House situation room.

"Where are you, McGarvey?" Murphy demanded.

"We're in a helicopter an hour and a half from Washington. What's the situation there, General? Have we exchanged shots with the Japanese?"

"It's more complicated than that now. You'd better tell me what you've come up with."

"Is the President there?"

"Yes, he is."

"Does he know what I've been working on?"

"Yes."

"Put this on the speakerphone."

"All right," Murphy said. "Okay, you're on."

"Mr. President, can you hear me?"

"Yes, we can, Mr. McGarvey. It's my understanding that you may have some information for me. But be quick about it. We are in a very difficult situation."

"Mr. President, the Japanese did not bring down our airplanes. They did not attack us."

"We know that," Lindsay said. "We have evidence that some of the sabotaged equipment aboard the Guerin fleet was of Japanese manufacture, but other more important elements were of Russian design."

"No, sir. That's wrong. I have a confession from one of the men who was responsible for the crashes. His name is Edward Reid. He worked with an engineer from an electronics company in California and an officer from the former East German intelligence service. Reid has told me how he did it, and why."

"He must have been working for the Russians," the President said. "At this moment the Russians are attacking Hokkaido in force."

"The attack is in retaliation for the Tatar Strait incident, Mr. President. The Russians do not want a war with Japan."

"The war is with us," Lindsay said. "Prime Minister Enchi has formally asked for our help."

"Call President Yeltsin. Tell him that we know who sabotaged our fleet, and to back down."

"I have spoken with him. He promised to withdraw his forces, but he lied."

"They could be experiencing technical difficulties," McGarvey insisted. His head was spinning. It was becoming increasingly difficult for him to hang on. "Think it out, Mr. President. Reid has no reason to work for the Russians. And the Russians have no reason to go to war with us over Japan. Just the opposite is true."

"I appreciate what you've done, Mr. McGarvey. But you cannot know all the facts. I do."

"I don't think so, Mr. President."

"You're wrong."

* * *

"Conn, sonar. I have torpedoes in the water. Five, no six. Range above thirty thousand meters. They've just gone active."

"Our torpedoes?" Lestov demanded.

"Aye, Captain. Range and bearing match the two Japanese destroyers."

"It has finally begun," Savin said.

"Fire tube one, fire tube three," Lestov ordered. "And then get us the hell out of here."

"Fire one . . . fire two!" the weapons control officer, Lieutenant Zukko, responded. Seconds later the two cruise missiles were launched.

"Crash-dive the boat, make your depth one thousand meters, make your speed forty-five knots."

Murphy held his finger on the mute button. "I think we should listen to him, Mr. President."

"I did listen," Lindsay said. "The Russians continue to press the attack against Hokkaido, despite Yeltsin's promise to withdraw his forces. The vital part of the system that brought down our fleet was Russian designed. And Mr. McGarvey just told us that Edward Reid worked with a former officer of the Stasi—a service, need I remind you, that was de facto an adjunct of the Soviet KGB."

"McGarvey knows the Russians . . ."

"Are you saying that he's done a better job than the CIA? Because, General, you've told me that you could produce no clear evidence *against* Russian involvement."

"In this case, Mr. President, perhaps he has."

"I have two sub-sea missile launches," the Viking leader ELINT officer reported.

"Do we have a positive fix on the target?" the pilot, Lieutenant Frances Kane, demanded.

"Aye, Skipper. Twenty thousand yards, bearing two-six-zero degrees. She's diving."

Kane hauled the twin-turbofan ASW aircraft in a

sharp turn to the left, her stomach tight. This was her first actual combat mission.

"Holy shit! Those are nukes!"

Two missiles had just surfaced and streaked to the south on long fiery tails.

"Skipper, I confirm the launch of two SS-NX-21 Russian missiles! They are nuclear!"

"Get that off to Sugar Hill, and prepare to launch two Mark 46 torpedoes on my command," Lieutenant Kane said. The crazy bastards. "Estimate time to impact?"

"Less than two minutes," the ELINT officer reported excitedly.

"Stand by," Kane said. She pulled the Viking back to the right, away from the coast, so that they would not be blinded by the flash. "Did you get that to Sugar Hill?"

"Aye, aye!"

"Mac, do you have Reid with you?" Murphy asked.

"Yes."

"Okay, I'll clear it for you to land here behind the White House. An escort will be waiting to bring you down to the situation room."

"You'd better try to calm everybody down, General. I'm sure about this one. Reid was trying to engineer public sentiment against the Japanese, but he wasn't working for the Russians."

Secretary of Defense Landry was on another telephone. His face turned white. "Mr. President, the Russians have launched two nuclear missiles against Hokkaido from one of their submarines in the strait."

Lindsay was silent for several seconds. "That is a clear declaration of war against Japan, and against us."

"No!" McGarvey shouted.

Murphy realized that he'd left the line open and that McGarvey had heard everything. He reached out for the disconnect button.

"It's a mistake, General!" McGarvey shouted. "Somebody made a mistake!"

"The launches were clean," Lieutenant Zukko reported.

"Time to impact?" Lestov asked. Everyone was braced against the steep dive angle.

"Impact now!"

"Eliminator Leader, this is Peregrine Able Leader. Those weren't nukes! They were conventional explosives!"

It took just a moment for the news to sink in. "Does Sugar Hill copy?" Lieutenant Kane radioed as she reversed course in a savage turn back toward the Russian submarine's position.

"Eliminator Leader, this is Sugar Hill. We copy!"

"We have target acquisition," the Viking's weapons officer reported.

"Stand by to launch torpedoes on my mark," Kane ordered. "Fire one . . . fire two!"

Landry was on a direct circuit to Admiral Ryland aboard the *George Washington*. He got the word on the missile strikes within seconds of impact.

"Mr. President, they were not nuclear missiles. Al Ryland says they were conventional high explosives. Not nuclear!"

The President recovered before anyone else. "What was their target?"

"The radar station at Wakkanai," Landry said. "We're engaging that submarine and two other submarines that are attacking a pair of Japanese destroyers."

Murphy put McGarvey back on the speakerphone.

"Mr. President, order everyone to stand down," McGarvey shouted.

Lindsay looked accusingly down the table at his DCI. "The attack may not have been nuclear, but it was an attack against one of our allies."

"Yes, Mr. President, but it was nothing more than a retaliation for Tatar Strait. It's gotten out of hand. Stop it now before it's too late."

"Cut that circuit," Lindsay ordered.

Murphy reached for the disconnect button.

"Please, Mr. President, I'm begging you," McGarvey pleaded. "Set up a three-way circuit between yourself, President Yeltsin, and Prime Minister Enchi."

"Now, General!" Lindsay roared.

"Mr. President, talking is better than fighting! Enough people have died! End it now! At least try to end it now, for Christ's sake, unless you're afraid to make a decisive move for once in your career—"

Murphy punched the disconnect button.

Lindsay's face turned red. "Let me talk to Admiral Ryland. I'm ordering our forces to DEFCON ONE."

The button on the President's console for the National Security Agency lit up. He hesitated a moment before pressing it.

"Mr. President, we've finally intercepted an ELF message from the Russian Pacific Fleet Headquarters in Vladivostok. All their submarine forces have been ordered to disengage immediately."

"Is it a trick?" Lindsay asked.

"Sir, the codes are correct. We're evaluating the order as genuine."

The President hesitated a moment longer.

"Call President Yeltsin and Prime Minister Enchi," Harold Secor suggested. "Admiral Ryland is standing by for your orders, but he'll wait. The delay will only be minimal."

"The Japanese have asked for our help."

"Yes, Mr. President," Murphy agreed. "I think you're in a position now to do just that."

"Who attacked us?"

"Mr. McGarvey gave us the answer. We'll sort out the details later. Let's step back from the brink before it's too late."

Lindsay studied the faces of his advisers. Normal color was returning to his face. "Very well," he said.

"We can stop the killing," Secor prompted gently.

Lindsay sat up straighter. "Send the order for our

forces to stand by. Then set up a conference call with President Yeltsin and Prime Minister Enchi."

"Yes, Mr. President," Murphy said, breathing the biggest internal sigh of relief in his life.

"Two American Mark 46 torpedoes have gone active," the *Strelka*'s chief sonar operator reported.

"Range and bearing?" Lestov demanded. They'd not counted on the Americans to enter the fight.

"Above and on our port quarter. Captain, they are in pinging mode! They have us!"

"Release countermeasures! Come right to one-eight-zero degrees."

"Conn, communications. We are receiving an ELF message from Pacific Fleet ordering us to disengage immediately!"

Lestov looked across the attack center at his XO. "Too late," he mouthed the words.

"They're close!"

The torpedoes hit, one after the other, breaching the *Strelka*'s hull, breaking her in two. The forward half of the warship, containing the control center and most of the crew, lazily rolled to starboard and headed down to the bottom of the sea, her waterproof bulkheads failing like dominoes in a row as the pressure increased beyond design limits.

FORTY-FIVE

Night had somehow turned to day. When McGarvey awoke in the hospital he looked up into the eyes of Dominique. She smiled uncertainly, distantly.

"Hello," she said.

"Hello to you. How are you feeling?"

"I'm supposed to be asking that question."

"I'll live," McGarvey said. He felt stiff, his mouth pasty, his eyes filled with hot sand, and his head splitting with a booming headache.

"I heard everything aboard the helicopter. What you said, what you did." She looked away for a moment, overwhelmed by everything she'd gone through.

McGarvey reached out and touched her hand, but she flinched away.

"They came very close to succeeding, didn't they? We almost went to war."

"Yes."

"But you stopped it. Nobody would listen, so you had to finally force them into it. Is it always that way?"

"Sometimes," McGarvey replied tiredly. He wanted to tell her everything, but she didn't deserve that burden. He was like a soldier home from the battlefield who refuses to talk about his experiences, in part because he does not want to relive the horrors, in part because there is no way to make anyone who'd not been there understand.

When he awoke briefly, she was gone, and he drifted off to sleep again.

"Stan!" Carol Moss called urgently from the cockpit.

Liskey roused himself from a troubled few hours sleep and hurried aft to the companionway. He'd not bothered to take off his wet foul-weather gear in case he'd have to go topside in a hurry. But the motion of the boat was much easier. And the setting sun, now that the skies had started to clear, was red and gold and purple on the western horizon.

"What?" he said, when he followed her open-mouthed gaze. Fifty yards downwind the gray mass of what he recognized was an American Knox-class frigate rose like the Great Wall of China. The number 1088 was painted on her bow, but there was no name.

Two officers stood on the starboard wing off the bridge. One of them raised a bullhorn. "Hello, *Fair Winds!*"

Liskey cupped his hands over his mouth. "Hello, Navy!"

"Do you require assistance?"

Liskey started to shout an answer, but Carol touched his arm.

"We don't need any help, do we, Stan?" she asked. "We went through all that, and now it's okay?"

"It's up to you, Carol."

"We came out to sail. To be together."

Liskey cupped his hands over his mouth again. "Negative, Navy! We're just fine!"

"Where are you heading?"

"South."

One of the officers ducked back onto the bridge for a few moments. When he came back he took the bullhorn. "The weather is clearing. Long-range forecast looks good. Do you need any supplies?"

"No, thanks!"

"Good sailing, *Fair Winds.*"

"Thank you," Liskey shouted. "Can you tell us what happened this morning?"

The officers heard him, he was sure of it, but they didn't answer, and the frigate slowly pulled away, thoughtfully waiting until it was a half-mile off before accelerating.

They watched the warship until it disappeared over the horizon, leaving them alone on the sea.

"South," Carol asked. "Back to Okinawa?"

"We'll take our time," Liskey replied. "You said something about a ten knot breeze in a sheltered cove?"

Murphy showed up at the hospital on Wednesday as McGarvey was checking out over the doctor's protests. His bodyguard stood watchfully to one side. It had been a busy few days, and the strain showed on the DCI's face.

"Every time we underestimate you, we end up with egg on our faces," he said, helping McGarvey with his coat.

"Have you come to apologize?" McGarvey asked.

"No."

"Well, at least that's honest."

"The President asks that I convey his thanks. It was close."

"Has everything settled down?"

"For the time being. But our relationship with Japan has been strained, even if it wasn't Enchi's government. We're still figuring out what to do. Half the country is calling it another Pearl Harbor, and the other half thinks it's our own fault. The disintegration of the family has turned us into the most violent country in the world."

"Live by the sword, die by the sword?"

"Something like that," Murphy said. "But how did you figure it out when everything pointed toward the Japanese?"

"It *was* a Japanese plot. But they didn't push the button on the Guerin flight to Dulles. They weren't ready. It meant someone else was involved, and Yamagata was just as desperate to find out who it was, and why, as I was."

"How the hell did Reid stumble onto it?"

"Ask him."

"For profit? Was that it?" Murphy asked.

"And idealism," McGarvey explained. "He's convinced that we're going to have another war with Japan. He wanted to wake us up to the fact, so that we'd do something about it before it's too late. Thing is, I think he's right."

"Even if that's true, we won't do anything about it."

McGarvey shrugged. "Am I under arrest?"

Murphy shook his head. "No. But I'd like you to come in for a debriefing."

"Give me a few days."

"Fair enough," the DCI said. "Can I give you a lift?"

"NTSB," McGarvey said. "Socrates and some of the others are meeting with the board."

"Did you hear about Al Vasilanti? He died last night in his sleep. Heart attack."

"I'm sorry. He was a good man."

"A lot of good people are dead. They're still identifying bodies."

They walked out of the hospital and got into Murphy's limousine. The sun was out, and the city looked lovely under the fresh blanket of snow.

"How's Howard Ryan?" McGarvey asked.

"He got in over his head. Thanks for saving his life."

"He should look for a new line of work."

"He's a good attorney."

"But a lousy spook," McGarvey said. He watched out the window for a few seconds. "Have you spoken with JoAnn Carrara?"

"Not yet," Murphy said.

"He was a good man."

"One of the best. Dick Adkins will do okay for us. He and Phil were close."

McGarvey looked at Murphy. "It goes on, doesn't it?"

Murphy nodded. "Howard's internal investigation into your background is finished. We didn't come up with much of anything, except that we made a mistake firing you over that Santiago assignment."

"I don't want the job, General."

"I wasn't offering you a job, Mac. I'm just telling you that those records . . . all the records . . . are being sealed for fifty years."

"Thanks," McGarvey said.

"Take care of yourself," Murphy told him in front of the NTSB headquarters downtown.

"I'll try."

Reid stood on the edge of the chair in his holding cell thinking about the future. He'd told his interrogators everything they wanted to know within the first few hours. But they'd recoiled from him as if he were a poisonous snake. He'd seen the look in their eyes. There'd be more questions, of course, because it was impossible for people like them to understand anything in more than small bites.

He'd managed to tear several long strips out of his bed sheet, which he had fashioned into a long rope, a simple slip knot forming a noose at one end. Standing on a chair he'd tied the other end of the rope to the ceiling grille that covered the single light bulb. With the noose around his neck, all he had to do was kick the chair away and in a few minutes he would be dead. Only a few minutes of pain and it would be over.

He contemplated his own death. Not such a frightening idea, although he didn't relish the idea of pain.

But another idea came to mind. They'd not allowed him to see a television news broadcast, nor had they brought him a newspaper, despite his repeated, and he felt reasonable, requests. They were frightened of him, which on reflection he thought was a good thing. It meant that although they might not understand, at least they were listening.

There would be more questions, more answers. And almost certainly there'd be a public trial at which he would be allowed, by law, to state his case.

Twenty-six hundred people had been killed at Pearl Harbor, and the war with Japan had resulted. At least that many men, women, and children had given their lives on Sunday across America. But their deaths would be wasted unless he remained alive to get this message to his countrymen. This time he would make certain that the tragedy would not be repeated. This time twenty-six hundred deaths would be used to *prevent* war with Japan.

Reid smiled as he reached up to slip the noose from around his neck. He would become their advocate. It was the least he could do for them and his country.

His left foot slipped and in panic he kicked the chair out from under him. The pain was sudden and intense. He thrashed blindly, trying to find a foothold, his fingers clawing uselessly at the fabric biting into his neck, cutting off his air, cutting off the blood supply to his brain. It wasn't fair! He wasn't ready to die! He had so much to live for now! So much he had to tell his fellow

Americans! Somebody would come to help him! They had to come now! His vision blurred, and he knew that he was dying. No one was coming. No one cared.

The fifth-floor auditorium in the Department of Transportation on Independence Avenue was nearly full. As chief investigator for the NTSB, Sam Varelis, an unlit cigar clamped between his teeth, sat at the head table, along with representatives from the Federal Aviation Administration, the FBI, and the House Subcommittee on Aviation. George Socrates stood at the podium explaining how the sabotaged engines had caused catastrophic wing failures that brought the airplanes down. Behind him a slide of an uncowled Rolls-Royce engine was projected on a large screen. As the Guerin engineer spoke, he used a light pencil to point to the various critical components in the engine.

"It'll be a long time before we recover, if we ever do," Newton Kilbourne said, sitting next to McGarvey at the back of the auditorium.

"I heard about Al Vasilanti," McGarvey said after a couple of minutes.

"It was more than he could take. He was from the old school where honor and fair play still meant something." Kilbourne nodded toward Socrates. "We'll figure it out so that it won't be so easy the next time."

"Don't believe it."

"We're coming up with a redundant cross-check system. Anything fails for any reason, no matter how slight, and the on-board monitors will catch it and automatically kick in the fix."

"If you design it, someone will find a way around it."

Kilbourne looked at McGarvey. "They won't go through ATC either. We'll have that covered."

"Then they'll plant a bomb, or shoot it down with a missile, or hijack the flight. If they want you, they'll get you. No way of stopping them, at least not one hundred percent."

"You didn't do such a hot job," Kilbourne retorted,

but he backed off immediately. "Shit. I'm sorry, Mac. You were right from the beginning. You and Dave Kennedy."

"Doesn't give me much pleasure."

"No, I suspect it doesn't. I'm sorry."

"You were doing your job," McGarvey said.

"And you were doing yours, only I didn't want to listen."

"It's a problem we all have, Newt." McGarvey got up.

"Aren't you going to stick around?"

"I have a couple of things to do. You people know the situation now. As you say, you'll figure out how to build a safer airplane."

"That's not the problem," Kilbourne said. "The problem is figuring out how to make a safer world."

"That's a thought," McGarvey said tiredly. He started to go, but Kilbourne stopped him.

"Dominique wants to see you."

McGarvey looked down at him. "She tell you that?"

Kilbourne shook his head. "Not in so many words. But she does."

"Sure," McGarvey said.

"Did he make a difference, Mac?"

McGarvey sat at the kitchen counter drinking a cup of coffee laced with brandy that JoAnn Carrara had fixed for him. "Of course he did."

"Are you sure? You're not lying to me? Because Phil said that you were one of the few men he knew who never lied about anything important. Have any of you made the slightest bit of difference?"

"We won the Cold War."

She waved it off. "So many innocent people were killed on Sunday. Are you saying it was just an act of terrorism?"

"That's exactly what it was, JoAnn."

"Funny, I don't know if I can believe you."

"Phil did."

"It could have been worse?"

"A lot worse," McGarvey said.

She brushed a strand of hair from her forehead, and managed a slight, off-center smile. "Thanks, Mac." She looked toward the den where her children were watching television. "You can find your own way out?"

"I think so."

"You won't mind?"

"Not a bit."

Finally he drove over to the Watergate. He parked in the visitors lot and took the elevator upstairs. He'd thought about returning to his classes at Milford, but it wouldn't be fair to Dominique. She was confused and frightened, as she had every right to be. Her carefully constructed world had been torn apart. It was as if she'd been living in a small town that was safe from the real world, and one morning she'd awakened to find out that a mass murderer had been living next door all along.

He rang the bell. There was so much that he wanted to explain to her, but he wasn't quite sure that she would understand any of it. His first wife, Audrey, hadn't, and she'd drunk herself to death. Nor had his second wife, Kathleen, understood, but she'd been smart enough to walk away before she was destroyed. He wondered now if he was in fact doing Dominique any favor by coming here.

He rang the bell again, and then listened at the door. But he could hear nothing inside the apartment. It was possible that she'd gone back to her brother's house in Detroit. She'd felt safe there. But there were other, darker possibilities.

McGarvey pulled out his gun, his stomach in a knot, and using the key Dominique had given him, unlocked the door. Standing to the side, he pushed the door open with his toe. The apartment was in darkness.

He slipped inside and, keeping low, made his way down the hall to the living room. It was night, but enough light came through the big windows for him to see that she wasn't at home.

"Dominique?" he called softly. There was no answer. He checked the kitchen and bathroom, then held up at the bedroom door which was slightly ajar. The apartment was utterly still.

"Dominique," he called. He closed his eyes for a moment, steeling himself against whatever he might find. In his mind's eye he could see a legion of bodies in great piles and in trenches. It was like seeing a film made of the Nazi death camps after the war. Only these bodies were his responsibility.

He pushed the door open. Dominique sat cross-legged in the middle of the bed. She wore jeans and a sweatshirt, and she held a gun in her lap.

Relief washed over him. He holstered his Walther, then went to her and took the pistol out of her hands and put it aside.

She looked at him, her eyes sparkling. "I wanted to kill him."

"It's over," McGarvey said. "No more killing."

Her lip curled. "He called me his 'dear little girl.' He asked if you'd told me that the killing never stops. He said it was in our nature."

"Stop it."

"You believe that, don't you?" she said. "Because now I do. And if I would have gotten the chance I would have killed him without even thinking about it. And I would have enjoyed it." Her mouth twisted into a hard, ugly grimace.

McGarvey wanted to take her in his arms, but she was so fragile he was afraid she would break. He touched her face, and she shivered. "You don't believe that."

"Oh, but I do. You were right."

"No."

"Then have the decency to explain what happened on Sunday before you leave me again." She looked into his eyes earnestly. "Because either you're an incredible cheat and liar, or what you've done with your life—what you're still doing—is some kind of horribly macho bullshit game." She shook her head, as if she were trying to pull herself out of a daze. "Talk to me, Kirk. Tell me things. Mueller did. Make me see where I'm wrong, before you go."

"I'm not going to leave you," McGarvey said, hating the lie.

"Yes, you are. And the reason you're going to leave is because you love me."

"No."

"As long as I'm with you, I'll never feel safe. But when you're gone, it's much worse."

"Everything will be okay now," McGarvey said. He started to leave, but she took his hand and held him back.

"Not yet," she said softly. "I want you to stay, for just a while."

McGarvey felt as if he were falling into her eyes.

"I love you," she said. "Just for a little while."

"It won't work."

"We'll make it work," Dominique said. "I'll try, you'll try. Maybe it'll be different this time. Maybe you can stop running, and maybe I can stop being afraid. That's worth trying, isn't it?"

He took her into his arms, finally, and she was careful not to hold him where he was wounded.

"You love me," she said. "That's enough for now. The rest will come."

Sokichi Kamiya sat on his haunches in front of a low table on the broad teak deck overlooking the peaceful garden. A slight breeze caused the chimes in the gnarled tree to tinkle gently. He contemplated the rock, "future" and "hope," as he thought about his long life in the service of the *Yamato Damashi*—the soul of Japan.

Chi, jin, yu. Wisdom, benevolence, and courage.

He opened his spotlessly white kimono, pulled his arms out of the sleeves, and tucked the sleeves beneath his knees so that he would not fall backward in death.

* * *

WHEN HONOR IS LOST, 'TIS A RELIEF TO DIE.
DEATH'S BUT A SURE RETREAT FROM INFAMY.

He sat at peace with himself for a long time. With a heightened sense of awareness, he could hear the wind in the trees farther down in the valley. He could hear the water gurgling in the pond. And when the morning sun began to rim the horizon, he smiled.

He took the *wakizashi,* which was a nine-and-a-half-inch razor-sharp knife, from its sheath, wrapped a white cloth around its handle, and placed its point against the left side of his abdomen.

IT IS TRUE COURAGE TO LIVE WHEN IT
IS RIGHT TO LIVE,
AND TO DIE ONLY WHEN IT
IS RIGHT TO DIE.

He plunged the knife to the hilt into his body and, mindless of the horrible pain, drew it slowly to the right while turning it over, so that in the end he cut straight up.

David Kennedy sat across the dinner table from his wife, Chance. The doors were locked, the telephone shut off, the lights turned low.

"I'm sorry," she said.

"Neither of us did very well. But we'll get past this."

"Will we, David?"

"If we want it badly enough."

"That easy?"

He shook his head. "It won't be easy, but I don't want to toss away what we had."

"Now that Al is gone, you've got a struggle ahead of you."

"I'm resigning. I think I can go back to work for NASA."

"No," Chance said sharply. "If you give up now they will have won. Everything." She looked away for a moment. "It'd all be for nothing."

"My marriage is more important."

"Our marriage," Chance corrected, looking into his eyes. "Don't ever forget it. I won't."

The Guerin P/C2622 majestically touched down for a landing at Portland International Airport, six weeks to the day after the air disasters that had brought the United States, Russia, and Japan to the brink of war. A huge crowd waited in the grandstands in front of the terminal to watch the boarding ceremonies for her maiden flight to Honolulu.

Incredibly, in that short time, the country had gotten back on its feet, and many of the 2622's systems had been redesigned and rebuilt to include Kilbourne's redundant cross-check system. She was the most sophisticated, and now the safest, airplane that ever flew.

"Al should have been here for this," David Kennedy said.

"He knew you wouldn't quit," McGarvey replied. He shaded his eyes against the bright sun as he watched the magnificent machine turn onto the taxiway. Even on the ground she looked like she was flying at the edge of space.

"We would have, except for you."

"It doesn't stop here."

"I know," Kennedy said, a dark look momentarily passing over his features. "But the next time we'll be ready."

McGarvey looked at Dominique, and she smiled radiantly, only the slightest hint of fear and uncertainty at the corners of her eyes. He couldn't help himself from thinking that they were still so terribly naïve that they actually hoped their troubles were behind them.

Kilbourne and Socrates came over as the big hypersonic airliner turned onto the ramp and came to a halt in front of the grandstands, *America* painted in bold blue letters across her fuselage.

"That was Al's idea, naming her *America,*" Kilbourne said. "He told me that it would mean hope, promise for the future, fair play, and honesty."

Kennedy smiled. "We don't always get it right."

"But we do most of the time," Kilbourne said.

Dominique squeezed McGarvey's arm. Then again, McGarvey thought, maybe it was he who was naïve. Maybe they were right after all.

I thank the following relatives, friends, advisers, and colleagues for their generous, expert help in writing this book. The mistakes are entirely my fault.

Peter Bagley
Bruce Carlson
John DelGaizo
Laurel Erickson
John Foggia
Bob Gleason
Kevin Hagberg
Laurie Hagberg
Joe Jerick
Richard Martinez
Kenneth Nebel
Nancy Nebel
Robert Roningen
David Scorse
Paul Vesterstein

TOR BOOKS

☑ Check out these titles from
DAVID HAGBERG